THE

STAR TREK
THE NEXT GENERATION®

COMPANION

THE

STAR TREK
THE NEXT GENERATION®

COMPANION

BY LARRY NEMECEK

POCKET BOOKS

New York   London   Toronto   Sydney   Tokyo   Singapore

POCKET BOOKS, a division of Simon & Schuster Inc.
1230 Avenue of the Americas, New York, NY 10020

 STAR TREK is a Registered Trademark of
Paramount Pictures.

This book is published by Pocket Books, a division of Simon & Schuster Inc., under exclusive license from Paramount Pictures.

ISBN: 0-671-88340-2

First Pocket Books trade paperback printing of this revised edition
May 1995

10 9 8 7 6 5 4 3 2 1

POCKET and colophon are registered trademarks of
Simon & Schuster Inc.

Printed in the U.S.A.

This book is lovingly dedicated:

To the memory of the man who dreamed he could fill us with wonder again,
Eugene Wesley Roddenberry;

To those involved at every turn in making sure that dream stays alive;

and

To those who most helped me achieve *this* dream by sacrificing a
large part of our first year together:
my own Janet and Andrew, Sarah and Nathan.

"Fate protects fools, little children, and ships named
Enterprise."

—Riker, "Contagion"

Acknowledgments

A reference book this complex has come together from so many sources and so many roots that dozens of people had a hand in it. For starters, thanks go out to Geoffrey Mandel, wherever you are, for letting a kid from Oklahoma know he could add to the hunt for *Star Trek* background way back in the late 1970s, when everything was so much simpler—until the best-laid plans fell through; to my mom and dad, who helped get the Macintosh hardware that made my return to Trek research a reality; and to all those fans at home and around the world whose feedback was so appreciated on my yearly self-produced *TNG* concordances.

A special thank-you also goes to those on the home front: Mike and Tamara Hodge, for the long-distance and last-minute missing credits cut by the local TNG affiliate; Mark Alfred, for more of the same; and, at the ol' *Norman Transcript*, to my boss Jane Bryant for understanding about my "other job," co-workers Ed Montgomery for the baseball trivia, Charles Stookey for my start with Macs, Jan Burton for support "above and beyond," and Karen Dorrell for trivia, tapes, and too many details to even remember.

I also wish to thank my agent, Sherry Robb, and my Pocket Books editor, Dave Stern, as well as those who will use this work and take the time, I hope, to forward any suggestions or corrections, and the like.

At the source, of course, are those connected with ST:TNG and Paramount Pictures past and present who toil long hours behind those studio walls. From the *past*: Eric A. Stillwell, trying to keep up with all my day-to-day questions of the ongoing series; Richard Arnold, spending countless hours by phone helping check the minutiae of Trek stories during the *TNG* concordance years; Ed Milkis, recalling his TNG efforts on very short notice; and Bob Justman, graciously sharing more of his personal memos and recollections from TNG's formative stage than I ever expected.

And my gratitude to those at 5555 Melrose Avenue *today* who cared so much and provided invaluable help: Carla Mason and Paula Block in Paramount Licensing; Junie Lowry-Johnson's casting office and J. R. Gonzalez; Matt Timothy in Paramount Research; the assistants who "hold the fort": Heidi Julian, Terri Martinez, Kim Fitzgerald, Lolita Fatjo, Kristine Fernandes, and Maggie Allen; Guy Vardeman; and Michael Okuda, Rick Sternbach, Rob Legato, Brannon Braga, Jeri Taylor, and of course, Michael Piller and Rick Berman.

Finally, to all those on TNG's creative team whom time and circumstances prevented me from talking with personally: thanks for sharing your thoughts and memories in previous interviews—and I look forward to the day we *can* meet.

Contents

Introduction

It would be an understatement to say that long-time Trekfans were wary when plans for a new *Star Trek* series were first announced. Even as episodes of *Star Trek: The Next Generation* (TNG) began airing, debates raged in many circles, egged on by the mainstream press, as to how there could ever be a new Trek without Kirk & Co., much less without William Shatner & Co. I was personally thrilled to see the mythos back in weekly production in any form as long as the right people were in charge, but the situation raised a different question in my own mind: which was the bigger challenge—competing with a legend twenty years later, or creating, selling, and maintaining an unappreciated classic in the first place?

That question led to an overall look at the differences in our world at the time each Trek series was born. There were the contrasting "big picture" political and sociological implications of the 1960s and 1980s, to be sure, but the most immediate differences were on the living room level: VCRs in most every U.S. household in the 1980s, fax machines, home computers and bulletin board services, cable television and syndicated programming, and of course an army of fans already in place, fed by two decades of familiarity with the earlier series.

Could the original series have been born in a similar test tube of almost impossibly high expectations? While classic *Star Trek* didn't come with a pedigree and, in fact, suffered through two pilots before finally being sold to a network, it shared many traits with its offspring: a grueling first-season in-house shakedown, hours of backbreaking work by its creator and staff, fre-

netic last-minute rewrites, and shooting on a tight budget.

(By the way, those who have only come into the *Star Trek* fold since the debut of TNG and have not yet discovered its forebear are missing out. Besides an entirely new world of people and adventures, those early shows are the key to an appreciation of the dozens of loving tips of the hat among the background details laid in by TNG's creators.)

Though the new kid on the block has actually been around for only five years now—six since development first got under way—the world is moving fast, and it's not too early for a book like this, since the show has picked up more fans as it has "lived long and prospered."

Still, this *Companion* is not meant to be an exhaustive work on all facets of TNG's production history, the past credits of its stars and creators, and the greater implications of every story. It can't be; it's simply too soon for that, although writers are hard at work now, and more in-depth coverage will surely follow. Neither is this work a tabloid tell-all on the clash of egos and personalities that inevitably occurs when so much is expected of a mere television series.

What we do have here is a handy guide to the first five seasons of the new *Star Trek* show, as well as a brief look back at TNG's evolution that I hope will add to your enjoyment of the series.

This book was a labor of love. Enjoy!

LARRY NEMECEK
Norman, Oklahoma
July 1, 1992

REBIRTH

Could lightning strike twice? The

bombshell announcement that posed that question and simultaneously ended fifteen years of rumors was delivered officially by Mel Harris, then president of Paramount Television Group, during a studio press conference on Friday, October 10, 1986, in Los Angeles.

"Twenty years ago, the genius of one man brought to television a program that has transcended the medium," Harris said. "We are enormously pleased that that man, Gene Roddenberry, is going to do it again. Just as public demand kept the original series on the air, this new series is also a result of grass roots support for Gene and his vision."

The new series would come to be called *Star Trek: The Next Generation*. The syndicated hour-long drama with an all-new cast would be introduced in a two-hour pilot movie in September 1987, and that would be followed by twenty-four one-hour episodes budgeted at one million dollars each, with Roddenberry as executive producer.

1

"Wait a minute," fans said. "An all-new cast? New actors playing the old familiar roles of Kirk, Spock, and McCoy?" That issue had been hotly debated among both fans and studio executives whenever talk of a new *Star Trek* came up.

No, Harris said, this new series would be set "a century after Kirk and Spock." Harris mentioned that the earlier heroes had trekked "two hundred years into the future." That remark, of course, revealed the uncertainty of the evolving TNG time frame as well as the confusion that still reigned over the exact era of the earlier series—a mystery that was finally solved once and for all in the movie *Star Trek IV: The Voyage Home:* the original series took place in the late twenty-third century.

As if to repeat Paramount's emphasis on who would be in charge, a studio spokesperson reassured the press that day that the new series would adhere to Gene Roddenberry's "vision, credibility, and approach." It might have been enough to say that "the Great Bird of the Galaxy"—a nickname given to Roddenberry by original series producer Robert H. "Bob" Justman—had come home to roost.

Even so, it was something of a miracle that Roddenberry even considered coming back to the weekly grind of churning out a quality series, especially in light of the bumps and bruises of budget battles and network hassles in the 1960s and the fact that the original show's syndicated success in the 1970s yielded few financial or professional rewards.

"It was a hard time for me," Roddenberry recalled later, speaking of the seventies. "I was perceived as the guy who had made the show that was an expensive flop, and I couldn't get work. Thank God college kids discovered the show, because I made enough money lecturing to pay the mortgage."[1]

Roddenberry came close to doing a remake of the Kirk-era series with *Star Trek II*, but that project was abandoned in 1977 after the landmark SF movie *Star Wars* premiered. The short-lived series idea gave way to plans for a splashy big-budget theatrical release, but Roddenberry relinquished direct control of the films after *Star Trek: The Motion Picture* drew the disdain of critics and many fans alike—the result of a host of problems he often had no control over. Then, in 1986, there was a reunion party for the twentieth anniversary of *Star Trek*, and the emotions that were rekindled in some of the original production staff gathered there really got the ball rolling once and for all on a new Trek television series. Earlier that spring, Roddenberry had turned down the concepts for a remake that were pitched by studio executives flushed with optimism over the hit they knew they had with *Star Trek IV*—until they unexpectedly agreed with his claim that the only one who could do *Star Trek* right was Roddenberry himself.

"I said absolutely not, no way," he recalled. "The first show took too much out of me. I didn't see my family for two years.

"It was only when the Paramount people agreed with me and said a sequel was probably impossible anyway that my interest was piqued."[2]

Why a *new* series? Local stations had bombarded Paramount with requests for new episodes, studio executives said at the time of the initial announcement. More bluntly, an all-new cast and setting would provide fresh, less costly, and longer-lived actors to take advantage of the never-ending appeal of the Trek phenomenon—and that phenomenon was already quite obvious to a studio with one eye on the steady *Star Trek* profits and the other on the mounting ages and salaries of the original cast and their limited availability.

Roddenberry, too, knew a weekly series with the original players was impractical, but he couldn't see recasting the roles—a point on which most fans agreed with him—and so the decision was made to set the new series sometime in the more distant future and to create a whole new set of characters.

"I don't think we need a retread crew with people playing the same kinds of roles," Roddenberry said then. "I'm not at all sure we'll have a retread Vulcan. I would hate to think our imagination is so slender that there aren't other possibilities to think about."

A year later, after the debut of the new series, he seemed even more certain about that decision. "How can you get the best writers and the best directors and tell them to do a retread?" he said.

"To get the kind of energy and enthusiasm we needed, you have to have new characters and a new series." Still, he acknowledged later, such a path in light of the original show's popularity had constituted "a considerable risk."

The embryonic series had a handle on characters and format, but would there again be bitter ongoing duels with network accountants and censors? For Roddenberry, it was just as well that all four networks, including the fledgling Fox, eventually turned down the new series. All had been intrigued, but none would commit itself to a full twenty-six-hour first season, an unchanging time slot, and an intense promotional campaign. "Nobody was going to give it the same kind of attention and care that we could give it," Mel Harris said later, calling Paramount's Trek franchise "one of our family jewels."

"I'm happy we're not on the network," Gene Roddenberry said. "It's one more level of censorship and so on that I don't have to deal with. I'm still bruised from some of those 1966 battles!"

Bob Justman, who had begun with Roddenberry on the original pilot for *Star Trek* in 1964 as first assistant director and wound up as associate producer by series' end, recalled some of those battles while reflecting on why he and others from the old show would take up the banner once again.

"When I left *Star Trek* in 1968 it was a disaster," Justman said. "It was a failure as far as the network was concerned, and the industry. . . . So I had a need to return to prove that the show did have value and was successful and that you can go home again and prove to the people who doubted you that there was value there all along, that this was a worthwhile—if you'll pardon the pun—enterprise."[3]

So the motivation and the assurances and the basic blueprint were in place. Now all Roddenberry and Company—whoever they were to be—needed was the other 98 percent of the series. They had to tackle the fine points of twenty-fourth-century characters and technology updates, as well as the twentieth-century dilemmas surrounding budgeting, special effects, organizing a crew, and topping a classic. Those were the issues that had to be faced as Roddenberry, armed for once with complete studio backing, began assembling a team and organizing his ideas for the first TNG writers' guide—the series "bible."

In the beginning, the new series didn't even have a name. In an October 24 memo, Justman suggested forty-four series titles. *Star Trek: The Next Generation* was not on the list, although a couple came close: "The New Generation" and "The Second Generation." The first-draft series bible of November 26 carried the ST:TNG moniker, but another Justman memo, dated December 15, suggested nineteen more possible titles. Earlier, on October 31, he had even suggested just keeping the title *Star Trek* and letting the obvious differences between the two shows clear up any confusion.

Creation in Flux

As good as the original *Star Trek* had been, even the most devout fan had to admit it was far from perfect in both execution and concept. Even as Roddenberry faced the challenge of making *The Next Generation* click, he was aware that few creators ever got a chance to improve on their earlier successes. The problems of time, budget, and censorship might have disappeared, but how could he improve the series itself?

David Gerrold, writer of the classic Trek episode "The Trouble with Tribbles," pointed out many of the original Trek's problems in his book *The World of Star Trek*. For one, there was the folly of beaming a starship captain right into the middle of an unknown, possibly dangerous situation week after week. Not only did it make the drama too easy, it simply wasn't very practical—or prudent. Then there was the duration of the ship's mission and its impact on crew members of both sexes. How did humans, single and married, deal with such a career? Still another plot device overused for jeopardy's sake was the failure of technology on a recurring basis, including the good old transporter. Why would anyone want to use devices with such a high failure rate?

Roddenberry and his team also had to deal with the "simple" problem of updating the starship, the technology, and the crew. How much of the old series' familiarity had to be retained to make it *Star Trek*? And how many changes had to be made, especially with a new set of character relationships, to make TNG stand alone?

To sound out his ideas, Roddenberry first gathered around him a small circle of people he knew he could depend on, those who had helped spark the triumph of the original Trek. That group included Roddenberry's former co-producer, Bob Justman, as well as Eddie Milkis, a onetime Trek associate producer who had gone on to produce hit series like *Happy Days* and *Laverne and Shirley* and numerous films. David Gerrold was also on Roddenberry's team. The new think tank hit the ground running, screening SF films like *Blade Runner* and *Aliens* and meeting for daily brainstorming lunches at the Paramount commissary.

Memos began flying back and forth between the two small offices TNG then occupied in Building L on the Paramount lot. On October 17, 1986, alone—barely a week after the new series was announced—Justman proposed three concepts: a so-called Noah's Ark premise that involved crew members bringing their families along; the use of an android as a regular character, and an idea that would grow into the holodeck concept. The next day he was summarizing the group's suggestions for developing new hostile or friendly alien races while also surmounting Roddenberry's aversion to retreads by suggesting a Klingon marine as a regular character. On October 20 he wondered if his android character might provide a Spock-like mystique for the new series.

From those early brainstorming sessions came a few ideas that, in hindsight, might be labeled as clinkers: on October 18 Justman suggested a female science officer in the mold of Sean Young, possibly part Vulcan and Spock's great-great-granddaughter, or a recent Academy grad who is Kirk's great-great-granddaughter.

"It was a very homogenous kind of thing," Milkis said of the creative mix at work. He recalled that it was Justman who always kept and filed the memos. "We all had input and built off the ideas of each other. Nobody really takes particular credit for anything."

"Gene was very wise," Justman said. "He would listen to people—[some] that he trusted and some that he didn't know—but he would make up his own mind about everything. And if he liked something, then he'd make use of it, and if he didn't he'd throw it away. But Gene had definite ideas; he always had definite ideas!"

After weeks of listening—and working with Gerrold on the text—Gene Roddenberry emerged on November 26, 1986, with a twenty-two-page writers' bible that described and explained the characters, sets, and terminology and laid down the format the series would follow.

Actually, some of the flaws in the old series, made obvious to fans and critics alike by fifteen years of reruns, were to have been corrected in the abortive 1970s series *Star Trek II*. That show, for example, was to have fought the old captain-in-danger weakness by having First Officer Will Decker lead most landing parties while Kirk stayed aboard. So, in a November 8, 1986, memo, Justman proposed that this Starfleet directive be credited to Jean-Luc Picard, who recommended it when he was first officer of *Stargazer* after his captain was killed in a tragic beam-down. The scenario was never fully fleshed out, but finally mentioned in Season 6 ("Tapestry"/241).

Roddenberry was also adamant in his insistence that the new series would not rely on failed technology as a plot device week after week. "Although this creates some additional difficulty in maneuvering our people into danger," he wrote in the infant writers' guide, "story believability demands that our twenty-fifth-century technology be at least as capable as our twentieth-century technology in this area—perhaps not such a difficulty if one realizes that twenty-fifth-century villains are no doubt capable of technological countermeasures."

His mention of the twenty-fifth century, by the way, was no mistake. At this stage the new show *was* set in that time frame.

The starship in the new series was first designated as NCC-1701-7, but the generational notation was later changed to a letter, following the pattern established in the recently released feature film *Star Trek IV.* The new ship was made the eighth *Enterprise,* NCC-1701-G.

One sign of the changes that had occurred between Kirk's era and Picard's was on page 1 of the new writers' bible, where it was stated that 19 percent of the Milky Way galaxy had been charted in this new century, compared to only 4 percent in Kirk's time.

But, more important, GR had always insisted that *people* be at the heart of any Trek yarn, and it was in the arena of human interaction that the differences in TNG would be most striking. While Kirk's crew was on a five-year mission, the new starship was to be outfitted for an assignment of ten years or longer. Because of that, officers and crew would be allowed to bring their families along, and that in turn created the need for a ship twice as long and eight times the volume of the original *Enterprise.* This new ship would have a whole community of services to support its population. More than ever before, the starship truly would be a city in space.

"Most twenty-fifth-century humans believe that 'Life should be lived, not postponed,' " the new bible stated, reiterating Starfleet's view that "people need people . . . in both family and community life, as well as other agreeable forms of human bonding." Of course, this wasn't a new concept. "The old navy sometimes took families along," Roddenberry later pointed out. "The wagon trains going west took families, of course."

Star Trek's creator also coined the term "Technology Unchained," referring to it as a concept used by twenty-fifth-century poets to describe how technical improvement in their era had moved beyond developing *things* that were smaller or faster or more powerful, in favor of concentrating on quality of life improvements.

TNG's holodeck (shown here in the episode "Code of Honor") was a concept refined from earlier Trek incarnations.

The Great Bird of the Galaxy further emphasized this point in the design of a new larger, brighter, and less "battleship-sterile" starship, with the original *Enterprise*'s dials and gauges largely replaced by flat, programmable supercomputer access panels.

One unique and dramatic use of technology to improve the quality of shipboard life was the holodeck. This had its roots, again, as far back as a never-realized concept postulated for the 1960s series—a holographic entertainment center. This idea, called the "rec room," was a major plot point in one of the animated *Star Trek* shows, "The Practical Joker," but the idea of combining transporters and replication with a hologram system was not fully developed and finally filmed until TNG was born.

Finally, the writers' guide opened with the familiar "These are the voyages" prologue, another link to the past, but it ended by promising to go "where no *one* has gone before," a far less sexist phrase than the famous "no *man*" tag line that was still being used in the Trek films of the 1980s.

Assembling the Team

With a writers' guide in hand, Roddenberry turned to filling out a production staff to further flesh out the writers' bible and get the series pilot rolling. Trek veterans Justman, Milkis, and Gerrold were soon joined by newcomer Robert Lewin as a writing producer. This new position represented the division of responsibility needed on a complex show like *Star Trek*—a division that Roddenberry had first conceived of for the 1970s series.

Lewin, the first top-level staffer on the new series not associated with original Trek or any of its film sequels, joined the staff in January after being recommended by Justman, who had worked with him on *The Man from Atlantis*. The producer of *The Paper Chase* and the writer of hundreds of episodes for series like *Gunsmoke*, *The Rifleman*, and *Rawhide* told his new boss he didn't know much about Trek or about science fiction and was told that he was wanted as a good character writer.

Dorothy "D.C." Fontana, who served for two years as story editor on the original Trek and penned the introduction of Spock's parents in the popular "Journey to Babel" episode, was hired by early December of 1986 to write the series' two-hour pilot script. She later became an associate producer at GR's invitation after he assured her the tone of this series would follow a new trail, not that taken by the movie features.

The initial design staff was also assembled from a crew of familiar names. Andrew Probert and Rick Sternbach, who were artists and fans as well as Trek movie contributors, were among the first to be signed on. Sternbach recalls pulling his car off the freeway when he heard the news of Trek's revival on the radio. He called Susan Sackett, GR's personal assistant, from the first available phone.

Probert, who was responsible for the final look of the starship *Enterprise* in the first film, had also worked on *Battlestar Galactica*, *Airwolf*, and *Streethawk*, and on the movie *Indiana Jones and the Temple of Doom*. Sternbach was assistant art director for Carl Sagan's Emmy-winning *Cosmos* series on PBS and later worked on TV's *Greatest American Hero* and the movies *The Black Hole* and *Halloween II*.

From the field of television commercial production in his native Hawaii came scenic artist Michael Okuda. His design submissions had impressed the producers of *Star Trek IV: The Voyage Home* and led to his being added to the TNG staff later in 1986 as a scenic artist. Okuda was in charge of designing the distinctive graphic look of consoles, computer readouts, door labels, and so forth for Starfleet and for alien cultures.

What was seen as merely a bonus in the beginning—the background in science and aerospace that all three men brought to their TNG jobs—later turned out to be a great asset. Their contributions eventually went far beyond their job descriptions. They helped enliven one of Gene Roddenberry's oldest maxims by offering viewers some real science, without hitting them over the head with it.

GR tapped original Trek costume designer Bill Theiss to plan Starfleet's new look, and Milkis and Justman helped bring in art director Herman Zimmerman.

"Bob and I together work[ed] very well," Milkis recalled. "He and I totally supervised the development of the physical look of the show and hired the people. And then things would reach a point from time to time where we'd take them in to Gene and get his okay."

As the team began feverishly working on the first-draft bible, memos that had been flying since October were being updated in light of the new questions that popped up daily. Lewin had a box taped to his desk just to hold them all.

Early in the process, egged on by fan and press reaction to the thought of a new Trek without the old cast, Roddenberry decided to completely avoid such original-series aliens as Romulans, Klingons, and even Vulcans. That worry proved groundless by midway through the first year, however, as new races, both friendly and

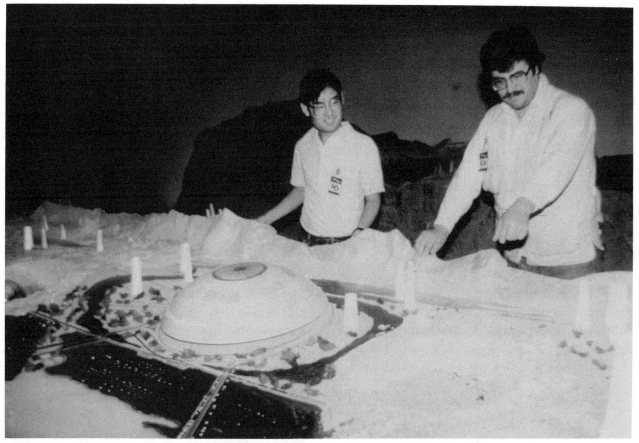

Mike Okuda and Rick Sternbach view the Mordan city, the last landscape model built for TNG.

hostile, began appearing. By the time the first revision of the writers' guide was completed in February 4, 1987, some 907 officers and family members were said to be aboard the new *Enterprise*, now designated as the fifth one so named, NCC-1701-D. The final first-season writers' guide of March 23 later increased the number of shipboard personnel to 1,012, its final mark, and honed the time frame to seventy-eight years after Kirk and Spock.

By mid-January 1987 Fontana's first draft for the two-hour pilot telefilm "Encounter at Farpoint" was well underway. While it was the staff's chief concern, advance scripts for the early first-season schedule were already being prepared by Gerrold and John D.F. Black, another veteran of the original series.

After working in separate quarters and one-on-one for weeks, the new series production team met as a full unit for the first time on February 18, 1987, having just received Fontana's first draft for "Farpoint" only a few days earlier. Gathered around the table with Gene Roddenberry were Justman, Milkis, Lewin, Fontana, Gerrold, Theiss, Sackett, GR's attorney–business manager Leonard Maizlish, Zimmerman, Probert, Sternbach, and Okuda; Herb Wright, another writing producer like Lewin, would soon be added. The staff discussed details of the show— such as the look of the new communicators, phasers, and tricorders—and specific production problems stemming from Fontana's pilot script.

Finally a fifty-five-page first-season writers' and directors' guide was issued on March 23. This, too, was largely assembled by Gerrold and the staff and then polished by Roddenberry himself.

Of Stars and Starships

As the heart and soul of the new series continued to evolve over that winter of 1986–1987, so did its physical presence on the Paramount lot. Mindful that the budget constraints could be even more of a problem than they were in the sixties, Milkis and Justman as early as October were scrounging all they could from the existing inventory of Trek's feature films, even to the point of merely re-dressing sets and miniatures and rehashing optical effects.

Justman recalled the day the two men were allowed to view the movies' standing sets to see what use they could make of them. "Cats inhabit studios. They live on the stages," he said, laughing. "And since this stage hadn't been shot on in a long time it was *shat* on by a whole bunch of cats!"

"It was horrendous," Milkis agreed. "You couldn't even walk on the stage!"

Eventually, as Gene Roddenberry's new concept of "Technology Unchained" evolved, a new *Enterprise* became a necessity. Though many of the film sets would be refurbished, the new look and feel of the twenty-fourth century would be fully symbolized by the bridge set, historically the most-filmed area aboard the starship.

The Great Bird had originally wanted a huge forward viewscreen four times the size of its predecessors, with a conference table right on the bridge,[4] but those ideas gradually changed over the winter. A large open command area replaced the table, and the observation lounge became a separate room just "behind" the bridge.

The final layout reflected Roddenberry's belief that the *Enterprise*'s basic functions should be automated. The simple conn and Ops (for "operations") forward stations left their operators free for less mechanical tasks such as discussion and investigation. Probert had also designed a transporter just off the bridge, but GR wanted the characters to have conversations en route to the transporter room, so that idea was dropped.

In a memo dated November 9, Justman first proposed creating a captain's ready room, a space close to the bridge where the crew could have private conversations. (Similar areas are used by today's navy). Roddenberry initially agreed with Probert, who proposed placing the office so that it opened onto the upper bridge level for more dramatic impact. But it was eventually moved down to its current location to provide a shorter, more direct route to the command chair.

In addition to the center seat, Probert included some other touches that would ring true to longtime fans: a dedication plaque and ship silhouettes on the walls, and a red warning sensor flasher at the base of the viewscreen. Improvements over the old design included more than one turbolift shaft and, in response to gibes about its ancestor's comfort, a bathroom! Though no actual set was built, a door labeled "Head" was tucked out of sight in the aft starboard alcove leading to the conference lounge. The ready room got a private washroom as well.

The result was an *Enterprise* bridge set that, thanks to its nine-foot-tall viewscreen and sprawling overhead window, seems immense. In reality, however, it's only thirty-eight feet wide, the same width as the original, but it is two feet longer and has a fourteen-foot ceiling. The side ramps and various levels add to the illusion of height.

Next, Probert turned his attention to the starship itself. Having done the final reworking of the TV-to-film refit of the old *Enterprise*, he largely based its Galaxy-class cousin—as the new design came to be called—on a "what if?" painting of an all-new starship he did shortly after the first film. Here again, the lines of the final model suggest that art and technology have merged into a design of sleeker, rounder contours, with windows—lots of them, in various sizes and shapes—to keep the crew and passengers in touch with their environment. Still, the overall design is dominated by the familiar sublight-driven saucer section and the battle module with warp nacelles.

Probert built into this starship a major concept that was mentioned first for TNG in the final writers' guide, though it dates back to earlier Trek incarnations. It is the *Enterprise*'s ability to separate its two main sections in time of emergency or attack and then later reconnect. Ship separation was referred to in the original series as well—in "The Apple," when a planet-bound Kirk tells Scotty to "jettison the nacelles and get out in the saucer section if you have to"—but it was never shown because of budgetary restraints.

The film *Enterprise was* built to separate, but the feature was never utilized.[5] Even TNG's "ship sep" feature was not approved by the studio until well into the pilot's development because of the extra expense in optical effects and filming models.

Drawings of the new 1701-D, dated December 8, 1986, eventually graced the cover of the final first-season "bible" and first appeared to fans in Gerrold's July 1987 column in *Starlog* magazine. Probert later said his biggest challenge was to produce a starship that looked as good in two pieces as it did in one.

At the same time he urged that a battle bridge be added: in effect, an update of the old Constitution-class starship's auxiliary bridge, relocated atop the battle module's cobra head and given a direct emergency turbolift from the main bridge. A March 23 sketch for this concept reveals how it was done: the set of the film *Enterprise*'s bridge would be inexpensively redressed—the first of many such times that would happen on TNG. Meanwhile, Zimmerman's new main bridge, ready room, and senior quarters/corridor sets began going up in March on cramped Stage 6, where they would stay a year before being located for good on adjacent Stage 8 once the *The Colbys*' mansion set was dismantled after that series' cancellation.

Meanwhile, on Stage 9, most of the movie ship's other standing sets were being re-dressed and expanded. The main engineering area, with

The "new" *Enterprise* (*below*) and its bridge (*opposite, both shots*) retained the feel of their forebears, while evoking Roddenberry's "Technology Unchained": a harmony of science and quality of life.

many of its components repainted and its spaces enlarged, acquired the Starfleet Command console from *Star Trek IV*, which was soon referred to as "the pool table." McCoy's movie sickbay lost two office walls. One, a bank of consoles, became the back wall of the engineer's office looking onto the main reactor. The other, the wall of stored samples, eventually turned up as the rows of access plates in the transporter room.

As another money-saver, the first-season observation lounge was a make-over of the movie sickbay. Its windows were covered with carpet for the medical scenes. (A new lounge was built for season two.) Finally all the connecting corridors were made longer and widened for TV use by removing the film sets' A-frames. The multipurpose cargo bay–shuttle bay–holodeck–gymnasium set would be erected, over time, from scratch.

Thus, with construction dating back to the first Trek film and the aborted 1977 series, the Stage 8–9 complex houses what Paramount veterans like to point to as the oldest standing sets in Hollywood!

Zimmerman's crew cabins, carved from the movie-set captain's quarters, were built for complete versatility. Upward-sliding walls and modular wall units could be reversed to suggest a dormlike, mirror-image floor plan from use to use.[6] The windows were later backed by velvet star backdrops—initially hand-cranked, later motorized—to avoid costly visual effects when the ship was not at warp.

Just as the original series had done twenty years earlier, TNG erected on nearby Stage 16 a multilevel canyon-cave set, made of reinforced concrete, to represent planet interiors and exteriors. This set came complete with an area capable of holding water for a "lake" and a gigantic white backdrop that could reflect colored lights to represent any planetary sky color. Because of the hostile environments and strange habitats represented there, the cast and crew soon began to refer to Stage 16 as "Planet Hell."

Meanwhile, Sternbach stayed busy updating Trek's famous props and equipment while Okuda began developing the "look" of TNG's graphics and its new generation of computers. Though

Note minute changes in the first-version tricorder (*above*) and its successor (*below*).

The "dustbuster" Phaser II (*above, left*) gave way to a more angular design (*right*) in Season Two, while the first phaser rifle (*below*) since the second original Trek pilot appeared in Season Four.

they would be modified later after filming began, the tricorder, hand phaser I, and pistol phaser II were all completed in the sketches dated February 6, which Probert prepared for construction bidders. Originally the communicator was to be a wrist device, as in the first Trek movie and outlined in the first two TNG writers' bibles, but their function was later built into a new metallic Starfleet insignia worn on the chest. A personal monitor tied in to the ship's computer, not unlike the perscan biomonitor buckles of the first film, was also made a part of the new communicator. The design of the new medical syringe was inspired by a present-day commercial inhaler.

While the full-scale environments of TNG

were under construction, the miniatures also began to take shape. These models and special optical effects had to be completed on time, on budget, and on the mark in order to meet the expectations of an audience grown accustomed to the optical effects of the feature films.

Early on, a new process was adopted so that TNG could compete for top quality while adhering to a television budget and schedule. All optical effects would be composited digitally on one-inch videotape so as to avoid the slower and more costly process involved in using film stock—not to mention the rapid deteriorating quality of film from one generation to the next when building composites. All live action shot on film would be transferred to tape as well for final editing.

For a time, Milkis revealed, he and Justman considered using only computer-generated effects and miniatures. One company even ran several tests using the old *Enterprise* design to demonstrate the look that could be produced by computers. "It was incredibly good," Milkis recalled, "and it took some real thinking on our part, but ultimately we decided that if something ever happened to that company and they couldn't deliver, then we'd have nothing. We were very concerned about that, and ultimately they did go out of business."[7]

Finally, he and Justman turned to Lucasfilm's legendary Industrial Light and Magic (ILM) to provide the models of the new *Enter-*

prise—a two-foot version and a six-foot model with modules that actually separated. They were built from Probert's specs and cost about $75,000. Work on the models got under way in March 1987 by an ILM crew of six headed by Greg Jein, a veteran maker of Trek models since the first movie, and Ease Owyeung.

Even before that work got under way, TNG's producers had looked down the road and decided they could get more FX bang for the buck by building a library of stock shots that could be reused with each other or with new footage each time a different effect was needed.

But after getting budget-busting bids back from four or five effects houses, Justman recalled that ILM, through lucky timing, gave the infant series another break. The famous shop found itself idle for about six months between major motion picture jobs with a lot of overhead to carry—a plant and lots of one-of-a kind personnel.

"What they decided was to make a bare-bones bid, enough to keep their doors open and keep everyone on that they needed," Justman said. "Oh, it was a tremendous bid. I couldn't believe it was so cheap! But it was ILM, you know? The best in the business!"

One new effect, described in a March 15 Justman memo, would come to be a signature of the new series: its own warp-speed jump. The Trek filmmakers had experimented with different types of animation, but Justman considered the results "too cartoony." So the producer got ILM and TNG's own Rob Legato—hired by new post-production supervisor Peter Lauritson to supervise TNG's in-house video effects—to design and film what came to be called the "rubber-band effect." It was a look that Doug Trumbull had actually sought for the first motion picture but had to abandon when he ran out of time: the saucer stretches out until the rear end snaps forward to catch up with it in a huge flash of light, which then fades to reveal the starship, long disappeared.

ILM's credit remained throughout the series' end titles, owing mainly to the use of that sole effect. "The reality of the situation is that they did effects for the pilot, but even then they just did the raw material; our team composited them," Lauritson noted. "And everything beyond the pilot we have addressed ourselves; they sent us the film, Paramount transferred it to video."

Throughout all this, fans had only the tantalizing snippets of news in the mainstream and industry press to keep them posted on the evolving show—along with the ever-active rumor mill via fan clubs, newsletters, and computer bulletin boards. In his *Starlog* magazine column, Gerrold sought to reassure the faithful that this new Trek would be faithful to the Great Bird's vision of the future. "Should the new *Enterprise* find itself in a military situation," he wrote, "then it will be seen as a *failure* of the ship's *diplomatic* mission."[8]

Then, as the rumblings mounted from those who had condemned the show months before it had even evolved, much less aired, Justman took it upon himself to appeal to fans directly. "I'd heard that we were 'ripping off our own show,'" he recalled. "Now there's a quote!"

Although he had never been a guest at a Star Trek convention in his life, Justman spoke at the April 18 Equicon in Los Angeles. There he thanked the attendees for keeping the Trek concept alive for twenty years against all odds, and he asked them to "hang in there with us, please" on this new venture. "If we fail, it won't be for lack of trying," he told the crowd. "So please bear with us if the new *Star Trek* doesn't always meet your expectations. Our little show has become a legend, and it's hard to live up to a legend. We're trying hard. We want to succeed. We want to excel. We hope we can. We're sure going to try."

Drafting a Crew

In creating the new *Enterprise* crew, Gene Roddenberry and his team continued to distance TNG from its forebear by striving to shed the familiar and dominating duality of the Kirk-Spock relationship. This time they chose to divide the attributes of that dynamic pair among the new characters so that they could assemble an ensemble cast in the style of 1980s TV dramas like *Hill Street Blues*, *St. Elsewhere*, and *L.A. Law*.

The first casting call went out to talent agencies on December 10, 1986. That outline now serves as a sort of historical snapshot, a first official look at the characters as they were shaping up. Here it is, as published in one fanzine newsletter,[9] with the original spelling, punctuation, and capitalization intact:

TO: ALL TALENT AGENCIES
RE: PARAMOUNT "STAR TREK: THE NEXT GENERATION"
1-HR. SERIES FOR SYNDICATION
2-HR. TV MOVIE TO START END OF MARCH
24 1-HR. EPISODES TO START END OF MAY
Exec. Producer: Gene Roddenberry
Supv. Producer: Eddie Milkis
Producer: Bob Justman
Director: TBA
Casting Director: Helen Mossler
Casting Assistant: Gail Helm
WRITTEN SUBMISSIONS—ONLY—TO: HELEN MOSSLER, PARAMOUNT, BLUDHORN 128, 5555 MELROSE AVE., LOS ANGELES, CA 90038
PLEASE BE ADVISED THAT WE DO NOT HAVE A SCRIPT YET AND ARE JUST IN THE PRELIMINARY CASTING STAGES.

SEEKING THE FOLLOWING SERIES REGULARS:
CAPT. JULIEN PICARD—A caucasian man in his 50s who is very youthful and in prime physical condition. Born in Paris, his gallic accent appears when deep emotions are triggered. He is definitely a 'romantic' and believes strongly in concepts like honor and duty. Capt. Picard commands the Enterprise. He should have a mid-Atlantic accent, and a wonderfully rich speaking voice.
NUMBER ONE (A.K.A. WILLIAM RYKER)—A 30–35 year old caucasian born in Alaska. He is a pleasant looking man with sex appeal, of medium height, very agile and strong, a natural psychologist. Number One, as he is usually called, is second-in-command of the Enterprise and has a very strong, solid relationship with the Captain.
LT. COMMANDER DATA—He is an android who has the appearance of a man in his mid 30's. Data should have exotic features and can be anyone of the following racial groups: Asian, American Indian, East Indian, South American Indian or similar racial groups. He is in perfect physical condition and should appear very intelligent.
LT. MACHA HERNANDEZ—26 year old woman of unspecified Latin decent who serves as the starship's security chief. She is described as having a new quality of conditioned-body-beauty, a fire in her eyes and muscularly well developed and very female body, but keeping in mind that much of her strength comes from attitude. Macha has an almost obsessive devotion to protecting the ship and its crew and treats Capt. Picard and Number One as if they were saints.
LT. DEANNA TROI—An alien woman who is tall (5'8–6') and slender, about 30 years old and quite beautiful. She serves as the starship's Chief Psychologist, Deanna is probably foreign (anywhere from Italian, Greek, Hungarian, Russian, Icelandic, etc.) with looks and accent to match. She and Number One are romantically involved. Her alien "look" is still to be determined.
LESLIE CRUSHER—An appealing 15 year old caucasian girl (need small 18 or almost 18 year old to play 15). Her remarkable mind and photographic memory make it seem not unlikely for her to become, at 15, a Starfleet acting-ensign. Otherwise, she is a normal teenager.
BEVERLY CRUSHER—Leslie's 35 year old mother. She serves as the chief medical officer on the Enterprise. If it were not for her intelligence, personality, beauty and the fact that she has a natural walk of a striptease queen, Capt. Picard might not have agreed to her request that Leslie observe bridge activities; therefore letting her daughter's intelligence carry events further.
LT. GEORDI La FORGE—a 20–25 year old black man, blind from birth. With the help of a special prosthetic device he wears, his vision far surpasses anything the human eyes can see. Although he is young, he is quite mature and is best friends with Data. Please do not submit any 'street' types, as Geordi has perfect diction and might even have a Jamaican accent. Should also be able to do comedy well.

These initial descriptions of the characters would undergo further revisions as the new production team bandied ideas about and, later, when actors began auditioning for the roles. Not the least of these changes would be the addition of the Klingon, Worf.

"Kirk came out of an earlier time in my life when I was pretending to be part of my macho southern background, and [the character] reflects some of that," Gene Roddenberry would later tell an interviewer. "Macho feelings about women, and so on. But in twenty-five years, my feelings have changed enormously about those things and I think Picard represents that. He's more mature."[10]

The back story for Picard—given a French heritage in homage to the many Gallic explorers, including Jacques Cousteau—was set down in the very beginning and mentioned a twenty-two-year stint as mission commander of the USS *Stargazer*. His first name, as well as the spelling of Riker, would not take on their eventual form until sometime between the February 4 revision of the writers' guide and the final version dated March 23. At that point, however, the captain was given the nickname Luke.

The first-draft "bible" mentions the historical British navy tradition of calling the first officer "Number One," but neglects to point out the usage in *Star Trek*'s own history. In the very first 1964 Trek pilot, "The Cage," Captain Pike's right-hand officer was a woman known only as Number One. Also, Riker and Troi's past relationship was originally described as "intimate," but it was changed to "unconsummated" in the March guide, as he was said to be torn between his feelings for her and a perceived need for detachment in his career. Along with an action-oriented command style and a healthy libido, Riker also shares with predecessor Kirk the middle initial T, although his actual middle name was not chosen until late in the series' run ("Second Chances"/249).

The first real character dynamic to emerge in this early memo-writing phase, after that of Picard and Riker, centered on Picard and Wesley—ironic in view of many fans' later disdain for the teenager. The latter two roles, incidentally, carried the names as early as November 8, according to a Justman memo, despite the December 15 mention of a girl, "Leslie."

"I identify probably more so with Wesley because he is me at seventeen," Roddenberry would say later. "He is the things I dreamed of being and doing."[11] This closeness to the character would color how Wesley was handled, even after GR's death ("Journey's End"/289).

Actually, the issue of whether the teenager would be a boy or a girl was bandied about for some time. According to Justman, the character began as a male called Wesley—GR's own middle name—even though he pushed to make the teenager a girl. The female character remained through the October 26 bible and the casting call, but had been changed back to the boy, Wesley, for good by the time the February 4 revision was completed.

"I thought, Jeez, anybody and everybody has had boy teenagers; let's do a girl," Justman recalled. "Let's explore the problems that female adolescents go through, because that's never done. . . . Then Gene switched it back to Wesley because he felt there would be a wider range of stories available dealing with the character if he were a male instead of a female."

What might surprise those who later objected loud and long that Wesley was too young and inexperienced for bridge duty is the fact that their arguments had been foreseen. Despite the character's brilliance, "The question will be raised as to why he was selected for this all-important mission rather than someone older who would have the maturity and experience which he has not, as yet, attained," Justman wrote in a memo to GR way back on November 12. "Because of his youth, Wesley Crusher has not yet had to learn to go with the herd and compromise his thinking just because compromising is easier and more socially acceptable. He has the ability to grow with the job and to devise new approaches and new capabilities for whatever unforeseen events we encounter. In effect he is a one-man 'think tank' without preconditioned limitations."

Though it was dropped before the final writers' guide was issued, one new development—a landing-envelope forcefield for away teams on inhospitable planets—was suggested at one point as a Wesley creation to help explain why he holds such a unique position. Coming up with a reason for Wesley's special status that viewers would accept proved difficult for writers and producers alike.

Although it was not mentioned in the casting announcement, Justman and the staff had worked out the story of Wesley's father Jack being killed under Picard's command and the dilemmas that posed for the captain, Wesley, and his mother. In fact, Beverly Crusher at first was referred to only in relation to Wesley and didn't rate her own page of background notes until the final writers' guide edition.

Only a few other role changes were made by the time of the February 4 revision: Geordi has the rank of ensign and Troi is promoted to lieutenant commander, though she is still referred to as the chief psychologist.

The cocky yet insightful Lieutenant (j.g.) Geordi La Forge was named for a quadriplegic fan, George La Forge, who died in 1975 after having endeared himself to Gene Roddenberry and much of fandom. The character's eventual rank was established later on.

Though her alien roots are not explained in detail on the call sheet, presumably for simplicity's sake, Troi was described in the very first bible as a quarter-blood Betazoid who possessed some telepathic powers due to her "Starfleet officer grandfather having lived on Betazed with one of its humanoid females." In the final draft (most likely with the first-season script for "Haven" in progress) her heritage was changed to half-blood Betazoid, her Starfleet father having lived with her mother on Betazed.

The new female security chief's name evolved from Macha Hernandez—inspired by Jenette Goldstein's tough space marine Vasquez in 1986's *Aliens*—to Tanya (for two days around March 13) and finally to Natasha "Tasha" Yar, coined by Lewin from the Balkan battle of Baba Yar. (The inspiration would come full circle after Goldstein appeared in the first TNG movie.)

Of all the new regulars it was probably the android Data whose premise changed the least. A Starfleet graduate and the highest scorer ever on the Turing Test of Sentience, he is on an eternal quest for the impossible goal of knowing what it is to be human. Roddenberry admitted that this character sprang from Questor, a similar android seeking its creator in his well-received yet unsold 1974 TV pilot movie, *The Questor Tapes*. From the beginning, Data and Geordi are said to be close friends—a virtual "walking library" (Data) and a "walking tricorder" (Geordi).

There were a number of unrealized details in these early character bios that now seem curious:

- Data was assembled by an alien race, his name rhymes with "that-a," and he "usually" avoids the use of contractions.
- Riker "doesn't fully appreciate the female need to be needed."
- Macha-Tasha considers Wesley-Leslie "the childhood friend she never had."
- Picard has visited Tasha's homeworld, which failed due to "environmental disasters and fanatical leaders."
- Riker is privately called William by Picard and Bill by "female friends."
- Geordi's shipboard specialty is listed as "the starship school for children."

Interestingly enough, the evolution of the regular characters went hand in hand with that of the bridge layout, as Justman and Milkis wrote GR that perhaps some of the regular characters needed more efficient on-screen development time. On the eve of the February 4 revisions, Data was to occupy the command circle with Picard and "Ryker," but the two producers realized that Troi would be strengthened both in her shipboard role and as a character if she took the third central seat. From there she could also advise Picard during Riker's absence on away missions.

A second point concerned Tasha (then called Macha) and Geordi, who also were homeless as to duty station. To remedy that, Tasha was made tactical officer and given one of the two forward seats, placed similarly to those in the original series, apparently before the new bridge's tactical horseshoe console was conceived. Geordi is suggested as her partner up front, allowing him character-development exposure that might be lost if the conn and Ops positions were staffed by extras only.

Justman, with Milkis, also proposed that Data be allowed to roam from one aft console to another as an information provider. The android was later stationed at forward Ops to fulfill this function, however, and the rear bridge duty appears to have been Worf's original assignment once he was added to the cast. During the ongoing brainstorming, two ideas were suggested but not adopted: that Data remain aboard during away missions, and that Geordi serve as an ombudsman who would speak to the captain about the concerns of the thousand-plus aboard—a duty eventually and informally seen as Troi's.

Worf, the lone Klingon in Starfleet, almost suffered from Gene Roddenberry's insistence that "no old races"—that is, alien races that appeared in the original Trek—be featured at first in order to distinguish TNG from its predecessor. As noted, Justman was among those lob-bying for a "Klingon marine," a concept the Great Bird finally agreed would show in the most obvious way the difference between this generation and the last—detente and even alliance with the Klingon Empire.

Still, Worf is absent throughout the evolving first-season bible and, though the character was written into the April 13 final draft script for "Farpoint," he is not present in the initial cast portrait that was taken on the Planet Hell set on June 1. Perhaps the first published word of his existence appeared in Gerrold's July 6 *Starlog* column only a month before the series debut.

Faces for the Names

As preliminary casting began in March 1987, one of the earliest of the inevitable staff shake-downs occurred, one that would have long-term implications for the series: producer Eddie Milkis was replaced by Rick Berman.

Having begun in the fall of 1986 as the studio's TNG liaison, Berman came aboard early in 1987 to take over for Milkis, who had decided to check out early on his one-year contract. "By that time I'd decided I had to get back to my other commitments," Milkis said. "But it was a very, very easy transition. Rick was very up-to-the-minute; he was in total sync with us."

Berman had come to Paramount from Warner Brothers in 1984 and performed a succession of studio roles: director of current programming, executive director of dramatic development, and finally vice president of "longform and special projects"—miniseries, TV movies, and then "the new Star Trek." He shared the title of supervising producer with Justman as "Encounter at Farpoint" prepared to shoot.

"I had been Paramount's 'studio guy' for the series for about two weeks when Gene Rodden-berry asked me to lunch, and it was love at first sight," Berman recalled. "He went to the studio and said, 'Can I have him?' and they said yeah."

And that, he added warmly, was the beginning of a relationship with GR that was "very special," although at the time Berman had no idea he'd end up as the "new" Great Bird in a few years.

Berman's track record for quality work and a caring attitude had already been established. He had produced informational projects for TV such as HBO's *What on Earth* and the award-winning PBS special *The Primal Mind*. He was also an Emmy-winning executive producer of ABC's *The Big Blue Marble* from 1977 to 1982.

"He was just perfect," Justman recalled in an interview on March 20, 1992. "We couldn't have found someone better to do the show. He's a perfect executive producer, and a perfect hands-on producer at the same time. My only fear is that he's going to overwork himself!"

So now it was Justman and Berman who set to work casting the regulars, screening their choices with Paramount casting agents before presenting them for GR's approval and eventually a final nod from the studio.

Finally, on May 15, Paramount announced the cast of largely unknown actors who would become "The Next Generation." Most news accounts emphasized LeVar Burton in the role of

Bob Justman's choice for captain, Patrick Stewart (*above, left*), finally won the job; Jonathan Frakes (*above*) received special coaching from the Great Bird himself during auditions; while Brent Spiner (*below*) brought his extensive stage, mime, and musical experience to the role of the android Data.

Geordi La Forge, thanks to his high-profile role in the landmark miniseries *Roots*.

The news reports also mentioned a longtime member of the Royal Shakespeare Company and occasional movie actor, Patrick Stewart, as the new Captain Picard, and Jonathan Frakes, best known for his role in the two *North and South* miniseries, as Riker. The main Associated Press dispatch didn't mention the remaining cast members but did note that the show had been sold in 150 markets and would reach 90 percent of U.S. viewing households.

The story of how Stewart landed the center seat was quick to take its place in TNG lore. As Justman loves to tell it, only weeks into the show's development Justman and his wife attended a dramatic reading at UCLA in which Stewart took part. Inspired by the Englishman's performance, Justman suddenly turned to his wife and said, "I think we have just found our captain!" Later he would say, "I'd never thought of him before, but once I saw him, that was the captain in my mind. I just couldn't shake it. I've never been so sure of anything as I was with that."

Still, Roddenberry had his heart set on a French actor for the role, and Justman knew it. He set up a meeting among Stewart, Milkis, and GR soon after "discovering" the actor, urging that he be included in the cast somehow—and even wrote in an October 17 memo that Stewart at least be considered for the part of Data! After that, the audition process went on, with Justman and later Berman persisting in the campaign to cast Stewart as captain.

"We couldn't find anyone who would satisfy Gene—or ourselves, really—who was good enough," Justman went on. "And finally at the end Gene relented and said, 'Well, let's go with Patrick. He's our best choice.' See, Patrick didn't fit his concept, but once he decided that Patrick was the character, he wrote the character for Patrick!"

Stewart, known in the United States mainly for his role as Sejanus in the highly acclaimed BBC-PBS miniseries *I, Claudius* and for supporting roles in the films *Dune* and *Excalibur*, has said that his naïveté about Trek's impact allowed him to avoid any apprehension about tackling the new show—that is, until a friend floored him by asking how it felt to be playing "an American icon."

Frakes, whose TV credits also included *Bare Essence, Paper Dolls, Falcon Crest,* and *The Doctors,* survived seven auditions in six weeks to finally claim the role, and has credited GR with making him his favorite and doing a little coaching on the side. At the time he was ironically linked with another up-and-coming genre TV star. "I had just finished a stage play with Ron Perlman called *My Life in Art,*" Frakes said in an interview. "I played a goat who became a man and ends up starring on Broadway; Perlman played a theater director. We both got something good out of it—I got *Star Trek* and he got *Beauty and the Beast.*"

Unlike those of any of the rest of the cast, the background stories on Deanna Troi and Tasha Yar came to be inexplicably intertwined with the actors who would play the roles. Londoner Marina Sirtis had been denied meaty roles in her native land because of her good looks. She had been in America barely five months when she tried out for TNG as the security chief, while

At first, Marina Sirtis read for the role of Macha Hernandez, not the Betazoid counselor Deanna Troi.

Denise Crosby—Bing Crosby's granddaughter—was reading for the Troi role.

Berman and Justman liked both actresses in those roles, but eventually GR switched them, deciding Sirtis's appearance was better suited to the empathic alien counselor than to the Latino security chief. "Once we had an 'exotic' for Deanna Troi, it seemed logical that we should have a different physical type for the head of security," Justman recalled. "We didn't want to have another brunette." At that point Macha Hernandez became Natasha Yar, who was given a Ukrainian background to match Crosby's blond hair. The final decision came in early May—just as Sirtis was packing to return home to England to restock her nest egg.

Sirtis's prior credits included *The Wicked Lady* with Faye Dunaway and *Death Wish 3* opposite Charles Bronson and TV guest spots on *Hunter* and *The Adventures of Sherlock Holmes.* Along with numerous TV guest-star credits and a role on *Days of Our Lives,* Crosby, a Hollywood native, had film roles in *48 HRS., Desert Hearts,* and *The Man Who Loved Women,* and she makes no apologies for a funky 1979 pictorial layout in *Playboy* during her "rebellious period."

Brent Spiner, who became Data, grew up in Houston, Texas. He moved up through the off-

When Denise Crosby (*above*) was cast as the *Enterprise's* security chief, the producers changed the character's name to Tasha Yar.

Thanks to his exposure in the miniseries *Roots*, LeVar Burton (*above*) was the most recognizable "name" in the new cast; Gates McFadden (*below*) had worked in dance, mime, and with Jim Henson's Muppets before being cast as Dr. Beverly Crusher.

Broadway and Broadway ranks, winning roles in such musicals as *Sunday in the Park with George, The Three Musketeers,* and *Big River.* He appeared in Woody Allen's *Stardust Memories* and, perhaps most memorably for sitcom fans, as a luckless hick in a recurring role on *Night Court.*

LeVar Burton auditioned largely because of the suggestion of Justman, who had once worked with him in a TV movie pilot called *Emergency Room.* Included in its cast was Gary Lockwood, star of *2001: A Space Odyssey* and the original Trek's second pilot, "Where No Man Has Gone Before." Along with his *Roots* credentials, Burton had hosted the PBS youth series *Reading Rainbow* for five years and in August 1988 would devote a segment of the PBS show to a peek behind the scenes of his famous "other job."

Gates McFadden came to the role of Dr. Beverly Crusher as a New York–based world veteran of the stage, mime, dance, and improvisation. She had also been on *Another World* and *The Edge of Night* and had served as choreographer and director of puppet movement for Jim Henson's *Labyrinth.* A student of mime and theater with Jacque LeCoq in Paris, she later served on several university faculties for theater arts.

Wil Wheaton had been best known as Gordie in *Stand by Me* before becoming young Wesley Crusher.

Michael Dorn brought so much presence to the character of Worf that the Klingon was soon made a regular.

Despite a disastrous first callback that convinced him he'd lost the part, Wil Wheaton, a veteran of film since he began appearing in commercials at age seven, was asked back for another try and wound up landing the role of Wesley Crusher. Highly acclaimed by moviegoers and critics alike as Gordie in Rob Reiner's *Stand by Me*, Wheaton had also appeared in *The Last Starfighter, The Buddy System,* and the telefilm *The Young Harry Houdini.* His voice was heard in *The Secret of NIMH,* and he was a guest on numerous series.

Casting delays didn't help clarify the early unsure status of Worf. Justman recalled that one trim black actor after another was auditioned—blacks being considered mainly to simplify the application of the dark Klingon makeup—before finally settling on the stage-trained Michael Dorn, who was free of any so-called street accent. The part was first conceived as a recurring role in seven of thirteen episodes for a couple of years,

according to Berman, but was expanded after filming and editing of "Farpoint" began and the producers decided that Worf had presence.

"I did not wear makeup," Dorn said of his audition, "but I took on the psychological guise of a Klingon. I walked into Paramount in character. No jokes. No laughing with the other actors. I sat by myself waiting for my interview. When my turn came, I walked in, didn't smile, did the reading, thanked them, and walked right out."[12] And eventually got the job.

A native of tiny Luling, Texas, Dorn was raised in Pasadena, California, and played in rock bands when he was in college, where he became a fan of the original Trek and drifted into acting. He was previously best known for his three years as a costar on *CHiPS.* On the big screen he played a small part as Apollo Creed's bodyguard in *Rocky.* The sash he would initially wear on the new series was the original Trek Klingon prop, explained as an heirloom.

Countdown and Launch

As work began shifting from an emphasis on the show's background to the specifics of the pilot episode, which was due to begin filming on May 29, 1987, members of the creative staff that would make this Trek fly were quickly getting their feet wet. One of the miracle workers who'd come aboard to crank out the magic under TV's many limits was makeup designer Michael Westmore, the 1981 Academy Award winner for *Mask*. On the Monday after his Thursday interview, when Westmore had to decide in an hour's time to give up his lucrative features work to take on TNG's challenges, he hit the ground running and plunged into not only screen tests but such crucial basics as Worf's Klingon look and Data's android appearance.

"Data's went through about twenty-four makeup tests over three days before the camera," Westmore said. "We went through all colors—pink, green, blue, different metallics. The choice got down to the color he is now, and battleship gray"—Justman recalled it as "bilious bluish gray." The makeup designer preferred the gold look that emerged but recalled: "Gene was leaning toward gray, but in talking with him, and Rick Berman, we kinda swayed him in the other direction." It remained relatively unchanged: the famous gold-beige contact lenses, an opalescent base, gold powder, and dyed black hair with a penciled-in hairline that requires an hour in all to apply.

In contrast, the original design for Worf's makeup, a two-and-a-half-hour application that dropped to almost two hours over time, would become only the first step in a search for the best look that subtly evolved over the life of the series; by Season 2 Westmore had broadened his forehead so it would not look so "busy." GR initially wanted Worf's hair short to reflect the no-nonsense military look of Starfleet, Westmore recalled, but from hair designer to hair designer it gradually lengthened over the years until actor Dorn finally got his wish for something different in Season 6 ("Face of the Enemy"/234).

To make TNG's Klingons distinct in general from those of the feature films, Westmore added a nose piece that continues the forehead ridge—a design inspired by dinosaur vertebrae. A unique set of crooked teeth was cast for each speaking actor, but the designer soon came to regret his early policy of casting each forehead with a different ridge pattern.

Meanwhile, other design work still had to be nailed down, such as Geordi's VISOR—Visual Instrument and Sight Organ Replacement—which provided with pain a full-spectrum electronic kind of "sight." After the art staff had spent three months on designs that could work, Michael Okuda one day brought in—as many fans quickly guessed—a girl's plastic hair barrette, and it was a hit! Remanufactured to fit LeVar Burton's face, it still included some of Sternbach's designs.

It was also during this time that the final look, or set dressing, of the various standing sets was refined by Zimmerman and his set decorator, original Trek vet John Dwyer. Echoing a memorial from the first Trek movie, the main wall of the conference lounge (originally dubbed the "ready room" when that set was called the "away cabin") was decorated with half-relief sculptures of the various *Enterprise* namesakes since the World War II American naval carrier, all in fiberglass-covered foam. They remained until after Season 4, when *ST VI* removed the ship wall to re-dress the set, but the stored ships returned in the finale flashback ("All Good Things . . ."/298).

In Picard's office, Zimmerman and Dwyer came up with the tome of Shakespeare (see notes, "Hide and Q"/111), the "batwing" desk, and the wall fishbowl with a rare tropical lionfish soon nicknamed "Livingston," after unit production manager and future producer David Livingston. "David's a super-nice guy. . . . He was trying very hard to be stern and nobody really believed it," recalled Dwyer. "So when this fish comes up and it sees you, up go *its* defenses; it's always doing this and always facing you and it kinda reminded us a little bit of David." Other long-running details included a crystal sailing ship that remained until late in Season 6 (see "The Chase"/246), Probert and Sternbach's original painting of the *Enterprise*, and their model of the *Stargazer*, Picard's prior ship. Their *Stargazer* work model, whose design was not accepted until needed in filming, actually had no stenciled ship name and carried the number NCC-7100—not that of the ship nor, supposedly, the class ship *Constellation*, NCC-1974 (see "The Battle"/110).

As the work of carving out a new series went on, Paramount TV chief Mel Harris in early August spoke via satellite with those at the 170 initial stations that would carry the new series to more than 94 percent of TV households in the United States. Introducing a slick production featuring footage from the yet-unaired pilot and the new sets as background, he described for this business-oriented audience the commercial merchandising, media publicity, and promotional efforts—themed "The 24th Century is about to begin!"—for what he called "some of the best-looking television anywhere on anybody's air this fall."

And the "final secret weapon" in this "unprecedented" effort? A one-minute commercial for TNG that would open some 2 million copies of the hit *Star Trek IV* videocassette, due for release just days before the new series' debut. Harris estimated that this message alone would be seen by over a quarter of all American TV households in just the first month of release.

Who needs an old network, anyway?

The Response to "Farpoint"

For all the pressure, work, and long hours, the result seemed to please most critics. Ed Bark of the *Dallas Morning News*, writing for the Knight-Ridder-Tribune service, thought the pilot "soared with the spirit of the original," coming off as a "fine redefining of a classic and a considerable breakthrough for non-network syndicated television." Don Merrill in *TV Guide* proclaimed that TNG "is a worthy successor" to the original and said GR had "lost none of his ingenuity or his taste in selecting stories." On the other side, while John J. O'Connor in the *New York Times* hoped "that things would get a little livelier in coming weeks," he may have needed to do his homework: in discussing the "new" technology of the show he included the "doors that open and shut effortlessly"!

And then there was the most important judge of all—the audience. Thanks to the lore of the original series, the heavy advance promotional campaign, and maybe even the often skeptical press, "Encounter at Farpoint" beat its prime-time network competition in Los Angeles, Dallas, Seattle, Miami, and Denver. This time around, the audience ratings *would* be on Trek's side, and despite a few rough times early on, the new series would never have to look over its shoulder again.

Notes

1. Interview by David Schonauer, New York Times News Service, March 1988.

2. Schonauer, ibid.

3. "Inside 'Star Trek: The Next Generation,'" Mark A. Altman, *Galactic Journal*, No. 23, Winter 1988, p. 42.

4. Photos of a model of this early design are in *Starlog*, No. 118, May 1987, pp. 14–15.

5. Dan Madsen, *Official Fan Club Magazine*, No. 60, February-March 1988, p. 3.

6. Zimmerman also designed the senior officers' quarters with a window wall that could be tilted to simulate an outer location in either the upper or the lower half of the saucer. His Ten-Forward and observation lounge followed over hiatus, before he and Dwyer's departure for *Star Trek V*.

7. A similar incident occurred with the first optical-effects house used on the original series, Milkis recalled, but at least the models that had been built could be photographed by someone else.

8. David Gerrold, *Starlog*, No. 118, May 87, p. 15.

9. *The Propagator*, March 1987, Vol. 2, Issue 30; Lisa Wahl, editor; Hawthorne, Calif.: Mark "Adam" Baum, contributor, cited copies he'd received from "friend of a friend" employee at an unnamed L.A. talent agency.

10. *OFCM*, No. 70, Oct.-Nov. 1990, p. 4.

11. Ibid.

12. Marc Shapiro, *Starlog*, No. 124, Nov. 1987, p. 50.

ENCOUNTER AT FARPOINT

Production No.: 101–102 (as two separate episodes)/721 (as two-hour TV movie pilot) ▪ Aired: Week of September 28, 1987

Stardate: 41153.7 ▪ Code: ef

Directed by **Corey Allen**
Written by **D. C. Fontana and Gene Roddenberry**
Music by **Dennis McCarthy**

GUEST CAST
Q: **John de Lancie**
Groppler Zorn: **Michael Bell**
Admiral Leonard H. McCoy, retired: **DeForest Kelley**
Conn Ensign: **Colm Meaney**
Mandarin Bailiff: **Cary-Hiroyuki**
Main Bridge Security: **Timothy Dang**
Bandi shopkeeper: **David Erskine**
Female computer ensign: **Evelyn Guerrero**
Drugged military officer: **Chuck Hicks**
Lieutenant Torres: **Jimmy Ortega**

The *U.S.S. Enterprise*, NCC-1701-D, one of the new Galaxy-class starships, is launched with veteran Jean-Luc Picard in command and facing a puzzling first mission. While picking up new crew members from Deneb IV on the rim of explored space, they must figure out how the low-technology Bandi there could have built the gleaming new Farpoint Station they now offer to the Federation for use as a base.

The new ship is almost sidetracked permanently by a being claiming to be part of an all-knowing super race known as "the Q." This Q, who considers humanity too barbarous to expand further, hijacks Picard's command crew and sentences them to death in a kangaroo court. Picard is able to save their lives only by offering to prove humanity's worth during his ship's upcoming mission to Farpoint.

Freed by Q and allowed to arrive there, the crew can find no explanation for the Bandi's mysterious new technology until a vast alien ship appears and opens fire on the old Bandi city. Q tries to goad Picard into firing on the newcomer, but the *Enterprise* away team finds that the attacker is actually a sentient life-form trying to free its mate from the Bandi's clutches.

Initially, Q (John de Lancie) tried to condemn Picard and all humanity.

Unlike original Trek, TNG's pilot depicted many of the characters' first meetings.

Farpoint Station, it turns out, was built entirely by this enslaved creature. As the freed aliens leave the planet, a disappointed Q vows he'll be back to test humanity yet again.

For the first time, a Trek pilot had been presold as a series, shifting the pressure from selling the show to introducing the characters. But that by no means simplified the work of the writers.

Fontana's more action-oriented original outline concerned a being captured by a simian race known as the Annoi. The captors built an orbiting gun platform around the alien, intending to use it to fuel their dreams of expansion, while feeding their prisoner just enough of the mineral balmine to keep it alive. The USS *Starseeker* arrives with the *Enterprise,* but is destroyed after opening fire when the Annoi demand the two crews beam down, surrender, and become balmine gatherers. As part of an away team sent to

DeForest Kelley's one-hundred-thirty-seven-year-old "Admiral McCoy" provides a surprising and poignant send-off on TNG's maiden voyage.

disable the platform, Troi makes mental contact with the captive entity and persuades it to crash-land on the planet, where her people will help it to free itself by leading a prisoners' revolt. In later drafts the people would come to be called the Annae and the starship opening would be deleted, but many of the plot points and character introductions can be seen in this earliest concept.

Gene Roddenberry added the Q subplot, partly because of indecision over the length of the pilot. "Gene wanted an hour show, but the studio wanted a two-hour movie," as originally announced, Berman recalls. "They tried to get him to agree to a ninety-minute show as a compromise, but they eventually won out." According to Justman, both the ship separation sequence and a touching scene in which an aged Admiral McCoy meets Data were a help in filling out what Fontana had intended to be a ninety-minute script.

"As I had feared, the show was woefully short when we cut it together," Justman said. He added that director Corey Allen's typically faster-than-usual scene pacing increased their difficulties. "In order to make the show two hours we had to skillfully edit it and cut it not as tight as we ordinarily would for pace. So at times that two hours drags a bit here and there.

Despite that, the final version is missing a short scene that was included in the final draft script dated April 13. In that scene Riker is introduced to Geordi and an enthusiastic ensign named Sawyer Markham. Riker overhears the ensign calling Picard "the old burrhog" when the *Enterprise* is overdue.

Other slight changes from the final draft script: Torres, the crewman frozen by Q, was initially named Graham; Troi, too, was frozen by Q after rushing to Tasha's aid; and Picard's tag line, "Let's see what's out there," was added.

The dates of the new United Nations and its demise are initially 2016 and 2049, changed to 2036 and 2079 during filming. Though sixties Trek indicated that Earth avoided a nuclear war, references to a "post-atomic horror" here would be cemented further ("Up the Long Ladder"/144, "A Matter of Time"/209). Deneb IV hosted a wild shore leave for Kirk and Gary Mitchell in the second Trek pilot.

The Fontana-written McCoy scene is in the final draft script, though the "old country doctor" is given the age of 147, not 137, and is identified merely as "Admiral"—presumably to keep the cameo scene a secret, and it largely worked.

"It was a late addition," Justman said later of the McCoy scene. "I think it had been on Gene's mind, and he invited De to lunch and he said, 'How would you feel about it?'—expecting De to say no—and De said, 'I'd be honored.' And not only that, but he refused to take any more than SAG scale [Screen Actors Guild base salary]. He could have held us up for a lot of money, but he didn't. And it really got to me; it was a beautiful, beautiful scene."

"I just wanted scale, to let it be my way of saying thank-you to Gene for the many good things he has done for me," Kelley said later.

Actor Colm Meaney, who didn't get a regular role in the original casting call but won the role of the battle bridge conn ensign, would return once ("Lonely Among Us"/108) before landing, in Season 2, the role of Chief Miles O'Brien and, in 1993, joining spinoff *Deep Space Nine*. The Dublin native and Irish National Theatre vet had stage roles in London, New York, and Los Angeles and played an English thief on *One Life to Live*. After

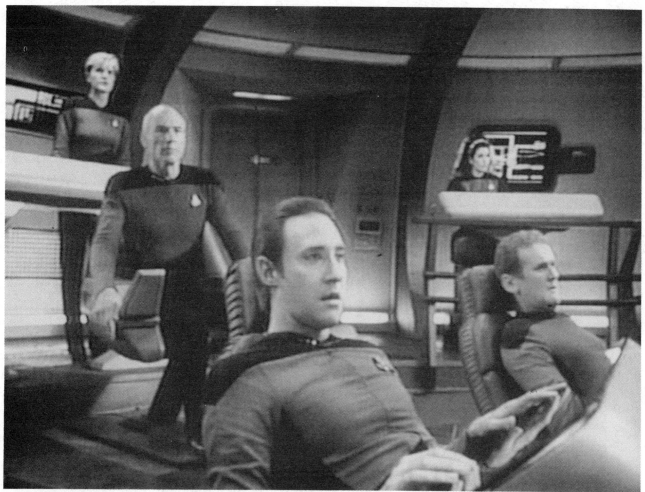

Though his role remained nameless for one and a half seasons, Colm Meaney's O'Brien appeared on the Battle Bridge in "Farpoint."

he settled in Hollywood, his later film career included *Far and Away, The Commitments,* and *The Snapper.*

The first TNG guest star and soon to be its first recurring guest, John de Lancie had acted since age fourteen and attended Juilliard, even though he didn't take up the profession full-time until the late seventies. De Lancie collected a good share of guest roles in film and TV, but he achieved his widest fame thanks to a three-year stint as villain-turned-comic inventor Eugene on the daytime drama *Days of Our Lives.* Berman later recalled that it was Leonard Maizlish, GR's attorney, who first recommended the actor. Also, Michael Bell later appeared in "The Homecoming" and "The Maquis, Part II" on spinoff *Deep Space Nine.*

Already being pumped up as the new alien threat, the Ferengi, too, are mentioned, although they would not be seen until the third regular episode aired (and the fifth filmed).

One scene in "Farpoint" was shot on location in Los Angeles' famous Griffith Park: the scene at the holodeck stream where Riker and a soggy Wes meet Data.

And the cannibalizing of old *Trek* sets continued: part of the

Klingon Bird of Prey sickbay from *Star Trek III* was turned upside down to become part of Zorn's council room wall.

Interestingly enough, the end credits were on a crawl but would be listed on cards screen by screen for the remainder of TNG's run. Also, the opening credits do not include the name of the character along with each actor's name, as they would later.

For trivia's sake, aside from Troi's appearance in it here, the final bridge scene shows Tasha as the only other regular of either sex to wear the "skant" unisex miniskirt uniform; Troi would return to regulation wear by a fluke in Season 6 ("Chain of Command, Part I"/236). And, indicating that the time frame of the series was still not set, Data refers to himself as a member of the "Starfleet Class of '78," but his graduation date is later set via data screen as 2345 ("Conundrum"/214*).

---

*Note: Numbers following episode titles are production numbers: episodes in this book will be discussed in production order.

FIRST SEASON

After its successful launch, TNG faced

the even larger task of staying on schedule while fleshing out the new mythos, meeting all expectations, and silencing its naysayers. Although the budget would be upped to $1.5 million per episode by year's end, the season would prove to be a shakedown cruise for the 129 full-time actors, producers, crew, staff, and designers aboard.

Filming began on July 6, 1987, for the very first hour-long episode, "The Naked Now," only ten days after "Farpoint" wrapped and with very few alterations in the series' infant format. One change concerned the character of Deanna Troi. Deemed too "loose" and cheerleaderlike in her skant, she was given a nonregulation uniform and a severe bun hairstyle. At the same time, Troi's telepathic abilities were softened to mere empathy with most species—a lessening blamed on her half-human genes—to avoid the emotional soliloquies even the actress cringed over in "Farpoint."

Still, the writing staff would continue to find the Troi char-

The first season "Smoky Bridge" cast shot (*opposite*)—this time with Worf.

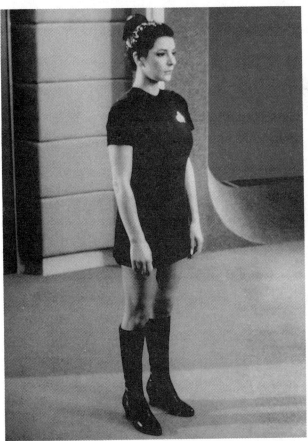

An unused post-pilot Troi look: both the "bun" *and* the "skant."

acter one of the hardest to write for. According to Marina Sirtis, the character was almost dropped in November after Troi went unused in four shows: "Hide and Q" (111), "Datalore" (114), "11001001" (116), and "Heart of Glory" (120).[1]

Despite those who complained of a copycat format and episodes, ratings began to rise as soon as the series hit the air. "The Naked Now," the first regular installment, would continue the pilot's success by taking its time slot in Boston, Denver, and Houston, according to A. C. Nielsen. *TV Guide* reported on December 26 that thirteen ABC affiliates and two with CBS had dumped their network programming to carry TNG in prime time, and perennial sixth-place Chicago station WPWR-TV jumped to the number two slot at 6:00 P.M. on Saturdays with TNG—an 1,100 percent ratings increase.

However, because TNG was syndicated, its

success would take some time to catch the attention of both the industry and the public at large since the series never showed up in the weekly Nielsen Top 10 lists. For a nationwide gauge, a composite had to be compiled by weighing the demographic figures in each market against those of other series.

The studio reported that fan mail was running 95 percent in favor of the new show, while the Colorado-based *"Star Trek: The Official Fan Club"* reported a 90 percent approval rate in mail from members. So much for the worry that TNG couldn't hold its own without rehiring the original actors or recasting the 1960s roles. This was a great relief for Paramount and all concerned, considering their investment of money *and* Trek's good name.

But then reports began to surface regarding the turnover in the writing staff that had been under way since before cameras rolled on "Farpoint." After Milkis's exit, Gerrold left in May of 1987, before weekly production began, although he received a "program consultant" credit through the seventh show filmed, "Lonely Among Us" (108). At the time he said he was leaving to write and produce a four-hour CBS science-fiction miniseries called *Trackers*, but later Gerrold let it be known he was upset about "promises made and not kept." He was appar-

Troi's first-year "severe" look.

Data and Worf, successors to Spock's logical and alien mystiques, in a scene cut from "Coming of Age."

ently referring to the shelving of an allegorical script he'd written about AIDS, called "Blood and Fire."

Fontana became the next in a long line of writers who grew upset with the extensive rewrites on this incarnation of Trek. She remained through October and was listed in the credits until her tenure ended completely after "The Big Goodbye" (113).

For the last top member of the old guard that had originally breathed life into TNG (aside from GR), departure was a health matter. Justman had signed on for a year, but unlike Milkis he had included a second-year pickup option in his contract. Midway through season one, though, he let it be known he wanted to reduce his work load. "I was still motivated, it was a good show, but I was just working myself into a dither; I was very tired and very cross," he said later. And he soon grew angry: he demanded and received a front-page apology from *Daily Variety*—the first in the trade paper's history—a day after it ran a story saying he'd been fired amid a "big shakeup at Star Trek."

The studio agreed to his request to cut back to handling only casting, rewrites, and editing in a consulting-producer role for the last eight

shows of the season, beginning with "Coming of Age" (119). With that, the staff was restructured. Berman received the title of co-executive producer, Maurice Hurley became the new writing producer, and David Livingston was promoted to line producer after having been hired by Justman as unit production manager for the pilot. Hurley, who had come aboard as a writer-producer at the start of weekly production with "The Naked Now" (103), left Universal to come to TNG after having worked on staff during the debut years of *Miami Vice* and *The Equalizer*.

Carrying the title of producer were writers Lewin, who stayed all season long, and Wright, who remained on staff from the pilot through "Skin of Evil" (122) in January 1988, when he left to become creative consultant on Paramount's *The War of the Worlds*.

Johnny Dawkins was credited as story editor in "The Naked Now," "Code of Honor," "Where No One Has Gone Before," and "Too Short a Season" (103, 104, 106, and 112). The title then went unused until the restructuring caused by Justman's leaving, when Richard Manning and Hans Beimler took over the chore until the end of the season (and later returned to serve in a similar capacity during the show's run). In the interim, Greg Strangis worked as creative consultant on "The Big Goodbye," "Datalore," and "Angel One" (113–115) before he, too, left to develop *The War of the Worlds*.

This revolving door for writers began to be blamed for the perceived lack of continuity on the series. Though most fans stayed patient, as reflected in the ratings, some criticized the lack of growth and interplay between the characters, as well as the thin or too crowded story lines.

After his departure a year later, Hurley talked about the story-writing system, which he had tried to change during his tenure. This system included a pattern of memo-writing among the story staff. "In the beginning there was a lot of [plot] clutter," Hurley said. "Too many ideas being thrown into one script. . . . There was a tendency to do a real quick wrap-up. Too much in the bag, trying to fill the bag too full."

"We were trying hard to put our house in order during the first season," Berman recalled.

"The writers were being rewritten by Gene, and there was a lot of tumult because people didn't know where they stood."

Why so many story problems? The most obvious reason was the sheer enormity of developing stories that were entertaining and thought-provoking while staying true to GR's unique unifying vision of Trek. The most frustrating thing for writers was his ban on interpersonal conflicts among the crew, based on his belief that such petty and ego-driven problems would be a thing of the past by the twenty-fourth century.

"Yes, there was a lot of rewriting done and it bruised some egos," Hurley would say later, chalking it up to typical first-year growing pains. "But I think it was really necessary."[2]

Even Hurley professed his disbelief in what he called GR's "wacky doodle" hope-filled future vision, but he acknowledged that viewpoint was what defined Trek. "You suspend your own feelings and your own beliefs and you get with his vision—or you get *rewritten*."[3] Ironically he would soon find himself clashing with more than one writer over just how to interpret that vision.

Actually, the original *Star Trek* had undergone exactly the same tortuous search for stability during its formative year—pages rewritten the day and even the hour before they were to shoot, and so on—but the older series spent its lifetime crying for attention while it remained largely unexamined under the microscope of fans and the Hollywood press that later magnified everything that was done—or rumored to have been done—on TNG.

Eventually, as an embryonic continuity eventually surfaced, the revolving door slowed down—or at least seemed to. Hannah Louise Shearer, teleplay writer on "When the Bough Breaks" (118), was named to the new position of executive story editor beginning with that episode. Two shows later, Tracy Tormé—a *Saturday Night Live* and *SCTV* veteran with TNG credits already on "The Big Goodbye" (113) and "Haven" (105)—was added in that same position. Shearer, whose background included producing *Emergency!*, *Knight Rider*, and *Quincy* and writing for *Cagney and Lacey* and *MacGyver*, served with Tormé through the rest of the season.

But delays due to last-minute rewrites took

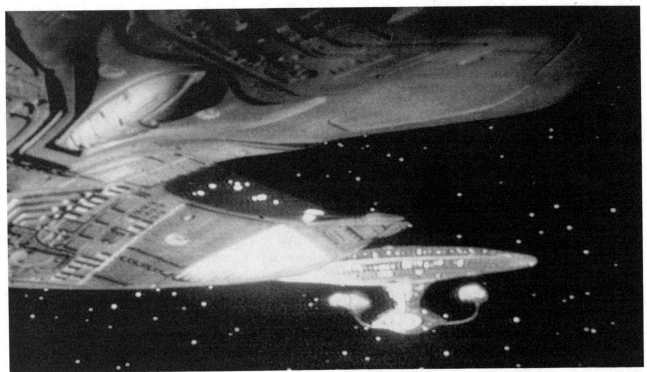

Andy Probert designed the underbelly of the Ferengi "Marauder" with its own (as-yet-unseen) shuttlecraft.

up only a part of each TNG episode's production schedule. Each show requires about sixteen weeks from the commitment to develop a story idea to the time its post-production optical effects, music, and titles are added, and each in turn overlaps the others in various phases of evolution. On any one day, according to Berman, one show is being filmed live, writing or design work is in process on upcoming scripts, and segments already shot are being edited and having FX, sound, music, and titles added.

A TNG director usually has only seven days to shoot about fifty-five pages of script. That means shooting eight or nine pages a day. The design staff gets about two weeks' notice on a script prior to shooting—or, as Zimmerman put it, "ten working days to do the thinking, drawing, construction, and get it ready to shoot." For the producers during the first season, that meant days stretching from 5:00 A.M. to 9:00 or 10:00 P.M., while the actors and stage crews were at it from 6:00 A.M. until 6:00 to 10:00 P.M. or later.

Meanwhile, Legato realized that the original idea of a library of optical-effects shots wouldn't save much time and money after all. "The plan was to take the library shots from ILM and add about five per show," he explained. "That was probably a little naive. . . . Then the pilot needed two hundred and ten FX shots, the second show had seventy-five, the third eighty, and so on, so by the sixth or seventh show we found it was cheaper just to 'trick' [custom-shoot] each one out."

Eventually, dropping the library concept allowed more movement in FX scenes, because elements freshly photographed—a ship, a planet, a nebula—didn't have to be static to match one element that had been shot for an earlier show. "Since we're filming [what amounts to] a feature a week, you need specific shots—a ship thrown into orbit, a Wizard of Oz head," Legato explained. "If you want to do it right and do it effectively, you've got to shoot it and do exactly what you want done. It's really less work and more powerful visually and dramatically."

And less work would quickly become crucial, as the shorthanded visual-effects chief nearly drove himself to exhaustion by handling the stu-

dio work solo through the pilot and the first nine episodes. "It got to where they'd finish live shooting at ten P.M., I'd go from there to work in the lab until five A.M., and they'd be ready to start live shooting again in another hour." Legato sighed. "We weren't just doing the work—we were learning *how* to do the work."

The last straw came when "The Last Outpost" (107) was moved up in the production schedule with 110 effects shots, right after the backbreaking visuals required for "Where No One Has Gone Before" (106).

"The effects budgets were running $100,000 over and we had a meeting to discuss why," Legato recalled. "I finally said, 'Look, this is costing $2,000 an hour just for me to sit here.' They said, 'How do you figure that?' and I told them that's how much the overtime and lab cost with me sitting there and not out working. Finally an executive said, 'Well it's obvious you need more help!' and that's how we got Dan!"

Dan Curry, mirroring Legato's role, would begin on the tenth hour-long show filmed, "Too Short a Season," (112) and alternate episodes with him to split up the work load. For the second season, each was promoted to visual effects supervisor and given his own associate. Gary Hutzel was hired to work with Legato, and Ron B. Moore became Curry's assistant.

About that time Legato also at last persuaded the producers to let him head a second-unit camera crew to film the special live-action shots needed for FX interfacing—like those before the blue screen in which live action will be mated with background paintings or visuals, and close-up inserts of computer displays and hands on controls. "If a director shoots something and doesn't understand how the visual effects tie in, you have to go back and repair that, and it costs more anyway," he noted.

Practically all the animated computer displays are matted in because the screens are usually not bright enough to be seen. Some live action is done on set, though—as when a finger traces a path shown by the display. Created by Okuda with Macintosh animation software, the sequences, like other second-unit shooting, use actors' photo doubles to save time and money.

Because of what they had to accomplish every week, TNG's visual-effects staff soon became pioneers in video special effects equipment and techniques for the entire industry. For example, Hutzel developed an inexpensive and quicker method of filming revolving planets by using slides of them projected on a dome, providing five or six finished sequences in an hour.

Regardless of how it stacks up against the original show in other areas, TNG wins hands down in series continuity. While *Star Trek* did a miraculous job for its day in keeping its back story intact, that effort simply pales next to the effort put forth by Sternbach, Okuda, and Probert (before he left at year's end to join Disney's *Imagineering* subsidiary) in matters of historical and technological consistency. They began injecting and describing what might be called preemptive backgrounding, or the anticipation of background needs, before the demand for it cropped up in a particular script. Okuda and Sternbach would later be rewarded for their efforts and officially given the added title of technical consultants with early script input.

By year's end, TNG would finish with a 10.6 rating—or about 9.4 million households watching from 210 local stations—and rank first among eighteen- to forty-nine-year-olds, the prime demographic group sought by advertisers. Beyond the United States and Canada, in eight European and Asian countries where first-run airing was initially restricted, TNG picked up a direct $2 million in videocassette sales by its first summer hiatus.

Though comparisons to the old show persisted, by season's end TNG had developed an identity all its own. *TV Guide* writer Gary D. Christenson compared the differences between the two Treks with the differences in his generation of Americans: "*Star Trek* depicted us in reckless youth, with a starship captain who tamed space as vigorously as we laid claim to the future. . . . *Star Trek: The Next Generation* reveals the child grown—a little more polished, but also more complacent. And if there's a bit of gray and a wrinkle or two, so much the better."[4]

THE NAKED NOW

Production No.: 103 ■ Aired: Week of October 5, 1987	
Stardate: 41209.2 ■ Code: nn	

Directed by **Paul Lynch**
Teleplay by **J. Michael Bingham**
Story by **John D.F. Black and J. Michael Bingham**

GUEST CAST
Chief Engineer Sarah MacDougal: **Brooke Bundy**
Assistant Engineer Jim Shimoda: **Benjamin W.S. Lum**
Transporter Chief: **Michael Rider**
Kissing crewman: **Kenny Koch**
Conn: **David Rehan**
Engineering crewman: **Skip Stellrecht**

A hauntingly familiar disease is unleashed aboard the *Enterprise* after it makes contact with the *Tsiolkovsky*, a now-dead research ship that had been investigating a nearby star's collapse. Those afflicted act intoxicated and mentally unstable.

As Dr. Crusher races to find a cure, the disease's symptoms ring a bell with Riker, who goes looking through decades of records with Data until they realize that the original *Enterprise* encountered much the same disease.

But the old cure doesn't work, and before Dr. Crusher can discover why, her afflicted son helps disable computer control, putting the ship at the mercy of the nearby collapsing star. Eventually almost the entire crew—including the doctor, Picard, Yar, and Data—come down with the virus.

Finally Data and Chief Engineer MacDougal hold off illness long enough to subdue Wesley; the android then uses his speed and dexterity to restore the computer memory in a desperate race against time to get the ship functioning in time to avoid a head-on collision from a chunk of the former star.

After a working cure is finally discovered, the crew ruefully gets on with life.

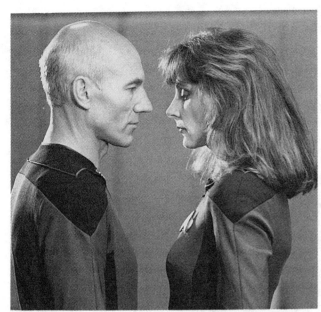

The Tsiolkovsky virus: a close call for Picard and Crusher.

This episode, filmed in six straight days through a Saturday to refine the new work schedule, sparked the first fan outcries that many TNG plots were being lifted from original-series stories. In this case, however, that was exactly what GR wanted: a story, like "The Naked Time" of 1966, in which the wants and needs of new characters could be quickly revealed to a new audience. Black, listed here as coauthor, wrote the original; J. Michael Bingham is Fontana's pseudonym. "It was an homage, not a copy," Berman said of the episode. "We even mentioned the old *Enterprise* and its remedy, which doesn't help our crew . . . after all."

This era's story roots go back to the opening thirteen pages of an unfinished teleplay GR began called "Revelations." The same opening points are included, except that Geordi makes a move on Tasha, who is the next to get the *Tsiolkovsky* virus even though she brushes him off. Fontana initially turned out a teleplay with a harder edge; Data turns down Tasha's advances but becomes a "perfect little boy" so as to become human a là Pinocchio; Troi bemoans an empath's lack of mental privacy among hundreds of humans; Riker fears a lonely captain's career; and Picard worries over the families he has aboard his ship.

Brooke Bundy's onetime appearance as Chief Engineer MacDougal began a season-long parade of characters in that position. Rider began a three-show stint as the first regular yet unnamed transporter chief, then a security guard; the Picard-Crusher tension would go unresolved until Season 6 ("Attached"/ 260).

Beginning an Okuda tradition, a bridge dedication plaque identifies the *Tsiolkovsky* as an Oberth-class vessel (the miniature a minor re-dress of the *U.S.S. Grissom* in *Star Trek III*), launched from a descendant of today's Russian Baikonur Cosmodrome; little did anyone know then how dated the USSR reference would soon be! A copy of the plaque was sent to the Kaluga Museum in the hometown of the starship's namesake, space pioneer Konstantin Tsiolkovsky.

CODE OF HONOR

Production No.: 104   ■   Aired: Week of October 12, 1987
Stardate: 41235.25   ■   Code: ch

Directed by **Russ Mayberry**
Written by **Katharyn Powers & Michael Baron**

GUEST CAST
Lutan: **Jessie Lawrence Ferguson**
Yareena: **Karole Selmon**
Hagon: **James Louis Watkins**
Transporter Chief: **Michael Rider**

A plague on Styris IV sends the *Enterprise* to the only known source for an organic vaccine, Ligon II.

Negotiations go smoothly for the vaccine until the planet's chief, Lutan, suddenly kidnaps Yar after being impressed by both her beauty and her strength. To get her back, Picard must abide by the Prime Directive and the Ligonians' strict patience and code of honor—and Yar must combat Lutan's current "First One" wife, who now feels her honor challenged, in a fight to the death.

Picard tries every diplomatic trick in the book, but he is finally left to hope that Yar can score a hit in the poison-tipped glavin combat. She does, and the fighters are beamed aboard, where Dr. Crusher concocts an antidote to the Ligonian poison.

Not only is honor served and Yar rescued, but wife Yareena's "death" satisfies tradition. Alive in reality, though, Yareena transfers her land and property rights to Lutan's lieutenant Hagon when she claims him as her new husband, in effect dethroning the chief. But Lutan takes it all in stride with Ligonian pride and calls the orderly transfer far more "civilized" than the *Enterprise* crew's society.

Amused but wiser, the crew warps out to help fight the plague.

Writer Katharyn Powers, an original-series fan and a veteran of series such as *Kung Fu, Logan's Run,* and *Fantastic Journey,* had known D. C. Fontana for some time when she got invited to pitch

Yar fights to the "death" against Yareena (Karole Selmon).

story ideas for the new show. She and writing partner Michael Baron initially tried to base the Ligonian "honor is all" culture on that of the Japanese Samurai, using a reptilian race called the Tellisians.

Not everyone was pleased with the results, though. Tracy Tormé, an eventual writing staffer, later said he was embarrassed by the show's "1940s tribal Africa" view of blacks and by the fight's uncanny resemblance to the win-or-die battle between Kirk and Spock in "Amok Time" in 1967.

The yellow-on-black grid of the empty holodeck wall made its debut here, but a phonelike programming unit used by Tasha—a seeming redundancy with vocal commands—was never seen again. Tried here and once more—in "The Last Outpost" (107)— before being scrapped was the building of Picard's extreme pride in his Gallic heritage to the point of humorous defensiveness in his banter with Data—an echo of the original series' recurring "Russian joke" with young Chekov, who believed his motherland was the home of all discoveries and inventions.

Fred Steiner made a onetime musical contribution to TNG with this episode, the only composer from the original series to do so.

Haven

Production No.: 105   ■   Aired: Week of November 30, 1987
Stardate: 41294.5   ■   Code: hv

Directed by **Richard Compton**
Teleplay by **Tracy Tormé**
Story by **Tracy Tormé and Lan O'Kun**

GUEST CAST
Lwaxana Troi: **Majel Barrett**
Wyatt Miller: **Rob Knepper**
Victoria Miller: **Nan Martin**
Steven Miller: **Robert Ellenstein**
Mr. Homn: **Carel Struycken**
Valeda Innis: **Anna Katarina**
Wrenn: **Raye Birk**
Ariana: **Danitza Kingsley**
Transporter Chief: **Michael Rider**

At planet Haven, Picard and his crew meet up with Lwaxana Troi, Deanna's mother, who blusters aboard when her late husband's best friends, the Millers, insist on seeing the childhood genetic bonding vows consummated between Deanna and their son, Wyatt.

Deanna dutifully agrees and comes to find Wyatt a good companion, much to *imzadi* Riker's confusion. Wyatt is puzzled because Deanna is not the blonde he has seen in visions since childhood.

The wedding plans go on despite the mothers-in-law's comical feuding—until a number of plague-ridden Tarellians, long thought dead, show up at Haven. Wyatt, a doctor, finds the blonde girl of his visions is a Tarellian; she had pictured him in her dreams for years as well without knowing why.

Wyatt apologizes to Deanna and shocks his parents by following his perceived destiny at last: joining the Tarellians to help them and his love find a cure.

Picard is glad to get his counselor back and to see Lwaxana's flustering flirtations end.

Troi ponders the marriage her mother (Majel Barrett) helped arrange.

This episode, which barely resembles Lan O'Kun's original story called "Love Beyond Time and Space," became the ticket that won Tracy Tormé a place on the writing team. After impressing the staff without making a story sale, the son of singer Mel Tormé was contacted in a last-ditch try to save O'Kun's concept. Tormé played up the in-fighting between the families to a caustically comic intensity that was later softened and edited out, to his regret.

Majel Barrett was hardly a newcomer to the Trek universe, having portrayed Nurse Christine Chapel in the 1960s series and Dr. Chapel in the first and fourth movies—and having been Gene Roddenberry's wife for nearly twenty years. Here she began what turned into a yearly visit as the "Auntie Mame of the Galaxy" and the bane of Picard's existence as well as her daughter's.

Troi here calls Riker "Bill"—the second (after "The Naked Now") and last time any of the regulars does so in the series. This also marks the last time she would use the Betazoid word for "beloved," *imzadi,* until the end of the second season (in "Shades of Gray"/148)—a barometer for the direction their relationship would take.

In one of the loveliest coincidences of Trek trivia, Richard Compton found himself directing this episode exactly twenty years to the day after appearing in a one-line walk-on role on the old show—as Lieutenant Washburn, a member of Scotty's team trying to repair the dead *Constellation* in "The Doomsday Machine."

Where No One Has Gone Before

Production No.: 106 ■ Aired: Week of October 26, 1987
Stardate: 41263.1 ■ Code: wn

Directed by **Rob Bowman**
Written by **Diane Duane and Michael Reaves**

GUEST CAST
Kosinski: **Stanley Kamel**
Traveler: **Eric Menyuk**
Maman Picard: **Herta Ware**
Lieutenant Commander Argyle: **Biff Yeager**
Crew member: **Charles Dayton**
Ballerina: **Victoria Dillard**

The brave new warp theories of a supposedly brilliant Starfleet consultant go awry when the "expert" plunges the ship first into a neighboring galaxy and then into a dimension where the physical and mental worlds converge.

The trouble turns out not to be with expert Kosinski's theories but with his mysteriously meek "assistant," whose race can travel among dimensions and times.

The strain of propelling the entire ship, though, has put the so-called Traveler gravely near death—threatening to strand the *Enterprise* forever. And in this nether-space, crew members begin seeing alternate realities that threaten their sanity as well.

Finally it is discovered that Wesley's friendship has a curative effect on the Traveler; he strengthens the alien just enough to get the ship home.

Before he does so, though, the Traveler advises Picard secretly of Wesley's prodigious abilities and urges him to not let them go undeveloped. With a proud mother standing by, Wesley is promoted to acting ensign by Picard, and his Academy training begins.

Even though producer Maurice Hurley did numerous uncredited rewrites on their script, Duane and Reaves's initial story survives as adapted from her Kirk-era novel, *The Wounded Sky,* in which an unusual alien resembling a glass spider performs warp experiments that mix physics with metaphysics and strand the original *Enterprise* far from home.

In the original teleplay, Kosinski was responsible for both the warp effects and the accident; he also had a son who felt he spent more time on his career than with him. The crew was in awe of Kosinski in the original script, and the hallucinations were even more bizarre, including the image of Jack Crusher appearing to both Picard and Beverly. The starship reappeared within a monoblock, or cosmological egg, and in exploding it to escape, the starship in effect caused the birth of a new universe. Significantly, the *Enterprise* has been missing for six days and the captain orders that the next day be observed as a day of rest!

The Traveler role was a consolation prize of sorts for Eric Menyuk, who only weeks before had come close to winning the part of Data. An original Trek fan at age six, he picked up drama in college and went from Boston-area theater to TV guest work in *Hill Street Blues, Matlock, L.A. Law,* and *Cheers,* among others.

Justman has said that hiring twenty-eight-year-old Rob Bowman to direct this segment was one of his proudest achievements on the show; Bowman was called in to replace Daniel Petrie, who dropped out to film the movie *Mystic Pizza.* It was a terrifying time for young Bowman, who wanted to make a good impression on his first assignment and overcome any doubts about his youth. Once he got his script, he worked for twenty days before filming began. He walked around the sets in off-hours, using storyboards and blocking out scenes to prepare his action lines and camera angles. Bowman went on to become one of the infant series' most prolific directors.

Wesley and the Traveler
(Eric Menyuk).

The episode's dazzling optical effects were quite literally homemade, Legato recalled. "We got the usual kind of vague explanation for the end-of-the-universe visuals in the script," he said. "But I did it simply, at home in my basement, with water. I had always noticed water reflections on the wall, so I shot multiple layers of that through dissolved Mylar bits. It was peculiar and bizarre. And I used little suspended moving Christmas tree lights for the little blinkies."

Worf's pet targ is actually a Russian wild boar named Emmy Lou, wearing a Theiss-designed original. "That pig smelled horrid," laughed Justman. "A sweet-sour, extremely pungent odor. I showered and showered, and it took me a week to get rid of it!"

Biff Yeager debuts here as the longest-running chief engineer of the first season, although Riker introduces him as "one of our chief engineers"; Dennis "Danger" Madalone, seen here as the sciences division ensign terrorized by his own self-conjured fire, is a stuntman who began getting screen credit as stunt coordinator in Season 3 and portrayed various unlucky crew members. Picard's mother picked up a first name in "Chain of Command, Part II" (237); Herta Ware played Jack Gilford's dying wife in *Cocoon*. Menyuk, who was featured in 1994's *The Air Up There*, returned as the Traveler twice later ("Remember Me"/179, "Journey's End"/272), while Kosinski's unexplained square rank pip was never seen again.

THE LAST OUTPOST

Production No.: 107 ■ Aired: Week of October 19, 1987
Stardate: 41386.4 ■ Code: lo

Directed by **Richard Colla**
Teleplay by **Herbert Wright**
Story by **Richard Krzemien**

GUEST CAST
Letek: **Armin Shimerman**
Mordoc: **Jake Dengel**
Kayron: **Tracey Walter**
Portal: **Darryl Henriques**
DaiMon Tarr: **Mike Gomez**

History is overshadowed by danger as the *Enterprise* readies for the first Federation contact with the Ferengi, the supercapitalists of the galaxy, while chasing one of the vessels to retrieve an outpost's stolen T-9 energy converter.

The chase ends abruptly when both ships find themselves immobilized over an unknown planet, which turns out to be an outpost of the long-dead Tkon Empire. A joint mission to inves-

The first meeting with Ferengi: Armin Shimerman (rear), Jake Dengel (left), and Tracey Walter.

tigate is arranged, but the Ferengi double-cross Riker's team and stun them.

An automated Tkon "portal" guard emerges from his centuries-old sleep and challenges the two sides. The childish Ferengi tire him, but Portal is finally impressed by Riker's wisdom and Federation ethics, and he frees both ships.

This ambitious yet uneven introduction of the Ferengi unfortunately failed to live up to all the advance buildup about the "new alien threat." As developed by Herb Wright and Gene Roddenberry, the Ferengi debuted in fur wraparound outerwear and used blue energy-bolt whips that were never seen again after the unsatisfying steel spring became an eleventh-hour fix when the original design was not delivered on time to use. According to Zimmerman, the Ferengi's poor eyesight accounts for their beady eyes and brightly lit ship interiors; to compensate, their huge ears help provide better hearing[5]—and an erogenous zone (Ménage à Troi"/172, "Chain of Command, Part I"/236).

Their ship, inspired by a horseshoe crab on Wright's desk, was designed by Andy Probert (who added the forward "earwig" pincers) and built by Greg Jein.

Richard Krzemien's initial story concerned a planetary caretaker named Dilo, precursor to Portal, as a latter-day Rip Van Winkle who slept while his empire fell. Riker's concluding request to beam over several replicated Chinese finger puzzles to the pesky Ferengi echoes Scotty's solution at the end of "The Trouble with Tribbles": sending the prolific fur balls detested by Klingons to their ship. The Tkon Empire seal that appears in the revolving holographic display is also seen as the blade design on Portal's staff.

By 1993, greater things in Trek awaited most of the Ferengi-playing actors here: Walter and Gomez resurfaced in "Rascals" (233), while Shimerman—after a run as Paskall on *Beauty and the Beast* and an uncredited TNG debut ("Haven"/104)—would go on to become the first actor to play a second Ferengi ("Peak Performance"/147) and the first regular Ferengi anywhere as Quark on eventual spinoff *Deep Space Nine*. Also, Henriques would play Romulan ambassador Nanclus in *ST VI*.

Mike Okuda's Ferengi insignia stems from a design literally meaning "dog eat dog," colored green for greed, envy, and the color of money. Also debuting here, Michael Westmore added, is the system by which the insignia tattooed on a military Ferengi's right lobe roughly denotes rank: from no "rocker" hashmarks up to three.

LONELY AMONG US

Production No.: 108 ■ Aired: Week of November 2, 1987
Stardate: 41249.3 ■ Code: la

Directed by **Cliff Bole**
Teleplay by **D. C. Fontana**
Story by **Michael Halperin**

GUEST CAST
Ssestar: **John Durbin**
First Security Guard: **Colm Meaney**
Assistant Chief Engineer Singh: **Kavi Raz**

The spat between two neighboring planets would be almost comical if it weren't for the *Enterprise*'s serious task of transporting their ambassadors to Parliament, a UFP diplomatic outpost.

En route there, the ship passes through a strange energy cloud, and puzzling malfunctions start to occur. Worf and Dr. Crusher then show bizarre personality shifts while attending to them.

After an assistant engineer is murdered while inspecting the malfunctions, Data adopts the methods of Sherlock Holmes. But Troi's hypnosis of Crusher and Worf reveals that they have accidentally taken aboard a long-lonely life-force. The creature is now looking for a host body to return it to the energy cloud.

The crew is shocked when the being chooses Picard as its host. After apologizing for the damage it caused, the alien has Picard resign his command and divert the ship back to the cloud—where it beams out as pure energy.

Just as Riker is about to take over the stunned ship, Troi senses that the union did not work. Sure enough, Picard uses the transporter circuits to rematerialize in his human form.

Once back, the tired captain gives Riker the job of keeping the cannibalistic races' diplomats from eating each other.

Michael Halperin's original story contained the final basic plot, but a dilithium breakdown on the starship was the subplot. The diplomatic conference was added by Fontana, as in her 1967 original-series script, "Journey to Babel." Halperin's story ended with Picard, his ship basically powerless, bringing the energy creature home by using the slingshot time-traveling effect seen in various Trek episodes and *Star Trek IV.*

This show was the first of many TNG treks for director Cliff Bole, a veteran of *The Six Million Dollar Man, V,* the new *Mission: Impossible, Paradise,* and every other *Vega$* shot. Bole recalled that the show got mail criticizing its depiction of what amounted to cannibalism on the part of the carnivorous doglike Anticans.

Seen as a still-unnamed security ensign was actor Colm Meaney of "Farpoint," where he'd been a command-division ensign; at least here he'd been given the mustard-colored uniform he began to sport in Season 2 as O'Brien, the transporter chief; the flap over his rank was yet to come ("Family"/178, "Schisms"/231). Uncredited as the lead Antican (unnamed but called "Badar N'D'D" in the script), Marc Alaimo played the first of many Trek

Rivan (Brenda Bakke) gives Riker a feel for life among the Edo.

aliens leading up to eventual spinoff DS9's Gul Dukat ("The Neutral Zone"/126, "The Wounded"/186, "Time's Arrow"/226).

Finally, the archenemy Antican and Selay are seen in close proximity with no problem in the background of "Tapestry" (241), supposedly some thirty-five years before this time. Both Anticans ("Captain's Holiday"/167, "Unification I"/208, and spinoff DS9) and Selay ("Ménage à Troi"/172) later turn up solo as background extras.

TNG's dress uniform, designed to evoke memories of the deck waistcoats of the eighteenth-century British navy, made its debut here. The look would be slightly altered the following season: the gold edging would be reduced in width, and the front flap would follow the collarbone panel line instead of spiraling down from the collar. Two nice visual effects are seen in this episode: the stars warping by outside the ready room window, and their reflection on the desktop.

A few odd notes: one of the scenes in which Kavi Raz could be seen as Singh in the background had to be reshot when the actor wasn't available, so a wig on a chair was used as a stand-in! Okuda and Sternbach winced at the use of the transporter in this early story as a life-pattern restorer, so they came up with the official explanation that the system had come under the unique electromagnetic influences of the cloud-entity. A clunker of a prop that would not be reused after this episode is Beverly Crusher's surgical cap with its bizarre eyepiece.

The debut of TNG's dress uniform, from "Lonely Among Us."

JUSTICE

Production No.: 109 ■ Aired: Week of November 9, 1987
Stardate: 41255.6 ■ Code: ju

Directed by **James L. Conway**
Teleplay by **Worley Thorne**
Story by **Ralph Wills and Worley Thorne**

GUEST CAST
Rivan: **Brenda Bakke**
Liator: **Jay Louden**
Conn: **Josh Clark**
Mediators: **David Q. Combs, Richard Lavin**
Edo girl: **Judith Jones**
Nurse: **Brad Zerbst**
Edo boys: **Eric Matthew, David Michael Graves**

The pastoral planet of Rubicun III beckons after the *Enterprise* delivers a party of colonists to the nearby Strnad system. Rubicun's healthy people—the Edo—and their ways of love and open sensual pleasure make this planet seem like the perfect R-and-R stop.

But trouble looms in paradise after Wesley inadvertently chases a ball into one of the Edo's always shifting forbidden zones, drawing the planet's simple punishment for every crime—death. Dr. Crusher is furious, but Picard feels helpless under the Prime Directive.

As the captain pleads for Wesley's life, a machinelike being begins to orbit the planet and sends a probe to scan Data's brain. Proclaiming itself the Edo's god, the being demands that the *Enterprise* people leave its "children" alone—and take the Strnad colonists back, too.

The Edo are shocked that the once-friendly visitors protest their law; one Edo is even given the chance to see her "god," much to the machine-being's displeasure.

Finally Picard agrees to take the boy from his Edo captors by force. He confronts the Edo, who cave in but bitterly taunt the crew with their own law.

But "God" won't let the crew beam back. Picard argues that when laws are absolute there can be no real justice, and this convinces "Him" to let them go on their way.

John D.F. Black put his pseudonym, Ralph Wills, on this script, which as aired bears only slight resemblance to the story on terrorism he originally pitched. His first treatment featured the colony of Llarof where random "punishment zones," originally designed to fight anarchy, are now enforced for any offense and, it turns out, against only those not deemed immune from the law. An *Enterprise* guard, protecting two children on shore leave who happen upon a crime scene, is shot dead by an overzealous local cop, who in turn is killed on the spot by his dutifully law-abiding partner.

In Black's first draft Picard refuses to back the first of the timid rebels who want a change, but he finds a loophole just as the rebels' army wins out and reestablishes order. Black's second draft saw the rebel leader Reneg put on trial and executed for treason, with Picard musing that the people have the right to decide their own justice without interference. Later major rewrites by Worley Thorne and Gene Roddenberry would add the "Edo-lord" and the culture's preoccupation with sex.

"Justice" was the first episode to feature location shooting since the brief holodeck scene in "Farpoint" (102). The Edo exteriors were shot at the Tillman Water Reclamation Plant in Van Nuys, a north Los Angeles suburb (see "The First Duty"/219), and Wesley's fall was filmed at the Huntington Library in Pasadena.

Director James L. Conway, an original-series fan who had directed everything from Sunn Classics' pseudo-documentaries to Westerns to horror movies to industrial films, had just completed a *MacGyver* at Paramount when he was chosen to direct for TNG. Brad Zerbst became the first actor to play a recurring med tech or nurse in sickbay; his unnamed part lasted through two more shows, "Heart of Glory" (120) and "Skin of Evil" (122). And a character trademark, Worf's curt one-liner, began here with his observation on the friendly, mostly nude Edo: "Nice planet!"

THE BATTLE

Production No.: 110 ■ Aired: Week of November 16, 1987
Stardate: 41723.9 ■ Code: ba

Directed by **Rob Bowman**
Teleplay by **Herbert Wright**
Story by **Larry Forrester**

GUEST CAST
DaiMon Bok: **Frank Corsentino**
Kazago: **Doug Warhit**
Rata: **Robert Towers**

While waiting to meet the Ferengi, Picard is amazed when his old ship, the *Stargazer*, turns up.

But the unusual headache he's having increases when DaiMon Bok of the Ferengi welcomes him as the hero of the Battle of Maxia, the incident in which Picard had to abandon the *Stargazer* after it was mysteriously attacked.

To his own's crew's amazement, Bok presents the derelict starship to Picard as a gift—most unmercenary for a Ferengi. But there's method in his madness: at Maxia, Bok's son was the other captain, who was killed after attacking the *Stargazer*. Bok has forged log tapes on *Stargazer* showing Picard firing first.

As Riker, Data, and La Forge work to clear their captain, Wesley finds that energy waves from the old ship match Picard's brain scan. He has stumbled onto the other part of Bok's trap—a mind-control device planted among Picard's old belongings.

Aboard his old ship, Picard is reliving the Battle of Maxia, and is about to use the acclaimed "Picard maneuver"—but with the *Enterprise* cast as the enemy ship. Data devises a defense for the tactic, and Riker breaks through to Picard, who destroys the device.

Before leaving, they see Bok removed from command for insanity—demonstrated by his giving away the *Stargazer*.

The Ferengi fare better in their second appearance, but their "silliness quotient," as Rick Berman put it, made them a "disappointment as a major adversary." Larry Forrester's first story outline included several scenes aboard the Ferengi ship, but they were dropped and the chance to provide some insight into their culture was lost. The nine years in Picard's life between the *Stargazer* and the *Enterprise* have been undetailed, although some incidents from his other command have come to light ("The Measure of a Man"/135, "Allegiance"/166, "The Wounded"/186)—including Jack Crusher's death ("Family"/178, "Violations"/212, "Attached"/260).

In his second directorial outing Rob Bowman particularly enjoyed working with Stewart, who had the stage all to himself during filming of the ghostly *Stargazer* battle scenes. The director used a Steadicam in these sequences to evoke an unsteadiness—the first such use on TNG—and Legato shot each of the *Stargazer* bridge crew separately with fog and filters, which were video-composited in later.

The *Stargazer* bridge was a re-dress of the Trek movies' original; the four-foot filming model was built anew by Greg Jein from Probert and Sternbach's design after they persuaded the producers not to use the movie-style 1701-A's craft. That choice was made so late it forced the name of the new ship's class: "Constellation" neatly fit over "Constitution" when LeVar Burton had to redub the scene after filming.

A long-running joke had its roots in this episode: the gesture Stewart makes as he pulls his uniform's shirtwaist down when rising soon came to be called the "Picard maneuver." The episode also provides one of the most offbeat moments in the first and only "blooper reel" of outtakes to be leaked so far. While exploring a darkened corridor of the *Stargazer* as Data, actor Brent Spiner shines his light across that starship's dedication plaque and stammers in his best Jimmy "It's a Wonderful Life" Stewart voice: "For God's sake, Mary, they built this thing in Bedford Falls!"

Kazago (Doug Warhit) examines Data.

HIDE AND Q

Production No.: 111 ■ Aired: Week of November 23, 1987
Stardate: 41590.5 ■ Code: hq

Directed by **Cliff Bole**
Teleplay by **C. J. Holland and Gene Roddenberry**
Story by **C. J. Holland**

GUEST CAST
Q: **John de Lancie**
Disaster survivor: **Elaine Nalee**
Wes at 25: **William A. Wallace**

The meddling, troublesome Q returns just as the *Enterprise* is racing to help a disaster-struck mining colony—but this time his target is Riker.

The alien creates a bizarre test for the first officer and his away team by sending fanged humanoids in Napoleonic costumes to attack them. Then he tempts Riker with the Q's power and lets him use it to restore Worf and Wesley, who were killed in the "skirmish."

Riker is worried about the power's influence on him, and when the *Enterprise* reaches the survivors of the mining disaster he refuses to help revive a dead girl.

Guilt over that leads him to yield to the power, and when Q presses him to grant his friends' wishes, Picard does not object: sight for La Forge, adulthood for Wesley, a Klingon mate for Worf, humanity for Data. But, as Picard has predicted, they all turn down the gifts because of their origin—Q.

Riker understands the lesson, and a humiliated Q gets "called home" by his continuum for losing the bet. Riker's power and the crew's wishes all disappear.

Maurice Hurley used his pen name, of C. J. Holland, on this episode, a move he later called a "misunderstanding" over Gene Roddenberry's extensive rewrites. That issue was soon resolved, and in fact proved to be a turning point in the way scripts would be handled. Hurley's original story postulated that there were only three Qs but that a hundred thousand residents lived on their dying planet. Those residents needed assistance to escape their dying world.

Riker is on the spot during Q's (John de Lancie) second appearance.

Returning director Cliff Bole, who noted that the series was still trying to find its tone with this show, had prepared by reviewing Q's previous appearance in "Farpoint." However, once the episode began shooting, he found that de Lancie's affinity for the character and the actor's sheer talent made much of that work unnecessary.

It is during the head-to-head battle of wits between Picard and Q in the ready room that the title of the captain's prized display book can be read: *The Globe Illustrated Shakespeare*. What isn't so clearly visible is that the book, as usual, is opened to Act III, Scene 2, of *A Midsummer Night's Dream*, with two illustrations showing.

Although Q refers to the Federation "defeating" the Klingons, later events, such as those in "Heart of Glory" (120), suggest he is being typically sarcastic. As hinted at in "Justice" (109), Klingon foreplay is seen here as rough, at Michael Dorn's suggestion, with extra Faith Minton as the first Klingon "warrioress" depicted in TNG. In a later episode, "The Dauphin" (136), Worf would imply that it is the male who is submissive.

An admiral's dress uniform is briefly seen here for the first time, before the duty uniform debuted in "Too Short a Season" (112). As worn by Q, it has wider gold braid for the tunic flap and collar.

TOO SHORT A SEASON

Production No.: 112 ▪ Aired: Week of February 8, 1988
Stardate: 41309.5 ▪ Code: ts

Directed by **Rob Bowman**
Teleplay by **Michael Michaelian and
D. C. Fontana**
Story by **Michael Michaelian**

GUEST CAST
Admiral Mark Jameson: **Clayton Rohner**
Anne Jameson: **Marsha Hunt**
Karnas: **Michael Pataki**

Rapidly growing younger, Admiral Jameson (Clayton Rohner) draws Dr. Crusher's concern.

A hostage situation on Mordan IV brings the *Enterprise* and Admiral Mark Jameson, who successfully negotiated a peace there forty years earlier, back for another case.

Unknown to Starfleet and Federation historians, Jameson actually appeased the planet leader Karnas with arms for his hostages then but kept the Prime Directive by supplying all his enemies, thus sparking four decades of civil war. Karnas doesn't need Jameson to negotiate on behalf of hostages now; the invitation is just a ruse to get him there so the governor can exact his revenge.

But the wheelchair-bound admiral has another surprise, which he has kept secret even from his wife, Anne. Another planet, grateful for Jameson's diplomacy, has revealed their de-aging compound to him, and he has been using it.

His youthfulness startles his wife and the crew until the overdoses start to backfire: his body can't take the strain.

Meanwhile, Picard arrives at Mordan and confronts Karnas with the truth, but the leader wants Jameson and doesn't believe the young man he sees before him is his enemy of so long ago. Only Jameson's display of their blood-cut scar convinces an amazed Karnas, but by now even vengeance is futile: the governor allows Jameson to die as his wife watches, and the admiral is buried on Mordan IV at her request.

Michael Michaelian's original story used the reverse aging device to deal with the issue of male menopause. In that version Jameson helps Governor Zepec and his rival, the high priest, sit down to peace talks and does not die at the end. Instead, he regresses to the age of fourteen and loses all memory of his wife. Fontana tightened up the terrorism trap as the dramatic story's lure and had Jameson die for having tampered with nature.

Rob Bowman, the director, remembered being excited about working on weekends with actor Clayton Rohner to build up the character of Jameson, but otherwise he recalled the show as a "sit-and-tell" script that was long on dialogue. Other problems with this episode included a sub-par makeup look for the aged admiral Jameson and a malfunctioning $10,000 wheelchair.

Michael Pataki had previously played another K-role on the original Trek: that of Korax, Captain Koloth's aide who taunts Scotty and Chekov in "The Trouble with Tribbles."

This show marks the first appearance of a Starfleet admiral in TNG and of his duty uniform, which would eventually be redesigned thrice more. Little used here is a miniature of the Mordan city, built by Okuda and Sternbach—the last such model used in favor of matte paintings until Season 6 ("Birthright"/242–243). Note the wall behind Karnas' desk, lined with "old-style" phasers from the 1960s and the Trek movie eras; the Portal's Tkon-style staff from "The Last Outpost" (107) also hangs there.

THE BIG GOODBYE

Production No.: 113 ■ Aired: Week of January 11, 1988
Stardate: 41997.7 ■ Code: bg

Directed by **Joseph L. Scanlan**
Written by **Tracy Tormé**

GUEST CAST
Cyrus Redblock: **Lawrence Tierney**
Felix Leech: **Harvey Jason**
Lieutenant Dan Bell: **William Boyett**
Whalen: **David Selburg**
Lieutenant McNary: **Gary Armagnac**
Desk Sergeant: **Mike Genovese**
Vendor: **Dick Miller**
Jessica Bradley: **Carolyn Allport**
Secretary: **Rhonda Aldrich**
Thug: **Erik Cord**

Data and Beverly Crusher's lark on the holodeck almost turns deadly.

Protocol is all to the insectoid Jarada, who insist that they be greeted successfully in their own tongue without fail before diplomatic relations can begin. It has been twenty years since the Federation last tried to contact them, and the demise of the Starfleet vessel that failed is a tale so horrible that no one wants Data to repeat it.

To relieve the stress of his preparations, Picard tries a little role-playing in his favorite holodeck program, a 1940s hard-boiled detective named Dixon Hill. He is so excited after a short

Picard-as-Dixon Hill reads of his client's murder, while Data and Whalen (David Selburg) look on.

holodeck visit that he takes Data, Dr. Crusher, and literary historian Whalen back with him.

But a long-range Jaradan scan glitches the holodeck programming, and the game turns deadly: Whalen is shot by mobsters, and the party is trapped with no exit. Wesley and La Forge try to make repairs, but a wrong move would kill the players.

Finally the holodeck is opened, and the mobsters gleefully leave, intending to plunder the *Enterprise*, but of course they dematerialize. Hill-Picard's police friend, in a metaphysical twist, ponders about reality for holodeck inhabitants as he watches them go.

Still in his trench coat, Picard emerges from his stressful play at last and delivers the Jaradan greeting perfectly, to his bridge crew's applause.

This 1940s-style romp that ponders the question of existence became an instant hit with the fans and an award-winner as well. Tracy Tormé credits the initial idea of Picard's detective fantasy

It takes a holodeck glitch that creates the image of an ice planet to convince Cyrus Redblock and henchman Felix Leech (Lawrence Tierney and Harvey Jason, *rear right*) and Lt. McNary and the thug (Gary Armaganal and Erik Cord, *rear left*) that they are not real. Meanwhile, Beverly tends to literature historian Whalen's (David Selburg) gunshot wound.

on the holodeck to Roddenberry and the staff, but Tormé added some *film noir* references, including Redblock and Leech as echoes of the Sydney Greenstreet and Peter Lorre characters from *The Maltese Falcon.* He also included a metaphysical twist at the end, when the holodeck creations become self-aware.

Rob Bowman had been set to direct the segment, but it was given to Joe Scanlan at the last minute, when problems developed with "Datalore" and the two were switched in production order. The director joined Tormé in suggesting that the 1940s scenes be filmed in black and white, but Berman and Justman disagreed, noting that the holodeck could not change the real Picard and crew.

The episode was "jeered" by *TV Guide* as too derivative of an original-series episode, "A Piece of the Action," a comic turn that featured a planetary culture based on 1930s gangland Chicago. Tormé and most of fandom disagreed. The writer felt the comparison was based merely on the appearance of "three-piece suits." Eventually those suits were good enough to help snare an Emmy award for series costuming, and "The Big Goodbye" was chosen by the George Foster Peabody Award Board for its "best of the best" award—the first for an hour-long first-run drama.

The private eye was originally named Dixon Steele, an homage to the character in Tormé's favorite Bogart movie, but he was told to change it because of its resemblance to the title of a TV series, *Remington Steele.*

The Jarada themselves became a casualty of budget prob-

lems; in the finished episode, they are only heard, not seen. Tormé had done a terrific amount of work on the aliens, creating a hive mind culture he wanted desperately to depict. Still, Marina Sirtis, as Troi, gets a chance to do some linguistics coaching in this episode, and Spiner, McFadden, and Stewart all get to display their rarely used comedic talents. One detail in this script almost equals the "Chinese rice picker" explanation of Spock's ears from the original-series "City on the Edge of Forever," and that is the explanation of Data's skin color: "he's from South America"!

A good VCR will reveal the detailed period graphics Okuda created for the Dixon Hill computer file. Tormé is credited as the author of "The Big Goodbye," Hill's debut, purportedly published in *Amazing Detective Stories* magazine in 1934 and followed by the novel *The Long Dark Tunnel* in 1936. According to his business card, Hill's office address is Room 312, 350 Powell, Union Square, San Francisco, Calif., phone PRospect 4631. The London Kings baseball shortstop who broke DiMaggio's hitting record in 2026 is later identified as Harmon "Buck" Bokai on spinoff DS9.

Hill's gal Friday goes unnamed but becomes Madeline in their other reincarnations, ("Manhunt"/145, "Clues"/188); actors Boyett ("Time's Arrow, Part II"/227) and Selburg ("Frame of Mind"/247) would return, while the Jarada would be mentioned just once more ("Samaritan Snare"/143). Ironically, the song "From Out of Nowhere" is heard as Picard enters the holodeck for the first time—a Bob Justman touch.

DATALORE

Production No.: 114 ■ Aired: Week of January 18, 1988
Stardate: 41242.4 ■ Code: da

Directed by **Rob Bowman**
Teleplay by **Robert Lewin and**
Gene Roddenberry
Story by **Robert Lewin and Maurice Hurley**

GUEST CAST
Lieutenant Commander Argyle: **Biff Yeager**

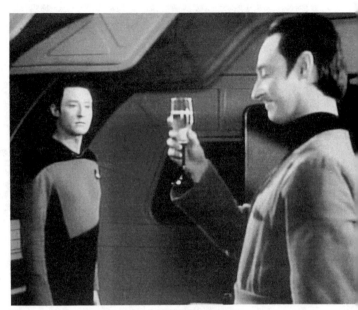

Data (left) confronts his android brother, Lore.

Data experiences an almost human expectancy when the *Enterprise* returns to his "home" planet in Omicron Theta to discover the secret behind the disappearance of its 411 colonists twenty-six years before.

An away team finds the lab of the reclusive Dr. Noonian Soong, a renegade Earth scientist who originally built a "twin" of Data's named Lore. Over time, the crew learns that Lore was disassembled at the demand of the colonists for being "too perfect." Data was the second model.

Lore's disassembled parts are found, rebuilt, and reanimated aboard the ship. But the reason for the android's original disassembly soon becomes clear—he turns Data off and assumes his identity. He then summons the huge life-draining crystal entity that destroyed the colony years before after being lured there by him as revenge for his disassembly.

Wesley senses the switch, but no one listens to him until it's almost too late. Finally his mother learns the truth and reactivates Data, but by then the crystalline being is almost upon the ship.

The two androids fight each other in a cargo bay until Lore is thrown into a wide-dispersal transporter beam. The crystalline being now has no contact with the *Enterprise*, and it departs.

By the end of season one, this episode was being cited by Berman as the one that changed the most from its inception. Lore was originally a female android, a non-lookalike love interest for

Data. Her job was to go out and repair dangerous situations à la Red Adair, the oil well fire fighter. It was Spiner who suggested the old "evil twin" concept.

Because of the delays caused by rewrites, Rob Bowman landed this segment instead of its predecessor, switching with Joe Scanlan when the two stories traded places in the shooting schedule. Though he regretted losing a chance to direct "The Big Goodbye," Bowman and Spiner met the challenge of "Datalore" and its troubled history head on. They produced a winner, thanks in no small part to an extra eighth day of shooting and to Spiner's virtuosity in the dual role.

The original back story of Data's creation by an alien race was tossed out. What emerged in its stead was the story of an android who originated in the laboratories of the Federation's most brilliant cybernetics expert, Dr. Noonian Soong. Data's positronic brain—an homage to the late sci-fi writer, Isaac Asimov—was foreshadowed as early as October 28, 1986, when Justman suggested in a memo that the author's "Laws of Robotics" be used and that a spoken credit be given. We discover in this episode that Data spent four years at Starfleet Academy, three years as an ensign, and ten or twelve years in the lieutenant grades. We also learn that only Beverly Crusher knows about his off switch. Two additional stories, "Brothers" (177) and "Silicon Avatar" (204), eventually stemmed from this episode. In addition, we learn that there is an "emergency close" vocal command that can shut the turbolift doors in a second, and that a phaser beam can be trapped within a transporter beam if timed just right. This episode would be the last of Yeager's two stints as Chief Engineer Argyle, though he had been mentioned in "Lonely Among Us" (108).

In a rare verbal blooper, Riker drops a digit from his away team log stardate, giving the date as 4124.5—the style used in the original Trek's stardates.

ANGEL ONE

Production No.: 115 ▪ Aired: Week of January 25, 1988
Stardate: 41636.9 ▪ Code: ao

Directed by **Michael Rhodes**
Written by **Patrick Barry**

GUEST CAST
Beata: **Karen Montgomery**
Ramsey: **Sam Hennings**
Ariel: **Patricia McPherson**
Trent: **Leonard John Crowfoot**

Troi and Yar lead the away team on the matriarchal Angel One.

Searching for survivors from a freighter that's been missing for seven years, the *Enterprise* visits the matriarchal planet Angel I and gets a frosty reception from its female leaders. Riker especially seems out of place as Yar and Troi handle the diplomacy, but he finds a more personal way to gain leader Beata's trust.

Survivors are found, but they refuse to return. They have taken wives from among outcasts on the planet who don't like the status quo: dominant women and submissive men.

Back aboard *Enterprise* crises break out as a virus from a holodeck file ravages the ship and Starfleet wants a response to a reported Romulan incursion near the Neutral Zone.

The renegade women are discovered and sentenced to death along with their Federation mates as enemies of society. Riker wants to intercede and violate the Prime Directive by beaming the outcasts aboard, but with the epidemic in full swing, Dr. Crusher forbids it.

Finally both dilemmas are resolved: the doctor finds an antidote to the virus, and Riker persuades Beata to forgo the death penalty. She allows the group instead to be exiled to a remote part of the planet, and the *Enterprise* warps out to counter the reported Romulan activity.

Heavy rewrites changed Patrick Barry's original story—a direct, action-filled allegory on apartheid using the sexes instead of the races to make its point. In the original, Riker beams down with an otherwise all-female away team and stops the leader, "Victoria," from striking him. Tasha immediately phaser-stuns Riker to prevent his on-the-spot execution by the natives. Data, with his machine nature, is held in higher esteem than Riker, who is thrown into jail with other slaves on the eve of a revolt led by the marooned human, Lucas Jones. Jones is killed after a verbal attack on Victoria, and his death inspires the rebels to strike at last as the *Enterprise* leaves. A recovered Picard, the only one taken ill in this version, is reassured by Number One that the members of his team were only witnesses to, and not instigators of, the uprising.

Except for a nice scene in which Troi and Tasha get to guffaw at Riker's revealing outfit, the revised teleplay is a one-note morality tale with yet another shipboard disease as the subplot. Director Michael Rhodes, a four-time Emmy winner on the series *Insights*, came to his TNG assignment as part of a deal with the series *The Bronx Zoo*, also shot at Paramount. He recalls that he gave Wil Wheaton his first starring role, in a 1981 ABC After School Special.

Two notes of interest in this episode: Troi remarks that Angel I's matriarchal oligarchy is "very much like" Betazed; and the Romulans are mentioned for the first time in TNG, as a reported threat in the Neutral Zone. And for students of stage design, Herman Zimmerman's cleverly designed Stage 16 sets, which were used as Soong's lab in the preceding episode, were re-dressed here and would be altered throughout the rest of the season to get even more mileage out of his budget.

11001001

Production No.: 116 ▪ Aired: Week of February 1, 1988
Stardate: 41365.9 ▪ Code: oo

Directed by **Paul Lynch**
Written by **Maurice Hurley and Robert Lewin**

GUEST CAST

Minuet: **Carolyn McCormick**
Commander Quinteros: **Gene Dynarski**
Zero One: **Katy Beyer**
One Zero: **Alexandra Johnson**
Zero Zero: **Iva Lane**
One One: **Kelli Ann McNally**
Piano Player: **Jack Sheldon**
Bass Player: **Abdul Salaam el Razzac**
Drummer: **Ron Brown**

The *Enterprise* visits Starbase 74 for an upgrade to the ship's computer facilities—a task that will be performed by the Bynars. They are a race grown so dependent upon computers that they work in pairs and communicate directly in binary language.

While the crew puts in for shore leave, Riker tries out a new holodeck program for a New Orleans jazz bar where he can play trombone. There he meets Minuet, a sultry brunette and the most realistic character a holodeck ever created.

Soon Picard joins them, and he is amazed at the difference the Bynars' upgrade has made—Minuet is almost too good. The reason why is soon discovered: the Bynars were using Minuet as a decoy, while faking a magnetic shield breakdown to empty the ship. The aliens' ruse works and they hijack the *Enterprise* to take them home.

To avoid its capture Picard and Riker program the ship to self-destruct. But when they emerge on the bridge, they find the Bynars not defiant, but dying.

The aliens feared an electromagnetic pulse from a nearby nova would ruin their world's master computer, so they wanted to "borrow" the *Enterprise*'s—the only mobile memory core large enough. But the pulse has already hit.

Now that they understand the problem, the officers use the ship's computer to help rejuvenate the Bynars. But Riker discovers his Minuet is gone and can't be re-created.

Another sign that both script quality and overall continuity were on the rise was this tale by Maurice Hurley and Robert Lewin in which we finally get some insight into Riker's character. The story even allows Jonathan Frakes to demonstrate his real-life trombone playing. His rendition of "The Nearness of You" would be repeated later ("Conundrum"/214), and Minuet would appear again in "Future Imperfect" (182). Number One's relationship with Minuet and his feelings about it showed that Frakes could do things with Riker if given the chance, and the Bynars and their troubled homeworld computer proved to be one plot frame that worked.

The four actors used for the Bynars were all women dancers whose voice track was mechanically lowered in pitch; initially, covert dialogue among them was designed to be subtitled. Gene Dynarski should be familiar to longtime Trek fans as Ben Childress in "Mudd's Women" and Krodak in "The Mark of Gideon" from the 1960s series. His character, who says he headed the team that put the *Enterprise* together, is given the first name of Orfil in the script.

This episode features several subtle optical effects. The *Enterprise* seen outside a Starbase 74 window is reflected in the wall controls, and Probert's painting of the docked *Enterprise* includes matted-in figures walking through the gangway tunnel. The shots of the planet Tarsas III, its moon, and the orbiting starbase are

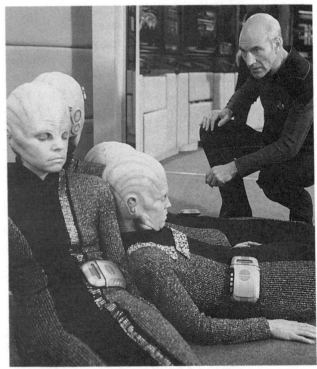

The Bynars are found near death after hijacking the *Enterprise*.

stock shots reused from *Star Trek III*. The autodestruct sequence is much more informally worded than the three-person code used in the Kirk-era's "Let That Be Your Last Battlefield" and in *Star Trek III*, and for the first time an emergency evacuation of the starship is shown. Also, a scene with a nonspeaking character named Dr. Terrence Epstein, a twenty-six-year-old research hero of Beverly's, was cut to save time, and he became only a mention.

HOME SOIL

Production No.: 117 ■ Aired: Week of February 22, 1988
Stardate: 41463.9 ■ Code: hs

Directed by **Corey Allen**
Teleplay by **Robert Sabaroff**
Story by **Karl Guers, Ralph Sanchez, and Robert Sabaroff**

GUEST CAST
Kurt Mandl: **Walter Gotell**
Louisa Kim: **Elizabeth Lindsey**
Bjorn Benson: **Gerard Prendergast**
Arthur Malencon: **Mario Roccuzzo**
Female Engineer: **Carolyne Barry**

The *Enterprise* is asked to check up on a remote terraforming station on Velara III that is working to transform the supposedly lifeless planet into a fertile, habitable Class M world.

But during the visit, an engineer is mysteriously killed when the laser drill in the hydraulics room goes berserk. Minutes later, Data narrowly avoids the same fate. As he and La Forge check it out, they discover what comes to be called a microbrain.

This unusual inorganic entity is a real lifeform native to the planet. As Dr. Crusher and Data investigate the aliens, the tiny being declares war on the humans. By pumping and desalinating the Velarans' narrow subsurface water ecosphere, the terraformers were killing its race.

The power it draws is strong enough to deflect the ships' transporter beam. Finally it is deduced that the microbrain is photoelectric, and a shutdown of power weakens it enough so that it can be sent home.

Data and La Forge discover the tiny crystalline Velara III lifeform dubbed "microbrain."

In doing so, Picard's crew promises to abide by the Velarans' request for no UFP contact for three hundred years. The planet is quarantined.

This story's theme of unintended destruction echoes that of original Trek's "Devil in the Dark," in which a silicon-based mother creature attacks the miners who are unknowingly taking her eggs. This TNG, however, was a lackluster show, which Hurley recalls as the one where just about everything that could have gone wrong did—including pages having to be rewritten the day before shooting. About the best thing this episode has going for it is an explanation of terraforming and the Velarans' name for humans: Ugly Bags of Mostly Water. Walter Gotell, who plays Mandl, will be remembered as General Gogol in the James Bond films. An unused matte painting of the Velara III station, complete with parked shuttlecraft, was prepared by Andrew Probert.

The crew finds the microbrain's growth in sickbay amazing.

WHEN THE BOUGH BREAKS

Production No.: 118 ■ Aired: Week of February 15, 1988
Stardate: 41509.1 ■ Code: wb

Directed by **Kim Manners**
Written by **Hannah Louise Shearer**

GUEST CAST
Radue: **Jerry Hardin**
Rashella: **Brenda Strong**
Katie: **Jandi Swanson**
Melian: **Paul Lambert**
Duana: **Ivy Bethune**
Dr. Bernard: **Dierk Torsek**
Leda: **Michele Marsh**
Accolan: **Dan Mason**
Harry Bernard: **Philip N. Waller**
Toya: **Connie Danese**
Alexandra: **Jessica and Vanessa Bova**

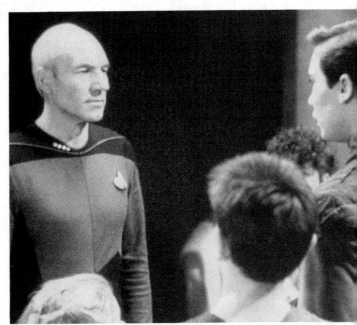

Retrieving the kidnapped children from Aldea provides a challenge for both Wesley and Picard.

The *Enterprise* stumbles across the planet Aldea, a world completely cloaked from outsiders by a powerful force-shield. But the find is no accident: the seemingly friendly Aldeans kidnap seven youngsters, including Wesley, from the ship to perpetuate their race.

Parents begin to panic as all attempts at negotiations fail. The Aldeans, convinced they are permanently sterile, stubbornly offer only to trade for the children. As a show of force, their defense system knocks the *Enterprise* three days' distance with one bolt.

But there Wesley finds holes in the Aldeans' technology: their age-old Custodian supercomputer shows wear and tear, and no one now knows how to maintain it. A secret scan by his mother shows the race is dying from radiation poisoning due to an ozone leak caused by their shield.

When Wesley organizes a hunger strike, Picard and Dr. Crusher are asked down to the planet for help. Riker and Data use the opportunity to secretly beam into a computer center, and, backed with control of the cloaking shield, the *Enterprise* crew is finally able to convince the Aldeans of the nature of their true problem.

Picard pledges UFP aid to help them regain their ecology and their health.

This was an opportunity to utilize those often ignored shipboard families that Shearer initially pitched to Fontana, and it was this story that helped win her a spot on the writing staff. A subplot involving ship separation and the saucer being held hostage was phased out to focus on the main story.

The nonspeaking young hostages included Wil Wheaton's younger siblings, Jeremy and Amy, as Mason and Tara; makeup designer Westmore's daughter MacKenzie played Roe. Hardin would return to TNG as Mark Twain ("Time's Arrow"/226–227), while Paul Lambert later appeared in "Devil's Due" (187).

This was another script in which Legato would provide an impressive yet inexpensive FX solution to a story need: the Aldean computer's power room. "The script called for a 'little black box' power station, but that wasn't enough," he said. "It needed to be something that left you awestruck—but how, on a low budget?"

First Legato had a two-foot-tall model of a reactor and a cavern-shaft built with a ledge. Then he shot actors against a simple black background with a single hard white light rising on them, as if from a door opening from floor to ceiling. Next he burned their image into the black side of the model to establish the scale for a few seconds before camera picked up the live-action shooting on the set. "At three thousand dollars it was much cheaper than compositing the scene with mattes," he added.

Coming of Age

Production No.: 119 ▪ Aired: Week of March 14, 1988
Stardate: 41416.2 ▪ Code: ca

Directed by **Michael Vejar**
Written by **Sandy Fries**

GUEST CAST
Admiral Gregory Quinn: **Ward Costello**
Lieutenant Commander Dexter Remmick: **Robert Schenkkan**
Mordock: **John Putch**
Lieutenant Chang: **Robert Ito**
Jake Kurland: **Stephen Gregory**
T'shanik: **Tasia Valenza**
Oliana Mirren: **Estee Chandler**
Technician No. 1: **Brendan McKane**
Technician No. 2: **Wyatt Knight**
Rondon: **Daniel Riordan**

As Wesley prepares to beam down to Relva VII to take his long-awaited entrance exam to Starfleet Academy, Picard's old friend, Admiral Quinn, beams up for surprise business that he won't explain: a tough interrogation of the captain's senior officers.

Wesley learns despite losing an Academy opening to the Benzite Mordock (John Putch).

Meanwhile, Wes consoles his friend Jake, who didn't make the final cut, and begins his grueling challenge while meeting the other candidates. He's in a neck-and-neck race for the single Academy slot open, and he's nervous about the infamous psych test.

Picard, along with Riker and the crew, grow increasingly bitter over the demeanor of Remmick, Quinn's probing aide, but the admiral won't talk until he's ready. He suspects a conspiracy growing within Starfleet, and he had to test Picard's loyalty . . . before offering to make him commandant of the Academy.

Picard is flattered but wants to think it over. In the meantime, Wesley returns rejected: his success on the psych test gave him food for thought, but he came in a close second in the competition. After consoling Wesley and saving a dejected runaway Jake from a near-fatal shuttle crash, Picard decides to stay on board.

This episode provides further evidence that Wesley was already being better written as a character, thank you, and the title is indicative of TNG's emerging self-confidence as well as the story. The show marks a number of firsts for the series: the first Vulcan in a speaking role, the first retrospective look at the crew's new starship as seen through Remmick's prying eyes, the first attempt at a true continuing plotline—threads of which would be picked up in "Conspiracy" (125)—and the debut of TNG's shuttlecraft.

A filmed scene cut for time showed Wesley's friends helping celebrate his sixteenth birthday, with predictably pithy comments from Worf and Data about human rituals (see photo, page 29). We learn Wesley enjoys his equivalent of today's computer bulletin boards, while the head of Starfleet Academy is called a "commandant," later changed to "superintendent" ("The First Duty"/219).

Original Trek fan Robert Schenkkan, whose well-received turn as inquisitor Remmick netted him a return for "Conspiracy" (125) along with veteran actor Costello, won a Pulitzer for his epic nine-part play *The Kentucky Cycle*. Ito was Jack Klugman's sidekick on *Quincy*, Putch played another Benzite ("A Matter of Honor"/134) and was in *Generations*, and Riordan was a Bajoran guard in spinoff DS9's "Progress."

The tale of this first appearance of the shuttlecraft, initially named the *Copernicus III* by Probert, is another uncanny echo of the original Trek. In both series, the building of a full-scale shuttlecraft was put off for budgetary reasons until writers made the craft an integral part of a story so that it had to be built. In the original Trek, that episode was appropriately titled "Galileo Seven." In this case, though, to save money, only a quarter of the shuttlecraft filming set was built. Added sections were made for specific story requirements during the next season, as money allowed.

Unfortunately, piecemeal construction could not match the expensive formed curves seen in Probert's miniature, and the full-scale mock-up eventually looked nothing like the small-scale model. Because of that, the majority of the live shuttlecraft filming needs would be met by the quick-and-dirty "shuttlepod" seen first in "Time Squared" (139) and later by the Magellan-class craft "Daimok" (202), though the original would turn up occasionally when a whole view wasn't needed ("The Host"/197).

HEART OF GLORY

Production No.: 120 ▪ Aired: Week of March 21, 1988
Stardate: 41503.7 ▪ Code: hg

Directed by **Rob Bowman**
Teleplay by **Maurice Hurley**
Story by **Herbert Wright** and **D. C. Fontana**

GUEST CAST
Commander Korris: **Vaughn Armstrong**
Lieutenant Konmel: **Charles H. Hyman**
Commander K'Nera: **David Froman**
Kunivas: **Robert Bauer**
Nurse: **Brad Zerbst**
Ramos: **Dennis Madalone**

Responding to signs of a battle in the Romulan Neutral Zone, the *Enterprise* finds only a battered Talarian freighter and—thanks to La Forge's new VISOR's visual feed—three Klingons, one near death. Their leader, Korris, explains that the ship was attacked by Ferengi and they were beamed away just before the ship exploded.

But after their comrade dies and Picard assigns Worf as a guide, the two survivors proclaim their hatred of the UFP-Klingon Alliance; they want to reclaim what they call the true Klingon warrior spirit. They appeal to Worf to listen to his heart and give up his life with the humans; the Starfleet Klingon is torn by their words.

Meanwhile, a Klingon Defense Force cruiser approaches and explains what really happened: the Klingons are rebels, who hijacked the Talarian freighter and destroyed a Klingon ship sent to pursue them. The two Klingons are detained, but they escape later with a homemade weapon; one is killed.

Korris, threatening to destroy the warp intermix chamber in Engineering, demands to be given the battle section and tries again to sway Worf, who tries to talk him out of sabotaging the ship. Korris lunges, Worf fires—and it is over.

The Klingon captain is impressed by Worf, but the lieutenant politely turns down his invitation to serve in the KDF fleet, electing to remain aboard the *Enterprise*.

At last—a Klingon show! Hurley, who spent just two days creating a teleplay based on Fontana and Wright's premise, was proud of this first-year episode, which finally shed some light on Worf's background and on the current Klingon-Federation relationship. The seeds of the Klingon saga to come are planted here with the story of Khitomer and the Romulan betrayal, and Dorn truly gets a chance to shine. This tale of personal conflict does for Worf what "The Naked Time" did for Spock back in the early days of the first series.

What may be overlooked in the later introduction of Worf's foster parents from Earth ("Family"/178) is the revelation here that he grew up with them on the farming colony of Gault and had a foster brother, still unseen, who joined him at Starfleet Academy but later left to return to the farm.

Klingon renegades Korris (Vaughn Armstrong) and Konmel (Charles H. Hyman) tempt Worf to join them.

Bowman said he lost his late-season fatigue in the excitement over this script. Again he used the Steadicam aboard the disintegrating *Batris*. He designed an elaborate sequence of vertical shots for the final battle in the multi-decked main engineering section, and he toughened up the Klingon Konmel so that three phaser hits were needed to bring him down.

Footage of the old *K'tinga*-class Klingon cruiser is lifted straight from the first Trek film. The Klingon phrases spoken here were written without any particular pattern by Hurley, but most later Klingonese would come from Mark Okrand, the linguist who developed the alien tongue for the Trek movies and wrote *The Klingon Dictionary*. The freighter *Batris*, an oft-reused miniature, is labeled a Talarian craft; the race would be somewhat fleshed out later ("Suddenly Human"/176).

Dennis Madalone here appeared in the second of many stunt roles as various crew members; he was first seen in "Where No One Has Gone Before" (106). Outside of Trek Robert Bauer, a drummer, was in a band (The Watch) with bass guitarist Michael Dorn for a time.

THE ARSENAL OF FREEDOM

Production No.: 121 ■ Aired: Week of April 11, 1988
Stardate: 41798.2 ■ Code: af

Directed by **Les Landau**
Teleplay by **Richard Manning & Hans Beimler**
Story by **Maurice Hurley & Robert Lewin**

GUEST CAST

The Peddler: **Vincent Schiavelli**
Captain Paul Rice: **Marco Rodriguez**
Chief Engineer Lieutenant Logan: **Vyto Ruginis**
Ensign Lian T'Su: **Julia Nickson**
Lieutenant (j.g.) Orfil Solis: **George de la Pena**

The *Enterprise* is sent to the planet Minos to search for the missing USS *Drake*. The famed world of arms merchants hails the ship with a commercial for weapons, but surprisingly the sensors show no sentient life on the planet.

On Minos, Riker meets the *Drake*'s captain, an old friend, but quickly realizes he is dealing with a holographic projection. It transforms itself into a small flying fighter drone that encases Riker in a stasis field. The drone is destroyed, but increasingly smarter ones appear.

While fleeing them, Picard and Dr. Crusher

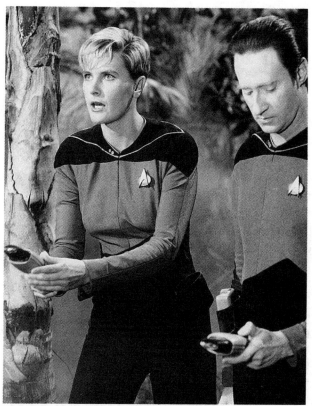

Yar and Data confront the Echo Papa 607's killer drones.

fall into a cavern; she's hurt and they can't get out. Above them, Data, Riker, and Yar fight off the drones, but one of them goes into orbit to attack the *Enterprise*. Left in command there, La Forge must contend with not only a green helm crew but also a pompous engineer who wants command. After separating the ship, he leaves orbit to devise a defense.

In the cavern, Picard stumbles onto the core of the mess—an automated "ultimate defense" system, which he realizes was probably responsible for killing the Minosians as well. La Forge pulls a tricky atmospheric tactic to destroy the attacking probe, just as Picard discovers the attack is an automated demonstration and ends it.

This episode was originally conceived as a Picard-Crusher love story, but Lewin recalled that Gene Roddenberry changed his mind and opted instead for this extremely ambitious action-adventure yarn/morality tale about arms merchants. Les Landau, an assistant director who became the first of many production staffers allowed to direct, suggested that it be Beverly Crusher and not Picard who is hurt in the fall into the pit, putting the captain in a "fish out of water" situation.

This fast-moving hour for once made good use of the entire ensemble, and gave Geordi his first shot at command. We learn a bit about Beverly's grandmother, not followed up until the series' last year ("Sub Rosa"/266), and for the last time until Season 4 we see a ship separation. Marco Rodriguez later played a Cardassian ("The Wounded"/186).

Stewart and McFadden endured flea-infested sand in the cave pit, built on the cargo bay set rather than on Stage 16. Riker gets in a good joke, telling the Rice image he's from the *U.S.S. Lollipop*—"a good ship."

SKIN OF EVIL

Production No.: 122 ■ Aired: Week of April 25, 1988
Stardate: 41601.3 ■ Code: se

Directed by **Joseph L. Scanlan**
Teleplay by **Joseph Stefano and Hannah Louise Shearer**
Story by **Joseph Stefano**

GUEST CAST
Armus: **Mart McChesney, voiced by Ron Gans**
Lieutenant Commander Leland T. Lynch: **Walker Boone**
Nurse: **Brad Zerbst**
Lieutenant Ben Prieto: **Raymond Forchion**

Tasha meets her fate against Armus (Mart McChesney, voiced by Ron Gans).

Troi and her shuttle pilot are pulled off course. They crash on Vagra II, the home of the sadistic being Armus, created from the cast-off sins of his race and then abandoned.

An away team beams down to rescue the counselor, but Armus and a forcefield of his creation are in their way. Then, acting out of sheer malice, the black oozing form of goo tortures Riker, taunts La Forge and Data—and kills Yar.

Worf, who is now acting security chief, and Wesley discover that Armus loses his power when provoked. Using that weakness, Picard is finally able to get his people out, but not before trying to reason with Armus one more time. He even has the splintered shuttle destroyed to prevent Armus from leaving the planet.

Back on board the *Enterprise*, crew members play a recorded hologram of Yar's will and her last thoughts to her friends. All of them—even Data—derive strength during their grief from their friendship with the security chief.

Long before this episode was filmed, rumors were flying about the manner of Denise Crosby's departure and the reasons for it. She was, after all, the first regular Trek character ever to be permanently killed off—the movies' resurrection of Spock notwithstanding. Thanks to media reports, it became widely known that Crosby was dissatisfied with her role's development and had asked to bow out on friendly terms so that she could pursue a film career. Shearer, who was handed the task of rewriting the original draft by *Outer Limits* veteran Joseph Stefano, said the in-house debate on the nature of her exit finally went the way Gene Roddenberry wanted, with a "senseless" but typical sudden death befitting a security chief. Originally, Tasha's demise came much earlier in the episode and the focus was more on the Armus creature than on the crew's reactions to their comrade's death.

"Gene felt we couldn't kill the creature, because it is not up to us as human beings to make a moral judgment on any creature that we encounter, because we are not God," said Shearer, charged with devising a satisfactory punishment without resorting to "eye for an eye" justice for the alien.

Everyone involved in this episode knew that the look and mechanics of the alien villain Armus had to be believable if the story was to work. "You're talking about a living tar pit," recalled Legato, who felt the episode was the series' biggest special-effects flop. "It's not attractive if you do it *well,* and if it's even worse it's not even that." Director Joe Scanlan, though noting the ironic and "wonderful intellectual quality" of Armus, told the staff: "If we don't make this monster believable, we are in deep shit."[6]

A surrealistic mime-type actor modeled on the Mummen-schanz group was the original concept for Armus. This was later changed to a more concrete "shroud" creature that would draw its oil slick up off the ground when arising. A plan to achieve this effect by reversing the film of a melting ten-inch figure on a hot plate had to be discarded. Finally, a grave-size pit ten feet deep was dug on the Planet Hell set and a hydraulic step was used for the rising-up effect. A mix including Metamucil was used for the black goo. Scanlan recalls that the "oil" was so heavy that actor Mart McChesney's suit began to disintegrate and new ones had to be built overnight. At one point he had to wear an open-backed costume in scenes where his back wouldn't show!

Recalling the final memorial scene, Scanlan said he filmed Tasha's "hologram tape" two ways: straight ahead, as if looking into her "holo-camera" (his preference), and the version used, in which she nods to each listener. "Don't ask me how she knew where they'd be standing," he said.[7] Still, if the sadness of the scene looked tearfully real, it was: Yar's death and Crosby's departure were sad for the actors as well as for the characters. Marina Sirtis began sobbing during reaction takes as her friend cued her from off-camera, leading Frakes and the others into one of the most moving scenes shot for the young series.

Ironically, Crosby said later that if scenes like the opening between her and Worf had been written more often, she would not have asked to leave the show. She would soon have second thoughts about departing the series, though, and would eventually find herself back in TNG through some of the most bizarre plot twists even Trek had ever come up with.

SYMBIOSIS

Production No.: 123 ■ Aired: Week of April 18, 1988
Stardate: unknown ■ Code: sy

Directed by **Win Phelps**
Story by **Robert Lewin**
Teleplay by **Robert Lewin, Richard Manning, and Hans Beimler**

GUEST CAST
Sobi: **Judson Scott**
T'Jon: **Merritt Butrick**
Romas: **Richard Lineback**
Langor: **Kimberly Farr**

While studying drastic solar flares around De-los, the *Enterprise* picks up a confusing distress call from a disabled freighter in the system. Only four of its six passengers are beamed away in time because the crew members insist on sending over the cargo first.

The survivors are from two neighboring worlds, Brekka and Ornara, and the cargo is felicium, a drug grown only on Brekka, which cures a two-hundred-year-old Ornara plague. The two haggard Ornarans demand the shipment; the Brekkians insist the deal's off.

The desperate Ornarans convince Picard to mediate; he gets them one dose apiece. But Dr. Crusher realizes the "cure" is a narcotic. The Brekkians have kept the unknowing Ornarans addicted for profit for two centuries!

Crusher demands to let the Ornarans know, but Picard cites the Prime Directive. He does find a solution to the dilemma, however: he refuses

Merritt Butrick returned to Trek as T'Jon, one of the "addicted" Ornarans.

to repair the Ornarans' remaining freighters. Now no trade in the low-technology system will occur and the Ornarans, although they will suffer withdrawal, will conquer their addiction.

This episode will likely be remembered for three things: the teaming of two *Star Trek II* actors in guest roles, the late Merritt Buttrick (his name was misspelled in the credits as "Merrit") and Judson Scott; the overbearing Nancy Reagan–era "Just Say No" anti-drug speech Tasha gives Wesley; and the *real* last scene for Denise Crosby.

Buttrick, who reprised his role as Kirk's son in *Star Trek III*, was already showing the ravages of the AIDS he died of a year later, in March 1989. Judson Scott, uncredited in *Star Trek II*, was the lead in the series *The Phoenix*; uncredited here was Kenneth Tigar as Margan, an Ornaran leader.

Because this story was filmed *after* "Skin of Evil" but would air *before* it, Crosby's real last scene came in the cargo bay in Act V: she's seen wildly waving goodbye from behind a console just as the corridor doors close behind Picard and Crusher! Even so, the odd stardates for "The Big Goodbye" and "The Arsenal of Freedom" mean that both shows feature Tasha even though they "occur" *after* her death!

WE'LL ALWAYS HAVE PARIS

Production No.: 124 ■ Aired: Week of May 2, 1988
Stardate: 41697.9 ■ Code: wa

Directed by **Robert Becker**
Written by **Deborah Dean Davis** and **Hannah Louise Shearer**

GUEST CAST
Jenice Manheim: **Michelle Phillips**
Dr. Paul Manheim: **Rod Loomis**
Gabrielle: **Isabel Lorca**
Lieutenant Dean: **Dan Kern**
Edouard: **Jean-Paul Vignon**
Francine: **Kelly Ashmore**
Transporter Chief Herbert: **Lance Spellerberg**

The romance that didn't quite click: Jenice Manheim (Michelle Phillips) and Picard.

While the ship is traveling to Sarona VII for shore leave, a bizarre time loop distortion causes a literal déjà vu effect on the *Enterprise*. Soon after this, the ship receives a distress signal from Dr. Paul Manheim's science outpost on Vandor IV.

They rescue Manheim and his wife, Jenice, who turns out to be an old love of Picard's. But the nonlinear time experiments Manheim and his now-dead team were conducting not only ended in disaster on Vandor, but were responsible for the disturbance that the *Enterprise* experienced earlier. Those disturbances now threaten to spread and rip open the interdimensional fabric of space.

Manheim himself is dying, since his body can't deal with the strain of partial interdimensional existence. On top of that, Picard's unresolved feelings for Jenice—he stood her up in Paris to ship out with Starfleet twenty-two years ago—are left hanging by a therapeutic session on the holodeck. Even Dr. Crusher finds herself jealous of Jenice.

Finally, using Manheim's directions, Data beams into the Vandor lab to reseal the center of the dimensional breach with a hunk of antimatter; although he finds himself in three time continuums at once, he sorts it all out and succeeds.

Manheim is instantly cured, and he and Jenice prepare to begin his work again. And this time, thanks to the Parisian holodeck program, Picard gives Jenice a proper good-bye.

———

If this story doesn't quite come off as another *Casablanca* (the source for the episode's title), it's not surprising. Shearer and her friend Deborah Dean Davis, who originally pitched the idea, wrote the script on five days' notice, aiming for an "utterly romantic" story, but she says the teleplay was "toned down 75 percent."[8]

As late as the final draft, dated February 22, Jenice's name was Laura, Riker was Picard's fencing partner, Paul Manheim was much more of a loose cannon, Picard and Jenice actually spent a night together, and Troi confronted Beverly about her feelings for the captain, which she had not yet sorted out. The crew reversed the Manheim effect by first bypassing a multilevel laser-guided security system; Worf then held open a door to cool an overheated silolike power room while Riker scaled the tower to switch out a chip and Data input commands to the system below.

Completed just a week before filming began, the revised script suffered again when the Writers Guild strike of 1988 shut down production on the climactic scene—Data's repair of the ripped time stream in Manheim's lab—because the dialogue and special effects had not yet been tied down!

"We just ran out of script," Legato recalled. "It was one of those 'We'll fix it when we get there' things, and suddenly we were there, and the writer was out on the picket lines. The director had never worked with effects before; I had to do it. I ran over to Rick Beman's trailer and said, 'We're out of script!' We spent forty minutes. We got the writer on the phone and Rick would say, 'Well, *if* you weren't on strike, the character might say this' and the writer'd say yes or no. I had to make up [the direction] on the spot; I came out with handwritten notes. I figured out how to shoot the three Datas in different time streams with a whip-pan instead of an effects shot."

Shearer and others complained that a lack of chemistry between Jenice and Jean-Luc diluted the story's romantic feel, but Michelle Phillips, who played Jenice, felt the problem lay in the story's conception; while her character wanted to see Picard again, and was quite willing to tease him, she was also fully committed to her husband and had been for a long time.

Phillips, an original-Trek fan who was one of the Mamas and the Papas, a 1960s group, began her acting career in 1970. Her roles include the miniseries *Aspen,* the film *Bloodlines,* and one season on *Knots Landing.* Rod Loomis, who acted in his first play while in the army, is best known for playing a confused Dr. Sigmund Freud in *Bill and Ted's Excellent Adventure.* Lance Spellerberg appeared a year later as the same transporter chief, Ensign Herbert, in "The Icarus Factor" (140).

The matte painting of twenty-fourth-century Paris seen in the holodeck nicely combines the old Eiffel Tower with a new antigrav craft flying by; it would later be used outside the Federation president's office in *ST VI.* Eduoard's Okudagram menu included joke items such as Croissants D'ilithium, Targ Klingon à la Mode, and Tribbles dans les Blankettes.

CONSPIRACY

———

Production No.: 125 ▪ Aired: Week of May 9, 1988
Stardate: 41775.5 ▪ Code: co

———

Directed by **Cliff Bole**
Teleplay by **Tracy Tormé**
Story by **Robert Sabaroff**

———

GUEST CAST
Admiral Savar: **Henry Darrow**
Admiral Quinn: **Ward Costello**
Lieutenant Commander Dexter Remmick: **Robert Schenkkan**
Admiral Aaron: **Ray Reinhardt**
Captain Walker Keel: **Jonathan Farwell**
Captain Rixx: **Michael Berryman**
Captain Tryla Scott: **Ursaline Bryant**

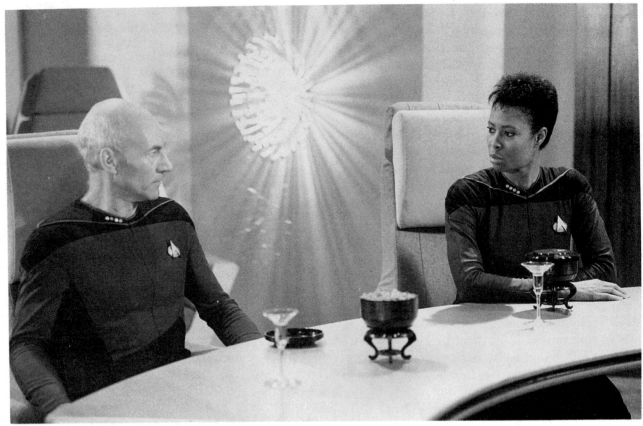

Picard realizes alien invaders have also possessed Captain Scott (Ursaline Bryant).

Picard is disturbed when his old friend Walker Keel summons him to a secret meeting with two other captains on a deserted planetoid, but he warily agrees. The subject? The trio's suspicion, much like Admiral Quinn's on Relva VII, that a conspiracy is spreading within Starfleet. Picard is skeptical until Keel's ship explodes and Data finds a disturbing pattern among command orders. Picard makes a decision: the *Enterprise* will return to Starfleet Command on Earth to check the suspicions firsthand.

Three top admirals, including Quinn, greet the ship with surprise and invite Picard and Riker down for dinner to discuss their concerns. But something does not feel right.

Then all hell breaks loose: the crew discovers that Quinn, aboard the *Enterprise* for a visit, is controlled by a tiny intelligent parasite, whose presence is revealed only by a quill-like protrusion from the host's neck.

Picard walks into a trap set by the other two admirals and Remmick, Quinn's former aide,

but a fake "quill" on Riker helps him foil the ambush. Soon the admirals are dead, along with Remmick, who housed the mother creature.

Quinn is cured and Starfleet saved, but the aliens' source and purpose remain a mystery.

This, the first moody episode of the series and one of its darkest ever, almost didn't come to be. The idea began as a one-sentence idea from Gene Roddenberry called "Assassins," which Robert Sabaroff fleshed out to a thirty-page treatment. Unfortunately it was deemed too expensive to produce, and Tormé got the assignment of starting the process all over again. Tormé said some on staff thought his treatment too dark, too bizarre; the assignment was going to someone else until GR read and loved it.[9]

Planned to push the limits as a hard-edged thriller, the story was originally inspired by *Seven Days in May*, and the conspirators were not aliens but members of a faction within Starfleet—all Picard's friends—who rebel against the Prime Directive and Federation-wide complacency following the Klingon detente. Ironically, although GR ruled against painting Starfleet in such dark colors, just such a conspiracy within the service later became a major plot point in the movie *Star Trek VI: The Undiscovered Country*.

The mail brought some cries against the gory scenes of death and worm-eating, but Tormé took issue with *Variety* for labeling it TNG's "most notorious" episode so far. Remmick's "hosting" of the mother alien and his exploding head were added later in post-production; originally, Picard and Riker were to meet up with the full-grown mother creature.

Henry Darrow, the first to play a speaking Starfleet Vulcan character and deliver the legendary neck pinch in TNG, has a long résumé that includes roles in the daytime soap *Santa Barbara* and the part of Manolito on the 1960s series *High Chaparral*. Jonathan Farwell, whose character introduced Jack Crusher to Beverly, was another longtime Trek fan and veteran guest star. He appeared in *The King and I* opposite Yul Brynner and on *The Young and the Restless*.

The Probert-designed Ambassador-class starship was first mentioned here as Keel's ship, the *Horatio* already having been designated as the *Enterprise*-C's class ("Yesterday's Enterprise"/163). The FX shots of Earth and spacedock and the matte painting of Starfleet Command were all from the Trek movies; the banquet room's heavy doors with inset etched-glass ovals would be used on the standing set for Ten-Forward, which was built during hiatus.

Though the story left room for a sequel, the parasites have never been seen again.

THE NEUTRAL ZONE

Production No.: 126 ▪ Aired: Week of May 16, 1988
Stardate: 41986.0 ▪ Code: nz

Directed by **James L. Conway**
Television story and teleplay by **Maurice Hurley**
From a story by **Deborah McIntyre & Mona Glee**

GUEST CAST
Commander Tebok: **Marc Alaimo**
Sub-Commander Thei: **Anthony James**
L. Q. "Sonny" Clemonds: **Leon Rippy**
Clare Raymond: **Gracie Harrison**
Ralph Offenhouse: **Peter Mark Richman**

As the *Enterprise* awaits Picard's return from a special briefing, Data can't resist investigating a three-hundred-year-old capsule that floats by. Three humans are found frozen inside the capsule. They are the only survivors of the fad of cryogenic preservation for the terminally ill.

But the last thing Picard needs is a sideshow of relics; his return brings news of disappearing

The first glimpse of Romulans in fifty-three years: Thei (Anthony James) and Tebok (Marc Alaimo).

outposts and the suspicion that at long last the Romulans are returning to activity along the Neutral Zone.

The revived humans have their own problems: a broker demands access to his money, a homemaker misses her kids, a bored country singer wants to party. Picard relies on Troi and Data to help solve their problems while he deals with another challenge: a cloaked Romulan ship, the UFP's first contact with its old foes in fifty-three years. A tense exchange yields the information that outposts are disappearing on the Romulan side of the Neutral Zone as well. The two sides agree to exchange information in the future, but the Romulans leave no doubt they mean to be reckoned with again.

With tensions eased somewhat, the *Enterprise* heads back, arranging a long ferry ride to Earth so its three new passengers will have enough time to get used to their new home century.

Hurley recalled putting this script together in a day and a half, a rushed and possibly unrefined casualty of the continuing Writers Guild strike. Originally, the rendezvous with the Romulans had been discussed as the first of a multi-part story that would have united the two governments against the newly discovered Borg, who were developed as a replacement for the disappointing Ferengi. The strike nixed that idea, though, and the Borg had to wait (Q Who/142). References to the pattern of their destruction, however, remained in the script. The subplot of the revived twentieth-century Americans—criticized by some as too reminiscent of the original Trek's "Space Seed"—came from a fan story by Deborah McIntyre and Mona Glee.

Peter Mark Richman once starred in the series *Cain's Hundred* and has racked up more than five hundred television guest roles, from *The Twilight Zone* and *Perry Mason* to *Bonanza* and *Mission: Impossible* and even to *Three's Company*, where he played Suzanne Somers's father. Leon Rippy appeared in both parts of *North and South* with Jonathan Frakes and in Steven Spielberg's *The Color Purple* as the storekeeper with eventual TNG cast member Whoopi Goldberg.

Sharp-eyed fans may notice a longer-than-usual shot of a skant-wearing female sciences officer departing a turbolift. That's Susan Sackett, a writer and Gene Roddenberry's personal assistant since 1974. She got the walk-on after winning a bet over losing weight. A TNG staff member until GR's death in late 1991, she would later contribute two episodes with writing partner Fred Bronson ("Ménage à Troi"/172, "The Game"/206).

In this episode Data makes history of another kind when he mentions the current Earth year as 2364—yet another sign that after more than twenty years, the many loose ends of Trek's background were being tied down once and for all. We also learn from Data here, ironically, that television had "died out" by 2040.

Finally, fans knew the Romulans' boast—"We're back!"—was no idle threat when their new vessel, eventually dubbed a Warbird, turned up here. Probert's size-comparison sketch comparing it to the 1701-D is dated March 25, 1988, and the miniature, which Greg Jein built, was released a year later by AMT as a plastic kit, along with the Ferengi and Klingon Bird of Prey vessels. The ships boast the new Romulan crest: a stylized bird of prey clutching the twin homeworlds of Romulus and Remus, one in each claw.

All the models were enhanced by Legato's first use of a moving camera on TNG for visual-effects sequences, allowing objects to move in relation to one another as the crews began getting away from the lock-off static shots needed in compositing the old stock-library elements.

Notes

1. Dave McDonnell, *Starlog*, No. 133, August 1988, p. 24.

2. Mark Dawidziak, *Cinefantastique*, March 1989, p. 26.

3. Eduard Gross, *Starlog*, No. 152, March 1990, p. 29.

4. *TV Guide*, July 23, 1988, p. 40.

5. For a visual evolution of the Ferengi through Probert's sketches, see *OFCM*, No. 60, February-March 1988, p. 7.

6. Gross, *Starlog*, No. 135, October 1988, p. 45.

7. Gross, p. 48.

8. Mark Altman, *Cinefantastique*, March 1989, p. 61.

9. Altman, p. 61.

PRODUCTION STAFF CREDITS— FIRST SEASON

(In usual roll order; numbers in parentheses refer to episode numbers.)

Main Title Theme: +**Jerry Goldsmith and** *****Alexander Courage**
Music: **Ron Jones (103, all even-numbered episodes, 106–126, except 112); Dennis McCarthy (101–102, all odd-numbered episodes, 105–125); George Romanis (112);** *****Fred Steiner (104)**
Director of Photography: **Edward R. Brown, A.S.C.**
Production Designer: **Herman Zimmerman**
Editor: **Tom Benko (101–102, 107, 110, 113, 116, 119, 122, 125); David Berlatsky (105); J. P. Farrell (103, 106, 109, 112, 115, 118, 121, 124); William Hoy (108, 111, 114, 117, 120, 123, 126); Randy Roberts (104)**
Unit Production Manager: **David Livingston (101–118); Kelly A. Manners (119); Bruce A. Simon (120); Sam Freedle (121–126)**
First Assistant Director: **Les Landau (101–102, 104, 106, 108, 110, 112, 116, 118, 124, 126);** *****Charles Washburn (103, 105, 107, 109, 114); Babu (T.R.) Subramaniam (111, 113, 115, 117, 119, 121, 122, 125); Bruce A. Simon (120, 123)**
Second Assistant Director: **Babu Subramaniam (101–110); Brenda Kalosh (109–114); Bruce A. Simon (111–118); Larry M. Davis (115–122); Bob Kinwald (119–122); Robert J. Metoyer (123–126); Adele G. Simmons (123–126)**
Costumes: *****William Ware Theiss, Executive Consultant (EMMY WINNER: "The Big Goodbye" [113])**
Art Director: **Sandy Veneziano (101–109, 120–126)**
Assistant Art Director: **Gregory Pickrell (110–118)**
Visual Effects Coordinator: **Robert Legato (101–111, 113, 116, 118, 120, 122, 124, 126); Dan Curry (112, 114, 115, 117, 119, 121, 123, 125)**
Post-Production Supervisor: **Brooke Breton**
Set Decorator: *****John Dwyer**
Makeup Supervisor: **Michael Westmore**
Makeup Artist: +**Werner Keppler (EMMY WINNER: "Conspiracy" [125])**

Hair Designer: **Richard Sabre**
Hair Stylist: **Joy Zapata (101–105); Carolyn Ferguson (106–126)**
Production Assistant: +**Susan Sackett**
Consulting Senior Illustrator: +**Andrew Probert**
Illustrator: +**Rick Sternbach**
Scenic Artist: +**Michael Okuda**
Set Designer: **Richard McKenzie (101–122); Louis Mann (123–126)**
Script Supervisor: **Cosmo Genovese**
Special Effects: *****+**Dick Brownfield**
Costume Supervisor: **Janet Stout (101–106); Elaine Scheiderman (107–115); Ed Sunley (117–126)**
Key Costumer: **Phil Signorelli (114–116); Richard Butz (117, 120, 122, 124); David McGough (118, 119, 121, 123, 125, 126)**
Camera Operator: **Lowell Peterson (101–102)**
Property Master: **Joe Longo (101 and all even-numbered episodes); Alan Sims (all odd-numbered episodes except 101)**
Chief Lighting Technician: **Richard Cronn**
First Company Grip: **Brian Mills**
Sound Mixer: **Alan Bernard, C.A.S. (all except 114); Dean Gilmore (114)**
Music Editor: **John LaSalandra, S.M.E. (101–114); Gerry Sackman (115–124)**
Supervising Sound Editor: **Bill Wistrom (101–118, 120–121, 123–125)**
Sound Editor: **James Wolvington; Mace Matiosian; and Wilson Dyer (105, 112–126) EMMY WINNERS (with crew): "11001001" [116])**
Casting Executive: **Helen Mossler**
Casting Associate: **Elisa Goodman (120–126)**
Production Coordinator: **Diane Overdiek**
Construction Forepersons: **Steven Monroe and John Clayton (101–102)**
Construction Coordinator: **Al Smutko (103–126)**
Special Visual Effects: +**Industrial Light and Magic (ILM) a division of Lucasfilm Ltd.**
Video Optical Effects: **The Post Group**
Special Video Compositing: **Composite Image Systems**
Editing Facilities: **Unitel Video**
Post-Production Sound: **Modern Sound**
Casting: **Junie Lowery**

[*] denotes a veteran of the original Trek series; [+] indicates a veteran of one or more Star Trek films.

SECOND SEASON

Its shakedown season over, TNG was on its way as not only a worthy successor to its namesake but also a commercial hit, ending its debut year as the number one first-run hour-long series in syndication and the number three syndicated show over all, behind game show kings *Wheel of Fortune* and *Jeopardy*.

Unfortunately, what precious momentum had finally built up during the stretch run of season one would now be lost through no fault of the staff: a strike by the Writers Guild went unsettled for six months through spring and summer, delaying the TV industry's fall 1988 schedule. Having already caused problems during the tail end of the premiere year, the strike forced the studio to cut TNG's second season back from twenty-six shows to twenty-two, and even at that the writing staff had to dig out the decade-old scripts in storage from the abortive *Star Trek II* series to see what might be usable (see "The Child"/127).

Many changes were made for the show's sophomore year. A

63

Second-season group portrait *(opposite)*. Gates McFadden (Dr. Crusher) is gone, replaced by Diana Muldaur's Dr. Pulaski.

new doctor, Diana Muldaur's Katherine "Kate" Pulaski, came aboard to replace Gates McFadden's Beverly Crusher. Also added to the cast was longtime fan Whoopi Goldberg as Guinan, hostess in the new Ten-Forward lounge; her character was named for the popular Prohibition-era nightclub owner "Texas" Guinan. Commander Riker gained a beard when the one Jonathan Frakes sported over hiatus caught the fancy of the producers, and Wesley got a new, West Point–inspired uniform. Geordi was promoted to chief engineer, ending the revolving door of guest roles there, and Worf's promotion to security chief was made permanent. The Klingon also got a new, twenty-pound baldric sash, and Troi finally got a much-welcomed wardrobe and hairstyle change, ending her affectionate cast nickname of "old bunhead."

McFadden's departure was said to be no reflection on her as an actress. "There were those who believed at the end of the first season that they didn't like the way the character was developing, vis-à-vis Gates's performance, and managed to convince Mr. Roddenberry of that," Rick Berman said years later, adding: "I was not a fan of that decision." By way of contrast, the new doctor, Kate Pulaski, was created somewhat in the image of Bones McCoy, as crusty and transporter-wary, and the second-season writers' guide even gave her three children by three different men. But while the sparks she brought were welcome, the handling of the change angered many fans and fired up the show's first real protest letter-writing campaign.

In addition to having guest-starred as two doctors on the original series—Dr. Anne Mulhall in "Return to Tomorrow" and Dr. Miranda Jones of "Is There in Truth No Beauty?"—Muldaur had most recently spent one season in a recurring role on the short-lived but highly acclaimed series *A Year in the Life*. Although she's no stranger to Broadway and film, she is perhaps best known for her TV work: regular stints on *McCloud* and *Born Free* and guest spots on series such as *Murder, She Wrote, Hart to Hart, The Master, Charlie's Angels*, and a Gene Roddenberry pilot, *Planet Earth*. She was also the first woman to be elected president of the Academy of Television Arts and Sciences, the organization that awards the Emmys. Runner-up for the part of Kate Pulaski, a choice that Berman recalled as "a very tough decision," was Christina Pickles, a regular on *St. Elsewhere*.

But while the switch in doctors got most of the fans' attention, the world at large was taking note of the new *Enterprise* bartender. The addition of Goldberg, a longtime Trek fan, to the cast was even more serendipitous. The news of Denise Crosby's departure prompted Goldberg to let the producers know—through her friend LeVar Burton—that she'd like to join the cast. Disbelieving, they ignored her until she finally called the TNG office and said, "Hey, I know I'm no blonde, but . . . !"

A 1991 Academy Award winner for *Ghost* and an Oscar nominee and Golden Globe winner for *The Color Purple*, superstar Goldberg also has an Emmy nomination and a Grammy on her résumé. She credits Nichelle Nichols, who played Uhura, original Trek's communications officer, as a childhood inspiration for her. In addition to the acting awards, she has been honored in many ways for her devotion to causes. Those honors include the 1989 Starlight Foundation Award as Humanitarian of the Year for her work in behalf of children, the homeless, human rights, and AIDS.

Both Diana Muldaur and Whoopi Goldberg received "special guest appearance" billing at the end of the opening guest credits. Muldaur declined the offer to be listed with the regular cast in the opening title.

Meanwhile, there were further changes in the writing staff as the series tried to generate some energy once the writers' strike finally ended. Robert Lewin left the series over discomfort with GR's constant writer rewrites and a perceived drift away from character-driven shows. Hannah Louise Shearer also left, though she contributed a story during each of the next two seasons ("Pen Pals"/141, "The Price"/156).

Along with Gene Roddenberry, of course, the returning team included Rick Berman and Maurice Hurley, Peter Lauritson, David Livingston, and, also on the writing side, Tracy Tormé, who later relinquished his title of co-executive story editor for the looser status of a "creative consultant" after a clash with Hurley over the script for "The Royale" (138). Meanwhile, Burton Armus began the second season as a producer, but relinquished that role for the season's last nine segments to Robert L. McCullough after overlapping with him on "Time Squared" (139).

That episode was also the last show for staff newcomers John Mason and Mike Gray, who had served as writing coproducers for the first thirteen shows of the year. Beginning two episodes later with "Pen Pals" (141), two positions for executive script consultants were created and filled by Hans Beimler and Richard Manning, longtime Trek fans who had been story editors for the last eight shows of season one. In addition, Leonard Mlodinow and Scott Rubenstein

By Season Two a moving "star field" was added outside the windowed sets.

worked as story editors from "The Outrageous Okona" (130) onward until Melinda Snodgrass, a science fiction novelist, was added in that capacity after selling the impressive script for "The Measure of a Man" (135). After four more shows, Mlodinow and Rubenstein left, and Snodgrass, another original series fan, carried the title alone for the rest of the season.

Around the sets modifications took place as well: the bridge was fitted with new, swiveling Conn and Ops chairs that had a less severe backward slant; the captain received a more distinctive command chair that better fit Stewart's body, with armrest panels permanently mounted open instead of hinged; and, to allow the new chief engineer an occasional piece of the bridge action, the aft stations were also redesigned. From portside inward, the outer three stations were now Engineering, Environment, and Mission Ops rather than Environment, Emergency Manual Override, and Propulsion Systems. The custom-built observation lounge now included built-in viewscreens, and Sternbach contributed the painting behind the bar in the new Ten-Forward lounge: an abstract portrait of the Milky Way galaxy.

As TNG settled in and found its stride, confidence rose in all quarters, including those of hardworking art staffers Sternbach and Michael Okuda. Both enjoyed inserting in-jokes, homages, and occasionally pure double-talk into a

Whoopi Goldberg on the set with her "inspiration," Nichelle Nichols.

TNG graphic or design when they could get away with it. In particular, Sternbach turned his interest in *animé,* or Japanese animation—an adult, well-crafted genre that has its own large following of fans—into innocuous and barely visible references in graphics and props.

Among other staff changes here, Zimmerman recommended as his successor veteran production designer Richard James, who worked temporarily at first until Zimmerman opted not to return after *Star Trek V.* James, who had prior genre work on *Battlestar Galactica* as well as other series and films like *Silkwood* and *Local Hero,* brought along set decorator Jim Mees to replace John Dwyer, who left with Zimmerman. Breaking in with the Norman Lear sitcoms, Mees had jumped to Paramount with *The Bronx Zoo.*

Worf received a literal facelift when Westmore simplified his forehead ridge piece, heeding actor Michael Dorn's plea for an application change to help end a forehead skin rash. The actor began wearing a headband under the head piece and the "forehead" was glued down only around its edges—although that cut down the facial expressions that could be reflected in the prosthetics.

THE CHILD

Production No.: 127 ■ Aired: Week of November 21, 1988
Stardate: 42073.1 ■ Code: tc

Directed by **Rob Bowman**
Written by **Jaron Summers & Jon Povill and Maurice Hurley**

GUEST CAST
Lieutenant Commander Hester Dealt: **Seymour Cassel**
Ian Andrew Troi: **R. J. Williams**
Transporter Chief: O'Brien: **Colm Meaney**
Miss Gladstone: **Dawn Arnemann**
Guinan: **Whoopi Goldberg**
Young Ian: **Zachary Benjamin**
Engineering Ensign: **Dore Keller**

The *Enterprise* is ferrying samples of a deadly plasma plague for study when Troi stuns the crew by announcing she's pregnant.

What she describes as a glowing white light impregnated her during sleep. According to new chief medical officer Kate Pulaski, the fetus will grow full term in just thirty-six hours. As Picard and his officers debate the security concerns raised by the "invader," Troi announces flatly she's having the baby.

The counselor has a remarkably easy birth—her son, Ian, appears completely harmless but continues his unusual growth rate, aging eight years in twenty-seven hours.

Almost oblivious to all of this is young Wes Crusher, who seeks counsel from the mysterious new Ten-Forward hostess, Guinan, about whether to join his mother, who has left to head Starfleet Medical. He finally decides to stay on board.

Meanwhile, one of the plague samples inexplicably begins to grow—threatening to break its containment and infect the crew within two hours.

It turns out that Ian—or at least, the life-force that took the form of the human child to learn more about humans—is a stimulus for the viral sample's growth. A tearful Troi watches Ian revert to his real form; the virus stops growing, and the ship's mercy mission can be finished.

During the writers' strike, "The Child" was chosen from among the old unused *Star Trek II* series scripts to be turned into a season opener, although Hurley stated his rewrites proceeded from premise, not from the original outline.[1] Instead of Troi, of course, in the original tale the "immaculate conception" happens to the first Trek movie's Deltan navigator Ilia—yet another parallel between the two female characters, who already share an empathic trait and similar onetime love interests, Decker and Riker. That original final draft story of January 9, 1978, opened with the same glowing light that was used here, but in that case the fast-growing baby was causing the ship's hull to turn to powder. Overseen by a nearby probe via an "umbilical" scanner beam, the child was being made to develop through its race's past stages of evolution prior to noncorporeality.

Director Rob Bowman got permission to film this season opener with extra cameras and equipment, including the impressive opening shot, and he praised Marina Sirtis for rising to the challenge of an expanded role. With Troi naming her son after her father, we learn that Mr. Troi was Ian Andrew—finally depicted in the final season ("Dark Page"/259).

Wesley asks Guinan whether he should join his mother at Starfleet Medical.

Epsilon Indi, a star spied by Wesley out Ten-Forward, was home to extinct pirates in 1968's "And the Children Shall Lead"—and to the Andorians in fan nonfiction. Cited on the Okudagrams as four associates working on the mutated strain are "Drs." Bowman, Hurley, Summers, and Povill (the latter pair the writers of the original story), and a likeness to the "Legato infection" or "Hutzel infection." Seymour Cassel's familiar face was lately in the films *Dick Tracy, Honeymoon in Vegas,* and *Indecent Proposal.*

Overlooked later, Guinan in her debut answers Wesley's direct question about knowing Picard during his *Stargazer* days ("The Battle"/110) by saying she "never knew the captain until I came on board"—and doesn't seem to be misleading him (see notes, "Time's Arrow, Part II"/227).

WHERE SILENCE HAS LEASE

Production No.: 128 ■ Aired: Week of November 28, 1988
Stardate: 42193.6 ■ Code: ws

Directed by **Winrich Kolbe**
Written by **Jack B. Sowards**

GUEST CAST
Nagilum: **Earl Boen**
Ensign Haskell: **Charles Douglass**
Transporter Chief: **Colm Meaney**

En route to the Morgana Quadrant, the *Enterprise* suddenly finds itself inside a black void without form or dimension—a void that is unending and inescapable, no matter which direction the ship turns.

A sister ship, the USS *Yamato*, appears in the void, and Riker and Worf investigate. But the ship is part of the trap, and the men find themselves in a maze of repetition that nearly drives Worf mad with its illogic.

Finally the presence behind the void appears: Nagilum, an entity who wants to study humans' reaction to death.

The superalien, who appears on screen only as vaguely humanoid facial sections separated by darkness, announces he will use from one-third to one-half of the crew for his experiments. After much soul-searching, Picard regretfully begins the autodestruct sequence with Riker, and later outwits images of Troi and Data sent by the alien to argue against the move.

With just two seconds to spare before autodestruct, the soft-voiced entity suddenly frees the ship, saying he has learned enough about human nature by watching the crew's preparation for death. In one final debate, a relieved Picard tells Nagilum that they do have one trait in common: curiosity.

Trapped in Nagilum's void, Picard's officers weigh their options.

TNG newcomer Winrich Kolbe, whose distinctive accent earned him a nickname, "the Baron," on the set, put his years of directorial experience to good use in fighting the claustrophobia of this budget-minded "bottle show." Penned by *Star Trek II* coauthor Jack Sowards, the only scenes that take place off the *Enterprise* are aboard a sister ship!

According to Hurley, this superalien's name is the reverse spelling (minus one *l*) of Mulligan. The name was chosen because actor Richard Mulligan, the star of *Soap* and *Empty Nest*, was originally sought to play the role.

This episode also introduces Worf's soon-to-be-famous holodeck combat-calisthenics program, which will be seen later in "The Emissary" (146) and "New Ground" (210). The autodestruct sequence seen in "11001001" (116) is repeated here, but with a flexible countdown time; the device has not been used since. Whether included as yet another homage to the original *Star Blazer's* flagship or even its namesake, the World War II Japanese battleship, the starship *Yamato's* NCC number given here was 1305-E. In a rare continuity error, the number was changed nine shows later, in "Contagion" (137) to 71807.

ELEMENTARY, DEAR DATA

Production No.: 129 ■ Aired: Week of December 5, 1988
Stardate: 42286.3 ■ Code: ed

Directed by **Rob Bowman**
Written by **Brian Alan Lane**

GUEST CAST
Moriarty: **Daniel Davis**
Lestrade: **Alan Shearman**
Ruffian: **Biff Manard**
Prostitute: **Diz White**
Assistant Engineer Clancy: **Anne Elizabeth Ramsay**
Pie Man: **Richard Merson**

After the *Enterprise* arrives three days early for a scheduled rendezvous, La Forge persuades Sherlock Holmes fan Data to use the extra time playing the role of the detective on the holodeck, with the engineer as Watson.

But Holmes's original cases are no challenge to Data's memory, so Dr. Pulaski—who has yet to accept the android as anything more than a machine—challenges him to solve a new, computer-generated case. La Forge obliges by programming a case that's a challenge match for Data: a Professor Moriarty who takes on consciousness. Holmes's archenemy not only kidnaps Pulaski in a bid to become real, but also threatens to take over the *Enterprise* with a Victorian gadget that can control the ship from within the holodeck.

In top hat and tails, Picard enters the program to confront Moriarty and convinces him his plan is useless because of the construct's true nature. A mellowed Moriarty, already transcending his character's fictional bounds, relents but asks to be recalled if a process for solidifying holodeck creations into real matter is ever found—and the captain agrees.

Data's initial fascination with Sherlock Holmes ("Lonely Among Us" /108) goes a step further here, as does the planned Pulaski-Data friction. The ending originally filmed was dropped from the version aired: the paper with Moriarty's sketch of the *Enterprise* is

Data proves his Holmesian prowess to Pulaski, while La Forge's Dr. Watson looks on.

significant not because of what he's drawn but for the fact that it exists off the holodeck. Picard is then aware that the character can somehow be saved, as opposed to the gone-awry holodeck images of "The Big Goodbye" (113), and so his explanations to Moriarty were seen as a lie by Gene Roddenberry, who didn't want Picard to stoop to deception. The climax leaves the ship's fate purely up to the captain's persuasiveness and Moriarty's newfound good sense.

To make up for having lost "The Big Goodbye" the previous season, director Rob Bowman grabbed this period piece when offered a choice of early-season shows. The wondrous Victorian London set was built on Stage 16 in just three days. Workers toiled around the clock with fiberglass and plaster to build the street, two side alleys, the warehouse, a wharfside, and the entrance to Moriarty's lair, and after two days of filming the over-budget $125,000 set all came down again.

Sadly, the popular Holmes milieu will likely not be used again on TNG for legal reasons. After this segment aired, Paramount received notice that the Arthur Conan Doyle estate still owns a percentage of the rights to the Holmes character, after nearly a century, and would require a usage fee if it was ever used again.

Anne Elizabeth Ramsay's character, Engineer Clancy, turned up again later as a command-division bridge ensign at the conn in "The Emissary" (146).

THE OUTRAGEOUS OKONA

Production No.: 130 ■ Aired: Week of December 12, 1988
Stardate: 42402.7 ■ Code: ok

Directed by **Robert Becker**
Teleplay by **Burton Armus**
Story by **Les Menchen, Lance Dickson, and David Landsberg**

GUEST CAST
Captain Thaduin Okona: **William O. Campbell**
Debin: **Douglas Rowe**
Kushell: **Albert Stratton**
Yanar: **Rosalind Ingledew**
Benzan: **Kieran Mulroney**
Lieutenant B. G. Robinson: **Teri Hatcher**
The Comic: **Joe Piscopo**
Guinan: **Whoopi Goldberg**

Near the twin Madena planets, the *Enterprise* picks up young trader Thaduin Okona while helping him repair his small craft. The roguish charmer quickly makes friends, especially among the female crew members.

Intrigued by Okona's wisecracks, Data lets Guinan talk him into a stint on the holodeck as a comic. He conjures up a twentieth-century comedy club and a stand-up of the day to coach him.

Meanwhile Picard faces a confrontation that's more of a headache than a crisis: the two hotheaded leaders of Madena's twin worlds are demanding Okona's hide. Straleb's ruler accuses him of stealing their sacred Jewel of Thesia, while Atlec's raves that Okona made his daughter pregnant.

Picard faces the exasperating prospect of the two tiny vessels actually opening fire on his ship or each other, until an inquisitive Wes Crusher persuades the trader to "fess up."

Okona baits the Straleb leader's son into admitting everything: the two fearful children used Okona as go-between for their romance and used the jewel as a nuptial vow.

With the two planets now bound for union, a Data despondent over his bad luck with humor unintentionally spouts a Gracie Allen nugget—and cracks up the bridge.

Destined to soar three years later in Disney's *Rocketeer,* William O. Campbell—no relation to the same-named actor behind the original Trek's Squire Trelane and Klingon Captain Koloth—had almost been cast as Riker when the regulars were being assembled. Rick Berman, echoing Justman's recollection, said that the studio executives, who had the final say, considered their runner-up "too soft." Funny, if a bit predictable, and helped by the misplaced arrogance of the two planet's leaders, this teleplay by producer Burton Armus features a main plot that actually has to compete for attention with the subplot of Data's holodeck comedy adventures.

Joe Piscopo, the *Saturday Night Live* veteran, does a good turn as a buck-toothed Jerry Lewis character. Lewis himself was to have played the part, but a schedule conflict with his guest spot on the show *Wiseguy* got in the way.

In-jokes include the Charnock Comedy Cabaret sign, which honors crew paint foreman Ed Charnock, Jr., and a holodeck menu of "humorists" taken from the office phone directory for the TNG staff, producers, and aides; the file chosen is actually that of visual-effects associate Ronald B. Moore. And when Data asks for the funniest performer available, those listed besides "Stano Riga"—seen only briefly—include the Great Bird himself as well as Maurice Hurley and Farouk El-Baz, a planetary geologist at Boston University who, during his NASA days, worked with Berman on a documentary and who later had a shuttlepod namesake in "Time Squared" (139).

Of the three vessels seen, Okona's *Erstwhile* is a re-dress of the Talarian *Batris* ("Heart of Glory"/120); Debin's Atlec ship is the merchant ship from *Star Trek III,* with more length; and Kushell's Straleb ship was new, a design Rick Sternbach said was simply modeled after "a big Easter egg."

Another of Greg Jein's contributions turns up here in the background: a tridimensional chess set that's a tip of the hat to its original-Trek cousin. This set, however, features among its pieces the Jupiter II spacecraft from *Lost in Space* for bishops. The kings are modeled after the robot from that same old sci-fi series.

Data experiments with humor.

THE SCHIZOID MAN

Production No.: 131 ■ Aired: Week of January 23, 1989
Stardate: 42437.5 ■ Code: sm

Directed by **Les Landau**
Teleplay by **Tracy Tormé**
Story by **Richard Manning and Hans Beimler**

GUEST CAST
Dr. Ira Graves: **W. Morgan Sheppard**
Lieutenant Selar: **Suzie Plakson**
Kareen Brianon: **Barbara Alyn Woods**

Kareen (Barbara Alyn Woods) and the crew find Data unconscious.

Dr. Noonien Soong may have been Data's "father," but the brilliant Dr. Ira Graves turns out to be Soong's mentor and Data's "grandfather."

Graves is dying of a terminal illness when the *Enterprise* answers his young female aide's call for help on their secluded research world.

Once he arrives on the planet, Data becomes close to Graves, leading the genius to reveal his last breakthrough: a device capable of transferring a human personality into a computer.

Graves dies, and his assistant, Kareen Brianon, is evacuated. But Data begins to act irrational, even accusing Picard of lusting after the beautiful Kareen. A diagnostic check of Data reveals nothing, but Troi performs a psych test that shows two competing personalities fighting to control Data: his own and Graves's.

Meanwhile Kareen is shocked when Graves-Data tells her of the transference, his love for her, and his plans to make her immortal by transferring her consciousness into another android body—which she refuses to consider.

That triggers his violent denial of the wrongness of his plans. After unintentionally crushing her hand, he hides in Engineering, rendering La Forge and an aide unconscious before Picard discovers him.

Graves knocks Picard out for arguing for the release of Data's body, but when the captain comes to, he finds the cyberneticist has reconsidered—and put himself into the *Enterprise* computer as simple data.

The tale of Ira Graves and the transfer of his intellect into Data began with Richard Manning and Hans Beimler, who wrote a concept called "Core Dump." During the rewrite process, this concept was combined with a separate but similar story that Tracy Tormé had pitched. In that tale, "Ménage," a woman comes aboard who once had a triangular love affair with two men from Omicron Theta, the now-dead colony whose memories are stored within Data ("Datalore"/114). The memories grow so strong when Data is in her presence that the two men's personalities fight for control of him.

The role of Kareen was the first that onetime Chicagoan Barbara Alyn Woods auditioned for when she arrived in Los Angeles—a departure from the "bimbos and wild girls" that, in her words, she had played in films and guest TV. Sheppard was later a Klingon commander in *Star Trek VI*.

Suzie Plakson's Dr. Selar was the first female Vulcan officer ever heard in Trek, but the actress would later go on to infamy on TNG as a member of another alien race in "The Emissary" (146) and in "Reunion" (181). Tormé has since revealed that he wanted to develop a romance between Selar and Worf, but that suggestion was nixed. Suzie Plakson counted the national tour of *Stop the World, I Want to Get Off*, opposite Anthony Newley, as a highlight among her improv comedy, regional theater, Broadway, and off-Broadway credits. After guest spots on *Murphy Brown* and *Beauty and the Beast*, a recurring voice on *Dinosaurs*, and the film *My Stepmother Is an Alien*, she landed a regular role on *Love and War*. Still, Dr. Selar would remain aboard by mention ("Tapestry"/241, "Suspicions"/248, "Sub Rosa"/266, "Genesis"/271).

A subplot in Tormé's script involved Data's lack of ego; trimmed along with several of the scenes featuring Data's beard was the original tag scene—already a legendary TNG story—in which he is seen trying yet again to emulate an admired and respected crew member. In this scene, to Picard's chagrin, the android is bald.

Loud as a Whisper

Production No.: 132 ■ Aired: Week of January 9, 1989
Stardate: 42477.2 ■ Code: lw

Directed by **Larry Shaw**
Written by **Jacqueline Zambrano**

GUEST CAST
Riva: **Howie Seago**
Warrior/Adonis: **Leo Damian**
Woman: **Marnie Mosiman**
Scholar: **Thomas Oglesby**
O'Brien: **Colm Meaney**
Warrior No. 1 (Blond Solari leader): **Richard Lavin**
Warrior No. 2 (Brunette Solari leader): **Chip Heller**
Lieutenant (Traitor Solari): **John Garrett**

His Chorus dead, Riva (Howie Seago) ponders his next move.

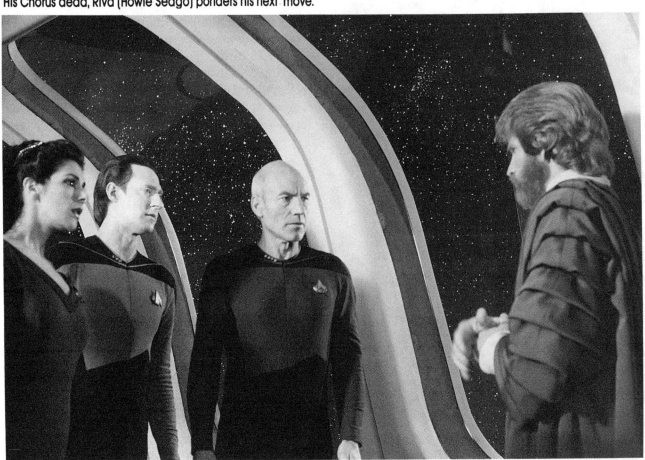

To help settle a civil war, the *Enterprise* is sent to retrieve the great Ramatisian mediator Riva, whose résumé extends to negotiating early UFP-Klingon treaties.

The crew is surprised to learn, though, that Riva and his ruling family were born deaf and use a three-member telepathic chorus to communicate: the Woman, the Scholar, and Warrior/Adonis. The latter informs Troi that Riva is taken with her.

But an incident on strife-torn Solais V wrecks the peace mission and Riva's self-confidence as well when a terrorist opens fire, killing the chorus.

The loss sends Riva into a fit of grief and helplessness. Data learns to read his frantic signing, but Picard cannot draw Riva out. When the mediator even refuses Troi's attempts to help, she opts to try the mission herself.

Plying Riva for negotiating hints, she inspires him to use his own main strategy: "turn a disadvantage into an advantage."

Reinvigorated, Riva beams down alone, determined to start from scratch and teach both Solais factions his sign language, no matter how long it takes.

Howie Seago, who is actually deaf, met with the producers during the writers' strike to suggest a show built around a deaf actor as a guest star. This episode is the result, and in it Seago helped to change what he felt was a dangerous myth regarding deaf people: the first draft's premise had his character learning to speak overnight after the failure of a mechanical translator he used to communicate with his chorus. The day before shooting he suggested an alternative scenario, where after the killing of his chorus Riva stays on Solais V to teach the combatants sign language. To his surprise the idea was eagerly accepted; the supportive mail from both deaf and hearing people seemed to bear out the wisdom of that idea.

Marnie Mosiman kept her TNG guest role in the family: she's the wife of John "Q" de Lancie. Richard Lavin had previously appeared as the second mediator in "Justice" (109).

LeVar Burton campaigned for a time to let Geordi's sight be restored so that he as an actor could use his expressive eyes, and Pulaski's line about perhaps doing so surgically seems to be a preparation for that. Despite some alternate universes ("Future Imperfect"/182, "All Good Things . . ."/277–78), it would never happen—and Burton came to suggest he stay blind but replace the VISOR with cloned implants to keep Geordi as a role model for all handicapped people, much as Uhura of sixties Trek became an inspiration for Whoopi Goldberg, other blacks, and indeed all women.

Look quick: Riva's "indigenous rock" table includes markings alluding to Kei and Yuri (more *animé!*), and one of Riva's hand signs to Data is the Vulcan spread-fingered greeting turned sideways! The mediator's youthful appearance is somewhat baffling, however. Like Sarek later (171), Riva is credited with many of the early UFP-Klingon treaties.

UNNATURAL SELECTION

Production No.: 133 ■ Aired: Week of January 30, 1989
Stardate: 42494.8 ■ Code: us

Directed by **Paul Lynch**
Written by **John Mason and Mike Gray**

GUEST CAST
Dr. Sara Kingsley: **Patricia Smith**
Transporter Chief: **Colm Meaney**
Captain Taggert: **J. Patrick McNamara**
Transporter Ensign: **Scott Trost**

Answering a distress call from the USS *Lantree*, the *Enterprise* finds by visual scans that the supply ship's entire crew has died of old age.

Mysterious "hyperaging" has also hit the ship's last stopover, the Darwin genetics lab, where the stricken staff begs to have its genetically bred "superchildren" rescued, after assuring the *Enterprise* crew the children do not carry the disease.

A skeptical Picard wants the children checked anyway; to avoid crew contamination Data pilots a shuttle so that Dr. Pulaski can examine one child in isolation.

But the youth and his "siblings" turn out to be infected, and the crew is shocked when Pulaski herself is quarantined at Darwin to help with the cure research.

Picard is not willing to accept the loss of his chief medical officer. He pushes his people to modify the transporter biofilter to screen out the virus. A hair sample finally provides the necessary pre-infection DNA, and the doctor and the lab staff are eventually cured.

Sadly, the fate of the Darwin youth cannot be so easily reversed, and because of the health threat, the "superchildren" must be isolated forever.

Dr. Pulaski shows the effects of the Darwin viral hyperaging.

In one last gesture, the *Enterprise* returns to the *Lantree* and solemnly atomizes the plague ship with full Starfleet ceremony.

An echo of an original-series episode, "The Deadly Years," this story almost let the proverbial "cat out of the bag" by using the transporter to reconstruct a "younger" Dr. Pulaski. To avoid a stream of endless complications (unlimited duplication of the characters, for one), specific limitations were later laid down on the use of this technology. The script is the only dual effort by John Mason and Mike Gray during their half-season stint as coproducers.

TNG's first named shuttlecraft is called the *Sakharov*, in honor of the late Soviet physicist and human rights advocate Andrei Sakharov, and a little more interior space has been added.

The Darwin "superchildren" were originally to have appeared nude and the extras were asked to shave from the neck down. But the use of transparent furniture quickly nixed that idea, and costumes were hastily made as the extras endured stubble itch. The youth who was brought aboard the *Sakharov* was played by actor George Baxter and had a name, David, but in a budget crunch all his lines were cut to save money.

A MATTER OF HONOR

Production No.: 134 ▪ Aired: Week of February 6, 1989
Stardate: 42506.5 ▪ Code: mt

Directed by **Rob Bowman**
Teleplay by **Burton Armus**
Story by **Wanda M. Haight, Gregory Amos, and Burton Armus**

GUEST CAST
Ensign Mendon: **John Putch**
Captain Kargan: **Christopher Collins**
Lieutenant Klag: **Brian Thompson**
O'Brien: **Colm Meaney**
Tactics Officer: **Peter Parros**
Vekma: **Laura Drake**

In a new exchange program, Riker becomes the first Starfleet officer to serve aboard a Klingon vessel. He throws himself into the job, taking a crash course in Klingon culture and cuisine from Worf.

Meanwhile, the same program brings the young Benzite Mendon aboard the *Enterprise* but a cultural difference nearly destroys the ship when he lags in reporting the presence of hull-eating bacteria.

Aboard the Klingon cruiser *Pagh*, Riker uses Worf's lessons to gain respect from his new captain and subordinates. He enjoys a hearty meal with the *Pagh* crew and banters with its women, but the discovery of the bacteria on the Klingon ship leads its captain, Klag, to brand Riker a traitor and order an attack on the *Enterprise*.

Riker uses an emergency transponder given to him by Worf to beam Klag off the bridge when he dismisses the *Enterprise*'s warnings—making

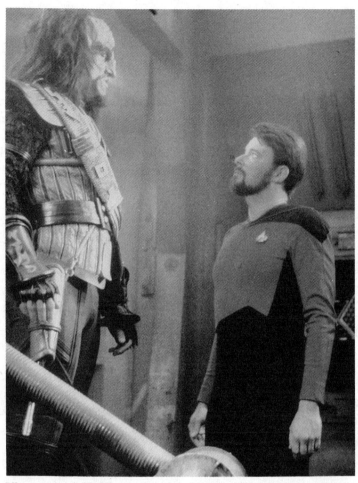

Riker confronts his Klingon "captain," Kargan (Christopher Collins).

Riker captain long enough to demand the "surrender" of the Starfleet ship to preserve the Klingons' honor.

A shrewd student of culture, Riker takes an uppercut from the returned Klag to let him regain his crew's respect, and Mendon makes amends by helping find a solution to the bacteria, saving both ships.

Maurice Hurley intended this story to be a reverse spin on Worf's situation aboard a human ship, and it became one of the bright spots of the second season, scoring a 12.2 rating—TNG's highest to that point—on the Nielsen Television Index used for syndicated programs. This episode gave Jonathan Frakes his meatiest role to date; he and director Rob Bowman both sank their teeth into it. "Every day it was Jonathan and I doing high-fives and trying to put forth on film all the energy and the spirit and adventure that was in that script," the director said. In one particularly nice scene Riker trains on the firing range as he tries to become ambidextrous in his use of the phaser.

Klingons are heard here to use kilometers as a unit of measure, even though kellicams had been used in *Star Trek III* (and later in "Redemption"/200). The heart of a targ, Worf's onetime pet ("Where No One Has Gone Before"/106), is a delicacy here, as well as its milk ("In Theory"/199); *gagh* (pronounced "gawk")—actually long brown noodles and root vegetables, according to prop master Alan Sims—is "best served live," while rokeg blood pie, later learned to be a Worf favorite ("Family"/178), was actually bottoms-up turnips and roots in pumpkin pies, all dyed red. As usual, the show ran long and one cut scene used a miniature for the Bird-of-Prey's engineering room.

After seven outings, Meaney's character finally gets a last name, O'Brien; another two years would pass before viewers learned his first and middle names (178). Vekma's fellow female Klingon, a nonspeaking character, is named Zegov. And John Putch, who appeared as Ensign Mendon, made TNG trivia history by becoming the first guest star to appear twice as a member of the same alien race but in a different role (see "Coming of Age"/119); how convenient that some Benzites really do look alike.

THE MEASURE OF A MAN

Production No.: 135 ■ Aired: Week of February 13, 1989
Stardate: 42523.7 ■ Code: mm

Directed by **Robert Scheerer**
Written by **Melinda M. Snodgrass**

GUEST CAST
Captain Phillipa Louvois: **Amanda McBroom**
Admiral Nakamura: **Clyde Kusatsu**
Commander Bruce Maddox: **Brian Brophy**
O'Brien: **Colm Meaney**
Guinan: **Whoopi Goldberg**

Data's rights as a sentient being are questioned when Commander Bruce Maddox, a cyberneticist, wants to disassemble the android to make duplicates for Starfleet.

When Maddox seems uncertain of his ability to reassemble Data, the *Enterprise* second officer refuses to submit to his experiment and resigns from Starfleet. But that resignation is made moot when Maddox gets a ruling that the android is Starfleet property under a three-hundred-year-old law.

Picard is ready to tackle that decision in a court of law, but the insufficient legal staff at the new starbase forces Riker to serve as both prosecutor and defender. On top of that, the base's judge advocate general, Captain Phillipa Louvois, is an old flame of Picard whose zeal in handling the USS *Stargazer* inquiry years before split them up.

Riker, warned to do his best or see a summary judgment in Maddox's favor, dramatically proves that his second officer is just a machine by removing one of Data's arms and then turning him off completely.

Picard has all but conceded until Guinan helps him see that Maddox's plan for an army of androids without rights would amount to slavery.

Confident again, Picard successfully argues that all beings are created but not owned by their creator. Later he and Louvois agree to a dinner date, while Data assuages Riker's guilt for taking part in the prosecution's case.

Below: Picard argues Data's rights before Commander Maddox (Brian Brophy) and Captain Louvois (Amanda McBroom). *Opposite; top:* Captain Louvois ponders her decision. *Bottom:* Riker "proves" Data is nothing but a machine.

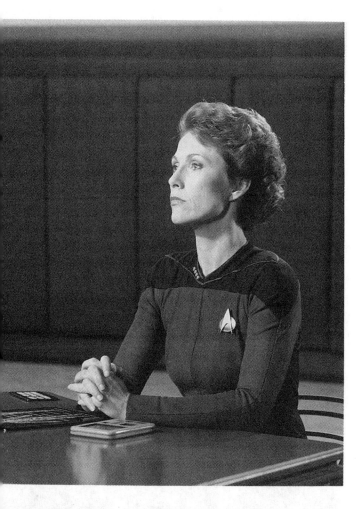

Writer Melinda Snodgrass drew on her own experience as an attorney to craft this timeless tale of personal rights. This episode, which marked her TV debut, was nominated for a Writers Guild award. Now an established SF novelist, Snodgrass hit the *New York Times* best-seller list with her first book, *Tears of the Singers,* also set in the Trek universe. She has coedited the Wild Cards SF book series with friend and fellow SF-fantasy author George R.R. Martin, a producer on TV's *Beauty and the Beast.*

Guest star Brian Brophy, who may be best known to genre fans as Traker from *Max Headroom,* earlier played a doctor on the "good" side of the research ethics question in the film *Paranoia.* His Maddox character, who is actually more impulsive than villain-ous, has since popped up occasionally. In "Data's Day" (185) he is corresponding with the forgiving android all the way from the Daystrom Technological Institute—an homage to computer gen-ius Richard Daystrom from the 1960s episode "The Ultimate Com-puter."

Amanda McBroom, a longtime Trek and SF fan, had a recur-ring role on *Hawaii Five-O* and won the 1980 Golden Globe for co-writing "The Rose," the hit Bette Midler song from the movie of the same name. A Broadway actress, she had guested on *M★A★S★H, Hart to Hart, Remington Steele, Magnum P.I.,* and *Taxi.*

During the trial, Data is forced to reveal his on-off switch to Picard and Riker ("Datalore"/114) as well as his intimate encounter with the late Tasha Yar in "The Naked Now" (103); he keeps a small copy of the hologram she recorded for her memorial service. Here we learn that Data's Starfleet awards include deco-rations for valor and for gallantry; the Medal of Honor, with clusters; the Legion of Honor; the Starcross; and three others seen in a case. His computer file, as viewed by Riker, refers to the android as NFN NMI Data; the initials stand for No First Name, No Middle Initial. And, for computer buffs, Data's storage capacity is said to be 800 quadrillion bits, with a rating of 16 trillion operations per second!

The regular poker game among Picard's officers is seen here for the first time, as is the redesigned flag officer's uniform. An attempt is also made—here with a novel and later, in "Up the Long Ladder" (144), with love poetry—to reestablish an ethnic-pride joke for Worf and the Klingons, a successor to the original Trek's Russian joke for Chekov and the short-lived French joke for Picard.

The Okudagram starmap originally seen behind "mother creature" Remmick ("Conspiracy"/125) is used for the last time on TNG in this show's courtroom, though it later turned up as a wall chart in spinoff DS9's classroom. Meanwhile, the Daystrom Institute would become a twenty-fourth-century Trek staple ("Booby Trap"/154, "Captain's Holiday"/167, "Data's Day"/185, and DS9's "Q-Less").

THE DAUPHIN

Production No.: 136 ■ Aired: Week of February 20, 1989
Stardate: 42568.8 ■ Code: dp

Directed by **Rob Bowman**
Written by **Scott Rubenstein and Leonard Mlodinow**

GUEST CAST
Anya: **Paddi Edwards**
Salia: **Jamie Hubbard**
O'Brien: **Colm Meaney**
Crewman Aron: **Peter Neptune**
Anya as Teenage Girl: **Mädchen Amick**
Anya as Furry Animal: **Cindy Sorenson**
Ensign Gibson: **Jennifer Barlow**

A diplomatic mission provides the setting for Wesley's first romance when the ship must ferry home a princess and her overprotective guardian.

As Troi worries that the two passengers are not what they seem, Wesley seeks advice on how to handle his emotions. Meanwhile, the princess's guardian Anya grows irrational at any hint of danger to Salia.

When Anya transforms herself into a dangerously violent creature to challenge Worf, Dr. Pulaski realizes that Salia's people are allasomorphs, or shape-changers.

To avoid a fight, Picard orders Wesley to stay away from Salia, but Wesley cannot, and their meetings continue until Anya discovers them. When Salia matches Anya's transformation with one of her own, Wesley is stunned, and he deserts her.

Wes at first rebuffs Salia's apologies for having deceived him, but he finally overcomes his pride and brings her a peace offering: another bowl of the chocolate mousse they once enjoyed together.

This simple story by the early-season story editors at last gives Wesley a contemporary problem and his first romance. It was a special thrill for Wil Wheaton: not only was it the sixteen-year-old's

first screen kiss but actress Jamie Hubbard was ten years his senior! "Dauphin" (pronounced doe-fan') incidentally, was the title given to the eldest son of the king of France from 1349 to 1830. The original Trek had included at least two references to shapeshifters: the people of Antos IV in "Whom Gods Destroy" and the Vendorians in "The Survivor," an episode of the animated series.

Seen only briefly here, Mädchen Amick—Hubbard's runner-up for the role of Salia—would go on to much more exposure as Leo Johnson's unfortunate wife Shelly on *Twin Peaks.*

The folks at the Post Group stayed extra busy with "The Dauphin," adding a seventh twenty-hour day to their week to create the shape transformations and the world the young couple visits on the holodeck. Two of the ten shots required for the Rousseau V asteroid ring required over 110 layers each, while some twenty-five steps were needed for each of the allasomorphs' seven transformations. Still, Rob Bowman thought the monster outfits looked cheap and reduced their screen time as much as possible.

An unusual touch is seen in Wes Crusher's quarters: just as Anya resumes her shape, you can see on the shelf behind her a display cube with an old-style Kirk-era phaser and communicator.

Wesley with his first love (Jamie Hubbard).

CONTAGION

Production No.: 137 ■ Aired: Week of March 20, 1989
Stardate: 42609.1 ■ Code: cg

Directed by **Joseph L. Scanlan**
Written by **Steve Gerber and Beth Woods**

GUEST CAST
Captain Donald Varley: **Thalmus Rasulala**
Sub-Commander Taris: **Carolyn Seymour**
Tactical Ensign: **Dana Sparks**
O'Brien: **Colm Meaney**
Doctor: **Folkert Schmidt**

Crossing the Neutral Zone to answer an SOS from the USS *Yamato,* the *Enterprise* arrives in time to see widespread computer malfunctions destroy its sister ship.

When log tapes from the *Yamato* reveal that its captain had tracked the mythical planet Iconia to this location, Picard has his ship retrace the *Yamato's* course: discovering the secrets of the extinct Iconian civilization would be worth risking an encounter with the Romulans. But after the same computer malfunctions begin to plague the *Enterprise,* La Forge realizes that an Iconian probe's energy burst infected the *Yamato* with a computer virus that rewrote that ship's control software. By downloading the *Yamato's* logs, the *Enterprise* has now become infected as well.

A desperate Picard beams down with Worf and Data to a control tower on long-dead Iconia, where they discover a time gateway. There Data becomes infected with the Iconian virus as well.

Meanwhile, the crew is forced to raise shields and strand the away team when a Romulan ship suddenly attacks the *Enterprise.* But Riker soon learns the enemy vessel is also crippled by the virus.

Picard decides to destroy the control tower and the remaining Iconian probes, but first returns Data and Worf to the *Enterprise* through the time gateway. Once Data arrives back on

Iconia's computer virus infects Data as well as his ship.

board ship, his self-correcting function eradicates the Iconian virus in his system; that reminds La Forge that the ship's computers have the same capability.

The *Enterprise* regains transporter capability in time to rescue Picard from the planet below. The Romulans, of course, offer no thanks for the virus cure that saves them as well.

Appropriately enough, the story was conceived by a fan and computer technician (Beth Woods) who at the time worked on the Trek offices' computers. It also introduced Picard's interest in archaeology ("Captain's Holiday"/167, "Qpid"/194, "The Chase"/246, "Gambit"/256–257, and "Bloodlines"/274). Carolyn Seymour would turn up as a different alien ("First Contact"/189) and another Romulan ("Face of the Enemy"/240).

This segment features Picard's first oral food-slot order for "Tea, Earl Grey—hot," and the first-ever name of a Romulan ship in twenty-three years of aired Trek: *Haakona*. A familiar character, Commander Bruce Maddox, is already being mentioned as a genius after his debut earlier in the season in "The Measure of the Man" (135).

Rick Sternbach designed the Iconian gateway with lots of Japanese inscriptions that refer to numerous *anime* titles and characters. And the names of the show's cowriters, Steve Gerber and Beth Woods, can barely be seen in the list of *Yamato*'s log entries, as the ship's first and second officers.

THE ROYALE

Production No.: 138 ■ Aired: Week of March 27, 1989
Stardate: 42625.4 ■ Code: ro

Directed by **Cliff Bole**
Written by **Keith Mills**

GUEST CAST
Texas: **Nobel Willingham**
Assistant Manager: **Sam Anderson**
Vanessa: **Jill Jacobson**
Bellboy: **Leo Garcia**
O'Brien: **Colm Meaney**
Mickey D: **Gregory Beecroft**

Puzzled by the recovery of a chunk of a twenty-first-century Earth spacecraft, Worf, Data, and Riker beam down into the middle of the lone structure they find on the nearest uninhabited planet.

After passing through a revolving door set in an otherwise black void, they cannot escape from what appears to be a resort casino named the Hotel Royale.

Bizarre scenes now unfold before them: a clichéd love triangle, gamblers who invite the Starfleet men to join them, and finally the discovery of a twenty-first-century American astronaut's remains in a hotel suite.

There Data also finds a book entitled *The Hotel Royale*, and the pieces of the mystery begin to fall into place.

By reading the astronaut's diary, the away team learns that aliens found his disabled ship and created a world in which he could live out his life. Unfortunately they used the badly written pulp mystery as their model.

As the love triangle resolves itself yet again with a mobster gunning down a bellboy, the trapped crewmen find a way to break the time-loop trap. Using the novel's ending, in which foreign investors buy the Royale, Data returns to the craps tables and breaks the bank, angering the casino characters but allowing the away team to exit for beam-up.

This story was supposed to be surreal, but if it comes across as merely unfocused, it's not surprising. The name of writer "Keith Mills" is a pseudonym of Tracy Tormé, who reportedly removed his name from the script after Maurice Hurley objected to its surrealism, comedy, and subtle satire. Hurley later said he thought it too derivative of the copycat aliens in the original-Trek episode "A Piece of the Action." The original story was good, but it was a budget-buster, according to director Cliff Bole. Later, Bole was reminded of his years directing *Vega$* when the "Royale" script took a budget cut that resulted in a casino built out of "curtains and some tricks."

The dispute led Tormé to leave active staff duty and take on a looser, nonexclusive role as a creative consultant with a commitment to just three more episodes; he would complete only one, "Manhunt" (145).

In the original final draft of "The Royale," completed on January 10—one of two scripts that had won Tormé a staff job during TNG's first season—the astronaut survivor was actually the last of his crew of seven to die. His image was then kept alive in this macabre setting, to be entertained by the captured *Enterprise* party. In the end, as with Pike and Vina in the original-Trek pilot, "The Cage," a dead away team crew woman is retained to keep the astronaut company after the unseen casino manager agrees to tell the story and release the crew.

In that early draft Dr. Pulaski at one point was supposed to say,

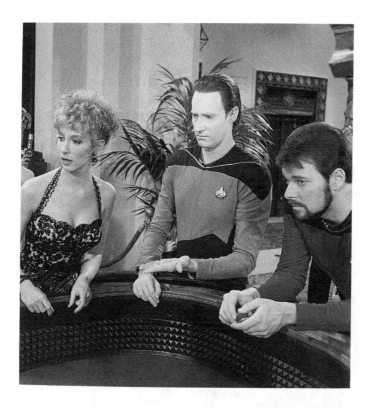

Data's high rolling
intrigues Vanessa
(Jill Jacobson).

"I'm a doctor, not a magician"—harking back to DeForest Kelley's
Dr. McCoy, but that line was lost in the revisions.

Lending sparkle to this outing is veteran character actor Nobel
Willingham, who has played many film and TV roles. He appeared on *Northern Exposure* in 1992 as Maurice Minnifield's
former U.S. Marine commander.

Despite the story's unevenness, much Federation and Earth
history is revealed here. As seen in Colonel Stephen Richey's
uniform patch, the United States is said to have had fifty-two states
in the years between 2053 and 2079, the year the "new" United
Nations fell—see "Farpoint" (101). Richey's flight, launched on July
23, 2037, and overseen by NASA with its 1970s-era logo, was the
third to try to push outside the solar system. Given the series' date,
according to "The Neutral Zone" (126), his death 283 years earlier
would have occurred in 2082.

By the way, for math fans: the missing proof for Fermat's Last
Theorem, devised by the seventeenth-century inventor of differential calculus and differential geometry, would show that $x^n +
y^n = z^n$ where $n>2$ and x, y, and z are whole numbers. This too
may be dated soon: Princeton University professor Andrew Wiles
claimed in 1993 to have discovered a proof to the famous puzzle,
and within a year had worked out the one snag pointed out,
winning tentative early backing for his solution among academi-
cians.

TIME SQUARED

Production No.: 139 ▪ Aired: Week of April 3, 1989
Stardate: 42679.2 ▪ Code: tm

Directed by **Joseph L. Scanlan**
Teleplay by **Maurice Hurley**
Story by **Kurt Michael Bensmiller**

GUEST CAST
O'Brien: **Colm Meaney**

In a bizarre turn of events, Picard is confronted
by his own double from six hours into the future,
out of phase and disoriented after being recovered from a shuttlecraft that has recorded the
Enterprise's destruction in a vast energy whirlpool.

The double Picard, dazed in a nightmare
world, cannot communicate what happened, and
the real-time captain begins to fear that the ship
will become trapped in a time loop.

When the energy whirlpool appears on schedule and the *Enterprise* cannot escape, Picard al-

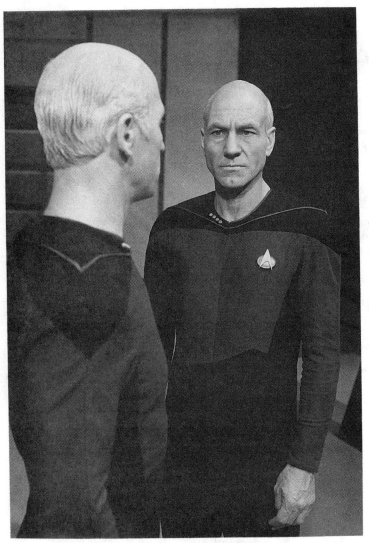

Stewart poses with his photo double/future self.

stand-alone episodes. "Time Squared" would segue into "Q Who" (142), in which the mischievous superalien is revealed as the cause of the vortex. That plan was scrapped at Gene Roddenberry's insistence, Hurley has said, and so adds confusion to the ending. "Why would going into the vortex's center save you?" Hurley asked. "It doesn't make sense. But it does if Q is pulling the strings." Still, the writer said his intent was to do a time-travel story involving just six hours, not "500 or a 1,000 years."

A cheaper alternative to the full-size shuttlecraft, the low-budget shuttlepod, debuted here. The vessel is named for one-time NASA scientist Farouk El-Baz, who had earlier received a tip of the hat in "The Outrageous Okona" (130). According to Michael Okuda, the professor sounded very surprised the morning he called in from Boston University after he and his children had seen the show for the first time!

This segment also mentions the slingshot time-travel method used in the original Trek and in *Star Trek IV,* and introduces Riker's fondness for cooking.

THE ICARUS FACTOR

Production No.: 140 ■ Aired: Week of April 24, 1989
Stardate: 42686.4 ■ Code: if

Directed by **Robert Iscove**
Teleplay by **David Assael and Robert L. McCullough**
Story by **David Assael**

GUEST CAST
O'Brien: **Colm Meaney**
Kyle Riker: **Mitchell Ryan**
Ensign Herbert: **Lance Spellerberg**

almost becomes bogged down with indecision and second-guessing.

Energy bolts attacking Picard lead Troi to suggest it is he the whirlpool wants, but when his double tries to leave the ship, Picard decides his departure "again" will only perpetuate the cycle. After stopping "himself" with a phaser stun, he orders a full-speed course directly into the vortex. After one more moment of self-doubt, the double Picard, his craft, and the whirlpool all vanish, leaving *Enterprise* alone and on course, just as before.

This story—originally titled "Time to the Second"—began as the first of what Maurice Hurley had planned as two consecutive but

When Riker is offered command of his own ship, the *Enterprise* heads for Starbase Montgomery to meet with the civilian strategist who will brief him on the assignment. That strategist turns out to be his father, Kyle, whom Riker hasn't seen in fifteen years. Time has not softened the first officer's hostility toward the older man, and he summarily rejects his father's efforts at reconciliation.

As Dr. Pulaski—an old flame of Kyle's—and Troi ponder why Number One is so bitter, Wesley, La Forge, and Data try to diagnose the reason for Worf's increased tenseness.

Pain-dealing holodeck Klingons help Worf celebrate his
Age of Ascension.

When they discover that Worf is out of sorts because he missed a ritual marking the decade since his Age of Ascension, they surprise him by setting up a reenactment of the Klingon spiritual rite on the holodeck.

As Troi and Pulaski compare notes on "their men," Riker's continued rebuffs lead Kyle to challenge his son to an anbo-jyutsu match—a martial art the younger man never beat him at.

The two finally resolve their feelings for each other, and Number One stuns the bridge crew by revealing his intention to turn down the offered command post and remain aboard *Enterprise*.

___

Here's another case where a subplot—Worf's Age of Ascension ceremony on the holodeck—almost overshadows the main story line, the return of Riker's father. The segment is good in that it reveals Number One's back story and brings Pulaski closer into the fold of characters, but it's hard to compete with Klingon heritage for sheer interest.

Here Riker for the second time refuses a command post, this

one on the *Aries*. We learn that his mother died when he was two and he left home at age fifteen. The almost forgotten Riker-Troi relationship gets a shot in the arm here as he confides to her his fears about advancement—and she and Pulaski compare notes about men.

The Tholians, a hot-planet race with a possible hive-mind culture who were introduced in an original-series episode called "The Tholian Web," are mentioned here in connection with a conflict a dozen years earlier—an attack that almost killed Kyle Riker and introduced him to Pulaski. The Tholians would occasionally pop up in conversation later on, in "Peak Performance" (147) and "Reunion" (181).

This show's hoopla included a visit by the *Entertainment Tonight* cameras, who were following *ET* host and unabashed Trek fan John Tesh through the two hours of makeup necessary to turn him into one of Worf's Ascension Chamber tormentors. Tesh, all six feet six of him, is the Klingon closest to the viewer on the left. Thanks to the "Klingon shortage" caused by the simultaneous shooting of *Star Trek V*, wardrobe was running low and two of the Klingons got to wear old *Planet of the Apes* boots!

Longtime character actor Mitchell Ryan who plays Kyle Riker, may be best known as the villain in *Lethal Weapon*. Lance Spellerberg appeared as Chief Herbert once before ("We'll Always Have Paris"/124). And, as with the Iconian artifact in "Contagion" (137), Sternbach filled the anbo-jyutsu mats and gymnasium set pieces with a myriad of *animé* references in Japanese.

PEN PALS

Production No.: 141 ▪ Aired: Week of May 1, 1989
Stardate: 42695.3 ▪ Code: pp

Directed by **Winrich Kolbe**
Written by **Melinda M. Snodgrass**
Story by **Hannah Louise Shearer**

GUEST CAST
Davies: **Nicholas Cascone**
Sarjenka: **Nikki Cox**
Hildebrandt: **Anne H. Gillespie**
O'Brien: **Colm Meaney**
Alans: **Whitney Rydbeck**

The *Enterprise* command staff decides it is time to give Wesley a real test of responsibility: oversight of a team checking into dangerous geological events in the Selcundi Drema system.

As the acting ensign seeks advice in picking and leading his team of older subordinates, a member balks at running a lengthy test Wesley feels is necessary. After soul-searching and a pep talk from Riker, Wesley gets the test run with no problem.

Meanwhile, Data interrupts Picard's holodeck horseback ride to admit he has contacted a young girl on one of the unsafe worlds, Drema IV.

Although he wanted only to reassure the girl after picking up her lonely broadcasts for help when her world became unstable, Data now fears—and Picard agrees—that his contact may violate the Prime Directive.

After a lively staff debate on the issue, Picard agrees to let Data bring the young girl, Sarjenka, aboard as Wesley's team tries to reverse the volcanic stresses that are about to wreck the planet.

Standing next to Data, Sarjenka watches from the bridge as the plan works and Wesley's team celebrates. Picard then orders Pulaski to "wipe" Sarjenka's short-term memory, and when Data takes her home she remembers nothing of her "pen pal" or of the ship that saved her.

Melinda Snodgrass, who adapted Hannah Louise Shearer's original story treatment, has called this Data's "age of innocence" story. The android had carried on a dialogue with Sarjenka for eight weeks without reporting it, much as he would later do while developing his protégé in "The Offspring" (164). In "Pen Pals," however, the writers had to limit the two characters' closeness, because Nikki Cox's orange makeup became smudged so easily on contact.

Just as she had turned to her roots in the legal profession for "The Measure of a Man" (135), Snodgrass revealed her love of horses—and Patrick Stewart's excellent horsemanship—in Picard's equestrian holodeck visit. This scene was the only location shoot of the season, filmed at a ranch near the L.A. suburb of Thousand Oaks.

A frightened Sarjenka (Nikki Cox)
won't leave her friend Data's side.

Sharp-eyed fans should spot one of the few TNG props not designed by Sternbach: the "spectral analyzer" used in the geology lab. This device was originally the "oscillation overthruster" sought by the evil red Lectroids in *The Adventures of Buckaroo Banzai Across the Eight Dimension*. Other homages to *Buckaroo Banzai* were planted throughout the series by the art staffers, most noticeably as passing references in graphics, as in "Up the Long Ladder" (144), for one.

 WHO

Production No.: 142 ■ Aired: Week of May 8, 1989
Stardate: 42761.3 ■ Code: qw

Directed by **Rob Bowman**
Written by **Maurice Hurley**

GUEST CAST
Q: **John de Lancie**
Ensign Sonya Gomez: **Lycia Naff**
O'Brien: **Colm Meaney**
Guinan: **Whoopi Goldberg**

On the edge of UFP space, the *Enterprise* encounters its old nemesis, the superbeing Q, whose anger at being refused a crew post leads him to hurl the ship into unknown space. There, they encounter a new threat—the Borg.

As the ship discovers planet after planet ravaged like those in the Neutral Zone whose destruction was first blamed on the Romulans, Guinan—an old foe of Q as well—tells Picard of the Borg's deadly attacks on her people.

Suddenly two Borg beam over from their cubelike ship to drain information from the starship's computers, ignoring the crew and quickly learning to blunt phaser attacks.

Their vessel then locks on Picard's ship and slices out a core of the saucer, killing eighteen. A brief skirmish leaves the Borg ship damaged, and Riker takes advantage of the lull to lead an away team over.

What they find is a half-humanoid, half-robotic race living as a group mind intent only on destruction and gaining technology. They also find that the Borg ship is regenerating itself.

Sure enough, the fight resumes and the *Enterprise* is soon on the brink of defeat, its shields

Data, Riker, and Worf get their first look at the Borg.

and warp drive gone. Picard admits to a gloating Q that humans can't yet handle all that the cosmos might yield—that he needs Q's help. Satisfied, the superbeing returns the *Enterprise* to its own corner of the galaxy—and vanishes.

Later a reflective Picard tells Guinan that the near-fatal Borg encounter may have been just the jolt a complacent Federation needed.

Recurring character Q takes a back seat here to Maurice Hurley's long-delayed new Federation opponents, the Borg, who were originally envisioned as a season-opening threat (see "The Neutral Zone,"/126). The new cybernetic race was meant to provide the hard-core danger the Ferengi couldn't deliver. "If somebody's interested in gold, they're not much of an adversary," Hurley said of the greedy little race. "We can make gold in our replicator."

Although the Borg began as a race of insects, a concept dropped for budget reasons, their relentless mentality survived. Guinan was not present at the time, but we learn it was the Borg who scattered and virtually killed off her people a century earlier—an event that drives the plot of the first TNG movie, *Generations*—and leaves perhaps her only prejudice ("I, Borg"/223). In this episode Guinan also engages in a defiant, barb-trading standoff with Q that will come back to haunt him later in "Deja Q" (161). Also, Guinan's office is seen for the first and only time in TNG history.

Pulling the props, wardrobe, and optical effects together for the Borg's physical look was a herculean task and a learning experience, to put it mildly. The Borg armature forearm, for example, weighed about forty pounds. Some of their outfits came from the makers of the "steel suits" for *Dune* and *Batman*. Because the show went over budget by about $50,000, a planned eighth day of live shooting was dropped, and for a time, according to Rob Bowman, "we didn't know day to day if we were making a stinker or a winner."

Meanwhile, it was effects expert Dan Curry's time to shine, along with associate Ron Moore. They won an Emmy nomination for bringing the Borg ship to life. The models for the ship were built by Starlight Effects from the simple embellishments that Rick Sternbach and Richard James had created based on the description of the cubical ship given in the script.

Making his debut as a stuntman extra as the "baby Borg" was Sam Klatman, the son of Carol Eisner, David Livingston's secretary. Lycia Naff, who played a three-breasted mutant woman in *Total Recall*, showed enough comic potential in this show to be written in again in the next episode, but her character was dropped after that appearance.

SAMARITAN SNARE

Production No.: 143 ■ Aired: Week of May 15, 1989
Stardate: 42779.1 ■ Code: ss

Directed by **Les Landau**
Written by **Robert L. McCullough**

GUEST CAST
Grebnedlog: **Christopher Collins**
Reginod: **Leslie Morris**
Surgeon: **Daniel Benzali**
Ensign Sonya Gomez: **Lycia Naff**
Biomolecular Specialist: **Tzi Ma**

As Wesley prepares to take more Academy tests at Starbase 515, Picard suddenly elects to join him for the long shuttle ride after a heated argument with Pulaski.

Aboard *Enterprise*, Riker underestimates the slow-witted Pakleds, who kidnap La Forge after Number One allows Geordi to beam over to give the obese scavengers a hand with their ship.

During the shuttle ride Picard finally opens up enough to explain his reason for making the trip—surgery to replace a defective cardiac unit—and leaves Wesley spellbound with the tale of the shore leave brawl as a young officer that nearly got him killed.

Meanwhile, the Pakleds demand that *Enterprise* release all of its computer information to them. As the crew considers a show of force to rescue Geordi, Riker learns Picard is near death after surgery.

Anxious to reach their captain, the crew members trick the Pakleds with the "crimson force field"—a ruse—and rescue Geordi.

Picard awakens in post-op to learn of his close call—and to find that an amused Pulaski is the specialist who pulled him through.

Created by TNG's late-season producer McCullough, the Pakleds, with their sniffly, slow-minded ways—an allusion to fans, or to materialistic Americans?—have to be among the most humorously bizarre aliens ever created for Trek. Geordi gets a chance in the spotlight in this episode, and the "crimson force field" harks back to the corbomite trick twice used by Kirk in the 1960s.

Christopher Collins had turned up in the TNG universe once

La Forge finds the Pakleds (Leslie Morris and Christopher Collins) harmless at first.

before, as the Klingon captain from "A Matter of Honor" (134), and played aliens on spinoff DS9's "The Passenger" and "Blood Oath." Lycia Naff had been in "Q Who" (142).

Listen carefully to the tale Picard tells Wesley about his early exploits and you'll hear the alien ruffians called Nasicaans—a rare verbal *animé* reference. Also heard are references to the Jarada from "The Big Goodbye" (113), to a recreation facility named for twentieth-century astronomy artist Chesley Bonestell, and to Epsilon 9 as the site of a new pulsar cluster, though no direct connection is made to the same-named communications relay station in the first Trek movie. Picard also mentions that the Klingon-UFP alliance is only twenty or so years old.

For this episode the art staff almost got a chance to bring to life the designed but as yet unbuilt captain's yacht, but budget constraints led to the use instead of an executive shuttle for Picard and Wesley's trip.[2] A rare slipup: Wes tells the control booth that he is departing Shuttle Bay 2 in Shuttle Number 2 when he's actually in the *Sakharov* (Shuttle Number 1) in Shuttle Bay 3, as indicated on the bay floor.

Picard's artificial heart and a replay of his Nausicaans incident became the basis of an entire Q episode in Season 6 ("Tapestry"/241), while the Pakleds were never again a major focus—except to rescue Lore offscreen in "Brothers" (177)—but did turn up in the background of *Deep Space Nine*.

UP THE LONG LADDER

Production No.: 144 ■ Aired: Week of May 22, 1989
Stardate: 42823.2 ■ Code: ul

Directed by **Winrich Kolbe**
Written by **Melinda M. Snodgrass**

GUEST CAST
Danilo O'Dell: **Barrie Ingham**
Granger: **Jon de Vries**
Brenna: **Rosalyn Landor**
O'Brien: **Colm Meaney**

Stellar flares are about to destroy the Bringloidi homeworld when the *Enterprise* rescues the colony, populated by a simple but lively people long ago forgotten except for fragmentary post-holocaust records.

The Bringloidi bring along their livestock and set up camp on a cargo bay. Riker is soon keep-

Riker and Brenna (Rosalyn Landor) take a shine to each other.

ing company with the bumbling leader's lovely but feisty daughter.

Then Picard and Data learn that the colonists' were one of two groups to settle in this solar system. The *Enterprise* heads off to warn the other of the danger.

Soon they find the Mariposans, an entire society composed of clones from the five crew members who survived the original colony ship's crash landing.

Now fearful of degeneration due to replicative fading, the Mariposans beg for fresh DNA from the *Enterprise* crew. But the idea is repugnant to the Starfleet people—just as the idea of sex is to the Mariposans—and they decline.

Desperate, the colony leaders kidnap Riker and Pulaski and collect DNA cells. But the two return to destroy the maturing bodies of the clones and bring a compromise suggestion from Picard: rejoin the Bringloidi, their original fellow colonists, and breed on a resettlement world.

Snodgrass's story, originally titled "Send in the Clones," began as a look at immigration and the "we don't want their kind here" prejudice, but the author admits it lost something in the push-and-shove of rewrites and budget limits. Still, she recalls the story drew some flak from two different directions. Right-to-life advocates objected to the pro-choice "I'm in charge of my body" sentiment espoused by Riker (intended) in denying the Mariposan permission to use his body for cloning, and Irish Americans protested

what they felt was a stereotypical portrayal of the Bringloidi (unintended, since Irishman Hurley conceived their look). The original title, a pun on the title of the Sondheim song "Send in the Clowns," actually survived until well after the scripts were printed.

The pregnant Bringloidi woman was no fake: prop man Alan Sims' wife was two weeks overdue with her baby at the time. The Sims family actually bred the African pygmy goats used in the scene. Mention of Earth's recovery from World War III in the early 2100s and the European Hegemony as the first stirrings of world government later that century seem to jive with Earth's twenty-first-century "post-atomic horror" of "Farpoint" (101–102) and "nuclear winter" ("A Matter of Time"/209), apparently separate from the Eugenics Wars of 1967's "Space Seed" in 1992–96; the reference there could be the "Third World" War, since most of Khan's people came from non-Western nations. In 1968's "Return to Tomorrow," Kirk said Earth had managed its nuclear crisis more wisely than ravaged planet Arret; "Bread and Circuses" set out that some 37 million died in World War III.

An Okudagram seen here—Picard's search menu for Ficus sector launches—includes several humorous references. There's the SS *Buckaroo Banzai*, captained by John Whorfin with a "missi⁻ to Planet 10, Dimension 8"; and two other ships are the *animé*-r . .ed *Urusei Yatsura* and the *Tomobiki*, the setting of "Urusei." Then there are mission assignments such as "diplomatic mission to Alderan," a Star Wars homage, and the one given "Commander Gene Roddenberry" to "explore strange new worlds."

Though it can barely be glimpsed, Picard overlooks on this screen the very launch he's looking for: the sixth line is for the SS *Mariposa*. Beyond the data he reads aloud, another chart shows the ship to be a DY-500 class vessel owned by OCC, launched November 27, 2123, with U.N. registry NAR-7678 and powered by—yes—yoyodyne pulse fusion. According to the 1960s "Space Seed" episode, the DY-500 class dates back to the early twenty-first century, making it a decades-old model by the time of this launch.

Manhunt

Production No.: 145 ■ Aired: Week of June 19, 1989
Stardate: 42859.2 ■ Code: mh

Directed by **Rob Bowman**
Written by **Terry Devereaux**

GUEST CAST
Lwaxana Troi: **Majel Barrett**
Slade Bender: **Robert Costanza**
Mr. Homn: **Carel Struycken**
Rex: **Rod Arrants**
O'Brien: **Colm Meaney**
Scarface: **Robert O'Reilly**
Madeline: **Rhoda Aldrich**
Antedian Dignitary: **Mick Fleetwood**
Transport Pilot: **Wren T. Brown**

While picking up Antedian delegates on diplomatic escort duty, the *Enterprise* is graced once again by Troi's mother, Lwaxana, who checks aboard this time with full ambassadorial status as a delegate.

Her daughter is dismayed to learn that Lwaxana is not only chasing Picard again but is in the midst of the Betazoid "Phase"—a midlife female cycle that quadruples (at least) the woman's sex drive.

Picard escapes from Lwaxana's dinner-for-two trap and flees into the holodeck to hide out and play Dixon Hill, his favorite gumshoe.

Lwaxana moves on to a short-lived engagement with Riker, then tracks both men down on the holodeck, only to fall for the program's bartender.

Meanwhile, in sickbay the fishlike Antedians have remained in a trance, their race's preferred state for deep-space travel. Upon arrival at the Pacifica conference site, they awaken and prepare to beam down just ahead of Lwaxana.

The whole flight having been a waste of time for her, Troi's mother finally shows off her telepathic powers by casually pointing out that the two Antedians are assassins carrying undetectable explosives with which to bomb the conference.

With security officers sheepishly standing by, a departing Lwaxana manages to redden her old friend Picard's face one more time.

Tracy Tormé once again used a pseudonym to protest the revisions of this episode, which turned out to be his TNG swan song. He had conceived of this show as a sequel to two of his first-

Even Dixon Hill and Madeline (Rhonda Aldrich) can't shake Lwaxana Troi (Majel Barrett).

K'Ehleyr (Suzie Plakson) participates in Worf's holodeck "calisthenics."

season episodes, a chance to bring back both Lwaxana Troi and Dixon Hill. The show, designed as a Majel Barrett vehicle, was also the last for prolific director Rob Bowman until season four's "Brothers" (177). Particularly funny were Riker's reaction to the thought of Troi's sex drive quadrupling during the Phase and the scene in which the holodeck character, Rex, realizes that he doesn't know his last name.

In that fiction-within-fiction of the Dixon Hill world, we learn his drink is "scotch, neat," and that secretary Madeline's is "rye and ginger." The holodeck villains, though, come from yet another story, "The Parrot's Claw" (see "The Big Goodbye"/113). Tormé, who based this plot roughly on *Farewell, My Lovely*, had included several Chandleresque voice-overs for Picard/Hill that were removed to avoid confusion with the captain's logs. The escapism is nicely underscored by the use of three pop standards "Moonlight Serenade," "How High the Moon," and "Let's Get Away from It All."

Longtime Trek fan Mick Fleetwood of Fleetwood Mac became the second rock music figure to appear as a guest star on TNG, though as the piscean Antedian terrorist in disguise he kept a much lower profile than did Michelle Phillips in the earlier episode (124). Fleetwood, by the way, shaved off his trademark beard to accommodate the makeup, which took 2½ hours to apply.

THE EMISSARY

Production No.: 146 ■ Aired: Week of June 26, 1989
Stardate: 42901.3 ■ Code: em

Directed by **Cliff Bole**
Teleplay by **Richard Manning and Hans Beimler**
Story by **Thomas H. Calder**

GUEST CAST
K'Ehleyr: **Suzie Plakson**
K'Temoc: **Lance le Gault**
Admiral Gromek: **Georgann Johnson**
O'Brien: **Colm Meaney**
Ensign Clancy: **Anne Elizabeth Ramsey**
Tactical Crewman: **Dietrich Bader**

Sent to assist the *Enterprise* in stopping a pre-alliance Klingon sleeper ship that could awake to prey upon helpless UFP worlds is a special envoy from the Klingon Empire—a half-human, half-Klingon female named K'Ehleyr.

K'Ehleyr, whose advice to destroy the ship is rejected by Picard, turns out to be a former lover of Worf's. He resists her playful advances, finally revealing his pent-up feelings left over from their last parting.

Later K'Ehleyr tries out Worf's holodeck combat program to relieve her mounting stress. Finding her there and joining in the fight, a battle-roused Worf grabs K'Ehleyr and they consummate their passion.

The couple's newfound intimacy is shattered, though, when she storms out after refusing Worf's marriage proposal traditionally offered after making love.

K'Ehleyr's original mission finally brings the two back together. The cruiser's crew awakens before being intercepted, and Picard lets Worf and K'Ehleyr masquerade as the *Enterprise*'s commanders.

Worf doesn't blink in the ensuing standoff and pulls off the ruse, winning kudos from his captain. Seeing K'Ehleyr off privately to take command of the ship, he at last agrees with her that neither will be complete without the other.

Worf's well-ordered life is disrupted by the first in a long series of complications when Suzie Plakson's dynamic K'Ehleyr steps back into his life with this story. Credit director Cliff Bole with the Klingon's crushing hand-holding, which draws blood. The popular Plakson played a Vulcan doctor earlier in the series, in "The Schizoid Man" (131) and would return as the ill-fated K'Ehleyr again, in "Reunion" (181).

Footage of the Klingon K't'inga-class vessels is recycled from the first Trek movie, which makes sense: a seventy-five-year-old ship would still have been in use four years after the events of the *Star Trek II-III-IV* trilogy, in 2286, using TNG's years as mentioned in "The Neutral Zone" (126). K'Ehleyr arrives in a probe that was re-dressed from Spock's photon-torpedo coffin from *Star Trek II* and *III*.

The Okudagram seen here gives K'Ehleyr several other holodeck exercise options: scuba diving, Hanauma Bay, Earth; Klingon Rite of Ascension Chamber, mentioned in "The Icarus Factor" (140); Shi-Kahr Desert survival, Vulcan, from D. C. Fontana's animated Trek episode, "Yesteryear"; carnival celebration, Rio de Janeiro, Earth; racetrack, Longchamps, France, Earth; and two Dixon Hill mysteries, "The Long Dark Tunnel" and "The Black Night."

Worf's calisthenics are seen in two other episodes, "Where Silence Has Lease" (128) and "New Ground" (210).

Anne Elizabeth Ramsey, who plays Clancy, was earlier seen as an assistant engineer in "Elementary, Dear Data" (129), although the actress's name there was "Ramsay."

PEAK PERFORMANCE

Production No.: 147 ■ Aired: Week of July 10, 1989
Stardate: 42923.4 ■ Code: pk

Directed by **Robert Scheerer**
Written by **David Kemper**

GUEST CAST
Sirna Kolrami: **Roy Brocksmith**
Bractor: **Armin Shimerman**
Ferengi Tactician: **David L. Lander**
Ensign Nagel: **Leslie Neale**
Ensign Burke: **Glenn Morshower**

To prepare for the Borg threat, Picard asks for a master Zakdorn strategist to oversee a battle simulation he will wage against Riker, who will command the revived derelict USS *Hathaway*. Strategist Sirna Kolrami, who predicts that Riker has no chance, is also a champion at the game Strategema. His shockingly easy defeat of Data leaves Pulaski and others fuming at the tactician's arrogance.

Meanwhile, Riker realizes his ship's hope in the "battle" is his own flair for off-beat tricks. With the help of a dilithium sliver from Wesley's science project, his crew stands ready.

Riker scores an early hit using the holographic image of a Romulan warbird as a distraction, but the games turn deadly when Picard mistakes an incoming Ferengi ship for another illusion. Its attack leaves his weapons fused in the harmless war games mode.

The Ferengi demand the secret weapon they surmise the *Hathaway* must be holding and threaten to destroy both vessels. But, using its jury-rigging, the older ship fakes its "shooting" in the split second as it warp-jumps, startling the materialistic Ferengi into withdrawing when they can't fathom its illogical destruction.

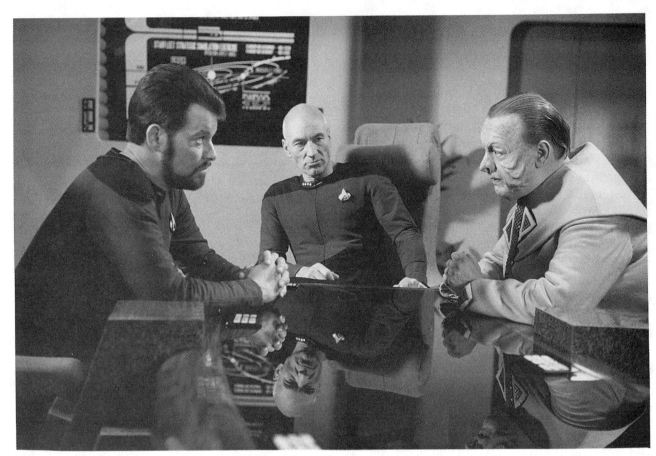

Kolrami (Roy Brocksmith) briefs Picard and Riker on the war games.

Meanwhile, Data gets a Strategema rematch with Kolrami. This time he coolly plays only for a draw and "wins" when the frustrated Zakdorn loses his patience.

———

The Ferengi return to grace here as comic foils, and they wear a more refined uniform to boot; note the yin-yang collar pips signifying rank. Armin Shimerman, the second to play two Ferengi roles ("The Last Outpost"/107), later starred as a third—Quark on spinoff DS9. Brocksmith later had recurring roles on *Picket Fences* and *Lois & Clark,* while Zakdorn would again be seen ("Ménage à Troi"/172, "Unification II"/207) and heard ("Unification I"/208).

The antimatter shards seen in this episode are actually blue candle wax, the *Hathaway*'s bridge is yet another re-dress of the film set, and the Tholians—referred to in "The Icarus Factor"/ (140)—are mentioned again here, this time as a "victim" of Riker's quick thinking during an Academy simulation. This story also includes the first known name of a Ferengi ship, the *Kreechta.* The acronym LCARS, seen prominently on *Enterprise* computer screens here and in other segments, stands for Library Computer Access-Retrieval System.

More Okudagrams with in-jokes and *animé* references: Kolrami's briefing chart calls the war games Operation Lovely Angel and lists Kei and Yuri as proper names of the three Braslota planets, along with Totoro. The *Hathaway*'s plaque, showing it was built at Copernicus Ship Yards of Luna (Earth's moon), carries two *Buckaroo* references: Yoyodyne Propulsion Systems is the builder, and the motto is the film's catch line, "No matter where you go, there you are."

SHADES OF GRAY

Production No.: 148 ▪ Aired: Week of July 17, 1989
Stardate: 42976.1 ▪ Code: sg

Directed by **Rob Bowman**
Written by **Maurice Hurley, Richard Manning, and Hans Beimler**
Story by **Maurice Hurley**

GUEST CAST
O'Brien: **Colm Meaney**

A painful thorn in the leg snagged during a planetary survey turns deadly for Riker when it is found to carry an organism that attacks his central nervous system.

When Riker falls into a coma and his vital signs plummet, Pulaski realizes that the invading microbe cannot be separated from the nerves it has wound itself around.

The chief medical officer is finally able to stabilize its spread, but not until it has actually reached Riker's brain. In a desperate try, she uses a tearful Troi's help in electronically stimulating his brain to help fight off the growth.

When Troi senses that Riker's romantic dreams promote the microbe's growth, she and Pulaski begin trying to stimulate the negative memories, including a recollection of Tasha Yar's death, to slow the organism. Pulaski finally decides to risk the potentially fatal all-out induction of Riker's most primitive emotions; after his body is racked with convulsions, the organism is defeated and disappears.

The neural stimulator proves to be Riker's only hope for surviving the Suratan microbe.

A limp "clip show" finale to the season, "Shades of Gray" is probably the weakest Trek script ever written for either generation; even writer Maurice Hurley agrees that it was "terrible, just terrible." Hurley wrote the hurried script—designed as a budget-conscious "bottle" (all-shipboard) show—on his way out the door after deciding to leave the series. Even Rob Bowman's touch as director couldn't save a show that only took three days to shoot; production assistant Eric Stillwell searched through tapes and came up with scenes representing Riker's memories to pad out the show.

For the record, those scenes included the momentary aloneness of away team command ("The Last Outpost"/107); fond first memories of Data ("Farpoint"/101); flirting with Guinan ("The Dauphin"/136); and a possible good-bye with Deanna ("The Icarus Factor"/140). More erotic memories include his times with the Edo ("Justice"/109), Minuet ("11001001"/116), Beata ("Angel One"/115), and Brenna ("Up the Long Ladder"/144). When his recollections turn increasingly negative, they cover his grief at the death of Yar ("Skin of Evil"/122) and Troi's "son" ("The Child"/127); violence at the hands of the Pagh's officer Klag ("A Matter of Honor"/134); the alien-controlled Admiral Quinn ("Conspiracy"/125); and the primal survival urge when threatened by T'Jon ("Symbiosis"/123), the Ferengi ("The Last Outpost"/107), and Armus ("Skin of Evil"/122); the possible autodestruct of the *Enterprise* ("11001001"/116), his near-death on the exploding *Batris* ("Heart of Glory"/120), and a rapid-fire mélange of many crises, including those involving Remmick ("Conspiracy"/125), the Tsiolkovsky virus ("The Naked Now"/103), the Solari traitor ("Loud As A Whisper"/132), and the infected *Lantree* ("Unnatural Selection"/133).

The drug tricordrazine—also used in "Who Watches the Watchers" (152) and in "Yesterday's Empire" (163) is a likely descendant of cordrazine, the drug that fired McCoy with enough hysterical paranoia to change history in the original-Trek episode "City on the Edge of Forever."

Notes

1. Edward Gross, *Starlog* No. 152, March 1990, p. 32.
2. Mike Okuda and Rick Sternbach, *The Star Trek: The Next Generation Technical Manual*, p. 64. Pocket Books, 1991.

PRODUCTION STAFF CREDITS— SECOND SEASON

(In usual roll order; numbers in parentheses refer to episode numbers.)

Casting: **Junie Lowery**
Main Title Theme: **Jerry Goldsmith, **Alexander Courage**
Music by: *Ron Jones (all even-numbered episodes, 128–146 except 136); *Dennis McCarthy (all odd-numbered episodes, 127–147 (plus 136)
Director of Photography: **Edward R. Brown, A.S.C.
Production Designer: Richard D. James (EMMY NOMINATION: "Elementary, Dear Data" [129])
Editor: *Tom Benko (127, 130, 133, 136, 139, 145, 148); Monty de Graff (142); *William Hoy (128, 131, 134, 137); Jon Koslowsky (140, 143, 146); Bob Lederman (129, 132, 135, 138, 141, 144, 147)
Unit Production Manager: *Sam Freedle
First Asst. Director: *Les Landau (127, 129); Merri D. Howard (all even-numbered episodes, 128–148); *(as 2nd AD) Robert J. Metoyer (odd-numbered episodes, 131–147)
Second Asst. Director: *Robert J. Metoyer (127–129); *Adele G. Simmons (130–148)
Costume Designer: Durinda Rice Wood (EMMY NOMINATION: "Elementary, Dear Data" [129])
Starfleet Uniforms: *William Ware Theiss
Original Set Design: *Herman Zimmerman
Visual Effects Supervisor: **Robert Legato (all odd-numbered episodes, 127–147 except 145); **Dan Curry (all even-numbered episodes, 128–148; EMMY NOMINATION, "Q Who" [142]); Coordinator: Gary Hutzel (145)
Post Production Supervisor: Wendy Neuss
Set Decorator: Jim Mees
Script Supervisor: **Cosmo Genovese
Special Effects: **Dick Brownfield
Property Master: **Joe Longo (all odd-numbered episodes, 127–147); **Alan Sims (all even-numbered episodes, 128–148)
Makeup Supervisor: **Michael Westmore (EMMY NOMINATION (with crew): "A Mother of Honor" [134])
Makeup Artists: **Gerald Quist; Sue Forrest-Chambers (127–133); Janna Phillips (134–149)
Hair Designer: **Richard Sabre (EMMY NOMINATION (with crew): "Unnatural Selection" [133])
Hair Stylist: *Carolyn Ferguson (127–132); Georgina Williams (133–148 except 136); Shirley Crawford (136)
Production Associate: **Susan Sackett
Senior Illustrator: **Rick Sternbach
Scenic Artist: **Michael Okuda
Set Designer: *Richard McKenzie
Construction Coordinator: **Al Smutko
Sound Mixer: *Alan Bernard, C.A.S. (EMMY NOMINATION, drama series: "Q Who" [142])
Chief Lighting Technician: **Richard Cronn
First Company Grip: **Brian Mills
Costume Supervisor: *Janet Stout
Key Costumer: Cha Blevins (127, 129–133); Alison Gail Bixby (128)
Costumer: Amanda Chamberlin (134, 137, 139, 148); Charmaine Nash Simmons (135, 138, 140, 142, 145); Kimberly J. Thompson (136); Cha Blevins (141, 144, 146); Carol Kunz (143, 147)
Music Editor: *Gerry Sackman
Supervising Sound Editor: **Bill Wistrom (EMMY NOMINATION (crew): "Q Who" [142])
Sound Editors: **James Wolvington; **Mace Matiosian; *Wilson Dyer
Post Production Sound: **Modern Sound
Casting Executive: **Helen Mossler
Production Coordinator: **Diane Overdiek
Casting Associate: **Elisa Goodman
Computer Monitors: Sony Corp. of America (131–148)
Special Visual Effects: **Industrial Light and Magic (ILM) a division of Lucasfilm Ltd.
Additional Motion Control Facilities: **Image "G"
Video Optical Effects: **The Post Group
Special Video Compositing: **Composite Image Systems
Editing Facilities: **Unitel Video
Research: Eric A. Stillwell (148)
Entity" Animation Sequence: Stokes/Kohne Associates, Inc. (127)

---

[*] denotes a first-season staffer; [**] denotes the only credited or co-credited person ever in that position.

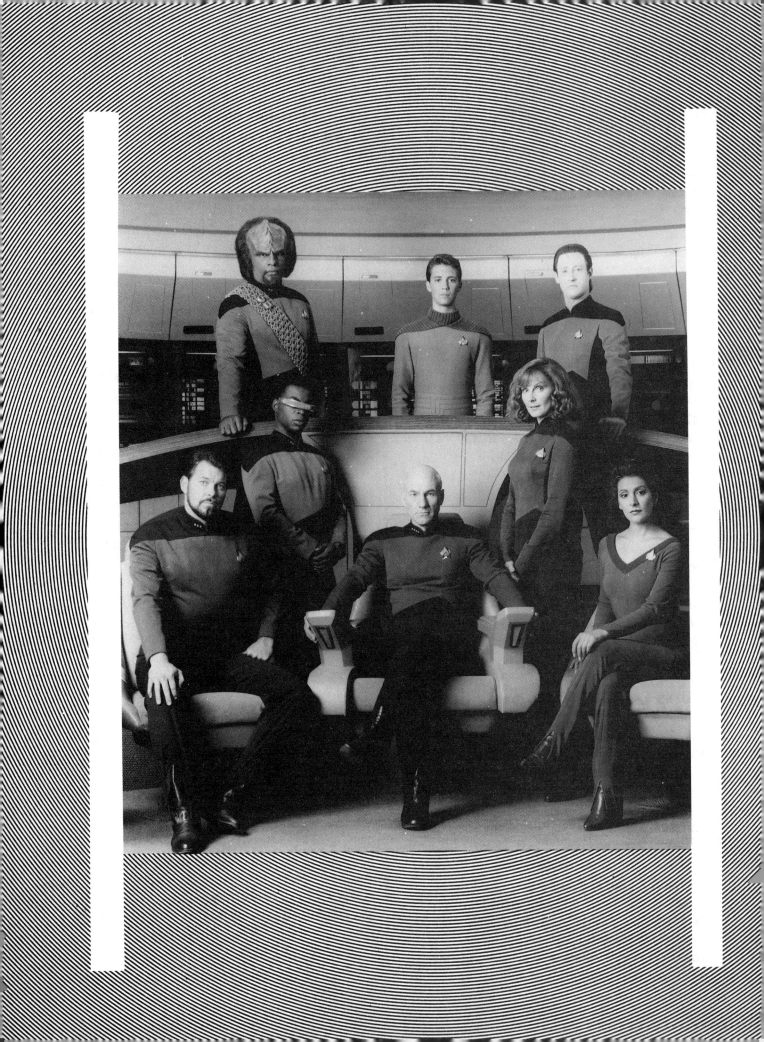

THIRD SEASON

If TNG's first season showed the birth
pangs of creation and its second creaked with growing pains,
then season three was the flowering of adulthood for a series
grown confident at last of its direction, its roots, and its synthe-
sis. "The stories this year are well-written, thought-provoking
and entertaining," Jerry Buck of the Associated Press wrote of
the third season. The show's success could be measured in more
concrete ways as well, as throughout the season the series built
on its opening 10.8 viewer rating and added to its affiliation of
235 stations, already the highest among syndicated shows.

Much of the credit for the show's new-found confidence goes
to the new head of the writing staff, Michael Piller. After
Maurice Hurley left, Michael Wagner served briefly as coexecu-
tive producer before recommending Piller, his *Probe* series
associate, for the job.

"We did have a lot of chaos in the second season," Rick
Berman recalled. "Maurice was at the helm and we had a lot of
turnover among the writers. Then Michael and I took over the
helm in the hiatus and things settled down."

The third-season cast shot (*opposite*); mother and son are
reunited as Gates McFadden (Dr. Crusher) returns.

Piller recalls it wasn't quite so easy at first. "That was a panic-driven season—we were 'riding the rims,' as we called it," he said. "I can't claim full credit for [the success]; we had a lot of good writers here.

"I will claim credit for my contribution, which is that I just have an idea for what I think makes a good dramatic story, and that I can help the flow of development in the room [at writing staff meetings]."

Piller took over beginning with "The Bonding" (153)—thanks in no small part to his and Wagner's "Evolution" script (150), which made a good impression on Roddenberry and Berman, now the real chief of day-to-day operations as the Great Bird eased away from hands-on duty.

"I take great pride in trying to protect Gene's universe, which I feel after four years is mine as well," Berman said later. "Gene has come to trust me and because of that his involvement can be lessened without any conflict."[1] After getting the new series off the ground and solidly on course, GR was affectionately likened by one staffer to the queen of England: proudly surveying, and still involved with, all that he had set in motion.

Piller was a New York native who originally worked in local TV news. After arriving in Los Angeles, he began reading scripts and learning about writing while working first as a censor and then as a programmer at CBS for series ranging from *The Dukes of Hazzard* and *The Incredible Hulk* to *Cagney and Lacey*. Thinking he could do as well, he wrote and sold a script each for *C&L* and *Simon and Simon*, then left the network and joined the staff of *Simon*, where he went from writer to producer in three years, working for a time with Maurice Hurley.

Helping to ease his transition were Hans Beimler and Richard Manning, who came back for the whole season while changing their title during the hiatus from executive script consultant to coproducer. Melinda Snodgrass, promoted to their old title from story editor, was joined on the staff by Ira Steven Behr as a writing producer beginning with the year's ninth show, "The Vengeance Factor" (157). Also having a hand in scripts were Richard Danus, who helped with "Booby Trap" (154) and became

Patrick Stewart gets to act in his beloved Shakespeare as a holodeck actor with Data (from "The Defector"/158).

executive story editor from that point through "Yesterday's Enterprise" (163), and Ronald D. Moore, a talented fan whose dream came true when his spec script for "The Bonding" got him hired as story editor beginning with "Sins of the Father" (165).

On-screen, the creative staff's efforts produced a year of highlights that saw Beverly Crusher return to the *Enterprise*, her son get promoted to full ensign, the captain slug a terrorist on his bridge, Riker and Troi finally find time for a kiss, Worf get disgraced, Data find himself "with child," Geordi change his luck with women, and more and more being revealed about O'Brien—but not his first name!

The year-long letter-writing campaign to return Gates McFadden to the show was not directly mentioned when a change of heart in the great "chemistry experiment" over TNG's doctors was announced. "Diana Muldaur is a marvelous actress and it's obvious that I think so because I've used her many times," Roddenberry would say later. "But it's all just chemistry. Beverly had that little something. . . . Somehow the way the captain bounces off her works well. It works with Muldaur, too, but it just seems to work a little more with Crusher."[2] He would also say, "It was always our intention to leave the door open for her to return to the show."[3]

"It was our opinion, Gene's and mine, that the Pulaski role was not working out either," Berman said. "And rather than going and looking for a third doctor in three years, we approached Gates about coming back, and she very graciously did."

McFadden, by the way, had not been idle during her year off. She had appeared in two movies, *The Hunt for Red October* (though much of her part ended up on the cutting-room floor) and *Taking Care of Business* (with John "Q" deLancie as a subordinate), and she had starred in an off-Broadway play, *To Gillian on Her 37th Birthday*. Muldaur would go on to create a similarly crusty, though ill-fated role, that of Rosalind Shayes on *L.A. Law*.

As the writing staff began to find its rhythm at last, the production office quietly went about its business. Retaining administrative oversight of special effects, associate producer Peter Lauritson was promoted to the new title of coproducer after the fourth episode, "Who Watches the Watchers" (152). Also, beginning with "Captain's Holiday" (167), Michael Okuda and Rick Sternbach would add technical consultant to their art titles, cementing the unofficial role as science experts they had been performing for the writers ever since the pilot.

David Livingston continued his role as cost estimator and Berman's liaison to all the non-effects departments. Producing an episode from script started now with early casting concept sessions involving Piller, the writers, and casting director Junie Lowry-Johnson; she did the actual casting with Berman and the episode's director. Newly hired costume designer Bob Blackman was then involved, after which Livingston would oversee early production meetings with the design and FX staff, the writers, Berman, and Piller. Livingston then kept tabs on all the ideas springing into action—production designer Richard James's set concepts, Westmore's makeup plans, hairstyles, Sternbach and Okuda's ideas—and made a last-minute check-in with all of them two days before principal filming began.

Blackman was among a slew of new people who came aboard for the third season, replacing his departing friend Durinda Rice Wood. One of his first tasks was to oversee the cast's long-sought end to the original uniforms. Made of spandex that had to remain taut, the hot one-piece jumpsuits actually led to fatigue and lower back pain among the actors. The new outfits cost $3,000 each and were phased in only for those above ensign rank. They were made of "breathable" wool gabardine and kept to a one-piece version for the women because of the design line.

A new main title greeted viewers beginning with the third season, featuring an incoming route from outside the Milky Way rather than a departure angle from the solar system. Also, a four-foot filming miniature of the *Enterprise* was built at mid-season, first turning up in "The Defector" (158). Though smaller, it was actually more detailed and for the first time accurately depicted the front Ten-Forward windows.

Mark "Sarek" Lenard is visited by Walter "Chekov" Koenig.

THE ENSIGNS OF COMMAND

Production No.: 149 ■ Aired: Week of October 2, 1989
Stardate: 43133.3 ■ Code: ec

Directed by **Cliff Bole**
Written by **Melinda M. Snodgrass**

GUEST CAST
Ard'rian McKenzie: **Eileen Seeley**
Haritath: **Mark L. Taylor**
Kentor: **Richard Allen**
O'Brien: **Colm Meaney**
Gosheven: **Grainger Hines**
Sheliak: **Mart McChesney**

The reclusive Sheliak Corporate breaks its 111-year silence with the Federation to demand that Tau Cygna V, ceded to it by treaty, be cleared of a human settlement within three days.

Forgotten by the UFP, a strayed colony ship deposited settlers there ninety years earlier. They have tamed the desert and now number over 15,000. News of the colony is doubly surprising, since the settlers had to adapt to the fatal hyperonic radiation that bathes the planet.

Because of that danger, Data is sent to announce the evacuation. But he runs up against a stubborn leader, Gosheven, who shrugs off the unseen Sheliak's threat and won't budge despite his people's growing qualms. Picard and Troi ask for a delay from the Sheliak, but the presumptive race is as stubborn as the Tau Cygnans.

Data gets nowhere in his mission, despite the help of a farsighted Cygnan woman, Ard'rian, until he finally shows the settlers the danger they face by launching a frightening, though restrained, show of force.

Picard congratulates Data on the creativity of his effort after achieving a victory of his own—beating the arrogant Sheliak with their own treaty to get the evacuation delayed.

A shocked Ard'rian (Eileen Seeley) watches Gosheven (Grainger Hines) threaten Data.

Though filmed first, this segment was aired after "Evolution" opened the third season. Director Cliff Bole once again came up against the budget ax as he watched his episode take a $200,000 cut at the last minute, although the impact doesn't seem as drastic as it did on "The Royale" (138). In fact, a story line with more romantic overtones between Data and Ard'rian seems to have been the main casualty, leaving the issue of Data in command of reluctant charges to be explored more forcefully later in "Redemption," II (201).

As happens occasionally, credit for a major guest player did not appear on screen. Actor Grainger Hines' dialogue all had to be dubbed in by another actor, and he asked that his name be pulled. Back under the monster suit is Mark McChesney, who played Armus in "Skin of Evil" (122). Data's oft-seen evolution as a violinist, one of many arts he tackles to study humanity, begins here ("Sarek"/171, "In Theory"/199, "Lessons"/245, "Inheritance"/262). O'Brien is seen playing the cello here as well.

In another example of intergenerational continuity, the old duotronics computers that Ard'rian refers to as her guess for Data's control basis is the system installed aboard Kirk's *Enterprise,* a contemporary of her colony ship. Invented by Dr. Richard Daystrom, it was the success he was trying to surpass with multitronics at the time of the 1968 episode "The Ultimate Computer."

Data's shuttlepod is named for Ellison Onizuka, one of the seven real-life astronauts who died aboard the U.S. space shuttle *Challenger* when it exploded after launch in 1986. During filming, Tibet's exiled Dali Lam and his entourage of monks—all of them Trek fans—visited the sets and surrounded Brent Spiner as Data on one of the colony village's sets to pose for a photo.

Stubbs has come on board with a specially designed probe, set to be launched to study the once-in-a-lifetime stellar explosion of a neutron-supergiant binary. The project is threatened, though, by malfunctions of the *Enterprise*'s main computer core.

The reason for those malfunctions? Wesley's science project, in which he allowed two medical microbiotic "nanites" to interact. The creatures bred and escaped into the ship's computer core, which they are now "eating." Attempts to placate or talk to the nanites are thwarted when an obsessed, impatient Stubbs sterilizes a core element of nanites with a gamma radiation blast.

But the nanites' deadly response—they shut down the ship's life-support system—convinces even Stubbs they are intelligent, and he apologizes to them after Data volunteers himself as a face-to-face communication conduit.

Satisfied with the goodwill shown them, the high-order nanites want only to keep "exploring" and ask for an uninhabited world to colonize. They even help reconstruct the ship's computer in time to make Stubbs's project a success.

The script that brought Michael Piller into the TNG fold was designed as a "growth show" for Wesley, and on his own initiative Piller added the plot points about Beverly Crusher's reappear-

EVOLUTION

Production No.: 150 ■ Aired: Week of September 25, 1989
Stardate: 43125.8 ■ Code: ev

Directed by **Winrich Kolbe**
Teleplay by **Michael Piller**
Story by **Michael Piller and Michael Wagner**

GUEST CAST
Dr. Paul Stubbs: **Ken Jenkins**
Guinan: **Whoopi Goldberg**
Nurse: **Mary McCusker**
Crewman No. 1: **Randal Patrick**

What starts out as a science project in genetics for Wes almost dooms not only scientist Paul Stubbs's lifelong project but the ship itself.

The nanites, through Data, confront Dr. Stubbs (Ken Jenkins).

ance when it became clear this episode would actually lead off the season.

One scene cut for time's sake included a corridor conversation between Wesley and his friends, pointing up how immersed in work and cut off from social life he'd become. Scott Grimes as Eric and Amy O'Neill as the blond Annette were to be given credit until their lines were cut, but they can be seen in the crowd Beverly eyes suspiciously in Ten-Forward at show's close.

Piller delved into his own love of baseball to round out the similarities between Wesley and Stubbs (played by Ken Jenkins), whom he envisioned as a forecast of the hard-driven, often friendless youngster at age forty. The players Stubbs refers to brought about the climax of the classic 1951 National League playoff when Bobby Thomson of the New York Giants broke open the tie game with a homer off Brooklyn Dodgers pitcher Ralph Branca, bringing in runners Whitey Lockman from first and Alvin Dark from second. Wesley's interest in baseball was mentioned long ago in "Justice" (109), although we learn here that his late father taught him the game. We also discover that Guinan was married at least twice and has "a lot" of children, one of whom is several hundred years old.

Stubbs's "egg" satellite module was reworked from the viral containment unit built for last season's opener, "The Child" (127); the computer core access is built on the old movie bridge set. A nice touch is the warning sign in the shuttle bay: "Warning: Variable Gravity Area."

THE SURVIVORS

Production No.: 151 ■ Aired: Week of October 9, 1989
Stardate: 43152.4 ■ Code: sv

Directed by **Les Landau**
Written by **Michael Wagner**

GUEST CAST
Kevin Uxbridge: **John Anderson**
Rishon Uxbridge: **Anne Haney**

Answering a distress call from Delta Rana IV, the *Enterprise* arrives to find the planet ravaged and its 11,000 colonists dead—except for two elderly botanists, Rishon Uxbridge and her unfriendly husband, Kevin. The two say they don't know why they were spared death, but they refuse to be evacuated.

An away team finds Delta Rana IV's survivors don't want to be rescued.

Then the massive ship that leveled the planet reappears, beginning a cat-and-mouse game with the *Enterprise* that leads Picard to suspect a connection between the heavily armed mystery ship and the Uxbridges. The aliens cripple the *Enterprise* in battle, then return to blast the Uxbridges' home; in turn, the Federation starship destroys them.

Picard has the couple beamed up to the bridge against their will. There Kevin finally reveals the truth. He is actually a Douwd, an immortal superalien disguised as a human, but in all the fifty-three years they've been married, he has never revealed that fact to his wife.

His credo against killing would not let him defend the planet against the aliens, a warrior-like race known as the Husnock, and his wife is actually just an image after she too died in the fighting.

Her death enraged Kevin, who used the powers he had always denied himself and blinked out the lives of all fifty billion Husnock instantaneously, without thinking.

Stunned at Kevin's crime and sobered by his shame, Picard knows there is no court that can try Kevin and he leaves the Douwd to his own thoughts and conscience—alone.

In Michael Wagner's only solo writing effort during his short-lived tenure as a producer, veteran actor John Anderson brings great dignity and mystery to the man whose grizzled exterior masks a sad and amazing story—though the actor has since revealed he almost didn't take the role due to the death of his own wife only a year earlier.

A day of location shooting of the Uxbridges' house was done at a beach house in Malibu; the moving master shot with the beam-in effect, a first for Trek, had the house matted into the landscape painting.

The Husnock warship, built by Tony Meininger, was one of the first not designed by a member of the TNG art staff. "Usually there just isn't time to put into designing them if they're just a 'ship-of-the-week' that's going to be re-dressed later anyway," said Rick Sternbach, adding that decisions on re-use are made by the alternating TNG visual-effects teams headed by Dan Curry and Rob Legato and their model contractors.

The mention of Andorian renegades marked the first time the antennaed, blue-skinned aliens of original Trek, who debuted in 1967's "Journey to Babel," were brought into the TNG era.

WHO WATCHES THE WATCHERS?

Production No.: 152 ■ Aired: Week of October 16, 1989
Stardate: 43173.5 ■ Code: ww

Directed by **Robert Wiemer**
Written by **Richard Manning and Hans Beimler**

GUEST CAST
Nuria: **Kathryn Leigh Scott**
Liko: **Ray Wise**
Dr. Barron: **James Greene**
Oji: **Pamela Segall**
Fento: **John McLiam**
Hali: **James McIntire**
Mary Warren: **Lois Hall**

A failing reactor at a hidden cultural observers' post on Mintaka III draws the *Enterprise* to that world to render assistance. Before the starship arrives, however, the reactor explodes, injuring three scientists and causing their "duck blind" screen to fail.

An away team is sent to the planet. They successfully rescue two of the scientists but cannot find the third, a man named Palmer. But one of the natives, Liko, witnesses the landing party's beam-up, and as a result falls, critically injuring himself. Dr. Crusher beams him aboard to save his life, a Prime Directive violation that angers Picard. A memory wipe doesn't take after Liko is returned home, and he begins telling his brethren that the old god-legends they gave up ages ago were true after all—and their "Overseer" is "the Picard."

Riker and Troi beam down in native disguises to find Palmer, but when the Mintakans find the missing scientist first, even their leader, Nuria, begins to believe Liko's tales.

Riker escapes with Palmer, but Troi is trapped and kept behind as a possible sacrifice. Liko now desperately wants "the Picard" to bring his dead wife back to life.

Picard risk further contamination by bringing Nuria aboard to prove he is mortal, a tactic that almost fails until she sees he cannot save one of the scientists from dying.

Picard bids good-bye to the Mintakans (Ray Wise, Pamela Segall, and Kathryn Leigh Scott).

This time, shooting in 100-degree heat for two days, the hardworking cast and crew were joined by the local snakes, scorpions, and bees—meaning no attractants like deodorant or perfume could be used.

Viewing the story as a morality tale, first-time TNG director Wiemer shot his Mintakan scenes as tableaux, reminiscent of medieval morality plays. Among the guest cast, *Twin Peaks* fans remember Ray Wise as Leland, Laura Palmer's possessed father. Wise also appeared in O'Neill's *The Hairy Ape* with Frakes in New York. Kathryn Leigh Scott later portrayed Maggie Evans, the love of vampire Barnabas Collins in the short-lived *Dark Shadows* remake, while James Greene played the more than friendly elevator operator on *The Days and Nights of Molly Dodd*.

Rick Sternbach has said he based the design of the protruding scope used in the "duck blind" on the video cameras used by the TMA-1 team in *2001: A Space Odyssey*. Using Trek's own background well, Picard and Beverly refer to the memory-wipe technique that Dr. Pulaski used in "Pen Pals" (141). The disguised Troi and Riker also use subcutaneous transponders, just as Kirk and Spock did in 1968's "Patterns of Force."

THE BONDING

Production No.: 153 ■ Aired: Week of October 23, 1989
Stardate: 43198.7 ■ Code: bo

Directed by **Winrich Kolbe**
Written by **Ronald D. Moore**

GUEST CAST
Lieutenant Marla Aster: **Susan Powell**
Jeremy Aster: **Gabriel Damon**
Lieutenant O'Brien: **Colm Meaney**
Teacher: **Raymond D. Turner**

Meanwhile, lightning storms prompt a hysterical Liko into almost sacrificing Troi before Picard arrives. The native, disbelieving his "god's" claims of mortality, shoots Picard with an arrow, drawing blood.

Although the Mintakans are aware of the outworlders now, Picard leaves them with the knowledge that the rational path is the one they should follow—and the "duck blind" is dismantled.

If the rocky crags of Mintaka III look familiar to longtime Trek fans, it's no wonder: they're the Vasquez Rocks, a county park that was the site of location shooting for several original-series episodes: "Arena," "Friday's Child," "Shore Leave," and "Alternative Factor."

A routine mission to explore the ruins of the Koinonian civilization ends in tragedy when a bomb left over from that people's long war explodes, killing ship's archaeologist Marla Aster.

Now Picard and Troi must comfort her twelve-year-old son, Jeremy, who has already lost his father. The tragedy evokes emphatic feelings from Wesley and Worf, who led Aster's away team.

But just as the shock is beginning to wear off, the boy's mother reappears and transforms the Asters' shipboard cabin into their old home back on Earth, bringing joy but confusion back into Jeremy's life.

Jeremy Aster (Gabriel Damon) considers the alien posing as his late mother.

Aimed at showcasing the often overlooked families aboard the *Enterprise*, Ronald Moore's first script for TNG shows his flair for creating characters. Here he brings together three who lost one or both parents at an early age—Wesley, Worf, and Jeremy Aster—in such a touching fashion that the science subplot of the overly solicitous alien is almost overshadowed. With very little rewriting—though originally, Jeremy himself programmed a holodeck to re-create his mother—the final version reflects the first-draft spec script that caused an enthusiastic Michael Piller first to commission "The Defector" (158) and later to offer Moore a staff job.

Along the way, this story reveals that Worf was six years old when his parents were killed at Khitomer ("Heart of Glory"/120) and that Wesley was less than twelve when his father Jack was killed.

BOOBY TRAP

Production No.: 154 ▪ Aired: Week of October 30, 1989
Stardate: 43205.6 ▪ Code: bt

Directed by **Gabrielle Beaumont**
Teleplay by **Ron Roman, Michael Piller, and Richard Danus**
Story by **Michael Wagner and Ron Roman**

GUEST CAST
Dr. Leah Brahms: **Susan Gibney**
Lieutenant O'Brien: **Colm Meaney**
Guinan: **Whoopi Goldberg**
Galek Dar: **Albert Hall**
Christy Henshaw: **Julie Warner**

Data discovers that Jeremy's "mother" is actually an energy being from the planet below. After it is trapped aboard ship by forcefields, the creature says it wants only to care for the boy, since the long-dead race it once shared the planet with was responsible for Marla Aster's death.

Picard argues that humans must endure suffering and pain along with joy, while Troi points out how Jeremy can never have a full life in the artificial environment.

The alien relents after Wesley and Worf tell their stories, and the Klingon leads the boy through the "R'usstai" bonding ceremony, making them brothers.

The crew see a seldom-revealed side of Picard as the captain gleefully leads an away team to explore an ancient Promellian battle cruiser. They find the ship intact, with all hands long dead, at the site of the battle that annihilated the Promellian race and its enemy, the Menthars.

But the mystery behind the ship's fate becomes all too clear when the *Enterprise* crew members realize they are being trapped by the same Menthar energy-draining device that snared the Promellians.

As ship reserves drain away, La Forge comes across the original plans by the Galaxy-class designers. He then re-creates one of them, Dr.

Leah Brahms, as an interactive holodeck character to help him find a way to escape the Menthars' trap.

La Forge, who has been a little unfortunate of late in his dealings with women, finds himself strangely drawn to "Leah" as they fight the clock in search of an answer.

Finally they hit on the idea of using one quick blast to free themselves; then they shut off all power.

Finally, Picard takes the helm himself and deftly slingshots his ship around a last stray asteroid, after which the *Enterprise* destroys the entire booby trap.

Originally Picard was to have become involved with Leah Brahms's holodeck simulacrum, but Michael Piller changed that to the more logical choice of Geordi, whom the writer likened to the guy who fumbles around women but is "in love with his '57 Chevy." This was the first TNG episode directed by Gabrielle Beaumont and the first episode ever directed by a woman. Richard Danus was invited to join the staff as executive story editor after helping out on the rewrite, which foreshadows not only Geordi's second try with Christy in "Transfigurations" (173) but the

eventual appearance of the real Leah Brahms in "Galaxy's Child" (190).

This episode also provides another tiny peek into Guinan's background: she reveals she is first attracted to men's heads, especially bald ones, since a bald man helped her through a painful time—but there's no clear indication that she means Picard. The art staff originally wanted the holodeck model to be a mockup of an actual warp engine, but time worked against that idea and yielded the compromise sliding panels seen. The Promellian ship *Cleponji* is a re-dress of the Husnock ship seen in "The Survivors" (151).

On the holodeck, Geordi meets a simulated Dr. Leah Brahms (Susan Gibney).

THE ENEMY

Production No.: 155 ■ Aired: Week of November 6, 1989
Stardate: 43349.2 ■ Code: en

Directed by **David Carson**
Written by **David Kemper and Michael Piller**

GUEST CAST
Centurion Bochra: **John Snyder**
Commander Tomalak: **Andreas Katsulas**
Lieutenant O'Brien: **Colm Meaney**
Patahk: **Steve Rankin**

Answering a distress call from the border world Galorndon Core, an *Enterprise* away team finds a crashed Romulan craft and an injured survivor. La Forge loses contact with the rest of the away team and can't be located due to the planet's severe electrical storms.

Picard and Riker suspect the small craft was spying, since it was destroyed after crashing, but its mother ship's Commander Tomalak smilingly insists that his man—one man—was merely swept off course.

Meanwhile, efforts to rescue La Forge center on a neutrino beacon that can transmit through a break in the storms. But La Forge soons discovers what the crew above can't: there is a second Romulan, Bochra, who captures the chief engineer.

La Forge finally convinces Bochra that they must work together to survive, especially since

La Forge and Riker on the latest "Planet Hell,"
Galorndon Core.

neer's unique abilities, shortcomings, and sense of humor well. In an early draft he was joined on the planet's surface by Troi, who had to incapacitate the Romulan.

Another story point—that of Worf letting a Romulan die by refusing to donate blood—met resistance from the writing staff and from Dorn himself when Piller first suggested it. But allowing it to stand reveals how the series was beginning to get an alien perspective on Worf. It also shows that these "perfect" twenty-fourth-century characters could come into conflict with one another after all. And, with an audience still close to the conflicts of Kirk's earlier era, Riker's gentle reminder to Worf that Klingons once hated humans as much as they now hate Romulans is a nice way to set this Trek generation apart from the last. Beverly's shock at Worf's stand is likewise a reflection of polite human society's reaction; we also learn that she had never operated on a Romulan before.

Andreas Katsulas makes the first of four TNG appearances as the quintessential Romulan Tomalak ("The Defector"/158, "Future Imperfect"/182, "All Good Things . . ."/277–278); he also was the "one-armed man" in 1993's *The Fugitive* and Narn Ambassador K'Gal of *Babylon 5.* John Snyder·would later play a human ("The Masterpiece Society"/213), while Galorndon Core would again prove strategic ("Unification II"/207). This debut version of the palm beacons required a sometimes-visible cable that ran inside the actors' sleeves to an off-camera power source.

their nervous systems are degenerating due to the planet's magnetic fields.

Tension mounts topside as Worf, the only possible blood donor, refuses to provide the injured Romulan with a necessary blood transfusion, and Picard won't order him to do so. Tomalak enters Federation space, against Picard's wishes, to pick up his man.

The Romulan dies just as his ship arrives for a fight, but the two lost below are found just in time, allowing Picard to drop shields for beam-up—and show goodwill.

War is averted and Tomalak, still feigning innocence, is curtly escorted back to the Neutral Zone.

David Carson left a declining industry in his native England and got this episode as his first directing assignment, having worked with Sirtis on one of the many Sherlock Holmes episodes he'd helmed. The second Geordi show in a row uses the chief engi-

THE PRICE

| Production No.: 156 ■ Aired: Week of November 13, 1989 |
| Stardate: 43385.6 ■ Code: pr |

Directed by **Robert Scheerer**
Written by **Hannah Louise Shearer**

GUEST CAST
Devinoni Ral: **Matt McCoy**
Premier Bhavani: **Elizabeth Hoffman**
Seth Mendoza: **Castulo Guerra**
Dai Mon Goss: **Scott Thompson**
Dr. Arridor: **Dan Shor**
Leyor: **Kevin Peter Hall**
Lieutenant O'Brien: **Colm Meaney**

Troi falls for the charismatic Devinoni Ral, a soft-spoken yet determined negotiator who comes aboard the *Enterprise* to bid on an apparently stable wormhole found near Barzan II.

The wormhole allows almost instant travel to

an unexplored corner of the galaxy, and the Barzan hope that proceeds from its sale will bolster the economy of their poor planet.

Ral, a human working for another world, arouses concern when he anticipates another bidder's fears and eases him out. Then the Ferengi crash the talks and secretly make the Federation delegate too ill to finish bidding. In a pinch, Picard makes Riker take that job, hoping that the commander's poker instincts will see him through.

To check the primitive Barzan probe's report, Data and La Forge take a shuttlepod through the wormhole; the protesting Ferengi send one of their own as well. But after the Starfleet officers emerge in the wrong area, they realize the wormhole does change endpoints, and they escape just before it collapses—stranding the pooh-poohing Ferengi far from home.

Ral finally confides the secret of his success to Troi: he too is part Betazoid. She clears her conscience by revealing this to all after the Bar-

zan accept his bid—and sadly discover the wormhole is no good anyway.

Ral tells Troi he needs her to be his conscience, to help him change, but they part, with her reminding him she's already got a counselor's job.

Despite the advance hype about Troi's "bed scenes"—a first in the Trek series—the finished product didn't quite live up to the rumored raciness. Other scenes, though, are wonderful: the lovers' debate on the ethics of being Betazoid among non-empaths; Beverly and Deanna's workout gossip, in which we learn that the doctor dated Jack Crusher for months ("Conspiracy"/125); and more good comic Ferengi scenes, including Goss's crashing of the wormhole negotiations.

Matt McCoy, who worked with Jonathan Frakes on Dreamwest, brought a slick yet sympathetic air to the role of the galactic manipulator who finally meets his match. A veteran of the Neighborhood Playhouse in New York, he later had regular roles on We've Got It Made, Penn 'N' Ink, and Hot Hero Sandwich and starred in the films Deep Star Six and Police Academy V and VI. Kevin Peter Hall, who died after this episode was filmed, stood seven feet four and had donned the alien suit for the original

Counselor Troi is seduced by Devinoni Ral (Matt McCoy).

Predator movie and the Bigfoot costume for *Harry and the Hendersons.* In the script, Ral's traveling companion, quickly tossed aside for Troi, is named Rojay.

A re-dressed set for Troi's office turns up here after its debut in "The Icarus Factor" (140). For trivia fans, its location is given as Deck 8/3472, while her quarters are at Deck 9/0910. This story also introduces Troi's love of chocolate, heard often ("Deja Q"/161, "The Game"/206, "Violations"/212, "Imaginary Friend"/222, "Man of the People"/229, "Liaisons"/254, "Parallels"/263); she says her passion for Ral exceeds even her early years with Riker ("Second Chances"/250). The European Alliance, mentioned as Ral's birthplace, is likely a successor to the European Hegemony of two hundred years earlier ("Up the Long Ladder"/144).

Though elusive here, a stable wormhole did become a historic find on spinoff DS9. The Ferengi ship here is first called a "Marauder," while a Ten-Forward crewwoman's rebuke of Goss's advances leads to his subtle gesture harking back to an original Ferengi concept: the male's large sex organ.

Mystery surrounds the talks between Brull (Joey Aresco) and Marouk (Nancy Parsons).

THE VENGEANCE FACTOR

Production No.: 157   ■   Aired: Week of November 20, 1989
Stardate: 43421.9   ■   Code: vf

Directed by **Timothy Bond**
Written by **Sam Rolfe**

GUEST CAST
Yuta: **Lisa Wilcox**
Brull: **Joey Aresco**
Marouk: **Nancy Parsons**
Chorgan: **Stephen Lee**
Volnoth: **Marc Lawrence**
Temarek: **Elkanah J. Burns**

The *Enterprise* traces an attack on a Federation science outpost back to Acamar III. There, Picard discovers responsibility for the attack lies with the Gatherers, a thieving band of renegades who split off from Acamarian society a hundred years ago. The captain decides to bring an end to the raids by healing the split between the two groups.

Marouk, Acamar's leader, agrees to offer amnesty to the renegades; Brull, the first Gatherer chief they encounter, admits a yen for peace himself.

Unknown to all, Yuta, the chef-taster to Mar-

ouk, is actually an assassin who's been cellularly altered to live for centuries. Her only purpose in life is to kill off members of the Lornack clan who massacred her own Tralesta clan.

Riker is attracted to Yuta but puzzled by her sadness over her inability to love. Thanks to Data and Dr. Crusher's research, he discovers that she murdered a Lornack among Brull's pack, and another one fifty-three years ago, among countless others.

Brull leads Picard and Marouk to his chief, Chorgan, and final talks commence, though stormily. Just in time, Riker learns that Chorgan is the last Lornack and dramatically saves him from Yuta by downing her with three phaser shots.

The talks succeed, and the two groups of Acamarians are reconciled, but peace is the last thing Riker feels.

Veteran actress Nancy Parsons welcomed the chance to play a matriarchal monarch after becoming famous to millions of moviegoers as Coach Balbricker in the *Porky's* series, while Lisa Wilcox counts among her credits a three-month stint on *General Hospital.* She also survived encounters with Freddy Krueger in parts 4 and 5 of *A Nightmare on Elm Street.* Mallon, the nonspeaking blond Gatherer whom Brull puts in charge after he leaves, was played by Sirtis's boyfriend, Michael Lamper; the two were married in June 1992.

The fusion reactor seen here is the same one used in "Who Watches the Watchers?" (152), but it's been re-dressed with more stick-on panels and labels. It is established in this episode that Data is indeed stronger than Worf.

THE DEFECTOR

Production No.: 158 ■ Aired: Week of January 1, 1990
Stardate: 43462.5 ■ Code: df

Directed by **Robert Scheerer**
Written by **Ronald D. Moore**

GUEST CAST
Sub-Lieutenant Setal (Admiral Jarok): **James Sloyan**
Commander Tomalak: **Andreas Katsulas**
Admiral Haden: **John Hancock**
John Bates: **S. A. Templeman**
Michael Williams: **Patrick Stewart**

While fleeing his own people across the Neutral Zone in a small scout, a low-level Romulan tactical clerk asks for asylum, bringing with him shocking news: the Romulans plan to retake that buffer area after almost two hundred years.

Can Picard trust the defector? A probe finds some cloaklike spatial disturbances at the Nelvana III site mentioned by Setal, the defector, but this evidence of his good faith is fragile at best—certainly not reason enough to justify crossing the Neutral Zone and risking war.

Then the lowly clerk reveals himself as the Romulan admiral Jarok, and provides Picard with defense and planning data he has seen. His defection, he says, was prompted by the blind aggression of the new Romulan command—and by concern for his daughter's future if a senseless war breaks out.

But the truth is revealed when the *Enterprise* risks a Neutral Zone encounter: no invasion is planned; the signs of activity were faked. Three warbirds decloak and demand that the *Enterprise* surrender. Jarok, already in disfavor for his protests, has been used.

All seems lost until, on a prearranged signal, three Klingon ships appear. With the odds reversed, the warbirds leave, but the Romulan admiral knows what his fate will be. He is found in his cabin, dead by suicide, leaving only a letter that Picard wistfully hopes can be delivered to his home someday—in peace.

Surprisingly enough, what writer Ronald D. Moore calls "the Cuban Missile Crisis at the Neutral Zone" at one point during rewrites became a love story between Crusher and Jarok. That angle was eventually written out except for the scene in which she treats the Romulan in sickbay. A planned Sherlock Holmes teaser with Data was cut just two days before filming began due to a lawsuit, Piller recalled, and he turned to Stewart as company scholar for help in picking out a replacement. They decided on Henry V, with a heavily made-up Stewart in the role of Michael Williams, one of the soldiers.

Adding to the tension and tragic nature of James Sloyan's performance and the story were the visual effects, which gave us for the first time in any Trek a glimpse—almost a travelogue—of Romulus. Also new for this episode were the Romulan scout vessel and the third and final version of the Starfleet admiral's uniform.

A puzzling reference into Trek's own history is the mention of renewed Romulan bitterness over their "humiliating" defeat at the Battle of Cheron, apparently fought during the original Earth-Romulan War a century before Kirk's time and first mentioned in "Balance of Terror" in 1966. Two seasons later, however, in 1969's "Let That Be Your Last Battlefield," Cheron was an unknown but long-dead world where two advanced native races had destroyed each other over racial bigotry.

More trivia: Jarok is unable to synthesize Romulan ale, referred to as illegal decades earlier in *Star Trek II*. The *Hood*, spoken of here, was Riker's prior assignment, as mentioned in "Farpoint"

The Romulan Admiral Jarok (James Sloyan)—torn between his duty, and his conscience.

(101) and an original Kirk-era starship, from 1968's "The Ultimate Computer." And in a rare verbal homage to *animé,* the alleged base site, Nelvana III, takes its name from a famous Canadian animation studio.

THE HUNTED

Production No.: 159 ■ Aired: Week of January 8, 1990
Stardate: 43489.2 ■ Code: hu

Directed by **Cliff Bole**
Written by **Robin Bernheim**

GUEST CAST
Roga Danar: **Jeff McCarthy**
Nayrok: **James Cromwell**
Lieutenant O'Brien: **Colm Meaney**
Zaynar: **J. Michael Flynn**
Wagnor: **Andrew Bicknell**

The *Enterprise* is relaying reports to back up Angosia III's application to join the Federation when it stumbles across an ugly skeleton in the planet's closet: the treatment of its war veterans.

A tenaciously cunning escapee from a lunar prison colony turns out to be Roga Danar, one of the top soldiers for the victorious planet in the Tarsian War. Now branded a murderer by the Angosians, he turns out to be a patriot who was turned into a killing machine by his government through biochemical and mind control.

Warned to shy away from this internal affair, Picard learns from Prime Minister Nayrok that the prison was constructed as a colony for those super-soldiers who could not re-adapt to peacetime civilian life.

Picard's hands are tied, and he is about to hand Danar over to the Angosians when the soldier escapes from a transporter beam, beginning a chase that ends when he commandeers a police vessel.

From there Danar attacks the prison, setting

Rampaging superkiller soldier Roga Danar (Jeff McCarthy) is finally subdued.

his fellow veterans free to march on Nayrok's government and demand treatment. Held at gunpoint, the dour Nayrok now asks for help but is shocked when Picard beams up, "agreeing" that the debate is an internal matter.

If Nayrok's rule survives, Picard says, Angosia will be a welcome addition to the UFP.

This analogy to ignored Vietnam veterans was to have hit even closer to home with a planned Rambo–style eruption when the soldiers stormed the capital, but time limits and a budget crunch would again play a part in reducing an episode directed by Cliff Bole. The result is a bit anticlimactic but funny, too, as the Prime Directive for once provides both a pretext for a fast getaway and an opportunity for local action.

On the trivia side, the "Jefferies tube" crawlways mentioned here are another homage to sixties Trek. That show's circuitry access area carried the name of Matt Jefferies, art director and designer of the original *Enterprise.* An actual set for this century's version, though, would have to wait another season, until "Galaxy's Child" (190). In another Trek first, the daring Danar breaks free of a transporter beam—supposedly due to a chemical that interferes with the signal—and powers up a transporter with a phaser's power pack. Also, the security section cell here takes on its standard look after debuting in a humbler version ("Heart of Glory"/120). James Cromwell later was a Yridian ("Birthright"/242–243).

THE HIGH GROUND

Production No.: 160 ■ Aired: Week of January 29, 1990	
Stardate: 43510.7 ■ Code: hi	

Directed by Gabrielle Beaumont
Written by Melinda M. Snodgrass

GUEST CAST
Alexana Devos: **Kerrie Keane**
Kyril Finn: **Richard Cox**
Waiter (Katik Shaw): **Marc Buckland**
Policeman: **Fred G. Smith**
Boy (Ansata): **Christopher Pettiet**

While helping victims of a terrorist bomb blast on nonaligned Rutia IV, Dr. Crusher is taken hostage by one of the terrorists, Kyril Finn. Finn is fighting for the independence of his people, the Ansata.

Aiding the abduction and all their other terrorist acts is dimensional-shift beaming, a mostly untraceable technology whose use came with a high cost: it breaks down body chemistry and is fatal if used too often.

Finn plans to keep Crusher for her medical skills and as a bargaining chip to increase Federation pressure on the Rutians to settle the conflict with his people.

Local police chief Alexana Devos, saddened but steeled to her job, is infuriated when Riker wants to bargain for Crusher. Angered by the medical aid brought to the Rutians by the *Enterprise,* Finn leads a raid to bomb its warp chamber. His plans are foiled by a cool-headed La Forge, but the Ansatan leader manages to get away with Picard as a second hostage.

Data and Beverly tend to the wounded on Rutia IV.

After Wes develops a scan for the dimensional beaming and locates the Ansata underground base, the hostages are freed—but not until Devos kills Finn just as he's about to shoot the captain.

Devos is coldly defensive: it's better for Finn to die than to live as a prisoner. The crew leaves, thankful for their liberated officers but sobered by the unlikely prospects for peace anytime soon on the troubled planet.

Written in response to the producers' request for another action-adventure script, Snodgrass had to come up with the concept of dimensional shifting to meet Gene Roddenberry's concern that the terrorists have a logical way to defeat the *Enterprise*'s vast array of technology.

Originally conceived of as a parallel to the American Revolution, the Ansata rebels' cause was changed to resemble that of Northern Ireland, according to Snodgrass, although Finn's reference to himself as a latter-day Washington stayed in. (During the episode, Data reveals that the reunification of Ireland on Earth occurs in 2025.)

Stewart's campaign to give Picard's character more action and romance may have begun to bear fruit by this time. The normally stoic captain belts a terrorist on the bridge of the *Enterprise*, foreshadowing his encounter with the Borg later on. The story also provides this season's version of the ongoing tease of Beverly's interrupted confiding to Picard, begun in "Arsenal of Freedom" (121). We also learn that she hails from North America.

DEJA Q

Production No.: 161 ▪ Aired: Week of February 5, 1990
Stardate: 43539.1 ▪ Code: dq

Directed by **Les Landau**
Written by **Richard Danus**

GUEST CAST
Q: **John de Lancie**
Guinan: **Whoopi Goldberg**
Dr. Garin: **Richard Cansino**
Bre'el Scientist: **Betty Muramoto**
Q2: **Corbin Bernsen**

As if Picard didn't have enough headaches trying to keep Bre'el IV's moon from crashing into the planet, Q shows up, claiming to be powerless. The alien says he's been evicted by the Q Continuum for his past mischief.

Data is assigned to keep an eye on Q, whose story no one believes—until a gaseous Calamarain life-form catches up with Q to exact a little

Another Q? Corbin Bernsen plays the bearer of good news for Q (John de Lancie).

revenge. Realizing Q really is defenseless, Data gets a severe electrical shock trying to protect him from the Calamarain.

Q is moved by the android's sacrifice for him and steals a shuttlecraft to lure away the Calamarain so the *Enterprise* can lower its shields and get on with trying to save Bre'el IV.

But just as Picard tries to talk Q out of sacrificing himself, another Q arrives in the shuttle to say the Continuum was pleased with Q1's selfless act. The visitor restores his powers—on a probationary basis.

Overjoyed, Q celebrates by providing a mariachi band, cigars, and women for the bridge crew. Furious again, Picard orders him off the *Enterprise*—but not before Q rewards Data with a one-time belly laugh as a lesson in humanity.

As Picard is wondering whether Q is finally going to learn a lesson himself, the impish being returns with a warning: "Don't bet on it."

This story, midyear staff writer Richard Danus's only solo effort, provided some of the best comic scenes in either Trek series. After five appearances, de Lancie said his hardest TNG scenes yet to film were the bridge scenes, which went on from 7:00 A.M. to 11:00 P.M. on Thanksgiving eve. Not only did his simulated trumpet playing require several takes, but after finding no way to fake the scene in which he appears suspended in the nude, he finally just did it *au naturel*.

The script originally told the story of a looming Klingon-Federation war that was actually caused by Q, who *faked* his loss of powers and then later rushed in to become a hero. Piller said GR suggested the portrayal of a godlike creature cut down to size. Most scenes are played for laughs, especially that ending, with the mariachi band, blondes, and cigars—although Q's reunion with Guinan leaves the viewer with chills when Guinan tries to stab Q with a fork.

Best known for his well-regarded performances as divorce attorney Arnie Becker on *L.A. Law*, Corbin Bernsen has said he took the role of Q2 not so much as a fan of Trek but to be a part of its legacy and its humanistic outlook.

The Berthold rays used by the Calamarain's scanning beam were referred to in 1967's "This Side of Paradise." We also learn in this story that Data requires no food but occasionally "eats" semiorganic nutrient suspension in a silicon-based liquid medium to "lubricate his biofunctions." He too is well aware of Troi's chocolate habit (see notes, "The Price"/156).

A MATTER OF PERSPECTIVE

Production No.: 162 ■ Aired: Week of February 12, 1990
Stardate: 43610.4 ■ Code: mp

Directed by **Cliff Bole**
Written by **Ed Zuckerman**

GUEST CAST
Krag: **Craig Richard Nelson**
Manua Apgar: **Gina Hecht**
Dr. Nel Apgar: **Mark Margolis**
Lieutenant O'Brien: **Colm Meaney**
Tayna: **Juli Donald**

A routine stop at a science station is anything but that when the wife of the lone researcher accuses Riker of having murdered her husband, who was killed in an explosion seconds after the first officer's departure.

Dr. Nel Apgar had been doing research for Starfleet on Krieger waves, a potential new source of energy. Apgar's wife, Manua, says Riker tried to seduce her, and his assistant backs up her claim that Riker and Dr. Apgar exchanged angry words during Number One's visit. Other evidence shows that an energy beam that struck Apgar and caused the explosion originated at Riker's beam-out point.

That is enough for Tanugan Inspector Krag to extradite Riker. Convinced of his first officer's innocence, Picard persuades Krag to use the holodeck to re-create the events prior to the explosion.

Riker is finally vindicated after La Forge, Data, and Wes look into a mysterious periodic energy burst that pulses through the ship. It turns out to be Krieger waves from the lab's ground-based generator, which is still switched on.

Actually the researcher had already made his breakthrough but was secretly trying to develop a new weapon he could sell on his own to the highest bidder. Fearing that Riker knew, Apgar aimed to disrupt Number One's beam-out with the generator—but the waves were deflected back into the lab instead, setting off the explo-

Geordi and Riker confront Tayna (Juli Donald) and Dr. Apgar (Mark Margolis).

sion. With Apgar's plot exposed, Krag drops the charges.

This episode's major plot device—having an officer accused of murder—recalls Scotty's dilemma in original Trek's "Wolf in the Fold," but the use of the holodeck to re-create the scene of the crime adds an interesting twist. Director Cliff Bole enjoyed what he called "our little trilogy," another conceptual device that foreshadows episodes to come, including "Cause and Effect" (218), while filming one of the most claustrophobic bottle shows ever.

After Data's unintentionally harsh criticism of the captain's artwork in the show's teaser, Picard has never been seen painting again. And in a moment that barely keeps the Riker-Troi relationship afloat, the counselor can be seen squeezing Number One's hand when he is cleared.

The mention of duranium is a throwback to an original-series episode, "The Menagerie": here the metal is still said to be an important alloy in starship hulls and interior walls.

YESTERDAY'S ENTERPRISE

Production No.: 163 ■ Aired: Week of February 19, 1990
Stardate: 43625.2 ■ Code: ye

Directed by **David Carson**
Teleplay by **Ira Steven Behr, Richard Manning, Hans Beimler, and Ronald D. Moore**
Story by **Trent Christopher Ganino and Eric A. Stillwell**

GUEST CAST
Lieutenant Tasha Yar: **Denise Crosby**
Captain Rachel Garrett: **Tricia O'Neill**
Lieutenant (j.g.) Richard Castillo: **Christopher McDonald**

A living ghost from the past, the *Enterprise*, NCC-1701-C, lost with all hands twenty-two years ago, emerges from a temporal rift. In "real" history, that ship answered a Klingon outpost's distress call, paving the way for the current union of the Federation and the Klingon Empire. By journeying through the temporal rift, the older ship has missed its appointment with

destiny and created an alternate time line; in this universe, where Tasha Yar is still alive and well, the *Enterprise*-C was not destroyed, and the Klingon-Federation detente never occurred. Instead, the two governments are engaged in a decades-old conflict that has claimed the lives of billions.

Only Guinan detects the changes in history. She tells Picard that the war, his dark and somber battleship, and time itself are "wrong" and that he must return the old *Enterprise*-C through the temporal rift to meet its intended fate.

Among the older ship's officers are Captain Rachel Garrett and helmsman Richard Castillo, who falls in love with Tasha. Picard, to the disbelief of his officers, is finally convinced of the truth of Guinan's story and prepares to send the *Enterprise*-C back through the rift. Then Garrett is killed in a Klingon attack; to take her place, Yar (who has learned of her senseless death in the "real" time line) volunteers to go back with the doomed ship; Picard reluctantly grants her permission to do so.

Attacked by three Klingon ships, the *Enterprise*-D holds out just long enough to allow its predecessor to enter the temporal rift. History immediately resumes its normal course, a change that goes unnoticed by all—except Guinan.

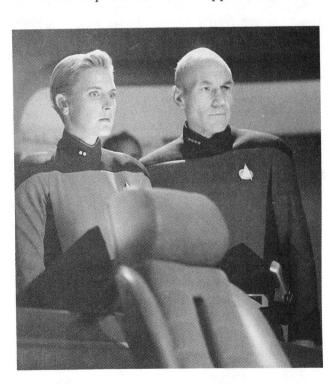

In spite of the multitude of writing credits, which suggest a patched-together episode, this show is continually cited as one of TNG's most popular and most powerful. Yet according to story writer Eric Stillwell, the writing staff didn't think the show would work because its teleplay was written by committee and rushed to final draft in just three days to meet a pushed-up shooting schedule. This was necessary because Whoopi Goldberg's and Denise Crosby's schedules made them unavailable during the original filming window in January.

"Most of the writers were not very happy with the script," said Stillwell (a gofer during TNG's first two seasons and a script coordinator for the next three, listed as a pre-production associate in the credits). "They thought it was going to be horrible, because they don't like having to write [something] and make it work in three days."

The tale actually began as an idea pitched by Trent Christopher Ganino a year earlier, in which the *Enterprise*-C comes forward in time and, while not changing the future, forces Picard to decide whether or not to reveal their fate to them before sending them back. Among the characters that would not survive to the final draft was Capt. *Richard* Garrett, whose last name was taken from a pizzeria in Ganino's hometown, San Jose.

Later on, Ganino and Stillwell joined forces on another alter-

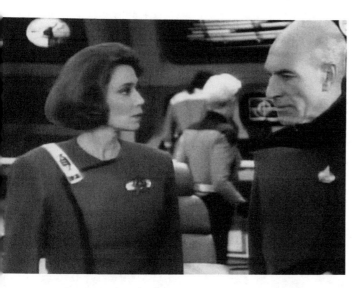

both Sarek and the Guardian—which he called a "gimmick" from the original series—but urged them to combine the story with Ganino's *Enterprise*-C tale, enlarging Tasha's part and bringing in Guinan. After eight days of brainstorming the eventual story emerged, with a female captain who dies to make room for Tasha's sacrifice and a more "honorable" death.

After another rewrite the regular staff took over and each wrote an act, with Piller sharpening Guinan's role in the incident and Ron Moore contributing the Yar-Castillo romance. Moore also stated that time constraints cut his own plans for a longer, bloodier ending for the alternate *Enterprise*-D, in which Data was electrocuted, Wesley's head blown off, and so on; of the sequence, only Riker's death was retained. Piller voluntarily took his name off the credits to meet the stringent Writers Guild credit limit of four names.

As in original Trek's "Mirror, Mirror," little touches are used to subtly point up the differences between the real and alternate universes: the substitution of "military log" for captain's log, "combat date" for stardate, and the absence of a counselor and a friendly Klingon. On the bridge, steps replaced the side bridge ramps, the captain's chair was more thronelike, and sidearms were the norm. Other nice touches: Dr. Selar—an allusion to "The Schizoid Man" (131)—is heard being paged, as is Lieutenant Barrett, an homage to Gene Roddenberry's wife, Majel Barrett.

Both 1701-C guest stars were already Trek fans. McDonald, whose TV and film roles include *Thelma & Louise,* was among those in the running in 1986 to be cast as Riker. O'Neil, another TV and film vet, won the Drama Critics Award and Theatre World Award for her Broadway lead in *Two by Two* and later played a Klingon in "Suspicions" (248). The Narendra outpost honored Moore friend and later science advisor/story editor Naren Shankar. Two TNG firsts here are designer Bob Blackman's use of the film-era costumes sans shirt, and—finally—Greg Jein's model of Andy Probert's Ambassador-class design. Look for the final scene's blooper when "normal" Geordi wears "alternate" uniform cuffs.

nate time line story that used material from three original Star Trek episodes. A Vulcan team on an archaeological mission accidentally change history through the Guardian of Forever ("City on the Edge of Forever") when Surak, the founder of Vulcan's peaceful, logical way of life ("The Savage Curtain") is killed. His absence leads to a "new" time line in which the violent Vulcans join with their brethren, the Romulans, in a super empire, wiping out the Klingons and turning on the Federation. After being captured as a spy, Spock's father, Sarek ("Journey to Babel" and *Star Trek III, IV,* and *VI*), persuades Picard to let him takes Surak's place in the past, restoring the time line.

"We thought it would be really cool that someone from the future would replace someone in the past, and I always thought it was funny that their names were so similar, anyway," Stillwell said. But after hearing that idea, Michael Piller nixed the use of

Scenes from an *Enterprise* that never was: Tasha and Picard (*opposite*) confront a mysterious intruder from the past; (*above*) Picard and Garrett confer on how to save history; (*below, left*) Castillo and Tasha steal some of what little time they have left; while Riker (*below, right*) is only one of many to die in the alternate timeline.

THE OFFSPRING

Production No.: 164 ■ Aired: Week of March 12, 1990
Stardate: 43657.0 ■ Code: of

Directed by **Jonathan Frakes**
Written by **Rene Echevarria**

GUEST CAST
Lal: **Hallie Todd**
Admiral Haftel: **Nicolas Coster**
Lieutenant Ballard: **Judyanne Elder**
Ten-Forward Crew: **Diane Moser, Hayne Bayle, Maria Leone, and James G. Becker**
Lal as Robot: **Leonard John Crowfoot**

Data and his "daughter," Lal (Hallie Todd).

Data sparks another legal row over the status of androids when he innocently sets out to further his creator's work. He builds a "child" whom he names Lal—Hindi for "beloved."

Troi and the others are delighted when Lal chooses a human female form; her personality soon blooms, despite growing pains. But Picard is not so pleased that she was developed in secret, and has a hard time calling her Data's "child" even though the elder android duplicated his own neural nets for Lal's.

Still, the captain becomes a firm ally of the androids when Admiral Haftel of Starfleet Research insists that Lal should develop in a lab rather than aboard a ship. Despite the protests of Picard, Data, and Lal herself, Haftel perseveres—especially after he finds the new android in Ten-Forward, where Guinan and Data thought she could best study humans.

But then Lal, who shows she can go beyond Data's programming by using contractions, grows too quickly when the stress of the fight over her future leads her to develop emotions—a new trait she finds she physically can't handle.

Haftel and Data unite to repair the damage to her system, but it is too great. Data, the supposedly unemotional android, bids his dying child good-bye and then tells his grieving shipmates that Lal will always live on in their memories.

Hallie Todd, who played Joe's daughter on the Showtime series *Brothers*, is the real-life daughter of Ann Morgan Gilbert who played next-door neighbor Millie Helper on the old *Dick Van Dyke Show*. She turned in a charming and poignant performance as Lal, the spark that aided Frakes's long-sought turn in the director's chair and made viewers forget that android rights had been addressed only a year earlier in "The Measure of a Man" (135).

After producer Rick Berman told him he'd "have to go to school" before directing a show, Frakes spent over three hundred hours observing editors, watching other directors, going to the dubbing stage, attending seminars, and reading. "I think the producers were hoping I'd lose interest, but I didn't," he once said, and judging by his subsequent directing assignments ("Reunion"/181, "The Drumhead"/195, "Ethics"/216) their reaction to his initial turn in the director's chair must have been positive. This script was the first TNG sale for Echevarria, who joined the writing staff to season five.

Daytime viewers may recognize Nicolas Coster from his current role on *Santa Barbara*. Leonard John Crowfoot, in an uncredited role as the robot Lal, endured much less anonymity and special makeup during an earlier guest turn on TNG ("Angel One"/115). Once again the Daystrom Institute ("The Measure of a Man"/135) pops up; Haftel is mentioned as working at a Daystrom annex on Galor IV.

Rob Legato used a rare motion-control camera onstage for the sequence in which the robot Lal is picking holographic self-facade options. This scene includes the first appearance of an Andorian on the series.

Sins of the Father

Production No.: 165 ▪ Aired: Week of March 19, 1990
Stardate: 43685.2 ▪ Code: sf

Directed by **Les Landau**
Teleplay by **Ronald D. Moore and W. Reed Morgan**
Based on a teleplay by **Drew Deighan**

GUEST CAST
K'mpec: **Charles Cooper**
Commander Kurn: **Tony Todd**
Duras: **Patrick Massett**
Kahlest: **Thelma Lee**
Transporter Technician: **Teddy Davis**
Assassins: **B. J. Davis and Chris Doyle**

The *Enterprise* receives a Klingon exchange officer on board who turns out to be the younger brother Worf never knew he had. The officer, Kurn, tells Worf their family name is about to be shamed: their dead father, Mogh, has been branded the traitor behind the Romulan attack at Khitomer that killed thousands and left Worf and Kurn orphans.

With Picard's backing, Worf returns to challenge the accusations before the Klingon High Council, even though the penalty for an unsuccessful appeal is death. Shortly after their arrival, however, Kurn is attacked.

Worf had used his brother as his advocate before the council, so he asks Picard to replace him. Together they locate Worf's childhood nurse, whose tale forces the revelation of the real truth in a closed-door meeting with aging council leader K'mpec.

It was the father of Duras, Worf's accuser,

Worf and Kurn (Tony Todd) face the High Council with Picard.

and not Mogh who was the traitor. Worf and Picard are stunned when told that the truth, if exposed, would plunge the Klingon Empire into civil war.

K'mpec sadly prepares to carry out the death sentence until Worf, putting his people ahead of himself, agrees to drop the challenge and be publicly branded an outcast and coward—and to live on for another day to clear his father's name.

This landmark show gave the Trek audience its first-ever look at the Klingon homeworld, and won art direction Emmys for production designer Richard James and set decorator Jim Mees. Worf's discommendation amounted to his being branded a coward, one without honor. The withdrawal of his win-or-die Council appeal left him a nonperson in Klingon society. Worf would carry the emotional baggage of this episode through the beginning of the fifth season.

Perhaps best known as Sergeant Warren in Oliver Stone's *Platoon*, actor, playwright, and longtime Trek fan Tony Todd has played many stage, TV, and film roles. He auditioned four times for guest spots on TNG before he scored with the part of Kurn, who would return later in the series to help reclaim the family honor in "Redemption" (200) and "Redemption II" (201).

Veteran actor Charles Cooper brought pride and forbearance to the role of the elder Klingon—traits that, because of a weak script, he was unable to show off in the part of General Korrd in the movie *Star Trek V*. In uncredited roles are stuntmen B. J. Davis and Chris Doyle as Duras's assassins.

The simple Klingonese words and phrases spoken here and in future episodes were all coined by linguist Marc Okrand. They include *Qapla'!* (success), *mev yap* (That is enough!), and *cha'Dich* (literally, second—the ritual defender-supporter). When Kurn and Picard accept Worf's invitation to join him, they reply, *"jIlajnes. ghIj qet jaghmeyjaj"* (I accept with honor. May your enemies run with fear.)

Curiously, often overlooked is the actual name of Duras's father, Ja'rod—mentioned only once here and never in succeeding stories. A briefly seen computer display reveals that the *Intrepid*—another ship renamed for a Constitution-class vessel (from 1968's "Immunity Syndrome")—was commanded by Captain Drew Deighan when it reached Khitomer on SD 23859.7—perhaps a descendant of the writer of the spec script this episode sprang from.

ALLEGIANCE

Production No.: 166 ■ Aired: Week of March 26, 1990
Stardate: 43714.1 ■ Code: al

Directed by **Winrich Kolbe**
Written by **Richard Manning and Hans Beimler**

GUEST CAST
Kova Tholl: **Stephen Markel**
Esoqq: **Reiner Schöne**
Cadet Mitena Haro: **Jocelyn O'Brien**
Alien No. 1: **Jerry Rector**
Alien No. 2: **Jeff Rector**

Picard is kidnapped and replaced with a double whose actions test the loyalty of the *Enterprise* crew. Meanwhile, the real captain is trapped with three other hostages in a bizarre cell and must devote his time not only to escaping but to keeping the peace among his cell mates.

The false Picard arouses suspicion when he orders a close look at a well-known yet dangerous pulsar without telling Riker, joins in the officers' poker game, leads the crew in a drinking song, and seduces Dr. Crusher.

The mystery behind his kidnapping is revealed when one of the real Picard's cell mates, disguised as a Starfleet cadet, mentions a classified mission only Picard's crew knew about, leading him to finger her as the enemy in their midst. She transforms herself into an energy-being, and is joined by two others of her race. Their captives were being studied for their reactions to authority, like lab rats.

The captain and the aliens return to the *Enterprise* just as Riker is leading a "mutiny" against the impostor, who is then transformed into another one of the energy-beings. Picard then gives the energy-beings a taste of their own medicine by trapping them in an energy field. He releases them only after lecturing that their "research" amounts to kidnapping and is immoral.

Another turn on the old "kidnapped for alien experiments" theme (also seen in the original-series episodes "The Cage," "The Me-

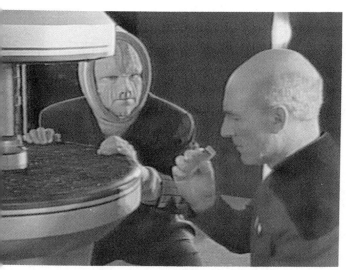

Picard studies his piece of nourishment as fellow hostage Kova Tholl (Stephen Markel) looks on.

nagerie," and "The Empath," among others), this segment still provides its own little gems: the false Picard's wooing and then dropping of a stunned Beverly, and his leading Ten-Forward in a drinking song and a round of ales. For the record, the song is "Hearts of Oak," first performed in 1770 with lyrics by David Garrick and music by Dr. William Boyce.

Haro's costume is our first look at a modern Academy cadet uniform and only our second at the Bolians ("Conspiracy"/125), whom we learn are from Bolarus IX. Picard visited Esoqa's anarchic world, Chalna, twelve years earlier as captain of the *Stargazer*—or a year before that ship's loss ("The Battle"/110). Tholl hails from the second planet of Mizar, the ancients' name for Zeta Ursa Majoris—the larger of two optical binary stars in the second position inward on the Big Dipper's handle. Picard's cabin is seen to be at Deck 9/3601.

CAPTAIN'S HOLIDAY

Production No.: 167 ▪ Aired: Week of April 2, 1990
Stardate: 43745.2 ▪ Code: cp

Directed by **Chip Chalmers**
Written by **Ira Steven Behr**

GUEST CAST
Vash: **Jennifer Hetrick**
Ajur: **Karen Landry**
Boratus: **Michael Champion**
Sovak: **Michael Grodenchik**
Joval: **Deirdre Imershein**

The crew needles Picard into taking a much-needed rest, but the galaxy's most reluctant vacationer soon finds himself in the middle of an adventure the likes of which he'd never get into aboard ship.

In rapid succession, he meets two Vorgons from the twenty-seventh century, traveling back in time to locate the superweapon Tox Uthat; Sovak, a Ferengi interested in buying the artifact; and Vash, a brash, striking woman whose late boss was an archaeologist also searching for the Uthat.

According to the Vorgons, Picard is destined to find the Uthat. He agrees to honor their request to return the Uthat to them and their time, but he doesn't count on falling for Vash on their overnight hike to get the artifact.

They are joined by a leering, armed Sovak, but their long dig at the presumed burial site yields nothing. Picard finally realizes that Vash found the Uthat a week ago and staged the dig to get Sovak off her trail.

She recalls how Vorgons are said to be thieves, not retreivers, and Picard has the returning *Enterprise* destroy the Uthat once and for all while beaming it up.

The Vorgons depart, while Picard and Vash muse whether they'll see each other when the alien thieves try again—in time.

This story, the first-unit debut of assistant director Chip Chalmers, grew out of Stewart's desire for more "sex and shooting" for the captain. It also introduced the off-mentioned Risa resort, a Fantasy Island-type getaway spot that apparently can meet needs even a holodeck can't satisfy.

According to Michael Piller, the first draft of the story concerned only the group's search for an ancient artifact à la *The Maltese Falcon*, but at Ron Moore's suggestion the time-travel element was added. The off-ship opening was a first for the series, but an echo of that scene planned to close the show—implying that the Vorgons were already returning to try again—was cut when it became too confusing.

Hetrick, a former model and commercials actress, followed to TNG her onetime *L.A. Law* costar Corbin Bersen (she played Arnie Becker's wife Corinne) and returned in sequels "Qpid" (194) and DS9's "Q-Less" as Vash—named by Behr for Susan Vash (rhymes with "dash"), his former show *Once a Hero*'s casting director and a friend of his wife. Grodenchik was another Ferengi on TNG ("The Perfect Mate"/221) and then won the role of Rom on DS9.

Other races seen in the Risian lobby are an Andorian, a Vulcan, and an Antican ("The Last Outpost"/108). The Daystrom Institute, spoken of in "The Measure of a Man" (135), is mentioned

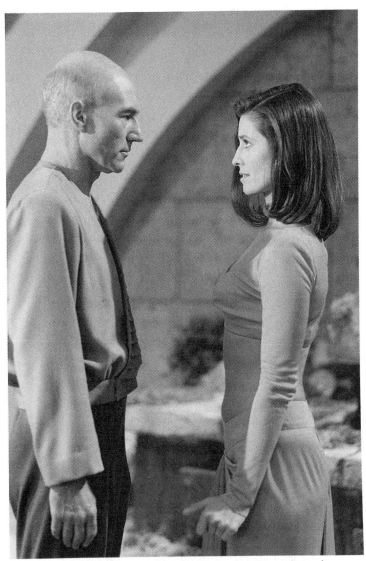

Vash (Jennifer Hetrick) proves an attractive enigma for a vacationing Picard.

TIN MAN

Production No.: 168 ■ Aired: Week of April 23, 1990
Stardate: 43779.3 ■ Code: ti

Directed by **Robert Scheerer**
Written by **Dennis Putnam Bailey** and
David Bischoff

GUEST CAST
Captain Robert DeSoto: **Michael Cavanaugh**
Romulan Commander: **Peter Vogt**
Lieutenant O'Brien: **Colm Meaney**
Tam Elbrun: **Harry Groener**

again when Vash promises to turn over the Tox Uthat. For the record, the Risian idol of sexuality is a *horgh'an,* and the state one hopes it brings is *jamaharohn.*

Notice the cave in which the treasure hunters all converge. The set is enlarged by a matte painting, but not the typical kind. As he would throughout the series on his shows, visual-effects supervisor Dan Curry created this background with pixels instead of pigment, and his computer-painted matte was then digitally blended with the live action.

The *Enterprise* takes on board a Betazoid first-contact specialist, Tam Elbrun, to establish relations with a creature known as Tin Man—an alien life-form resembling an organic spaceship. This seems like a straightforward task—except that the Romulans also wish to contact Tin Man, and have sent two warbirds to carry out that assignment.

Elbrun is an unusually powerful telepath; on their way to rendezvous with the creature, he tells his old friend Troi about the pressure he feels as a result of being constantly bombarded by voices in his head. Troi sympathizes, but when Elbrun hints that he has already made contact with Tin Man, a suspicious Riker recalls that Elbrun's last assignment caused the death of forty-seven Starfleet officers.

Just as the *Enterprise* arrives in the star system in which Tin Man has taken up orbit around an incipient supernova, one of the Romulan ships opens fire on them and on the creature, intending to prevent the two from making contact. At Elbrun's mental suggestion, the creature destroys the Romulan warbird with a shock wave. Picard wants Elbrun to coax Tin Man into a safer sector, but the lonely alien has come to this system intending to die in the upcoming explosion. Beaming over with Data to make physical contact, Elbrun establishes an immediate rapport with the creature.

As the second warbird prepares to open fire on Tin Man, the creature emits a shock wave that sends the *Enterprise* and the warbird hurtling

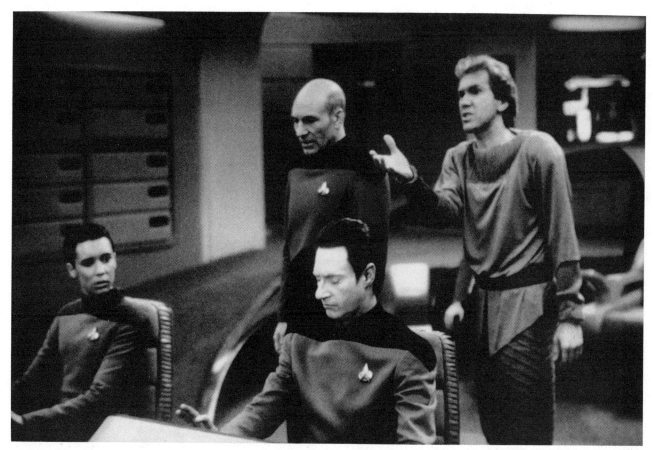

Betazoid Tam Elbrun (Harry Groener) is the crew's troubled contact with "Tin Man."

through space, away from both it and the exploding star. Later it returns Data to the *Enterprise*. The android tells the crew that Elbrun has decided to remain with Tin Man, the two of them having found peace and comfort with each other.

___

Based on "Tin Woodman," a 1979 Ace book by Dennis Putnam Bailey and David Bischoff, this spin on the familiar alien encounter was the first for new composer Jay Chattaway, who late next season would take over Ron Jones's slot in alternating episodes with Dennis McCarthy. The show also gives us more background on the Betazoid race, as we learn that their mental powers, which usually blossom during adolescence, can be emotionally unsettling if they are present at birth.

Harry Groener played the insecure nerd Ralph on NBC's *Dear John* and later won a Tony for his lead in the musical *Crazy for You*; here, his role was the first male Betazed seen on TNG. Also, "Ensign Russell" is longtime extra Carl Banks.

Staying true to TNG's own background story, the *Hood* here is commanded by Captain DeSoto. Riker's previous commander was mentioned by Picard way back in "Farpoint" (101–102). A script line, later deleted, revealed that the two captains had once served together as lieutenants. We also learn, in "Ménage à Troi" (172), that Troi studied psychology at the University on Betazed, where she met both Tam and Riker.

The interior sound of Tin Man—"Gomtuu" in his native tongue—was actually based on the noises in sound-effects editor James Wolvington's stomach, recorded through a stethoscope. The model was another Rick Sternbach creation built by Greg Jein. It was designed in homage to the thermal pods in *Buckaroo Banzai*. Rob Legato created the organic chair that seems to form out of Tin Man's very structure by reversing a time-lapse sequence of a melting wax chair.

HOLLOW PURSUITS

Production No.: 169 ▪ Aired: Week of April 30, 1990
Stardate: 43807.4 ▪ Code: hp

Directed by **Cliff Bole**
Written by **Sally Caves**

GUEST CAST
Lieutenant (j.g.) Reginald Barclay: **Dwight Schultz**
Lieutenant Duffy: **Charley Lang**
Lieutenant O'Brien: **Colm Meaney**

Geordi experiences problems with one of his engineers, Reg Barclay, (nicknamed "Broccoli" by the crew), a nervous, shy officer who retreats to the holodeck when he can't handle real life.

After Barclay botches an antigrav repair diagnosis, Picard urges Geordi to find the man's strengths and bring him out. What the chief engineer finds is a host of holodeck fantasy programs ranging from the seduction of Deanna Troi to the casting of La Forge, Data, and Picard as Three Musketeers who are no match for Barclay's swordplay.

Meanwhile, during a routine transport of medical samples to help stop a plague, systems such as the replicator, transporter, and warp drive begin to show flaws. Suddenly the matter-antimatter injectors freeze open, catapulting the ship forward with a sudden burst of warp speed. *Enterprise* then continues to accelerate; if Geordi can't find a way to slow it down, the starship will self-destruct in minutes.

It is meek Barclay who realizes the problem stems from a little-used substance leaked from the medical-sample containers and then spread by crew members to the affected systems. That known, La Forge is able to unstick the injectors and get the ship back under control just in time.

Infused with confidence from his performance, Barclay decides to bid his holodeck fantasies good-bye once and for all, except—he smiles to himself—for program 9.

A critic-pleasing tour de force for actor Dwight Schultz—remembered by many as "Mad Dog" Murdoch, the manic pilot from *The A Team*—this story answered the questions of viewers who'd won-

Only in fantasy can Barclay (Dwight Shultz) deal with his crewmates.

dered if even twenty-fourth-century Starfleet officers were beyond the temptations of overdosing on holodeck fantasy, or "holodiction." Schultz had been a longtime Trek fan and, like Whoopi Goldberg, had asked to do the show if the right part came along.

While this episode provided the regular actors with some real change-of-pace scenes—including Wesley as a pie-eating Gainesborough "Blueboy" and Troi as the sheer-robed "goddess of empathy"—those involved in this show deny they intended to make a comment aimed at Trek's more obsessive fans. Again it seems a holodeck program cannot be secured against intrusion—as in "Manhunt" (145), "The Emissary" (146), "Cost of Living" (220), "Relics" (230), "Ship in a Bottle" (238), and "Emergence" (275), among others.

We learn more about Guinan's background here: her nonconformist slant and her mother's misfit brother, Terkim. Trivia note: the test objects made of "duranium," also mentioned in "A Matter of Perspective" (162), that O'Brien uses on the malfunctioning transporter are actually U.S. Navy sonar buoy transport cases.

Data confronts The Collector, Kivas Fajo (Saul Rubinek).

THE MOST TOYS

Production No.: 170 ■ Aired: Week of May 7, 1990
Stardate: 43872.2 ■ Code: mo

Directed by **Timothy Bond**
Written by **Shari Goodhartz**

GUEST CAST
Kivas Fajo: **Saul Rubinek**
Palor Toff: **Nehemiah Persoff**
Varria: **Jane Daly**
Lieutenant O'Brien: **Colm Meaney**

Data is presumed lost by a shocked crew who watch his shuttlepod blow up while returning from dealer Kivas Fajo's ship.

Saddened, his shipmates go on to their mission, little knowing that Fajo staged the "disaster" so he could add Data to his prized galaxy-wide collection of stolen one-of-a-kind artifacts.

Fajo's comic manner hides a cunning side unhindered by ethics or conscience. Determined to break the android's resistance to being "collected," he is humiliated when Data won't "perform" for a friend and rival.

Though Fajo's assistant, Varria, seems loyal to him, Data senses she feels as trapped as he does. When Fajo finally breaks Data by threat-

ening to kill Varria with a painful, banned disruptor beam, she finally agrees to help the android escape. But Fajo heads them off and kills Varria. Data gets control of the weapon, but Fajo taunts the android because of his directive against killing for no reason.

Meanwhile, the *Enterprise* officers have been researching Fajo's record and have guessed the truth regarding Data's disappearance. As they prepare to rescue him, sensors reveal a weapon being fired—a subject Data is surprisingly close-mouthed about, even after Fajo is arrested and his prize stolen collection confiscated.

An interesting story from a spec script that pushed Data to the brink of murder for a logical reason, "The Most Toys" was struck by tragedy early in the filming. Originally, the actor chosen to play Fajo was well-known little person David Rappaport, star of the series *The Wizard* and a veteran of many films and guest roles, including two memorable appearances on *L.A. Law* as a scrappy defense attorney. But Rappaport attempted suicide over the weekend after two days of filming and was hospitalized. Shortly afterward he died as a result of a second attempt. "Of course it left us very sad," Rick Berman recalled.

Left with unusable footage, the producers huddled, then hired Saul Rubinek and had him into fittings for a new costume by noon on the following Monday, although promotional photos of Rappaport in the role had already been sent out. Considering the short notice, Rubinek, a busy Canadian actor, did a remarkable job of making the quirky role his own. In the expected grief over Data's loss, Worf has a nice moment when he actually confides to Troi that his assignment at Ops is the second time he's filled in for a fallen comrade, after Tasha Yar.

This story's shuttlepod, the *Pike,* was the first on TNG actually named for a fictional person. Fans of the 1960s Trek series know that Christopher Pike was James T. Kirk's predecessor as captain of the original starship *Enterprise.* He was seen in the first pilot, "The Cage" and again later, in "The Menagerie."

The Varon-T disruptor appears to be the same prop as one of the smaller weapons Sovak used in "Captain's Holiday" (167). When Data fires it just as he is beamed out, we learn the transporter is capable not only of detecting weapons but of shutting them down as well. We also learn that Data has never killed anything. Here we see that the android has added to the mementos revealed during his human rights hearing in "The Measure of a Man" (135): a deck of poker cards and chips, his violin, and the painting he was working on in "Tin Man" (168). Fajo's lapling, a puppet, was built by makeup designer Michael Westmore.

Sarek

Production No.: 171 ■ Aired: Week of May 14, 1990	
Stardate: 43917.4 ■ Code: sa	

Directed by **Les Landau**
Written by **Peter S. Beagle**
Story by **Marc Cushman and Jake Jacobs**

GUEST CAST
Sarek: **Mark Lenard**
Perrin: **Joanna Miles**
Ki Mendrossen: **William Denis**
Sakkath: **Rocco Sisto**
Lieutenant O'Brien: **Colm Meaney**
Science Ensign: **John H. Francis**

Renowned Ambassador Sarek of Vulcan is about to oversee the completion of his career's crown-

Perrin (Joanna Miles) comforts her ill husband, Sarek (Mark Lenard).

ing achievement: the establishment of relations between the Federation and the Legaran.

But while being ferried to the meeting site aboard the *Enterprise*, Sarek weeps during a Mozart concert. The Vulcan has developed Bendii syndrome, an Alzheimer's-like disease that can erode an aged Vulcan's emotional control.

Sarek unknowingly begins projecting his lack of control onto others: Wes and La Forge fight, Dr. Crusher slaps her son, and a brawl breaks out in Ten-Forward. But Sarek's Vulcan and human aides remain in denial until Sakkath, a young Vulcan, admits he has been "propping up" Sarek's control so the Legaran mission could continue.

Confronted by that fact and Picard's insistence that he face reality, Sarek erupts in a fit of anger that even he admits proves the captain's point. The Legaran, who have been dealing with Sarek for years, will talk only to him, so as a last resort to avoid canceling the mission the captain proposes a Vulcan mind-link to share his mental control with Sarek during the negotiations.

The Vulcan agrees, and Dr. Crusher braces Picard—who always wanted to know the remarkable Vulcan better—for the onslaught of Sarek's life of repressed emotions. He is reduced to rage and sobs, but he survives the pressure as Sarek completes his mission.

After being written out of "Yesterday's Enterprise" (163), Mark Lenard here reprises the role he first played in 1967's "Journey to Babel." His appearance is the first major unifying event tying together the old and new Trek eras since McCoy's cameo in the "Farpoint" pilot (101–102).

According to Michael Piller, the original story concerned the mental problems of an ambassador other than Sarek; from there, the writing staff moved to the problems of the aging, then added the Vulcan loss of control and the telepathic "bleeding." Using Sarek was the last logical step in maximizing audience involvement and impact. "It brings home the idea that even the greatest of men is subject to illness," Piller said.

Lenard's work is complemented by the mind-meld scene in which Stewart *is* Sarek with a brilliant portrayal of pent-up emotional anguish. Though Sarek's famous son Spock is later seen to be very much alive ("Unification"/207–208), Behr recalled the battle at the time just to *mention* the character at all, with caution still in place about dealing with the original series. Picard does say he attended the wedding of "Sarek's son" as a lieutenant, though again Spock is not specified.

References are also made to "Journey to Babel"'s Coridan issue and to Amanda, Sarek's first wife, played by Jane Wyatt in the 1960s and in *Star Trek IV*. Given the human life span, it was

decided that Sarek would have remarried; his second wife is played here by veteran actress Joanna Miles, a new kid on the Trek block. As Riker learned in school, Sarek is given credit, among other things, for the early Klingon-Federation treaties—credit that he shares with Riva ("Loud as a Whisper"/132).

On the trivia side, note the scroll given Picard by the Mintakans ("Who Watches the Watchers?"/152) is seen draped over his chair in this episode. And for music lovers: the first selection played at the Mozart concert is the String Quartet No. 19 in C Major, also known as "The Dissonant," while—in a blooper—the second is actually by Brahms, the andante moderato movement from his Sextet No. 1 in B-flat Major.

MÉNAGE À TROI

Production No.: 172 ■ Aired: Week of May 28, 1990
Stardate: 43930.7 ■ Code: me

Directed by **Robert Legato**
Written by **Fred Bronson & Susan Sackett**

GUEST CAST
Lwaxana Troi: **Majel Barrett**
DaiMon Tog: **Frank Corsentino**
Dr. Farek: **Ethan Phillips**
Nibor: **Peter Slutsker**
Reittan Grax: **Rudolph Willrich**
Mr. Homn: **Carel Struycken**

Picard and Betazoid officials have their doubts about allowing Ferengi to take part in a biannual Betazed trade conference, but it seems to come to a smooth conclusion for all except Lwaxana Troi, Deanna's mother, who is followed by a pesky lovestruck DaiMon Tog.

Riker and Troi stay behind for a rare romantic shore leave on the planet while their ship finishes a routine assignment. But just as Lwaxana interrupts once again to nag her daughter about settling down, Tog appears and kidnaps all three, determined to use Lwaxana's telepathic skills for his own profit—and to make her his mate.

Riker and Troi outfox their guards and try to secretly signal their ship while Lwaxana keeps both Tog and her conscience at bay. Meanwhile, Wesley is due to leave to take his Starfleet Academy orals but stays behind at the last minute to

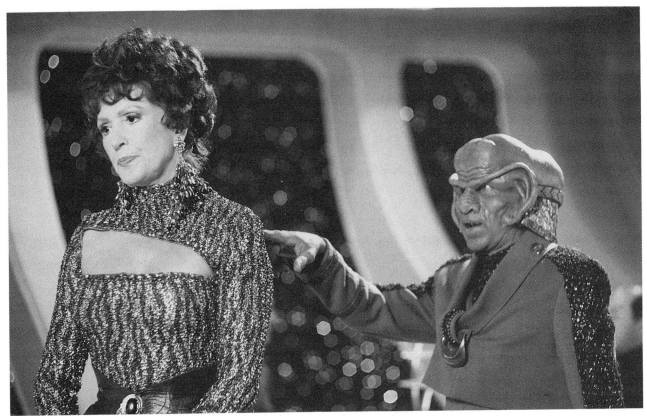

Lwaxana Troi (Majel Barrett) can't escape an obsessed Tog (Frank Corsentino).

help decode Riker's signal, which later earns him a field promotion to ensign.

Tog's doctor suspects their escape attempt almost too late, but Lwaxana, already in pain from his mind probes, asks him to let Riker and Deanna go free while she stays behind.

Then, with the young officers safely back aboard the *Enterprise*, Lwaxana signals the captain, her old would-be flame. Picard plays along by pretending to be her jilted lover. His performance is good enough to scare Tog into giving her up without an incident.

R**ob** Legato crossed over from his position as supervisor of visual effects to direct this episode, which included the first-ever look at the Betazed surface. Actually the Betazed scenes were filmed on location at the Huntington Library Botanical Gardens in San Marino, an L.A. suburb. Legato recalls that the show was thick with visitors, including Gene Roddenberry, since it was the first sale for his assistant, Susan Sackett, and also the yearly vehicle for GR's wife, Majel Barrett. To mark Wesley's promotion to full ensign at show's end, the Great Bird presented actor Wil Wheaton with his own ensign's bars, earned in the U.S. Navy thirty years earlier. General Colin Powell, chairman of the Joint Chiefs of Staff, was on hand for the ceremony.

Sackett recalled that the comic idea began with an O. Henry short story, "The Ransom of Red Chief"—the tale of a hostage nobody wanted. Still, aside from the moment when Riker and Troi are about to share their first on-screen kiss, the most memorable scene may be the one in which Picard mangles his beloved Shakespeare volume to get Lwaxana back.

Nearly abandoned as adversaries, here the Ferengi are developed even further in a tale recalled later by Lwaxana in DS9's "The Forsaken." Their four-node brains resist empathic contact by Betazoids and other races—which leaves Troi's earlier sensing of Bok ("The Battle"/110) unexplained—and their erogenous ears are sensitive to stroking, or *oo-mox* (also in "Chain of Command, Part I"/236 and DS9's "Q-Less"). Corsentino, after Armin Shimerman and Max Grodenchik, became the third to play more than one Ferengi ("The Battle"), while Slutsker would later join them ("Suspicions"/248, "Bloodlines"/274) and Phillips would win the role of Neelix on *Voyager*. The Ferengi phaser debuts here, while another anime joke creeps in: Tog's code is "Kei-ee, Yur-ee. . . ."

The USS *Bradbury*, of course, is named for the great science fiction writer Ray Bradbury, while "Cochrane distortion" pays homage to the discoverer of the space warp, Zefrem Cochran, mentioned in 1967's "Metamorphosis."

Michael Westmore peppered the trade delegates with a Klingon female and uniformed male, a Vulcan woman, a Selayan, a Zakdorn male, two Bolian females, and a Mizarian male, along with the Algolian musician. And yes, body doubles were used for Barrett and Sirtis in the nude scenes.

Grax knew Lwaxana's "first" husband, who was not Troi's dad,

Ian ("The Child"/127, "Dark Page"/259), unless she reverted her last name later; she says her first was "not much of a conversationalist," a cold view in light of her memories (259). Ian may even have been her third, if Zon, her next lover briefly mentioned, was a husband.

TRANSFIGURATIONS

Production No.: 173 ■ Aired: Week of June 4, 1990
Stardate: 43957.2 ■ Code: tf

Directed by **Tom Benko**
Written by **Rene Echevarria**

GUEST CAST
"John Doe": **Mark LaMura**
Commander Sunad: **Charles Dennis**
Christy Henshaw: **Julie Warner**
Lieutenant O'Brien: **Colm Meaney**
Nurse Temple: **Patti Tippo**

A severely injured humanoid—known as "John Doe" because of his amnesia—is found in the wreckage of an escape pod. After being linked to Geordi's nervous system to initially stabilize his body functions, the man recovers much faster than expected.

The good-natured John brings an unusually strong sense of serenity and confidence to those around him: La Forge, for one, who resumes his romance with a onetime holodeck date.

But as he recovers, John Doe is racked by fits of pain marked by a glowing energy burst within him.

The mystery man also demonstrates incredible healing powers, but increasingly severe bouts of pain frighten him into trying to steal a shuttlecraft. After he is subdued, John tells Picard he knows he is a threat to the crew and asks to leave.

The truth is revealed when a Zalkonian ship approaches and demands that the *Enterprise* turn John over to them. When the alien captain uses a paralysis beam against the *Enterprise*, John's memory finally returns. He frees the crew from the beam's effects. Then he explains that

he is among the first of his people to have taken the next step up the evolutionary ladder: transmutation into a being of pure energy. He is also the only survivor of his fearful government's attempt to exterminate this new life-form on their world so as to preserve their own power.

John now completes his transformation into an energy-being and prepares to return to his people and tell them of their own coming rebirth.

Longtime TNG film editor Tom Benko, brought onto the series by Corey Allen when he directed the pilot, got his own chance to break into directing with this simple piece, Rene Echevarria's second. The episode was originally designed as a love story for Beverly Crusher, but that plot would have to wait another year for "The Host" (197). Benko had previously sold scripts to *Magnum P.I.* and *The Fall Guy* and directed the second unit for *The Rockford Files*, *Kojak*, and *Battlestar Galactica*.

With Geordi gaining new confidence with women, the returning character of Christy gained a last name, Henshaw ("Booby Trap"/154). The shuttlepod *El-Baz* is also in "Time Squared" (139) and "Descent" (252–253), while motor-assist bands were used again in "Ethics" (216). Surprisingly, the alien's last scene was done live with actor LaMura donning a flourescent orange suit that literally glowed on the special film used and required little touch-up.

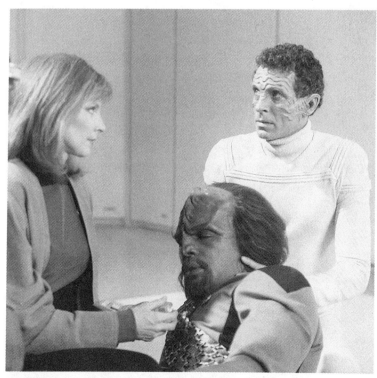

The evolving "John Doe" (Mark LaMura) brings Worf back to life.

THE BEST OF BOTH WORLDS

Production No.: 174 ■ Aired: Week of June 18, 1990
Stardate: 43989.1 ■ Code: bb

Directed by **Cliff Bole**
Written by **Michael Piller**

GUEST CAST
Lieutenant Commander Shelby: **Elizabeth Dennehy**
Admiral J. P. Hanson: **George Murdock**
Lieutenant O'Brien: **Colm Meaney**

The Borg are suspected of having caused a Starfleet colony's utter destruction, and Starfleet sends its best tactician to deal with the threat.

Riker and Borg expert Lt. Commander Shelby (Elizabeth Dennehy) investigate the destruction of Jouret IV.

Lieutenant Commander Shelby, who proves to be as smart and ambitious as she is beautiful, lets Riker know she wants his job. Riker refuses the latest command offered him, setting the stage for mounting friction, which heats up when Shelby tells him he's gone soft and lost his edge.

Meanwhile, the Borg finally appear and demand that Picard personally surrender to them. Thanks to Shelby's quick-witted strategy, the *Enterprise* breaks away and hides out in a sensor-blinding nebula to buy time for repairs and strategy.

La Forge and his team devise a weapon using the main deflector, but the ship will have to drop out of warp to use that power supply. The weapon is only part finished when the Borg find the ship, beam over, and kidnap Picard. The aliens then set course directly for Earth.

Shelby leads an away team to find Picard, who is already being assimilated by the Borg. As Locutus, he will serve as the cyborg race's speaker with humans.

Shelby's team does enough damage to force the Borg to drop out of warp, but they cannot retrieve Picard. Returning to the *Enterprise*, they find Geordi's jury-rigged weapon ready at last. The engineer insists they must fire on the Borg immediately or lose their only chance to destroy the invaders.

This spectacular movie-quality offering, the first true two-parter in this series, is still perhaps TNG's proudest achievement. Michael Piller, who says he didn't know how the saga would end when he first sat down to write it, began with the need for a cliff-hanger and came up with the Borg plot to kidnap Picard—after having tried all season long to work up a new story about the cyborg race.

Needing a so-called Queen Bee among the Borg collective for dramatic storytelling needs, Piller came up with the idea of Picard's abduction. Originally, he intended for Data and Picard to be "Borgified" into one unit. The later addition of Riker's career-advancement quandary gave Jonathan Frakes a chance to do some of his best work as Riker. For Piller personally, the subject matter was timely, coming as it did at his own contract-renewal time.

"When [Riker] talked to Troi about 'Why am I still here?' and she's telling him, 'because you're happy,' that was a conversation I had with myself several times during the course of writing that show," Piller confided. He elected to stay on in the seat he still occupies as the series enters its sixth season.

The exceptional guest cast includes Elizabeth Dennehy, the daughter of actor Brian Dennehy, and George Murdock, a vet-concede that TNG had finally arrived. Over that summer of 1990, fan debates raged, computer bulletin board lines hummed, and fanzine letter-writers argued, fueled by rumors that Stewart's contract talks with Paramount had stalled: Would Shelby die while saving Picard? Would Picard die heroically? Would Riker be promoted to captain? Would Shelby become his first officer? Paramount's publicity department ran its first-ever promotional campaign for a single TNG episode since "Fairpoint"; ads and radio spots were specially prepared for the season opener.

Now only one question remained: could anybody write an ending that would live up to all the hype?

Kidnapped from his own bridge by the Borg (*above*), Picard has no idea of the fate that awaits him (*right*).

eran of years of character roles. Trek fans may recognize Murdock as the "godhead" from *Star Trek V: The Final Frontier,* he was also the doctor on *Battlestar Galactica.*

The freighter *U.S.S. Lalo* had reported the Manheim time loop effect ("We'll Always Have Paris"/124); the *Melbourne,* which became the third command Riker had turned down, was in "11001001" (116) and is seen in DS9's pilot, "Emissary." A nice continuity touch that would be repeated later is the addition of Riker's trombone to his cabin, but a continuity gaffe has Riker and Shelby leave the main bridge for the battle bridge by way of the normal forward turbolift instead of the direct connection to starboard. We also hear that Picard "recruited" Riker as first officer and promoted him, a story fleshed out later in "The Pegasus" (264).

All in all, so great was the impact of "The Best of Both Worlds" that even the hardest of the hard-core original-Trek fans had to

Notes

1. Marc Altman, *Cinefantastique,* Oct. 1991, p. 18.
2. *Star Trek: The Official Fan Club Magazine,* Oct./Nov. 1989, p. 4.
3. *Star Trek: The Official Fan Club Magazine,* Aug./Sept. 1989, p. 9.

PRODUCTION STAFF CREDITS— THIRD SEASON

(In usual roll order; numbers in parentheses refer to episode numbers.)

Casting: (*) **Junie Lowery**

Main Title Theme: (*) **Jerry Goldsmith**, (*) **Alexander Courage**

Music: (*) **Ron Jones** (all even-numbered episodes, 150–174 except 168); (*) **Dennis McCarthy** (all odd-numbered episodes, 149–173; EMMY NOMINEE: dramatic underscore, series: "Yesterday's Enterprise" [163]); **Jay Chattaway** (168)

Director of Photography: **Marvin Rush**

Production Designer: ** **Richard D. James** (EMMY CO-WINNER: art direction, series: "Sins of the Father" [165])

Editor: **Daryl S. Baskin** (171); (*) **Tom Benko** (151, 154, 157, 160, 163; adds ACE: 166, 169); **Howard S. Deane**, ACE (172); (*) **J. P. Farrell** (150, 153, 156, 159, 162, 165, 168, 174); ** **Bob Lederman** (149, 152, 155, 158, 161, 164, 167, 170, 173; EMMY NOMINEE: single camera production editing, series: "Deja Q" [161])

Unit Production Manager: **Merri D. Howard** (+)

First Asst. Director: **Chip Chalmers** (all even-numbered episodes, 150–174 except 164, 168); **Brad Yacobian** (all odd-numbered episodes, 149–173); **Bruce Alan Solow** (166, 168); **Adele G. Simmons** (+) (162)

Second Asst. Director: ***Adele G. Simmons** (all but 162); **Jeff Cline** (162)

Costume Designer: **Bob Blackman**

Original Starfleet Uniforms: (*) **William Ware Theiss**

Visual Effects Supervisor: (*) **Robert Legato** (all even-numbered episodes, 150–174 except 170) (EMMY CO-NOMINEE: special visual FX "Tin Man" [168]); (*) **Dan Curry** (all odd-numbered episodes, 149–173 except 169) (EMMY CO-NOMINEE: special visual FX: "Deja Q" [161]); *** Gary Hutzel** (+) (170); **Ron Moore** (+) (169)

Post Production Supervisor: ***Wendy Neuss**

Original Set Design: (*) **Herman Zimmerman**

Makeup Supervisor: (*) **Michael Westmore** (EMMY CO-NOMINEE: makeup, series: "Allegiance" [166])

Set Decorator: **Tom Pedigo** (149–155); ** **Jim Mees** (156–174) (EMMY CO-WINNER: art direction, series: "Sins of the Father" [165])

Senior Illustrator: (*) **Rick Sternbach** (added Technical Consultant, 165–67)

Scenic Artist Supervisor: (*) **Michael Okuda** (added 167; EMMY CO-NOMINEE: special visual effects: "Tin Man" [168])

Set Designer: **Gary Speckman**

Script Supervisor: (*) **Cosmo Genovese**

Special Effects: (*) **Dick Brownfield**

Property Master: (*) **Joe Longo** (all odd-numbered episodes, 149–173); (*) **Alan Sims** (all even-numbered episodes, 150–174)

Construction Coordinator: (*) **Al Smutko**

Hair Designer: **Vivian McAteer** (EMMY CO-NOMINEE: hairstyling, series: "Hollow Pursuits" [169])

Hair Stylist: **Barbara Lampson** (149–158, 160, 162, 164–174), **Rita Bordonaro** (163) (both, EMMY CO-NOMINEE: hairstyling, series: "Hollow Pursuits" [169]); **Tim Jones** (159, 161)

Makeup Artists: ** **Gerald Quist** (all but 174), **June Abston-Haymore** (both, EMMY CO-NOMINEES: makeup, series: "Allegiance" [166]); **Hank Edds**, S.M.A. (174)

Visual Effects Coordinator: **Ron Moore** (all odd-numbered episodes, 149–173 except 169; EMMY CO-NOMINEE: special visual effects: "Deja Q" [161]); **Gary Hutzel** (all even-numbered episodes, 150–174 except 170; EMMY CO-NOMINEE: special visual effects: "Tin Man" [168]); NONE on 169–170

Sound Mixer: ***Alan Bernard**, C.A.S. (EMMY CO-NOMINEE: sound mixing, drama series: "Yesterday's Enterprise" [163] with re-recording mixer crew)

Chief Lighting Technician: **Buddy Bowles**

First Company Grip: **Bob Sordal**

Costumers: ** **Amanda Chamberlin** (all odd-numbered episodes, 149–171); ** **Kimberly Thompson** (150, 153, 156, 159, 162, 165, 168, 171, 174); **David Velasquez** (150, 152, 154, 156, 158,

160–173); Camille Argus (149, 152, 154, 157, 160, 163, 166, 169, 172); Kris Jorgensen (151, 155, 158, 161, 164, 167, 170, 173); David Page (162, 164, 166, 168, 170, 172); Norma Johnson (174)

Music Editor: *Gerry Sackman (EMMY CO-WINNER: sound editing, series: "Yesterday's Enterprise" [163])

Supervising Sound Editor: (*) Bill Wistrom (EMMY CO-WINNER: sound editing, series: "Yesterday's Enterprise" [163])

Sound Editors: (*) James Wolvington; (*) Mace Matiosian; *Wilson Dyer (EMMY CO-WINNER: sound editing, series: "Yesterday's Enterprise" [163])

Post Production Sound: (*) Modern Sound

Production Associate: (*) Susan Sackett

Production Coordinator: (*) Diane Overdiek

Post Production Associate: Terry Martinez (151–174); Heidi Julian (+) (161–174); Wendy Rosenfeld (161–174)

Pre-Production Associate: ( ) Eric Stillwell (+)

Casting Executive: (*) Helen Mossler

Assistant Scenic Artist: Cari Thomas

Stunt Coordinator: Dennis Madalone (all but 156, 158, 168, 172)

Research Consultant: Richard Arnold (uncredited first two seasons)

Computer Monitors: (**) Sony Corp. of America

Lenses and Panaflex Cameras: (**) Panavision

Special Visual Effects: (*) Industrial Light and Magic (ILM) a division of Lucasfilm Ltd.

Additional Motion Control Facilities: (*) Image "G"

Video Optical Effects: (*) The Post Group

Special Video Compositing: (*) Composite Image Systems

Editing Facilities: (*) Unitel Video

The number of * denotes the company or staffer's prior initial season of screen credit in that position; ( ) denotes an original credited or co-credited person in that position; a (+) following indicates prior TNG work in another position.

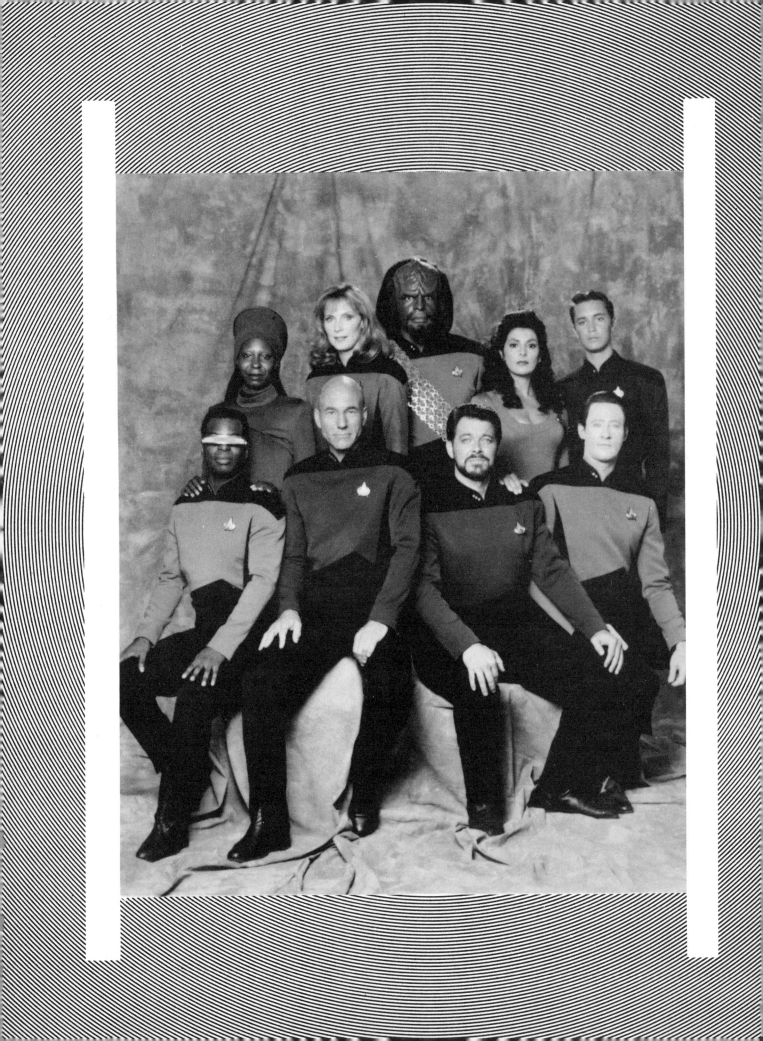

FOURTH SEASON

By the time of its much-heralded fourth-season opening, TNG had come so far from its splashy yet wobbly origins that even the original era's movie series had a hard time keeping up. Where once the "new show," fearful of suffering in comparison, avoided using original Trek's established aliens, now Romulans, Klingons, Cardassians, and Borg were being woven into a backdrop whose scope could only have been dreamed of by fans during the rerun and movie years of the seventies and early eighties.

After resolving "The Best of Both Worlds" cliffhanger, season four quickly became known as the sequel season: returning guests ranged from the Traveler, K'Ehleyr, and Duras to Leah Brahms, Lore, Vash, and Reg Barclay. Jack Crusher, Minuet, and Noonien Soong also reappeared, as did Q and Lwaxana Troi, with Tasha Yar's sister Ishara and mystery daughter Sela thrown in for good measure. In all, nine of the season's first eleven shows concerned family.

TNG made history within the Trek mythos when its widely

The fourth-season publicity shot (*opposite*), including recurring guest star Whoopi Goldberg as Guinan.

publicized eightieth episode, appropriately titled "Legacy," was filmed, breaking the seventy-nine-show record of the original series. The season-ending cliff-hanger, "Redemption," would be TNG's one hundredth completed hour.

Records of a more significant type were being broken as well. During the February 1991 sweeps month, "Devil's Due" (187) drew the series' highest-ever Nielsen rating of 14.4, breaking the record of 14.0 set in November 1987 during season one. And in January, members of Viewers for Quality Television quickly voted TNG the first non-network series to make the group's list of fully endorsed television series—after VQT leaders had been persuaded by members to put the show on their ballot despite its syndicated distribution.

But there was still a long way to go before the industry's old prejudices against science fiction in general and TNG in particular completely melted away. The series again won only two Emmys from among its many technical nominations and none on the so-called creative side despite such excellent actors as Patrick Stewart and Brent Spiner.

"Because our show doesn't air on one of the traditional networks, we continually face the frustration of being an anomaly," Rick Berman said in accepting the VQT award. "We hope other organizations will follow . . . in acknowledging our show, which an increasing number of viewers have obviously been enjoying for four seasons regardless of where they watch it."

Amid the grand epics and "comeback" shows, the 1701-D family found time to continue its own evolution: the fourth season showed us an Academy-bound Wesley, Data's first romance, Picard reconciling with his brother, Troi losing her empathic powers, Riker confronting fatherhood, Beverly falling in love (at last!), Geordi's VISOR turning against him, more shocks and sorrows for Worf and his loved ones, and O'Brien getting not only a name but a wife as well.

Credit some of that to the calmest hiatus yet for the series, thanks to the return of most of the staff—led again by Michael Piller, now settling into his second year, and Rick Berman, whose name joined Gene Roddenberry's in the closing credits as a fellow executive producer.

On his second directorial stint, Frakes shares a laugh with Dorn and Suzie Plakson ("Reunion"/181).

While many third-season staff writers left to work on other projects, Ronald D. Moore returned and added "executive" to his story editor title, sharing the position with newcomer Joe Menosky. They—along with supervising producer Jeri Taylor, who came on board after she helped rewrite "Suddenly Human" (176)—turned in their share of rewrites in tandem with writers who were new to the show. Among those new writers were David Bennett Carren and J. Larry Carroll, who wrote "Future Imperfect" (182) and joined the staff as story editors on the next episode, "Final Mission" (183). "Future Imperfect" marked the last show for producer Lee Sheldon, who wrote "Remember Me" (179); he was the latest in a long line to decide that writing for TNG was not for him.

"There are people who could be Emmy Award–winning writers on a lawyer show or a police drama," Rick Berman once said, "who just can't grasp what it is to write for a somewhat stylized twenty-fourth-century world where the conflict between characters is very, very subtle. There are a lot of writers who just don't get it, or who have a lot of difficulty at it. It's nothing to do with how smart they are, or how good they are, but how they fit into writing *Star Trek*."

Piller described how a process called "breaking the story" is applied to a premise or outline once it goes to development. "I don't like to get stuck in details," he explained. "I encourage the writer, after the sale, to 'hug' the whole concept—get your 'arms around it,' get it into five or six double-spaced pages with a beginning, middle, and end, what you want to accomplish, and your major character arc (the path of an individual's changes due to that story's new experiences). If you can tell that and have a real solid foundation—*then* we start talking about details."

From there, Piller said, the staff and any outsiders involved sit down and begin the show's most collaborative process. Using a marker board, they go through each writer's proposed story, seeing if it holds up to group scrutiny by diagramming and defining four to five "beats," or major plot moments, in each act. From there the story is sent back to the assigned writer to be turned into a first-draft teleplay. Even for those scripts that survive this process, however, the route to final draft might take months or even years.

"I always tell the writers what they leave with from here is just a road map for the story," Piller added. "I really believe first of all in listening to the characters—they may not want to follow that map. You may get to a point where they want to 'turn left' when you thought they were going to turn right!" While the writers were busy honing their act in the Hart Building, just across the studio street in the Cooper Building first-season veterans David Livingston and Wendy Neuss were being promoted: he by dropping the "line" from "line producer," and she by joining the senior ranks in moving up from post-production supervisor to associate producer. They and the rest of the staff would work hard to keep production values as high as possible, especially given the spate of money-saving bottle shows that marked the second half of season four—the result of a studio effort to improve Paramount's finances in early 1991—while saving up the budget for the fourth-season cliff-hanger, "Redemption" (200).

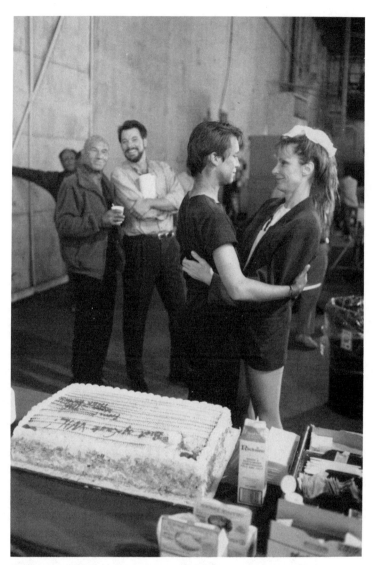

"Mom" and "son" embrace at Wil Wheaton's good-bye party.

THE BEST OF BOTH WORLDS, PART 2

Production No.: 175 ■ Aired: Week of September 24, 1990
Stardate: 44001.4 ■ Code: b2

Directed by **Cliff Bole**
Written by **Michael Piller**

GUEST CAST
Lieutenant Commander Shelby: **Elizabeth Dennehy**
Admiral Hanson: **George Murdock**
Lieutenant O'Brien: **Colm Meaney**
Guinan: **Whoopi Goldberg**
Lieutenant Gleason: **Todd Merrill**

Hopes are dashed when the *Enterprise*'s jury-rigged deflector-dish weapon fails to stop the Borg, who go on to obliterate a Starfleet armada on its way to Earth.

At the same time, Borg have tapped into Picard's knowledge of Starfleet defenses and human nature. A single tear is his only reaction to the DNA rewrites and bio-implants that have transformed his body.

Now captain of the *Enterprise*, Riker at first can't shake off the feeling of doom pervading the ship. But, inspired by Guinan's advice to turn the tables on the Borg by using their own hostage, he and Shelby, now serving as his first officer, design a daring plan. They kidnap Picard so that Data can try to tap into the Borg collective consciousness.

The going is slow, but just as Riker is prepared to give up hope and ram the Borg ship directly, Picard fights through to give Data one simple Borg network command: "Sleep."

Now dormant, the Borg experience a power feedback that destroys their ship. A shaky Picard begins his rehabilitation, thankful for his escape but deeply troubled by his experiences.

Though the logic of the Borg's demise in Data's lab is irrefutable, writer Michael Piller and director Cliff Bole both felt that this sequel did not live up to its setup. Piller has said he waited until he

Crusher and Troi look for signs of Picard in Locutus.

returned to the lot in late July to sit down to wrap up the story—and the idea of using the Borg's interdependency as a weakness hit him just two days before filming was to start.

Despite the rumors over the summer, the talk about making the strong-willed Shelby a regular in the wake of Wesley's upcoming exit eventually evaporated. A succession of female conn officers would follow until the semi-regular Ensign Ro came aboard in the fifth season in an episode named for her (203). Meanwhile, amid all the swashbuckling, hand it to the women of this crew for saving humanity: it is Beverly who discovers the Borg's fatal flaw, and it's Troi who realizes that Picard is fighting through his programming.

Though her background remains murky, Guinan delivers an intriguing line when she tells Riker that her relationship with Picard goes "beyond friendship and beyond family." And Todd Merrill would be back to play Gleason later in "Future Imperfect" (182), though with a change in rank and duty assignment.

In another bow to series continuity, Piller's teleplay proposes using nanites as a weapon against the Borg ("Evolution,"/150) and in throwaway references, mentions Barclay's name ("Hollow Pursuits"/169, and "Nth Degree"/193). After its breakthrough use here, the main deflector dish would be utilized again in other episodes, albeit with more mixed results ("The Loss"/184, "Night Terrors"/191, "Nth Degree"/193, "A Matter of Time"/209). Data's cybernetics lab where Picard is brought, yet another re-dress of the old movie bridge, was the site where Lal was born and died ("The Offspring"/164). And we learn that a shuttle can carry its own small transporter system.

Though less favored by Rob Legato and Dan Curry and largely unused since the appearance of its four-foot cousin in season three, the original six-foot *Enterprise* model had to be hauled out of storage for the ship-separation sequence in the Borg battle, since it was the only version built in two sections. The various battle effects and Borg visuals are motion-picture quality, but again TNG struck out with the Emmys for special effects. Part 2 was nominated, but it won no awards in that category. The episode did snag Emmys for sound editing and for sound mixing, as well as a nomination for art direction.

Almost lost amid the saga and special effects in Part 2 are the slew of new starship designs—admittedly not seen here in good shape—that were crew-designed and built by "kit-bashing"—combining parts from available kits to assemble an all-new model. Among the new ships were the Cheyenne-class *Ahwahnne*, the Challenger-class *Buran*, the Springfield-class *Chekhov*, the Freedom-class *Firebrand*, the Niagara-class *Princeton*, and, as mentioned by Shelby, the New Orleans–class *Kyushu*, the Nebula-class *Melbourne* (later seen in "Future Imperfect"/182 and "The Wounded"/186), and the Rigel-calss *Tolstoy*, for the author of *War and Peace* but renamed the *Chekhov* in the final draft. Some of the dead hulks can even be seen with their hulls' lifeboat hatches open—a Greg Jein touch. Rick Sternback also revealed that the Mars Defense Perimeter ships—basically unmanned bombs—were based on the submarine model used in *The Hunt for Red October,* and quickly dubbed the "Blue-gray October."

In a later episode, "The Drumhead" (195), Admiral Satie would put Starfleet's loss at 39 ships and nearly 11,000 lives; Shelby says it should take less than a year to "get the fleet back up," though the loss definitely leaves Starfleet shorthanded, as we see in "The Wounded" (186).

Although wrecked starships won't be found there, the site of the armada's massacre is an actual star: Wolf 359 is the third-closest system to Sol, after Alpha Centauri and Barnard's Star—just 7.6 light-years from our solar system or, in Trek terms, a journey of about thirty-six hours at warp nine.

SUDDENLY HUMAN

Production No.: 176 ■ Aired: Week of October 15, 1990
Stardate: 44143.7 ■ Code: sh

Directed by **Gabrielle Beaumont**
Teleplay by **John Whelpley and Jeri Taylor**
Story by **Ralph Phillips**

GUEST CAST
Captain Endar: **Sherman Howard**
Jono: **Chad Allen**
Admiral Connaught Rossa: **Barbara Townsend**

The *Enterprise* discovers a failed Talarian craft adrift with five unconscious teenage boys, one of them human.

Raised a Talarian and known as Jono, the human checks out as Jeremiah Rossa, kidnapped a decade earlier when his parents were killed and his colony attacked by Talarians.

But Jono is the adopted son of Talarian Captain Endar, who by custom raised him after his own son was killed. He threatens war when the boy's human grandmother, a Starfleet admiral, asks that he be brought back home.

The boy also shows signs of having been abused, but Endar says the scars are only reminders of a rough-and-tumble Talarian boyhood. With Jono at the age of decision, Endar and Picard finally agree to let him decide his own fate. Photos help him recall his parents and the attack. But Jono is so agonized by the choice before him that he tries to avoid it by killing Picard so that he will be put to death.

Seeing that, Picard realizes Jono should remain with his adopted people and returns him to a grateful Endar.

Picard tries to help Jono (Chad Allen) choose between his native and adopted cultures.

A budget-saving bottle show sandwiched in among this season's ambitious early stories, "Suddenly Human" stirred rumors throughout Trek fandom that it would address the issue of child abuse. Instead, it deals with the emotions and decisions faced by broken families and by cultures in collision.

Viewers may remember young Chad Allen as the autistic son of the doctor played by Ed Flanders on *St. Elsewhere.* He shares some fine moments with Picard who once again must confront his discomfort with children ("Farpoint"/101, "Disaster"/205). Under Troi's gentle probing, the captain wonders if the feeling stems from his lack of friends as a duty-driven child who early on wanted to be in Starfleet. His brother later speaks of Jean-Luc's childhood in "Family" (178).

"To us, it was the issue of the foster parent, having raised and nurtured the child, having as much right to custody as the natural parent," said writer Jeri Taylor. Taylor, who had been recommended by short-time producer Lee Sheldon before his exit, won

an ever-expanding staff job as a result of this script. She came from a line producer's background on series such as *Quincy, Magnum P.I., In the Heat of the Night,* and *Jake and the Fat Man,* but knew nothing about Trek until she took a crash course by watching all prior TNG and original-series episodes as well as the motion pictures.

Originally, Taylor named these aliens Phrygians, but after Okuda suggested that a once-mentioned race be used instead, the staff chose the otherwise undescribed builders of the Batris ("Heart of Glory"/120). The look of Endar's warship, *Q'Maire,* is based on the big galactic patrol vessels of E. E. "Doc" Smith's Lensman series, Sternbach revealed. The training ship, with its two great power panel "sails," harks back to the early wind-powered Coast Guard trainers. Although neither was based on the often-re-dressed Probert-designed freighter, their armament—like that of the *Batris*—includes "merculite rockets."

Judging by the art department's galactic "map," Talarian space lies adjacent to that of the Federation, opposite Klingon and Romulan territory. A historical note: the evidence given here indicates that Starfleet's uniform style changed sometime between Wesley's birth ("Family"/178) and the tape of Jono's parents, thirteen to eighteen years prior to this episode.

BROTHERS

Production No.: 177 ■ Aired: Week of October 8, 1990
Stardate: 44085.7 ■ Code: br

Directed by **Rob Bowman**
Written by **Rick Berman**

GUEST CAST
Jake Potts: **Cory Danziger**
Lieutenant O'Brien: **Colm Meaney**
Willie (Potts): **Adam Ryen**
Ensign Kopf: **James Lashly**
Lore/Dr. Noonian Soong: **Brent Spiner**

A boy's practical joke backfires, leaving his younger brother dangerously ill. But as the ship rushes toward a nearby starbase with the medical facilities the boy needs to survive, Data inexplicably malfunctions. The android isolates himself on the bridge and changes course. It turns out that Data has been automatically and unknowingly "called home" to the lab world of his reclusive creator, Dr. Noonian Soong.

Soong has at last perfected an "emotions" chip for Data, but the android and his creator are both surprised when Lore, Data's "older

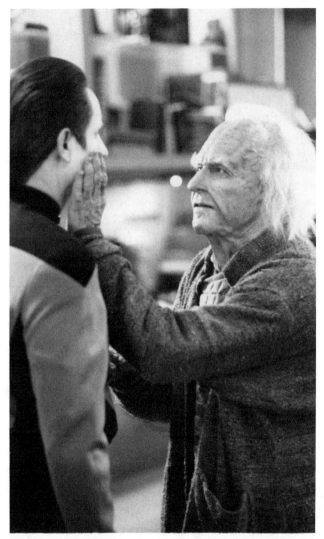

Data at last meets his creator, Dr. Soong (Brent Spiner).

back Lore ("Database"/114) for this story of Data finally meeting his creator, but then, at Piller's suggestion, he changed his mind, providing Spiner with the rare opportunity to play three roles. For a time, however, veteran actor Keye Luke—an original-Trek guest in "Whom Gods Destroy"—was considered for the role of Soong, Berman revealed.

Rob Bowman, who had directed Lore's first story and was once TNG's most active director, returned to the show after a year away working for series like *Alien Nation, Baywatch,* and *In the Heat of the Night.* Piller recalled that Bowman, Legato, and Spiner worked on the elaborate Stage 16 lab set for three days before shooting began, taping off the floor and blocking out the action for camera moves, as if they were preparing a stage play or a multi-camera TV show. This is rarely done on TNG, but it was needed here to avoid costly downtime with a whole crew standing by.

During the filming in Soong's lab, Legato recalled, Spiner would shoot one day as Lore-Data and the next as the elderly scientist. Some shots, as when Soong grasped his creation's cheeks, were done inexpensively "in the camera" without post-production compositing by placing the Soong's bent elbow below the frame line. On "Soong" day, after four hours of makeup, Spiner was shot with his arm going down; on his "Data" day, the film was reshot with a photo double's hand coming up to grasp his face.

"It was difficult," Spiner recalls, "because I had to hear dialogue that I hadn't read yet coming out of somebody else's mouth before I would get to it. [I had] to remember where I was when I was Data, and so on."[1] To help him, the set was closed during the two and a half days when Spiner soloed.

True to Lore's story of having been picked up by Pakleds, he wears one of their outfits (143). Among other continuity threads picked up here: Data whistles the same halting version of "Pop Goes the Weasel" he tried in the pilot, "Encounter at Farpoint" (101–102), and "Often Wrong" Soong mentions the Crystalline Entity ("Datalore"/114, "Silicon Avatar"/204), whom he refers to as the "giant snowflake." At his creator's death Data finally calls the old man Father.

brother," who was left to drift in space some years earlier, responds to the same signal.

Lore disables Data and tricks Soong into installing the chip in him, then goes on a rampage, fatally injuring the doctor. Help arrives, but Soong insists on being left behind after Lore escapes.

The young boy is rushed to the starbase to receive medical care, leaving Data to ponder the emotions he could have had, his late "father," and the strange bond between him and his "brother."

Making his debut as a TNG writer, Rick Berman, in the relatively calm hiatus after the third season, finally had the chance he'd always wanted. Initially, he had rejected the idea of bringing

FAMILY

Production No.: 178 ■ Aired: Week of October 1, 1990
Stardate: 44012.3 ■ Code: fa

Directed by **Les Landau**
Written by **Ronald D. Moore**
Based in part on a premise by **Susanne Lambdin**
and Bryan Stewart

GUEST CAST
Robert Picard: **Jeremy Kemp**
Marie Picard: **Samantha Eggar**
Sergey Rozhenko: **Theodore Bikel**
Helena Rozhenko: **Georgia Brown**
Louis: **Dennis Creaghan**
Lieutenant O'Brien: **Colm Meaney**
Guinan: **Whoopi Goldberg**
Jack R. Crusher: **Doug Wert**
René Picard: **David Tristin Birkin**

With the *Enterprise* in dry dock for repairs after the Borg attack, Picard, full of doubts about himself and his abilities, beams down to Earth to visit his family's French vineyards. He has not been home in nearly twenty years, since a falling-out with his brother.

Meanwhile, Worf's visiting foster parents are saddened at his coldness, but they are comforted by Guinan's reassurances. They let their gruff but grateful son know they support him, as they always have, and they know he did not deserve his recent discommendation by the Klingons.

Dr. Crusher shares the literal ghost of her late husband, Jack, with the son he barely knew, by letting Wes view a stored holotape Jack made just after Wesley's birth.

Picard is made welcome by Robert's family and meets his nephew, a youngster whose dream of being in Starfleet echoes Picard's own wishes at that age. To his surprise, the captain finds himself tempted to leave Starfleet to head up a planned continent-raising project on Earth, but his brother, after a fight, reminds Picard that

Picard and his family—nephew Rene (David Tristin Birkin); sister-in-law Marie (Samantha Eggar); and brother Robert (Jeremy Kemp).

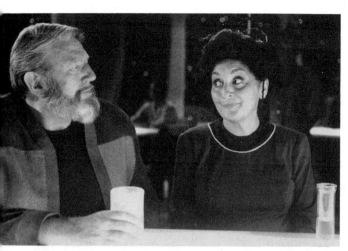

Sergey (Theodore Bikel) and Helena Rozhenko (Georgia Brown) visit foster son Worf.

wherever he stays, he must come to terms with the self-doubt and guilt caused by the Borg incident.

The captain beams back aboard *Enterprise*, which then leaves orbit, having been far more healed than the ship itself.

***

A daring departure for the series, "Family" is the only installment in Trek's twenty-five-year history with no scenes on the bridge. Airing right after the season-opening cliff-hanger resolution as an epilogue to the Borg two-parter, Ronald D. Moore's introspective character story was controversial even among the writing staff. Unfortunately it was the lowest-rated show of the season, even though it gave a deeper insight into more of the show's characters than virtually any other segment.

Michael Piller suggested a third segment in a proposed Borg trilogy. When that was rejected, Piller lobbied for a follow-up that would at least let Picard heal his emotional wounds on-camera after his virtual rape by the Borg. At first Berman agreed to it but insisted that a science subplot be used to round out the show. After weeks of trying various story lines that just didn't work— including a child stowaway, and a paranoid's nightmare of disappearing crew members, a story line that was used on its own in "Remember Me" (179)—Berman relented and allowed the other family-theme subplots to fill out the hour.

The lush Emmy-nominated photography in this episode was enhanced by a distinguished guest cast and two days of location shooting. The Picard family home in Labarre, France—where the hard-driven young Jean-Luc was class valedictorian, school president, and a star athlete—was actually a private residence in Encino. The vineyard scenes were shot at a private dryland operation near Lancaster in the extreme heat southwest of Edwards Air Force Base. Dan Curry digitally manipulated a matte painting background to match the windblown vineyards in the live foreground shots.

And what a cast, all with years of stage and film experience!

Samantha Eggar and Jeremy Kemp would pack enough star power into any episode. Theodore Bikel, an internationally known folksinger as well as an actor, and Georgia Brown are two of the biggest stars of Yiddish theater. Their presence initially caused some studio concern that Worf's parents might become comically "Jewish," but as Piller says the finished product "treads the line" of universal humor—and it led to a return visit by Brown in "New Ground" (210). Still, no mention is made of the Rozhenkos' own son, described by Worf in "Heart of Glory" (120), or of their years on the farming planet Gault.

Some sequences with Wesley's father, taken from Susanne Lambdin's premise after dozens of Jack Crusher spec scripts had been received through the years, were cut to save time. Piller remembers that the holotaped speech really hit home for him, arriving soon as it did after the birth of his own daughter.

In an unused sequence from the final-draft script Jack says he's about to report to the *Stargazer* and that Wesley "R." Crusher—a name later seen in Beverly's personnel file in "Conundrum" (214)—was named for Jack's grandfather, Richard Wesley Crusher, who gave Jack his first flying lesson. We also learn that a great-grandfather had a painting on exhibit in the Prado Museum in Madrid, Spain. Other Trek continuity touches in the scene included mentions of a Crusher who was a horse thief on Nimbus III (the planet in *Star Trek V*), another who served as a Confederate soldier at Bull Run, and a third who died at Station Salem One, referred to in "The Defector" (158) as the site of an enemy surprise attack à la Pearl Harbor during an unmentioned war.

Jack Crusher wears the old-style uniform of a lieutenant (j.g.) in the holotape, but his locker with his last effects is labeled with the rank of lieutenant commander and the middle initial *R*. Beverly recalls that he proposed to her when she was in medical school. As a dream image, Doug Wert would appear as Jack Crusher again in "Violations" (212).

After two seasons the full name of Colm Meaney's character is finally revealed: Miles Edward O'Brien, the name of a little boy Rick Berman knew. Curiously, Worf's foster father, a Starfleet veteran, mistakes O'Brien for a noncommissioned crew member, even though he clearly wears the two solid pins of a lieutenant, just as Sergey's own son does. The "chief" in O'Brien's title refers not to a rank, like chief petty officer, but to his duty position as transporter chief.

Trivia notes: the captain's ditty bag is stenciled simply with his name and title, Jean-Luc Picard, Captain; the bottle of family wine given to him by Robert is later seen stored and then shared in upcoming shows ("Legacy"/180, "First Contact"/189); the *Intrepid*, Sergey's old ship, had already been mentioned as the one that found Worf at Khitomer some twenty years earlier ("Sins of the Father"/165); Riker once enjoyed Worf's favorite food, rokeg blood pie ("A Matter of Honor"/134); Guinan's "prune juice" remark refers back to her gift to Worf ("Yesterday's Enterprise"/163); and Picard tells his friend Louis of the starship's efforts to stabilize the tectonics of Drema IV ("Pen Pals"/141).

REMEMBER ME

Production No.: 179 ■ Aired: Week of October 22, 1990
Stardate: 44161.2 ■ Code: rm

Directed by **Cliff Bole**
Written by **Lee Sheldon**

GUEST CAST
The Traveler: **Eric Menyuk**
Commander Dalen Quaice, M.D.: **Bill Erwin**
Lieutenant O'Brien: **Colm Meaney**

After welcoming her mentor, Dr. Quaice, an elderly man sadly reflecting on the loss of his wife and friends, Dr. Crusher visits her son in the engineering department. Wesley is working on a warp-field experiment. As Beverly watches, the project aborts in a brief flash of light. The moment is forgotten until, one by one, Quaice, her staff, and even the senior bridge officers begin to disappear. Those who remain, even Data, know nothing about the vanished.

But it is actually Dr. Crusher who has disappeared—into an alternate universe. Aboard the "real" *Enterprise*, the Traveler reappears to let Wesley know that the experiment is to blame. He, La Forge, and Data try to retrieve Dr. Crusher, but their efforts appear to her as a vortex that she resists being sucked into.

After even Picard vanishes and the universe begins eroding away, Dr. Crusher figures out what has happened. This "world" is ruled by the thought in her mind at the time of the failed experiment: the loss of friends and loved ones.

Realizing the way back to the real world is the site of the flash, she dashes back and falls into Wesley's arms just as her "new world" collapses.

Marked by the return of Eric Menyuk as the Traveler, this budget-minded bottle show actually served as a delightful showcase for the talents of Gates McFadden as Dr. Crusher soloed in her own decaying universe during about 40 percent of the script. The actress absolutely shines as she deals with increasing double-talk from Data and Picard, her own fear of insanity, and the prospect of being left with the humorless computer as her only companion.

We also learn more about Beverly's background, including the fact that she interned with Dr. Quaice only fifteen years ago—in other words, after Wesley was born. She repeats her recurring opening line to Picard when they are both alone on the bridge ("Arsenal of Freedom"/121, "The High Ground"/160).

McFadden performed all her own stunts for the swirling-vortex effects sequences, including the most outlandish maneuver—when she appears to be sucked out horizontally by the vortex while clutching the back of a chair. Rob Legato had a chair mounted on the wall, and McFadden hung down out of the chair. Legato used compressed-air machines and other devices to animate the scene; the footage was then matted in at a 90-degree angle. Only days after that strenuous shoot, McFadden learned she was pregnant—see "The Host" (197).

This story, Lee Sheldon's only contribution to the series during his short tenure as producer, began as a subplot for "Family" (178) in which crew members begin to disappear because of a wormhole. But, according to Piller, the staff felt there was not enough room for both story lines in that script, and the "Remember Me" material was cut loose to be developed on its own.

The "cochrane," by the way, is used here as a unit of measure of subspace field stress. The term was coined by Rick Sternbach and Michael Okuda as yet another homage to Zefren Cochran, the discoverer of space-warp physics—see "Ménage à Troi" (172). Mention is made here of Kosinski, the Traveler's original companion ("Where No One Has Gone Before"/106) and Dr. Selar ("The Schizoid Man"/131); we also learn that the *Enterprise* was carrying 1,014 people, including Dr. Quaice, when it docked at the starbase.

The Traveller (Eric Menyuk) returns to help Wesley retrieve his mother.

LEGACY

Production No.: 180 ■ Aired: Week of October 29, 1990
Stardate: 44215.2 ■ Code: le

Directed by **Robert Scheerer**
Written by **Joe Menosky**

GUEST CAST
Ishara Yar: **Beth Toussaint**
Hayne: **Don Mirault**
Lieutenant O'Brien: **Colm Meaney**
Tan Tsu: **Vladimir Velasco**
Coalition lieutenant: **Christopher Michael**

Déjà vu sets in when the *Enterprise* attempts to rescue two Federation engineers lost on the late Tasha Yar's planet, Turkana IV. There they are surprised to discover her sister, Ishara, involved with one of two warring factions.

One faction, the Alliance, has taken the ship's engineers hostage: their rival, the Coalition, offers to help retrieve the engineers and volunteers the services of Ishara as a guide.

Ishara beams aboard the *Enterprise*, where Picard tries to reverse Ishara's view of her sister as a runaway and a quitter, and Data finds his memories of Tasha rekindled by Ishara, who shows some interest in joining Starfleet.

What Riker and Picard don't know is that the plan Ishara helps them devise is also meant to defeat the proximity detectors both Turkana factions agreed to years ago, so Ishara can disable the Alliance's power plants and cripple their defense.

Ishara leads the rescue effort but is stopped by Data at the reactor, where he dares her to shoot him. She is about to do so when Riker stuns her, then tells Data he's just learned about betrayal.

An allegory on gang warfare with added complications provided by Tasha's previously unknown sister, Joe Menosky's first script for the series will forever live in the annals of TNG trivia as the eightieth episode—the one that broke the record of the seventy-nine-episode run of the original series. To help mark the milestone, the cast and staff wrapped the filming with a party, reported by *Entertainment Tonight,* and a cake adorned by the art staff's special congratulatory logo.

Tasha Yar was given even more background history in this outing. We learn that her parents were killed in cadre crossfire just after Ishara was born, about four and a half years after Tasha. Also, Picard says he asked Tasha's former captain to transfer her to his command when the new *Enterprise* was about to be launched.

The starship *Potemkin,* the last to have contact with Turkana IV, was a former assignment of Lieutenant Riker's mentioned in "Peak Performance" (147), and a namesake of a Kirk-era starship seen in "The Ultimate Computer."

As his predecessor had done in season one, production designer Richard James made the precious budget for sets go farther by ingeniously re-dressing the Borg ship interiors, left standing on Stage 16's Planet Hell, for use as the Turkana underground tunnel complex. He would also make good use of them in several episodes to come, as would happen with the hostages' escape pod off the *Arcos,* a Sternbach design that would be re-dressed often ("Family"/183, "A Matter of Time"/209).

Data learns about betrayal from Yar's troubled younger sister Ishara (Beth Toussaint).

Reunion

Production No.: 181 ▪ Aired: Week of November 5, 1990
Stardate: 44246.3 ▪ Code: re

Directed by **Jonathan Frakes**
Teleplay by **Thomas Perry, Jo Perry, Ronald D. Moore, and Brannon Braga**
Story by **Drew Deighan, Thomas Perry, and Jo Perry**

GUEST CAST
K'Ehleyr: **Suzie Plakson**
Gowron: **Robert O'Reilly**
Duras: **Patrick Massett**
K'mpec: **Charles Cooper**
Alexander: **Jon Steuer**
Security Guard: **Michael Rider**
Transporter Chief Hubbell: **April Grace**
Klingon Guard #1 (Duras aide): **Basil Wallace**
Klingon (Vorn) Guard #2: **Mirron E. Willis**

The ill-fated K'Ehleyr (Suzie Plakson) presses Worf about their son.

Ambassador K'Ehleyr, Worf's half-human former love, beams aboard the *Enterprise* with two pieces of shocking news: Klingon leader K'mpec has been poisoned, and the young boy with her is her son—and Worf's.

K'mpec wants Picard to help him perform the ritual selecting a new leader. After revealing his suspicion that one of the contenders poisoned him, he tells Picard that no one on the Klingon Council can be trusted. One contender for the throne is Duras, who hid his own father's guilt by accusing Worf's father of being the Romulan collaborator in the Khitomer massacre.

Picard stalls for time as Duras and his rival, Gowron, beam aboard the *Enterprise* for the succession ceremony. Worf opts not to acknowledge his son so as to save him from the family's dishonor. K'Ehleyr's efforts to research the truth lead to her murder by Duras; he in turn is killed by a vengeful Worf.

Gowron is named leader of the Klingon Empire as a somber Worf sends Alexander off to be raised by his own foster parents on Earth.

In directing this chapter in Trek's ongoing Klingon saga, Jonathan Frakes again drew a no-lose episode for his second directorial outing, with actors like Patrick Massett, Suzie Plakson, and Charles Cooper at his disposal. Despite the multiple writing credits, the story shines. It also takes a lot of chances, including the deaths of both K'Ehleyr and Duras. Michael Piller and Ronald D. Moore defended the decision to kill off Worf's popular mate, who in an earlier draft had a relationship with Duras. We "wanted to get to a place where Worf was going to take Duras apart, and there's no good reason for him to do it unless she dies," Piller said.

And what a time for Worf! In one fell swoop he learns he has a son, his mate is killed, and he in turn kills her murderer and his family's accuser; he then sends his newfound son off to live with his own foster parents.

This episode is not exactly a vacation for Picard, either. It's a tribute to both actors and to the writers that what would always have been thought inconceivable is completely believable here: a human from the Federation choosing the next leader of the Klingon Empire!

For summer intern Brannon Braga, sitting down with Ron Moore to hash out the teleplay as his first TNG writing credit was an "illuminating, exhilarating" experience. Braga, who arrived with a strong production background from Kent State and the University of California at Santa Cruz, had produced music videos but got his first writing job as a member of the TNG staff for season five.

Dan Curry, nominally the visual-effects supervisor on alternating shows, drew on his martial arts background to design Worf's *bat'telh* weapon and helped Michael Dorn develop the unique movements used in wielding it.

Like his Klingon counterparts Plakson, Massett, and Cooper, Robert O'Reilly was also a TNG veteran, although he was first seen not as a Klingon but as Scarface, one of the hoodlums in "Manhunt" (145). Michael Rider, who plays an unnamed security guard in this show, was seen as a transporter chief in the several early pre-O'Brien shows (103–105).

During K'Ehleyr's briefing, we learn that the territories of the Ferengi and the Tholians border those of the Klingons and the Federation. And the *sonchi* pain sticks are ceremonial versions of those used for Worf's Rite of Ascension as seen in "The Icarus

Factor" (140). However, K'mpec—who is revealed to have led the Klingon Empire longer than anyone else in history—says his people and the Romulans have been "blood enemies" for seventy-five years, even through Worf once said that the two were still allies at the time of the infamous Khitomer massacre.

To this point budget constraints had forced the staff to use the two Klingon vessels from the films, but TNG finally got its own Klingon ship, the *Vor'cha*-class attack cruiser that debuted here. Roughly three-quarters the length of a Galaxy-class starship, the three-foot model—designed by Rick Sternbach and built by Greg Jein—reflects the post-alliance era with warp nacelles that have a Starfleet look. Even its color is new, midway between the old Klingon dark green and the bluish white of Starfleet. Within a year the model was released as an AMT kit.

FUTURE IMPERFECT

Production No.: 182 ■ Aired: Week of November 12, 1990
Stardate: 44286.5 ■ Code: fi

Directed by **Les Landau**
Written by **J. Larry Carroll and David Bennett Carren**

GUEST CAST
"Ambassador" Tomalak: **Andreas Katsulas**
Jean-Luc/Ethan: **Chris Demetral**
Minuet: **Carolyn McCormick**
Nurse Ogawa: **Patti Yasutake**
Ensign Gleason: **Todd Merrill**
Transporter Chief Hubbell: **April Grace**
Transporter Chief: **George O'Hanlon, Jr.**
Barash: **Dana Tjowander**

"Admiral" Picard and his aide Troi (*above*) come aboard the *Enterprise* to sign a peace treaty with "Captain" Riker and the Romulan "Ambassador" Tomalak (Andreas Katsulas) (*below*).

After having passed out during a mission to Apha Onias III, Riker awakens to an unbelievable scene: sixteen years have passed; he's now captain of the *Enterprise* and a widower with a teenage son!

Dr. Crusher explains that during his mission to Alpha Onias III he contracted a virus that only recently became active; the virus wiped out his memory of the years since then. Riker also discovers that a peace treaty with the Romulans is about to be signed and that his onetime nemesis

Tomalak, now an ambassador, is on board the *Enterprise,* as is "Admiral" Picard.

But Riker senses something is wrong when the ship's computer takes an unusually long time to respond to his queries about his missing years. He then discovers that his late wife was Minuet, an ideal woman created for him by the Bynars.

When he confronts Tomalak with this knowledge, the scene dissolves into a Romulan holodeck, with only Tomalak remaining. Riker is then thrown into a dungeon with his "son," who turns out to be a boy who was captured by the Romulans.

The boy then helps him escape, but makes another reference to "Ambassador" Tomalak. Finally, the boy reveals the truth: he is an alien named Barash who captured Riker and devised the elaborate memory-loss scenario to have company during his exile. Riker then invites the youngster to return with him to the *Enterprise*.

Albeit in illusory form, "Future Imperfect" continued the family theme that marked the season's first nine shows. The episode also gave Frakes a chance to show he could invest Riker's character scenes with the same level of intensity Stewart had brought to Picard's in "Family" (178). The script gained perhaps its most poignant scene at the last minute, when for once the pace of filming was going too fast. Writers Larry Carroll and David Bennett Carren had to meet after hours with Rick Berman and Michael Piller to thrash out a new scene the night before it was to be shot. What evolved was the turbo-lift scene between Riker and his "son" in which Number One admits his fear of repeating his own father's mistakes as a parent—a satisfying echo of "The Icarus Factor" (140).

Their efforts won Carroll and Carren a spot on the writing staff that would last all season. Carren had written previously for *Starsky and Hutch*, the 1980s *Twilight Zone*, and the 1970s *Buck Rogers*. Carroll had been a film editor on the original *Texas Chainsaw Massacre* and had written low-budget films for independents and for Empire, including *Ghost Warrior*, which he also directed.

Back again, though only briefly, is Carolyn McCormick as Riker's onetime holodeck soul mate, Minuet ("11001001"/116). Another nice long-term continuity touch is Andreas Katsulas's third appearance as a Romulan villain ("The Enemy"/155, "The Defector"/158). Patti Yasutake began her continuing role as a nurse here. She would go on to acquire not only a name but even a personality by season five. And, though she was seen once before, and will appear in many shows to come, it is only in this episode that April Grace's character, a transporter chief, is given a last name: Hubbell.

The transporter chief of Barash's illusion is played by an actor whose background includes both space and fantasy, sort of: George O'Hanlon, Jr., is the son of talented voice actor George O'Hanlon, perhaps best known as Hanna-Barbera cartoon star George Jetson. Todd Merrill's character, Gleason, returns but seems to have been demoted since the Borg battle; here he is a services-division ensign rather than a command-division lieutenant (j.g.), as he was in the season opener, "The Best of Both Worlds," Part 2 (175). And under the Barash alien costume is an uncredited extra, Dana Tjowander.

Barash managed to conjure up a whole new look for the Federation in his future fantasy, including new Starfleet communicators (which were quickly put on sale by Trek merchandisers), a female Klingon ensign, and a Ferengi at the conn; a scar for Worf, a cranberry uniform for First Officer Data, a replacement for Geordi's VISOR, and a gray-streaked, married Troi as "Admiral" Picard's aide.

Some things weren't changed, though: Riker still had his trombone handy, kids still got hurt playing Parrises Squares, and Number One clearly managed to pass on his love of fishing to his son.

Tomalak's fantasy Romulan warbird, *Decius*, carries the name of the fatally injured aide to Mark Lenard's unnamed commander

in original Trek's "Balance of Terror," and we also learn that the original eight outposts along the Neutral Zone, seen in that 1960s episode, have grown to at least twenty-three. Once again, the original Borg interiors seen in "The Best of Both Worlds," Part 2 (175), came back to life, this time refigured by Richard James as the underground Romulan base. Next to an old twentieth-century Apollo lunar module, the other model in Riker's "future" ready room is the Nebula-class USS *Melbourne*, designed by Ed Miarecki.

FINAL MISSION

Production No.: 183 ■ Aired: Week of November 19, 1990
Stardate: 44307.3 ■ Code: fm

Directed by **Corey Allen**
Teleplay by **Kacey Arnold-Ince and Jeri Taylor**
Story by **Kacey Arnold-Ince**

GUEST CAST
Dirgo: **Nick Tate**
Chairman Songi: **Kim Hamilton**
Ensign Tess Allenby: **Mary Kohnert**

Wesley has finally been accepted into Starfleet Academy, but before he leaves, he is to accompany Captain Picard on one last mission.

They've been sent to mediate a miners' dispute, but the rattletrap of a shuttle sent for them malfunctions, and they crash-land on a desert moon. Their pilot, Dirgo, overconfident of his own planning and leadership abilities, didn't stock water, so the trio is forced to set out for some distant caves. Meanwhile, the *Enterprise* is summoned to remove an old garbage scow that is leaking radiation into a planet's atmosphere.

The crash-landing survivors finally find a fountain, but it is guarded by an energy sentry. An impatient Dirgo causes a rockslide that wounds Picard, then bullies Wesley into an attack on the sentry that results in Dirgo's death.

Riker and the crew struggle to finish their job and then go hunt for the missing shipmates. Meanwhile, Wesley works to keep Picard alive while figuring out a way to defeat the sentry. After forging new bonds with his nearly comatose captain, he does both—keeping himself and Picard alive until rescue finally comes.

An Academy-bound Wesley faces his biggest challenge yet in saving Picard's life.

Wil Wheaton bows out as a TNG regular in this story, giving what was probably his best performance of the series to date. He had asked to be let go so he could pursue the many film offers coming his way, but the door was left open for future appearances by finally shipping Wesley off to the Academy, as Gene Roddenberry had suggested. And in this last appearance, Wheaton didn't "save the ship," only his captain. "He directly saved the ship only one and a half times and had a hand in contributing to the solution of the problem two times! That's it!"[2] Wheaton once asserted, long accustomed to defending his character against some fans' scorn.

Corey Allen returns for his first directorial outing since the pilot and season one's "Home Soil" (117), just in time for two days of location shooting on the El Mirage Dry Lake Bed in San Bernadino County, east of Los Angeles. Jeri Taylor said the story, originally set on an ice planet where only Picard and Wesley crash-land, was changed to a desert locale because it was feared a Planet Hell ice-world set would be too hokey.

Nick Tate, who played Dirgo, is known best to genre audiences from his regular role on *Space: 1999.* Mary Kohnert would be the first of many (mostly female) replacements for Wesley at the conn, though her role would last only another episode.

The decrepid *Nenebek* shuttle, re-dressed from the SS *Arcos* escape pod in "Legacy" (180), features "archaic" labels and controls lifted from the present-day space shuttle by Michael Okuda. The episode's only headache was caused by the spring fountain, built indoors on Stage 16. Both live and optical effects for its shield at first failed to deliver. Finally, on two days' notice, Legato succeeded in devising what he called "an acrylic log" that rotated with reflective bits.

Trek continuity touches included Dirgo's use of "old-model" pistol phasers from *Star Trek III*; mention of the shuttle's duranium hull ("A Matter of Perspective"/162, "Hollow Pursuits"/169); and the use of hyronalin, first described in 1968's "The Deadly Years" as a treatment for radiation sickness. And Picard contributes a look forward and backward: while semiconscious he hums *"Auprès de Ma Blonde,"* the French song that he and his brother sang while drunk after their tussle in the mud in "Family" (178), and he tells Wesley about Boothby, the Academy's gardener, who would be seen a year later in "The First Duty" (219).

THE LOSS

Production No.: 184   ■   Aired: Week of December 31, 1990
Stardate: 44356.9   ■   Code: ls

Directed by **Chip Chalmers**
Teleplay by **Hilary J. Bader and Alan J. Adler
& Vanessa Greene**
Story by **Hilary J. Bader**

GUEST CAST
Ensign Janet Brooks: **Kim Braden**
Ensign Tess Allenby: **Mary Kohnert**
Guinan: **Whoopi Goldberg**

The *Enterprise* finds it cannot resume course after stopping to check out what appeared to be images in its path. At the same moment, Troi discovers her empathic powers have completely disappeared.

The roadblock is found to be a unique cluster of two-dimensional life-forms that have caught the starship up in their wake.

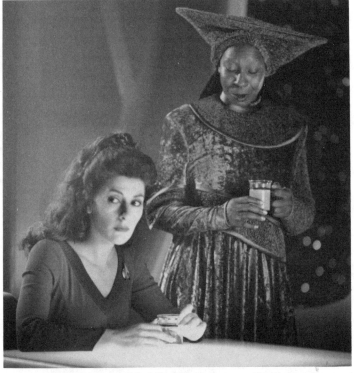

Guinan (Whoopi Goldberg) must counsel the counselor when Troi loses her empathic sense.

Meanwhile, Troi suffers denial, panic, and even anger at friends. Despite the protests of Guinan, Picard, and Riker that she still has her professional training to lean on, she resigns as ship's counselor. Then Data and Riker realize the creatures are heading for a cosmic string that would doom the starship, and a desperate Picard turns to Troi for help.

After trying to warn the creatures of the danger, she realizes they want to seek out the cosmic string. When Data creates a "dummy" string to the ship's rear, the creatures are confused and stop long enough for the *Enterprise* to break free.

Troi's powers come rushing back to her as she realizes that the strength of the two-dimensional creatures' feelings overwhelmed her powers. She resumes her job with renewed confidence in her abilities.

"The Loss" demonstrates that the TNG writers have finally learned to create conflict in Gene Roddenberry's perfect world by using outside stimuli. This episode gave Marina Sirtis a rare chance to stretch and shine as Troi—and made those weeks of almost being written out of the series in season one seem very far away indeed. Riker here calls Troi a "blue-blooded Betazoid" who's always had a unique means of control to fall back on, giving her character a subtext that was sadly lacking in the early years. Their relationship, long shunned or even denied by the writers, revealed here how well it could survive if it was shown and not just talked about. In this show we hear the Betazoid endearment, *imzadi,* for the first time in nearly two years since "Shades of Gray" (148).

Another landmark is Troi's conversation with Guinan. One of the few criticisms of the addition of Whoopi Goldberg's character is that Guinan seems to duplicate Troi's shipboard function, but in this case that "competition" is turned on its ear and used to great effect.

Writing intern Hilary Bader added the science subplot of the cosmic string, and Michael Piller revealed that for a time the staff even toyed with the daring idea of not giving Troi back her lost empathic sense. Sirtis has remarked that many fans with disabilities reacted warmly to her performance in this episode. Ironically, the episode that almost cost her her empathy is the one that begins by finally showing her counseling an adult crew member.

We learn that Betazoids' empathic abilities lie within the cerebellum and cerebral cortex, and that the Breen and others as well as the Ferengi cannot be sensed. Picard's equestrian interest ("Pen Pals"/141, *Generations*) is noted with a Kabul River Himalayan ride on the holodeck, and Kim Braden would later play his "wife" in the first TNG film.

A major concept in warp-drive design is introduced here by Michael Okuda and Rick Sternbach in a passing reference to the ship's structural integrity field, a force that keeps the ship intact under various inertial forces and stresses when the simple vacuum and null gravity of space aren't enough.

DATA'S DAY

Production No.: 185 ▪ Aired: Week of January 7, 1991
Stardate: 44390.1 ▪ Code: dd

Directed by **Robert Wiemer**
Teleplay by **Harold Apter and Ronald D. Moore**
Story by **Harold Apter**

GUEST CAST
Keiko Ishikawa: **Rosalind Chao**
Lieutenant O'Brien: **Colm Meaney**
Ambassador T'Pel (Sub-Commander Selok): **Sierra Pecheur**
Admiral Mendak: **Alan Scarfe**
Transporter Chief Hubbell: **April Grace**
V'Sal: **Shelly Desai**

The wedding party watches Miles (Colm Meaney) and Keiko O'Brien (Rosalind Chao).

Data's understanding of human behavior is put to the test when his friend Keiko Ishikawa gets cold feet on the eve of her wedding to Lieutenant O'Brien and calls off the ceremony.

Logically, the android reasons, if calling off the wedding makes her happy it will make O'Brien happy, too. Of course, when Data delivers the news to the transporter chief he quickly discovers otherwise. Geordi, however, assures him the ceremony will take place, so the android purchases a gift with Worf's assistance and takes dancing lessons from Dr. Crusher.

Meanwhile, the whole crew—except for Data—is made edgy by the presence of Ambassador T'Pel, a cooler-than-usual Vulcan en route to historic treaty negotiations with the Romulans in the Neutral Zone. But shortly after Data refuses to grant the ambassador access to security information for which she has not been cleared, she is killed in a mysterious transporter accident.

With her death, the treaty negotiations are called off, and the Romulans prepare to depart. But a probe, led by Data in his Sherlock Holmes persona, turns up signs that her death was faked. Confronted with this information, Romulan Commander Mendak reveals the truth: T'Pel was actually a deep-cover spy for his Empire.

The danger passed, the mood turns more joyful. Data walks his friend Keiko down the aisle, and she and O'Brien are married in a ceremony performed by Picard.

A marvelous and ambitious show relished by trivia fans, this day-in-the-life plot was the first attempted in any of Trek's various incarnations. Harold Apter first pitched the story during the third season, and various viewpoints including Picard's and that of the ship itself were considered for the narrative. Ronald D. Moore recalled that Data was the final choice because "he's the only one who's up twenty-four hours a day." Michael Piller then agreed with Rick Berman that at least one plot arc should run through the story, and the Romulan-Vulcan spy intrigue was added.

Director Robert Wiemer revealed that Brent Spiner and Gates McFadden worked up their own dialogue as well as their dance routine during after-hours rehearsals, and the lines they created were later accepted by the scriptwriters. The director, though, took credit for Data's "pasted-on" smile at the end of the dancing scene. Spiner—who, Wiener said, did "99 percent" of his own tap routine—was as good as his double but was modest enough to let the double perform to ensure the routine's quality.

The writing staff had toyed with the idea of a shipboard marriage for some time. Piller at one point even quietly inquired about marrying Picard off to provide some new story dynamics. Pairing O'Brien with the female conn officer slated to replace Wesley was also considered. Finally a wedding was proposed for the day-in-the-life story and Keiko was conceived. The part is played by Rosalind Chao, a close friend of Elizabeth "Shelby" Dennehy and an earlier candidate for a recurring role on the show. Chao is probably best remembered as Corporal Klinger's war bride on *M*A*S*H* and *After M*A*S*H*. Loads of *Enterprise* trivia can be found in this story. On SD 44390, for example, the 1,550th day since the starship's commissioning (SD 40759.5—or October 4, 2363, according to Okuda and Sternbach's technical manual. Data is still writing to Commander Bruce Maddox at the Daystrom Institute. For the first time, we see the android's cat, an idea Spiner proposed; the cat would get a name later, in "In Theory" (199). Data records that the starship's day included four birthdays, two transfers, four promotions, two chess tournaments, a secondary school play, a celebration of the Hindu Festival of Lights, various accidents, the birth of the Juarezes' baby, and the O'Brien-Ishikawa wedding.

Meanwhile, original Trek fans will note that Picard's wedding remarks are almost the same as those which Kirk used in 1966's "Balance of Terror." The Murasaki Quasar mentioned here is the same as Murasaki 312 from 1967's "Galileo Seven," Moore said. The Andorians are mentioned for the first time in a year ("The Offspring"/164) with their bizarre wedding ritual; likewise, the Bolians reappear (see "Schisms"/231) with Shelly Desai playing the first in a string of different Bolian barbers ("The Host"/197, "Ensign Ro"/203, "Schisms"). And the *U.S.S. Zhukov*, which ferries the Romulan spy, had been Barclay's last assignment ("Hollow Pursuits"/169). Alan Scarfe would return in "Birthright" (242–243).

The ship's arboretum, mentioned on several other occasions as a socializing site, makes its debut here—but as a work site for Keiko, a biologist. Another first is this show's glimpse of people "shopping" at the ship's replication center, where we discover Worf's appreciation of fine glass bird sculpture.

THE WOUNDED

Production No.: 186 ■ Aired: Week of January 28, 1991
Stardate: 44429.6 ■ Code: wo

Directed by **Chip Chalmers**
Teleplay by **Jeri Taylor**
Story by **Stuart Charno, Sara Charno, and Cy Chermak**

GUEST CAST
Captain Benjamin Maxwell: **Bob Gunton**
Keiko Ishikawa O'Brien: **Rosalind Chao**
Gul Macet: **Marc Alaimo**
Lieutenant O'Brien: **Colm Meaney**
Glinn Telle: **Marco Rodriguez**
Glinn Daro: **Time Winters**
Admiral Haden: **John Hancock**

Picard is shocked to learn a renegade Federation starship under the command of Captain Benjamin Maxwell is destroying Cardassian ships, threatening the fragile peace that the Federation and the Cardassian Empire have achieved after years of skirmishes.

He invites the Cardassian, Gul Macet, aboard to witness the pursuit of the ship, the USS *Phoenix*. Both watch in horror on long-range scan as two more Cardassian ships are destroyed.

O'Brien, Maxwell's former tactical officer, says he finds the decorated captain's acts hard to believe. Maxwell, he says, must have a reason for the attacks. Intercepted at last, Maxwell gladly comes aboard to tell Picard that he has proof the Cardassians are rearming for war.

Picard refuses and orders Maxwell to surrender, but he aims to fight until O'Brien breaks the standoff by beaming over and quietly persuading his old captain to give up. Macet is relieved, but Picard sternly warns him that despite Maxwell's crimes he knows he had the truth.

This wonderful show not only offered a tragic figure in Bob Gunton's Captain Maxwell but added long-overdue depth to O'Brien and introduced new adversaries, the Cardassians. Even the scientific deus ex machina—transporting through the one-fiftieth-of-a-second break in recycling shields—was well done. Note too the mention of the depleted post-Borg fleet and the shield-dropping prefix code, seen in *Star Trek II*.

While the philosophical conflict was between the two captains, it was O'Brien who butted heads with his counterpart Cardassian and sang an Irish song with his former commander—a gem of a scene suggested by Michael Piller (which Rick Berman picked)—helping to diffuse a tense situation and returning Maxwell to a sane but broken state. (The song, "The Minstrel Boy" by Thomas Moore, figured prominently in the movie *The Man Who Would Be King*.) We also learned that young Miles Edward O'Brien was a peaceful, nature-loving boy who never killed until a Cardassian patrol forced him to. Mentioning his stint as tactics officer on the *Rutledge* provided a nice setup for future bridge duty ("Redemption II"/201, "Disaster"/205).

Only Mark "Sarek" Lenard had played three different aliens in the Trek universe until Marc Alaimo did it here as a Cardassian, after stints as an Antican and a Romulan ("Lonely Among Us"/108, "The Neutral Zone"/126); he was next a human ("Time's Arrow"/226) before getting the recurring Cardassian Gul Dukat in spinoff DS9—but without the facial hair here, never seen again in the species. Rodriguez had been a human ("The Arsenal of Freedom"/121), while Hancock, seen in *A Soldier's Story*, *Foul Play*, and *L.A. Law*, died of a heart attack at home in late 1992 soon after costarring as bartender Ike Johnson on *Love and War*. Gunton, known for Broadway's *Sweeney Todd*, played a Maxwell whose Queeg-like turn echoed Matt Decker of 1967's "The Doomsday Machine."

In creating a new ongoing race, costume designer Bob Blackman and makeup designer Michael Westmore worked together

O'Brien (Colm Meaney) and Cardassian Daro (Time Winters) confront old prejudices.

to give the Cardassians an overall "snakelike" look; the dress helmets briefly seen here were never used again. Westmore based the unusual makeup and shoulder pieces, which take at least two and a half hours to apply, on a passing image that had struck him two years earlier: an abstract painting in a Ventura Boulevard store of a wide-shouldered woman with what looked like a spoon in the center of her forehead. Modelmaker Greg Jein built Ed Miarecki's original Nebula-class design ("Future Imperfect"/182) into the *U.S.S. Phoenix*, NCC-65420, while Rick Sternbach evolved the first Galor-class Cardassian ship seen, the *Trager,* from a pod ship to a scorpionlike design to the simple Egyptian-*ankh* look; Miarecki and Tom Hudson built it. The new race would be located "west" of the UFP on art department maps and sector numbers, opposite the Klingons and Romulans; their energy weapons were pink here but made to be amber afterward.

DEVIL'S DUE

Production No.: 187 ■ Aired: Week of February 4, 1991
Stardate: 44474.5 ■ Code: dv

Directed by **Tom Benko**
Teleplay by **Philip Lazebnick**
Story by **Philip Lazebnick and William Douglas Lansford**

GUEST CAST
Ardra: **Marta Dubois**
Dr. Clarke: **Paul Lambert**
Jared: **Marcello Tubert**
Devil Monster: **Thad Lamey**
Klingon Monster: **Tom Magee**
Marley: **William Glover**

An emergency transmission from a Federation science station sends the *Enterprise* to Ventax II, where Picard and crew discover a peaceful but meek people about to hand over their world to a woman who claims she is the planet's devil, Ardra.

It seems the pollution-plagued, war-torn Ventaxians generations ago made a pact with Ardra: a thousand years of peace and health in return for their eternal slavery. The Ventaxians had long thought the tale a legend until the shape-changing Ardra showed up.

Picard draws Ardra's wrath when he refuses her sexual advances, and she makes the starship "disappear." As La Forge races to discover a power source behind her "special effects," Ardra agrees to a legal contest on the real-enough contracts and her identity, with Data as magistrate.

Picard tries to convince the Ventaxian leader, Jared, that his people are responsible for their own prosperity, but when Ardra runs through her illusions again, Jared agrees to submit to her judgment.

Finally, La Forge locates her cloaked orbiting ship and enables Picard to tap into its power systems, revealing Ardra as just another con artist.

Picard must outwit Ventax II's "devil," Ardra (Marta Dubois).

Like "The Child" (127), this story predates TNG—to at least August 16, 1977, when the Lansford story turned up in a status memo for the 1970s *Star Trek II* TV series. Its "Devil and Daniel Webster" plot, originally unearthed during TNG's third-season story pinch, eventually bore the mark of a score of TNG staff writers. In the end, it was Trek fan and *Wings* staff writer Philip Lazebnick's comic touches that survived, along with Piller's idea of making the "devil" a female.

The 1977 outline reads like a 1960s Trek episode. In it a demonstrative Captain Kirk fast-talks planet Neuterr out of falling for an impostor's scam, exposing the "devil" as merely the mental energy of a surviving planetary elder and his original fellow council members.

Although familiar actresses like Stella Stevens and Adrienne Barbeau were considered, the role of Ardra went to Marta DuBois, Magnum's estranged wife on *Magnum, P.I.,* after several prior auditions. Paul Lambert had already played an Aldean ("When the Bough Breaks"/118).

Though some may regard it as the Klingon devil, Fek'lhr as seen here is carefully described as the guardian of Gre'thor, the hereafter where the Klingon dishonored go after they die. This is consistent with the fact that Klingons have no devil—a detail that was revealed in 1969's "Day of the Dove."

CLUES

Production No.: 188 ■ Aired: Week of February 11, 1991
Stardate: 44502.7 ■ Code: cl

Directed by **Les Landau**
Teleplay by **Bruce D. Arthurs and Joe Menosky**
Story by **Bruce D. Arthurs**

GUEST CAST
Lieutenant O'Brien: **Colm Meaney**
Ensign McKnight: **Pamela Winslow**
Madeline: **Rhonda Aldrich**
Guinan: **Whoopi Goldberg**
Nurse Alyssa Ogawa: **Patti Yasutake**
Gunman: **Thomas Knickerbocker**

As the *Enterprise* is on its way to investigate a mysterious planet, a wormhole suddenly appears in the ship's path, knocking the crew unconscious. As they begin to come to, Data, who is immune to the wormhole's effects, tells them only thirty seconds have passed since their encounter with the phenomenon.

But soon evidence mounts that the crew was out for much longer—an entire day, in fact. A twinge of pain in Worf's wrist reveals a recent fracture, a botany experiment records a full twenty-four hours' growth, and the ship's chronometer has been tampered with.

A check of Data's systems shows nothing wrong, but an analysis of the probe he sent shows it was rigged to send false information.

Picard finally orders the crew to proceed to the mystery planet, over Data's objections. The android refuses to say why, but he does tell Picard the captain himself ordered him to lie.

Suddenly a being called a Paxan inhabits Troi's body. Data then explains the truth: the horribly isolationist Paxans stun intruders and send their ships on their way, but Data's presence foiled their plan. The *Enterprise* did go to the planet, but the Paxans demanded the starship be destroyed. Picard, though, won agreement to a short-term memory wipe for all the crew, with Data ordered to keep the secret.

During the second visit Picard assures the Paxans that the bugs in his plan can be worked out so that their existence will remain a secret.

Story creator Bruce D. Arthurs proved it can be done: the fan and Phoenix, Arizona, mail carrier had his spec script for TNG bought and turned into an episode, helped along by a rewrite that won Joe Menosky a staff job. Michael Piller called this bottle-show mystery, which includes the first appearance of Dixon Hill since "Manhunt" (145) in season two, one of his favorites for the season.

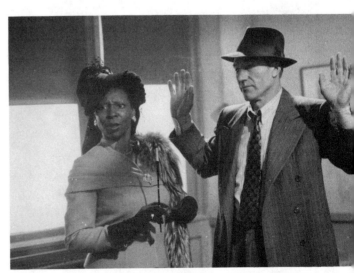

Guinan (Whoopi Goldberg) doesn't share Picard's thrill at playing detective.

Notice director Les Landau's use of longer and more fluid camera takes for the flashbacks, in contrast with a choppier style with more cuts back and forth for real time.

In addition to bringing back Rhonda Aldrich as Madeline, Dixon Hill's secretary, this segment includes the only mention of Nurse Ogawa's first name—Alyssa. There's also a fleeting glimpse of a t'ai chi class led by Worf, with Riker, Troi, and Geordi among the participants. We also learn the transporter trace records can be used to determine elapsed time judging by cellular cycle, and that a ship's clock exists apart from the chronometer—which only La Forge and Data can reset—used by the computer system. Wormholes have previously been seen in *Star Trek: The Motion Picture,* and Data mentions having encountered them twice in his own career: during the Barzan affair in "The Price" (156) and during his service aboard the *Trieste,* mentioned already as a previous assignment ("11001001"/116).

FIRST CONTACT

Production No.: 189 ▪ Airdate: February 18, 1991
Stardate: Unknown ▪ Code: fc

Directed by **Cliff Bole**
Teleplay by **Dennis Russell Bailey, David Bischoff, Joe Menosky, and Ronald D. Moore**
Story by **Marc Scott Zicree**

GUEST CAST
Chancellor Avill Durken: **George Coe**
Mirasta: **Carolyn Seymour**
Berel: **George Hearn**
Krola: **Michael Ensign**
Nilrem: **Steven Anderson**
Dr. Tava: **Sachi Parker**
Lanel: **Bebe Neuwirth**

Krola (Michael Ensign) is not about to let "aliens" on his world.

A reconnaissance mission on the planet Malcoria III goes disastrously wrong when Commander Riker (in native disguise) is injured and taken to a native hospital. There, Malcorian doctors soon uncover his true identity.

To prevent worldwide panic, Picard and Troi beam down to meet with the astonished planet's leader. But though Chancellor Durken and his science minister Mirasta (in charge of Malcor's fledgeling space program) are both convinced by the *Enterprise* crew's message of peace and friendship, Durken's security officer Krola remains suspicious. After Riker unsuccesssfully attempts to escape from the hospital, Krola steps in to interrogate him, using potentially lethal drugs.

When his questioning proves fruitless, Krola stages his own death and makes Riker appear to be the executioner, hoping both to prevent the aliens from gaining a foothold on his world, and to quash Mirasta's dreams of space exploration. Dr. Crusher beams in, however, bringing both Riker and Krola back up to sickbay, where she convinces Durken of what really happened.

Though the Chancellor is satisfied of the Federation's good intentions, he realizes his people aren't ready to accept the idea that they aren't alone in the universe yet. Durken quietly puts his world's nascent space program on hold—while granting Mirasta's wish to leave with the starship.

Michael Piller had to persuade Rick Berman to let him bend the rules and tell this story—for the first time in Trek's twenty-five years, the teaser of 1967's "Tomorrow Is Yesterday" notwithstanding—from an alien culture's point of view. The gamble worked to perfection in this homage to the classic 1951 science fiction movie *The Day the Earth Stood Still*, which gave us a look at what must be an ongoing process within the Federation. We also learn that a bungled first-contact mission was the reason behind decades of Klingon-Federation conflict.

The multiple teleplay credits include versions by "Tin Man" (168) scriptwriters Dennis Putnam Bailey and David Bischoff and another by Ronald D. Moore and Joe Menosky that tried to use the point of view of the *Enterprise* crew after Marc Scott Zicree—author of *The Twilight Zone Companion*—first pitched this basic story idea during season three.

Throughout its evolution, the idea took many twists and turns. It was considered for the season-end cliff-hanger and, in a version called "Graduation," as Wesley's swan song in which he was to stay planetside permanently after a cultural-contact mission. One rejected concept, according to Zicree, had the new space travelers finding out about the Federation by taking in Picard & Co.'s crippled shuttlecraft. In another, the members of the contact team become celebrities.

The excellent cast includes George Coe, perhaps better known in genre circles for his old *Max Headroom* role as Network 23 president Ben DeVore; Carolyn Seymour, who played Romulan Sub-Commander Taris in "Contagion" (137); and Bebe Neuwirth, a longtime fan who plays Dr. Lilith Crane on *Cheers*. Here she's a Malcorian nurse in a late-draft cameo, written with her in mind; she offers to help Riker escape if he'll fulfill her greatest fantasy: to make love to an alien. Did Riker—or didn't he? Well, he escapes somehow!

Clever use is made here of Malcorian medical and anatomical terms that sound almost authentic: "cardial organ" for heart, "costal struts" for ribs, "terminus" for foot, and "renal organ" for kidney.

GALAXY'S CHILD

Production No.: 190   ■   Aired: Week of March 11, 1991
Stardate: 44614.6   ■   Code: gc

Directed by **Winrich Kolbe**
Teleplay by **Maurice Hurley**
Story by **Thomas Kartozian**

GUEST CAST
Dr. Leah Brahms: **Susan Gibney**
Ensign Rager: **Lanei Chapman**
Ensign Pavlik: **Jana Marie Hupp**
Guinan: **Whoopi Goldberg**
Transporter Chief Hubbell: **April Grace**

La Forge's joy at finally meeting Dr. Leah Brahms, the Galaxy-class engine designer whose holodeck image he once fell in love with, turns to ashes when she finally comes aboard the *Enterprise*. The real Dr. Brahms is cold and highly critical of the field changes Geordi has made in her original designs.

Meanwhile, the discovery of a new alien life-form ends in tragedy when the creature is accidentally killed. When the saddened crew members realize the entity was pregnant, Worf and Dr. Crusher free its baby with a phaser-fired "cesarean section." The newborn attaches itself to the starship and drains energy from what it believes is its mother.

La Forge and Dr. Brahms set to work to "wean" the baby, Geordi having only recently discovered that his dream woman is in fact mar-

La Forge and Dr. Brahms (Susan Gibney) find neither is what the other expected.

ried. Their fresh start as friends is derailed, however, when she finds his old holodeck program and is infuriated to learn that he used her as a fantasy object.

As other alien adults approach from their native asteroid field, the energy drain on the ship grows critical. Finally the two engineers rise above their friction to devise a sour harmonic frequency, which breaks the link between the *Enterprise* and the baby just in time. The crisis past, Geordi and Leah find they can laugh about their feelings now—as friends.

The use of computer animation produced a very believable alien baby and adults in this story, written from Thomas Kartozian's outline by former producer Maurice Hurley, with uncredited assist from Jeri Taylor on the Geordi–Leah Brahms reunion and Ron Moore on the tale of "Junior." The chemistry between LeVar Burton and Susan Gibney was strong enough to lead many fans to hope for a return by the engineer if she ever becomes unattached.

Jana Marie Hupp, seen here as Ensign Pavlik, would fare much worse in a fifth-season episode, "Disaster" (205). The Jefferies tubes, named for original-series art director Matt Jefferies, are finally seen here, after having been mentioned during the third season in "The Hunted" (159).

In a rare blooper, "Junior" is seen attached over the starboard shuttle bay, which is spoken of as Shuttle Bay 2 even though it has always been identified in drawings as Shuttle Bay 3.

NIGHT TERRORS

Production No.: 191 ■ Aired: Week of March 18, 1991
Stardate: 44631.2 ■ Code: nt

Directed by **Les Landau**
Teleplay by **Pamela DouglasJeri Taylor**
Story by **Shari Goodhartz**

GUEST CAST
Keiko O'Brien: **Rosalind Chao**
Andrus Hagan: **John Vickery**
Ensign Gillespie: **Duke Moosekian**
Ensign Peeples: **Craig Hurley**
Ensign Kenny Lin: **Brian Tochi**
Ensign Rager: **Lanei Chapman**
Lieutenant O'Brien: **Colm Meaney**
Guinan: **Whoopi Goldberg**
Captain Chantal R. Zaheva: **Deborah Taylor**

The *Enterprise* finds the starship *Brattain*, missing for several weeks, adrift in space. The entire crew save the ship's Betazoid counselor, is dead.

While the crew is investigating the incident, odd events begin to occur. Troi is tormented by nightmares, and La Forge can't restart the *Brattain*'s engines. Dr. Crusher suggests that the irritability among the crew might indicate a repetition of whatever happened to the now-dead science vessel. Picard decides to leave the area only to discover the *Enterprise*'s engines don't work either.

Data, unaffected, theorizes the ships are caught in a Tyken's Rift, a spatial rupture that is draining their energy. La Forge fails in an attempt to dislodge them. Dr. Crusher finds that the crew's depression and shakiness stem from dream deprivation, and Troi realizes that her colleague's nightmares mirror her own; she wonders if they could be an attempt at communication.

While brainstorming with Data, Troi guesses that her nightmare images come from a ship trapped on the other side of the rift. The other ship is asking for their aid in freeing both vessels with a release of hydrogen; the *Brattain* crew died before they could figure it out.

Troi tries to reach the other ship in a dream while Data vents all the ship's stored hydrogen. Just as their attempts seem to have failed, there is a giant explosion and the ship is thrown free.

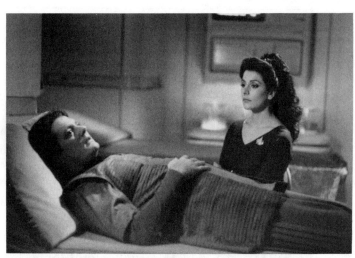
Troi ponders the Tyken's Rift trap with a tormented Betazoid (John Vickery).

Though it's regarded as the clinker of the fourth season by many fans and by those involved, this script—from a story by Shari Goodhartz, who penned "The Most Toys" (170) during season three—does let Troi save the ship for once. The story suffered from time problems, among other things. Michael Piller recalled that the energy and pace were so slow that the episode ran nine minutes over and had to be severely cut.

After "flying" in a suspended harness during the filming of this episode, Marina Sirtis joked that her plea for more action scenes for Troi had backfired—she is deathly afraid of heights. The scenes, shot throughout an entire day of second-unit production, "seemed like a great idea in the meetings," but were a "terrible" production mistake, Jeri Taylor said. Rob Legato was more blunt: "Horrible!"

Longtime Trek fans should recall Brian Tochi as young Ray Tsingtao in the original-series episode "And the Children Shall Lead." More recently he was the voice of Leonardo in the *Teenage Mutant Ninja Turtles* movies and has appeared in everything from *Santa Barbara* to the last two *Police Academy* movies.

Michael Okuda's plaque for the *Brattain*—inexplicably labeled "Brittain" on the re-dressed *Reliant* miniature from *Star Trek II*—identifies the ship as NCC-21166 of the Miranda class, built at the Yoyodyne Division (another *Buckaroo Banzai* reference) over 40 Eridani-A (Vulcan's sun, according to Franz Joseph's 1974 *Starfleet Technical Manual*).

More in-jokes: TNG staffers' names can be seen in the explosives manifest that Data and Troi examine. Entries include Mooride Polyronite 4 (Ron Moore, visual-effects coordinator), Takemurium Lite (David Takemura, visual-effects associate), Neussite 283 (Wendy Neuss, associate producer), Bio-Genovesium (Cosmo Genovese, script supervisor), and Hutzelite (Gary Hutzel, visual-effects coordinator).

IDENTITY CRISIS

Production No.: 192 ■ Aired: Week of March 25, 1991
Stardate: 44664.5 ■ Code: ic

Directed by **Winrich Kolbe**
Teleplay by **Brannon Braga**
Story by **Timothy de Haas**

GUEST CAST
Lieutenant Commander Susanna Leitjen:
Maryann Plunkett
Nurse Alyssa Ogawa: **Patti Yasutake**
Lieutenant Hickman: **Amick Byram**
Transporter Technician Hedrick: **Dennis Madalone**
Ensign Graham: **Mona Grudt**

La Forge is disturbed to hear from former shipmate Susanna Leitjen that they are the only two members remaining from an away team sent to Tarchannen III five years ago.

The others are disappearing and apparently headed for the planet, initially investigated after a small colony disappeared there without a trace. On the surface, three shuttles but no life signs are found.

Leitjen tells La Forge she senses the others nonetheless. She then becomes unstable and has to be beamed to sickbay. Finding that Leitjen's blood chemistry has been altered, Dr. Crusher guesses the others have undergone the same process and have somehow been transformed

La Forge, almost entirely transformed into one of the ultraviolet light-beings of Tarchannen III.

into another species. Leitjen worries that the same thing will happen to her and La Forge. After she makes a dash to get off the ship, Geordi finds her skin broken out in blotches and her middle fingers fused together.

La Forge, working harder than ever, finds a shadow not noticed before on the team's original log tapes, indicating another entity nearby. Then he too falls ill and leaves the ship, evolving faster than any of the others.

Meantime, Dr. Crusher finds and removes a parasite from Leitjen that had been rewriting her DNA. They beam down to the planet's surface, where La Forge has been almost completely transformed; he is invisible except by ultraviolet light. Only his old friend's coaxing brings him back in time to remove the parasite.

Rescued from the slush pile of spec scripts, this story by fan writer Timothy de Haas originally concerned two non-regular crew members. The glowing transformed aliens gave Westmore, Blackman, and a company called Wildfire a chance to pioneer a remarkable optical effect using ultraviolet light. "MTV is using that a lot now," David Livingston said of the ultraviolet effect. "We didn't do it just to be glitzy—we did it because it tied in dramatically with the story."

Originally, Brannon Braga recalled, the script linked Geordi and Susanna romantically, but the word came down to give the engineer a break with his "failed love" record, which began in "Booby Trap" (154) and continued in "Galaxy's Child" (190). Braga said his first draft was more "horrific" with many more aliens on the surface, but Geordi wasn't transformed; keying the mood more to terror, of a type he described as "restrained and psychoanalytical," and involving Geordi in the emotional trauma of the change made the show click.

A nice continuity touch here is the use of the older-style uniforms, phasers, and tricorders for the visual log from the *Victory*'s away team five years earlier—note the opening stardate, 40164.7—with Geordi as a command-division lieutenant (j.g.) when he came from the *Victory* ("Elementary, Dear Data"/129). The shuttlepod *Cousteau* from the *Aries* carries its ship's number, NCC-45167; it was the first ship command offered to Riker, in "The Icarus Factor" (140).

After debuting in the sciences division ("Where No One Has Gone Before"/106) and dying in the guise of security noncom Ramos ("Heart of Glory"/120), stunt coordinator Dennis Madalone here became Transporter Chief Hedrick; he's listed as a transporter technician, but he wears an ensign's pip. Likewise, Yasutake's recurring character finally gained a last name, Ogawa, here after Beverly had already called her by her first name, Alyssa in "Clues" (188).

Extra Randy Pflug models the humanoid shape that Geordi creates from the cast shadow, while among those wearing the ultraviolet suits were Mark and Brian, two L.A. disc jockeys who had become NBC variety show hosts.

NTH DEGREE

Production No.: 193 ■ Aired: Week of April 1, 1991
Stardate: 44704.2 ■ Code: nd

Directed by **Robert Legato**
Written by **Joe Menosky**

GUEST CAST
"Einstein": **Jim Morton**
Cytherian: **Kay E. Kuter**
Lieutenant Linda Larson: **Saxon Trainor**
Ensign April Anaya: **Page Leong**
Lieutenant (j.g.) Reginald Barclay: **Dwight Schultz**
Ensign Brower: **David Coburn**

Sent to repair the malfunctioning Argus Array telescope, the *Enterprise* discovers an alien probe near the installation. An energy surge from the probe knocks out La Forge and Lieutenant Barclay, who have been sent to study it from a shuttle.

When they come to, both officers seem to be fine, but Barclay soon begins making leaps of insight and showing abilities he never had before. He describes how to destroy the probe when it grows dangerous and then how to fix the telescope in a fraction of the time he would normally need.

A scan of the lieutenant's brain tissue reveals an underlying physiological reason for his new abilities: he is rapidly evolving into the most advanced human ever seen. The crew is edgy about his new powers, but Barclay seems innocent enough.

Then the telescope's reactors begin to fail rapidly, and even Barclay is stymied. Just as the installation is about to explode, the computer blinks out and then comes back on line—speaking with Barclay's voice.

The transformed crewman saves the installation and then propels the ship to a point thirty thousand light-years away. Picard now fears Barclay's intentions but is reluctant to sever the lieutenant's link to the computer, fearing it might kill him.

Suddenly the image of a smiling alien appears. His race, the Cytherians, studies other plot. He was proud of a camera shot on the bridge in which he rejected a series of close-ups in favor of a long continuous roll from one speaker to another.

This segment demonstrates how Gates McFadden's pleas to round out Beverly's character with "comedy and hobbies" were finally being met. We see her interest in the theater here on top of past glimpses of dance, in "Data's Day" (185), and biology in "Clues" (188). Michael Piller credited Rick Berman with suggesting the *Cyrano de Bergerac* scene between Barclay and his teacher, the "drama doctor."

Geordi and Barclay's shuttlecraft here is the *Feynman,* named for 1965 Nobel laureate physicist Richard P. Feynman. The "ODN bypass" mentioned concerns the optical data network, the starship's multiplex data transmission system. And the graviton concept, used by the Cyterians to bring their subjects home for study, was first used by the two-dimensional creatures in "The Loss" (184).

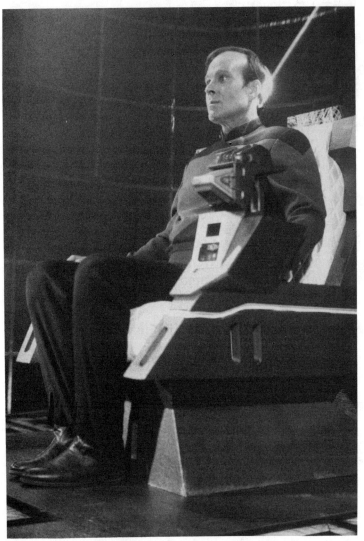

Supermind or superthreat? Barclay (Dwight Schultz) interfaces with the computer.

civilizations by transforming them using the probe, and then bringing them to their home system. Barclay is restored to normal as Picard agrees to be scanned in exchange for information about the Cytherians.

Looking for a vehicle to bring back popular guest star Dwight Schultz and his milquetoast character, the staff decided on Joe Menosky's idea of an episode focusing on superintelligence. Rob Legato made good use of his effects background here in his second outing as a director, using live lasers to "connect" Barclay to the ship's computer on the bare holodeck.

Legato recalled how the pages for the final scene arrived the day of shooting on this ever-changing script, making the alien a floating head whose purpose was much more benevolent than in earlier drafts—an attempt to get away from the standard hostage

PID

Production No.: 194   ▪   Aired: Week of April 22, 1991
Stardate: 44741.9   ▪   Code: qp

Directed by **Cliff Bole**
Teleplay by **Ira Steven Behr**
Story by **Randee Russell and Ira Steven Behr**

GUEST CAST
Vash: **Jennifer Hetrick**
Sir Guy: **Clive Revill**
Q: **John de Lancie**
Servant: **Joi Staton**

Picard is nervous enough while preparing his keynote speech for the Federation Archaeology Council. Then in quick order he's visited by Vash, a mischievous female archaeologist he met on vacation on Risa and then by the pesky superbeing Q.

A spat erupts when Picard finds out that Vash is setting off for an illegal dig and she discovers he never mentioned her to his friends. Q, a secret witness, decides to return the favor Picard did him a year ago by getting the stubborn lovers to admit their feelings for each other—in a special simulation of Sherwood Forest, that he creates.

With the couple cast as Robin Hood and Maid Marian and Picard's senior officers as Merry Men, Q becomes the sheriff of Nottingham. He

Third-season producer and Vash creator Ira Steven Behr suggested Camelot as the best off-ship locale for Randee Russell's original Picard-Vash-Q triangle until Piller suggested this venue, in vogue with the Kevin Costner movie. The romp included Worf's "I am *not* a merry man!" and his smashing of Geordi's mandolin: a Behr homage to *Animal House.* We also get hints about the Picard-Beverly duo after "The Naked Now" (103) and the tease of "Allegiance" (166); the capper would be "Attached" (260).

The expansive castle set was really made up of several inexpensive foreground set pieces shot through a long lens, noted director Cliff Bole; a day's worth of location shooting at Descanso Gardens northeast of Glendale provided Sherwood Forest. Due to a stunt quarterstaff mixup, Frakes suffered a cut eye when his weapon broke under a broadsword blow just as he turned in to it.

Throughout the series, Picard had been shown as Jeffersonian in his interests in history, science, and literature—as well as archaeology (see notes, "The Chase"/246). Among the symposium's delegates can be seen an Algolian ("Ménage à Troi"/172), a Bolian (see notes, "Schisms"/231), and a Vulcan. Q and Vash's fate is unveiled later in "Q-Less" during spinoff *Deep Space Nine's* first year.

Picard as Robin Hood, and Vash (Jennifer Hetrick) as Maid Marian.

Q (John de Lancie) becomes the Sheriff of Nottingham to repay his "debt" to Picard.

challenges the captain to risk his crew's lives for the woman he loves. Picard sets out to rescue Vash, claiming he'd do the same for anyone else.

But "Marian" rejects his rescue, turning him in and agreeing to marry her captor, Sir Guy. Q is delighted until he sees her send a note to the crew for help; he then turns her in as well.

Heads are about to roll when the Merry Men come to the rescue; Picard, a skilled fencer, skewers Sir Guy. The game is over.

Back on the ship, Vash announces she plans to travel through the galaxy with Q. An uneasy Picard admits the two do have much in common—just before he kisses Vash good-bye and they promise to meet again.

THE DRUMHEAD

Production No.: 195 ▪ Aired: Week of April 29, 1991
Stardate: 44769.2 ▪ Code: dr

Directed by **Jonathan Frakes**
Written by **Jeri Taylor**

GUEST CAST
Sabin Genestra: **Bruce French**
Simon Tarses: **Spencer Garrett**
Lieutenant J'Ddan: **Henry Woronicz**
Admiral Thomas Henry: **Earl Billings**
Admiral Norah Satie: **Jean Simmons**
Nellen Tore: **Ann Shea**

An explosion in the *Enterprise*'s dilithium chamber begins a trail of intrigue that leads Worf to suspect a Klingon exchange officer. Noted investigator Admiral Norah Satie comes out of retirement to help conduct a probe of the incident.

The Klingon, J'Ddan, admits to smuggling plans to the Romulans but denies any role in the explosion. Satie's Betazoid aide, Sabin, senses he's telling the truth; the Admiral begins to hunt for co-conspirators.

During the investigation Sabin senses that med tech Simon Tarses is lying about some part of his testimony. Even after the explosion is found to have been an accident, Satie bullies Tarses into admitting a forebear was Romulan, not Vulcan as he had once sworn.

Picard, uncomfortable with Satie's tactics,

Sabin (Bruce French) and Norah Satie (Jean Simmons) lead a latter-day Inquisition.

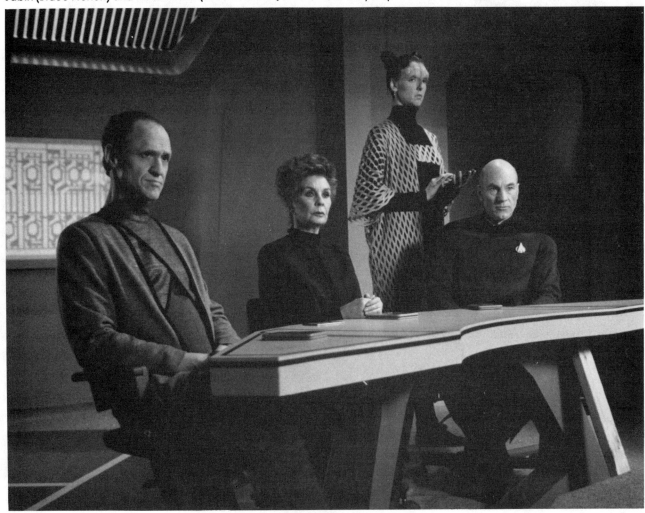

meets with Tarses to confirm the man's innocence, and then the captain openly challenges Satie. She vows to bring him down before visiting Starfleet admiral Henry.

Picard's reluctance to participate any further in Satie's hearings leads her to question him as a possible traitor. When Picard uses her famous father's words to rebut her charges, she begins a groundless tirade, accusing him of violating the Prime Directive. Her rage shocks everyone in the room, disgusts Admiral Henry, and breaks up the witch-hunt at last.

What was to have been a money-saving "clip show"—(like the second-season finale "Shades of Gray") turned into one of the season's most chilling episodes. Determined to mount a meaningful story on a slim budget with no visual effects, Berman and Piller turned to this tale, which rings with echoes of the McCarthy hearings and the Salem witch-hunts.

Jeri Taylor's script, the one she is most proud of, was inspired by a Ronald D. Moore idea called "It Can't Happen Here," and echoes the groundless investigation of Picard from season one "Coming of Age" (119) and weaves in references to his abduction by the Borg in "The Best of Both Worlds" (174–175), the alien parasitic invaders "Conspiracy" (125), the T'Pel-Selok spy scandal in "Data's Day" (185), and the developing Klingon-Romulan intrigue. And it still came in $250,000 under budget!

In his second directorial outing, Jonathan Frakes recalls he had a good time and wasn't too intimidated by the presence of Oscar nominee Jean Simmons, with whom he had worked on *North and South.* The acclaimed actress, a longtime unabashed Trekker, also played the matriarch of the Collins family in the short-lived revival of *Dark Shadows.*

After twenty-five years of Trek, we finally learn that the Federation's governing document is called a Constitution, and its various Bill of Rights is composed of Guarantees, the seventh roughly corresponding to the U.S. Fifth Amendment's ban on self-incrimination. Also, Tarses's birthplace on the Mars Colony was noted in the original Trek as the home of the Fundamental Declaration of the Martian Colonies, mentioned in 1967's "Courtmartial" as a landmark in interstellar law.

Satie's ferrying starship, the *Cochrane,* is of the Oberth class (a modified *Grissom* from *Star Trek III*), like the *Tsiolkovsky* from "The Naked Now" (103) and another namesake of the warp-drive discoverer "Ménage à Troi" (172). And Picard isn't the only one with a reputation as an advocate: Riker seen previously in a lawyer's role in "Angel One" (115) and "The Measure of a Man" (135) is chosen to defend first Tarses and then Picard.

On the tech side, we learn here that an individual communicator provides a traceable ID on computer and other system use and that the dilithium "cradle" ("Skin of Evil"/122) is called the "articulation frame"—a defective one was installed during the post-Borg refit in "The Best of Both Worlds," Part 2 (175).

And for pure trivia fans: Picard says he took command of the *Enterprise* on Stardate 41124; that was after the ship was commissioned on SD 40759.5, inscribed on the bridge plaque, and before the first aired captain's log entry of SD 41153.7, in "Encounter at Farpoint" (101).

HALF A LIFE

Production No.: 196   ■   Aired: Week of May 6, 1991
Stardate 44805.3   ■   Code: hl

Directed by **Les Landau**
Teleplay by **Peter Allan Fields**
Story by **Ted Roberts and Peter Allan Fields**

GUEST CAST
Lwaxana Troi: **Majel Barrett**
Dara: **Michelle Forbes**
B'Tardat: **Terrence E. McNally**
Lieutenant O'Brien: **Colm Meaney**
Mr. Homn: **Caryl Struyken**
Dr. Timicin: **David Ogden Stiers**

Picard is nervous when Troi's mother returns for a visit, but this time the ebullient Lwaxana has set her sights on Dr. Timicin, a quiet scientist who's abroad to test stellar ignition theories that may enable him to save his world's dying star.

Timicin, who invested his life's work in the plan, is crushed when it eventually fails. Lwaxana can't understand why he's so despondent until he tells her he is nearly sixty, the age of the

Lwaxana (Majel Barret) questions Timicin (David Odgen Stiers) about his world's custom of ritual suicide.

resolution: a ritual suicide to save children the burden of their parent's aging.

Enraged, Lwaxana demands that Picard intervene. He can't, of course, so she turns on Timicin herself: why doom his entire world by committing suicide when his research is so close to success? At first he resists, but eventually he agrees with her and seeks asylum.

His decision causes an uproar among his people, and armed ships are sent to retrieve him. Timicin stands firm, though, until his daughter beams up to plead with him to stand by the heritage he taught her. Touched, he agrees, and tells a tearful Lwaxana that the revolutionary will have to be someone else.

Later, Timicin is surprised when Lwaxana shows up as he prepares to beam down. If she is one of his loved ones, she tells him, she wants to be there with all the others when he says good-bye.

Fans had looked forward to the guest appearance of *M*A*S*H* regular David Ogden Stiers in this outing, but it was Majel Barrett who surprised them by pulling off a well-done first look at the non-comic side of Lwaxana Troi; the segment features the two guest stars as perhaps no other TNG hour ever has. Its theme, the worth of older citizens and the problems of the aged, was handled in a thought-provoking way by Peter Allan Fields, who was hired as a staff writer the following season, and his partner Ted Roberts.

Though she had only one small scene, actress Michelle Forbes more than stepped out of the shadow of the two guest leads with her performance as Timicin's loving yet embittered daughter, Dara—so much so that she would land a new recurring TNG role in the coming season. A student at the Performing Arts High School in Houston, she moved to New York at sixteen to audition for a movie and wound up staying. She worked on *The Guiding Light* for almost three years and moved on to TV guest roles.

The mention of oskoid leaves dates back to Lwaxana's visit last year in "Ménage à Troi" (172) while her nickname for the security chief—"Mr. Woof"—first appears here. And Rigel IV, where Lwaxana says she once persuaded a young astronomer to name a star after her, was the home of Argelian administrator Hengist, who was possessed by the Redjac evil spirit in 1967's "Wolf in the Fold."

THE HOST

Production No. 197 ● Aired: Week of May 13, 1991
Stardate: 44821.3 ● Code: ho

Directed by **Marvin V. Rush**
Written by **Michel Horvat**

GUEST CAST
Governor Leka Trion: **Barbara Tarbuck**
Kareel: **Nicole Orth-Pallavicini**
Kalin Trose: **William Newman**
Nurse Ogawa: **Patti Yasutake**
Odan (Trill host): **Franc Luz**

Dr. Crusher falls in love with Odan, a Trillian mediator en route to settle a bitter dispute between Peliar's Alpha and Beta moons.

But while shuttling down to the surface he is mortally wounded by a marauding ship; in surgery his "Dr. Beverly" is shocked to find a parasite living inside him. Her surprise is compounded when she learns that Odan himself is the parasite occupying the host body in a joint symbiotic arrangement the Trill have used for generations.

As the dispute grows more intense, Riker volunteers to be Odan's host while a replacement is sent. Although Riker's human body adjusts to its new "co-tenant" Dr. Crusher cannot accept the first officer as her lover. Odan agrees to stay away.

The moons' delegates are just as uneasy about the situation, but Odan convinces them he can be trusted. Finally Dr. Crusher decides she can accept Odan, even in Riker's body, and they spend one more night together. Odan then settles the political dispute in a marathon session that greatly weakens Riker's body.

Dr. Crusher removes Odan to save Riker's body; both recover well. Then the expected Trill host body replacement arrives only to turn out to be female.

Crestfallen, Beverly admits she can't take Odan's constant changes. The two do, however, exchange vows of love before he leaves.

Crusher and Ogawa (Patti Yasutake) prepare a new host for Odan.

Another tale that could only be told in science fiction, Horvat's script gives Gates McFadden a rare chance to show Beverly as a woman of passion, and even dallies with homosexuality (more precisely, asexuality) until the doctor admits she is unable to accept Odan in a female form.

Marvin Rush, director of photography since season three, became the first of three in-house staffers in a row to get a turn in the director's chair. Rush started out on the original *WKRP in Cincinnati* as a camera operator before moving on to low-budget films and sitcoms such as *Dear John* and *Frank's Place*, where he caught the eye of the TNG staff. He recalls that much of his effort went into helping Franc Luz and Jonathan Frakes establish a continuity for Odan—and into disguising McFadden's seven-month pregnancy. James Cleveland McFadden-Talbot, her first son, would be born over the hiatus on June 10 in Los Angeles—a well-timed delivery.

In a nice echo of the workout scene from "The Price" (156), we now see Beverly talk to Deanna about her new lover. The scene is played out in the ship's barbershop, where we meet another Bolian barber, as in "Data's Day" (185) and "Ensign Ro" (203). An uncredited Robert Harper played the speaking role of Lathal Bine, representative from Peliar Zel's Beta moon.

The large shuttle seen here—named the *Hawking* for American physicist Stephen F. Hawking—is not new; it is the original full-scale set, little seen due to its piecemeal construction history ("Coming of Age"/(119).

THE MIND'S EYE

Production No: 198 ▪ Aired: Week of May 27, 1991
Stardate: 44885.5 ▪ Code: mi

Directed by **David Livingston**
Teleplay by **Rene Echevarria**
Story by **Ken Schafer and Rene Echevarria**

GUEST CAST
Ambassador Kell: **Larry Dobkin**
Taibak: **John Fleck**
Lieutenant O'Brien: **Colm Meaney**
Governor Vagh: **Edward Wiley**
Computer Voice: **Majel Barrett**

En route to a vacation and seminar on Risa, La Forge is kidnapped by Romulans as part of a complex plot to split the Federation-Klingon alliance.

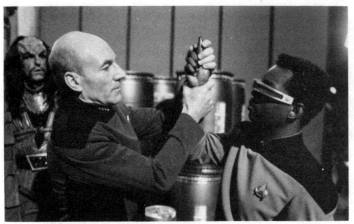

Picard disarms the mind-controlled La Forge and the Romulan assassination plot.

While he is gone, Klingon Ambassador Kell comes aboard the *Enterprise* to investigate a Klingon governor's charge that Starfleet is aiding rebels fighting for independence on his colony. La Forge, who returns with false memory implants of his Risa trip, and Data work to show that phaser rifles seized by Governor Vagh are really Romulan replications. Their work does little to change Vagh's mind, though, especially when a shipment of arms is detected being beamed from the ship.

The cargo was beamed over by La Forge, who is being mind-controlled by the Romulans. The engineer's next task: assassinate Vagh and split the Federation-Klingon alliance.

Kell, ostensibly the cool-headed mediator, turns out to be the Romulan sympathizer manipulating La Forge. Data, meanwhile, has been tracking strange E-band emissions and finally discovers what is going on, and warns Picard, who knocks La Forge's phaser fire astray just in time. Vagh is furious, but even more so when Data explains the story.

Kell's quick asylum request is refused by Picard and he uneasily departs in Governor Vagh's custody, while Troi sits down to the painful task of helping La Forge regain his memory.

Line producer David Livingston had come from ABC way back in February 1987 to be production manager for the "Farpoint" pilot (101–102). He got a powerful story for his first shot at directing: a retelling of *The Manchurian Candidate* that foreshadowed the mounting Klingon civil war that would reach its climax at season's end. It features a chilling depiction of Geordi's reprogramming aboard a warbird and the first use of his VISOR as the camera's point of view since season one's "Heart of Glory" (120).

Livingston, an unabashed fan of *The Manchurian Candidate*, tried unsuccessfully to get someone from the movie to appear in this episode as an extra. There's even an homage camera shot in which the possessed O'Brien is shot in Ten-Forward.

Geordi's preference for guitar music on his lonely ride is an echo from his dinner date with Leah Brahms in "Galaxy's Child" (190). His Shuttlepod 7 is the *Onizuka* from "The Ensigns of Command" (149), formerly Shuttle 5, which was seen earlier as the *El-Baz* in "Time Squared" (139).

For some time Rick Sternbach had played with various designs for a phaser rifle, and when it was at last needed for this show Livingston made the final choice. And the first TNG look at the Klingon and Romulan transporter beams occurs here. The Klingon beam is a quick solid red wipe from top to bottom with a few residual gold sparkles; the Romulans use a green beam that dissolves rapidly with little shimmer.

The reality of the new Klingon Empire is artfully brought home when Vagh longs for the old days when an insurrection could be violently put down. Curiously, Krios may be a Klingon colony fighting for independence, but somehow it is also involved in a centuries-old civil war with Valt Minor, as seen in "The Perfect Mate" (221).

IN THEORY

Production No: 199 ■ Aired: Week of June 3, 1991
Stardate: 44932.3 ■ Code: it

Directed by **Patrick Stewart**
Written by **Joe Menosky and Ronald D. Moore**

GUEST CAST
Ensign Jenna D'Sora: **Michele Scarabelli**
Keiko O'Brien: **Rosalind Chao**
Lieutenant O'Brien: **Colm Meaney**
Ensign McKnight: **Pamela Winslow**
Guinan: **Whoopi Goldberg**

Data takes one more step on the road to understanding humanity when a shipmate, Jenna D'Sora, begins to view him as more than a friend.

The two had grown close while studying a dark-matter nebula, the *Enterprise*'s latest assignment. After getting mixed advice from his friends when she comes on to him, Data decides to pursue the relationship and creates a special program to provide a guide to love. He and Jenna have their ups and downs, and eventually his true nature gets through to her: his seemingly artificial behavior is, of course, artificial.

Meanwhile, a Class M planet in the nebula suddenly winks out and then reappears. Data theorizes that the nebula causes pockets of deformed matter that phase out anything they contact, and with his ship's vital areas endangered, Picard orders the *Enterprise* out of the nebula.

But the starship is too large to sense and dodge the pockets, so the captain pilots a scout shuttlepod himself to relay back course directions. His craft is nearly lost, but the ship breaks clear at last.

That crisis over, Jenna tells Data she now realizes she went from one unemotional boyfriend to another who was even more so and now she wants to break the pattern. He agrees and erases his special program without a second thought.

Following up on Jonathan Frakes's lead, Patrick Stewart became the second cast member to direct an episode. The story chosen for Stewart's debut was a no-fail Data show by Ronald D. Moore and Joe Menosky that confronted questions about the android and love that TNG had backed away from in "The Ensigns of Command" (149).

Television SF watchers will recognize Michele Scarabelli as Sam Francisco's wife Susan on *Alien Nation*. A name for Pamela Winslow's character had been mentioned during the Paxan affair in "Clues" (188). Among the uncredited extras were Ritt Henn as the alien bassoonist, Phil Mallory as the French horn player, Gary Baxley as engineer Ensign Thorne, and Georgina Shore as the ill-fated Lieutenant (j.g.) Van Mayter.

The O'Briens turn out to be a musical family with Keiko on clarinet and Miles on cello ("The Ensigns of Command"/149). Meanwhile, Data is seen to have learned to play the oboe and the flute as well as the violin (149, 171, 245, 262); his cat, first seen in "Data's Day" (185), gets the name Spot here (see notes, "Birthright, Part I"/242). Longer-term Trek notes include Saurian brandy (repeated in "Bloodlines"/274), referred to in 1966's "The Enemy Within," among others; milk from a targ, the Klingon boar that can either be a pet (106) or food source (134); and transparent aluminum, subject of some necessary historical meddling by Scotty and McCoy in *Star Trek IV*. Also, this story's shuttlecraft was the *Voltaire*.

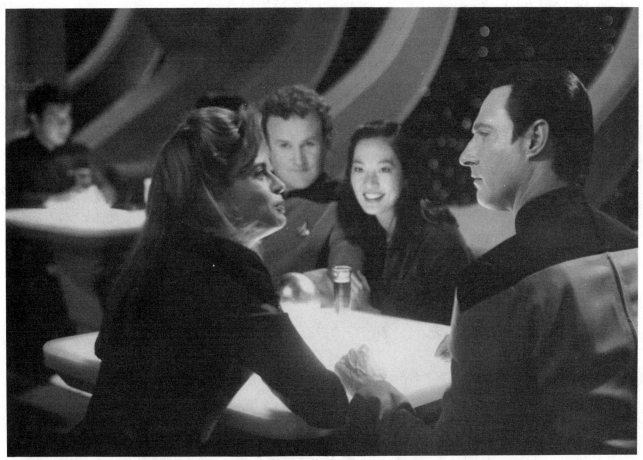

Jenna D'Sora (Michelle Scarabelli) decides Data is the man for her.

REDEMPTION

Production No.: 200 ■ Aired: Week of June 17, 1991
Stardate: 44995.3 ■ Code: rd

Directed by **Cliff Bole**

Written by **Ronald D. Moore**

GUEST CAST
Gowron: **Robert O'Reilly**
Captain Kurn: **Tony Todd**
Lursa: **Barbara March**
B'Etor: **Gwynyth Walsh**
K'tal: **Ben Slack**
General Movar: **Nicholas Kepros**
Toral: **J. D. Cullum**
Guinan: **Whoopi Goldberg**
Klingon First Officer: **Tom Ormeny**
Computer Voice: **Majel Barrett**
Commander Sela: **Denise Crosby**

In his role as Arbiter of Succession, Picard returns to the Klingon homeworld to oversee Gowron's installation as emperor. The captain also urges Worf to confront Gowron over his family's discommendation.

En route, the starship is intercepted by a Klingon vessel bearing Gowron, who informs Picard that a faction of the Empire, led by the family of the dead Duras is mounting a rebellion against his throne. Picard refuses to get involved, though: he won't risk dragging the Federation into a Klingon civil war.

In turn, Gowron refuses to restore Lieutenant Worf's family honor, citing the need to shore up his own power. Worf's younger brother, Kurn, wants to join the rebellion against Gowron, but the lieutenant persuades him not to do so—the family will back Gowron, for now.

Then Duras's bastard son, Toral, makes a surprise claim to the throne, backed by his powerful family, including Duras's sisters. But Picard, knowing full well their Romulan ties, rejects their claim to the throne.

As Worf again presses Gowron to restore his

Worf gets a moving farewell when he resigns to fight in the Klingon civil war.

Klingon traitors: B'Etor (Gwynyth Walsh), Toral (J. D. Cullum), and Lursa (Barbara March).

family name, Duras's forces ambush them; only Kurn's timely appearance saves them from defeat.

Gowron is installed as leader, and restores Worf's honor. Feeling the tug of his heritage, the lieutenant resigns his Starfleet commission.

Meanwhile, members of the Duras family meet with their Romulan backers, who include a woman who looks amazingly like Tasha Yar. . . .

Opening the final chapter of the Klingon trilogy that began with "Sins of the Father" (165) and "Reunion" (181), Ronald D. Moore's epic provided this season's cliffhanger: Worf's departure from Starfleet to fight alongside his brother and Gowron to preserve the Klingon Empire. The return of Denise Crosby, already hinted at in "The Mind's Eye," would not be explained until the conclusion that launched season five.

Also returning were actors Robert O'Reilly ("Reunion"/181) and Tony Todd ("Sins of the Father"/165); with his rise in stature, Gowron has upgraded his Bird-of-Prey *Buruk* for the *Bortas,* a Vor'cha-class attack cruiser. Barbara March is the wife of Alan Scarfe ("Data's Day"/185, "Redemption"/200-201).

Guinan continues to be full of surprises, as she again proves to be no slouch with a weapon, a skill we first saw in "Night Terrors" (191); she actually tops Worf's score on the phaser range.

We learn that the UFP-Klingon alliance treaty includes a pledge of mutual defense. And we are told that Worf's son, Alexander, who first appeared in "Reunion" (181), is already having a hard time on Earth, foreshadowing his return next season in "New Ground" (210). Gowron's father is M'Rel—though once again, Duras's name is used for his family in place of Ja'rod, as in "Sins of the Father" (165). A script description that was not included in the show's dialogue reveals that K'tal is the longest-serving member of the Klingon High Council, which here is given eight members besides him.

Bob Blackman's costume designs include a revealing bustline for the Duras sisters' standard Klingon outfit that quickly came to be known among fans as "Klingon kleavage"—but those on the show attest that, like Ricardo Montalban in *Star Trek II,* neither actress used chest padding.

And for the truly trivial: note the use of "kellicams" as the Klingonese unit of distance (established in ST III) is renewed here (see "A Matter of Honor"/134), and Movar's title, "general"—the first ever non-naval rank used for a Romulan.

Notes

1. *Star Trek: The Official Fan Club Magazine,* Oct./Nov. 1991, p. 4.

2. *Star Trek: The Official Fan Club Magazine,* Dec. 1990/ Jan. 1991, p. 3.

PRODUCTION STAFF CREDITS—FOURTH SEASON

(In usual roll order; numbers in parentheses refer to episode numbers.)

Casting:(*) Junie Lowery-Johnson, C.S.A.; Ron Surma

Main Title Theme: (*)Jerry Goldsmith, (*)Alexander Courage

Music: *** Jay Chattaway (179, 197, 199); (*)Ron Jones (all odd-numbered episodes, 175–195 except 179); (*)Dennis McCarthy (all even-numbered episodes, 176–200)

Director of Photography: ***Marvin Rush (EMMY NOMINEE: cinematography, series: "Family" [178]

Production Designer: **Richard D. James (EMMY NOMINEE with art staff: art direction, series: "The Best of Both Worlds" Pt. 2 [175]

Editor: *Tom Benko, ACE (177, 180, 183, 189, 192, 195, 198); ***J. P. Farrell (175, 178, 181, 184, 187, 190, 193, 196, 199); *William Hoy (186); **Bob Lederman (176 with Stephen Tucker, 179, 182, 185, 188, 191, 197, 200); Stephen Tucker (176 with Bob Lederman, 194)

Unit Production Manager: ***Merri D. Howard (+)

1st Asst. Director: ***Chip Chalmers (176); ***Brad Yacobian (all odd-numbered episodes, 175–199); Doug Dean (all even-numbered episodes, 178–200)

Second Asst. Director: *Adele G. Simmons

Costume Designer: ***Robert Blackman (EMMY NOMINEE: costume design, series: "Devil's Due" [187]

Set Decorator: **Jim Mees

Visual Effects Supervisor: (**)Robert Legato (+) (all odd-numbered episodes, 175–199 except 189) (EMMY CO-NOMINEE with FX crews: special visual FX: "The Best of Both Worlds" Pt. 2 [175]); (**)Dan Curry)(+)(all even-numbered episodes, 176–200 except 192); *Gary Hutzel (+) (189); ***Ron Moore (+) (192)

Senior Illustrator/Technical Consultant: (*)Rick Sternbach

Scenic Artist Supervisor/Technical Consultant: (*)Michael Okuda

Make-up Designed and Supervised: (*)Michael Westmore (TWO-TIME EMMY NOMINEE (with crew): makeup, series: "Brothers" [177], "Identity Crisis [192]

Visual Effects Coordinator: ***Ron Moore (all even-numbered episodes, 176–200 except 192); ***Gary Hutzel (all odd-numbered episodes, 175–199 except 189)

Set Designer: ***Gary Speckman

Assistant Art Director: Andy Neskoromny

Original Set Design: (*)Herman Zimmerman

Original Starfleet Uniforms: (*)William Ware Theiss

Script Supervisor: (*)Cosmo Genovese

Special Effects: (*)Dick Brownfield

Property Master: (*)Joe Longo (all odd-numbered episodes, 175–199); (*)Alan Sims (all even-numbered episodes, 176–200)

Construction Coordinator: (*)Al Smutko

Assistant Scenic Artist: (***)Cari Thomas (dropped Assistant beginning 190)

Hair Designer: Yolanda Toussieng

Hair Stylist: ***Rita Bordonaro [Bellissimo after 191] (175–196); Bill Howard (175); Kim Santantonio (176–98); NONE on (200)

Makeup Artists: **Gerald Quist, ***June Abston-Haymore

Sound Mixer: *Alan Bernard, C.A.S. (EMMY WINNER: sound mixing, series: "The Best of Both Worlds" Pt. 2 [175]

Chief Lighting Technician: ***Buddy Bowles

First Company Grip: ***Bob Sordal

Costumers: **Mandy Chamberlin (all even-numbered episodes, 176–200); **Kimberly Thompson (all odd-numbered episodes, 175–199); Charles Evan Drayman (all odd-numbered episodes, 175–197); David Roesler (199); ***David Page (174, 178); Carol Kunz (182, 200); Maurice Palanski (even-numbered episodes from 184–198, except 182)

Visual Effects Associate: David Takemura (175–200 except 180, 191)

Music Editor: ***Gerry Sackman**

Supervising Sound Editor: **(*) Bill Wistrom (EMMY CO-WINNER: sound editing, series: "The Best of Both Worlds" Pt. 2 [175]**

Sound Editors: ***James Wolvington; *Mace Matiosian; *Wilson Dyer (EMMY CO-WINNERS: sound editing, series: "The Best of Both Worlds" Pt. 2 [175]**

Post Production Sound: **(*)Modern Sound**

Production Associate: **(*)Susan Sackett**

Production Coordinator: **(*)Diane Overdiek**

Post Production Associate: *****Terry Martinez, ***Heidi Julian (+), ***Wendy Rosenfeld**

Pre-Production Associate: **(***)Eric Stillwell (+)**

Casting Executive: **(*)Helen Mossler**

Stunt Coordinator: **(***)Dennis Madalone (+) (all except 176, 182, 184–187, 190–191, 195–196, 198)**

Research Consultant: **(***)Richard Arnold (uncredited first two seasons)**

Lenses and Panaflex Cameras: **(**)Panavision**

Special Visual Effects: ***(*)Industrial Light and Magic (ILM) a division of Lucasfilm Ltd.**

Additional Motion Control Facilities: **(*)Image "G"**

Video Optical Effects: **(*)The Post Group**

Special Video Compositing: **(*)Composite Image Systems**

Editing Facilities: **(*)Unitel Video**

Prosthetic Electronics: **Michael Westmore II (177, 180)**

Choreographer: **Gates McFadden (+) (185)**

Lasers Provided by: **Laser Media Rentals (193)**

The number of * denotes a returning company or staffer's initial season of credit in that position; ( ) denotes they are an original credited or co-credited person in that position; a (+) following indicates prior TNG work in another position.

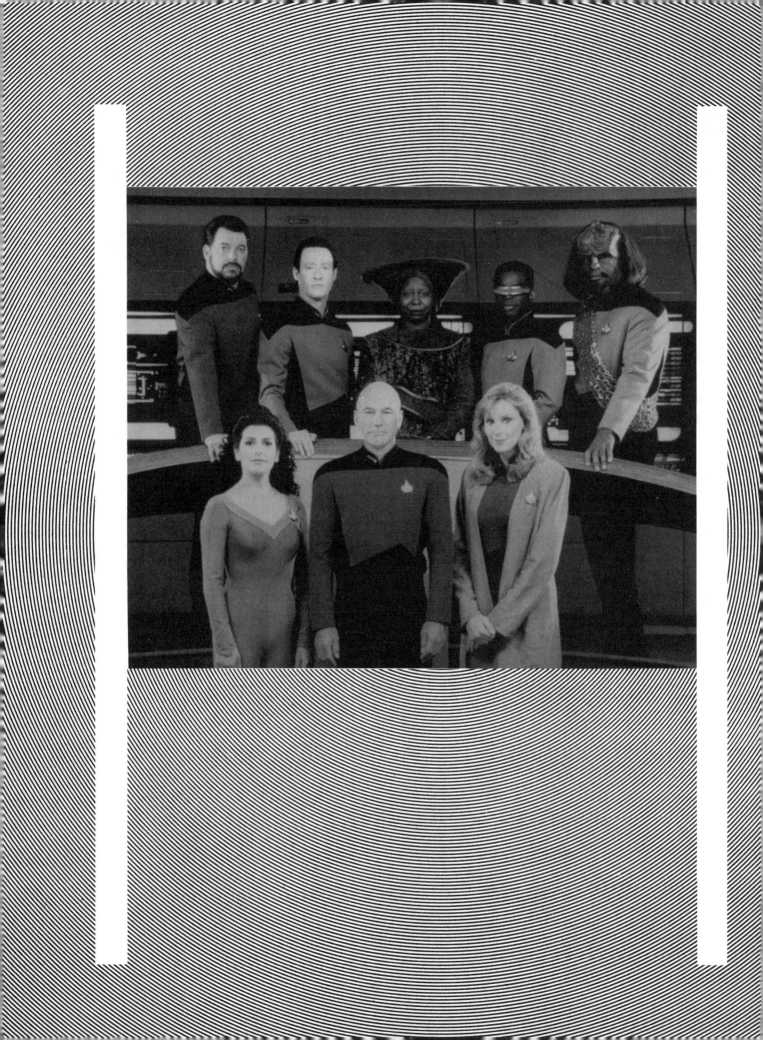

FIFTH SEASON

The fifth year of TNG would provide

more than its share of high points—and yet prove to be the show's saddest as well. The series enjoyed its share of the hoopla as *Star Trek*'s year-long twenty-fifth anniversary celebration climaxed in September, but that joy was overshadowed by the death of the Great Bird of the Galaxy on October 26, 1991, after a series of strokes.

Even though the debate will undoubtedly rage forever as to which Trek generation was better, both in its time and afterward, one thing is certain: buoyed by the two-part Spock episode "Unification" (207–208) and the anniversary celebrations during the November 1991 sweeps period, TNG's Nielsen ratings hit an all-time Trek high. In the key demographic group of men age eighteen to forty-nine the show received a rating of 14.6 against prime-time competition, with the composite for both sexes not far behind. Astoundingly, that rating left other major TV series in the dust. TNG beat *60 Minutes* (10.7), *Coach* (11.6), *Roseanne* (12.7), *Cheers* (12.8), and even *Monday Night Football* (13.9).

173

Fifth-season cast portrait (*opposite*); the departed
Wil Wheaton would guest-star twice.

In other words, as Matt Timothy of Paramount's research department put it, "If we were a network show we'd be showing up in the Nielsens' Top Ten every week."

TNG's ever-increasing popularity showed up in other ways as well. Echoing what happened on the old *Batman* TV series, more and more Hollywood stars began to seek guest spots on the show. Following in the footsteps of Corbin Bernsen, Bebe Neuwirth, Jean Simmons, and Mick Fleetwood in past seasons, distinguished guests in year five included Kelsey Grammer of *Cheers* and Paul Winfield, with Robin Williams, Elliott Gould, John Goodman, Christopher Lloyd, and others waiting in line. The fifth season, though, would be the first in which Q would not appear. "We had a couple of stories in development, but they just didn't work out," Rick Berman said.

One of the major reasons for the show's continuing success was stability in the ranks. For the first time, TNG's upper echelon stayed relatively unchanged all season long. Berman, Michael Piller, and Jeri Taylor retained their titles while Ronald Moore and Joe Menosky were promoted to coproducer. For a time they were joined by Herbert J. Wright, a veteran of the very first season who was coaxed back aboard for six episodes (213–218) before leaving again. His replacement was Peter Allan Fields, a veteran of *Columbo* and, with Piller, the short-lived *Helligan's Law*. Fields was invited to join the staff as an executive script consultant after writing the fourth-season Lwaxana Troi episode, "Half a Life" (196). On the production side, Peter Lauritson, David Livingston, and Wendy Neuss all returned, with unit production manager Merri D. Howard filling in on one show, "Power Play" (215), and receiving credit as a line producer.

Such was the closeness of the fifth year's writing staff that when mid-season burnout set in during the fall and neither staff nor freelancers seemed to have a new story idea, Piller offered his house in Mexico as the site of a weekend retreat to recharge their creative batteries. That weekend's brainstorming sessions provided the basis for a string of six episodes that closed out the season, from "The Outcast" (217) through "I, Borg" (223), with only one exception: "Imaginary Friend" (222).

The weekly episodes were being turned out for basically what they cost in 1987 dollars, according to Berman. "Aside from the salaries going up and the cost of living raises, we're still doing the show with the same budget—no more for sets or special effects. But," he added, "after five years we are spending it much more efficiently than we did in 1987."

For Season Five, a new "captain's jacket" was designed for Patrick Stewart.

REDEMPTION II

Production No.: 201 ■ Aired: Week of September 23, 1991
Stardate: 45020.4 ■ Code: r2

Directed by **David Carson**
Written by **Ronald D. Moore**

GUEST CAST
Commander Sela: **Denise Crosby**
Commander Kurn: **Tony Todd**
Lursa: **Barbara March**
B'Etor: **Gwynyth Walsh**
Toral: **J. D. Cullum**
Gowron: **Robert O'Reilly**
Captain Larg: **Michael G. Hagerty**
Admiral Shanthi: **Fran Bennett**
General Movar: **Nicholas Kepros**
Lieutenant O'Brien: **Colm Meaney**
Lieutenant Commander Christopher Hobson:
Timothy Carhart
Guinan: **Whoopi Goldberg**
Kulge: **Jordan Lund**
Hegh'ta Helmsman: **Stephen James Carver**
Ensign Craig: **Clifton Jones**

Having made good on his decision to leave Starfleet and fight at Gowron's side in the Klingon civil war, Worf begins to suspect Romulan involvement in the conflict when Duras's faction remains strong despite the loss of most of its weaponry to raids.

Picard finally decides to cast aside his noninterventionist stance. He advocates exposing Romulan support of the rebellious clan because a Duras victory would pose a threat to the UFP-Klingon alliance.

After winning approval for a nonaggressive blockade, Picard deploys a fleet along the Neutral Zone. His crew spreads out to lead the task force as the starships are joined by an active tachyon web, which will enable them to detect even cloaked warbirds. While Worf is kidnapped and tortured, Data faces his own test of command before a skeptical crew. He finally wins them over when his apparent disobedience to Picard helps plug a hole in the Federation's defenses the Romulans were about to exploit.

Exposed, the Romulans withdraw, leaving the Duras sisters helpless. They flee, leaving Toral behind as Gowron at last assumes leadership of his empire.

Worf, realizing he belongs to two different cultures, decides his place is aboard the *Enterprise*. Picard and crew are left to wonder how the late Tasha Yar could have borne Sela, the half-human Romulan commander—said to be Tasha's daughter—who led the operation.

Michael Piller said he initially thought of using the saga of the Klingon Empire and Worf as third season's cliff-hanger, but the Borg epic began to take shape at that time and he shelved the Klingon idea for a year. He praised Ronald Moore's treatment of the Klingons—here and in "Sins of the Father" (165) and "Reunion" (181)—calling them probably the most-explored alien culture in Trek.

"I've come to think of Part One as Shakespearean-style royal drama, *I, Claudius*-type intrigue at the highest levels," Piller said. "Here we add[ed] Data's command dilemma and the subplot of Sela that Denise Crosby came to us with." Data's leadership skills had already been tested on a smaller scale, of course, when he evacuated Tau Cygne V in "The Ensigns of Command" (149).

"In all of our two-parters, we always end up writing the conclusion after we return from hiatus," Berman recalled, and then deadpanned: "It's something we kind of look forward to over the summer!"

It was fitting that David Carson was chosen to direct this episode in which Sela is revealed to be Tasha's daughter; he, after all, had directed "Yesterday's Enterprise" (163), in which Tasha was sent back in time in the first place. Guinan's interest in Tasha Yar here was set up by that earlier episode's final sequence, where she asked Geordi about the late security chief. We learn

Sela (Denise Crosby) confirms the unbelievable: she's Tasha's daughter.

here that Sela is twenty-three, born a year after the 1701-C was retrieved twenty-four years ago—which works out to 2344, as reckoned with "The Neutral Zone" (126)—and that Tasha was killed in an escape attempt after four-year-old Sela turned her in. Chris Hobson is a longtime friend of Ron Moore; *Sutherland* extras "Keith" and "Terry" are his brothers. A clue is also given to the duration of the UFP-Klingon alliance when Picard says the Romulans have been undermining it for "over twenty years," in contrast to fifty-three years of no Federation-Romulan contact ("The Neutral Zone"/126).

Practically all of the staff's stockpiled ship designs make an appearance here in the Starfleet armada, including the Nebula-class *Sutherland*, Data's command, NCC-72015 (previously seen as the *Phoenix* in "The Wounded" (186). Riker's command, the *Excalibur*, is of the Ambassador class, like the 1701-C, and the USS *Tiananmen* commemorates the central Beijing square that was the scene of a bloody Chinese populist uprising in 1989.

DARMOK

Production No.: 202 ■ Aired: Week of September 30, 1991
Stardate: 45047.2 ■ Code: dm

Directed by **Winrich Kolbe**
Teleplay by **Joe Menosky**
Story by **Philip Lazebnik and Joe Menosky**

GUEST CAST
Tamarian First Officer: **Richard James**
Lieutenant O'Brien: **Colm Meaney**
Captain Dathon: **Paul Winfield**
Ensign Robin Lefler: **Ashley Judd**

The *Enterprise* tries for the eighth time in a century to contact the Children of Tama, a peaceful, well-intentioned advanced race whose language is indecipherable. Their words translate as descriptive phrases of people and places.

When the two races fail again in their attempt to understand each other, the Tamarians beam Picard and their own captain Dathon to a rugged planet nearby. The Tamarian ship blocks all attempts by the *Enterprise* crew to beam up Captain Picard.

A wary Picard, realizing Dathon means him no harm, accepts help to survive the night. He's still trying to fathom the Tamarian's purpose when the two are forced to combine their efforts to fight a predatory electromagnetic creature.

Above, Riker and the Tamarians dicker over their captains' safety and almost go to war when the starship makes a concerted effort to rescue Picard.

That attempt ends in failure, but not before Picard's momentary dematerialization allows the magnetic creature to critically injure Dathon. Finally Picard catches on: the Tamarians speak in abstract narrative images based in folklore. "Darmok and Jalad at Tenagra" learned to understand each other by facing a common foe—just like "Picard and Dathon at El-Adrel."

A second rescue attempt by the *Enterprise* succeeds in saving Picard from the creature, but the Tamarians are ready to open fire until the *Enterprise* captain speaks to them, praising their late leader. Contact having been successfully established, Picard is left to wonder if he would knowingly sacrifice his life for the sake of making contact with another race.

Picard and the ill-fated Dathon (Paul Winfield) learn to communicate against a common enemy.

Joe Menosky, who would leave the staff at season's end for a sabbatical in Italy, drew high praise from Michael Piller for the work he did bringing to life this episode, which Piller said had the longest gestation period of any episode during his tenure. The inability to communicate had been the central theme of a story by Philip Lazebnik, but it was Menosky who worked out the Tamarians' language of allusion and metaphor. He also changed the story's focus from a complex and confusing "ant farm" visit to an exploration of the two strong commanders, Picard and Dathon.

Ashley Judd, the youngest sister of Wynnona of the singing Judd family, makes her debut here as Ensign Lefler. She will pick up a first name and a love interest in "The Game" (206). We also learn that Data has met some 1,754 different races in his twenty-six years with Starfleet.

Outdoor scenes were shot over two days near the Bronson Caves, an area off the canyon below the famous Hollywood sign. Legato said the glowing creature, portrayed by stunt extra Rex Pierson, was realized with a less expensive version of the *Terminator 2*-type melting effects. Going from tape to film and back again, the creature was shot against a blue screen on fast video and developed on film 10 stops over the exposure.

Though its name is unseen, the *Magellan* shuttlecraft debuted here, giving the series a long-sought larger shuttle whose miniature matched its full-scale set. And in one of the series' rare effects bloopers, phaser fire is seen erupting from the forward photon torpedo launcher.

ENSIGN RO

Production No.: 203 ■ Aired: Week of October 7, 1991
Stardate: 45076.3 ■ Code: er

Directed by **Les Landau**
Teleplay by **T. Michael Piller**
Story by **Rick Berman and Michael Piller**

GUEST CAST
Ensign Ro Laren: **Michelle Forbes**
Keeve Falor: **Scott Marlowe**
Gul Dolak: **Frank Collison**
Orta: **Jeffrey Hayenga**
Transporter Officer: **Harley Venton**
Barber Mot: **Ken Thorley**
Admiral Kennelly: **Cliff Potts**
Guinan: **Whoopi Goldberg**
Computer Voice: **Majel Barrett**

After Bajoran extremists attack a Federation colony, Ensign Ro, a troubled young Starfleet officer, comes on board the *Enterprise*. The crew resents her presence: Ro was court-martialed after disobeying orders on an away team mission that led to eight deaths.

Starfleet Admiral Kennelly has pardoned Ro, who is also Bajoran, hoping she can help persuade the militant Bajoran leader Orta to call off the raids and agree to resettlement. The Bajorans were displaced from their home world by the Cardassians some forty years ago.

Already uneasy at Ro's presence, Picard angrily confines the ensign to quarters after she gets his away team taken hostage while tracking Orta. But Picard soon learns the Bajorans were not responsible for the raid on the Federation colony. Guinan then befriends Ro and persuades the ensign to reveal Kennelly's secret reason for sending her on the mission to Picard: in return for her freedom, Ro is secretly to offer Orta arms and ships, then allow his vessel to be destroyed by a Cardassian ship once he comes out of hiding. Kennelly will order the *Enterprise* not to interfere, in order to protect the peace treaty with the Cardassians.

Picard allows the plan to proceed, but with a twist: the Cardassians destroy an empty ship. At first furious, Kennelly is shocked to find the Cardassians staged the raid on the Federation themselves to enlist aid in destroying the Bajorans.

Afterward, Picard offers Ro a chance to remain in Starfleet—aboard his ship. She accepts.

This episode's roots were simple, according to Rick Berman: the show was specifically designed to introduce a sharp-edged character, an idea that had been floating around as far back as Wesley's departure from the conn seat a year earlier. "The other characters in the cast are relatively homogenous; some might even say bland," Berman explained. "So we wanted a character with the strength and dignity of a Starfleet officer but with a troubled past, an edge." The introduction of a strong woman often embroiled in conflict and her acceptance by the fans and writers was "one of our greatest achievements of the season," Michael Piller added. Michelle Forbes was asked back to play the new recurring character after making a strong impression as Timicin's daughter Dara in "Half a Life" (196).

Actor Harley Venton's character, a transporter officer, gets no on-screen name in either appearance, but he is named Collins in the script for this show and Hutchinson eight shows later, in "Hero Worship" (211).

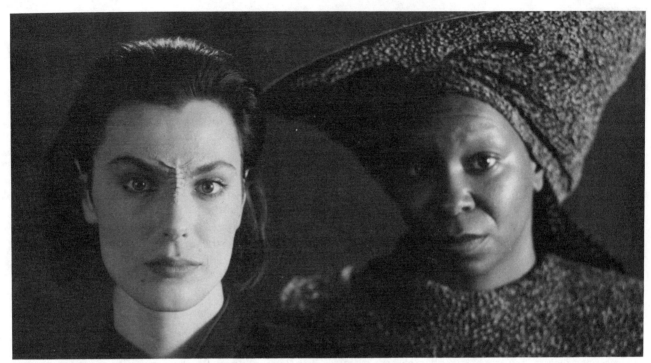

The troubled Ro (Michelle Forbes) finds a friend in Guinan (Whoopi Goldberg).

Though it was not known at the time it was written, this episode would lay much of the groundwork used for the new *Deep Space Nine* series, set aboard an abandoned Cardassian mining station in the Bajoran system. Here we learn that Bajor was annexed forty years ago (the DS9 pilot reveals it was occupied for twenty more earlier), that Ro served on the *Wellington* ("11001001"/116), that she is not the only Bajoran in Starfleet ("The First Duty"/219), and that she was forced at age seven to watch her father be tortured to death—a later story point ("Preemptive Strike"/276). Also, the Cardassian warship is christened the Galor class here.

The Bajorans, Berman added, were not modeled on any one real-life ethnic group: "The Kurds, the Palestinians, the Jews in the 1940s, the boat people from Haiti—unfortunately, the homeless and terrorism are problems [in every age]."

Scenes of the Bajoran encampment were shot in one day in Bronson Canyon near the area used in the preceding episode. Michael Westmore's subtle Bajoran makeup makes use of a nose-bridge piece reminiscent of those worn by actors who play Ornarans and Brekkians in "Symbiosis" (123).

SILICON AVATAR

Production No.: 204 ▪ Aired: Week of October 14, 1991
Stardate: 45122.3 ▪ Code: Si

Directed by **Cliff Bole**
Teleplay by **Jeri Taylor**
Story by **Lawrence V. Conley**

GUEST CAST
Dr. Kila Marr: **Ellen Geer**
Carmen Davila: **Susan Diol**

Riker and an away team are helping a group of colonists survey their new home when they are suddenly attacked by an old nemesis: the Crystalline Entity. All but two of the colonists and the away team are eventually rescued by the *Enterprise*.

Dr. Kila Marr, on the trail of the destructive alien ever since her son Renny was killed on Omicron Theta, now joins the starship in a hunt for the entity. Blaming Data for her son's death because his "brother" Lore lured the entity to Omicron Theta, Marr is ice-cold to the android until she learns he has the stored thoughts of the colonists—including her son. Through Data—who can even mimic his voice—she is able to relive her son's last few months of life.

Meanwhile, she and Picard clash over how to treat the Entity once it is contacted: the captain wants to try talking to it first, arguing the creature may not know it is killing. Marr simply wants revenge.

They lure the Entity with graviton pulse emissions, and the moment of truth arrives. The starship and the entity appear to be communicating—until Marr coolly and quietly raises the frequency of the pulse. The emissions shatter the entity.

Outraged, Picard can barely contain himself, but back in her quarters, Marr is strangely calm. She asks Data to talk like her son again, repeating that she "did it for him." As dispassionate as ever, Data tells her that Renny would be sad that his mother had ruined her career for his sake.

Just when the writers had decided on no more sequels and no more "cannibalizing," as Jeri Taylor put it, along came this premise by free-lancer Lawrence V. Conley, who took a bus down from Oregon to pitch the idea. "And of all the characters to bring back, who'd have thought the Crystalline Entity?" Taylor said. "But the *Moby-Dick* premise of this obsessed woman whose son's consciousness was stored in Data was too good to pass up."

It didn't hurt that the staff loved the title, Taylor adds, even though "no one ever knew exactly what it meant." One meaning of "avatar" is "the appearance on earth of a god in bodily form," but Taylor prefers another meaning: "a repository of knowledge," referring to Data.

The pastoral opening scenes of the Melona IV colony before its destruction were shot in a day at the Golden Oaks Ranch, also known as the Disney Ranch, in the Santa Clarita Valley north of Los Angeles.

The Entity's destruction, though, was accomplished by adding eighteen-inch miniature trees to the foreground after the live filming of the fleeing colonists. The light beam was animated on computer later, Rob Legato said, but the "sand trap" was actually a four-foot-wide tarp spread along the ground with air shot up from under it through the mesh. As with its first appearance, the Entity itself was generated entirely by computer.

DISASTER

Production No.: 205 ■ Aired: Week of October 21, 1991
Stardate: 45156.1 ■ Code: di

Directed by **Gabrielle Beaumont**
Teleplay by **Ronald D. Moore**
Story by **Ron Jarvis and Philip A. Scorza**

GUEST CAST
Keiko O'Brien: **Rosalind Chao**
Lieutenant Miles O'Brien: **Colm Meaney**
Ensign Ro Laren: **Michelle Forbes**
Marissa: **Erika Flores**
Jay Gordon: **John Christopher Graas**
Patterson: **Max Supera**
Ensign Mandel: **Cameron Arnett**
Lieutenant (j.g.) Monroe: **Jana Marie Hupp**

Riker and Data seal off survivors from the Crystalline Entity.

As Captain Picard is playing host to three young winners of a shipboard science contest, a catastrophe strikes the ship, causing violent power failures, total disruption of communications, and an almost complete shutdown of its systems.

On the bridge, Troi is shocked to find herself in command and facing a momentous decision; the disaster has weakened the magnetic containment field surrounding the ship's antimatter pods. An explosion could occur at any moment. Ensign Ro argues she must separate the saucer section immediately, while O'Brien points out that they have no way of knowing if anyone is still alive in Engineering.

On a ship in crisis, Worf delivers Keiko's baby.

A pitchman might best describe this plot as "Star Trek Meets *The Poseidon Adventure*," but Ronald D. Moore's teleplay as usual didn't miss many chances to let all of the regular characters grow by placing them in a fish-out-of-water predicament—especially Picard, who's trapped in a turbolift with three children, and Troi, who is forced to make life-and-death command decisions. Michael Piller remarked that his only hindsight regret was in seeing Ro "lose a rough edge" in her infant character development by apologizing so easily to Troi.

As usual in Hollywood, twins played the newborn Molly here and later ("Power Play"/215) before little Hanna Hatae took over the role a year later ("Rascals"/233) and into DS9. Beverly's drama coaching of Geordi from *The Pirates of Penzance* harks back to her arts roots (see notes, "Nth Degree"/185). And we learn that O'Brien's father with the roving eye ("Family"/178) is named Michael, while Keiko's father is Hiro.

In Ten-Forward, Riker, Data, Worf, and Keiko O'Brien, who is pregnant, treat the injured while Geordi and Dr. Crusher find themselves trapped in a cargo bay and threatened by a radioactive fire. And Captain Picard, his leg broken, is trapped in a damaged turbolift with three very frightened children.

While Troi struggles to come to a decision regarding saucer separation, Riker and Data decide to leave Ten-Forward for Engineering, where they will attempt to restore power. After being trapped in an access tube by an electrical current, Data is forced to sacrifice his body—but not his head—to allow them to continue. Meanwhile, Keiko shocks Worf by going into labor.

Picard and the three children attempt to reach safety as Dr. Crusher and La Forge decide their only hope of extinguishing the fire is to blow the airlock.

Riker reaches Engineering and uses Data's head to tap into the ship's control circuits, where he notes the failing pod field in the nick of time. Troi, seconds away from jettisoning the drive section, is overjoyed when power is restored. Picard and the children are rescued, La Forge and Crusher escape the cargo bay, and Keiko, with Worf's assistance, gives birth to a baby girl.

THE GAME

Production No.: 206 ■ Aired: Week of October 28, 1991
Stardate: 45208.2 ■ Code: gm

Directed by **Corey Allen**
Teleplay by **Brannon Braga**
Story by **Susan Sackett, Fred Bronson, and Brannon Braga**

GUEST CAST
Ensign Robin Lefler: **Ashley Judd**
Etana Jol: **Katherine Moffat**
Lieutenant Miles O'Brien: **Colm Meaney**
Nurse Alyssa Ogawa: **Patti Yasutake**
Cadet Wesley Crusher: **Wil Wheaton**
Ensign: **Diane M. Hurley**

During his first visit back aboard since entering the Academy, Wesley Crusher falls for a young engineering ensign, Robin Lefler, while the rest of the crew seem to fall for a new interactive video game that is worn over the eyes like antique eyeglasses and rewards the player with a pleasurable sensation.

Riker has brought the game back from his latest trip to Risa, and it proves so popular that Wesley and Robin begin to get the creeps. It seems as if the others are playing it all the time.

First step to mental addiction: Etana (Katherine Moffat) shows Riker her "game."

Indeed they are. Sensor scans show that the game induces a chemical release in the brain that leads to psychological addiction and interrupts higher reasoning processes. All of the crew members are affected except Data, who was mysteriously "injured" shortly after Riker brought the game on board. Wesley and Robin find the android, but cannot reactivate him. They decide to fake addiction to avoid suspicion. Shortly thereafter, Etana Jol, Riker's "date" on Risa, appears. She had passed on the game as part of a plan to conquer the Federation one starship at a time. She now orders an all too compliant crew to begin distributing the game to other vessels.

The crew soon catches on to Wesley and Robin's deception; they capture and convert Robin, who tells them where to find Wesley. As they're about to force him to play the game, Data emerges carrying a neuro-optic burst device. Its flash reverses the game's effects, robbing Etana of her would-be foot soldiers just in time.

Braga's first assignment on staff was to polish this comment on game addiction, which Susan Sackett and Fred Bronson, who wrote "Ménage à Troi" (172), had pitched the year before. "Wesley's come home and his family's out to get him" is how Braga summarized his more sinister treatment. He made a conscious effort to make Wesley "a little hipper," showing him as a ladies' man and a cadet capable of pulling a practical joke or two. Michael Piller, pleased with the treatment, said it also marked the birth of a good writer. "If you can get away with having Troi describe how to eat chocolate for thirty-five seconds so that it doesn't slow down the story, then you're doing something."

Pleased with Ashley Judd's first outing as Lefler ("Darmok"/202), the staff had been looking for a vehicle in which to bring her back, and this story seemed perfect. A hoped-for third appearance ("The First Duty"/219) didn't work out, though.

Wesley's Academy uniform—as did Haro's ("Allegiance"/166)—did not yet have the class rank pips established in "The First Duty." Jol's Ktarians were mentioned again ("The Game"/206, "Birthright, Part I"/242, "Timescape"/251, "Liaisons"/254, "Phantasms"/258, and *Generations*—the last as a Kirk-era reference), while actress Moffat turned up as a Bajoran widow later on DS9's "Necessary Evil." Troi's chocolate habit was not new (see notes, "The Price"/156).

UNIFICATION I

Production No: 208 ■ Aired: Week of November 4, 1991
Stardate: 45236.4 ■ Code: u1

Directed by **Les Landau**
Teleplay by **Jeri Taylor**
Story by **Rick Berman and Michael Piller**

GUEST CAST
Spock: **Leonard Nimoy**
Perrin: **Joanna Miles**
Capt. K'Vada: **Stephen D. Root**
Klim Dokachin: **Graham Jarvis**
Senator Pardek: **Malachi Throne**
Proconsul Neral: **Norman Large**
Romulan No. 1: **Daniel Roebuck**
B'Ijik: **Erick Avari**
Admiral Brackett: **Karen Hensel**
Sarek: **Mark Lenard**
Soup Woman: **Mimi Cozzens**
Computer Voice: **Majel Barrett**

Picard is shocked to learn that the legendary Vulcan scientist and ambassador, Spock, appears to have defected to the Romulan Empire.

While traveling to Vulcan, where Spock's equally legendary father, Sarek, lies near death, the captain learns that Spock may be working toward rejoining the Vulcan and Romulan peoples, who split aeons ago when the Vulcans adopted logic as the cornerstone of their civilization. Sarek's human wife, Perrin, reveals her bitterness at Spock's continued estrangement from his father, especially in her husband's last days. Picard is soon saddened to hear that Sarek has died.

After securing a cloaked Klingon ship and disguising themselves as Romulans, Picard and Data venture on to Romulus in the hope of meeting Spock's contact, Pardek, an aging peace advocate now back in favor. Neral, also an apparent reformer, has been elected proconsul.

Meanwhile, Riker and the crew track a Vulcan deflector stolen by the Ferengi. The search leads them to a ship junkyard, whose manager is surprised when several Vulcan vessels turn up

missing. Encountering an unidentified ship at one of the vanished ship berths, the *Enterprise* fires a warning shot at the mystery vessel—which promptly self-destructs.

On Romulus, Picard and Data are discovered and taken hostage, but their captors turn out to be members of Pardek's Romulan underground who help them, finally, to meet Spock.

If any doubts remained that TNG had become a worthy sequel to its namesake after five years, even the most skeptical diehard had to admit that Leonard Nimoy's presence as Spock quashed them. There had always been rumors that more of the original cast would turn up following De Forest Kelley's appearance in the pilot, and scripts had actually floated around to that effect. Tracy Tormé, for example, had been signed to do a second-season opener called "Return to Forever," bringing the movie-era Spock together with the Spock of the twenty-fourth century through the Guardian of Forever time portal from 1966's "City on the Edge of Forever." But, during the Writers Guild strike that summer, talks with Nimoy fell apart just as the outline was being finished, and the project never went any further.[1]

But things had changed in the intervening three years. Nimoy, an even hotter property than before, thanks to his success as a director of *Star Trek III* and *IV* and *Three Men and a Baby*, could not afford to ask much less than a salary that by itself would have soaked up most of the episode's budget. As *Star Trek VI: The Undiscovered Country* went into planning, Rick Berman said, the key turned out to be an idea of Paramount president Frank Mancuso's—"to somehow find a way to lock the two together" during Trek's silver anniversary.

On his deathbed, Sarek (Mark Lenard) tells Picard of his love for Spock.

Berman recalled that he and Nimoy talked about story ideas. After that "we structured a deal with him: he got very little, a little more than scale [union salary minimum]. But with Leonard as executive producer of *Star Trek VI*, what you had in essence was a cross-promotion. It made everybody happy."

Star Trek VI director Nick Meyer was brought in to discover ways to bridge references between the generations in his movie script and in "Unification," since the motion picture filmed long before the episode did. "Nimoy loved the idea of making slight references in the future" to the Kirk era, Berman recalled. The recent filming of the movie helped in other ways, too: the movie's Klingon Bird of Prey bridge and other sets on Paramount's Stage 5 were used for Picard and Data's cloaked ship in both segments.

Michael Piller was to have written the teleplay for both parts, but the time squeeze and the shift in production order proved too demanding and he offered Part I to Jeri Taylor. At first disappointed to do only the story setup, she had no idea how much a part of her life "Unification" would become. When Pocket Books called to suggest a novelization of the historic meeting of the Trek eras, Taylor—who wanted to break into books—asked for the job.

"The hitch was that I had thirty days to do it!" she said. "Yes, September 1991 was a month I'll never forget. I was writing Part One, I was writing the novel—it was like an endless finals week. You live on coffee, you're wired, you shut yourself off from family and friends: I had no other life but 'Unification'!"

Dokachin is the first speaking Zakdorn seen since Kolrami ("Peak Performance"/147), while actor Throne was twice a guest on Spock's other two-parter, 1966's "The Menagerie"—as Commodore Mendez and the original Keeper's voice in the first pilot "The Cage." Lenard provided the first death of a sixties-era Trek figure, after he and Miles had of course graced TNG's "Sarek" (171). Large took time out from *Phantom of the Opera* to play Neral; he would return as a Cairn ("Violations"/212) and a Kobherrian (DS9's "Duet").

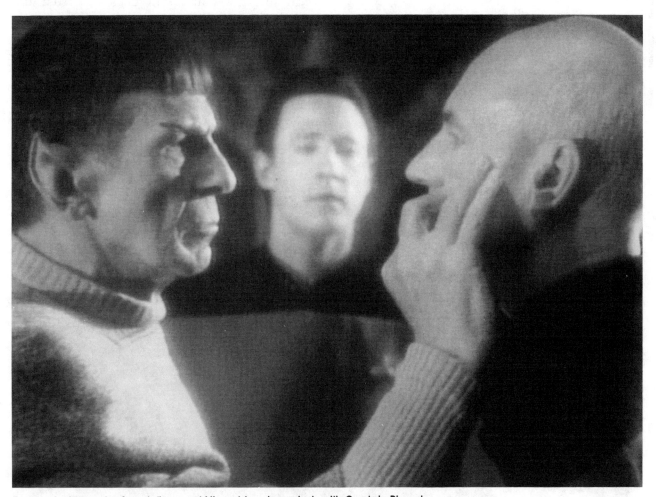

Former Ambassador Spock (Leonard Nimoy) touches minds with Captain Picard.

UNIFICATION II

Production No. 207 ■ Aired: Week of November 11, 1991
Stardate: 45245.8 ■ Code u2

Directed by **Cliff Bole**
Teleplay by **Michael Piller**
Story by **Rick Berman and Michael Piller**

GUEST CAST
Spock: **Leonard Nimoy**
Captain K'Vada: **Stephen D. Root**
Senator Pardek: **Malachi Throne**
Proconsul Neral: **Norman Large**
Romulan No. 1: **Daniel Roebuck**
Omag: **William Bastiani**
Romulan No. 2: **Susan Fallender**
Commander Sela: **Denise Crosby**
D'Tan: **Vidal Peterson**
Amarie: **Harriet Leider**

Having found Spock on Romulus, Picard must perform the uncomfortable task of telling the ambassador his father has died. The news, combined with Picard's attempt to fulfill his friend Sarek's requst by telling Spock of his father's love, breaks the tension between the two. Spock then reveals he is indeed undertaking an unauthorized mission to pursue the reunification of the Vulcan and Romulan peoples. While Data begins working to crack the Romulans' computer net, Picard confides to the ambassador that he mistrusts the Romulans.

Meanwhile, the trail of the missing Vulcan ships leads Riker to a Ferengi smuggler, who finally admits that Romulans are involved. Number One contacts Picard, who has met Proconsul Neral in person and still does not trust the Romulan's intentions.

Soon they find Spock has indeed been double-crossed: a proposed peace envoy of Vulcan ships is just a ploy staged by Commander Sela, Picard's Romulan nemesis in the Klingon civil war. She and Neral plan to send the stolen ves-

Betrayed by Romulan Senator Pardek, Data is captured.

sels filled with Romulan troops as a "Trojan horse"—a sneak attack to conquer Vulcan.

Sela captures Spock and the two disguised *Enterprise* crew members, but can't force the Vulcan to publicly endorse the phony peace mission. She then reveals a holotape in which the ambassador does just that. Left unguarded in her office, Spock and Data send a coded signal to Riker and use a holotape of their own to escape Sela and her guards.

When Riker intercepts the "peace envoy," the Vulcan ships are destroyed by their cloaked escorts to remove any trace of the mission. Spock decides to stay on Romulus and work with the underground for real peace. At the last he bids his father good-bye by sharing Sarek's previous mind-meld with Picard.

Pardek (Malachi Throne) and Commander Sela (Denise Crosby) mastermind a plot to destroy Vulcan.

Part 2's production number precedes that of the opening segment because it was filmed first to accommodate Leonard Nimoy's schedule. During his five days of work, the set was closed to visitors, although Rick Berman recalled that the week was like most others on the series. Nimoy has said that his TNG experience was a sentimental yet hectic reminder of his days of weekly television, a stark contrast to the more leisurely pace of motion picture production.

Michael Piller used the unification of Germany as his basic thematic metaphor but was disappointed that his teleplay couldn't provide more chemistry in the Picard-Spock scenes. "We got some good moments, and Leonard was splendid," he said, "but I thought a lot of it was flat, talky, and dull." The historic meeting of Data and Spock was one of his favorite scenes, though, and he took issue with fans who ridiculed the idea of a Romulan invasion force of only three ships bound for Vulcan. "That's the only way you *could* do it, with a Trojan horse," he said. "You couldn't launch an all-out attack."

With two episodes to spread the cost over, the size and scope of the Romulan street-office complex built on Stage 16 rivaled the Victorian London holodeck set in "Elementary, Dear Data" (129). Production designer Richard James also re-dressed the cargo bay—last seen as the control room of the attack cruiser *Bortas'* in "Redemption" (200)—to the Quaylor II piano bar seen here.

"One of the show's major strengths," observed Rick Sternbach,

"is how they can put these Tinkertoy set pieces together again and again in different ways and repaint them and come up with completely different looks."

The Vulcan ships were originals, built by Greg Jein from an original design by Sternbach, with a *Reliant*-like feel featuring long, pointed engine pods and a bridge-over-hull look. Urged to go for a more alien non-Starfleet look, Sternbach said he based the design on a central core surrounded by a wraparound circular generator.

Notable among the nonspeaking actors in the Qualor II bar scene—which includes Riker's Trek play on words, "Andorian Blues"—were Jerry Crowl as yet another background Antican, Shana O'Brien and Heather Long as Omag's women, Leonard Jones as the Zakdorn waiter, and April Rossi as an extra known as Space Hooker.

The title of this most unusual of all TNG episodes carries more than the usual layers of meaning. The hoped-for reunion between Romulans and Vulcans is only the first of many "unifications." Symbolically carried out through Picard's mind-meld with Spock, it extends not only to a posthumous reconciliation between Sarek and his estranged son but indeed to both incarnations of Gene Roddenberry's vision, *Star Trek* and *Star Trek: The Next Generation.* When this episode is viewed in tandem with *Star Trek VI,* it's clear the torch has been passed, and any breach that may have existed between productions and between fans has been closed.

A MATTER OF TIME

Production No.: 209 ▪ Aired: Week of November 18, 1991
Stardate: 45349.1 ▪ Code: ma

Directed by **Paul Lynch**
Written by **Rick Berman**

GUEST CAST
Dr. Hal Mosely: **Stefan Gierasch**
Berlingoff Rasmussen: **Matt Frewer**
Ensign Felton: **Sheila Franklin**
Female Scientist: **Shay Garner**

While trying to reverse the nuclear winter–type effects caused by a crashed asteroid on Penthara IV, the *Enterprise* is visited by a time-traveling historian from twenty-sixth-century Earth, Berlingoff Rasmussen.

The officers' initial suspicions give way to

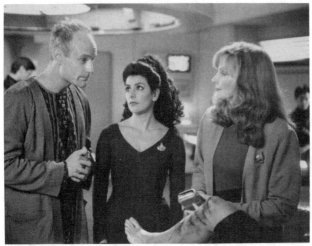

Supposed "time traveler" Rasmussen (Matt Frewer) doesn't impress everyone aboard.

impatience when Rasmussen asks repeatedly to see their "artifacts" and to have questionnaires filled out. Troi is convinced he is hiding something, but most crew members go along with his teasing and his annoying cheeriness.

The ship's first try at helping Penthara IV only makes matters worse; then La Forge comes up with an alternative plan that will either clear the atmosphere or burn it off entirely, killing every living thing on the planet. Desperate for help, Picard turns to Rasmussen, but the time traveler says he can't divulge the future. When the Pentharans agree to Geordi's plan so does Picard. Luckily, it works.

Rasmussen quickly moves to leave after the planet is saved, but Picard first demands he be allowed to search the time pod for items reported missing by his crew. The time traveler agrees to let Data enter because he can be ordered not to divulge any secrets of the future, but once the two are inside the pod, Rasmussen pulls a phaser and reveals he is really from the twenty-second century. He appropriated the real twenty-sixth-century time traveler's craft and came forward in time to gather trinkets—which now include Data—that he could claim to have invented.

But a suspicious Picard had Rasmussen's phaser deactivated. Helpless, Rasmussen is stranded in the twenty-fourth century when the pod's timed return mechanism whisks it away without him.

Rick Berman said he'd always been interested in the idea of someone traveling through time to steal Data, and he got the chance to do it in this, his second and last turn at TNG storytelling. "It's like imagining what Newton could have done if he'd had a calculator," Berman said. *Max Headroom's* Matt Frewer played it to the hilt, but one wonders about the outcome had Berman gotten to cast Trek fan Robin Williams, who had to turn it down while making *Hook.*

The effort to replace Wesley with a female conn officer had of course ended with the addition of Ro, but beginning here and for five shows this season, Sheila Franklin's Ensign Felton filled in as well. Though never spoken aloud, the name Felton appeared in all of the scripts she turned up in "New Ground," "Hero Worship," "The Masterpiece Society" and "Imaginary Friend" (210, 211, 213, and 222).

Among the tidbits of Trek information provided here: a phaser on maximum stun is required to stun Data; the Federation was founded after the Romulan War "The Outcast" (217); and phasers, medical forcefields, and the warp coil were all invented after the twenty-second century.

NEW GROUND

Production No.: 210 ■ Aired: Week of January 6, 1992
Stardate: 45376.3 ■ Code: ng

Directed by **Robert Scheerer**
Teleplay by **Grant Rosenberg**
Story by **Sara Charno and Stuart Charno**

GUEST CAST
Helena Rozhenko: **Georgia Brown**
Alexander: **Brian Bonsall**
Dr. Ja'Dar: **Richard McGonagle**
Kyle: **Jennifer Edwards**
Ensign Felton: **Sheila Franklin**
Computer Voice: **Majel Barrett**

Worf and Troi find newfound common ground over raising Alexander.

On the eve of testing the Soliton Wave, a historic new drive system, Worf receives an unexpected visit from his foster mother, Helena Rozhenko, and his son, Alexander. To Worf's surprise, Helena tells him that he must take custody of his son for the boy's own good.

The lieutenant soon discovers what his mother is talking about: he finds Alexander has been lying and acting up in class. After Worf threatens to send him to a rigorous Klingon school, Troi points out Alexander may be feeling neglected after his mother's death and his father's virtual abandonment of him.

When the Soliton Wave experiment goes awry and reaches power levels that could wipe out a colony in its path, the *Enterprise* must start a "backfire" effect, using its photon torpedoes. As they prepare to break up the wave, Alexander is visiting his favorite animals, unaware that the biolab is unprotected by shields. He is trapped there when the wave is penetrated; a fire breaks out in the lab, forcing Worf and Riker to rescue him.

Worf then realizes how much he would miss his son if he were sent away; Alexander agrees to remain aboard the *Enterprise*.

For the only time this season, the writing credits carried no staff names; still Michael Piller credited Ronald D. Moore with lending "a big hand" in the polishing of Grant Rosenberg's teleplay, taken from a story by TNG veterans Sarah and Stuart Charno, who wrote "The Wounded" (186).

After child actor Jon Steurer originated the role of Alexander in last season's "Reunion" (181), the slightly older Brian Bonsall—who'll best be remembered as Andy, the youngest Keaton in the later seasons of *Family Ties*—was brought in; he had the series track record desired for what was now to be a recurring role. Alexander's age became a topic of some discussion and not a little confusion when he first appeared in "Reunion" so soon after his apparent conception in "The Emissary" (146), but some clues are provided here. His birthday, the twenty-third day of Maktag, is a nice bit of trivia, but his stardate birth, 43205, falls during the time of season three's "Booby Trap" (154), only 304 stardate units after K'Ehleyr's first *Enterprise* visit and 1,041 units before the boy turns up with his mother later—although 1,000 units are generally considered to be a year. Of course K'Ehleyr's half-human makeup may have altered Alexander's maturation process from the Klingon norm.

A nice bit of continuity was provided by the Klingon legend of the fighting brothers Kahless and Morath, whose statue Worf refers to in his quarters. Kahless the Unforgettable was one of the evil images in an original-Trek episode, "The Savage Curtain," in 1969. The statue was a stock piece, but the figures "grew" Klingon ridges thanks to Michael Westmore's deft touch.

The experimental Soliton Wave glider is a re-dress of the Mars defense ships that were easily picked off by the Borg in "The Best of Both Worlds," Part 2 (175).

HERO WORSHIP

Production No.: 211 ■ Aired: Week of January 27, 1992
Stardate: 45397.3 ■ Code: hw

Directed by **Patrick Stewart**
Teleplay by **Joe Menosky**
Story by **Hilary J. Bader**

GUEST CAST
Timothy: **Joshua Harris**
Transporter Chief: **Harley Venton**
Ensign Felton: **Sheila Franklin**
Teacher: **Steven Einspahr**

The *Enterprise* is sent to check on the missing USS *Vico*, a research ship sent to explore the interior of a Black Cluster—the remains of hundreds of protostars. The cluster generates gravitational tidal waves that are capable of buffeting a starship but pose no real danger.

Data finds a lone survivor among the wreckage of the *Vico*, a boy named Timothy, who tells his rescuer an alien vessel destroyed the ship. The evidence soon indicates otherwise, however, and Troi urges Data to foster his friendship with the boy to get the real story. Timothy, meanwhile, is so impressed by Data that he takes to mimicking the android.

Picard orders his ship into the Cluster to further investigate the *Vico*'s demise, whereupon the shock waves surprisingly grow more intense.

The captain urges Timothy to recall what he can of his ship's destruction, but the boy steadfastly refuses to change his story of alien invaders, until Data tells him androids do not lie. Timothy then breaks down and says he destroyed the *Vico* by accidentally touching a console.

Incredulous, Picard, Troi, and Data convince him that cannot be, that his action was just a coincidence. Timothy has trouble believing them, however, especially when he hears more and more power being ordered to shields; he tells Data his ship did the same thing. As a huge wave approaches the *Enterprise*, Data finally realizes that all shields should actually be lowered: they're magnifying the waves' effect. Timothy decides to drop his android act, but he and Data vow to stay friends anyway.

This big Data–little Data episode provided a charming turn not only for the android but for ship's counselor Troi as well, expanding on the depiction of her duties. "Jeri Taylor and I say that since we've been here the counseling scenes have become much more numerous and realistic," Michael Piller said. "But that expertise doesn't come from practicing—it comes from being a patron!"

We also get a rare bit of Geordi background in this story, learning of a traumatic fire he suffered through at age five before receiving his first VISOR. The scenario was originally one of the memory scenes not used in "Violations" (212).

This time around, Harley Venton's transporter officer who also appeared in "Ensign Ro" (203), is named Hutchinson in the script, although the name remains unspoken. The USS *Vico* is a new model of *Star Trek III's Grissom*, built and detailed as a wreck by Greg Jein. The Breen, one of the races suspected of having destroyed the *Vico*, were mentioned in "The Loss" (184) as a race that could not be sensed telepathically.

Data and Timothy (Joshua Harris) study the art of painting.

Violations

Production No.: 212 ■ Aired: Week of February 3, 1992
Stardate: 45429.3 ■ Code: vi

Directed by **Robert Wiemer**
Teleplay by **Pamela Gray and Jeri Taylor**
Story by **Shari Goodhartz, T. Michael Gray and
Pamela Gray**

GUEST CAST
Keiko O'Brien: **Rosalind Chao**
Jev: **Ben Lemon**
Tarmin: **David Sage**
Dr. Martin: **Rick Fitts**
Inad: **Eve Brenner**
Lieutenant Commander Jack Crusher: **Doug Wert**
Crewman Davis: **Craig Benton**
Computer Voice: **Majel Barrett**

A forced memory: Beverly Crusher views her husband's corpse with Picard.

The *Enterprise* takes aboard three Ullians, members of a race of telepathic historians who do their research by probing their subjects' long-forgotten memories. Their leader, Tarmin, is surprised by the crew's reluctance to be probed, while his son Jev is embarrassed by his father's continued attempts to gain the crew's permission. That evening Troi has a flashback to a romantic encounter with Riker—but Jev replaces Riker in her memories. As she struggles against him, she lapses into a coma.

The same thing happens to Riker, who remembers a shipboard disaster that cost a crew member's life, and then to Beverly, who is forced to recall the time years ago when Picard took her to see her late husband's body.

Picard is increasingly suspicious of the Ullians, but they protest their innocence. Troi finally comes to and readily agrees to be mind-probed by Jev about the night she slipped into a coma. This time it is Tarmin who takes Riker's place in her dreams.

The elder Ullian is taken into custody, but when Jev visits Troi, the flashback returns and she realizes he's the real mental rapist. The timely appearance by Worf and Data saves her. Researching a history of similar comas on other worlds, they had discovered Jev was the only

Ullian present when all the incidents took place.

Tarmin apologizes for his son, saying he'd thought his once-violent race had put memory rape behind it.

This story began as the second outline TNG bought from Shari Goodhartz; the first was "Night Terrors" (191). This script evolved through numerous drafts, each of which approached the rape metaphor differently. Jeri Taylor and Pamela Gray, an intern, came up with the atypical science fiction angle of mental rather than physical assault.

"We had been doing so many political shows that the success of this one reminded us that maybe we could do more with the mental side of SF, exploring the bizarre possibilities of psychological dramas," Taylor said.

Lots of memory flashbacks were generated for every major character before those of Troi, Riker, and Beverly were chosen. One alluded to Ro's yet-unexplained trouble on Garon II, mentioned in "Ensign Ro" (203), while another involving Geordi's childhood brush with fire was so popular that Joe Menosky picked it up to use in the previous episode, "Hero Worship" (211). Goodhartz's first treatment had featured Miles O'Brien as victim.

Director Robert Wiemer sought and received permission from Rick Berman to use a number of different camera tricks to set apart the bizarre memory scenes implanted by Jev, then used conservative camera work in the "reality" scenes to heighten the contrast between the two. The tricks included the use of wide-angle lenses during Beverly's flashback; at one point both Gates McFadden and Patrick Stewart are sitting on the moving dolly (rolling camera crane), generating an eerie floating effect.

After several mentions and one false start ("Where No One Has Gone Before"/106), the time of Jack Crusher's death is finally established here, albeit vaguely. Actor Doug Wert makes a brief reappearance here in a casket, after having been seen earlier in "Family" (178).

The Riker-Troi flashbacks caused a stir of their own, Jeri Taylor remembered, from fans who were disappointed that later episodes did not continue the rekindled intimacy between the two (105, 148, 184). The fans had obviously missed the point that these scenes were flashbacks. In this sequence, though, we do learn that it was Troi who decided to cool their relationship for the sake of professionalism when they learned that they had both been assigned to the *Enterprise*.

Other trivia: Keiko's grandmother was named Obachan, and Geordi got his first pet—the Circassian cat mentioned in "Galaxy's Child" (190)—at age eight.

THE MASTERPIECE SOCIETY

Production No.: 213 ■ Aired: Week of February 10, 1992
Stardate: 45470.1 ■ Code: ms

Directed by **Winrich Kolbe**
Teleplay by **Adam Belanoff and Michael Piller**
Story by **James Kahn and Adam Belanoff**

GUEST CAST
Aaron Conor: **John Snyder**
Hannah Bates: **Dey Young**
Martin Benbeck: **Ron Canada**
Ensign Felton: **Sheila Franklin**

While monitoring the progress of a neutron star's core fragment, the *Enterprise* crew is shocked to learn of an unknown human colony on Moab IV, now threatened by the fragment—and even more surprised when the residents refuse to relocate.

Their leader, Aaron Conor, explains that the colony has been genetically planned and engineered to be the perfect society. Any contact with outsiders is bound to be corrupting. Conor reluctantly agrees to let *Enterprise* officers beam down to discuss the danger posed by the fragment.

The colony's chief scientist Hannah Bates begins working with La Forge to develop a tractor beam that will be powerful enough to deflect the core fragment. When Bates must beam aboard the *Enterprise* with Geordi to continue her research, Troi stays behind, fascinated by the soft-spoken Conor. After spending the night with him, she berates herself for allowing the brief affair, knowing her Betazoid DNA would not be welcome in the genetically closed colony.

Ironically it is the VISOR of an "imperfect" blind man that inspires the needed tractor beam enhancement; but to install the equipment necessary to deflect the fragment, fifty more people from the *Enterprise* will have to beam down.

Conor reluctantly agrees to their presence. The engineers' plan works, and the fragment is diverted. But the colony's problems are far from over. Hannah, after a taste of the outside world, decides to leave. She fakes an alarm to force evacuation, but Geordi sees through her ruse. Yet despite pleas from Conor and other colonists, Bates and twenty-three others decide to leave. Conor decides he can't stop them, despite the irreparable damage their departure will cause.

Picard is left to wonder which ultimately posed the greater threat to the colony, the core fragment or his ship's "help."

Aaron (John Snyder) and Martin (Ron Canada) describe their fragile society to Troi and Riker.

In the most reasoned and focused Trek position on selective human breeding since 1967's "Space Seed," Picard echoes the classic Roddenberry-inspired argument against eugenics as dehumanizing and a detriment to free choice. Michael Piller himself took over this script after it had passed through five other writers' hands over a season and a half. He struggled mainly with the question, "What exactly *is* a genetically engineered society?"

Hannah's laboratory, once again, was built over the frame of the old two-level movie bridge set with the "science lab" set pieces in place; her computers use black-on-white, almost Macintosh-like computer visuals.

CONUNDRUM

Production No.: 214 ■ Aired: Week of February 17, 1992
Stardate: 45494.2 ■ Code: cn

Directed by **Les Landau**
Teleplay by **Barry M. Schkolnick**
Story by **Paul Schiffer**

GUEST CAST
Commander Keiran MacDuff: **Erich Anderson**
Ensign Ro Laren: **Michelle Forbes**
Kristin: **Liz Vassey**
Crewman: **Erick Weiss**

After being scanned by an unknown alien ship, *Enterprise* crew members discover both their own and their computer's memories have been selectively wiped out.

Though they can't remember their names or their functions, they've all retained the knowledge necessary to operate the ship. They grope their way to some kind of structure: Worf assumes command; Data decides he's the bartender in Ten-Forward; and Ro feels attracted to Riker, Troi even more so. Finally the ship's computer is able to provide them with name, rank, and serial number; among the bridge crew is Commander Kieran MacDuff, listed as first officer.

The computer also reveals their mission: the *Enterprise* is part of a fleet fighting a decades-old war with the Lysians. Their current assignment, to be conducted under radio silence, is to destroy the aliens' Central Command.

Picard grows concerned, though, when the Lysian vessels they meet prove no match for his ship. His conscience finally forces him to call off the attack. Angered, MacDuff tries to assume control of the ship. Worf stuns him, and the phaser blast reveals that MacDuff is actually an alien.

Dr. Crusher soon restores the crew's memories, whereupon they identify MacDuff as a Sartaaran, a race that's been at war with the Lysians for decades. Despite their skill with computers and memory suppression, his race's weak weapons technology forced their thwarted hijacking of the *Enterprise*.

One of several amnesia stories from season four, this episode was put on hold for a year and then developed into this script, which Michael Piller felt didn't quite do justice to the original and fascinating tale of drafting soldiers by rewriting their memories. Staff and fans alike, though, loved the Riker-Troi-Ro triangle that emerged here, especially the fact that all three retained the memory of their past "interactions."

In his cabin, Riker plays few notes of "The Nearness of You," the song he played for Minuet on the holodeck in "11001001" (116), and looks over his *horgah'n* from Risa, first seen in "Captain's Holiday" (167).

Curiously, while the ships of the two warring sides were not new staff designs, the Lysian command center miniature dates all the way back to season one, when it was hazily photographed as the *Edolord* over Rubicum III in "Justice" (109).

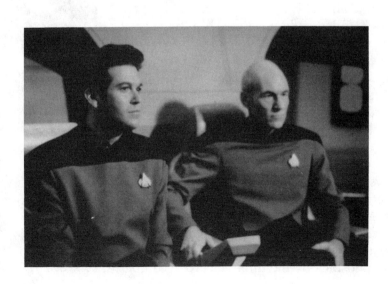

His memory erased, Picard doesn't suspect the true nature of his "Number One," Commander Kieran MacDuff (Erich Anderson).

POWER PLAY

Production No.: 215 ■ Aired: Week of February 24, 1992
Stardate: 45571.2 ■ Code: pw

Directed by **David Livingston**
Teleplay by **Rene Balcer, Herbert J. Wright, and Brannon Braga**
Story by **Paul Ruben and Maurice Hurley**

GUEST CAST
Keiko O'Brien: **Rosalind Chao**
Lieutenant Miles O'Brien: **Colm Meaney**
Ensign Ro Laren: **Michelle Forbes**
Transporter Technician: **Ryan Reid**
Computer Voice: **Majel Barrett**

After receiving an old-style distress call from a moon of Mab-Bu VI, previously thought to be uninhabited, and after learning also that magnetic storms prevent the use of the transporter, Riker, Troi, and Data take a shuttlecraft down to the moon's surface to investigate.

Stranded after the shuttle crash-lands, they are relieved when O'Brien risks his life to beam down to them. He brings along transport enhancers to enable them to beam back to the ship. As they depart, a strange cloud envelops all but the injured Riker.

Troi, Data, and O'Brien have been possessed by alien entities, who soon secure themselves in Ten-Forward with hostages—including a bewildered Keiko and little Molly—until Picard agrees to their chief demand: move the ship to the area over the moon's south pole.

The entities claim to be from the USS *Essex* and say they want only to be buried in peace. Troi, possessed by the spirit of Captain Bryce Shumar, says they were disembodied when their ship broke up over the moon two hundred years ago.

But their violence belies this story, and Picard eventually learns the truth: the entities were actually prisoners condemned to the penal colony Mab-Bu VI. They tried to possess the *Essex*'s crew and use that ship to escape—as they plan to do now with the *Enterprise* and its crew.

Taken hostage by the three, Picard accompa-

nies them to a cargo bay where the rest of the entities are beamed up. The captain then turns the tables, saying he will open the outer cargo bay doors and kill all of them, including himself, rather than allow the entities to take his crew. The entities relent, abandon their host bodies, and return to their prison.

Bearing a slight conceptual resemblance to an original-series episode, "Return to Tomorrow," another tale of alien possession, this story went through several script treatments by free-lancers before being assigned to Braga. Herb Wright brought in the ghost angle when the two teamed up for the version eventually used.

"It was supposed to be the ultimate bottle show, a tense psychological drama between Picard and the possessed Troi, crammed into one room, but it became one of the costliest of the year with the shuttle crash and the phaser fight," Braga said. "It has no socially redeeming value, but it sure is action-packed!"

"It was wonderfully directed," Michael Piller agreed, praising David Livingston for his second outing behind the camera. "That's why it was successful." Marina Sirtis finally got into some rough stuff, and Brent Spiner found an edge different from Lore's for his character as well. They and Colm Meaney invented nicknames for their "possessed" personae: Slugger, Buzz, and Slash.

Once again Planet Hell lived up to its nickname: filming spilled over an extra half-day on Stage 16, where Livingston recalled worrying about Spiner's contact lenses and where Sirtis got so dirty from the blowing sand she had to take a midday shower and get made up again.

Possessed by an alien entity, Troi terrorizes the *Enterprise*.

The crashed shuttlepod was the *Campbell*, named for pioneering science fiction author Joseph W. Campbell. Inspired by the movie *Cape Fear*, a 360-degree rotating camera was used to film the craft's interior crash scenes.

A bit of early Federation history is revealed here with the mention of the NCC-173 *Essex* and its ill-fated crew of 229. The end of service for the ship's Daedelus class is established as 172 years earlier, or 2196, and its specific loss over two hundred years prior to this episode means the Daedalus prototype was likely designed and commissioned well before the UFP's founding in 2161, as established in "The Outcast" (217). At the time of its loss, though, Starbase 12 is referred to as already in operation.

Finally, another bit of Klingon culture—their notion of spiritual possession, *Jat'yln*—is revealed here as well.

ETHICS

Production No.: 216 ■ Aired: Week of March 2, 1992
Stardate: 45587.3 ■ Code: et

Directed by **Chip Chalmers**
Teleplay by **Ronald D. Moore**
Story by **Sara Charno and Stuart Charno**

GUEST CAST
Dr. Toby Russell: **Caroline Kava**
Alexander: **Brian Bonsall**
Nurse Alyssa Ogawa: **Patti Yasutake**

Neurospecialist Dr. Toby Russell comes aboard to help treat Worf after an accident leaves the Klingon paralyzed from the waist down, but she and Dr. Crusher clash over Russell's proposal to use genetonic replication to replace his spine. Beverly considers the life-threatening procedure an unnecessary risk to her patient, who is in no danger of dying.

Worf feels that he is dead already; his shame at being helpless is so great he won't let Alexander see him. He even asks Riker to help him commit ritual suicide to avoid being pitied. Riker is torn, weighing his values against Worf's, until he learns that Klingon custom requires the son to assist in the ceremony anyway.

After Worf refuses to consider the partial mobility offered by neural implants, Beverly is shocked when Dr. Russell tempts him with her untried genetonic process. It has only a fair test

success rate and has never been tried with humanoids—and failure would mean death.

Meanwhile, during a rescue attempt, another of Russell's experimental techniques costs a patient's life. Angered, Crusher relieves her of all medical duty. But when Worf can't bring himself to ask Alexander to complete the suicide ceremony, both he and Beverly relent, and agree to try Dr. Russell's procedure.

The Klingon dies in surgery, but mourning turns to joy when a redundant Klingon body system kicks in. Worf again asks his son for help—but this time with his therapy.

This examination of medical ethics once again shows how conflict can be drawn out of the regulars using a guest star as catalyst. The story faced off not only the two doctors but Riker and Worf as well—seen here battling over Klingon ritual suicide. Picard's willingness to respect Worf's Klingon beliefs echoes his decision in "The Enemy" (155) not to force Worf to donate blood to a Romulan, but here the captain almost seems to be taking the easy way out, even given Trek's multicultural philosophy, in light of Riker's aggressive condemnation of suicide.

Seen again are the red surgical outfits used during Picard's heart surgery in "Samaritan Snare" (143). For much of the surgery sequence, Michael Dorn's photo double, Al Foster, stood in as the Klingon exo-backbone was glimpsed for the first time. We also learn about the redundancies of Klingon anatomy, discovering that Worf has twenty-three ribs, two livers, an eight-chambered heart, a double-lined neural pia matter, and of course a backup synaptic system.

Continuity with earlier Starfleet medical references was maintained with the use here of "motor assist bands" and the drugs inoprovaline in "Transfigurations" (173) and cordrazine in "Shades of Gray" (148). Other echoes of the past include Russell's ferrying

Alexander (Brian Bonsall) helps his paralyzed father choose life rather than ritual suicide.

ship, the *Potemkin,* mentioned in "Peak Performance" (147) as one of Riker's prior assignments and, in "Legacy" (180), as the last ship to visit Turkana IV. A gravitic mine, the Cardassian War leftover that does in the USS *Denver,* was referred to earlier in the Kobiyashi Maru scene in *Star Trek II.*

La Forge is seen briefly in the teaser sporting a beard—a test that the producers allowed LeVar Burton to try, once.

THE OUTCAST

Production No.: 217 ■ Aired: Week of March 16, 1992
Stardate: 45614.6 ■ Code: oc

Directed by **Robert Scheerer**
Written by **Jeri Taylor**

GUEST CAST
Soren: **Melinda Culea**
Krite: **Callan White**
Noor: **Megan Cole**

The J'naii, an androgynous race, ask the *Enterprise* for help in locating a missing shuttlecraft. An abnormality called "null space" proves to be the cause of its disappearance. Riker works to recover it with a J'naii shuttle pilot named Soren. The two become fast friends, even to the point of comparing their cultures' mating habits. Soren tells Riker that sexual preference is banned on J'naii and that all nonconformists are treated to a brainwashing "cure." Soren insists on coming along on the rescue mission with Riker, where "she" reveals the female tendencies she has always been too scared to admit.

Soren is injured on the flight, delaying their search, but now grows bolder and admits her feelings for Riker. He finds himself falling too, but they present a professional front while rescuing the shuttle and its near-dead survivors.

But after the two share a kiss at that night's celebration party, the J'naii Krite detects what's going on and takes Soren into custody with no warning. Enraged, Riker crashes Soren's "trial" and tries to defend her, but she admits her feelings in an impassioned plea for acceptance that falls on deaf ears.

Despite Picard's warnings that a rash act could ruin him, Riker tries to free her with

Worf's help, but it is too late: the "therapy" has already taken hold, and Soren renounces her feelings for him.

A bitter Riker returns to the ship and assures Picard his business on J'naii is finished.

For over twenty-five years Trek's two television series had pioneered the intelligent and fair-minded depiction of various sexes, races, and ethnic groups, including aliens. One notable and controversial exception, though, was homosexuals. With the relative freedom of expression granted TNG, various letter-writing campaigns over the years grew more and more insistent that one or more gay crew members be seen.

Jeri Taylor jumped at the chance to take on this teleplay, the first of the late-season run that emerged from the writers' Mexican weekend, and she brought to the script a real empathy for the feelings of the powerless and disenfranchised.

After the show aired, Taylor received mail from viewers who ranged all the way from fundamentalists on the religious right who thought the episode " 'should have been balanced with the other side,' whatever that means," to gays who thought the ending might be misinterpreted as "sanctioning" Soren's brainwashing therapy.

"I did get lots of thank-yous from both gay and straight people who appreciated the story as a science fiction treatment of the intolerance of choice and need as a tragedy," she said. "It really woke up the audience," Michael Piller agreed. "We didn't want to just blow off the issue by showing a same-sex couple holding hands in the corner." Added Rick Berman: "We thought we had made a very positive statement about sexual prejudice in a distinctively *Star Trek* way, but we still got letters from those who thought it was just our way of 'washing our hands' of the homosexual situation." TNG's executive producer added that he considered the letter-writing fan on any issue very rare—about one-tenth of a percent of TNG's total audience. And the massive write-in campaigns "where you receive three hundred letters with the same sentences" didn't carry as much weight as the simple individual letters.

Aside from the question of sexual preference, this story shows a maturity of another kind in dealing with Riker. He was the first regular to be out of control over an emotional attachment, other than Worf, whose actions were always explained away by his Klingon nature.

Riker brings out the forbidden "female" feelings of Soren (Melinda Culea).

A minor story throwaway line but a major point for trivia fans is the revelation that the UFP was founded in 2161. Michael Okuda, who calculated the in-house chronology of Trek events taken from series facts throughout the years, assumed the Federation was founded after the Romulan War, a century before Kirk's time, based on the statement in 1966's "Balance of Terror" that "Earth," not the Federation, fought the alien empire.

We also received a better view of the starship's *Magellan* shuttlecraft, first seen in "Darmok" (202). The J'naii shuttle *Taris Murn,* briefly seen, is the same craft used as the *Nenebek* in "Final Mission" (183) and as Rasmussen's time pod in "A Matter of Time" (209).

CAUSE AND EFFECT

Production No. 218 ■ Aired: Week of March 23, 1992
Stardate: 45652.1 ■ Code: ce

Directed by **Jonathan Frakes**
Written by **Brannon Braga**

GUEST CAST
Ensign Ro Laren: **Michelle Forbes**
Nurse Alyssa Ogawa: **Patti Yasutake**
Captain Morgan Bateman: **Kelsey Grammer**

The crew's regular poker game suddenly feels too familiar to Dr. Crusher, who experiences feelings of déjà vu that are at first puzzling and then maddening. Those feelings intensify when she is called away to treat La Forge for a minor but baffling dizziness. Preparing for bed, she hears strange voices in her cabin.

Meanwhile, the *Enterprise* is continuing to chart the Typhon Expanse when the ship's propulsion systems fail, hurling it onto a collision course with another starship that appears out of the void. Picard follows Data's advice to use the tractor beam to alter the other ship's trajectory, but the tactic fails. The ships collide, and both are destroyed. . . .

The regular poker game resumes, and this time Beverly is not alone in her feelings of déjà vu. After experiencing another cycle of destruction, she records the voices she hears in her room, which Data discovers are the echoes of their own conversations from past time loops.

As another cycle climaxes, Data plants a clue

The weekly poker game: Dr. Crusher's first clue to the Typhon Expanse's time loop.

for himself in the next time loop—recurring instances of the number 3. Realizing at the last second that the three refers to the pips on Riker's uniform and his plan to decompress the main shuttle bay to alter course, Data follows the first officer's suggestion rather than his own—and the loop is broken.

They find the *Enterprise* has been trapped for seventeen days, but Picard wonders how he will explain to the crew of the other starship, the *Bozeman,* that they have been caught for ninety years.

Braga, who said he'd always wanted to do a time-travel story without the cliché of the "screwed-up time lines," called this solo story the smoothest he had yet worked on, though it provided a challenge in drawing out the subtleties of the varying time loops. Beginning with what he called "the ultimate teaser," he was proud for once to be able to tie the poker game scene into the plot as a major point.

Kelsey Grammer became the third *Cheers* actor to enter the Trek universe—after Bebe Neuwirth in "First Contact" (189) and Kirstie Alley in *Star Trek II*—but his viewscreen scenes were all shot separately from the rest of the cast, again using the old movie bridge set re-dressed. The staff had wanted the first officer to the right of Bateman to be Kirstie Alley as Lieutenant Saavik, but the scheduling couldn't be worked out.

The USS *Bozeman* was a "new" Soyuz-class ship: the *Reliant* miniature from *Star Trek II* minus the roll bar and with new sensor turrets, docking port, and bridge. Originally the plan was to make the ship a 1960s-era, pre-movie Constitution-class starship, but budget demands put an end to that when the costs of creating and filming ship, props, and costumes were added up.

The enormous main shuttle bay was depicted for the first time in any form. It was actually a tabletop model built by Michael Okuda on which the two shuttlecraft were named—in lettering too small to be legible—the *Berman* and the *Piller!*

THE FIRST DUTY

Production No.: 219 ▪ Aired: Week of March 30, 1992
Stardate: 45703.9 ▪ Code: fd

Directed by **Paul Lynch**
Written by **Ronald D. Moore and Naren Shankar**

GUEST CAST
Boothby: **Ray Walston**
Cadet First Class Nicholas Locarno: **Robert Duncan McNeill**
Lieutenant Commander Albert: **Ed Lauter**
Captain Satelk: **Richard Fancy**
Superintendant Admiral Brand: **Jacqueline Brookes**
Cadet Third Class Wesley Crusher: **Wil Wheaton**
Cadet Second Class Jean Hajar: **Walker Brandt**
Cadet Second Class Sito: **Shannon Fill**
Cadet: **Richard Rothenberg**

En route to deliver the commencement address at Starfleet Academy, Picard learns that a horrifying accident has occurred. While rehearsing for the graduating ceremonies, a member of Wesley Crusher's five-person flight squadron has been killed.

A routine inquiry into the accident finds discrepancies between the cadets' filed flight plan and their testimony. Nova Squadron leader Locarno reluctantly reveals that the dead squadron member, Joshua Albert, panicked and caused the mishap. This news comes as a painful blow to his already grieving father.

But in a squadron meeting later, Wesley is angry. Locarno lied, he says. Joshua Albert

Picard (*below*) consults his old Academy mentor Boothby the gardener (Ray Walston) after the tragedy that threatens Wesley's young career. *Opposite, bottom:* The charismatic Locarno (Robert Duncan McNeill) tries to lead Wesley and Sito (Shannon Fill) astray by encouraging them to cover up their flight accident. *Top:* Picard helps Wesley choose the truth.

wasn't to blame. But the squadron leader makes an impassioned plea for the four remaining team members to stick together, pointing out that their careers will be over if they reveal the whole truth.

The next day, Wesley's testimony is countered by surprise evidence from a satellite. But to the surprise of both Picard and Beverly, he refuses to expain the discrepancy. Returning to the *Enterprise* after a talk with his old mentor, Boothby, Picard realizes that the accident occurred because Nova Squadron was practicing the Kolvoord Starburst, a spectacular exhibition of stunt flying banned for over a century, that would have made Locarno a living legend.

Picard confronts Wesley with the truth and says he will reveal it if Wesley doesn't. Despite a last-minute entreaty by Locarno to stand by his team, an anguished Wesley agrees that his first duty is to the truth. Locarno is expelled, while Wesley and his mates must repeat the past year and face the difficult time ahead.

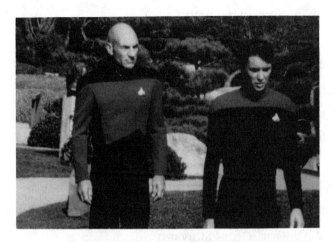

Satelk is the first Vulcan captain seen in TNG, while the presence of Cadet Sito proves that Ensign Ro is not the only Bajoran in Starfleet. While the exact date of Betazed's first participation in Federation affairs has yet to be pinned down, we do know that a Betazoid headed the Academy at least as early as Riker's years, set at 2353–2357 in the Okudagram bio files that Michael Okuda prepared for "Conundrum" (214); Picard's graduation with the "class of '27" is also included there. Earlier, the head of the academy was called "commandant" when the position was offered to Picard in "Coming of Age" (119).

The exterior views of Starfleet Academy, matted into the twenty-fourth-century Starfleet environs, were location scenes filmed one day at the Tillman Water Reclamation Plant in Van Nuys, the same site that provided the exteriors for Rubicun III in "Justice" (109). Notice the Academy flag flying half mast. Dan Curry added that to the exterior matte painting.

That little touch and the Academy seal on the flag itself were just two of many the staff threw in. The seal's equilateral triangle form, adapted by Michael Okuda from a design by Joe Senna, features the sun behind the Golden Gate Bridge in the logo's center; an animated version with the sun rising into place was considered but ultimately not used. The name "Starfleet Academy" adorns the left leg of the triangle while the bottom reads "San Francisco/MMCLXI," the Roman numerals for its founding date of 2161, the same as that of the Federation, as established in "The Outcast" (217). The right leg of the triangle bears the Academy's Latin motto, *Ex astra, scientia*," or "From the stars, knowledge"—quite a pacifist notion for what some might mistakenly regard as a military school. Okuda reports the motto is taken from that of the ill-fated Apollo 13, "*Ex luna, scientia.*"

The various sensor log tapes used in the inquiry were all computer-generated by Curry's team, including the brief tape of the cadets' ships in flight. Wesley's dorm room contains models of both an Apollo command-service module on display in the background and Kirk's original Constitution-class *Enterprise.*

The cadets' collar pips, descending among Nova Squadron from Locarno's four to Wesley's two, appear to be the same as the longer pins adorning the movie-era uniforms' white sleeve cuff. The inquiry's hearing bell was also used in the original series' official proceedings as seen in "Space Seed" and "Courtmartial." And the "Yeager Loop" maneuver pays tribute to an even earlier ancestor of TNG—Chuck Yeager, the pilot who first broke the sound barrier in 1947.

For over twenty-five years, Starfleet Academy had been talked about but never seen—until this story, developed during the writers' Mexican retreat by Ron Moore, who wound up in a philosophical argument with Michael Piller over Wesley's ultimate decision. "I thought he should choose the truth, and Ron thought he couldn't go back on his friends," Piller recalled. "Ultimately I gave the order to go with the truth—that's what I'd want my kids to do—but I think it shows how much we can get into these characters when we find ourselves debating the points they're arguing."

Boothby, of course, had twice before been mentioned by the captain—in "Final Mission" (183) and in "The Game" (206)—but was seen here for the first time. Ray Walston, immortalized forever in TV reruns as the title alien in the 1960s sitcom *My Favorite Martian,* commented that throughout his days of shooting, the cast and crew approached him with the old character's schtick of head antenna and finger-wiggling "levitation."

COST OF LIVING

Production No.: 220 ■ Aired: Week of April 20, 1992
Stardate: 45733.6 ■ Code: cs

Directed by **Winrich Kolbe**
Written by **Peter Allan Fields**

GUEST CAST
Lwaxana Troi: **Majel Barrett**
Alexander: **Brian Bonsall**
Campio: **Tony Jay**
Mr. Homn: **Carel Struyken**
Young Man: **David Oliver**
Juggler: **Albie Selznick**
Erko: **Patrick Cronin**
Young Woman: **Tracey D'Arcy**
Poet: **George Edie**
First Learner: **Christopher Halste**

After the *Enterprise* helps destroy a rogue asteroid, Troi's mother Lwaxana beams aboard and makes a surprise announcement: she is getting married—to a man she has never met!

As if worrying about her mother wasn't enough, Troi must also help Worf deal with his increasingly rebellious young son, Alexander. Matters worsen when Lwaxana persuades the young Klingon to join her in a holodeck mud bath amid a colony of artists and freethinkers, frustrating both Worf and Deanna.

Lwaxana reveals she will forgo the traditional nude Betazoid wedding at the request of her fiancé, Campio—whom she is shocked to find is stuffy and old.

Meanwhile, an increasing number of ship's systems are beginning to fail. The problem is eventually traced to metallic parasites the ship picked up after destroying the asteroid they were feeding on. In a race against time, Data barely gets the ship back to the creatures' home field and beams them away before life support breaks down, leaving him the only crew member conscious.

Disaster is soon averted, and Lwaxana is free to proceed with her wedding plans. But to her fiancé's surprise, and her daughter's delight, Lwaxana turns up at the ceremony wearing basic Betazoid—that is, in the buff—sending Campio running for home. Deanna then coaxes Worf to join her mother and Alexander for one last visit to the mud bath.

After coming on staff to fill the slot that Herb Wright's departure opened up, Peter Allan Fields created his second Lwaxana Troi tale in two years—one that truly revealed the character's "Auntie Mame" roots by pairing her up with a "corruptible" Alexander, confounding Worf and Troi alike. In fact, Michael Piller revealed that for a time the staff had toyed with the idea of a Troi-Worf relationship and had been building little moments into scripts to support that if it happened: their mutual concern with Alexander, for one, and Worf making Deanna the boy's guardian if he died during surgery in "Ethics" (216).

Tony Jay's role here as the elderly and distant Campio was not nearly as powerful as Paracelsus, the tunnel-dwelling villian he played in *Beauty and the Beast*. And only in a show like TNG could Majel Barrett as Lwaxana Troi talk to Majel Barrett as the voice of the *Enterprise* computer; that moment happens outside the holodeck before her first visit with the "little warrior."

The Wind Dancer balloon effect was simple to create, Legato explained. After filming a bowling ball without holes as if it were bouncing around, the face of a made-up clown was shot on a camera following in sync with the ball's white highlight spot, and the two images were mated.

Campio (Tony Jay) and Erko (Patrick Cronin) are shocked at Lwaxana Troi's decision to appear "au naturel," as per Betazoid wedding custom.

THE PERFECT MATE

Production No.: 221 ■ Aired: Week of April 27, 1992
Stardate: 45761.3 ■ Code: pm

Directed by **Cliff Bole**
Teleplay by **Gary Percante and Michael Piller**
Story by **Rene Echevarria and Gary Percante**

GUEST CAST
Kamala: **Famke Janssen**
Briam: **Tim O'Connor**
Par Lenor: **Max Grodenchik**
Alrik: **Mickey Cottrell**
Qol: **Michael Snyder**
Miner No. 1: **David Paul Needles**
Miner No. 2: **Roger Rignack**
Transporter Chief Hubbell: **April Grace**
Miner No. 3: **Charles Gunning**
Computer Voice: **Majel Barrett**

Kriosian Ambassador Briam arrives aboard the *Enterprise* with a peace offering from his people for the ruler of Valt Minor. The gift, Briam declares, is priceless, and is intended to end years of war between Krios and Valt Minor. Picard immediately orders the object, being delivered in a stasis field, off-limits to his crew.

En route to Valt Minor the *Enterprise* rescues two Ferengi from a shuttle in distress—an act of mercy that soon backfires when the Ferengi are caught attempting to steal the Kriosian gift. In the process, the stasis field protecting the item is shattered, revealing a beautiful and exotic woman, Kamala.

She is an empathic mesomorph, a genetic rarity among her people—such creatures are born only once every seven generations. Kamala can be what any man wants her to be. Educated to fulfill her role as peacemaker, she has been prepared from birth to bond with Valt's ruler, Alric. The Ferengi's interference has caused her to be released prematurely, and the ambassador insists she be confined to her room until Alrik arrives.

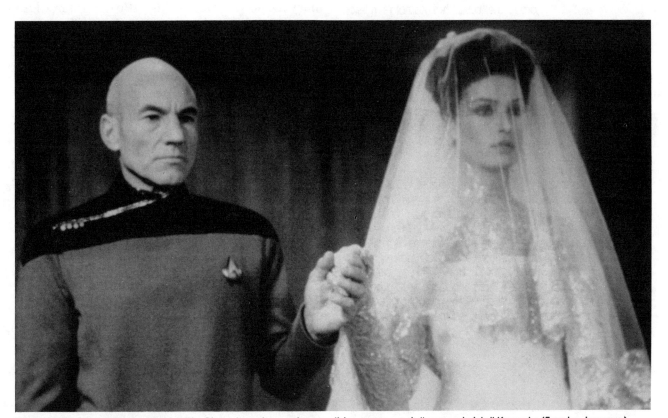

Knowing she's bonded to him for life, Picard must escort empathic mesomorph "peace bride" Kamala (Famke Janssen) "down the aisle" to marry another.

That move sets off Dr. Crusher, who complains to Picard that the entire affair smacks of prostitution. The captain gamely cites the Prime Directive, but understands the ambassador's request after seeing the effect Kamala has on his crew. When Briam is accidentally injured by the Ferengi, Picard is forced to turn to Kamala for help in performing his ambassadorial duties—and soon finds even his legendary resistance weakening. Kamala is drawn to him as well; she tells Picard he is the first man who has suggested she has value in and of herself.

Alric finally arrives and confides to Picard he cares more about treaties and trade than he does for his "peace bride." Just before the reconciliation ceremony, a sad Kamala tells Picard she has chosen to bond with him, rather than become the woman Alric expects her to be. She assures a visibly shaken Picard she'll carry out her duties nonetheless—as he will carry out his.

What could have been just another romance became a much more significant story, as this episode again used a science fiction premise to turn conventional wisdom on its ear.

"We have Beverly argue the point that Kamala's mission amounts to prostitution," Michael Piller noted. "And we have Picard taking the other tack: that whether or not we approve, we can't change or interfere with the way these people are. And if you accept Roddenberry's vision, which we are built on, you have to respect that."

The only writing pseudonym requested during Piller's tenure turned up here: "Percante" was actually his friend Reuben Leder, who disliked the rewrite done on his draft. The script included an unused optional fantasy scene in which Picard, just before the actual ceremony, daydreamed that he spoke out at the wedding to claim Kamala as his own.

For once we actually got to see the Picard-Crusher morning tea ritual referred to in "Qpid" (194), which, in its own way, shows how the two officers' relationship has matured over the years. We also learn that the young Jean-Luc spoken of in "Family" (178) hated piano lessons but briefly took them to please his mother.

The best line in the script almost went to Qol, upon his discovery in the cargo bay: "I must have lost my way—I was looking for the barbershop." But ultimately that honor belongs to a painfully aroused Riker, who wipes the sweat off his mustache after barely escaping Kamala and says, "If you need me, I'll be in holodeck four!"

IMAGINARY FRIEND

Production No.: 222 ■ Aired: Week of May 4, 1992
Stardate: 45832.1 ■ Code: im

Directed by **Gabrielle Beaumont**
Teleplay by **Edithe Swenson and Brannon Braga**
Story by **Ronald Wilderson, Jean Matthias, and Richard Fliegel**

GUEST CAST
Clara Sutter: **Noley Thornton**
Isabella: **Shay Astar**
Ensign Daniel Sutter: **Jeff Allin**
Alexander: **Brian Bonsall**
Nurse Alyssa Ogawa: **Patti Yasutake**
Ensign Felton: **Sheila Franklin**
Guinan: **Whoopi Goldberg**

Troi tries to assure an officer that the "imaginary friend" created by his little daughter, Clara, is a normal reaction to a childhood of constant change. But as the *Enterprise* prepares to explore the FGC-47 nebula, Clara's friend Isabella materializes. Soon she is getting Clara into all sorts of trouble, leading her into areas of the ship that are off limits to children, like Main Engineering and Ten-Forward.

Meanwhile, the *Enterprise* has become surrounded by strands of an inexplicable nature that are draining the ship's power. At the same time, Clara and Worf's son Alexander are becoming fast friends—until Isabella sabotages their relationship. Clara's playmate now turns even more frightening, telling the little girl that she and all of the others aboard are about to die.

Summoned by Clara's father to help, Troi tries to prove to Clara that her imaginary playmate can't hurt her—and is promptly stunned by Isabella. Picard realizes there is a connection between the energy drain his ship is experiencing and Clara's playmate, a fact soon confirmed by Isabella. She says her kind will feed off the ship's energy, rejecting Picard's offer of alternative sources. She says the ship deserves to be destroyed because of the way her friend Clara is

Picard finally learns why "imaginary" Isabella (Shay Astar) has disturbed Clara (Noley Thornton) and his ship.

treated. But ultimately she relents in the face of Clara's pleas.

As reflected in the credits, this was another script turned out after several tries by free-lancers. Braga chose to develop it in place of one of the year's abortive Q stories, and by the time it was finished, his original "negative attitude" toward the tale had turned around as much as the concept of the alien. Curious and benign in earlier drafts, Isabella took on more menacing *Bad Seed*-style traits in the finished script.

Guinan was not intended to be part of this show, but Whoopi Goldberg became available and was written in just days before filming. Originally her cloud-watching scene with Data was written for Beverly and Deanna and, later, for Guinan and Deanna. The Samarian coral fish she spies is likely from the same planet as the Samarian Sunset drink that Data prepared for Troi in "Conundrum" (214) after losing a bet. Guinan also talks of her own imaginary friend, a Tarcassian razor beast.

For the first time we hear about Geordi's parents. Both were Starfleet officers; his father was an exobiologist, and his mother a command officer, apparently once assigned to a Neutral Zone outpost.

I, BORG

Production No: 223 ■ Aired: Week of May 11, 1992
Stardate: 45854.2 ■ Code: ib

Directed by **Robert Lederman**
Written by **Rene Echevarria**

G U E S T   C A S T
"Hugh" Borg: **Jonathan Del Arco**
Guinan: **Whoopi Goldberg**

While surveying a cluster of systems for colonization, the *Enterprise* traces a distress signal to a small world, where they find crash debris and one survivor—a young Borg.

Fighting his impulse to let it die, Picard accedes to Dr. Crusher's humanitarian desire to care for the Borg. The rest of the crew are skeptical, especially Guinan, who points out that others of his kind will follow and learn of their presence if they take the young Borg aboard.

But cut off from his race's collective consciousness and influenced by the crew who help him survive and heal, the Borg known as "Third

La Forge fears for "Hugh" Borg's (Jonathan Del Arco) future.

of Five" becomes more and more of an individual. He eventually acquires a name—Hugh—and starts to refer to himself as "I" instead of "we."

His evolution affects the others, who had always viewed the Borg as an intractable, unrelenting foe. When even Guinan is thrown into doubt, Picard decides to visit Hugh himself. Assuming the role of Locutus, the captain is shocked to hear Hugh plead with him not to assimilate his "friends," like Geordi.

The captain calls off a plan to plant a virus in Hugh to disable his race, figuring that the concept of the individual could be just as effective. Hugh himself opts to return to the crash site, and his newfound friend La Forge goes with him. Will Hugh's new memory and sense of self remain intact? Hugh returns to his stoic Borg de-

meanor when others of his race arrive, but the glance he shoots Geordi at beam-up is telling: he'll remember.

The clamor for "another Borg show" had swelled ever since the third-season cliff-hanger "The Best of Both Worlds" (175–176), but the dilemma facing the production and writing team was obvious: when your all-out foe is so dangerous that you barely escape him once, what can you do for an encore? And how can you afford to film it?

Rene Echeverria's tale—Michael Piller's favorite of the season and the one he called "everything I want *Star Trek* to be,"—found answers to both questions by serving up a young Borg story that still packed a lot of emotional wallop. Robert Lederman, one of TNG's three rotating film editors since the second season, became the only new director to get a shot this year after last season's flood of rookies behind the camera.

Jeri Taylor, who provided uncredited help in polishing the script, commented that the story meant "we can never treat the Borg the same way again." Guinan may never be the same again, either; aside from Q, the Borg were about the only thing that could shatter her aloofness and calm detachment. But one by one we saw her and all the regulars, including Picard, examine their own prejudices. "Just when you think it's safe to hate the Borg," Piller says, "we make you look him in the eye and ask if you could still kill him."

THE NEXT PHASE

Production No.: 224 ■ Aired: Week of May 18, 1992
Stardate: 45092.4 ■ Code: np

Directed by **David Carson**
Written by **Ronald D. Moore**

GUEST CAST
Ensign Ro Laren: **Michelle Forbes**
Mirok: **Thomas Kopache**
Varel: **Susanna Thompson**
Transporter Chief Brossmer: **Shelby Leverington**
Parem: **Brian Cousins**
Ensign McDowell: **Kenneth Messerole**

Picard offers aid to a wrecked Romulan science ship, but the rescue mission ends in tragedy when Ro and La Forge apparently die in a transporter accident.

The two rematerialize on board the *Enterprise*

but somehow remain unseen. Ro thinks she is dead when she discovers that she can pass through walls and that others can walk through her.

She locates La Forge, who wants to find a reason other than death for their state, and they learn their presence causes chroniton particles, a harmless by-product of cloaking devices. They soon deduce the truth: thanks to an ill-fated test by the Romulans, they are cloaked!

As the *Enterprise* delivers an energy beam to the Romulan vessel to help it power up, Data attempts to clear the ship of a series of puzzling chroniton fields using an anyon beam. The android is puzzled, however, when new fields keep popping up all over the ship. Ro and La Forge are trying to get Data's attention by leaving lots of "tracks" so they can warn him of the Romulans' plan to cause a residual feedback in the energy beam and blow up the starship once it goes into warp. Their task is made considerably more difficult, though, when they encounter a Romulan who is also cloaked. Finally La Forge and Ro discover a way to leave enough chronitons to force Data into using a maximum-level spray of anyon, causing them to reappear—right in the middle of their own memorial service, and in the nick of time to save the ship.

This was supposed to be a money-saving bottle show, but like "Power Play" (215), it turned into one of the year's most expensive—with characters actually running through the walls! Actually, the walk-through effect of the cloaked characters was straightforward but time-consuming, Rob Legato reported. The actors and set pieces were filmed in second-unit shooting before a blue screen backdrop and then carefully animated into the live action.

Lots of background bits adorn this story, including the fact that Picard first met Geordi during an unspecified inspection tour and that Geordi has known Riker longer than anyone aboard. We also learn about the two-hour Bajoran death chant, and we are given their word for spirits and souls, *borhyas*. At the same time it is revealed that Worf's people view an honorable death as joyful. Riker also gets another chance to play his trombone, and Picard delivers a rare reference blooper in the script, saying Ro's troublesome incident occurred at Garon IV instead of Garon II, as in "Ensign Ro" (203) and "Conundrum" (214).

The *Goddard* is the shuttle's name here, for American rocket pioneer Robert H. Goddard, while the Romulan science vessel miniature is a re-dress of Jarok's scout ship from "The Defector" (158). The Romulan ship ejects its off-line reactor core through the top instead of the bottom, as the Galaxy-class starship does. And for the truly trivial: for the first time since "The Defector" (158) two Romulan terms of measurement are given: *melakols*, a unit of pressure, and *kolems*, a unit of engine flow or frequency. And though no captain's log is heard establishing a stardate, the one listed on Ro's death certificate is 45092.4.

Ensign Ro and Geordi regain their solid form.

THE INNER LIGHT

Production No.: 225 ■ Aired: Week of June 1, 1992
Stardate: 45944.1 ■ Code: il

Directed by **Peter Lauritson**
Teleplay by **Morgan Gendel** and
Peter Allan Fields
Story by **Morgan Gendel**

GUEST CAST
Eline: **Margot Rose**
Batai: **Richard Riehle**
Administrator: **Scott Jaeck**
Meribor: **Jennifer Nash**
Nurse Alyssa Ogawa: **Patti Yasutake**
Young Batai: **Daniel Stewart**

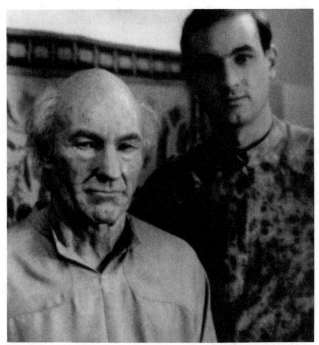

Like father, like son: Kamin and Batai (Patrick and Daniel Stewart).

While traveling between missions, the *Enterprise* encounters an unassuming-looking probe. It begins transmitting a nucleonic beam that manages to penetrate the shields and then lock directly onto Picard. The captain collapses to the deck, unconscious.

As Dr. Crusher works over him, the captain awakens to what seems to him a dream: he is on the drought-stricken planet Kataan, where he is an iron weaver named Kamin married to a young woman named Eline.

The days pass into years for him, and Picard finally accepts his new life as reality. Eline bears two children by him, the drought continues to get worse, and despite the support of his friend Batai, people laugh at his high-tech plans to provide relief.

Back on the *Enterprise* bridge, though, only a few minutes have passed, though Picard still lies unconscious. Growing more concerned for his captain's safety, Riker orders Data to break the beam. Its disruption nearly kills Picard, and it must be restored as the crew waits in frustration.

Meanwhile, the aging "Kamin" watches his children grow, his wife and friend die, and his planet dry up. Finally the truth is revealed: the Kataan sun is going nova, but without the means to evacuate, the planetary leaders have decided to gain immortality by launching records of their world in a probe and thus revealing their

story to some future historian. The probe, Picard realizes, is the very same one the *Enterprise* encountered what now seems to him like years ago. And he is the historian the Kataan were looking for.

To his bridge crew's relief, Picard awakes to the staggering realization that he has lived over thirty years in less than half an hour.

Combining the warmth of "Family" (170) with a science fiction plot twist worthy of "Yesterday's Enterprise" (163), this story proved to be one of the simplest and at the same time most mind-boggling episodes TNG would ever attempt. Here Picard experiences all the things Starfleet could never give him: a wife and children, stability, and a home.

The warm cinematography, designed to subtly imply the oncoming supernova of the Kataan sun, almost rivals that of "Family." What's amazing here, though, is that the exterior scenes of the Ressick community were all filmed on Stage 16 *indoors;* Marvin Rush's lighting can be credited for the beautiful illusion. There is one brief moment of location shooting, however, a pickup scene filmed after principal photography had closed: Picard's hiking scene, augmented by a matte-painting vista, was shot in nearby Bronson Canyon, also seen in "Darmok" (202) and in "Ensign Ro" (203).

Some appropriate casting was employed in this episode: Stewart's own son, Daniel, played the young Batai, Picard's Kataanian son, after several auditions for the show. Another piece of trivia: Margot Rose's résumé includes her role as one of two prostitutes in the film *48 HRS.:* her partner was Denise Crosby.

TIME'S ARROW

Production No.: 226 ■ Aired: Week of June 15, 1992
Stardate: 45959.1 ■ Code: ta

Directed by **Les Landau**
Teleplay by **Joe Menosky and Michael Piller**
Story by **Joe Menosky**

GUEST CAST
Samuel Clemens: **Jerry Hardin**
Bellboy: **Michael Aron**
Doorman: **Barry Kivel**
Seaman: **Ken Thorley**
Joe Falling Hawk: **Sheldon Peters Wolfchild**
Beggar: **John M. Murdock**
Gambler/Frederick La Rouque: **Marc Alaimo**
Scientist: **Milt Tarver**
Guinan: **Whoopi Goldberg**
Roughneck: **Michael Hungerford**

Called to the scene of excavations under San Francisco to investigate evidence of alien visitors in Earth's past, the *Enterprise* crew is amazed to find Data's head among artifacts dating back to the late 1800s. Triolic wave traces in the cavern point to Devidia II as the source of the relics. After journeying there, Picard sends an away team to investigate. The team discovers a time rift and traces of life-forms that are invisible to them.

Deliberately left off the team in an attempt by Picard to cheat fate, Data must now beam down to deal with what he theorizes is a slight time shift in the life-forms on the planet below—a shift that renders them invisible. Using a mobile forcefield that he sets to match the aliens' time shift, Data begins reporting back to the ship on what he sees. Then another time vortex opens up and sends the android to nineteenth-century San Francisco.

Thanks to poker winnings and a friendly bellboy, he quickly adapts and begins building a device with which to contact the *Enterprise*. Surprised to see Guinan in a local newspaper, he arranges to run into her, only to find that she has no recollection of him. She is not surprised, however, to learn that the two of them serve together in the future. Unfortunately, she is overheard by one of her guests—Samuel Clemens.

To uncover the suspected aliens' threat to history, the crew rig a large phaseable forcefield, just as Data had done. Then Picard, unnerved by cryptic words from "his" Guinan, leads the team into the vortex. . . .

Originally, TNG's "top two"—Rick Berman and Michael Piller—had decided not to end season five with a cliff-hanger, but the planned Trek spinoff series, *Deep Space Nine*, changed all that. "Because of all the attention *Deep Space Nine* was getting and the rumors that *Next Generation* would be shutting down, we wanted to send a message that this show was alive and well and continuing to grow," Piller said.

Surprisingly, "Time's Arrow" marked the first real time-trekking for this crew, holodeck and Q-fantasies aside. At first Piller said he wanted to bring the crew to the 1990s, but he discarded that idea because it had been done in *Star Trek IV*. The staff discussed the 1960s and the 1930s before deciding on the turn of the century. Piller said that before Joe Menosky went on sabbatical, he left notes on the concluding segment that would open TNG's sixth season come fall.

Three TNG veterans were among the guest cast: Ken Thorley had played chatty Bolian barber Mot ("Ensign Ro"/203, later "Schisms"/231); Jerry Hardin, sans the Mark Twain makeup, had led the sterile childnappers of Aldea as Radue ("When the Bough Breaks"/118); and Marc Alaimo, finally playing a human, followed his other alien stints ("Lonely Among Us"/108, "The Neutral Zone"/126, "The Wounded"/186); he would soon be DS9's Gul Dukat.

Trapped in the 1890s, Data hopes Guinan (Whoopi Goldberg) will be the key that gets him home again.

The San Francisco exteriors were shot on location at historic Pico House and along Olvera Street, the restored area near the first mission in old Los Angeles. Data's hotel room and gambling table were shot on a re-dress of a Stage 9 area and in the Planet Hell caves and caverns on Stage 16.

Troi's quote from Data regarding friendship is straight from his good-bye speech to Tasha's sister Ishara Yar in "Legacy" (180), and the marker beacons used to erect the large forcefield were seen before in "Power Play" (215).

As in the past two season-enders, few clues were provided for what a conclusion might bring. But a role seems assured for Hardin's Clemens character, who appears to be the owner of the pocket watch found among the artifacts, engraved "To S.L.C. with love, 30 November 1889."

Notes

1. *Starlog* No. 143, June 1989, p. 30.

PRODUCTION STAFF CREDITS— FIFTH SEASON

(In usual roll order; numbers in parentheses refer to episode numbers. Emmy nominees and winners not known at presstime.)

Casting: **(*)Junie Lowery-Johnson, C.S.A.; ****Ron Surma**

Main Title Theme: **(*) Jerry Goldsmith (*), Alexander Courage**

Music: *****Jay Chattaway (202, 204, 206 and all odd-numbered episodes 209–225) (*); Dennis McCarthy (201, 203, 205, 207 and all even-numbered episodes, 208–226)**

Director of Photography: *****Marvin Rush**

Production Designer: ****Richard D. James**

Editor: ***Tom Benko, A.C.E. (202, 205, 208, 211, 214, 217, 220, 223, 226); ***J. P. Farrell (203, 206, 209, 212, 215, 218, 221, 224); **Robert Lederman (201, 204, 207, 210, 213, 216, 219, 225); ****Steve Tucker (222)**

Unit Production Manager: *****Merri D. Howard (+)**

First Asst. Director: *****Brad Yacobian (all odd-numbered episodes, 201–225); ****Doug Dean (all even-numbered episodes, 202–226)**

Second Asst. Director: ***Adele G. Simmons**

Costume Designer: *****Robert Blackman**

Set Decorator: ****Jim Mees**

Visual Effects Supervisor: **(**) Robert Legato (+) (all even-numbered episodes, 202–226) (**); Dan Curry (+) (all odd-numbered episodes, 201–225)**

Senior Illustrator/Technical Consultant: **(*) Rick Sternbach**

Scenic Artist Supervisor/Technical Consultant: **(*) Michael Okuda**

Makeup Designed and Supervised: **(*) Michael Westmore**

Visual Effects Coordinator: *****Ron Moore (all odd-numbered episodes, 201–225); ***Gary Hutzel (all even-numbered episodes, 202–226)**

Set Designer: *****Gary Speckman**

Assistant Art Director: **(****) Andy Neskoromny**

Original Set Design: **(*) Herman Zimmerman**

Original Starfleet Uniforms: **(*) William Ware Theiss**

Script Supervisor: **(*) Cosmo Genovese**

Special Effects: **(*) Dick Brownfield**

Property Master: **(*) Joe Longo (201–205, 207, 209, all odd-numbered episodes from 217–225); (*) Alan Sims (206, 208, 210–215, all even-numbered episodes from 216–226)**

Construction Coordinator: **(*) Al Smutko**

Scenic Artist: **(***) Cari Thomas (+)**

Hair Designer: **Susan Carol-Schwary (201–216); *Joy Zapata (217–226)**

Makeup Artists: ****Gerald Quist, ***June Abston-Haymore**

Hair Stylist: **Gus le Pre (201–209); Patty Miller (210–226)**

Wardrobe Supervisor: *****Carol Kunz (+)**

Sound Mixer: ***Alan Bernard, C.A.S. (201–213, 217–226); Bill Gocke (214–216)**

Camera Operator: **Joe Chess, S.O.C. (214–226)**

Chief Lighting Technician: *****Buddy Bowles**

1st Company Grip: *****Bob Sordal**

Key Costumers: ****Amanda Chamberlin (all odd-numbered episodes from 201–223); **Kimberly Thompson (202, 204, 206 plus all odd-numbered episodes from 209–225);**

****Maurice Palinski (207 plus all even-numbered episodes from 208–226); Jerry Bono (all even-numbered episodes, 202–224, except 214); Mary Ellen Boché (203, 205, 225); ***David Velasquez (201); ****David Roesler (214); Phil Maldonado (226)

Music Editor: *Gerry Sackman

Supervising Sound Editor: (*) Bill Wistrom

Sound Editors: *James Wolvington; *Wilson Dyer; Dan Yale

Post Production Sound: (*) Modern Sound

Production Associate: (*) Susan Sackett (201–212)

Production Coordinator: (*) Diane Overdiek

Post Production Coordinator: (***) Wendy Rosenfeld (+)

Visual Effects Associate: (****) David Takemura

Production Associate: ***Terry Martinez (+), ***Heidi Julian (+)

Pre-Production Associate: (***) Eric Stillwell (+)

Casting Executive: (*) Helen Mossler

Stunt Coordinator: (***) Dennis Madalone (+) (201, 205, 207, 210–212, 214–217, 221–224)

Research Consultant: (*** Richard Arnold (201–214); (uncredited first two seasons)

Lenses and Panaflex Cameras: (**) Panavision

Monitors: (**) Sony Corp. of America (201, 202, 205, 206, 209–211, 214, 216, 219, 222)

Special Visual Effects: (*) Industrial Light and Magic (ILM) a division of Lucasfilm Ltd.

Motion Control Photography: (*) Image "G"

Video Optical Effects: (*) The Post Group

Special Video Compositing: (*) Composite Image Systems

Editing Facilities: (*) Unitel Video

Prosthetic Electronics: Michael Westmore II (218)

"Soliton Wave" Animation: Stokes/Kohne Assoc., Inc. (210)

The number of * denotes a returning company or staffer's initial season of credit in that position; ( ) denotes they are an original credited or co-credited person in that position; a (+) following indicates prior TNG work in another position

SIXTH SEASON

If the Great Bird's death the year be-
fore had loomed as perhaps the end of an era, the sixth season
of TNG—the last of the regular cast's original contract options,
back when a "new Star Trek" was still a shaky idea—sure
enough saw the birth of two events that would finally set the
future of the Star Trek franchise in the post-Roddenberry era.
And longtime fans of GR's vision and philosophy soon saw they
had little to fear.

There had been a few raised eyebrows when early press
reports described the new spinoff series *Star Trek: Deep Space
Nine*, announced midway through TNG's Season 5 for a January
1993 debut, as carrying a "grittier, darker tone" than the
usually bright Starfleet look of TNG. Michael Piller, who had
always reported to Rick Berman on TNG even after he shared
the title of executive producer, entered this new series with
equal billing as creator and executive producer—and both let
fans know they'd merely put GR's humanistic universe in collision with other cultures to see once again how it holds up.

DS9's debut had also been primed to quench Star Trek fans' never-ending thirst for more TV adventures in the Great Bird's mythos so the TNG cast could be readied for its certain future in theatrical movies. Piller, Berman, and even Roddenberry himself had long been peppered with questions as to Picard and Company's future on the silver screen—though they'd always noted that no feature would follow until the TV series had run its course, following the cast that blazed the trail a "generation" before them.

With the original contract options ending, rumors amid fans and the industry press surrounded the cast—especially Patrick Stewart—about their plans to return for an additional season, though Berman certainly talked of a possible seventh season and even an eighth, provided all the terms could be agreed on. But the future of the franchise finally came into focus in early April 1993 when GR's heir apparent formally announced a TNG theatrical feature by Christmas '94, shot after a brief respite following a moved-up seventh and final TV season. At the time, Berman said he was working on stories for two separate screenplays: one by former TNG associate Maurice Hurley, most recently a supervising producer on the latter-day *Kung Fu* series, and the other by ongoing staff writers Ronald D. Moore and Brannon Braga. And both, he added, could be structured to include some of the original Trek cast.

The immediate acceptance of DS9 by fans and new viewers—the pilot drew a syndication-high 18.8 for the season, thanks in no small part to TNG's lead—pointed up how it was not so long ago that even TNG had found it rough gaining acceptance from original Trek fans. And if a few "old-timers" still resisted, those not won over by the "Unification" two-parter had another generation-bridging event in the new season's "Relics" (230): a sentimental and effectively used appearance by James "Scotty" Doohan in which the engineering "miracle worker" is conjured up by inspired transporter jury-rigging and left in good health at tale's end to roam the era of both TNG and DS9. Its ratings weighed in at the time as the third-highest-rated episode in the series' history with a 13.9, after "Unification II" and the

1987 pilot. (As with "Devil's Due" in Season 4, the oddities of the late-winter February sweeps would give the uneven "Aquiel" (239) the season high with a 14.1.)

TNG's early season numbers were so strong that even baseball fanatic Piller was likely impressed with the studio's two-page color trade-magazine ad that boasted "Baseball's World Series lost to our worlds' series" above the image of the 1701-D streaking past a planet and a world-sized baseball. The ad revealed that TNG beat the six-game ratings average of the 1992 Series among all adults eighteen to forty-nine and both the adult and men-only brackets for the eighteen-to-thirty-four age group—by as much as twenty-three percent!

That success led to a November 6 *Los Angeles Times* feature examining why the series had suffered so little from the death of Roddenberry a year earlier, with the series' own average rating now at 13.5, or over twelve and a half million households—a twenty-two-percent jump during the early going of the sixth season over even the prior year's new highs, and domination for the fourth year of *Wheel of Fortune* in syndication. True, it was noted, TNG benefited in ratings numbers from being shown twice a week in about half its 248 markets of the time, but that didn't take away from the fact that the last half hour of "Rascals" (233) beat out the Monday-night competition on all four networks in the Los Angeles market. Other reasons cited for the ratings rise: the audience gained from increasing numbers of stations who "strip" TNG in daily showings, and the move into prime time by even more stations—including four network affiliates who dumped their own programming to air it!

Even the venerable New York Times Syndicate, offering features from articles to crossword puzzles for newspapers nationwide, got the message when it announced in February a weekly "Inside Trek" column for sale—a review of stars, plots, upcoming episodes, and even fandom; a year later, columnist Ian Spelling noted that the strip was running in around thirty-five papers. And more than ever, Trek entered the academic world with news reports of a Klingon Language Camp for linguists in Minnesota and a law-journal article examining the twenty-fourth-century justice system of Starfleet and the Federation. Outside academia, Star Trek's legendary galaxy of merchandising was on the boom too, as the studio estimated sales of all Trek products through 1991 had hit $2 billion. And Pocket Books—Trek's exclusive publishing licensee since 1979—noted in February of 1993 that its 100-plus Trek titles include sixty-four on the *New York Times* best-seller list.

Yet a third group of numbers also revealed what a phenomenon TNG had become—if it was still a secret. Lolita Fatjo, who had replaced Eric Stillwell as script coordinator for both series when he left to join Creation Entertainment at Season 5's close, reported that about three thousand scripts—both from pros and amateurs—had poured in to her office over the nine-month period. After outside readers compile a two-page "coverage" memo on each script, that will be perused by Piller, only one in two hundred writers sell, even the bare story premise, one in fifty is invited in to "pitch" one or more ideas to someone on staff, and less than one percent of them sell a teleplay. Still, several premises would be bought from thrilled amateurs all over the country during the coming year, providing still another way to keep the fans involved and the writing staff fresh.

And freshness would be at a premium as the usually quiet early-summer hiatus of 1992 took on a new fervency as much of the creative team worked double-duty shifts, especially at first, to plan for DS9's launch. "Some people have split their time between the series, but those who did so had put together a good enough staff of people over the past five and a half years and they rose to the occasion," noted Berman. For instance, David Livingston won the job of supervising producer on both series, while sole TNG title changes saw Peter Lauritson upped to producer's title, Unit Production Manager Merri D. Howard promoted to line producer, and associate producer Wendy Neuss now a co-producer.

Also, with fellow FX supervisor Rob Legato taking the title of visual effects *producer* with a move to *Deep Space Nine* and overseeing his own alternating crews, Dan Curry would do the same

by remaining with TNG. Now heading up alternate shows were five-year co-worker Ronald B. Moore, an FX veteran from the likes of *2010*, *Ghostbusters*, and *Poltergeist II*, and newcomer David Stipes, a twenty-four-year veteran of films, commercials, and movies such as the "V" sagas, *Tales of the Gold Monkey*, *The Flash*, *Creepshow*, and *Reel Genius*—including eleven years with his own firm (see "Conspiracy"/125)—who had once tried to get on during original *Trek*'s last season as a green college grad, then later worked with Curry at Universal and just missed a shot with DS9 when the TNG slot opened.

Michael Westmore, Bob Blackman, Rick Sternbach, Mike Okuda, and composers Jay Chattaway and Dennis McCarthy were among the others who toiled on both series, usually with split crews. Others won promotions, as rotating film editor J. P. Farrell did when he became supervising editor and allowed Berman to cut his previous time in the editing room from six sessions a week to just two.

"It's made long days even longer," Berman said of the dual-series load, "but I have managed to step back [from TNG] and limited but not eliminated myself from production and post-production. I'm amazed that I've made it through! And I can still be proud that we've put on forty-six hours of pretty good television in just eleven months." And Piller praised the advent of the dual production schedule for helping lift TNG out of the staid formula he feared it might fall into. "Rarely do you find a television show this late in its lifetime that continues to do fresh, challenging material like we do," he observed. "It's nice to see that the brotherhood of *Deep Space Nine* has contributed to *The Next Generation*."

Among the writers in the Hart Building, supervising producer Jeri Taylor won both a promotion to co-executive producer and the praise of both Berman and Piller at year's end for keeping the ship afloat while their attention was diverted. Thanks to Taylor's veteran hands-on experience, Berman was able to relinquish TNG's top casting decisions to her, while Piller began staying out of the infamous writing staff "break sessions" until after a story had been hashed out in detail on the wipe board. "Basically I approve the stories and give notes," Piller said. "They wrangle and I take the credit!"

"Michael did absolutely the right thing, which was to throw me into the water and refuse to rescue me," Taylor recalled with a laugh. "So I felt like I went down a couple of times and was choking on scum water but I finally learned to swim." Her touch was evident in subtle ways too, such as the "graying of Starfleet" aboard the *Enterprise* in Season 6 that followed her specific request in extras casting that not everyone aboard be "under thirty."

Initially, veteran writer-producer Frank Abatemarco had been hired on at Taylor's old title for Season 6 as her right-hand man. Abatemarco had scripts for *Equal Justice*, the latter-day *Mission: Impossible*, and *Cagney and Lacey* to his credit—the last a staff job where he first worked with Piller. "Frank is a wonderful writer—I've known him for years," Berman said. "He's done some of the best cop shows and movies-of-the-week of anyone I know." However, after thirteen episodes he would go the way of Michael Wagner, Lee Sheldon, and other professionals who just didn't fit the Star Trek system; Taylor noted, for one thing, that Abatemarco hadn't been asked to complete the usual "audition script" to gauge his future success writing in the Star Trek vein.

Joe Menosky, the two-year veteran who had worked up to co-producer with Moore, was offered a producer's job on *Deep Space Nine* but elected instead to take a break with an extended sabbatical overseas to "recharge his batteries," as Piller put it. Despite his absence, two scripts with his partial credit ("The Chase"/246, "Suspicions"/248) as well as a DS9 segment would resurface for infamous rewrites during Season 6 and even drew his hands-on attention during an unannounced trip home to work on a proposed TV pilot with Braga. "Joe just wanted out of Hollywood and loves it in Italy, where he has relatives," Taylor said. "He is one of a kind and he follows his heart."

Executive script consultant Peter Allen Fields did go on to become a co-producer on DS9, where he was joined by Ira Steven Behr, who had been so much a part of the TNG writing staff during Season 3 before leaving to work on a screenplay for a later-shelved Harrison Ford project.

Moore, whom Piller praised for taking up the slack after Abatemarco left, returned along with newly hired story editors René Echevarria—the busy freelancer whom Piller and then Taylor finally coaxed into moving out west from New York City to take the slot opened up by Fields' departure—and Braga, who had been on staff since his initial stint as an intern in Season 4. By year's end the latest junior member of the writing staff was science adviser and "The First Duty" co-writer Naren Shankar, another one-time intern who brought aboard his doctorate in engineering and physics when he was hired at midseason (after his "The Quality of Life"/235) to fill the last open slot.

Taylor said she gave a wide berth to her young staff, headed in age by Echevarria at thirty during Season 6. "I try to provide a nurturing atmosphere and let them feel safe that they can say anything, that we can fight and that dissension is desired because frequently you can get to a greater truth when you have people in conflict . . . and nobody's going to be demeaned or made to feel bad. It gets very alarming at times, it gets very exciting at times, because people feel things passionately and argue things passionately—and I become a referee after a while!"

Intent on getting away from the "soap opera" plots of the past year, the writers' new focus on "high-concept science fiction"—or "weird shit," as Piller put it—lasted through the first third of the season, which flowed from a series of Sunday-afternoon brainstorming sessions at Taylor's home that were modeled after Season 5's infamous yet highly productive "Mexican Incursion" writers' retreat. But then available premises and the crush of deadlines once again became the driving force behind what viewers saw from week to week. "You can say you want to do 'X' and you can write shows with more humor and you can give them a certain touch," Braga said, "but the stories come pretty much at random—more random than you'd think." And Berman added: "Everything goes in waves, like cop shows and Westerns. We can get too many Data shows, too many Klingon-Romulan shows, too many 'strange diseases.' My goal is just to turn out twenty-six good hours of television."

And by season's end, he and the rest of the staff could point to what they called the "most eclectic season ever" on TNG—and Piller could boast that for the first time a season passed without a single shipboard technological breakdown as a plot device. "What really works best for *Star Trek* is a mix of things," Taylor added. "This is a canvas that can contain many different kinds of stories, obviously, so I see no need to limit ourselves."

Limitless, yes, but with a vision grounded in continuity and plausible "extensions" of today's technology that GR had always insisted on—a tenet that long ago helped his creation become the darling of the "real" science community. Nowhere was that more apparent than the Paramount lot itself as Season 6 wound down—first with the walk-on role of onetime space-shuttle astronaut Dr. Mae Jemison in "Second Chances" (250), and then with physics genius Dr. Stephen Hawking, appearing as himself in the teaser of the season finale.

The new year of TNG would also reflect on-camera changes wrought by the coming of a sister series. By midsummer, after actors Colm Meaney and Rosalind Chao agreed to the move *and* the weekly commitment, plans called for Miles, Keiko, and little Molly O'Brien to transfer aboard the alien space station that would provide the format for *Deep Space Nine*. Both characters would continue to serve aboard the *Enterprise* until midseason, though, when a two-hour pilot like TNG's "Encounter at Farpoint" would launch the series. And by grounding the new Commander Sisko's background in the battle of Wolf 359 with the Borg ("The Best of Both Worlds, Part 2"/175) it allowed appearances in both past and present by Patrick Stewart's Locutus and Picard, helping christen the new show as a guest star to lend the needed continuity.

DS9 was originally planned to take a cue from its sister series in another way. Michelle Forbes, whose Ensign Ro character was talked about for a promotion and transfer to the station as its first officer, opted to shoot a motion picture

and not commit to the new weekly venture. Instead, Piller said, the door was left open for her to continue her recurring role aboard the *Enterprise*—though for Season 6 that amounted to only a cameo on "Rascals" (233), which ironically also provided the last pre-DS9 scene for Keiko O'Brien and one of only two appearances for the year by Guinan, thanks to Whoopi Goldberg's ever-burgeoning schedule. Also, though she turned up on DS9 in "The Forsaken," Lwaxana Troi was a familiar face completely absent from TNG in Season 6. Comparing the situation to the drought of Q stories the year before, Taylor said three Lwaxana scripts in development all fell through.

In contrast, young Brian Bonsall's busy career was not the only reason he would make only two appearances as Alexander this season: once again there was the desire to break away from the so-called personal "soap opera" stories that could be told on any contemporary program. "It was almost the sitcom thing, with the single parent and his trials and tribulations," Taylor said. "A few of those were a change of pace, but to make Worf a suburban dad did not seem to be serving him well." Although a line explaining Alexander's absence as a visit back home to Earth had to be cut for time, he is free to reappear if a story demands it "in a unique and special way"—as in "A Fistful of Datas" (234).

About the only real downer in the latest triumphant year of TNG was the series' continued snubbing in the so-called creative side of TV's Emmy Awards, such as acting, writing, and direction—a category whose mere connotation Berman outright rejected. "Why somebody decides writing a screenplay is 'creative' and somebody scoring a soundtrack isn't is just ego," he said.

"I'd like to think the Academy [of Television Arts and Sciences, awarders of the Emmy] is coming around, but we're a 'science fiction' show, a 'sequel,' and syndicated," he noted—all marks against the series in a system dominated by traditional network-oriented voters. "Anybody who watches it almost immediately becomes addicted to it," Piller added. "Unfortunately there's just not enough of them." The eye-opening success of DS9 is gradually helping to change that—"We've been on the business page more than the calendar section," he said—but with the clock ticking down to the big-screen transformation, Berman ironically noted that "TNG may not be around to enjoy the rewards of what it pioneered."

Before the season Piller had said no major character "arcs" were planned, but two of the regular cast marked milestones in their own lives as both LeVar Burton and Marina Sirtis got married during the year. The year also saw the death of Original Series and first-season TNG costume designer William Ware "Bill" Theiss, who died December 10 from complications arising from AIDS, and the posthumous awarding of NASA's distinguished Public Service Medal to Roddenberry at the close of the held-over *Trek* exhibit at the National Air and Space Museum in Washington, D.C.

TIME'S ARROW, PART II

Production No.: 227 ▪ Aired: Week of September 21, 1992
Stardate: 46001.3 ▪ Code: t2

Directed by **Les Landau**
Teleplay by **Jeri Taylor**
Story by **Joe Menosky**

GUEST CAST
Samuel Clemens: **Jarry Hardin**
Mrs. Carmichael: **Pamela Kosh**
Policeman: **William Boyett**
Jack (London) the Bellboy: **Michael Aron**
Dr. Appollinaire: **James Gleason**
Alien Nurse: **Mary Stein**
Young Reporter: **Alexander Enberg**
Guinan: **Whoopi Goldberg**
Male Patient: **Bill Cho Lee**
Computer Voice: **Majel Barrett**

Having traveled back to 1890s San Francisco, Picard and his senior officers go "native" to retrieve Data and stave off his apparent destruc-

tion while probing the real reason that the energy-consuming aliens found on Devidia II are coming to the Earth of that time.

When they find two of the aliens in disguise, sapping the energy from dying cholera victims in one infirmary, Dr. Crusher snatches their time-vortex "cane" after a group fracas, and they find Data.

Meanwhile, the curious Samuel Clemens—convinced that Guinan and the stranded Data are themselves an alien threat—follows the Starfleet group to the cave where Data's head will be found in the future. The crew has realized that the cave is the time-travel focusing device, but when the two aliens surprise them and grab back the cane, the resulting blast of the "time door" opening decapitates Data. Picard seems trapped when he alone doesn't make it back through to the twenty-fourth century, but he keys a crude escape message in Data's head that he hopes will be "found" later.

Data and Counselor Troi in 1890s garb.

Once reconnected, Data's "old" head recites Picard's message and the door is opened, but just far enough for one. A reassured Clemens volunteers to go back so Picard can return, and with all as it was. The aliens' doorway is destroyed—leaving no clue to their true motives.

"Any time you deal with time you're going to have complexities that are hard to grasp," Piller said. "But if you really look at that closely I think we got them all nicely stitched." Taylor, who modeled her mix of historical fact and fiction on the writings of E. L. Doctorow, was satisfied with the outcome but regretted how much the demanding writing distracted her from settling in with the staff right after hiatus. It would be the last cliffhanger conclusion whose writing would be put off until after hiatus—an "exciting" but "very scary" custom she was determined to end.

Regretting that more wasn't done with the 1890s period, Ron Moore said that one of the ideas dropped due to time and budget would have picked up the time-travel crew in various jobs after several months, centered around their meeting place at a wharfside café run by Picard where the running joke was how bad his food was.

More than ever before ("The Best of Both Worlds, Part II"/175, "Ensign Ro"/203), the facts of Guinan and Picard's first "true" meeting presented here mean that the "listener" was misleading Wesley Crusher when she told him at their first meeting that she'd "never met the captain before I came aboard" ("The Child"/127). In reality, all three top producers pleaded guilty to not realizing the line planted in Guinan's very first appearance, which predated all but Berman's tenure on the show.

While writer Jack London turned up as the bellboy, a sidelight to the use of Mark Twain, the "Judge Williams" and "General Mallory" mentioned were fictitious. Twain's reference to Halley's Comet harkens to his birth during its 1835 appearance and his famous comment that he "came in with the comet and will go out with the comet"—a prophecy of his 1910 death.

Hardin had not played Mark Twain before and was simply cast for the general physical type, Berman noted, but he became so enamored of the author that he created a one-man touring show. William Boyett had played a TNG cop in another past time—he was holodeck Lieutenant Dan Bell back in Season 1's "The Big Goodbye" (113). Repeat faces would include Enberg ("Lower Decks"/267) and Kosh ("All Good Things . . ."/277–278); extra Leonard Jones was the Bolian crew member spied by Twain, while O'Brien is spoken to but not seen.

Unlike Part I, the period scenes were shot not on location but right on Paramount's newly completed New York Street backlot; original plans called for using one at Universal, but with a few camera cheats and the removal of non-period fire escapes they made do. The scenes sported a horse-driven fire vehicle from a museum that had loaned it out for the first time ever thanks to "the power of the words 'Star Trek,'" noted production designer Richard James. Among the in-joke signs adorning the street were the "Okuda Laundry," "James Bank," and "Purser Carpentry," for TNG scenery shop foreman Tom Purser.

Visual FX supervisor Ron B. Moore noted that the many opticals here included new computer "morphing" by Joe Walter to clarify the ophidian snake-head cane's transformation first seen in Part I. Accomplished completely by computer were the arcs and sparks of Data's "invention" when disturbed by Clemens—a moving-camera shot—and Data's decapitation in the explosion, though Moore recalled the first take on the effect, as sometimes happens, proved comical until some extra animation touches and a change-up in speed were added to dull its effect. Smoke filmed through lighted holes in paper provided the main element for the vortex itself.

REALM OF FEAR

Production No.: 228 ■ Aired: Week of September 28, 1992
Stardate: 46041.1 ■ Code: rf

Directed by **Cliff Bole**
Written by **Brannon Braga**

GUEST CAST
Chief Miles Edward O'Brien: **Colm Meaney**
Nurse Alyssa Ogawa: **Patti Yatsutake**
Lieutenant (j.g.) Reginald "Reg" Barclay III: **Dwight Schultz**
Admiral Hayes: **Renata Scott**
Crew Member: **Thomas Belgrey**
Computer Voice: **Majel Barrett**

The ever-nervous engineer Barclay sees his victory of devising a method of boarding the disabled *U.S.S. Yosemite* turn sour when he confronts one of his worst fears—transporter beaming.

Emboldened by Troi's counseling, he makes it over to the dead ship but in mid-transport and discovers creatures living in the transporting beam that seemingly try to attack him when he transports back alone.

Knowing his own shaky reputation, Barclay keeps the story to himself until the spot on his arm where the creature touched him begins to glow. He finally reports the incident to a skeptical crew, but with O'Brien's help the determined engineer finds the creatures again during another trip.

Then Dr. Crusher discovers that his arm is radiating the same energy as a dead Yosemite crew member, and she realizes the glowing light

O'Brien doesn't believe Barclay's story of monsters in the transporter beam.

is a life-form trapped in Barclay's body. The only way to separate the form is in mid-beaming, while his molecules are disassembled, so he once again must confront his old phobia of molecular limbo.

Then, during the beaming, he not only doesn't panic but realizes he can grab the creature—who turns out, upon rematerialization, to be one of a lost Yosemite crewmen. The others are rescued too, and Barclay finds himself a hero after all.

Though wary of too much "tech" talk near the end, Braga enjoyed developing Barclay for this romp that updates for the twenty-fourth century the writer's own fear of air travel: "In some ways it's my most personal show to date, because I relate to Barclay—it comes from the heart!" The story, fleshed out from a premise Michael Piller initially felt was too close to the old *Twilight Zone* segment in which William Shatner sees a monster sitting on his airplane's wing, also provides the first TNG look at a transporter's guts and a beaming subject's point of view—and a little hypochondria with "transporter psychosis," first diagnosed in 2209, or within fifty years or so of the century-old system's origins ("The Masterpiece Society"/213). Braga's "multi-infarct dementia" would later resurface in his "Frame of Mind" (247), while the "plexing" gag was to have been repeated again in the final scene between Barclay and his spider.

After much testing and designing, various versions of the plasma creatures for Berman's final choice were designed by Dan Curry and built by modelmaker/sculptor Carey Howe. To avoid the need for motion-control or animation, Curry donned green tights to operate the creatures as a hand puppet against a green screen matte—and credited his tai chi for the slow and graceful movement he had to bring to the task.

O'Brien had borne full lieutenant's rank since Season 2 and was even addressed that way before he had a name ("Where Silence Has Lease"/128), but here he sports a single back-centered pip for the plot point that *Lieutenant j.g.* Barclay outranks him. Taylor said it had always been intended even before her tenure that O'Brien be a noncommissioned "chief petty officer," as Sergey Rozhenko noted ("Family"/178)—not a chief by position, as in "security chief"—and so this corrected an original miscue by the wardrobe department. Still, actor Meaney's unnamed character had been an ensign initially ("Encounter at Farpoint"/101, "Lonely Among Us"/108), indicating a promotion before the CPO rank flap arose. O'Brien, who hasn't received his promised promotion after transferring to *Deep Space 9* by year's end on that series, has been a transporter operator at least twenty-two years with nary an accident—which only occur about two or three times a decade at all, thanks to system redundancies. For the record, in "real" screen time Barclay is in the transporter beam about 105 seconds, not just thirty to forty as hoped.

The workhorse Grissom model from *ST III* turns up as the *U.S.S. Yosemite*, while Talarian hook spiders apparently share the homeworld of a race seen before ("Suddenly Human"/176). The dual-system linkup is not new ("Symbiosis"/123), while Crusher's cardio-stimulator is a smaller version of McCoy's from The Original Series (1967's "Journey to Babel"). O'Brien's throwaway reference to planet Zayra IV honors Zayra Cabot, Jeri Taylor's secretary at the time, while the dead Robert Kelly wears the oft-seen silvery scientists' civvies, first used in "Home Soil" (117), even though he's titled as a lieutenant.

Man of the People

Production No.: 229 ■ Aired: Week of October 5, 1992
Stardate: 46071.6 ■ Code: mn

Directed by **Winrich Kolbe**
Written by **Frank Abatemarco**

GUEST CAST
Ambassador Ves Alkar: **Chip Lucia**
Nurse Alyssa Ogawa: **Patti Yasutake**
Admiral Simons: **George D. Wallace**
Ensign Janeway: **Lucy Boryer**
Sev Maylor: **Susan French**
Jarth: **Rick Scarry**
Liva: **Stephanie Erb**
Ensign (Troi's): **J. P. Hubbell**
Computer Voice: **Majel Barrett**

Dr. Crusher is unable to explain the death of Ramid Sev Maylor (Susan French).

After the *Enterprise* assumes the transport of an ambassador to the site of an interplanetary war's peace talks, Troi begins aging rapidly and acting without abandon following the sudden death of the mediator's aged mother.

The woman had accused Troi of having designs on her son Alkar, a Lumerian, but after her strange death he refused an autopsy according. Upset at the woman's outburst and later death, Troi aids Alkar in what he says is his planet's "funeral ritual," which leaves her feeling odd and her libido running amok.

First she seduces a young ensign after both Alkar and Riker turn her down. Then, aging shocking she stabs Captain Picard—which leads him to order the dead woman autopsied over Alkar's objections.

It is found that Alkar and Troi actually shared a process that let him "dump" his negative thoughts in her in order to keep his mind clear for negotiating. The dead woman was not his "mother," just his previous victim.

Picard, angry at Alkar's nonchalant admission, waits until near the end of the successful talks before faking Troi's death. The broken "link" with Troi in mid-link forces Alkar to turn to one of his aides, whom Picard has beamed out—leaving Alkar to die in agony, aged just like his victims.

Piller and Moore, among others, praised Sirtis' "sexy but scary" scenery-chewing performance for lifting one of the season's early disappointments, an episode that shows the signs of being rushed into production one slot early when the next show, "Relics," had to be pushed back due to the schedule of James "Scotty" Doohan. With Abatemarco an experienced writer but the "new guy" on the block, the staff each took an act and pulled another committee-write to break the script for his treatment. "He was a seasoned veteran, but it wasn't a fair introduction for him," said Taylor, who was still preoccupied with the season debut at the time. "It remained for his later work for everybody to realize that perhaps this wasn't for him."

A Q story by Echevarria was considered for this slot, Piller revealed. The plot had the superbeing dividing the crew into twins representing opposite halves, but not just good/bad as in original *Trek*'s "Enemy Within"; in fact, the lack of agreement on what the two polarities should be is what bogged down the story.

This episode's closing is one of the warmest Riker-Troi scenes yet, her chocolate habit (see notes, "The Price"/156) is recalled, and the plot device of an autopsy ban would be used later in the season ("Suspicions"/248). Here Troi's quarters are seen to be Deck 9/0910, Worf's martial arts class ("Clues"/188, "New Ground"/210) is glimpsed again before gaining a name ("Birthright, Part II"/243), the biobed forcefield restraint is used again ("Time Squared"/139), and the extra playing Chief Daniels is seen with a solid ensign's pip, as per O'Brien's rank from the preceding episode. Past references include the cortical stimulator ("Ethics"/216,

"Inner Light"/225) and the stimulant inoprovalene ("Transfigurations"/173, "Ethics"/216), while mention of the drug cordrazine (see "Shades of Gray"/148) and the Federation Council date back to sixties Trek.

The voice of Captain Talmadge was provided by Terrence Beasor, who had previously given uncredited vocal life to aliens ("Skin of Evil"/122, "The Ensigns of Command"/149, "Devil's Due"/187).

RELICS

Production No.: 230 ▪ Aired: Week of October 12, 1992
Stardate: 46125.3 ▪ Code: rl

Directed by **Alexander Singer**
Written by **Ronald D. Moore**

GUEST CAST
Ensign Sariel Rager: **Lanei Chapman**
Ensign Kane: **Erick Weiss**
Captain Montgomery "Scotty" Scott, Ret.: **James Doohan**
Lieutenant Bartel: **Stacie Foster**
Waiter: **Ernie Mirich**
Computer Voice: **Majel Barrett**

The *Enterprise* crew is amazed by two simultaneous discoveries: an immense Dyson sphere (an artificially constructed habitat built around a star), and Starfleet engineering legend Montgomery "Scotty" Scott, kept alive for seventy-five years in molecular limbo within a transporter diagnostic loop aboard a shuttle crashlanded on the sphere.

But depression sets in for James Kirk's old "miracle worker" when an impatient La Forge blurts out that the old man is only "in the way" now. Drink in hand, a blue Scotty is joined during a holodeck look at his old Constitution-class bridge by an understanding Picard, who later urges his engineer to put Scotty to use in a check of the downed *Jenolen* shuttle.

Then things get rough when the Enterprise is drawn inside the sphere and Riker manages to pull the starship out of a deadly spiral into the sun, only to be threatened by its long solar flares once in a close orbit. Only later does the crew realize that a subspace frequency had activated the sphere's tractor beam, which pulled them inside, just as the *Jenolen* had done.

Back in the shuttle, it is Scotty who figures out a way to power it up to open the sphere's doors long enough to get the *Enterprise* out—and a split-second beam-out when the craft has to be blown clear.

Rejuvenated, Scotty is given his own shuttle—and a new sense of purpose.

Ron Moore's roots as a longtime Star Trek fan had never shown as brightly as in this instant classic, which included not only the appearance of Scotty, the third character from original *Trek* on TNG, but the use of the Dyson sphere as a plot device after it had been bandied about so long it had been almost a joke. And the icing on the cake was the appearance of the old Constitution-class bridge—and the struggle to get it on film has already become as big a tale in Star Trek lore as Scotty's appearance itself.

The original sixties bridge, struck not long after the series was canceled, in 1969, had been turned down for re-creation only a

Scotty on the holodeck version of the old *Enterprise* bridge.

year earlier due to money constraints ("Cause and Effect"/218), but this time Moore was determined to see it done. After a fully rebuilt set was scoffed at during early production meetings due to the cost of both materials and labor, it looked as though the latest movie-era version would be unpacked and used—unless, as graphic artist and fellow longtime Star Trek fan Mike Okuda recalled, a way could be devised to create the sixties bridge for the same amount of money. Michael Piller remembered that he huddled afterward with Jeri Taylor and Moore to suggest that they should come up with alternatives to present, such as renting a fan-built replica or using miniaturization.

That got the "think tank" juices flowing. Designer Richard James suggested using Scotty's single "pie wedge" station from the old bridge with a blue-screen matte from old film, and FX producer Dan Curry revealed his own Trek fan roots by recalling such a scene: the bare few frames of a mutiny-emptied bridge from "This Side of Paradise." They were brightened and lengthened by computer into a loop that is seen as Scotty enters the holodeck door. Only the turbolift alcove and engineering station were built anew, but James said that that alone meant hours and days spent in research on dimensions and colors which had to be refigured from film clips since no set plans existed. He, Curry, and cameraman Jonathan West even figured out the original camera angles and lenses so the new footage of Scotty, Picard, and the set would match seamlessly with the old. "They lit the set with color [in the sixties], and that threw us off trying to establish what color to paint our set," James said. "We had to look through old calendars and photographs—we were really back on the level of fans!"

Ironically, Okuda added, it took the discovery of fan Steve Horch's center console and captain's chair, built for display at conventions, to keep the project on budget. "We rented it and then enhanced it a little bit and he was happy with that," laughed James, who said the unexpected extra pieces gave more depth for director Singer to work with. James also designed the single-viewer upper panel so it could be changed out for the opposite two-viewer section behind Picard on reverse angles.

The total effect—the marriage of modern construction, research, and twenty-six-year-old footage—held up so well it fooled many viewers and even passed muster with visiting Original Series producer Bob Justman, who was amazed to point out only one small error: the carpet color. "They had that gray carpet but it looked rust," James recalled with a smile, "and I just assumed it was that because in those days that was such a common color. But he pointed it out and I said, 'Why didn't I call you?' And he laughed and said 'I don't know!'"

Even beyond the art staff, much of the creative team went above and beyond in their own way to make the segment special. Curry, for instance, recalled seeing a box in storage labeled "Star Trek Transporter Sparkle" from his days as an intern at Cinema Research Corp., and thus was able to retrieve the actual sixties-era photographic element from the original transporter glitter effect; to match it, co-producer Wendy Neuss hunted down the old transporter whine from studio archives (although technically both effects would have predated the changed look and sound of the movie-era Jenolen). Original Trek's live FX man Jim Rugg had given Greg Jen bridge buttons from his keepsakes for the consoles. "The people in the production department put in a lot of extra hours and a lot of free work because they really

wanted it to look good," Moore said. "They really wanted to sweat the details because they knew everyone was going to be watching us—it's the kind of thing you better not screw up or you're going to be hearing about every little thing!"

Through it all, Moore praised his two top bosses for standing by him to help present one of TNG's magical moments. "Michael and Rick were both very supportive and said 'All right, let's do it!' Two years ago they may not have, but I think the show has gotten to the point where they're more comfortable with the Original Series stuff. Here it was always just a question of money."

Moore reveals that the story had its roots as a uncredited premise bought from Michael Rupert about a crewman saving himself in a transporter loop, which Piller prophetically suggested could be a vehicle for returning a Kirk-era character if the chance ever arose again. "Everything gravitated toward using Scotty," he said. "McCoy is old ["Encounter at Farpoint"/101], Spock's playing James Bond on Romulus ["Unification I-II"/207–208]—and we couldn't do Kirk; it would raise too many other things. Nothing against the other characters, but Scotty seemed like the one with the most 'fun' quotient." Given a movie format, though, Shatner's Kirk would eventually cross paths with the TNG crew in Star Trek Generations.

So many lines are in-joke references to some of actor Doohan's best scenes in sixties Trek: the first Moore conceived was based on Scotty's reference to a beverage as only "It's green," from his duel of drinking in "By Any Other Name"; the line about needing thirty minutes to restart a cold warp engine is right from "The Naked Time"; and of course the Dohlman of Elas was the guest character of "Elaan of Troyius"—making, coincidentally, a sampling from each of original Trek's three seasons.

The writer mentioned two scenes he hated to lose: the "It's green" Ten-Forward scene with Data originally written for Guinan before her schedule ruled it out, and a filmed but cut-for-time scene just before that showed Troi's visit with Scotty after his blowup with Geordi. At first taken with "the lass" and her charms, Scotty indignantly declares that he's "not crazy" and tells her "I know what I need and it's not here!" before stomping off to the lounge. The three-page scene also revealed that counselors have been assigned to starships for about forty years—and explains why he gives Troi a kiss in what now seems to be her first appearance at story's end.

In contrast to the rest of the well-oiled episode, Moore sheepishly admits that nothing can explain how Scotty and Geordi were beamed through the Jenolen's shields in the climactic scene—a nominal violation of long-established Trek technology—unless the shield cycling technique O'Brien once used explains it away ("The Wounded"/230). "It's just a straight, flat-out mistake!" he admitted. "I didn't think about it, I didn't catch it, the producers didn't catch it, the technical consultants didn't catch it—it was just one of those things and a single line of dialogue could've explained it away."

Singer, a self-taught veteran of the craft with five features and 262 series episodes to his credit since moving out West from Brooklyn in 1959, knew full well how lucky he was to draw what he called "an instant classic" as his first-ever Star Trek assignment. An associate of both Rick Berman (on MacGuyver) and Jeri Taylor (In the Heat of the Night, Jake and the Fat Man), he had counted himself a science-fiction fan since his boyhood in 1938 but had never worked on a Star Trek series until now. So touching was the day's shoot on the old bridge set, he recalled, that both he and his less sentimental wife—not necessarily a Star Trek fan either—were moved to tears at the "mythic quality" of the moment and what it meant for American pop culture. Though he had not worked extensively with SF series lately, he breezed through the filming with the FX and art staffs helping out and was asked back for two more episodes in turn and three the next year. The *Jenolen* itself, NCC-2010, was named for some caves Moore visited during a convention trip near Sydney, Australia, which in turn provided its "Sydney class" designation. The craft actually began as the admiral's shuttle seen briefly in the opening of *ST VI: The Undiscovered Country,* built for the movie by former ILM modelbuilder John Goodson. Turned upside down with an added bridge module and Starfleet nacelles, the design was at one point a candidate for the new runabout vessel for DS9, said illustrator Rick Sternbach—and the forward and side windows in that craft's full-size cockpit set were based on it. The movie shuttle's three front windows were combined into two and the set was built around them. Greg Jein built the huge model of the Dyson sphere and doors, shot from various angles, with the interior supplied via a matte painting by Eric Chauvin. And the fate of the newly built bridge section? It was struck and given to DS9 and onetime TNG designer Herman Zimmerman for use in a planned *Star Trek* theme park.

Given that the current year is 2369 (dated from "The Neutral Zone"/125), it's apparent from clues here that Scotty was born in 2222 and disappeared at age seventy-two, after having served on eleven different ships. We also learn here that there is a Fleet museum which numbers a Constitution-class starship among its artifacts, and that isolinear chips debuted about "forty years ago," while transporters, sensors, and subspace radio have remained largely unchanged since Scotty's time and impulse engines have been little altered for two centuries—or the era of the first Romulan War. And we find out that synthehol is not all Guinan has available in the bar.

Also: Bartel is called a lieutenant although she wears an ensign's pip; the small *Jenolen* displays a graphic of a Galaxy-or other large-class starship's warp reactor; and the holodeck computer knows without asking that Scotty wants the Constitution-class version of his *Enterprise*'s bridge, even though the uprated ship of the first three movies was also known simply as NCC-1701—with no suffix letter.

SCHISMS

Production No.: 231 ■ Aired: Week of October 19, 1992
Stardate: 46154.2 ■ Code: sc

Directed by **Robert Wiemer**
Teleplay by **Brannon Braga**
Story by **Jean Louise Matthias & Ron Wilkerson**

GUEST CAST
Ensign Sariel Rager: **Lanei Chapman**
Mot: **Ken Thorley**
Kaminer: **Angelina Fiordellisi**
Lieutenant (j.g.) Shipley: **Scott T. Trost**
Crewman: **Angelo McCabe**
Medical Technician: **John Nelson**
Computer Voice: **Majel Barrett**

The crew is puzzled when various members report strange symptoms following a false-alarm "explosion" in a cargo bay, thought to result from La Forge's attempt to rechannel warp energy into the deflectors to more efficiently map an extremely dense cluster.

Riker reports extreme exhaustion, Worf and La Forge experience sharp pains and anxiety, and even Data has apparently "dozed off" for ninety minutes he can't account for. No medical reason can be found, although it is soon realized that all were involved with the call to the cargo bay.

After a particle stream from outside this universe is detected, signs point to abduction by aliens when one of two crew members initially found to be missing returns and dies in agony. Then Troi leads the affected crew members in a re-creation of what she finds to be a common description of what they fear: an alien lab of some kind.

Armed with a stimulant and a homing signal, Riker volunteers to track where the missing people are being taken. He awakes in the lab to find insectlike inhabitants there battling to close a "rupture" between universes that the *Enterprise* crew has tracked and now opened on their own. Riker finally grabs the last missing crewmate

Beverly is puzzled by the strange illness striking the crew.

and dashes back as the rupture closes, but the aliens' exact origin is never discovered.

This latest of Braga's darkly macabre outings and one of the "high concept" hard-SF stories sought early on, "Schisms" proved disappointing due to a scaled-back ending less costly to shoot than the one he had envisioned: a single insectoid claw around Riker's bed in the alien lab, with only a few sparse bits of light and the ever-present clicking sounds to break up the darkness. Veteran TNG director Bob Wiemer joined Braga and Michael Piller in their disappointment, saying the alien scenes were too "languid" and should have featured more cuts to aid in the off-balanced feeling. "There was a story consensus to do lighting control, smoke control, to limit what one saw, but it's always harder to paint with light when you're on the crush of time."

None of the three liked the look of the aliens and Piller said they wouldn't be back, despite the open ending. "I felt they

looked like monks—fish monks," Braga said, "and monks aren't terrifying." Still, the tale was a far cry from the last TNG effort of the Matthias-Wilkerson writing team ("Imaginary Friend"/222), and in his rewrite Braga was proud of the "creepiness" and atypical mysteriousness of the first three and a half acts that pushed the show's limits, his use of the holodeck as an investigative tool, and especially Data's bad poetry, the bulk of a light teaser in direct contrast to the dark story to follow. He hoped the verse would reappear again beyond ("A Fistful of Datas"/234).

On her fourth appearance, Lanei Chapman's Ensign Rager (first seen in "Galaxy's Child"/190) gets a first name, Sariel, while Trost's character Shipley would appear to have been promoted since he previously appeared as an ensign transporter operator ("Unnatural Selection"/133); Ken Thorley's Mot is put to good use again ("Ensign Ro"/203) as the series' latest Bolian ("Conspiracy"/125, "Data's Day"/185, and DS9's "The Forsaken"). We also learn that Data not only is "marked" by traces from a warp field whenever aboard a starship, but that he can record and file that data for retrieval.

Picard's Aunt Adelle's home cures are mentioned again ("Ensign Ro," "Cause and Effect"/218), as is the "FGC" catalog prefix for space phenomena ("Imaginary Friend"/222); Geordi's diagnostic device and Riker's arm beacon are props recycled from "Cause and Effect" (218), and tetryons would figure anew in another story ("Suspicions"/248). Though Cargo Bay 4 is on Deck 4 the indicator light in Main Engineering is seen to be below the battle bridge (Deck 8). Counting each grid as two feet square, the empty holodeck's opposite walls seen here can actually be figured to be at least sixteen feet high, twenty feet wide, and thirty feet long. And Braga revealed that the Amargosa Diaspora was named for a spot near Death Valley and his mother's onetime pet finch, while the character Kaminer was named for author Wendy Kaminer.

Riker's lateral abduction into the dimensional doorway—"Not another vortex!" groaned FX supervisor and "Time's Arrow, Part 2" veteran Ronald B. Moore—was accomplished by mounting a fast-speed camera atop a tower before blue screen and shooting down as a stunt man jumped off stiff-legged, then tilting the footage laterally for the playback at the slower film speed; it took three takes to get it right.

Co-producer Wendy Neuss, who counts overseeing sound effects mixing among her many duties, recalled that the funniest session of her tenure came as she, sound editor Jim Wolvington, and supervising sound editor Bill Wistrom brought to life the carefully crafted clicking language of the aliens. "We had decided what kind of clicks we wanted with Rick [Berman] and Peter [Lauritson] at the spotting session," she recalled. "Then the three of us actually sat there one night and wrote a script in English and then transposed it to 'clicks.' We wanted it to be organic, not synthesized, and we had a cadence to it; we decided where the clicks should be and what kind of feeling they should have. Then we brought in the group people to do it—so in addition to the individual clickers we had group clicking: you see five people clicking, really intently, like the professionals that they are. And I just had to leave the stage—that's when you think, 'I can't believe I'm doing this!'"

TRUE Q

Production No.: 232 ■ Aired: Week of October 26, 1992
Stardate: 46192.3 ■ Code: tq

Directed by **Robert Scheerer**
Written by **René Echevarria**
Based upon material by **Matthew Corey**

GUEST CAST
Amanda Rogers: **Olivia d'Abo**
Orn Lote: **John P. Connolly**
Q: **John de Lancie**

A young honor student's world is turned upside down when she realizes during her *Enterprise* stint that the powers she has been trying to ignore mean she is actually a member of the Q Continuum of superbeings.

Picard's old nemesis, Q himself, turns up to take the girl back with him but agrees to let the girl decide her own destiny with either humanity or the Continuum.

The girl, Amanda, is confused and torn between the newfound abilities Q tempts her with and her love for her old friends—even willing Riker into a romantic fantasy until its lack of reality grows disappointing. When Data discovers that her supposedly natural human parents were killed by an odd tornado on Earth, Q admits that the two were actually executed as renegades from the Continuum—and the same fate might befall Amanda.

Informed of this, the furious girl gets Q to back down to his original agreement—but he tells her that if she remains with humans she must pledge to give up her powers. That seems an easy task until Amanda can't help herself by intervening in a planetary disaster, and sadly realizes the best choice for all is for her to go live among her own kind.

Originally entitled "Q Me?" until well after live filming was finished, the first Q story in one and a half seasons on TNG did not come easy after various premises had been considered and discarded (a "Q Olympics" story and another with him creating doubles of the officers based on their opposite character poles)—but it did

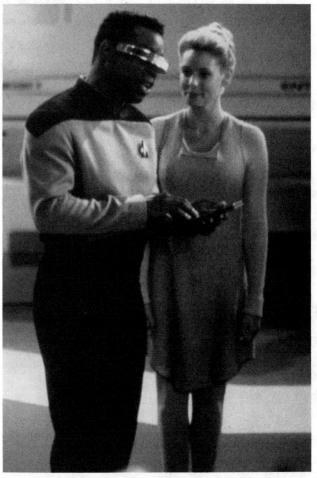

Geordi gives Amanda (Olivia D'Abo) a tour of the ship.

finally live up to Piller's goal of returning the super-alien to a more malevolent tone "so that he's just not there for the jokes." Showing how far the series' writing had matured since Season 1's "Hide and Q" covered much the same human-turned-god theme, the story mirrors that with the stress of adolescent-turned-adult.

The premise by seventeen-year-old Matt Corey from North Carolina had the guest role as a young man so he could play it, Taylor said. Despite its original plot involving Wesley Crusher, a teenage love affair, and an unwanted pregnancy, Echevarria noted it was "quite good"—and it provided a special thrill when Taylor let him call Corey to tell him of the sale. "It was kind of the mirror of three years ago, when Michael Piller called me one day—after more than a year of sending scripts to *Star Trek* and having them rejected—and then saying they wanted it."

Even then, Echevarria said his first show as a staff writer had its share of stress in working for the first time on deadline, and admitted with a laugh that he didn't even know that the various colors of script rewrite pages were coded to keep them in order. But the humor didn't suffer: for the young woman's character he had "sneaked" the name of Samantha—Elizabeth Montgomery's supernatural sitcom nose-twitcher of *Bewitched*—through several drafts before Rick Berman caught it.

If Amanda's holodeck fantasy with Riker seems more airy and offbeat than usual, it's due to the late decision by Piller to punch up the underlying tension by letting the audience hear just before that Q might kill her—a change made *after* the fantasy scene was filmed. As in "Relics," the single biggest scene cut for time involved Troi, who early on brought Amanda a vacationing crewman's dog named Henry to "dog-sit"; a scene with a puppy litter she conjured up was cut for time, although a white blur is visible next to Q on the sofa immediately after.

FX supervisor David Stipes recalled that the big challenge here was filming the warp-core breach, accomplished by having live FX man Dick Brownfield actually squirt the ever-useful liquid nitrogen onto the reactor set over specially appliquéd flashing bulbs. Animation to both widen and heal the breach was added by Digital Magic.

On the trivial side, it is spelled out that Jack Crusher died when Wesley was five and that a "Weather Modification Network" largely protects Earth from severe storms like tornadoes. Starbase 112 had been mentioned earlier ("Identity Crisis"/192), while the shuttlecraft, named for the twentieth-century pioneer atomic physicist, is seen to be Shuttlecraft 16 in the next outing, just before its destruction.

RASCALS

Production No.: 233 ■ Aired: Week of November 2, 1992
Stardate: 46235.7 ■ Code: ra

Directed by **Adam Nimoy**
Teleplay by **Allison Hock**
Story by **Ward Botsford & Diana Dru Botsford
and Michael Piller**

GUEST CAST
Chief Miles Edward O'Brien: **Colm Meaney**
Keiko Ishikawa O'Brien: **Rosalind Chao**
Ensign Ro Laren: **Michelle Forbes**
Young Picard: **David Tristin Birkin**
Young Ro: **Megan Parlen**
Young Keiko: **Caroline Junko King**
Young Guinan: **Isis Jones**
DaiMon Lurin: **Mike Gomez**
Berik: **Tracey Walter**
Morta: **Michael Snyder**
Alexander Rozhenko: **Brian Bonsall**
Guinan: **Whoopi Goldberg**
Kid No. 1: **Morgan Nagler**
Molly O'Brien: **Hana Hatae**
Computer Voice: **Majel Barrett**

After they are beamed off an endangered shuttlecraft through an energy field, Picard, Ro, Keiko, and Guinan are turned into the physical equivalents of twelve-year-old children. Their minds, though, are left intact.

As the cause is probed, the awkwardness is rampant: Picard turns over command to Riker when he realizes his commands seem odd, and O'Brien and his wife have their own personal life to sort out.

Life is complicated when renegade Ferengi in Klingon Warships disable the ship and declare it theirs, but the "youngsters" realize their advantage and gain control through the school's computer after the captain poses as Riker's son and Number One gets them secret access during a technobabble explanation for a confused Ferengi.

With computer access, the "children" beam in to surprise the occupying Ferengi and retake the ship, while O'Brien and Crusher help discover how to use the transporter to undo the masked effect on their genetic code that caused the incident in the first place. All are restored, including Ro—who finds she's become more at peace with the carefree childhood she was never able to have.

A story left over from last season—dubbed "The Year of the Child" by Piller—"Rascals" survived various rewrites to pose the old question about reliving childhood: Would anyone want to stay there? Jeri Taylor said she and Piller, the staff "elders," were the only two on staff who wanted to buy the idea—also an echo of animated Star Trek's "The Counter-Clock Incident"—which then led to numerous rewrites that no one could crack. Moore finally found the handle when the process drew a deadline as Whoopi Goldberg committed to doing the slot for Adam Nimoy, son of the famous Vulcan-playing actor. Everyone was bothered that the Ferengi takeover of the *Enterprise* came so easily, but as Taylor noted, "Would you believe four little kids could retake it from the Cardassians?"

The younger Nimoy, trained as an attorney, had decided to leave that career and built upon his familial show-business instincts, first through several UCLA extension acting and film master's classes, then by assisting Nick Meyer on *Star Trek VI*. "The day we wrapped that feature," he recalled, "I was in Rick Berman's office about observing directors on TNG." After doing so for Season 5, he got the nod here and, despite his rookie status, won praise from his boss, who noted that the "nightmare" of directing four child actors playing their first roles "would have been a challenge for Francis Ford Coppola!"

Aside from Ro's only appearance of the season, Keiko's last

Keiko and Ensign Ro
as children (Caroline
Junko King and
Megan Parlen).

before her *Deep Space 9* transfer with Miles and Molly, and the first of only two this year for Guinan (along with "Suspicions"/248) and Alexander (besides "A Fistful of Datas"/234), the cast featured many more subtle Star Trek faces: actors Snyder ("The Perfect Mate"/221) and Gomez and Walter ("The Last Outpost"/107) had all played Ferengi before; Birkin had been Picard's nephew Rene ("Family"/178); and young Isis Jones repeated her childhood impersonation of Whoopi Goldberg from the big-screen comedy hit of 1992, *Sister Act.* Birkin gets to perform numerous shirt-tugging "Picard maneuvers," while Megan Parlen pulls off one of Ro's single-heel hundred-and-eighty-degree turns just like Forbes.

With Ro's return to adulthood never shown, Taylor said that the staff toyed for a time with the idea of letting her choose not to. "Where else but on *Star Trek* could you do something like that?" she laughed. "But it seemed too drastic for us, and we were sort of squelched on that." We do learn here that Ro has an interest in biology, and that Guinan's father is still alive and over seven hundred years old (or at least two hundred during the "Time's Arrow" saga [226/227]). Another moment foreshadows Picard's nagging temptation to take up archeology full-time, later seen in "Suspicions" (248); the Professor Langford he mentions was named after a woman Moore was dating at the time—"She wasn't a fan and we stopped going out soon after, so I don't think she ever saw it!"—and was unintentionally used again next episode.

Moore pointed to Riker's scene confusing the Ferengi as his "Salute to Technobabble"—*Trek*'s unique tech talk that has bogged down more than one writer; listen closely and you can hear terms from the "Back to the Future" movie trilogy. He also owned up to inventing RVN—merely a pleasing-sounding set of letters he and Shankar hoped would go by so fast if didn't sink in—after Berman asked for something new other than DNA.

Also here: Guinan recalls her Tarcassian razor beast ("Imaginary Friend"/222); we learn that Miles and Keiko O'Brien take their coffee "with cream" and "double-sweet"; the built-in ship defense anesthizine gas is mentioned again ("The Hunted"/159, "Power Play"/215), as are the ruins of Tagua ("Qpid"/194); Shuttle Bay 2, the smallest, is only about twenty yards wide; Ferengi revere their children but never take them aboard service starships; and the Klingon Bird-of-Prey is christened the B'rel class—with the unlikely sight of Ferengi using the sparkly-red Klingon transporter. And in a minor blooper, the "young" captives' computer screen is labeled for "Classroom 7" while the room is referred to as "Schoolroom 8"; its computer design icon was the state fish of Hawaii, the reef triggerfish (Rhinecamthus aculeatus) or in Hawaiian, *humuhumu-nukunukuapua'a*. And its "periodic table" has only sixty-five cubicles instead of the 110-plus, with elements such as "Daffy Duckium," "Harponium," "Marxium," and "Grouchonium"; in-house homages like "Neskoronium" (for art director Andy); and categories like "World Series" and "Mega Series."

A FISTFUL OF DATAS

Production No.: 234 ▪ Aired: Week of November 9, 1992
Stardate: 46271.5 ▪ Code: fs

Directed by **Patrick Stewart**
Teleplay by **Robert Hewitt Wolfe and Brannon Braga**
Story by **Robert Hewitt Wolfe**

GUEST CAST
Alexander Rozhenko: **Brian Bonsall**
Eli Hollander: **John Pyber-Ferguson**
Annie Meyers: **Joy Garrett**
Bandito: **Jorge Cervera Jr.**
Computer Voice: **Majel Barrett**

With some spare time to enjoy, the *Enterprise* crew head in different directions: La Forge tests a hunch that Data can be used as a backup to the ship's computer, and Alexander coaxes his father and later Troi into taking part in an "Ancient West" holodeck role-play scenario he's written.

But after the test linkup to Data, minor glitches become obvious in ship's systems: the android's bad poetry showing up in a play script Dr. Crusher is rehearsing, for one. Far worse is what the holodeck gamers discover when Alexander is kidnapped by outlaws and the game won't stop: the weapons failsafes won't work and the "bad guys" confronting them one by one assume not only Data's look but his abilities!

Knowing they can only end the game by surviving till story's end, the outgunned Troi and Worf prepare for the inevitable gunfight, while back in "reality" Data begins lapsing into a Western drawl that tips off what the problem is; his memory has been crossed with the ship's holodeck database.

While La Forge works to repair it from outside, Worf saves himself from an ambush at the attempted hostage switch for Alexander by juryrigging a forcefield to repel the outlaws' bullets. Even that, though, cannot save him from the big pucker of the saloon owner Annie—who now also looks like Data.

Worf and Alexander on the holodeck version of the Old West.

This offbeat show, writer Wolfe's pitch script that got him hired to work on DS9, received a polish by Braga with a little help from Ron Moore and practically everybody—including, by the luck of the draw, an English Director named Patrick Stewart. "I'm not a Western fan, I never really saw Westerns," Braga observed, "and Patrick Stewart, a British guy who's not familiar with the Western genre—and here we are doing our big Western show! But, I think, we brought a fresh sensibility to it."

"Patrick approached this with such zealousness—he went out and rented two classic Westerns every night," Taylor recalled. "The next morning he'd come in and tell us what great ideas he'd had, and we could always tell just what he'd watched!"

Originally the story concerned a greedy land baron, but after Ira Stephen Behr's suggestion from the DS9 office down the hall they switched the homage plot to *Rio Bravo*. At first Worf was to play the Clint Eastwood "man with no name" type from the Sergio Leone "spaghetti Westerns" with Troi as a dance-hall girl and Alexander her son—complete with a Leone-parody title, "The Good, The Bad and the Klingon." But it was decided that the boy would likely write the program to feature himself, so he became a deputy to "Sheriff Worf" and Troi got the strong, silent role of Durango in a victory for off-type writing.

"This was a hoot! It was never meant to be anything more than old *Star Trek*," said Piller, who noted that the script met two of his pre-season goals: be more lighthearted and give Brent Spiner something more interesting to do. Braga said Data's bad poetry ("Schisms"/231) and Spot's cat food (version 127!) in the replicators were his way of making the shipboard scenes just as fun as the holodeck tale: "The tricky part was not to make it broad parody but make it believable Western storytelling and still have fun just from seeing the characters in those situations."

The opening big boots/little boots scene was right from Leone—whose Eastwood vehicle "A Fistful of Dollars" inspired the title—while the *Enterprise* flying off into the sunset at tale's end was just the right touch. Even the music had a familiar feel: harmonica virtuoso Tommy Morgan, veteran of all those distinctive Western soundtracks of the past, was brought in with his packet of hand-filed instruments to record the soundtrack, Peter Lauritson recalled. The uncredited "henchman" Nick Dimitri also is seen later as a taxi driver ("Emergence"/275), among other assignments, while, sadly, actress Joy Garret died the next year of liver failure.

Two fun scenes that had to be cut for time included a homage to "The Ransom of Red Chief" between Data/Bandito and Alexander as the testy captive, and a funny moment where Worf nearly shoots himself in the foot after a quick-draw lesson from Troi—which closes with Deanna trying a little therapy on the criminal son. Watch out too for the blooper when Worf's gun switches hand between takes.

Eli Hollander was named for one of Braga's film school professors at UC-Santa Cruz, and the place-names reflect hometowns of his family: his own Bozeman, Montana (see "Cause and Effect"/218), along with Rapid City and Deadwood, SD. "Miss Langford's House of Pleasure" was kept even though Moore forgot he'd suggested Langford for a name in the prior episode (seen "Rascals"/233), while the *Biko* pays homage to the slain black South African leader.

The exterior scenes were all filmed in a day on the Western Street at Warner Brothers' backlot, while the interiors were all built on Stage 16. Picard's Kataanen flute turns up for the first time since "The Inner Light" (225), so does a mention of Reg Barclay and the old *Grisson* miniature posing as the *Biko*. Meanwhile, La Forge is ribbed in the first of two consecutive episodes about Le Var Burton's beard, "Ms." is heard to be still in use in the twenty-fourth century, and we learn that Troi is a Western fan thanks to her late father's reading aloud when she was young. From his boorish start here, Riker's acting under Beverly's direction apparently takes off, judging by his later efforts ("Frame of Mind"/247); the Observation Lounge is not-so-subtly redressed as their rehearsal room. Finally, it seems programmer Alexander needs to study his Ancient West geography: a map of Arizona is seen hung in the sheriff's office in the supposedly South Dakotan town.

THE QUALITY OF LIFE

Production No.: 235 ▪ Aired: Week of November 16, 1992
Stardate: 46307.2 ▪ Code: ql

Directed by **Jonathan Frakes**
Written by **Naren Shankar**
Based upon material by **L. D. Scott**

GUEST CAST
Dr. Farallon: **Ellen Bry**
Transporter Chief Kelso: **J. Downing**
Computer Voice: **Majel Barrett**

During a status survey of the Tyrus VII-A orbital mining station and its new but lagging technology, center director Farallon unveils her "exocomp": a problem-solving "smart" computer tool that can make repairs where a living being can't go, such as inside the station's troubled power grid.

She wins a delay for Picard's report deadline in order to make station upgrade repairs by using the units. When one inexplicably fails, a curious Data checks out the "faulty" unit only to realize the exocomp had not malfunctioned, but was instead repairing itself after shutting down at the sign of danger—an act of survival that convinces him the "machines" are alive!

The stressed-out Farallon is skeptical but seems vindicated after a shipboard test with a simulated danger that the exocomp apparently doesn't recognize. Data later repeats the trial run on his own until he discovers the exocomp knew the danger was not real.

But before he can report, Picard and La Forge are trapped in yet another station accident. Recalling his own struggle for rights, Data locks out the transporters and refuses orders to use the exocomps as slaves to rescue them until Riker agrees to request their help. The three units agree and devise their own plan, but one must sacrifice itself in the successful rescue. All are saddened, but Data is satisfied he's made his point.

Dr. Farallon, developer of the Exocomp (Ellen Bry).

Shankar, like Ron Moore and René Echevarria an Original Series Star Trek fan, took on this story as an early-season reserve script for Taylor while still "only" the writing staff's science adviser; in L. D. Scott's original premise, the creatures Data stakes his career on were simply talking wall terminals and household appliances. Shankar's initial take on the "metacomps," as they were first called, was for something modular that would be added to existing tools "like a high-tech Transformer toy" and above all be alien and easily overlooked. (The name had to be changed when a real-life company by that name turned up.) He had hoped the eventual look of the aliens-to-be would not be "cute R2-D2-types," referring to the famous "droids" of the Star Wars film saga, since he felt the story could almost become a comment on aspects of the animal-rights movement: "As long as they're cute and fuzzy people respond, but if it's a nasty, ugly-looking thing they won't save it."

Rick Sternbach designed the exocomps, but budget allowed only two to be built; the shots of three included one composited in later, FX supervisor Ron B. Moore said. Amazingly, their every motion was propelled by a puppeteer with control rods who was "painted out" via computer in what had to be some of the series' most unnoticed effects; the bouncier approach won out over sophisticated motorized robots with jerky motion control, à la the saucers of *Batteries Not Included*.

Dr. Farallon was named not for the software company but for the islands off the San Francisco Bay area which the company was named for. Beverly's character gets a unusual twist—and a foreshadowing of the commando regimen to come next episode—when we learn she is taking *bat'telh* lessons from Worf; we also hear about her brunette experiment at age thirteen. For prop watchers, the particle fountain miniature is a new model touched up with cheap and quick detail and lighting by computer, while the lateral neon "blinky" units first seen in *Star Trek II: The Wrath of Khan* appear in yet another alien lab.

Having never gained approval to keep Geordi's beard permanently after his brief poker scene in "The Outcast" (217), LeVar Burton confronted the producers with a request they couldn't turn down: He wanted it for his wedding!

CHAIN OF COMMAND, PART I

Production No.: 236 ▪ Aired: Week of December 14, 1992
Stardate: 46357.4 ▪ Code: c1

Directed by **Robert Scheerer**
Teleplay by **Ronald D. Moore**
Story by **Frank Abatemarco**

GUEST CAST
Captain Edward Jellico: **Ronny Cox**
Vice-Admiral Alynna Nechayev: **Natalija Nogulich**
Gul Lemec: **John Durbin**
DaiMon Solok: **Lou Wagner**
Gul Madred: **David Warner**
Computer Voice: **Majel Barrett**

Shipboard routine is jolted with the sudden reassignment of Picard, Crusher, and Worf for a classified mission and the arrival of Captain Edward Jellico. Riker and La Forge in particular have a tough time getting used to the gruff Jellico, who is as hard on his crew as he is with the Cardassians he must negotiate with during a time of heightened tensions.

Meanwhile, the reassigned trio train and obtain transport for a secret search-and-destroy raid on the otherwise deserted Celtris III, where Starfleet fears the Cardassians are developing—

Beverly tries to find non-Starfleet transport to carry out the mission.

genetically engineered viruses that can wipe out all life in their path.

At a meeting intended to ease tensions, Jellico enrages Gul Lemec and his party with ploys at intimidation until the Cardassians reveal that they know of Picard's secret mission and walk out.

Meanwhile, the raiders discover that they've walked into a trap when they find nothing and realize the metagenics story is a hoax. Worf and Crusher are forced to escape without Picard, who is captured in the ambush and faces a Cardassian interrogator who promises to reward Picard's silence with death.

Aside from setting up a terrific battle of wills in its conclusion, this story also introduced the news of the Cardassians' Bajoran withdrawal to set up the events of DS9's pilot, airing less than a month later. In fact, Ron Moore revealed that the two-parter was meant to be a crossover (with the Solok scene written word-for-word for DS9 resident Ferengi Quark) until someone realized it would air before DS9 was out!

Moore said he took most interest in developing Jellico—whose name Abatemarco had lifted from the British fleet commander at World War I's Battle of Jutland. To make Jellico a mix of personable as well as irritating and "just different" qualities, Moore added aspects such as displaying his son's art and ditching Livingston, the ready-room fish (though it played more harshly than intended). A scene cut to save time, similar to one revealing his early warmth shown Riker, had Jellico tell Geordi that he'd played rugby at the Academy with the chief engineer's former captain

Zimbata from the *U.S.S. Victory* ("Elementary, Dear Data"/129, "Identity Crisis"/192). But again, the man who'd helped negotiate the Cardassian-UFP armistice only two years earlier ("The Wounded"/186) also carried a "captain on the bridge" formality and ordered "Get it done," his own catchline contrasting Picard's "Make it so."

Another contrast with Picard, Jellico's request that Troi wear a standard uniform while on duty, made good a goal that Moore had wanted to try and Sirtis was all too happy to oblige. With the disliked cheerleader-like "skant" uniform from the pilot a dim memory, she began here to alternate the standard uniform with her other outfits in future episodes.

Ronny Cox, who these days puts more time into his first love as a burgeoning country singer than acting, once played nice guys on the short-lived *Apple's Way* and *Cop Rock* series and the movie *Deliverance* but may be best known for his stern types: Eddie Murphy's boss in the *Beverly Hills Cop* films and the villainous executives in *Robocop* and *Total Recall*. Often combining his music with guest-starring roles—such as an *L.A. Law* segment with fellow country songster Pam Tillis—he offers here a unique mix of qualities that, despite a first glance, lived up to Moore's intent.

Actor Wagner later appeared as another Ferengi, Krax, in the first-season DS9 segment "The Nagus," while Durbin, as had castmate Marc Alaimo, emerged from under the alien masks of "Lonely Among Us" (108) to play a Cardassian. Nogulich's admiral would surface again in "Descent" (252) and throughout various crises ("Journey's End"/272, "Preemptive Strike"/276, and DS9's "The Maquis, Part II" and "The Search, Part II"), while—like Selar and Barclay—another past crew member would return by mention only: tactical officer McDowell ("The Next Phase"/224). There's also a glimpse into Starfleet training when Jellico is able to reassign a third of Geordi's engineers to security.

For trivia's sake: Riker graduated eighth in his Starfleet class of 2357 (as seen in "Conundrum"/214) and has been decorated five times, while Picard is the first on TNG to get a serial number, SP-

937-215, and be seen in a ship command-transfer ceremony; his marathon running is also recalled ("The Best of Both Worlds, Part 2"). The formal name of Cardassia for the aliens' homeworld is introduced, although "Cardassian Union" is used instead of "Cardassian Empire" here for the only time on either TNG ("Ensign Ro"/ 203) or DS9. Their hand weapon debuted here, described by Sternbach as a "copper-colored banana" and firing a purple beam, while their would-be metagenic weapon harkens back to the 1980s "clean" neutron bombs once hailed for killing armies while leaving infrastructure intact.

Seen before: the black commando fatigues ("The Outcast"/ 217), the shuttle Feynman shown as the original model from stock footage of being launched ("Unnatural Selection"/133), and the Torman IV matte painting, originally the Genome Colony ("The Masterpiece Society"/213).

Curiously, Solok wears a Ferengi uniform but no head tattoo, and is called a DaiMon but wears no "ying-yang" color rank; he was originally named "Selok," but that name had been used already ("Data's Day," 185). Also in the bar—where Beverly revives the stimulating art of *oo-mox* ("Ménage à Troi"/172)—are a Bajoran, a Mizarian ("Allegiance"/166), and a lavender-faced alien Westmore dubbed "Rotciv," a palindrome of the Algolian chimes musician from Season 4 dubbed "Victor" ("Ménage à Troi") after the extra who's under both makeups, Victor Sein. Reflecting its roots, the scene's tight angles are a try at concealing its real identity: the replimat corner of Quark's bar from DS9. Blond script typist Jana Wallace (namesake of longtime extra Guy Vardaman's persona in "Descent" [252]) is seen as a foreground extra in Ten-Forward's transfer-of-command scene.

CHAIN OF COMMAND, PART II

Production No.: 237 ▪ Aired: Week of December 14, 1992
Stardate: 46360.8 ▪ Code: c2

Directed by **Les Landau**
Written by **Frank Abatemarco**

GUEST CAST
Captain Edward Jellico: **Ronny Cox**
Gul Lemec: **John Durbin**
Gul Madred: **David Warner**
Jil Orra: **Heather Lauren Olson**
Computer Voice: **Majel Barrett**

Captured after the failed Celtris III raid, Picard tells all he knows about Starfleet motives in the area under effects of a truth drug. But his captor, Gul Madred, isn't satisfied and presses on with horrendous torture, both physical and psychological, to break the captain's will.

Meanwhile, after retrieving Worf and Dr. Crusher, new *Enterprise* captain Jellico refuses Riker's request for a rescue mission of Picard until they learn he is still alive. The new captain relieves Riker of duty after he opposes Jellico's trade admission to the raid for Picard's release. Then Jellico, over his senior staff's objections—orders a first strike readied on the theory that the Celtris III matter portends a Cardassian invasion.

Meanwhile, despite his beatings and captivity, Picard eventually holds his own in his battles of will with Gul Madred, his interrogator, and even wins a few, to the Cardassians' chagrin.

Aboard ship, Jellico swallows his pride to ask Riker to lead a mine-laying mission to stave of war, and uses the mines to bargain for Picard's release when the outraged Cardassians realize what has happened.

Having never succumbed to his captor, a weary Picard is returned and his command restored.

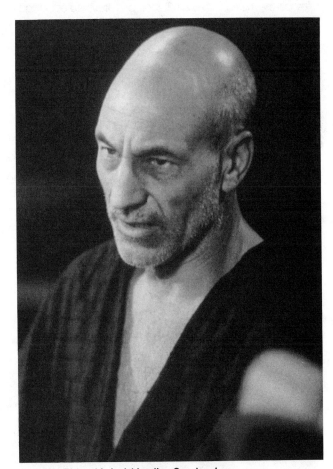
Captain Picard is held by the Cardassians.

Abatemarco had dug into the research books on everything from Amnesty International to the psychology of torturers, their methods, and their survivors for what he hoped would be a grander opus than the rushed "Man of the People" (229). As the scope of the project swelled (the episode was designed as a money-saver, and a bigger final confrontation between opposing ships had to be scrapped, Moore said), Piller and Berman suggested a two-parter, and Amnesty supporter Patrick Stewart threw his support into it—later to grow concerned when the inevitable rewrites came across and pleasing that its intensity not be diluted.

Of course it wasn't and the story—the first of two to be expanded to a two-parter this season—became a tour de force for Stewart in what many believed to be his most intense and focused acting on the series to date, if not in his career. (A method actor, Stewart, was at his insistence, nude during the one interrogation scene but performed that scene on a closed set.) "There's just nothing better than putting Patrick Stewart alone in a room with one other good actor and really letting him go for an hour," noted Piller, who took out a full-page ad in *Variety* to back an unsuccessful Emmy nomination for the actor. "It is not possible that there are five better male actors in this town than Patrick Stewart!" Taylor agreed. "It's probably his finest performance—he literally threw himself, physically and mentally, into that."

Warner, of course, included among his long career guest-starring roles in both the fifth and sixth Trek features—where his roles as the human St. John Talbot and the ill-fated Klingon Chancellor Gorkon combined here to make him another one of the few who have played multiple races in the Trek universe.

For the one-on-one scenes between Madred and Picard, designer Richard James provided a sparse interrogation-room set that was almost theatrical in its stark simplicity, with pools of light and tight lighting designed to provide the focus needed. He had originally planned a grand staircase for its entrance with a floating ceiling piece from which the captor would lord it over the captive, à la *Man of La Mancha*, but budget cuts dropped that back to the massive doors shown and the simple manacles, often reused ("Lower Decks"/267, DS9).

We are also given the up-by-the-military-bootstrap history of the Cardassians, see that Riker's cabin is Deck 9/Room 0912, and discover that the equivalent of today's Geneva accords on war is the Milky Way's "Seldonis IV Convention"—called the "Selonis" convention by Riker, thanks to a script typo. An unaired reference gives the Minos Korva colony a population of two million, while we do hear that Picard's mother's maiden name is "Gessard" and that the family sang after Sunday dinner—a nice touch setting up the captain's occasional lapses into song ("Family"/178, "Final Mission"/183).

SHIP IN A BOTTLE

Production No.: 238 ■ Aired: Week of January 25, 1993
Stardate: 46424.1 ■ Code: sb

Directed by **Alexander Singer**
Written by **René Echevarria**

GUEST CAST

Professor James Moriarty: **Daniel Davis**
Countess Regina Barthalomew: **Stephanie Beacham**
Lieutenant (j.g.) Reginald "Reg" Barclay III: **Dwight Schultz**
Gentleman: **Clement von Franckenstein**
Computer Voice: **Majel Barrett**

After a glitch turns up in Data and La Forge's "Sherlock Holmes" role-play holodeck game, Barclay, while making repairs, comes across the stored file of Holmes' fictional archvillain Professor Moriarty, accidentally given consciousness and intelligence four years earlier.

Incensed that he has been "forgotten," Moriarty astounds the naysaying officers when he walks off the holodeck, alive and whole! While the crew struggles to understand, he demands that his love, the Countess Regina Barthalomew, be made alive as well—taking control of the ship's computer from Picard until he agrees to do it.

Amid the effort—made more dire by the ship's dangerous proximity to two colliding gas planets to be studied—Data realizes that he and Picard are trapped in a holodeck simulation themselves that Moriarty devised: the professor isn't real, but he does have computer lockout on the ship and access to their program.

To outwit him, the officers create their own false reality and have Moriarty and the Countess "beamed" into it, ostensibly giving them a shuttlecraft in return for releasing ship control.

Once "launched," Moriarty returns control to Picard and the two lovers are allowed to roam forever in their own "reality" within a protected file.

Barclay (Dwight Schultz) and Data worry about regaining control of the ship.

dizzy: Ron Moore recalling diagramming the various universes as nestled boxes during the break sessions.

Schultz was booked to reprise Barclay when it was initially felt a character was needed who had not known about the first Moriarty encounter in Season 2, but that became a moot point and viewers—as well as director Singer, asked back after his first-ever TNG outing ("Relics"/230)—got to enjoy Schultz, Daniel Davis, and Stephanie Beacham—later of *SeaQuest DSV*—all in the same episode. Too, Echevarria mused, no one but Barclay could have made the whole episode's final punch line work.

Set decorator Jim Mees revealed that his crew had to please two masters of continuity when outfitting the 221-B Baker Street study—the original Doyle story descriptions as well as the previous scene in Season 2. For instance, the first set's wallpaper design had been discontinued in the past four years and could not be exactly matched.

Not to be overlooked, too, is FX supervisor David Stipes' sequence featuring the collision of the star and gas planet; Stipes which allowed him to bring in "real science." Designer Rick Sternbach said of the effect, "Our cry became 'This is not *Nova*,' " he joked, referring to the PBS science series, "but we wanted to be as accurate with the gas exchange as possible. A lot of testing ensued, along with the discovery of the need for longer than

After three years, it turned out that the perceived taboo in doing more Sherlock Holmes stories—first laid down in Season 3 (see "The Defector"/158) following the first Moriarty story a year earlier ("Elementary, Dear Data"/129)—had all been a mistake! "Apparently the Arthur Conan Doyle estate was irritated with Paramount because of [the movie] *Young Sherlock Holmes* and they said no more, ever," Taylor said. "Well, as in many walks of life it was never say never again; to my amazement they were willing to give us the characters for a very reasonable license fee."

Even with that hurdle cleared, a planned Moriarty script fell through and the idea languished until Piller told Taylor to ask about one of the three story ideas Echevarria had suggested during his very first pitch session during Season 3—a feat that amazed the young writer: "My God, the man's an elephant! He remembered that pitch?" Though not a Holmes story, the premise centered around a character on the holodeck who actually thinks he's aboard ship. While brainstorming at one of Taylor's Sunday sessions, Echevarria recalled, his hostess had just spoken of watching the first Moriarty episode and an idea to bring back the professor though alien embodiment when the two ideas struck him—solving the problem of getting Moriarty off the holodeck plausibly. Still, the nested universes kept even the writing staff

Dr. Moriarty (Daniel Davis) and Countess Regina (Stephanie Beacham) think they've escaped from the holodeck.

usual sequences—twelve seconds as opposed to the typical four-to-five-second shot."

For detail hounds, it is made clear in back-to-back shows that voice command codes are changed often: Picard's goes from "Delta-5" ("Chain of Command, Part I"/236) to "Epsilon 7-9-3" here. The pattern enhancers are old hat ("Power Play"/215, "Time's Arrow"/226, "Frame of Mind"/247, "Inheritance"/262), while the newer rear-entry live shuttle set doesn't match the stock footage of the Sakharov original (from "Unnatural Selection"/133). Other oddities: Picard orders a "Class A" probe be launched when all others had previously been designated with numbers, and the "real" Riker talks to the Holo-Generated Moriarty via the main viewer.

AQUIEL

Production No.: 239 ■ Aired: Week of February 1, 1993
Stardate: 46461.3 ■ Code: aq

Directed by **Cliff Bole**
Teleplay by **Brannon Braga & Ronald D. Moore**
Story by **Jeri Taylor**

GUEST CAST
Lieutenant (j.g.) Aquiel Uhnari: **Renee Jones**
Governor Torak: **Wayne Grace**
Commander Morag: **Reg E. Cathey**
Computer Voice: **Majel Barrett**

An odd mystery unfolds when La Forge, while replaying the personal logs of the missing lieutenant Aquiel Uhnari and befriending her dog—finds himself fall in love with her as he probes into the mysterious abandonment of her two-man relay station on the Klingon-UFP border.

With DNA residue found at the station, suspects yielded by her logs range all the way from the Klingon Morag, who had occasionally harassed her, to her own crewmate, Keith Rocha—until unexpectedly, the Klingon's superior delivers both Morag and Aquiel to the *Enterprise*, where she returns La Forge's affection.

Morag and Aquiel then become suspects in Rocha's disappearance, especially when the station crew's ongoing fights, Aquiel's quick temper, and her log tampering are revealed.

Despite La Forge's support, clues are pointing to Uhnari's guilt when the DNA residue shocks

Crusher by suddenly assuming the shape of her hand. Picard's staff realizes that a coalescent creature is at work and had taken the form of Rocha, then Aquiel's dog—and La Forge barely escapes the creature when it wants to kill him and take his form.

Her name cleared but her career tainted, Uhnari can only bid La Forge a fond farewell and hope the two can meet again.

This story, generally felt to be one of the few disappointments of the season, originally began as yet another try at providing Geordi a recurring romance while tying into Piller's suggestion of a mystery in the manner of the classic movie *Laura*—falling in love with someone who first appears to be dead and then turns up alive. "We now portray the twenty-fourth century as being full of single people," Taylor observed. "We lost the O'Briens [to DS9] and everybody else is footloose and fancy free. It seems to me that's not the only comment we should be making—that marriage and serious relationships DO survive into the twenty-fourth century. But how to tell a love story with an SF spin on it?"

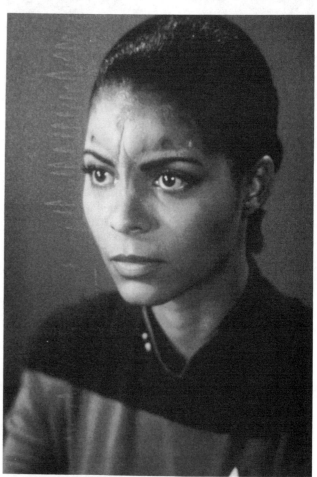

The beautiful Aquiel (Renee Jones).

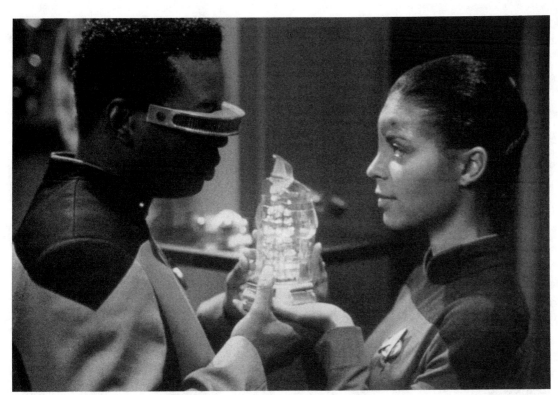

Geordi falls for Aquiel (Renee Jones).

Moore said the problem was that no one was ever satisfied with the person "whodunit." Aquiel was initially to have been the killer, but when the plot seemed to be veering toward a *Basic Instinct* clone, both the Klingon and the dead Keith Rocha—named by Moore for another one of his high-school friends—were in turn considered for the murderer and then dropped as seeming too obvious. "At one point," he recalled, "we finally said 'Why not the dog?' He had always been in the script; we had meant to leave him with Geordi from that time on."

Taylor praised actress Renee Jones but felt she had too much of a burden to live up to, and the chemistry with Geordi never clicked. "*Star Trek* sometimes does to actors what it does to writers—people who are very effective in one kind of thing feel very exposed," she said. "So I don't think this was quite her cup of tea." Despite TNG's ongoing tough luck with mysteries ("The Royale"/138, "A Matter of Perspective"/162), Taylor vowed to keep plugging away (see "Suspicions"/248). Even FX supervisor Ronald B. Moore commented he was not completely satisfied with the creature, a computer-generated effect subcontracted out that was delivered as promised but not in time to do any of the touch-ups to add the texture and motion he felt was needed.

To make the relay station, RS-47 was Letter on a redress of the module from the cryo capsule of "The Neutral Zone" (126), and carries it on its shuttle as well. We also learn that Geordi drinks iced coffee, and keeps a Phaser II in his quarters; that stored phasers are all set to Level 1; and there's been no Klingon raid on the UFP in "Seven years"—a fact Moore created to show that things can still be shaky in the Alliance. Also, Geordi learned Haliian and many other languages during his "Starfleet brat" childhood ("Imaginary Friend"/222), and the *Enterprise*'s com-

puter voice is also used on the station. Somewhat strangely: Dr. Crusher beams in meters away and on a different level from the rest of the away team during its first visit; Worf touches hot metal only seconds after he's cut through it with a phaser; Geordi has the same long artwork on his wall as Data has; and actress Jones has a minor blooper when she refers to Starbase "12" instead of 212.

Despite its faults, a sense of humor still reigned in "Aquiel": Moore said it was all he and Braga could do to *not* push for their preferred episode title of "Murder, My Pet!" And until the plot change made it moot, a planned closing scene had Data in Geordi's quarters, commenting with a matter-of-fact "Spot doesn't do that" as his friend ticked off his various newly discovered problems like chewed boots and soiled carpet. Finally, after Maura trots over to drool on his own boots, the android gets to deliver the punch line: "Geordi, I think I am a cat person!" Maura (played by Friday, a terrier mix) was also Commissioner Robert Scorpio's dog for four years on *General Hospital.*

"Aquiel" also marked the beginning of an in-house joke in the manner of original Star Trek's "Jefferies tubes" ("The Hunted"/159): the "Mees panel," a script note referring to set decorator Jim Mees' ongoing complaints about the cost—about $1,000—of detailing the interior of an opened wall console. "Ron Moore and I have had a long-standing running joke," he explained. "Every show he ever wrote they always ended up going into a panel and fixing something. And I said to him: 'Ron, do you know we're not on a real ship here? Do you know that if they pull that metal thing off there isn't anything there? It costs money to do it, it takes time to design these things!' So they now call them the Mees panels, because I've bitched and moaned so much!"

Face of the Enemy

Production No.: 240 ■ Aired: Week of February 8, 1993
Stardate: 46519.1 ■ Code: fe

Directed by **Gabrielle Beaumont**
Teleplay by **Naren Shankar**
Story by **René Echevarria**

GUEST CAST
Subcommander N'Vek: **Scott MacDonald**
Commander Toreth: **Carolyn Seymour**
Ensign Stefan DeSeve: **Barry Lynch**
Khazara Pilot: **Robertson Dean**
Corvallen Captain: **Dennis Cockrum**
Ensign McKnight: **Pamela Winslow**
Computer Voice: **Majel Barrett**

Kidnapped from a conference, Troi awakens to find herself aboard the Romulan Warbird *Khazara*, disguised as a Tal Shiar special intelligence officer and smack in the middle of a plot by the Empire's underground to smuggle out three high-level defectors to the UFP via a neutral Corvallen freighter.

At first, the dazed "Major Rakal" is dependent upon Subcommander N'Vek, her contact, as the usually soft-spoken counselor uses all her wiles in dealing with the ship's bitter and suspicious Commander Toreth, whose father was a midnight victim of the Tal Shiar.

After N'Vek destroys the Corvallens when Troi senses they are traitors, Toreth is furious when "Rakal" orders the Warbird to cloak and wait, buying time for a backup plan.

Meanwhile, the *Enterprise* has picked up a rare Romulan defector, whose message from Spock and the underground leads them to the wrecked Corvallen ship and then the cloaked *Khazara*—aided by a subtle signal from the Warbird's sympathetic engineer.

The stoic Toreth braces for a battle or a collision until Troi, having bolstered the wavering N'Vek, surreptitiously beams over the defectors. N'Vek is killed when Toreth senses the plan and retakes her bridge, but a relieved Troi is beamed home just in time.

This "fish out of water" plot, which Marina Sirtis herself felt was a series-long landmark for the character, began as a Dr. Crusher story until the staff realized Troi's empathy would make her better suited to espionage. Michael Piller, among those roundly praising both Sirtis and Seymour for their performances, recalled that a similar *Hunt for Red October*-style premise had been killed until the staff "cajoled" Rick Berman into giving it a try. (Ron Moore recalled that long-ago Q premise in which the whole crew is deposited on a Romulan Warbird had been discarded for its likeness to *Quantum Leap*.)

The prize to be delivered to the Federation evolved from a Romulan ship to actual *Romulans*—Vice-Preconsul M'Ret would have been just under Proconsul Neral of "Unification" (207–208); The Empire's underground and Spock's "cowboy diplomacy" phrase also hark back to that story. As Shankar rushed out the easy-flowing first-draft teleplay in six days from Echevarria's staff-generated story outline, at one point Piller had joked about allowing the Romulan "Popsicle people" to reveal that Spock tried to get out but didn't make it. "It was one of those craaaazy moments," Shankar added. "You can't kill somebody like that offscreen!" The writer also was pleased to break Troi out of the caregiver role for once, make the Romulans sympathetic, with a three-dimensional internal conflict, and create the first Federation defector ever seen. A trimmed scene follows defector DeSeve after the food units refuse his Romulan beverage and he struggles to remember "coffee."

Winslow had last appeared two years earlier as McKnight ("Clues"/188, "In Theory"/199), while Seymour makes her second appearance as a Romulan ("Contagion"/137) and her third overall on TNG ("First Contact"/189); McDonald would later turn up human in the second spinoff series *Voyager*'s pilot. Shankar said Seymour might reappear as Toreth; the name change came because it was initially assumed her earlier Romulan, Taris, had been killed. Toreth was created as a male, and Shankar recalled writing dialogue as if *Red October*'s Sean "Captain Ramos" Connery himself were delivering it—an interesting twist when the unchanged words were kept intact after the female-female conflict was hit upon. He named the Romulan's KGB-like "Tal Shiar," indicated by an extra strip on the chest sash's right side, as an homage to the "tal shaya," the fatal Vulcan neck-break created by D. C. Fontana for 1967's "Journey to Babel."

This story allows TNG's first real peek aboard a Warbird: the senior officers' "wardroom" mess is just off the small bridge (a nomenclature change since "Control Central" of 1969's "The *Enterprise* Incident") and the helmsman is dubbed the "pilot." We learn too that "Imperial Romulan Warbird" is the formal prefix for the ships, which use a forced quantum singularity as a power source and monitor their EM emissions while cloaked. Also, the cloak-detecting tachyon field ("Redemption, Part II"/201) is recalled, while the Corvallens' old Antares-class freighter is of different design than the Bajorans' flat angular ship of the same name ("Ensign Ro"/203).

Worf's ponytail debuted here but it was a long time coming, according to hairstylist Joy Zapata: she and Dorn had both long lobbied for it—"[Worf's hair] used to remind me of a Klingon that had gone to the beauty salon; it looked like Donna Reed!"—but in relenting Rick Berman didn't want it to look trendy, as if copied from 1992's *Last of the Mohicans* or any of the other long-hair look

Deanna Troi in disguise aboard a Romulan ship.

features out that year. "Now we tie it back, he carries himself differently—he's a whole different person." The two wigs, alternated for daily use, are made of hair sold by Russian children for the money and cost $5,000 each.

Amid a light FX show, supervisor David Stipes got director Beaumont to agree to let the ill-fated Nevek die a more gruesome, writhing death than usual on TNG when vaporized.

Tapestry

Production No.: 241 ■ Aired: Week of February 15, 1993
Stardate: Unknown ■ Code: tp

Directed by **Les Landau**
Written by **Ronald D. Moore**

GUEST CAST
Ensign Cortan "Corey" Zweller: **Ned Vaughn**
Ensign Marta "Marty" Batanides: **J. C. Brandy**
Nausicaan No. 1: **Clint Carmichael**
Penny Muroc: **Rae Norman**
Q: **John de Lancie**
Maurice Picard: **Clive Church**
Ensign Lean-Luc Picard: **Marcus Nash**
Computer Voice: **Majel Barrett**

After being gravely wounded by terrorists during a diplomatic mission, Picard awakens in a white limbo to find Q, his old nemesis, announcing that the captain's artificial heart has failed him—and that He, Q, is God.

Though Picard scoffs at that, he cannot deny the regrets he feels about his rambunctious younger years and wishes that he could change them. Instantly, Q whisks him back to the eve of one of his life's biggest turning points: the fight where, as a fresh-faced ensign just before shipping out, he was stabbed through the heart during a brawl with three large Nausicaans.

Determined to change history, Picard avoids the situation which caused the fight, Q returns him to the present once he escapes injury, where Picard finds himself a junior lieutenant in astrophysics, bluntly told by Riker and Troi that he plays it too safe to have a chance at command.

Pleading with his old foe, Picard begs Q to let him relive the fight so he can die rather than live his new dreary life. History is reset, the fight ensues, and Picard again falls to the Nausicaan—until he comes to back in sickbay, recovering from his wounds and actually grateful to Q for the new insight.

Based on a brief mention way back in Season 2's "Samaritan Snare" (143), Picard's Nausicaan encounter was actually just part of "A Q Carol," a Dickensian premise pitched years ago in which Q tours the "mistakes" of Picard's life: the stabbing, a family scene, and an event aboard the *Stargazer,* possibly Jack Crusher's death. Ron Moore said his longtime yen to do such a Capra-esque script led back to that old premise as a starting point, pruned down to only the Nausicaan incident that had always piqued his curiosity—although, as with Picard's brother ("Family"/178), we do get a taste of his father's disdain for a Starfleet career. The tale also reinforces the contrast in Trek's two captains, Moore noted: Picard was the hard-drinking womanizer who became studious, reserved, and cool, while Kirk was a bookworm at the Academy before becoming a hell-raiser later on. He felt the segment overall was better than his own "Relics," while Michael Piller had mixed feelings about it but took its popularity as a sign of audience interest in metaphysics and examining one's mortality.

But the premise behind Q's first tale since the pilot, whose title did not include his "name"—had murky roots. No one could remember the source of the "near-death white light" premise, especially after one pro with a similar old pitch passed on the claim; it was not until after the show aired that a heartbroken and disillusioned letter arrived from James Mooring, who'd actually pitched the exact same idea after submitting a spec script. With the first-season story-credit disputes ironically unknown to this staff, they immediately set out to settle up and make amends. "I talked to him, Ron talked to him," Jeri Taylor said, "and they paid him. He was very happy. All he wanted was acknowledgment of this, and we apologized profusely; I hope it restored his faith in our integrity, because we would never do anything like that intentionally."

Unaware of Bob Justman's formative idea to credit the ban on captains' dangerous beam-downs to Picard, Moore said the brief mention of just such an instance with Picard taking command was meant to show that his "twenty-two-year mission" on his old ship as laid out in GR's original Writer's Guide was not all spent as captain. Also, he added, the stabbing is *not* the major event Boothby talks of in "The First Duty" (219), and Jellico ("Chain of Command" 236–37) was his later-nixed first choice for *Enterprise's* captain in Picard's altered future.

Station Earhart, Picard's "laugh at death," and the Bonestell facility (filmed on an extra, non-Star Trek Stage 10) are taken right from "Samaritan Snare" populated by many of Michael Westmore's aliens from DS9, such as buck-"toothed" alien and the "tailhead"; a script note warns against the use of Ferengi before their discovery, but within inches of each other here are a remarkably calm Antican and a Selay—supposedly some thirty-five years before they make peace in "Lonely Among Us" (108). The nonspeaking Nausicaans are veteran TNG stunt men Tom Morga and Dick Dimitri, the latter seen sans makeup as the "henchman" with the Bandito ("A Fistful of Datas"/234) and the cabdriver of "Emergence" (275). Finally, Q may not be so omniscient: he says the just-graduated Picard is twenty-one in 2327 although his file says he was born in 2305 ("Conundrum"/214).

The jacket-style uniforms of the 2320s here feature a previously

Q lets Captain Picard visit his past.

unseen low-profile collar, rather than the plush ones of the Trek films and the later bare look ("Yesterday's *Enterprise*"/163). In that color style, Corty wears engineering gold, Marta has services blue-gray, and Picard, despite his later washout, has command white. Prop man Alan Sims said many of the odd "coins," glasses, and tableware were from a Paramount vault of long-stored *Ten Commandments* props.

Lines trimmed for time indicated that a third of Academy freshmen cadets don't make it and referred to Picard's superintendent as Admiral Silona, perhaps the Betazoid he once mentioned ("The First Duty"), and to "Scobee Hall," named for the captain of the ill-fated Challenger space-shuttle crew in 1986; another cut scene showed the low-ranking Picard reporting to a disinterested Geordi in Engineering, where engineer Duffy ("Hollow Pursuits"/169) is mentioned. Dr. Selar is also audibly resurrected ("The Schizoid Man"/131, "Yesterday's *Enterprise*"/163, "Remember Me"/179), while "Penny" was named for an older woman Moore himself had once dated; her reference to Rigel as her home may be Rigel IV, as with fellow humanoid Hengist of 1968's "Wolf in the Fold." Corey's posting, the *Ajax,* may be the one later worked over by Kosinski ("Where No One Has Gone Before"/106) and a part of Picard's blockade ("Redemption, Part II"/201).

BIRTHRIGHT, PART I

Production No.: 242 ■ Aired: Week of February 22, 1993
Stardate: 46578.4 ■ Code: bi

Directed by **Winrich Kolbe**
Written by **Brannon Braga**

GUEST CAST
Lieutenant (j.g.) Julian Bashir, M.D.: **Siddig El Fadil**
Jaglom Shrek: **James Cromwell**
Gi'ral: **Christine Rose**
Ba'el: **Jennifer Gatti**
L'Kor: **Richard Herd**

With the *Enterprise* docked at *Deep Space Nine* for a Bajoran aid mission, Worf is disturbed to learn from the moley Yridian Shrek that the Klingon's father may have survived the Khitomer massacre only to be held ever since in a Romulan prison camp—especially damning since an honorable Klingon would have died rather than be taken prisoner.

At the same time, a device found in the Gamma Quadrant that the station's Dr. Bashir brings aboard the Enterprise to test accidentally jolts Data, causing the android to shut down and experience a surreal vision of his creator "father," Dr. Soong.

Convinced by Bashir and La Forge that he was accessing images planted by Soong and in effect was "dreaming," Data is compelled to paint images he doesn't clearly recall, and for guidance asks Worf about a childhood vision the Klingon once described. The conversation convinces Worf to put conscience before pride, and he too sets out after his father, forcing Shrek to take him to the camp. Upon landing, he is stunned to be captured by the Klingons there, who have raised a new generation and don't consider themselves prisoners.

Meanwhile, Data opts for a new daily "dreaming" shutdown period after he takes flight as a bird image, and image of Soong promises he will grow to be more than a machine.

Intrigued with the *Bridge Over the River Kwai*-like conflict between inmate Worf and prison commander Tokath (played by Alan Scarfe, previously a different Romulan in "Data's Day"/185), Michael Piller suggested expanding this story to two parts—though Jeri Taylor recalled that the staff initially thought their boss's quiet and furrowed brow after their break session meant he didn't like the story at all! Two premises were woven together for the Worf story: One pitched by George Brozak about captured Klingons too proud to go home got Echevarria's interest but initially duplicated an MIA story in the works for DS9 that was later shelved. The other, from Daryl F. Mallett, Arthur Loy Holcomb, and Barbara Wallace, concerned the news that Worf's father Mogh might still be alive after Khitomer ("Sins of the Father"/165, et al.).

When Worf's capture was the moment chosen to climax the expanded first part and a B-story was needed to fill out the hour, the filler evolved under deadline desperation into the acclaimed sequence of Data's dreaming—a chance to expand the android's character with surreal images and metaphysical archetypes that Brannon Braga recalled coming up with while having pizza with Echevarria. Initially the bit had concerned "flatlining," Echevarria recalled, until just before "Tapestry" mined the subject. Many fans greeted the lack of a follow-up to the Data plot in Part II with disappointment, but the staff praised the outing and promised a follow-up story in this new area of Data's humanity—a plotline initially considered for the season's cliffhanger. He would eventually get a chance to follow up on the nightmare side of those dreams ("Phantasms"/258).

As usual, FX supervisor David Stipes used storyboards in creating the dream sequence—featuring an airbrushed nebula by his boss, Dan Curry. Like the character, his motif was "breaking free" of the mundane—in this case, camera angles—and he joined Braga in crediting director Cliff Bole for the lyrical quality of the bird flight sequence and in keeping consistent feel through both the live and FX sequences. Jim Magdaleno, Alan Kobayashi, and Mike Okuda of the TNG art department provided Data's paintings—except for a landscape Curry had done for the painting scene with Timothy in "Hero Worship" (211). Actor Brent Spiner was thrilled to take Data in a new direction, while the forties-ish Dr. Soong took far less effort to prepare than his initial appearance, though he wears the same lab wrap ("Brothers"/177, "Inheritance"/262").

Time constraints and a broken leg suffered by actor Cromwell (also in "The Hunted"/159) over the holiday break between the two segments' filming forced the trimming of the part of Jaglom Shrek—a name Braga coined from Henry Jaglom, independent film director, and the old Yiddish/Hebrew word for "shriek." A sympathetic scene in which he confesses he was once a prison camp inmate himself was lost, while another cut before filming would have contrasted with Worf's actions even more by having Shrek assassinated during a shipboard interrogation by one of the captured Klingons' grown sons who was determined not to hear the truth about his father. Shrek's craft was the old "alien shuttle" live set and miniature ("Legacy"/180, "Final Mission"/183, "A Matter of Time"/209, "Liaisons"/254, "Gambit, Part II"/257), re-dressed once again.

One of the oddest bits of casting here is the debut of the "new" Spot, since producers had lost track of the original source

Worf learns that his father may well be alive.

BIRTHRIGHT, PART II

Production No.: 243 ■ Aired: Week of March 1, 1993
Stardate: 46579.2 ■ Code: bi2

Directed by **Dan Curry**
Written by **René Echevarria**

GUEST CAST
Gi'ral: **Christine Rose**
Jaglom Shrek: **James Cromwell**
Toq: **Sterling Macer, Jr.**
Tokath: **Alan Scarfe**
Ba'el: **Jennifer Gatti**
L'Kor: **Richard Herd**

("Data's Day"/185) until the day of filming, when it was too late to change. The result was a breed change from Somal to mixed short-hair. With full-time prop master Alan Sims now using Rob Block's Critters of the Cinema for most animals, Brandy now would be "passive Spot," with backup "active" Abbott, eventually replaced once by Bud and for the duration by Monster—the animals "cast" by photo alone. "I did suggest they have Data give Spot away and get another cat (to cover the change), but they turned it down," Block recalled. The legendary Spot would be seen again in "Descent" (252–253), "Phantasms"/258, "Force of Nature"/261, "Genesis"/271, and *Generations*—and even undergo pregnancy after being male here!

We find here that Data does indeed "grow" hair, "breathe," and have a "pulse"; his room is still adorned with his Sherlock Holmes garb ("The Last Outpost"/107, "Elementary, Dear Data"/129, "Ship in a Bottle"/238), his violin ("The Ensigns of Command"/149, "Sarek"/171, "Lessons"/245, "Inheritance"/262), and the supposed "holodeck" Musketeer cap and foil ("Hollow Pursuits"/169). The *Merrimac*, mentioned briefly, was part of Picard's blockade ("Redemption, Part II"/201), and had provided transport for Wes Crusher ("The Game"/206) and Sarek ("Sarek"/171). Along with Bashir we get a glimpse of a Bolian and the recurring silent alien Morn from DS9, learn that the Ktarians ("The Game"/206, "Timescape"/251, "Liaisons"/254, "Phantasms"/258, *Generations*) had spacegoing technology three hundred years ago, and hear that the hammer is a Ferengi archetype for sexual prowess, building on that old joke (see "The Price"/156). And thanks to prior clues ("The Bonding"/153) we know that Worf was younger than six during the ritual hunt L'Kor speaks of.

Held captive by an unlikely, peaceful Romulan-Klingon colony on Carraya IV, Worf discovers that the tale of his father's survival that lured him there is untrue.

Kept hostage so the Klingons' survival during capture will not dishonor their survivors, Worf learns from Klingons L'Kor and Gi'ral of their eventual peace in the camp—and even Gi'ral's marriage to Romulan leader Tokath, somewhat of a rebel himself for keeping them alive and staying there with her.

But Worf, hating Romulans since his family's death at Khitomer, is disgusted by the intermarriage and his realization that their lovely daughter Ba'el, who was attracted to him, is a half-breed. An escape try foiled by the cynical young Toq leaves Worf a caged animal in the compound, but even more so he is disturbed to see the Klingon youths ignorant of their heritage. A wary Tokath and L'Kor allow his stories and teachings, even letting Toq go with Worf to take part in—and insure his return from—the Klingons' ritual hunt.

But Toq and the other youths grow so restless following his truths that Tokath sadly decides to kill Worf rather than lose the historic peace of the village. But the youths and the elders stand with Worf, who takes the youths with him under guise of "crash survivors" while keeping the elders a secret and their honor intact.

Though he had worked in live theater in college and had long been directing TNG second-unit and pickup shots, visual FX producer Dan Curry got his first crack at directing in the long form here and credited director of photography Jonathan West, sound mixer Alan Bernard, and Dorn himself for easing his transition. Sadly, he had to cut some seven minutes of character scenes due to time, including "steps" showing Worf and Ba'el's relationship, and the confrontation between Worf and Gi'ral in which the Klingon woman who married a Romulan stands up to the presumptuous interloper about her mixed-race marriage.

Surprisingly, Echevarria said that so much effort went into making both the Klingons and Romulans sympathetic here in the two-parter's main story arc that many fans felt Worf came off looking like a fascist racist who ruins a peaceful place. "His motives are in fact racist, when he's dealing with Romulans," the writer said. "But his actions are different; all he said was these people should know the truth and be free to leave. He never advocated violence and bloodshed." A smaller in-house debate raged over the depth of the Worf-Ba'el affair: whether a rendezvous would have been dramatically correct or too contrived for a one-hour episode.

Curry's hands-on mark shows up throughout the episode—and not just from throwing the spear through the wheel for the insert shot during the Klingon youths' game sequence. Drawing on the same background in swords and weaponry that produced Worf's *bat'telh,* he designed the blade for the *Gin'tak* spear (see notes, "Firstborn"/273), modeling it on the wavy-bladed Balinese *kris* dagger with the "capturing flanges" inspired by Northern Chinese weapons, while Sternbach designed the shaft. Curry's tai chi expertise also came to the fore when Worf's Klingon movement, first seen briefly in "Data's Day" (185), finally gets a name, *Mok'bara*—though a reference to Kahless as its creator was yet another cut for time. One of the most famous Klingon weapons, the spring-loaded dagger first seen in *ST III,* is finally christened here as a *D'k tahg.*

The Romulan fortress miniature, complete with computer animation that added tiny walking figures and flying birds, was computer-inserted into Laotian jungle photos Curry snapped in the sixties during his days in Southeast Asia. The large fortress live set, also designed by Richard James, built from a budget spread over two episodes; in one shot it appears to include a wheelchair-access ramp over a curbstone (though that's just for mundane camera work). With filming for the two episodes split by the December holiday break, all the live plants and trees from the substantial jungle and garden sets died untended on the dark, sealed-off soundstage and had to be replaced!

Listen for the blooper as Picard transposes two digits in his log's stardates, saying "46759.2" instead of "46579.2"; compared to Part I's stardate the difference means Worf was gone for over two months! Another curiosity is the location of the Carraya system, since it is seen on an Okudagraph map to be just outside Romulan space though apparently here not lying too far from DS9 in the

On the former prison planet, Klingons and Romulans live in peace.

Cardassian border area, which had earlier been set as on the opposite "side" of the Federation; the same map displays an unmentioned third star as "Echevarria." Throughout the two-parter the massacre at Khitomer (seen in the same map as *within* Romulan space) is referred to variously as occurring twenty-five, twenty, and twenty-three years ago, though by taking the period of "twenty years ago" literally in Season 3's "Sins of the Father" (165) only the latter can be correct. Further mythic conflict between Kahless and his brother Morath ("New Ground"/210, "Rightful Heir"/249, "Firstborn") is also featured. Among the guests, Alan Scarfe had played a Romulan already ("Data's Day"/185) while Richard Herd was well known to *V* and later *SeaQuest DSV* viewers.

With music composed by Jay Chattaway, Braga said it was the writing, broadcast, and residual payments for this episode's Klingon lyrics—along with those for the "Song of Aquiel" (239) and Data's bad poetry ("Schisms"/231)—that ironically won the self-described nonmusical Chattaway an invitation to join ASCAP, the songwriter/lyricist union. "We did a Klingon rap version of it too," co-producer and sound overseer Wendy Neuss recalled, and then joked: "I'm going to do an album someday, *Songs From Around the Universe.*"

Starship Mine

Production No.: 244 ■ Aired: Week of March 29, 1993
Stardate: 46682.4 ■ Code: st

Directed by **Cliff Bole**
Written by **Morgan Gendel**

GUEST CAST
Commander Calvin "Hutch" Hutchinson: **David Spielberg**
Kelsey: **Marie Marshall**
Devor: **Tim Russ**
Orton: **Glenn Morshower**
Neil: **Tom Nibley**
Satler: **Tim deZarn**
Kiros: **Patricia Tallman**
Waiter: **Arlee Reed**
Pomet: **Alan Altshuld**
Computer Voice: **Majel Barrett**

With the *Enterprise* shut down and its crew evacuated at the Remmler Array for a routine yet deadly baryon-purging sweep, the senior officers brace for a dreary reception at nearby Arkaria Base with Commander "Hutch" Hutchinson, known as the king of boring hosts.

Picard, anxious to slip away to get his saddle on the ship for some planetside riding, discovers a plot by six thieves to drain off the warp engine's toxic waste, trilithium resin, whose only use is as a weapon. Escaping capture, Picard begins a cat-and-mouse game on the lifeless, darkened ship as he escapes and slowly knocks off the gang one by one.

Picard knocks out the field diverter that would have protected the thieves from the sweep, sending them all scurrying to Ten-Forward to escape the beam. Back on the base, administrator Orton,—a co-conspirator—leads a takeover and kills Hutchinson, taking the senior officers hostage.

Gang leader Kelsey, after killing a cohort who'd rigged a stabilizer for the explosive resin, recaptures Picard but loses her last assistant to one of his booby traps. After they fight for the container, she grabs it and beams off to a waiting shuttle. Picard's pleas for help over his captured communicator are heard by his officers, who have turned the tables on their captors. The beam fades just as Kelsey's shuttle explodes—thanks to the stabilizer he removed during their melee.

This take on *Die Hard* was a violent action/adventure concept so far off the TNG norm that Jeri Taylor predicted it probably wouldn't have been done in years past. "It was very violent," Michael Piller agreed, "but it's good to have one of these kind in the mix [of stories]"; Stewart enjoyed the break from the "sitting and talking" norm and did several of his own stunts, as he had in "Tapestry." With only a slight rewrite by Ron Moore for budget needs—"all those stunts take forever to shoot—we're just not geared to it," he noted—the script from Morgan Gendel won praise as coming from one of the show's better outside writers. It was far afield from his last effort, the gentle "The Inner Light" (225).

Denied extras in the reception scenes due to cost, director Bole asked co-producer Wendy Neuss to round out the effect with background small talk among the regular cast—who had only the gabby Commander Hutchinson and two terrorist/servants to make up a formal occasion. In a unique move, Neuss virtually choreographed all the dialogue with a flowchart, tracking the cast involved even when not on camera and what they might be saying. She even had staff writers Brannon and Echevarria write scripted small-talk "walla" for the regulars, which led to the series' first-ever group "looping" (or redubbing) session by the cast at Modern Sound. Unfortunately, Neuss noted, most of that—Gates McFadden's improv with the waiter about him being an out-of-work actor, for one, and Braga's lines for Troi and Geordi about cheese logs, later deemed too over-the-top—will never see the light of day.

Picard's interest in horses was nothing new ("Pen Pals"/141, "The Loss"/184, *Generations*), but his apparent use of a Vulcan neck pinch is really supposed to be just a carotid-artery block; amid the chatter Data mentions the Sheliak ("Ensigns of Command"/149) and Hutchinson reveals he'd met Beverly during her stay at Starfleet Medical ("Evolution"/150). The matte shot of Arkaria Base was originally used as Darwin Genetics Research Station ("Unnatural Selection"/133) and would be reused again this season ("Descent"/252). And with the need for routine baryon "cleansing" of starships established, Geordi mentions that his starship gets double the number of warp-hours as is usual; it is also established that his VISOR comes with a pain-blocker. And for an odd bit of background, we learn that Phaser IIs are stored in Sickbay when Picard pulls one out of the same bin that Riker uses later ("Timescape"/251).

Filming the Remmler Array, as designed by Rick Sternbach and built by Greg Jein, proved tricky in itself since video of the eighteen-inch miniature had to be composited with the four-foot starship model. FX supervisor David Stipes revealed than an actual laser was used to scan the ship, its reddish glow serving as a target for the green-tinged animation added later. Curry's shuttle drone briefly seen was the same used earlier in "11001001" (116): a six-inch "quick-and-dirty" model with disposable Gillette razor handles as nacelles. Budget cuts also trimmed the look of

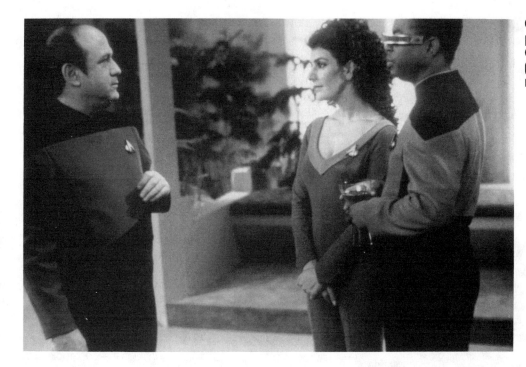

Geordi and Deanna are polite but bored at Commander Hutchinson's (David Spielberg) reception.

the male "shoelace eye" alien terrorist, whom Michael Westmore said was to have had a fuller face treatment. Kiros, the lesser female terrorist, was a Bajoran and was played by Patricia Tallman, a frequent stunt double—Crusher's, for example, in "Suspicions" (248). The later much-traveled cast also included Arlee Reed, script coordinator Lolita Fatjo's husband and later "human" ("Emergence"/275); Alan Altshud, a later Yridian ("Gambit, Part I"/256); Glenn Morshower, also seen as a bridge officer reincarnated from one *Enterprise* (*Generations*) to another ("Peak Performance"/147); and finally Tim Russ, who was not only the Klingon T'Rul in DS9's "Invasive Procedures" and a 1701-B crewman in *Generations* but played older Vulcan regular Tuvok on the second TNG spinoff, *Voyager*.

LESSONS

Production No.: 245 ▪ Aired: Week of April 5, 1993
Stardate: 46693.1 ▪ Code: In

Directed by **Robert Wiemer**
Written by **Ronald Wilkerson & Jean Louise Matthias**

GUEST CAST
Lieutenant Commander Nella Daren: **Wendy Hughes**
Computer Voice: **Majel Barrett**
Lieutenant (j.g.) Marques: **R. Cox**

The captain's usually solo personal life suddenly becomes a duet when his new chief of stellar sciences, Lieutenant Commander Nella Daren, checks in aboard his ship.

The lovely, intelligent woman is also an accomplished pianist, and after a concert Picard tells her of his Ressikan flute and the odd way he learned to play it. Their duets quickly lead to love: Troi assuages the captain's guilt about his command image, while an unintended incident between Nella and Riker leads the captain to remind her that in any choice between her and the ship, the *Enterprise* must come first.

But that credo is more than put to the test when the ship arrives to study the firestorms of Bersallis III. The scientific excitement turns tense when the storms threaten the UFP outpost earlier than expected, and Nella goes down with the teams when she and La Forge create a shield to cover the evacuation.

But Picard finds himself ordering Nella to her possible death when the teams must remain to control the shields manually. When she and her crew are presumed dead, it is all he can do to keep life going, but even her miraculous reprieve with a team member leads them both to realize they cannot remain lovers while working as commander and subordinate.

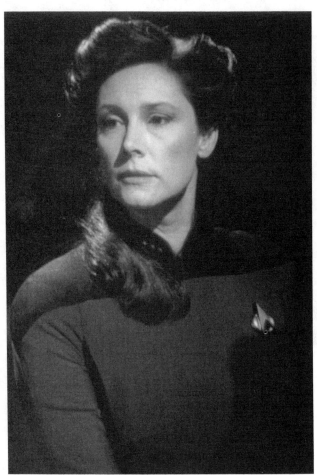

Commander Neela Daren (Wendy Hughes) captures Captain Picard's heart.

Nella opts for a transfer, noting that they must remain apart to keep their love alive.

A complete contrast from the Picard story just prior, this slice-of-life plot Michael Piller dubbed "Brief Encounter on the *Enterprise*" sparkles from the chemistry between Stewart and actress Wendy Hughes, most recently seen in *Homicide: Life on the Streets*. Ironically, Picard is seen wearing a shirt from "Captain's Holiday" (167), but unlike Vash, this time around the captain is given a real peer and equal in Nella Daren—a quality that Jeri Taylor felt gave the match-up "true substance and genuine warmth" the actors could play from. "The script was a pleasure and we had really turned-on performances," veteran TNG director Robert Weimer said. "If we'd had only moderate performances it would have fallen flat."

Taylor was pleased to be able to finally give freelancers

Ronald Wilkerson and Jean Louise Matthias a chance to take their story to the teleplay stage, after their previous two sales ("Imaginary Friend"/222, "Schisms"/231) were handed to a staff writer to save time through rewrites. René Echevarria did only a polish job on their final draft, a task Brannon Braga swapped off after his last uneven experience with a love story on "Aquiel" (239).

Because it was so much a part of the relationship's growth, the music recorded and played for this episode received extra special attention. Series composer Dennis McCarthy had dubbed a tape of professionals playing the music needed, but Taylor knew that such a straight treatment wouldn't work for the dramatic build and she called a Sunday huddle with him and producer Wendy Neuss. "The music had to reflect that she was making him feel comfortable and letting him kind of test these strange waters and being gentle with him, not overwhelming him with a 'look at me—see how good I am!' kind of attitude." The final product portrays what Neuss called "a real synergy, a constant feeding back, growing, getting better at what they do."

But if recording the music was one thing, shooting it was another. Keeping his filming angles simple and conservative to reflect the tone of the story, Wiemer still worked in tricks to disguise the live musicians playing for actors Stewart and Hughes: the unbroken piano pan and the up-through-the-clear-table shot disguised the likes of pianist photo-double Natalie Martin, who also recorded the music for Nella's instruments. Her husband Bryce has done the same for Picard's Ressikan pennywhistle "flute" ever since its debut in "The Inner Light" (225). Stewart did much of his own flute fingering in the "teaching" scene, with inserts photo-doubled in his quarters by Noel Webb and by John Mayham in the Jefferies tube, where Wiemer used a wide-angle lens in the crammed junction; an enormously long dolly he filmed retreating down the crawlway until the duo was just a spot had to be cut short for time. Webb also hand-doubled for Data's violin playing with Spiner's face onscreen as he, Nella, and musician extra Jan Kelly "performed" Chopin's "Trio in G Minor"—as a joke take, Neuss recalled, Webb's unused hand reached in as Data's "third" one to scratch the android's nose!

Picard's love of fencing ("We'll Always Have Paris"/124, "I, Borg"/223) and his early piano lessons ("The Perfect Mate"/221) are already known, as is Crusher's interest in ribosomal replication ("The Enemy"/155, "Ethics"/216). Some of the weapons used are a variation on Kivas Fajo's Varon-T ("The Most Toys"/170), and "Frere Jacques" harks back to "Disaster" (205).

Echoing the show's simplicity, Dan Curry and Ron Moore used a "low-tech" means of creating the Bersallis III firewalls by spilling liquid nitrogen onto black velvet draped over a big table and blown from behind by an air hose for the shimmering effect. It was later enhanced by computer before being painted into the background of the live-action "Planet Hell" trench. Look for the blooper of stars at rest outside Picard's quarters during a time of warp drive: the FX staff caught it in time but decided it wasn't worth the cost of a late fix.

THE CHASE

Production No.: 246 ▪ Aired: Week of April 26, 1993
Stardate: 46731.5 ▪ Code: cha

Directed by **Jonathan Frakes**
Teleplay by **Joe Menosky**
Story by **Joe Menosky & Ron D. Moore**

GUEST CAST
Humanoid: **Salome Jens**
Captain Nu'Daq: **John Cothran, Jr.**
Romulan captain: **Maurice Roeves**
Gul Ocett: **Linda Thorson**
Professor Richard Galen: **Norman Lloyd**
Computer Voice: **Majel Barrett**

Picard's old archaeology professor, Richard Galen, comes calling with a rare gift and a tempting offer: an archaeological hunt on a theory that, if proven true, would have galaxy-wide impact.

Galen is bitter and leaves the starship when Picard turns him down, but he regrets his tone only hours later as he lies dying, mortally wounded after his ship is raided.

Puzzled over what Galen was up to, Picard retraces their stops at empty or long-dead planets until the answer is realized: the "clues" he'd collected are from prehistoric DNA samples which fit into an overall pattern—but for what?

The missing pieces that would provide the answer arrive as a surprise: Cardassians and Klingons who are chasing Galen's work too. When Picard convinces them all that they all must pool their clues or fail, they find that the patterns link up to indicate star systems. The last DNA clue site is decoded but, due to a suspected double-cross, the Cardassians are fed the wrong destination and they take the bait.

At the site, the *Enterprise* crew discovers not only the last DNA needed and the nonplussed Cardassians, but a cloaked Romulan ship. While the others squabble, Picard and Crusher quietly add the sample and trigger the message: words from a long-dead race that had seeded the codes as a legacy across the various races' home plan-

ets—not a weapon or energy source, but a tie of commonality for the old foes to ponder.

Dubbed the most "Roddenberryesque" of TNG episodes by the staff, this background fan's delight pays homage to the unified view of life that the Great Bird infused his universe with. But writer Ron Moore wryly said that the episode might as well have taken its name from the year-and-a-half pursuit of a workable script from Menosky's original premise, concocted way back during the infamous Mexican staff retreat from Season 5. That idea, more in the manic comic mood of *It's a Mad, Mad, Mad, Mad World*, was constantly being rewritten, disapproved as "too cartoony" and shelved—until the desperation point of the season set in and premises became scarce. Jeri Taylor joked that she got yet another try at the show by letting Menosky take a crack at a draft while her boss was trying to lure the former staffer to work on *DS9* during one of his infrequent visits; in one of Piller's biggest about-faces, she recalled, he was so excited about the revised story he wanted to make *it* the season's cliffhanger!

Inspired by Carl Sagan's "Contact" story about a clue to the nature of the universe being discovered in an long calculation of *pi*, Moore said Menosky suggested using the gene code and DNA as message conduit. What finally sold Berman and Piller on the idea was the addition of the emotional stakes for Picard with his mentor's death: the original story opened with a Vulcan scientist not personally tied to anyone who sends a distress call that he's been surrounded by Klingon, Romulan, and *Ferengi* ships. "Riker beams over into this cramped little tiny shuttle, where everyone's yelling and trying to find things and the guy's dead," Moore recalled. "And then they zip away, and we're off and running with *Mad, Mad, Mad, Mad World*. It would have been a lot more comedic."

Frakes, in his second TNG outing behind the camera this year and sixth overall, strikes the right balance between mystery and science and keeps all of Trek's familiar aliens recognizable yet individualistic. It was a historic tale he drew: the first time that Star Trek's humanoids, Klingons, Romulans, and Cardassians appear together in the same scene, much less the same episode. (The budget-trimmed Ferengi and the written-out Vulcan would have made the party even bigger.) The Yridians, of course, were introduced in the guise of Jaglom Shrek just this season ("Birthright, Part I"/242); the wasplike ship debuting here was designed by Rick Sternbach and built by John Goodson, moonlighting from his ILM job. Among the other new looks are a sampling tube that connects directly to the tricorder and the first-ever view of a Cardassian female (in command, no less) and their transporter beam: free-form amber sparkles and arcs.

More than ever, we learn why archaeology is important to Picard ("Contagion"/137, "Qpid"/194, "Rascals"/233, "Chain of Command, Part II"/237, "Gambit"/256–257, "Bloodlines"/274) and hear again his regrets about his father ("Tapestry"/241, "Bloodlines"), while Beverly is seen right at home in Picard's quarters for their morning tea ("Qpid," "Perfect Mate"/221, "Lessons"/245, "The Chase"/246, "Attached"/260). At this point, seventeen aboard the *Enterprise* are said to come from non-UFP worlds; a short, funny scene cut for time would have established Bolius IX ("Allegiance"/166) as one of them, with barber Mott ("Ensign Ro"/

Cardassians and Romulans confront each other in the Vilmoran system.

203, "Unification I"/208, but spelled with two *t*'s here) among those whose DNA is sampled by Beverly. As hinted at previously ("Starship Mine"/244), we learn that the ship's constant and rapid use of high warp drive is not usual. Galen mentions both the Satarran ("Conundrum"/214) and, though its connection to DS9 is unspecified, a "Deep Space 4," the first record of a sister station; he indicates it on a map as somewhere beyond the Romulan Empire on the edge of explored space.

As a nod to *really* long-term Star Trek background fans, Moore said he'd considered but intentionally didn't specify that the DNA-coding aliens here were the Preservers, the unseen race from 1969's "The Paradise Syndrome" said to be seeding humanoids around the galaxy, so as to keep the suspense. "But this *could* be them and be internally consistent," he added. At least Salome Jens is no galactic stranger; she later turned up as one of Odo's shapeshifter species on DS9's "The Search."

FRAME OF MIND

Production No.: 247 ■ Aired: Week of May 3, 1993
Stardate: 46778.1 ■ Code: fr

Directed by **James L. Conway**
Written by **Brannon Braga**

GUEST CAST
Dr. Syrus: **David Selburg**
Administrator ("Lt.") Suna: **Andrew Prine**
Mavek: **Gary Werntz**
Inmate Jaya: **Susanna Thompson**
Wounded crew member: **Alan Dean Moore**

With a few days' rest before leading an undercover mission to rescue Federation hostages on the newly anarchic Tilonus IV, Riker takes on the demanding role of a mental-health patient turned prisoner in the play "Frame of Mind."

Haunted by the face of a strange alien lieutenant, Riker finds reality and theater shifting back and forth in a series of baffling segues as he finds himself first on the stage set and then in a real asylum, where his doctor—played by Data in the play—tells him to shed his "starship" fantasy. Haunted by doubt, and a recurring bleeding temple when he's on the starship, Riker is finally convinced that his Starfleet career is an illusion, the alien he saw is the clinic administrator, and that he will soon stand trial for murder.

Worf and Data retrieve him, but aboard ship he still refuses to believe he's a starfleet officer. Finally, when his temple continues to bleed despite Dr. Crusher's care, Riker senses he can't trust any of these "realities," and he mentally breaks through each one in turn to finally wake up on a lab table, a probe attached to his temple.

Eluding the Tilonians for an emergency beam-out, he realizes that the memories of his starship and the play were the only thing that kept him "sane" while he had been drugged by his captors.

A fellow inmate (Susanna Thompson) tries to convince Commander Riker he is insane.

After a drought of Riker stories in Season 6, Frakes won praise this time for his intense yet controlled performance on a roller coaster of a part in what Braga mused was his best work to date, using his favorite "underused" character: "Riker's a friendly character, he's the one human you can do humor with, you can do action—and here you can jerk him around and drive him crazy!"

Considering the late-season time crunch, it's amazing that this desperation premise to fill the slot when another story fell through works at all. Braga came up with the barest idea—"What if Riker wakes up in an insane asylum?"—and, due to the time crunch, took it right from a brief memo barely approved by a skeptical Piller and Berman into the most torturous yet creative break session this staff had ever seen. "We didn't have time to do a story, so we went ahead and 'broke' this . . . which is the most risky thing in the world to do," Jeri Taylor said. ". . . They're painstaking, they take days, and if you lose it you're doomed!" Finally, after three days in the same room, they let Piller in to hear the story and, hearing it fresh without a story outline, he was instantly hooked on what had emerged.

In an interesting twist, Braga noted that another challenge was to write the compelling last scene to the same-named play within the play—or, in other words, "write a famous play without ever

having been famous!" The writer also said he'd had second thoughts about his frequent use of the word "crazy" in light of current mental-health trends but decided to shrug it off. "People use this word, it's a good word, and I decided to use it," he said. "When you get too 'politically correct' it shows, and what's 'PC' today won't be five years from now. *Star Trek* is a show that transcends time, and we try not to date it."

Berman recalled that James Conway had been a well-received director way back in Season 1 ("Justice"/109, "The Neutral Zone"/126), but had simply been too busy in the nineteenth century as executive producer on *The Guns of Paradise,* among other projects, to "return" to the future before this skillfully handled outing. FX supervisor Ron B. Moore praised the cast, recalling how the five-minute scene with Riker and his mates as holograms was shot all in one take with just a little rehearsal and no slips—and then repeated perfectly for a second angle. The initial look of Riker's "immolation" was thought too similar to the *Time Trax* effect, so a simple fade-out was used; the "shards of glass" shatter was done by Joe Walter.

Like Barclay ("The Nth Degree"/193), the first known student in Beverly's new backstory of amateur theater, Riker too shows the miracles her coaching can do ("A Fistful of Datas"/234); for the performance she wears her off-the-shoulder dress from "Allegiance" (166). Through the makeup, two familiar TNG faces can be seen here: David Selburg was lit-historian Whalen in "The Big Goodbye" (113), while Susanna Thompson had earlier played Varel, the female Romulan officer of a disabled science ship ("The Next Phase"/224). Her inmate here mentions several "real" starships, the old *Yorktown* (from 1967's "Obsession") and the *Yosemite* ("Realm of Fear"/228). Another TNG vet, stunt coordinator Dennis Madalone (seen without makeup in "Identity Crisis"/192, among others), steps out once again as an extra as Mavek's assistant guard. And pattern enhancers have been used before ("Power Play"/215, "Time's Arrow"/226, "Ship in a Bottle"/238, then "Inheritance"/262).

Suspicions

Production No.: 248 ■ Aired: Week of May 10, 1993
Stardate: 46830.1 ■ Code: su

Directed by **Cliff Bole**
Written by **Joe Menosky and Naren Shankar**

GUEST CAST
Nurse Alyssa Ogawa: **Patti Yasutake**
Kurak: **Tricia O'Neil**
Dr. Reyga: **Peter Slutsker**
Dr. Jo'Bril: **James Horan**
Dr. Christopher: **John S. Ragin**
Dr. T'Pan: **Joan Stuart Morris**
Guinan: **Whoopi Goldberg**
Computer Voice: **Majel Barrett**

Dr. Crusher's foray into "science diplomacy" is cut short when the Takaran scientist Jo'Bril, one of those responding to her call to witness new shield technology developed by the Ferengi scientist Dr. Reyga, is killed while testing it.

Dr. Reyga vows to prove himself when Dr. Crusher stops the tests of the "metaphasic shield," designed to protect a vessel even within a sun's corona, but soon he is found dead of an apparent suicide. Crusher suspects foul play, especially after a Klingon scientist admits she threatened Reyga when the Ferengi accused her of sabotage in the first test.

Crusher wants to do an autopsy to gather clues, but Takahan customs—and thus the prime

directive as well—forbid it. She proceeds anyway, finds nothing, and is relieved of duty to await court-martial after Reyga's family and government protest her act.

With Guinan's reassuring advice to pursue her gut feelings, and with nothing left to lose, Crusher presses on. When Data guesses that a shield disruptor might leave tetryon traces, Nurse Ogawa risks her career to help Crusher find that tetryons were indeed present in Jo'Bril's body.

But it is not proof, and Crusher desperately tries one more route: testing the shield herself to see if only sabotage ruined the first test. It works, but Jo'Bril—actually alive thanks to the death-like self-stasis ability of his race—has stowed aboard to steal it for use as a weapon. During a fight Crusher gets the upper hand, Jo'Bril is killed—and Reyga's work is vindicated.

Dr. Crusher confers with Klingon scientist Dr. Kurak (Tricia O'Neil).

Like Marina Sirtis earlier, Gates McFadden finally gets the chance to step out in a nontraditional role with a story the staff dubbed "Beverly as Quincy," after Jack Klugman's great series about a crime-solving medical examiner (and one of Jeri Taylor's past producer credits). But if "Frame of Mind" had the longest single break session in recent TNG years, this tale started had the most break sessions—five through both seasons, by Shankar's tally, with three rewrites once in script form.

Menosky's original story—his second resurrected this year, after "The Chase"—had the same murder mystery of a Ferengi scientist but set up the shocking discovery that warp travel is pollution that rips holes in the fabric of space. Like Piller, Shankar took an interest in that environmental theme and its impact on the future Trek universe and he agreed to take on the reborn project—only to endure delay once again when everyone almost immediately agreed to rip out the eco-angle (later used anyway in "Force of Nature"/261) to focus on the mystery. It began as a Worf vehicle done in forties black-and-white film noir style with flashbacks, dissolves, and voice-over narration—styles that TNG had never used before (see notes, "Manhunt"/145) that finally got grudging one-time-only approval from Rick Berman. When the many Worf stories this season led to using another character, Ron Moore suggested Crusher as the focus and the search for a truly suspenseful mystery began anew; Piller's nixing of various drafts as too dull finally led to the twist of a victim being the perpetrator. "It was just a never-ending, never-waking nightmare," Moore recalled. "Keep the murder mystery, lose the warp thing, move Worf out, keep the flashbacks, loose the film noir, insert Beverly—it was just *arrgh!*" On top of it all, Taylor said, the crew learned early on that this show's slot would be the only other one for which Whoopi Goldberg would be available, leading to another series of rewrites.

The resulting science plot and mix of Trek aliens, as in "The Chase," works well under director Cliff Bole, by now TNG's most prolific with twenty-two episodes. James Horath, perhaps best known to soap-opera fans from his onetime role as Clay Alden on *Loving*, had since guest-starred on series like *The Commish* and *Highlander*, and returned to TNG as the human Lieutenant Barnaby in "Descent, Part II" (253). Other TNG vets included O'Neil ("Yesterday's *Enterprise*"/163) and Slutsker, here in one of his three Ferengi roles ("Ménage à Troi"/172, "Bloodlines"/274). Both portrayals reflect their cultures' disrespect toward scientists; the Klingon is the only one not accorded the title "doctor."

Past Trek "tech" abounds: real baryon particles ("Starship Mine"/244) and fictional tetryons ("Schisms"/231), the stimulant inoprovaline ("Tapestry"/241), "Man of the People"/229, et al.), the cortical stimulator ("Tapestry"), and—from 1967's "Journey to Babel"—the first TNG mention of the Vulcan Science Academy, where Sarek initially would have preferred young Spock devote his life rather than Starfleet. The ship's morgue is new (with its automated covers), and we discover the first shuttlecraft named for neither a real nor a Trek-fictional scientist/explorer: the *Justman*, paying homage to the sixties Trek and first-year producer. Other trivia: the *Enterprise* has at least sixteen numbered sciences labs, tennis is still popular in the twenty-fourth century, Ferengi don't allow autopsies before their elaborate death rituals and burial, and, as seen in an Okudagraph, the Takaran body has three hearts. Reflecting her interest, Beverly gets a set of theater masks on her walls, courtesy set decorator Jim Mees, and for only the second time we hear Nurse Ogawa's first name, Alyssa ("Clues"/188).

Hurdling his biggest FX challenge of this story, supervisor David Stipes portrayed the Vaytan sun's corona accurately with actual NASA footage.

RIGHTFUL HEIR

Production No.: 249 ■ Aired: Week of May 17, 1993
Stardate: 46852.2 ■ Code: rh

Directed by **Winrich Kolbe**
Teleplay by **Ronald D. Moore**
Story by **James Brooks**

GUEST CAST
Koroth: **Alan Oppenheimer**
Gowron: **Robert O'Reilly**
Torin: **Norman Snow**
Divok: **Charles Esten**
Kahless: **Kevin Conway**
Computer Voice: **Majel Barrett**

Left unsure of his beliefs after the "stranded" Klingon youths of Carraya IV embraced them so heartily—and with his job performance slipping—Worf wins a leave from the *Enterprise* to "seek Kahless," his peoples' mythic spiritual leader, on the planet where clerics await his promised return.

After ten days the dismayed Worf is ready to leave with no insights when suddenly Kahless appears, rallying those at the temple and planning to unite and uplift all Klingons again. Gowron, the High Council leader, asks the *Enterprise* to ferry Kahless back to Klingon space, to avoid arousing any more native passions until he can be checked out. There, Worf remains skeptical until various tests—including a DNA match with a blood sample on a sacred ancient knife—seem to rule out deception.

Worf is overjoyed, but Gowron is not about to hand over his hard-won government. When they meet at last, Gowron shocks the crowd by outfighting the "greatest warrior of them all."

At that, head cleric Koroth admits this Kahless is just a clone of the original, specially programmed with a memory taken from sacred texts. But with word of Kahless' devotion already spreading—and Worf agreeing that their people need a renewal of purpose—Gowron agrees to let this "heir" to Kahless rule as emperor and a moral authority, while he and the council retain their political power. Worf is crushed again until Kahless reminds him it's the words and teachings, not the man, that are important.

Emperor Kahless (Kevin Conway) returns.

Alluding to 1993's blockbuster film about the resurrection of dinosaurs from preserved DNA, James Brooks dubbed his premise "Jurassic Worf" when he pitched the idea of a cult of Klingons returning one of their mythic figures to life in similar fashion and passing him off as the real thing. But while Brooks' story was more concerned with intrigue and politics among the clerics, Moore said he was proud to take his story where TNG had practically never gone before: an examination of spiritualism and faith in the twenty-fourth century centered on Starfleet's lone Klingon. "Gene Roddenberry was very much a secular humanist, and I don't think that story would have worked with anyone else but Worf," Jeri Taylor added, noting that this script's break sessions opened up the staff's various views on religious faith and its place in TNG.

Not only does Moore get to flesh out the Klingons' hinted-at mythic legends by making Kahless the central figure, he also single-handedly converts the Klingon Empire into a constitutional monarchy! While Brooks had not used Kahless, Moore saw it as the chance to reveal another side of Klingon life apart and develop the character first presented in 1969's "The Savage Curtain" (albeit in original Star Trek's Klingon guise with pre-alliance description as the one who "set the pattern for his planet's ruthless tyranny"). Originally the Kahless legend included his Christ-like death by the tyrant Molor after an honorable promised return from one last night of wandering amid nature, but those stories from René Echevarria's "Birthright, Part II" were cut for time and Moore developed the messianic figure for his story needs here. Still, from that earlier script he picked up on Worf's vision of Kahless in the No'Mat lava caves, used Molor as a Kahless victim (later fleshed out in "Firstborn"/273), and pegged Worf's loss of faith to the Carraya IV experience. As a result, we now have Kahless and the Sto-Vo-Kor afterlife as the Klingons' contrast to Fek'Ihr and his realm of the dead dishonored ("Devil's Due"/187).

One point finally cleared up is the status of the Klingon Empire's "emperor." Gowron, who has grayed with the demands of office since last seen ("Redemption, Part II"/201), and K'mpec before him ("Sins of the Father"/165) had been called "Leader of the High Council" and Gorkon of ST VI was titled "chancellor"—but here we learn that the title hasn't been used in "three hundred years." A past reference in "Sins of the Father" to an emperor at the time of the Khitomer massacre was just a throwaway, Moore said, before the government was fully sketched out a year later ("Reunion"/181). Actor Oppenheimer later changed races to become the ill-fated Captain Keogh in DS9's "Jem'Hadar" segment.

For "missing trivia" buffs, lines in the cut scenes put Kahless' original death 1,547 years earlier—or A.D. 822; in another, Alexander's absence is finally explained as a visit back on Earth ("Family"/178, "Reunion"/181); a third deleted exchange mused whether the Kahless figure is a front for the Duras sisters ("Redemption"/200-201, *Generations*, DS9's "Past Prologue") or the "B'nok faction." Still onscreen are mentions of a coalescent creature ("Aquiel"/239), Worf's original Rite of Ascension ceremony, performed on the Home World ("Icarus Factor"/140), and that his brother Kurn ("Sins of the Fathers"/165) now has a seat on the High Council since the civil war ("Redemption"). And we learn that Kahless created the first *bat'leth* sword.

The Klingon temple, whose design was inspired by similar structures Dan Curry recalled from his days in the Himalayas, was an impressive set that the small screen did not do justice to. For one thing, over $4,000 alone went into the fat beeswax candles used on the set, according to set decorator Jim Mees.

SECOND CHANCES

Production No.: 250 ■ Aired: Week of May 24, 1993
Stardate: 46915.2 ■ Code: sd

Directed by **LeVar Burton**
Teleplay by **René Echevarria**
Story by **Michael A. Medlock**

GUEST CAST
Ensign Palmer: **Dr. Mae Jemison**

Returning to a planet outpost whose unstable atmosphere and infrequent transport window almost left him stranded while a lieutenant on the *Potemkin*, Riker is shocked to find a double of himself—created years ago by an odd transporter reflection.

Nervala IV's atmosphere allows only brief transporter use just once every eight years, and the *Enterprise* is back now for the same database sought earlier. But "Lieutenant Riker" 's appearance is more than just a scientific shock—it upsets Troi, since he's ready to resume the passion they shared at the time.

While Troi finally decides to renew the affair, the two Rikers clash on the current mission when Picard chooses "Lieutenant Riker" 's plan. Meanwhile, Number One gently reminds Troi that this one will likely become just as involved with his career as he did.

Back for a third and final try to retrieve the database, Commander Riker saves his twin from plunging to his death from a collapsed bridge in the outpost's underground caverns.

Safely aboard again, Lieutenant Riker is preparing for his new posting on the *U.S.S. Gandhi* when he receives two going-away gifts: a trombone, from his twin, and Troi's promise to consider marrying him in six months when he can have family aboard his ship. Until then, Commander Riker promises to watch over her, the same as always.

First-time director LeVar Burton won praise all around for his preparation and unruffled handling of one of the toughest of FX shows, one that turned the Riker character on its ear and finally satisfied the clamoring Riker-Troi romance fans. And, to unleash the two-Riker trick without a cheap tech breakdown as catalyst, Rick Berman and Michael Piller were adamant that the transporter mishap be established as a once-in-a-trillion occurrence due to Nervala IV's unique atmosphere. Echevarria, who recalled that the script practically wrote itself, relished once again getting to call a premise-pitcher about his story sale—though he recalled with a laugh that Medlock's tale of a Riker twin almost got him booted from the office until he added the hook: the premise of the renewed romance.

If Riker's future seems boggled by these events, consider what might have been: Taylor and the staff originally wanted to kill off *Commander* Riker, installing a hungry, career-climbing "young" Riker at the helm with Data as first officer—and greatly complicating Troi's life. Berman and Piller, eyeing the character's stability and its future in films, nixed that idea outright—and so it seemed that *Lieutenant* Riker would bite the dust until Piller suggested they salvage some of the unexpected and keep both alive: "I mean, what other show could do it?" he asked. At the time, Taylor said she had no idea what direction to take the twins in, but Thomas was to be featured in a third-year DS9 story called "The Defiant."

The brief appearance by Dr. Mae Jemison, who like Whoopi Goldberg credits Nichelle "Uhura" Nichols from original *Trek* as one of her inspirations, came at Burton's invitation and marked the first time any real-life space traveler had appeared on-

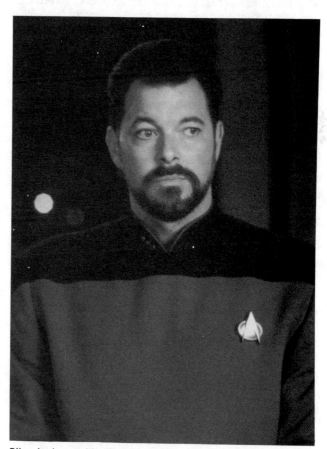

Riker is stunned to "find himself" on the planet Nervala IV.

camera in the Trek universe. Jemison, a general medical practitioner and the first black woman in space, had left her six-year NASA career by the time she appeared here to found a Houston-based communications company.

Echevarria said he created most of the Riker background here (especially that it was he rather than Troi who decided to cool their affair) but the group finally decided that "simplest was best" for a middle name. Taylor recalled that "Tecumseh" was among those considered—and, no, "Tiberius" (as in James Kirk) never was. Facts given here fit that Riker and Troi began their affair on Betazed as per "Ménage à Troi" (172) and that he had previously served aboard the *Potemkin* ("Peak Performance"/147), starting the day after their last time together at Betazed's Janaran Falls. No time span is given, but the two years they were apart (the difference in the eight-year Nervala cycle and Riker's six years on the 1701-D) is enough to include the rapid promotion he received after the Nervala mission (and presumably out of the mustard tunic of services) since he was quickly a lieutenant commander and the *Hood*'s first officer ("Encounter at Farpoint"/101-102).

For background buffs, Riker's chance to command the *Aries* and his rocky years with his father are recalled ("The Icarus Factor"/140), and a move from Worf's *Mok'bara* exercises gets a name: *Koh-man-ara.* Despite prior word of transporters being largely unchanged in recent decades ("Relics"/230), here we learn there have been advances enough just in the last eight years. And once again ("Imaginary Friend"/222) we learn that the Galaxy class was not the first to allow families on board: Troi could have joined Riker on the *Potemkin* two years before the 1701-D was launched. Past references include Riker's trombone ("11001001"/116, "Future Imperfect"/182, "The Next Phase"/224, "Thine Own Self"/268, "Timescape"/251) and Parreses Squares ("11001001," "Future Imperfect," "Silicon Avatar"/204, "The First Duty"/219).

Scheduling problems kept Jonathan Frakes from pre-recording his own trombone tracks for the Ten-Forward jazz quartet scene, but co-producer Wendy Neuss said he would likely do so in the future. Frakes got to join castmate Brent Spiner in the hassle of photo doubling and other FX needed to create a twin, though relying with much-praised success on the subtleties of acting with little aid from makeup. The collapsed bridge was built and filmed live in Stage 16's "Planet Hell" pit, with cavern depths added in the computer paintbox.

TIMESCAPE

Production No.: 251 ■ Aired: Week of June 14, 1993
Stardate: 46944.2 ■ Code: tms

Directed by **Adam Nimoy**
Written by **Brannon Braga**

GUEST CAST
Romulan/Alien: **Michael Bofshever**
Sickbay Romulan: **John DeMita**
Engineering ensign: **Joel Fredericks**

Returning by runabout from a conference, Troi, Picard, Data, and La Forge are puzzled by time "freezing" and "speeding up" around them until they discover it is due to temporal "pockets" that their runabout must dodge.

Even more shocking, they find their starship likewise frozen in time before a Romulan Warbird, a disruptor bolt partway to the starship's half-raised shields. Riker had reported moving to help a stricken Warbird, but—by adapting emergency transporter armbands to create skintight forcefields of "real" time—Picard and the others board the Enterprise where they find freeze-framed signs of apparent Romulan boarding and a warp-core breach in progress.

Visiting the warbird, they find an odd alien vortex in the engine core. After Data's tricorder sets off the vortex and time races forward and backward only to "freeze" again, with the *Enterprise* exploding and re-forming, they try to shift time backward far enough to prevent the breach.

Meanwhile, an alien from another time dimension reveals it is his young who are the "vortex," accidentally attracted to the core's artificial gravity well. They are the cause of the time pockets. Time is "reset" successfully, but one of the aliens—distracts Data long enough to allow the breach to re-form.

Picard has the runabout steered into the transfer beam's path to break it, sending the aliens back to their "time" and restoring his own.

occasional minor twitch can be seen here and there—watch how Nimoy avoided much of that problem with a constantly moving camera, establishing the "frozen" person and then moving on to provide the actor some relief.

For the first time we get a look at a Warbird's engineering room and the aft compartment of the runabout vessel created for DS9—which, oddly enough, was built on TNG's budget to help out its sister show. Designer Richard James and set decorator Jim Mees lamented that seven weeks went into the creation of the cockpit over on DS9, but he had only nine days to design *and* build the living quarters—and his crews worked round-the-clock at that.

On the trivial side: a clue to the rules of Parrises Squares ("11001001"/116, "Future Imperfect"/182, "Silicon Avatar"/204, "The First Duty"/219, "Second Chances"/250) is that an "old" player like Riker could "fall and break his neck"; the Ktarians ("The Game"/206, "Birthright, Part I"/242, "Liaisons"/254, *Generations*) appear to be respectable after all; we see Troi "plexing" when stressed ("Realm of Fear"/228); and the sickbay phaser bin ("Starship Mine"/244) is still accessible to anyone. Actor Bofshever also played Minister Toran in DS9's "The Storyteller" and an *Excelsior* engineer in *ST VI;* Spot is mentioned (see note, "Birthright, Part I"/242), as is Worf's "calisthenics" program ("Where Silence Has Lease"/128, "The Emissary"/146, "New Ground"/210). Two of the conference speakers' names, Wagner and Vassbinder, come from a onetime date and a high-school teacher of Braga's. And in what seem to be bloopers, the power-transfer beam ("The Next Phase"/224) emanates from the port side of the dorsal rather than the main deflector, possibly due to the needs of FX work, and we discover the bridge restroom is a Jefferies tube access point: the officers using the tunnels enter the bridge from that door in the aft starboard alcove.

An alien being masquerades as a Romulan.

"**A**t the end of 'Rascals' (233) we told Adam Nimoy 'We owe you one with grown-ups!' " Rick Berman said. "The joke was, my next one would be all animals!" Nimoy recalled. Whatever the case, the still-young director here went from the frying pan into the fire with what has been dubbed the most "techie" TNG episode ever to shoot, the first of two requiring eight and a half days to shoot.

When the planned story fell through for this slot, Braga again stepped in to complete a script and skipped the story-outline stage, going right to the break session to save time—just eight days before the first production meeting with the director. Inspired by the simple late-season premise "ship trapped in time like amber," pitched by Mark Gerhed O'Connell, Braga set out to top his own "Cause and Effect" of a season before (218) with another out-of-the-ordinary time story: "I wanted to do this as 'man against nature,' or 'man against time'," he said. "What *The Abyss* was to deep-sea diving, this would be to 'deep-time diving'"; in fact, "Deep Time" was almost the segment's title.

Bringing that "eerie ambience" of the teleplay to life became Nimoy's main goal, especially in his favorite moments: the frozen-time reaction and reveal shots aboard the runabout, inspired by old German impressionistic films like *The Hands of Dr. Mugabi.* Though the scenes of live "frozen" actors are tricky—and an

Descent

Production No.: 252 ■ Aired: Week of April 21, 1993
Stardate: 46982.1 ■ Code: de

Directed by **Alexander Singer**
Teleplay by **Ronald D. Moore**
Story by **Jeri Taylor**

GUEST CAST

Isaac Newton: **John Neville**
Albert Einstein: **Jim Norton**
Vice-Admiral Alynna Nechayev: **Natalija Nogulich**
Crosis: **Brian J. Cousins**
Professor Stephen Hawking: **Himself**
Bosus (1st Borg): **Richard Gilbert-Hill**
Tayar (2nd Borg): **Stephen James Carver**

Data plays poker with Isaac Newton and other great scientists.

Answering an outpost's distress call, the *Enterprise* finds an unknown alien craft in orbit, a litter of dead bodies in the nonstrategic station—and, finally, the Borg.

But these Borg are different: the plot strategy, seek vengeance rather than assimilation, have individual names—and look for Data, who kills a Borg in rage when he is charged. The other Borg and their ship retreat, leaving the android and his stunned friends to realize they have witnessed Data's first emotion.

As Data excuses himself from duty in a fruitless try at re-creating the moment, Admiral Nechayev arrives with a task force and gives Picard a dressing-down for his release a year earlier of "Hugh," and his giving up a chance to eliminate the Borg.

After re-creating the Borgs' transwarp travel vortex, the starship is boarded by two lone Borg who are easily stopped. The one captured taunts Data, urging him to act on the dark feelings that he is experiencing.

The two escape in a shuttlecraft and are traced to a sensor-shielded planet. Dr. Crusher is left in command when all but a skeleton crew leave the Enterprise to conduct a massive ground search. After tracking for hours, Picard's team is surprised by a mass of Borg—and shocked to see Data and his evil "brother" Lore, who proclaim they will destroy the Federation with their new army of followers.

Inspired by the film *Heart of Darkness,* this segment, which won much media attention for British physicist Stephen Hawking's cameo, takes its name from what Ron Moore called "Data's descent into darkness." Following up on the unknown fate of Hugh Borg a year ago ("I, Borg"/223), the story, which followed several failed cliffhanger ideas—including an early take on Data's dreams ("Birthright, Part I"/242) turning into nightmares—finally came together after the staff decided on a "mad Lore" premise, his first appearance in over two years ("Brothers"/177). Jeri Taylor, the only free hand at the time, was glad to get back into the story credits and said Moore's idea to use the Borg as a catalyst made a fine excuse for ending her ban on using the aliens. "I knew we couldn't simply do a Borg story just to do it and use them as villains, because after Hugh that was impossible," she said. "This was the exact right story." Still, at the time it left unrevealed the scope of the Borg change, reflecting Piller's view that the entire species not change too radically for now.

Hawking, a longtime Trek fan, planted the idea for his scene after visiting Paramount to shoot a promotional piece for the film of his best-seller *A Short History of Time.* While on a tour of the TNG sets, he asked to be taken from his wheelchair—a rare request—for a sit in the captain's chair and, as relayed through Leonard Nimoy, wondered if there was any way he could appear on the show! Writer Naren Shankar recalled that the search was on for a "profound" scene for him when Piller suggested the innocent premise of a poker game; Newton, of course, completely misses the reference to Mercury since he lived well before its discovery.

Actor Neville had starred in the movie *Baron Munchausen* and Jim Norton had played a holodeck Einstein once before ("Nth Degree"/193), while Cousins had earlier been seen as a Romulan ("The Next Phase"/224). Nogulich's Nechayev ("Chain of Command, Part I"/236, "Journey's End"/272, "Preemptive Strike"/276) and Data's cat Spot—were both TNG veterans; the unspecified Admiral Brooks Nechayev refers to had also been mentioned by Beverly ("Suspicions"/248). "Bosus" and "Tayar" are the two speaking Borg during the outpost melee; the "uncredited stunt roles of the dead" include Christine Bauer as Corelki, the guard in Riker's away team; Kenny Lesko as the Picard team's security guard handling a phaser rifle, only its second TNG appearance ("The Mind's Eye"/198, later in "Lower Decks"/267); and stunt coordinator Dennis Madalone, who took falls as both Data's Borg victim and the one beaming in with Crosis. And for true trivia fans: Longtime extra Guy Vardaman, who had been with the series since mid-first season in a variety of tasks on either side of the camera, finally picked up a character name: Lieutenant (j.g.) Wallace—a year later to gain a first name ("Eye of the Beholder"/270) and a place on the "new" bridge plaque ("All Good Things . . ."/277–78). This name and co-crewman Towles were named after TNG and DS9's two script typists, Daryl Towles and Jana Wallace (who'd been an extra in "Chain of Command, Part I"/236).

Starship naming history is also made here: The *Crazy Horse* is the first for a Native American, while the Excelsior-class *Gorkon*

paid homage to the slain Klingon chancellor of *ST VI*, replacing the *"Valiant"* in early drafts when Rick Berman asked for a first-ever alien namesake. The *Agamemnon* was named for British Admiral Nelson's ship, while the venerable shuttlepod *El-Baz* (from "Time Squared"/139, last seen in "Transfigurations"/173) reappears here. Even more trivia: Crosis' eyepiece is the same as the upper medallion on Worf's baldric, which has the pattern motion stilled to avoid distractions in close-ups; and again this season (after "Starship Mine"/244), the Darwin Station matte painting ("Unnatural Selection"/133) was used, here as the Ohniaka III outpost.

We learn that instant death in Klingons can be caused by shattering the cranial exoskeleton at the "tricipital" lobe; in Bajorans (as in the first uniformed Bajoran aboard since Ensign Ro was last seen), puncturing the heart's "lower ventricle" will do the same.

Moore praised Singer's handling of the action scenes as TNG's best ever, and their finished look was a milestone: After an earlier warm-up ("Birthright, Part I"/242), a proud FX supervisor David Stipes said the Ohniaka III station's terse hand-to-hand phaser battle he pieced together with film editor Steve Tucker used no live FX. For that, all the flames and sparks were added by computer in post-production—somewhat of a gamble, but a time-saver with no rigging explosives and touch-up of damaged set pieces needed. The "transwarp conduit"—a term Moore said had no relation to the once-mentioned technology of *ST III*—was yet another vortex effect, this time created live with lots of smoke and animated frame-by-frame with a sizzling effect by pushing increasing amounts of black confetti across an intensely backlit silhouette—a "lot of work," Stipes said, which characterized the extra time and budget bestowed on the cliff-hanger.

The finale's "swarm" of renegade Borg actually numbered just eleven—limited by the available wardrobe—but were multiplied thanks to four different FX split-screen overlays. Their new ship, built by Greg Jein, was designed by Dan Curry to reflect a typical Borg geometric outlook while being radically asymmetrical and includes recessed windows revealing layered girders and other structures. The "Borg Hall" exterior was a computer-retouched version of Brandeis Bardin Institute in Simi Valley, northwest of Los Angeles—the same structure used not only for Camp Khitomer's meeting hall in *ST VI* but as one destroyed (in miniature) by Stipes when handling effects for the film *Lawnmower Man.* The location shoot involved a very long day for the "hall" and planetside, all filmed by Jonathan West under a coral/amber filter for the bright atmospheric effect. Curry added another subtle alien touch: twin moons in the sky.

PRODUCTION STAFF CREDITS— SEASON 6

(In usual roll order; numbers in parenthesis refer to studio's episode numbers)

Casting: (*)Junie Lowery-Johnson, C.S.A.; ****Ron Surma

Music by: ***Jay Chattaway (228, 230, 232, 234, 236–37, 239, 242–44, 249, 252); (*)Dennis McCarthy (227, 229, 231, 233, 235, 238, 241, 245, 248, 250, 251); Don Davis (240)

Main Title Theme: (*)Jerry Goldsmith, (*)Alexander Courage

Director of Photography: ***Marvin Rush (227–228); Jonathan West (229–252)

Production Designer: **Richard D. James

Editor: *Tom Benko, A.C.E. (229, 232); ***J. P. Farrell (227, 230, 233, 236, 239, 242, 245, 248, 251); **Robert Lederman (228); David Ramirez (235, 238, 241, 244, 247, 250); ****Steve Tucker (231, 234, 237, 240, 243, 246, 249, 252)

Unit Production Manager: Brad Yacobian (+/***)

First Asst. Director: Jerry Fleck (all odd-numbered episodes, 227–251); Adele G. Simmons (+/*) (all even-numbered episodes, 228–252)

Second Asst. Director: Arlene Fukai

Costume Designer: ***Robert Blackman (EMMY NOMINEE: "Time's Arrow, Part II" [227])

Set Decorator: **Jim Mees

Visual Effects: Dan Curry (+/*)

Visual Effects Supervisor: Ronald B. Moore (+/***) (all odd-numbered episodes, 227–251); David Stipes (all even-numbered episodes, 228–252)

Post Production Supervisor: Wendy Rosenfeld (+/***) (Last name "Knoller" after 251)

Supervising Editor: John P. Farrell (+/***)

Senior Illustrator/Technical Consultant: (***)Rick Sternbach (+/*)

Scenic Artist Supervisor/Technical Consultant: (***)Michael Okuda (+/*)

Make-up Designed and Supervised By: (*)Michael Westmore

Visual Effects Coordinator: Phil Barberio (all odd-numbered episodes, 227–251); David Takemura (+/****) (all even-numbered episodes, 228–252)

Set Designer: ***Gary Speckman

Art Director: Andy Neskoromny (+/****)

Original Set Design: (*)Herman Zimmerman

Original Starfleet Uniforms: (*)William Ware Theiss

Script Supervisor: (*)Cosmo Genovese

Special Effects: (*)Dick Brownfield

Property Master: (*)Joe Longo (227); (*) Alan Sims (228–252)

Construction Coordinator: (*)Al Smutko

Scenic Artist: Jim Magdaleno (all odd-numbered episodes, 227–251); Alan Kobayashi (all even-numbered episodes, 228–252)

Hair Designer: Joy Zapata

Make-up Artists: **Gerald Quist, ***June Abston-Haymore

Hair Stylist: Patti Miller (228–35, 238, 240–42, 247–52); Candace Neal (227); Josee Normand (236, 237, 239, 241, 243–252)

Wardrobe Supervisor: ****Carol Kunz (+/**)

Sound Mixer: *Alan Bernard, C.A.S. (EMMY NOMINEE, with crew, sound mixing: "A Fistful of Datas" [234])

Camera Operator: *****Joe Chess, S.O.C. (227–230)

Chief Lighting Technician: William Peets (227, 228); R. D. Knox (229–252)

1st Company Grip: ***Bob Sordal (227–228); Steve Gausche (229–252)

Key Costumers: **Amanda Chamberlin (227); **Kimberley Thompson (all odd-numbered episodes, 227–251); *****Jerry Bono (228); *****Mary Ellen Boché (odd-numbered episodes, 229–251); David Powell (all even-numbered episodes, 228–252); Matt Hoffman (all even-numbered episodes, 230–252)

Music Editor: *Gerry Sackman

Supervising Sound Editor: (*)Bill Wistrom (227–237); Mace Matiosian (+/*) (238–252)

Sound Effects Editors: **James Wolvington (+/*) (227)**
Sound Editors: **Miguel Rivera; Masanobu Tomita; Guy Tsujimoto; *****Dan Yale (227–243); *Wilson Dyer (244–247); Ruth Adelman (248–252)**
Post Production Sound: **(*)Modern Sound**
Production Coordinator: **(*)Diane Overdiek**
Post Production Coordinator: **Dawn Hernandez**
Visual Effects Associate: **Edward L. Williams**
Production Associate: **Kim Fitzgerald (+/****)**
Science Consultant: **Naren Shankar**
Casting Executive: **(*)Helen Mossler**
Pre-Production Associate: **Lolita Fatjo (+/**)**
Monitors by: **(**)Sony Corp. of America (246)**
Stunt Coordinator: **(***)Dennis Madalone (229, 231–236, 241–243, 247–252)**

Lenses and Panaflex Cameras by: **(**)Panavision**
Special Visual Effects: **(*)Industrial Light and Magic (ILM) a division of Lucasfilm Ltd.**
Motion Control Photography: **(*)Image "G"**
Video Optical Effects: **Digital Magic**
Special Video Compositing: **(*)CIS Hollywood**
Editing Facilities: **(*)Unitel Video**

The number of * denotes a returning company or staffer's initial season of credit in that position; () denotes they are an original credited or co-credited person in that position; a (+) following indicates prior TNG work in another position

SEVENTH SEASON

When it was announced that Season 7 would be TNG's last, to make way for the long-requested feature film and the successor series *Star Trek: Voyager*, the idea that the beloved show was ending amid high ratings and critical acclaim still hit fans hard and left many in denial, often anger.

Signs of Star Trek's success were certainly everywhere, capped by the post-season breakthrough of an Emmy nomination for best dramatic series alongside the likes of *NYPD Blue*, *Picket Fences*, and *Northern Exposure*. For his part, Berman was proud that the show had come out on top despite having "three strikes against it": being science fiction, syndicated, and a sequel. "And we overcame all of those things," he said, "and we've given rebirth to *Star Trek*, a show that was very important to people, and 176 episodes later it's been embraced and welcomed by a lot more people and given them pleasure. That's a good feeling."

The depth of that popularity was evident all around.

Sparked in part by the success of the New York Times Syndicate's column by Ian Spelling, *TV Guide* began a science-fiction media column after offering a slew of high-selling Trek-related covers through the 1993–94 season. The eleventh-month Smithsonian Trek exhibit, described as the most popular in the history of the museum, had two thousand to three thousand visitors a day and racked up record-breaking sales in the gift shop before moving on to New York City's Hayden Planetarium. A touring exhibit called "Federation Science" was also making headlines as it left its native Oregon and inspired thoughts of similar events, including attractions at Paramount-owned theme parks. Finally, there was the June 13 *Wall Street Journal* cover story detailing the philosophical split in the effort to translate the Bible into Klingonese that grew out of the prior summer's Klingon language camp—though the TNG writing staff had long since moved away from using the "official" Marc Okrand linguistics created for the Trek feature films.

And what about ratings? Boosted by its own publicity campaign with local tie-ins and a gala studio preview for licensees, the finale "All Good Things . . ." drew a 15.4 rating and 26 share in the 36 metered Nielsen ratings markets to become the all-time first-run syndication *and* TNG leader, topping the pilot's 17.7 rating from 1987 and coming in first in 21 of 31 markets. According to Paramount Research figures it even beat network prime-time offerings in 13 of the 19 markets where it ran from New York City and Los Angeles to Miami, Boston, St. Louis, Denver, Charlotte, and San Antonio. Meanwhile, the studio reported that TNG's other "bottom line" showed sales of Trek-related merchandise topping $650 million overall as of spring 1994—including major lines of action figures and props from Playmates Toys and the ever-popular publishing line from Pocket Books, now closing in on 140 authorized titles and over $55 million in sales with some 70 on the best-seller lists.

But the question remained for fans, critics—and even cast members: How could such a popular entity leave the air at the height of its success? Some, like AP writer Scott Williams, wondered aloud that it all came back to the same old thing: money. "Paramount was looking at a 'mature asset' that could only get costlier," he wrote a week before the finale aired. "At the same time, its revenues would remain relatively flat. . . . Folding the TNG tent lets Paramount close its books on one set of syndication deals and open them, more profitably, on another."

Meanwhile back at the lot, the series-ending hoopla was but a distant din when the show's writers realized that the season was getting off to a surprisingly slow start—in part thanks to the creature that came to be called *Star Trek Generations*. Not only did its Thanksgiving 1994 release date push up the series' shooting schedule a month and cut short everyone's vacation, but Ron Moore and Brannon Braga, winning promotions to producer and co-producer respectively, took the month of May 1993 to go write the feature's first draft in Hawaii while the rest of the staff veterans got things running a week or two later: Jeri Taylor, now assuming more responsibility than ever as a full executive producer; René Echevarria, who added "executive" to his official story editor's title; and Naren Shankar, who got an onscreen credit as story editor. Replacing Shankar as science adviser was André Bormanis, a longtime fan, computer manual author, and onetime astronomy doctoral candidate with ties to both NASA and the needs of Hollywood, thanks to a partnership with screenwriter Steve Geller and past story pitches to Star Trek.

"They definitely did their series jobs," Echevarria said of Moore and Braga's "distraction." "But it was a priority for everybody to pull together and try to give them a little breathing room, if necessary, to get their job done." Piller, still spending two-thirds of his time getting *Deep Space Nine's* sophomore year rolling, felt TNG's early season also suffered from a letdown of another kind. "The fact that it didn't seem like there was a future took the wind out of our sails," he said. "But I think the pride factor kicked in about a third of the way into the season and we started doing some really top-notch stuff." At that point, he and Taylor discussed making the series' wrap-up episodes special by tying up a few loose threads—the roots of the eventual Wesley Crusher and Ro Laren stories—while using TNG's forum to introduce early backstory for *Voyager*, whose onrushing evolution was already well underway.

The series' finality also played at least a subconscious part as the seventh season evolved into sort of a family reunion with more of the regular cast's backgrounds finally being revealed through the dangling threads of real or imagined relatives: La Forge's parents, Tori's late father, Crusher's grandmother, Worf's once-mentioned foster brother, and even Picard's "son" and Data's "mother"! "You know, you could almost recite every day of Worf's entire life, and Geordi was the guy we knew the least about, so it became natural for us to flesh that out," Moore said.

"It was not our intent to answer every question and knit up every little mystery," Taylor added, noting that details such as Jack Crusher's demise would have to be left to future movies. "Still, I'm sure that underlying a lot of things was the awareness that it's our last season, and that may have allowed us to take some chances and do some things that wouldn't have been approved in earlier years." As the architect behind beefing up the women with Troi and Crusher in command roles, she also noted how something finally came of the long-teased Picard-Crusher attraction as well as the controversial Worf-Troi-Riker triangle first hinted at during Season 5. "People always give us more credit than we deserve, as if we have a map for each season—it's always so much more by the seat of our pants," she added. "You know, the stories come along and we say 'Aha! There's the chance!'"

The workload led to kudos from the bosses, with Piller again citing Taylor's "nurturing" of her staff. With the Moore-Braga duo busy working at year's end with the finale and Piller and Berman scrutinizing the last few episodes, Taylor again leaned heavily on the others and turned to other freelancers to help fill the bill. For instance, former staffer Joe Menosky's three scripts for TNG's last year were all completed, along with "Rivals" for DS9, without a trip back across the Atlantic from Italy. "We learned that it's possible to break a story here, fax it to Joe, have a phone conversation to flesh it out, and then two weeks later he sends us a script!" Taylor laughed.

The production side of the aisle had few shakeups as well—aside from brush fires and earthquakes—although visual effects producer Rob Legato's departure from *Deep Space Nine* to join the new company Digital Domain allowed Trek cohort Dan Curry to assume oversight of both series, setting up greater continuity with two alternating visual FX teams. For TNG, veteran Ron B. Moore supervised with Michael "B." Backauskas—an eighteen-year veteran who'd even worked on the first Trek feature in 1979 as well as the DS9 pilot—while supervisor David Stipes took on Joe Bauer as his coordinator. Both were joined by veterans Phil Barberio, moving over to become Curry's "roving fielder" as series coordinator, and associate Eddie Williams.

The coming of *Generations* meant further opportunities, with Peter Lauritson getting involved and reverting to a consulting producer's title on TNG as midseason on "Genesis" (266), leaving veteran Wendy Neuss to take on more overall post-production chores and move up "above the line" into the opening credits where residual fees are paid. Visual effects supervisor Moore also left to work on the feature at the same time, with his alternating slot split up among the rest of the staff late in the season. Also, with everyone doing triple duty costume designer Bob Blackman got help from Abram Waterhouse as co-costume designer. But by now, as TNG prepared to sail off into the rarefield subspace of the silver screen, the series' caretakers no longer worried much about the impact of the day-to-day changes; indeed, since DS9's launch—and especially during the protracted Viacom/QVC buyout war for Paramount in 1993—no one ever questioned the future of the Trek "franchise," as some perhaps ruefully had come to call it. "I said facetiously once that *Star*

Trek was bigger than Paramount," Majel Barrett Roddenberry once said, "and since then I've started to think back on that, because it's true: we've had *three* new groups (of owners/managers) come in, but they've changed and we're still here—we've been the ones to keep a roof over everyone's head!"

DESCENT, PART II

Production No.: 253 ■ Aired: Week of September 20, 1993	
Stardate: 47025.4 ■ Code: d2	

Directed by **Alexander Singer**
Written by **René Echevarria**

GUEST CAST
Hugh: **Jonathan del Arco**
Ensign Taitt: **Alex Datcher**
Lieutenant Barnaby: **James Horan**
Crosis: **Brian Cousins**
Transporter Technician Salazar: **Benito Martinez**
Goval: **Michael Reilly Burke**

With Dr. Crusher commanding the *Enterprise*, Picard and fellow captives Troi and La Forge hear Lore explain how their release of Hugh a year ago left a faction of the cyborg race in a vacuum of purpose that he and now the "emotional" Data can fill.

When Troi realizes that Data is showing only negative feelings, La Forge guesses that Lore must be using that part of Dr. Soong's emotion chip (actually intended for Data) as his means of control. But before La Forge can build a device to block Lore's control, he is led away by Data for more of Lore's attempts to transform organic beings into full androids—then wins a reprieve when Data's conscience kicks in.

In orbit, a Borg attack forces Crusher to leave behind some more of the crew, Riker and Worf are found by Hugh's Borg-in-hiding, who ditched Lore when his crude tests left many born mutilated. Meanwhile, Beverly uses metaphasic

shielding and a daring plan to destroy the Borg ship in a star's corona.

Hugh, at first bitter about being left adrift by the *Enterprise* crew, helps the group infiltrate the Borg complex. He leads a revolt just as Lore orders Data to kill Picard. Once bested, Lore is finally deactivated by his brother, who later keeps the emotion chip intact only at La Forge's insistence.

Despite producer Jeri Taylor's best intentions, this last cliffhanger wrap-up was not ironed out until after hiatus, and she and Echevarria both regretted having "too much story" so that not all of the plot lines, especially Hugh's ("I, Borg"/223), could be developed as much as desired. However, the shipboard plot with Beverly in command grew as it became more interesting.

"Part I left many balls in the air and I had to catch them," Echevarria observed. "We had a better idea of what this Part II was going to be like, but nothing turned out quite as simple as it had seemed." The first draft had Data shoot Lore in self-defense in an extended phaser battle, but Michael Piller wanted to avoid such an overt means and so the dismantling did the job instead. Taitt was Barclay in an early draft, but was dropped due to availability, expense, and the logic—as the writer pointed out—that "he's quite senior and would have been down there—foolishly—with everybody else!"

Director Singer, only the third to helm both segments of a TNG two-parter, easily recalled the one-day location shoot back at the distinctive Brandeis-Bardin Institute in 100 degree Simi Valley. "Those Borg extras were dying," recalled visual FX producer Dan Curry. "They had to wear black longjohns under those rubber suits." The Borg Hall interiors—actually a narrow three-wall set multiplied optically, as were the extras—were left standing over hiatus on Stage 16, but the caverns were built anew.

Here we learn, as Picard must have when he was Locutus ("The Best of Both Worlds"/174–175), that a tube carrying a silver liquid can disable a Borg when pulled from their headgear. "Of course, you don't want to imply that you can pull out any hose and they're down like an old car," Echevarria mused. Also, it is clarified that Hugh's local unit of Borg are the only ones affected by the "individuality" concept, and, via an Okudagram, that they are thought to originate in the Delta Quadrant. Data would later discover the memories on the emotion chip ("Brothers"/177) that Lore spoke of ("Inheritance"/262), and it all would become a major point again (*ST: Generations*); Data's "evil twin" uses his left index nail for a covert control switch, rather than his left thumbnail seen earlier ("Brothers").

Crusher's skills at bridge command would be explained later ("Thine Own Self"/268). Ironically, tactician Barnaby is played by James Horan, the same actor whose character almost killed her the last time the metaphasic shield came up ("Suspicions"/248); the solar-flare optical is the latest retouched reuse of an earlier element ("Redemption II"/201). Actor Burke later appeared on DS9 Cardassian pacifist Hogue in Season 2's "Profit and Loss," the unseen Lieutenant Powell speaking to Riker as a comm voice

Lore and one of his loyal Borg.

later becomes Ogawa's fiancé ("Lower Decks"/267) and husband ("All Good Things . . ."/277–278).

Once again, reflecting the confusion over O'Brien's initial pips and what a "chief" is ("Reai of Fear"/228, "Man of the People"/229, et al.), Crusher refers to Salazar as one though he's clearly a pipless NCO. And the adhesion strip formerly seen used to attach Starfleet comm badges ("The Naked Now"/103, "The Survivors"/151, "The High Ground"/160) is absent here—a likely advance in quartermaster and/or studio techniques.

LIAISONS

Production No. 254   ■   Aired: Week of September 27, 1993
Stardate: Unknown   ■   Code: ii

Directed by **Cliff Bole**
Teleplay by **Jeanne Carrigan Fauci & Lisa Rich**
Story by **Roger Eschbacher & Jaq Greenspon**

GUEST CAST
"Anna": **Barbara Williams**
Ambassador Voval: **Eric Pierpoint**
Ambassador Loquel: **Paul Eiding**
Ambassador Byleth: **Michael Harris**
Young boy (Eric Burton): **Ricky D'Shon Collins**

As part of a cultural exchange, Picard greets two Iyaaran ambassadors aboard ship before departing in their shuttle to meet with their leader.

Worf, already uncomfortable in diplomatic settings, is upset to be chosen as a host by Byleth, a surly type who comes to blows with the Klingon over poker. In contrast, Troi finds herself escorting the gentle Loquel, who seems to be gorging himself on pure sensations of food and drink.

En route to Iyar, Picard's shuttle crashes on a hostile world, and the Iyaaran pilot Voval is knocked out. After stumbling outside and collapsing outdoors, Picard awakes to find a human woman, Anna, caring for him inside a downed freighter. Apparently a crash survivor for seven years, a moody Anna ruins the shuttle's com panel when sent to retrieve it and then confides she loves Picard.

Initially sympathetic, Picard rails at the woman after he realizes he is not injured badly and that she seeks to keep him captive. She flees into the murky night just as Voval, very much alive, shows up at the freighter shelter and they set out after her.

Not until the "lovesick" Anna appears and

Anna (Barbara Williams) saves Picard's life, then won't let him leave.

in just eight days. Taylor was surprised Braga's odd humor didn't make the episode more popular, but for veteran director Bole the episode was "just flat not my favorite show," citing the many rewrites as deadlines loomed.

Actor Pierpoint became the second regular from the onetime Fox SF series *Alien Nation* to guest on TNG ("In Theory"/199)—his craft being the redressed "alien shuttle" (see "Birthright, Part I"/ 242 note)—while "Eric," who appeared twice again ("Masks"/ 269, "Firstborn"/273), was named for Braga's nephew. Propmaster Alan Sims recalled how, after he had bought chocolate-covered raisins for Loquel's poker-game snack, actor Eiding confided he was allergic to chocolate and caused a wee-hours run to an open candy store for an alternative snack. "He said he broke out in red hives but offered to eat it anyway," Sims said. "Now there's an actor who's grateful to be working!"

Braga also conjured up one of TNG's infamously confusing "T"-aliens, the Tarellians, with Picard's comment that Anna could not be of that race "unless you've lost two of your arms"—indicating it's possibly the species of bar pianist Amarie ("Unification II"/207), since a two-armed Tarellian was filmed but cut from the finale for time ("All Good Things . . ."/277–278). The plagued Tarellians ("Haven"/105) and warrior Talarians ("Heart of Glory"/120, "Suddenly Human"/176) are confusing enough, even without Dathon's Tamarians ("Darmok"/202), but Braga would later concoct the Tarellian "death syndrome" ("Genesis"/271) and "plague" ("All Good Things . . .").

After seven years, Worf, Deanna, and Beverly are finally seen in their dress uniforms; Worf's added Klingon sash scene evokes both Scotty's dress kilts and McCoy's dress-blues fussing (1967's "Journey to Babel"). Continuity hounds will also notice references to the Ktarians ("The Game"/206, "Birthright, Part I"/242, "Timescape"/251, "Phantasms"/258, *Generations*); Troi's chocolate habit (see notes, "The Price"/156); papalla juice, red here instead of clear ("Imaginary Friend"/222); a Tarvokian powder cake, rather than "pound cake" ("The Game"); Worf's battle "calisthenics" ("Where Silence has Lease"/128, "Emissary"/146, "New Ground"/210); Deck 12's stellar cartography ("Lessons"/245, "Homeward"/265, *Generations*) and Deck 8's unfinished nature, taken from the *TNG Technical Manual*. In a cut scene, Byleth had awakened Worf at 0500 for a tour of the arboretum, while later in a minor blooper he actually takes three poker chips during their game—not two as Worf claims.

Built by modelmaker Tony Doublin, new to TNG but a longtime associate of FX supervisor David Stipes, the freighter exterior scene was a six-by-sixteen tabletop model with crash-skid furrows and forced-perspective mountains only five feet away; Richard James' live interior featured a slanted "crashed" floor. The cliffs were another Doublin model, combined at Digital Magic with a Dan Curry computer matte painting and the filmed actors, smoke, and stage—with Picard being a late addition to clarify the scene. Anna's transformation to Voval came from an unused test element Curry had shot years before: the end result of a laser beam shot through melted plastic and bounced off white cardboard.

threatens to jump off a cliff does Picard discover the truth: Voval took Anna's form to learn about love, a concept alien to the Iyaarans—just as his shipboard cohorts wanted to study pleasure and antagonism.

Sixth-season interns Fauci and Rich took this teleplay out of the season's most arduous break session, building on Eschbacher and Greenspon's straight homage to Stephen King's *Misery*. "She" initially became a very balanced Starfleet officer, but Braga suggested hiking the character's angst a few notches to create more tension.

Originally the script had Taylor's B-story about Troi earning her commander's pips, but when the two plots didn't gel that line was ejected and saved for later ("Thine Own Self"/268), while Braga created the aliens' "testing" events in an uncredited rewrite done

INTERFACE

Production No.: 255 ■ Aired: Week of October 4, 1993
Stardate: 47215.5 ■ Code: in

Directed by **Robert Wiemer**
Written by **Joe Menosky**

GUEST CAST
Captain Silva La Forge image: **Madge Sinclair**
Admiral Marcus Holt: **Warren Munson**
Commander Edward M. La Forge, Ph.D.: **Ben Vereen**

After successfully testing a new interface that transforms remote sensor data into hands-on "reality" via his own VISOR inputs, La Forge is ready to take on the retrieval of the lost *U.S.S. Raman* trapped low in the atmosphere of gas giant Marijne VII.

But the mission is threatened when Picard breaks the news that the *Starship Hera* has been lost with all its crew—including its captain, La Forge's mother, Silva.

The engineer opts to press on with his *Raman* mission, noting that the device is designed to work with his unique anatomy. Just as he finds the crew of seven all dead, a fire flash leaves him with severe hand burns—even though the flash was merely relayed from the remote probe's inputs.

After Dr. Crusher adjusts the interface to prevent a reoccurrence, La Forge tells his father via subspace that he refuses to believe his mother is dead. Even so, he's startled to "find" her on the *Raman* during the probe's next run. "She" asks him to take the ship lower in the atmosphere, where her vessel is supposedly trapped.

Despite suffering neural shock in the exchange, La Forge, with Data's help, risks one more contact—countering Picard's direct order and the beliefs of his friends, who feel he's in hallucinatory grief. This time, he learns that his "mother" is really one of many fire-based life-forms who were trapped on the ship and will die if not returned to their home lower in the atmosphere—and he does so. Initially angry, Picard later relents and shares his sympathy.

Though it became the first installment of what writer-producer Ron Moore dubbed TNG's "Year of Lost Souls," Geordi's background finally comes to life in onetime staffer Joe Menosky's fifth-season pitch, whose heavy special effects portray a sometimes confusing point of view. "Using Geordi in place of the camera/probe was a difficult convention to establish," said director Wiemer, who noted it would have been "emotionally unrewarding" to show the reality of filming the remote probe with "Silva" while cutting back to Geordi in the lab for reactions.

The high-profile guest stars include Sinclair (the *Saratoga's* unnamed captain in *ST IV*) flying in from Jamaica and Vereen, whom Le Var Burton helped attract to the show, buying out a day of his Broadway show.

Originally Menosky had Riker in the virtual-reality suit, troubled by the death of his father and glimpsing scenes of their Alaska cabin, but Geordi was made the focal character because of Riker's mind trip late last season ("Frame of Mind"/247) because of the logic of the VISOR implants. René Echevarria did a late polish, while Riker's consolation of Geordi was a rare scene *added* for time and penned by Taylor, not filmed until three shows later. For his part, though, staff writer Naren Shankar wondered if the story's concept wasn't futuristic enough, and science adviser André Bormanis agreed: "There are prototypes of that kind of thing already, although tying it straight to the brain will take much longer."

Menosky coined the names of Geordi's sister Ariana and his mother Silva, although the name "Alvera K." was on a bio screen briefly glimpsed in "Conundrum" (214); Taylor thought "Silva" was

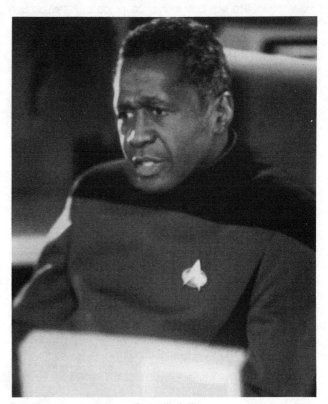

Ben Vereen appears as Geordi's father.

more "interesting" and didn't consider the other visible enough to change it. His father, addressed as "doctor," is not named here, though the earlier screen called him "Edward M." and the script gives his rank as commander. Both parents had already been referred to as an exozoologist and a command officer ("Imaginary Friend"/222).

The suit itself, designed by costumer Bob Blackman, carried "a prop man's nightmare," Alan Sims recalled: "blinky" sensors that each ran off its own watch battery and switch, requiring ten minutes in all to turn on or off between takes. "If I have any legacy it's the teasing from the actors—'Oh God, let's save Alan's batteries,'" he laughed. "But it's not the cost of the batteries—it's what happens when they run down and you have that delay to open 'em up and put in new ones."

Background fans: The *Raman*, named for a Nobel Prize–winning Indian physicist, has a gaseous rather than forcefield fire-suppression system ("Up the Long Ladder"/144) and carries Starfleet registry number NCC-29487 but has a crew dressed in "civvies"; Riker missed his mother and acted out when he started school; roller coasters are still known in the twenty-fourth century; *Deep Space Three*, in contrast to DS9, is headed by an admiral and is apparently near the Breen ("The Loss"/184, "Hero Worship"/211, *Generations*) and Ferengi; and the *Hera* had a mostly Vulcan crew, a century-old Starfleet practice (1967's "The Immunity Syndrome"). Also seen again is the oft-used biolab lift ("The Offspring"/164, "The Best of Both Worlds, Part 2"/175, *Generations*) dubbed by set decorator Jim Mees as the "*Rocky Horror* elevator" after the cult classic.

Visually, Wiemer and FX supervisor Ron B. Moore were disappointed that the elaborate probe miniature by veteran model-maker Brick Price was only seen once; producer Peter Lauritson regretted not getting to depict the trapped *Raman*. The hardest FX shot, Silva's transformation to flame, used torso-shaped shells of flash paper that live FX man Dick Brownfield had formed and dried around a mannequin; two were butted together so the flames would go the same direction. Geordi's walk-in wall of fire used the same effect as the Bersallis III firestorms ("Lessons"/245), although many of the flames were shot live—but not too close.

GAMBIT, PART I

Production No.: 256 ▪ Aired: Week of October 11, 1993
Stardate: 47135.2 ▪ Code: g1

Directed by **Peter Luritson**
Teleplay by **Naren Shankar**
Story by **Christopher Hatton and Naren Shankar**

GUEST CAST
Arctus Baran: **Richard Lynch**
Tallera: **Robin Curtis**
Vekor: **Caitlin Brown**
Narik: **Cameron Thor**
Yranac: **Alan Altshuld**
Admiral Chekote: **Bruce Gray**
Ensign Giusti: **Sabrina LeBeauf**
Bartender: **Stephen Lee**
Lieutenant Sanders: **Derek Webster**

When Picard disappears on an archaeological pleasure trip, the senior staff discover he was apparently vaporized weeks earlier by ruffians in a bar. Riker, who refuses to accept Picard's death until justice is served, forces a Yridian source to reveal the attackers' next likely stop, Barradas III.

There, La Forge finds the same kind of micro-crystalline damage found in the bar. Suddenly the group is ambushed by Picard's "murderers," who kidnap an injured Riker in a quick beam-up.

The "pirates" escape, but Data chooses to look for clues rather than pursue. Coming to, Riker discovers he is wearing a pain inducer, used for forced discipline by Baran, the leader of a mercenary band.

Riker is shocked to find Picard alive and posing as renegade archaeologist "Galen," who's at odds with Baran. Taking a cue from Picard, Riker assumes the air of a Starfleet "black sheep" and then repairs an engine problem that Picard had secretly caused so Riker could win the trust of Baran and the crew.

Data soon realizes the raiders have been hitting the ruins of a Romulan offshoot race and

Captain Picard is trapped aboard a pirate vessel.

pursues them to Calder II, where he's surprised to hear Riker order the *Enterprise*'s shields lowered. He does so as Picard, who won a reprieve against attacking the Starfleet outpost there, is forced by Baran to open fire on his own ship. . . .

This story, born from a sixth-season spec script from Iowa college student Chris Hatton, not only bore an all-star cast but truly went where no TNG story idea had gone before: breaking Gene Roddenberry's thirty-year ban on so-called "space pirate" stories. First Michael Piller and then Jeri Taylor mulled over the impossible, attracted by the premise of Riker seeking vengeance for Picard's death and the promise of an offbeat, less "talky," romp. As they warmed to it and Piller suggested it could hold up as an expanded two-parter, and finally Rick Berman called Taylor in to talk.

"Rick has a little bust of Gene Roddenberry on his desk," she recalled, "and he'd tied a little red bandanna around Gene's eyes and said, 'Gene *always* said he'd never do space pirates, and *this* is a space pirate story, and I don't want Gene to see this, or hear it!' " "I just blindfolded it as a joke one day," Berman added. "Whenever they come up with a story I don't think Gene would like I blindfold him when we discuss the story. . . . I take it on and off, depending on who's in here."

"We say we'll never do the 'rodeo' show and 'A Fistful of Datas' comes along," agreed writer Shankar, who acknowledged the show's popularity while still doubting it had had the "legs" to be expanded. "To me, it's one of the classic television problems: If you start off the show by saying the captain's dead, no one's buying it . . . and you're just marking time until the captain's

revealed"—in contrast to "The Best of Both Worlds," which occurred over hiatus when there were "legitimate" doubts about Patrick Stewart's return. Hatton, who beat the odds with a second story sale after this one ("Thine Own Self"/268), moved to Hollywood for a time to pursue writing but then returned home to finish his degree first. His original spec script followed Picard's point of view and didn't involve Riker.

The guest cast boasted many familiar faces: a return to Trekdom for Robin "Saavik II" Curtis after her *ST III* and *ST IV* appearances; veteran Richard Lynch, who had previously worked with Stewart onstage; and Sabrina "Sondra" LeBeauf of the eighties *Cosby Show*, whose character Giusti was named for a friend of Shankar. "Sabrina was a fan, and though she's a professional, I think sitting down at the controls of the *Enterprise* kinda unnerved her a little bit, but she picked it up and did fine," recalled postproduction producer Peter Lauritson, here directing his second TNG outing. Also, Altshuld was terrorist Pomet in "Starship Mine" (244), Brown had played Ty Kajada in DS9's first-season "The Passenger," Gray reprised Chekote from an earlier shot on DS9's "The Circle," and Lee had played Chorgan ("The Vengeance Factor"/157).

In contrast to his Hugo-winning directing opus ("Inner Light"/225), Lauritson noted the outdoor/action scope and visual FX team planning required in this segment. "I was really whipped after this one!" he laughed. "Directing is a tough job, and I really respect the guys who do a lot of it." Set decorator Jim Mees remembers the shoot too: his crew had to lug real rocks up from the studio in the heat and "build" the ruins.

Lauritson and Taylor praised Stewart's portrayal of Picard while she joked that Lauritson must have "saved up all the favors ever owed him" to afford the show's most extended phaser fight ever with over seventy phaser shots. All the explosions were done in post-production due to the fire-season ban on live explosive "squibs" at the location site at Griffith Park's Cedar Grove. In fact, his boss David Stipes noted that the fire ban meant all damage "stains" had to be painted on digitally, as did a fake rock blown up in front of Geordi's face—actually, on a blue screen set by live FX man Dick Brownfield and matted in. For orbital shots, the "Miradorn raider" from DS9's "Vortex" was seen over what began as four-by-five NASA Earth slides, used to provide more detail for closer shots.

Trivia fans will note: the first TNG use of DS9's gold-pressed latinum; Riker's serial number, only the second given for the regulars in the series, is SC 231-427, and his time on the *Hood* ("Encounter at Farpoint"/101-102, "Tin Man"/168, "The Pegasus"/264) and the Minos Korva crisis ("Chain of Command"/236-237) are recalled; Picard's alias "Galen" was his mentor archaeologist ("The Chase"/246); the Yridians ("Birthright, Part I"/242, "Suspicions"/248, and DS9) are readable by empaths, unlike Ferengi and others ("Ménage à Troi"/172); there's a UFP "Science Council" (repeated in "Force of Nature"/261) as well as an "Archaeological Survey"; and the Argus sector ("Nth Degree"/193, "Parallels"/263).

GAMBIT, PART II

Production No.: 257 ■ Aired: Week of October 18, 1993
Stardate: 47160.1 ■ Code: g2

Directed by **Alexander Singer**
Teleplay by **Ronald D. Moore**
Story by **Naren Shankar**

GUEST CAST
Arctus Baran: **Richard Lynch**
Tallera: **Robin Curtis**
Vekor: **Caitlin Brown**
Narik: **Cameron Thor**
Koral: **James Worthy**
Ensign Giusti: **Sabrina LeBeauf**
Commander Setok: **Martin Goslins**

Facing the defenseless *Enterprise* while posing as part of a mercenary crew, Picard and Riker play their parts by firing a low-level phaser burst that leaves the *Enterprise* unharmed but impresses the mercenary leader, Baran.

Data plays a hunch and lets the pirate ship escape but finds a coded message from Riker that details their next heading. Meanwhile, the Romulan Tallera forces Picard to reveal his true identity while explaining that she is actually a Vulcan agent sent to grab the crew's target: an ancient psionic superweapon wanted by Vulcan isolationists who wish to rid their world of its leaders and off-worlders.

At the rendezvous site, Baran sends a raiding party aboard the *Enterprise* to retrieve the last psionic resonator piece from a Klingon contact who'd been detained there. Riker, whose act has fooled Baran, is ordered to kill "Galen" but instead is "shot" on stun by Picard.

Learning that Tallera is actually among those who want the weapon, she and Picard expose each other to the crew. He is taken hostage while others go with both of them down to Vulcan for their money, where Tallera kills them with the resonator just as Picard realizes its power source is negative thought. He then alerts his would-be *Enterprise* rescuers. Left useless, the weapon is destroyed by the Vulcan government and Tallera is detained.

To flesh out Hatton's original hour-long story, Part II expanded upon the reason for the mercenaries' looting, the Vulcan subplot, and the appearance of Koral, the galaxy's tallest Klingon. Director Singer, who had done his continuity homework by visiting Lauritson's set during Part I, took his turn at enjoying the show's tone: a thankful change of pace that "took the onus off of being deadly earnest, deadly serious, and deadly complicated."

Star Trek fan and NBA star James Worthy's unforgettable appearance began with a chance meeting with the top Klingon of them all, Robert "Gowron" O'Reilly ("Reunion,"/181, "Redemption" I and II/200-201, "Rightful Heir"/249). He confided he'd always wanted to be on the show while they jokingly signed each other's trading cards during an airline flight. At O'Reilly's urging, Worthy met with Berman and Piller, who in turn asked Taylor about any suitable cameo parts—and the stoic, intimidating Koral was a perfect fit. "They asked if James Worthy could be written in and I said, 'Who?'—'cause I'm not a big sports fan," Moore laughed. "And then—'Oh! He's a Laker!' . . . We were looking for little filler plot elements to do anyway." Worthy's showing was a light-hearted lift for everyone, Singer said, and he noted that athletes are usually comfortable before the camera: "They're in show business, they don't freeze, and they take direction well." Still, prop man Alan Sims recalled that he seemed to be humorously intimidated by it all: "To him, the pressure of basketball was *nothing* compared to what it's like here."

Despite his mixed feelings about the show, Shankar enjoyed fleshing out the Vulcan subplot—in part based on Spock's admission in 1967's "Journey to Babel" that a Vulcan was quite capable of killing for a logical reason. "We went for people who very logically felt that Vulcan's 'problems' were linked to contamination by illogical people," the writer observed, "so in a logical

Captain Picard works with Tallera (Robin Curtis), a Vulcan agent.

sense you say 'Get rid of them.' . . . I just thought it was a very logical way to arrive at racism being the answer to your problems. It was a different but very believable tone for the Vulcans."

Reusing place names to increase believability, Shankar reprised Draken IV from his own script ("Face of the Enemy"/249) and intended to name Yadalla Prime "Yonada Prime" as the destination of the people in 1969's "For The World Is Hollow And I Have Touched The Sky" but it was changed due to the presumed Romulan origins required. Likewise, Barradas III was an homage to "Beratis," one of many names for the Jack the Ripper entity from 1967's "Wolf in the Fold." Moore named the Stone of Gol after the plateau of the Vulcan Masters where Spock studied in the first feature—leading Shankar to quip that the weapon might colloquially be referred to as the "Gol stone."

With Vulcan so little mentioned in much of TNG, Moore had a chance to tie up a few loose ends regarding the planet, such as its "founding" UFP status, the governing "Vulcan council" (a cut line) titled ministers, and the myths of Vulcan gods. Surak's Vulcan reformation of logic (from 1969's "Savage Curtain"), referred to here as the Time of Awakening, is definitely dated for the first time with a two-thousand-year-old time frame, but with the Debrune of Part I described as "a Romulan offshoot" and their Barradas III outpost dated to the same era, the Vulcan-Romulan schism would appear to predate Surak by several generations, at least. In any case, it confirms that all three races had starflight well before Earth did—curious, given that Romulans had no warp drive in their first televised appearance (1966's "Balance of Terror") and are said to have lost their twenty-second-century war to Earth because of it.

The psionic resonator was another late-developed detail but was scaled back from early plans to make it a killer of millions at one stroke. Prop man Alan Sims recalled that the Vulcan god of death (to the right on the back) was bald-headed until Rick Berman ordered that hair be etched on to avoid any resem-

blance to Patrick Stewart in the insert close-up! Its effect shot was completely computer generated, reported FX supervisor Ron B. Moore, whose initial was switched to "D."—as with the writer-producer—in a rare end-credits typo. The budget-minded cavern set won more praise from the director: "There's more invention in that show per dollar and per hour of labor than almost anything else I've ever seen," Singer said. "It is so extraordinary that the industry at large doesn't know that or appreciate that: Richard James is in a class with anyone in the world."

Trivia watchers will note Koral's "Toron-class" vessel is the alien shuttle re-dressed again ("Liaisons"/254), seen alongside the *Justman* ("Suspicions"/248); the "Judge Advocate General" harks back ("The Measure of a Man"/135), while the Federation-Klingon treaty is quoted for the first time. Finally, the brief TNG clip with Frakes and Spiner that was used for the 1993 MTV Music Video Awards was shot during a break in this episode.

PHANTASMS

Production No.: 258 ■ Aired: Week of October 25, 1993
Stardate: 47225.7 ■ Code: ph

Directed by **Patrick Stewart**
Written by **Brannon Braga**

GUEST CAST
Ensign Tyler: **Gina Ravarra**
Sigmund Freud: **Bernard Kates**
Admiral Nakamura: **Clyde Kusatsu**
Workman No. 1: **David L. Crowley**

La Forge is embarrassed by the ongoing failure of a newly installed warp core just as Data becomes troubled by disturbing nightmare images from his dreaming program.

From memories of eating a living cake in the shape of Deanna Troi to workmen apparently disrupting a plasma conduit, Data seeks out a Sigmund Freud holodeck program and even Troi herself for answers. Though wondering if he's developing human neuroses, Troi, like La Forge, dismisses Data's dreams as just a new level of humanity—until he drifts off during a work session, begins seeing eating and mouth images on crewmen and finally stabs Troi in the shoulder when he sees a mouth image there—even with his dream program turned off.

With Data confined to quarters and the new warp core still a problem, in sickbay Dr. Crusher finds an interphasic, leechlike creature on Troi at the point of her stab wound. She learns the creatures, largely invisible, are all over the crew and are fatally extracting cellular peptides.

Sensing that Data's dreams are a clue to their removal, Picard and La Forge enter a holodeck sequence connected to his dream program and encounter the images Data has been seeing. Upon awakening, the android successfully uses a high-frequency interphasic pulse to drive out the creatures, whose effects—including the warp-core failure—had been depicted in his dreams.

In his weirdly offbeat trademark style, staff writer Braga delved successfully into the nightmarish side of Data's dreams—a goal ever since he introduced the idea of dreams earlier ("Birthright, Part I"/242)—but around the set the episode went down in Trek lore as simply "the cake show." Perhaps the most infamous production headache since the first season's Armus creature ("Skin of Evil"/122), "the cake" reveals that even TNG's well-oiled production machine has its breakdowns.

"The episode was fun and easy and it turned out great," recalled the writer, who enjoyed taking jabs at Freud's theories, "but the cake was the big thing: the production team, for some reason, God bless 'em, it threw 'em for a loop." Never mind the old "saw a lady in half" magician's trick table, or the same gag used in one of his own low-budget student films or the Tom Petty Wonderland-themed rock video; from the first production meeting Braga had wanted a full-length, anatomically correct cake with more gore, but that was pulled back by Berman and simplified to what staff members *thought* they'd finally agreed on: a torso sheet cake on a cutaway table.

Prop man Alan Sims, who at first suggested building the cake right over Sirtis' body to employ her own limbs, told of a morning rush-hour call to his Santa Clarita baker after director Stewart, helming his fourth TNG outing, realized two hours before shooting that a "life-sized torso" wasn't that large after all; store-bought sponge cakes added on and color-matched frostings were the jury-rigged answer. "The producer's there now, the production manager's there now, everyone's upset, Patrick's upset," he recalled. "You *can't* see it before [shooting day], so that's why I ask these questions in the production meetings—'You want arms or you want it like a Venetian statue?'" "Dreams are not practical . . . because no matter what you do someone's gonna say 'Oh, that's not what I thought it was going to look like,'" agreed designer Richard James. "You virtually have to throw the head back because otherwise the head's going to be looking right into the cake . . . but they didn't want her 'thrown back.'"

"I think there was a little bit of panic that day" was producer Peter Lauritson's understatement, while set decorator Jim Mees was more blunt: "I thought everyone was going to kill each other! It was one of those things that if you could have you'd have pretended you were dying in a hospital rather than come to

In Data's dream, Deanna appears as a cake.

work!" And Dan Curry, who tried the "box" out himself, recalled that "if you put a prisoner of war in there you'd be put on trial for war crimes. . . . Marina (Sirtis) was a trooper about it."

Despite it all, Braga said he was more "stunned" that Data's stabbing scene of Troi was left in. "It's really a very shocking moment, very disturbing—I fully expected children in the audience to scream about Data hiding in the closet to their parents!" Lines cut for time featured Data's study of 138 dream theories, including Dr. Syrus of Tilona IV ("Frame of Mind"/247) and a banquet featuring Ktarian spice cake (see "The Game"/206) and a keynote speech on Bajoran aqueduct management (as in "Birthright, Part I"/242). Braga'd named Ensign Tyler after his girlfriend's niece, and pointed out that Data did not yet know he had a "mother" ("Inheritance"/262).

Kutsatsu reprises Nakamura, one of Starfleet's fifty-plus admirals, all the way from Season 2 ("The Measure of a Man"/135), while longtime con extra Joyce Robinson gets dubbed "Ensign Gates" here, an homage to actress McFadden. Also for the trivia buffs, Alexander is finally mentioned this season and said to like Riker's jazz ("11001001"/116, "Second Chances"/250), and the "new" hatch cover was meant to be an all-new reactor *core,* cut for budget; the metaphasic scanner prop ("The Next Phase"/224) is an anyonic scanner here.

Finally, in Data's room we see another casually stored phaser ("Aquiel"/239), Jenna's gift ("In Theory"/199), and his getups for Dixon Hill (see "11001001"/116) and Sherlock Holmes ("Elementary, Dear Data"/129, "Ship in a Bottle"/238); despite his bedtime ritual we know he needs no rest ("The Best of Both Worlds"/174) although he has tried it ("Tin Man"/168). Ongoing here are the jokes about Spot's pet-sitters ("Timescape"/251, "Genesis"/258), and his picky appetite, now up to feline supplement 125 from 74 ("Data's Day"/185, "Force of Nature"/251). And in the season's biggest blooper, the cat's clear status as a male here would soon change ("Force of Nature"/261, "Genesis"/258).

The surreal imagery translated into a full plate for the post-production teams, the most complex being the quick holodeck dissolve from Ten-Forward to Freud's office while Picard is talking on Data's "chest phone." Aside from director of photography Jonathan West and second-unit DP Tom DeNove matching lighting on the various sets to blue-screen shootings and to the half-second transformational cross-fade, the scene already required that prop man Alan Sims' telephone within a cast Data "chest" be matted in on the imaged Data, who himself would dissolve with the backgrounds and the phone receiver that Picard holds.

Modelmaker Tony Doublin created two different creature puppets for the episode, including cable-actuated foam models for the "mouths" initially five times larger than the finished shot and then scaled down, with the background blended digitally so even Geordi's skin muscles appeared to move. His interphasic creatures were originally much more complex, sporting visible tentacles and shot on two plates for a transparent "jellyfish" effect with internal organs visible on the fourteen-inch model. After the shots had all been filmed and composited, FX supervisor David Stipes recalled with a groan, the word came down to make them more mollusk-like with embedded tentacles and not so much movement apparent in "this" dimension—so the extras were all painstakingly "painted" out. "You can still see their guts moving but it's about a tenth of what we did," Stipes said.

Finally, the dream aura allows a reality warp on the sets: As Picard and La Forge round a corner to enter Ten-Forward, the wall of "fake" cabin doors can be seen backing up to the wall behind the bar.

DARK PAGE

Production No.: 259 ■ Aired-Week of November 1, 1993
Stardate: 47254.1 ■ Code: dk

Directed by **Les Landau**
Written by **Hilary J. Bader**

GUEST CAST
Ambassador Lwaxana Troi: **Majel Barrett**
Maques: **Norman Large**
Hedril: **Kristen Dunst**
Lieutenant Ian Andrew Troi: **Amick Byram**
Kestra Troi: **Andreana Weiner**

While escorting and tutoring the Cairn, a telepathic species who until recently had no concept of spoken language, the normally boisterous Lwaxana Troi seems tired when the group visits the *Enterprise.* Despite Lwaxana's playing matchmaker for her with Maques, a Cairn, Deanna is troubled by her mother's unusual moodiness and prods her to get a checkup.

Lwaxana is seen to be low on psilosynine, a Betazed neurotransmitter used in telepathy, but defies Crusher's order to avoid mental contact and collapses. Maques helps them learn that something has triggered a past event that Lwaxana had blocked into her metaconscious mind—the Betazoid protection from psychic trauma—and caused the comatose shutdown.

After assuring the crew that his presence is not the cause, Maques offers to act as a telepathic "bridge" so Troi can explore her mother's mind and unblock the damage. There she encounters images trying to drive her away: Picard, a wolf, and even her late father—as well as Hedril, a Cairn girl.

Still baffled, Troi reads her mother's diaries and finds seven years have been deleted by her mother. Using Maques as a telepathic bridge again, she uncovers her mother's self-guilt over the drowning of a previously unknown older sister, Kestra. After helping her mother say goodbye to her daughter and the guilt, Troi gives her grateful mother an old photo of the whole family

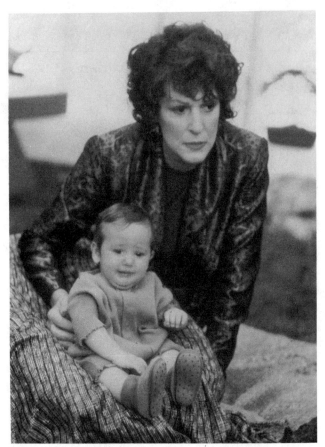

Lwaxana Troi (Majel Barrett) with Deanna Troi as a baby.

that Mr. Homn, their valet, had saved for just such an occasion.

The season's next "family reunion" not only featured Lwaxana Troi in another less "Mame"-like turn but finally gave a glimpse of Deanna's father, previously only hinted at ("Encounter at Farpoint"/101–102, "The Child"/127, "The Host"/197) but seen here to be a Starfleet lieutenant played by Byram Amick—who previously appeared as Paul Hickman, one of La Forge's former crewmates ("Identity Crisis"/192).

Bader kept retrying her basic pitch of a telepathic mental/emotional rescue through various guises—Crusher and another female doctor, then a Geordi story, then Crusher and Troi, then Troi and someone else, and then Lwaxana rescuing Deanna—before it took its present form. Taylor was glad to continue fleshing out the story behind the boisterous Lwaxana and to deliver the unique science-fiction "rescue"; the hard part for her and Bader, noted uncredited polish writer René Echevarria, was coming up with a dark enough secret that after seven years wouldn't portray Lwaxana "unsympathetically."

Echevarria's regrets were being told to tone down Maques' sometimes comical attempts at language into halting and simple pauses, and doing without location lakeside scenes in favor of the less-expensive arboretum set—which was larger than usual ("Data's Day"/185, "Imaginary Friend"/222) with its own pond this time. Bader had included the part of valet Mr. Homn but had to make him an unseen long-distance contact when Carel Struyken was not available; the staff was unaware that Deanna originally did not recognize Homn in the first Lwaxana story ("Haven"/105).

After "Phantasms," a move toward more fictional neural "tech" led to the uniquely Betazoid telepathic neurotransmitter psilosynine, the metaconscious, and the paracortex lobe of telepathy. Bader's one homage that stood was originally the "Lake El'Nar eddy," named for her late friend Eddie Elnar.

Actor Large had already played Romulan proconsul Neral ("Unification I-II"/208-7) and a Kobheerian captain on DS9's first-season "Duet." Young Kristen Dunst was also seen in 1994's *Interview with the Vampire*, while Teddy and backup Buck of Working Wildlife, the rented wolves who chased her and Troi, had played Two Socks in *Dances with Wolves* and were later in *The Jungle Book*. As usual the past two seasons, all the animals were arranged by Rob Block's Critters of the Cinema, who'd provided Data's most recent Spot as well as Simon, the mixed Pomeranian appearing as Kestra's dog.

Actually no chase was involved, since actors and most crew weren't allowed close to the trained but still-wild animals—"Nobody wanted to be there with the wolf except Dan Curry," Lauritson quipped. Instead, extensive split-screen shots against blue screen were used: for instance, Dunst actually petted not the wolf but the knuckle of a handy C-clamp stand, with the animal matted in later. To inject motion into otewise static lockdown shots, the camera panned with Troi running through a doorway, then locked down to film the wolf running through, apparently only a moment later.

Block revealed the wolf's growl was achieved safely by the "give-and-go" method: first the leashed wolf gets a lick of a bolted-down meaty bone before it is covered, then the cameras are readied to catch the animal's reaction when it is revealed again as a trainer moves as if to take it. Staring down the lens at that sight, "the second unit cameraman said he'd never been more scared in his life," Sims recalled. As with all animal shots, an American Humane Association offical was on hand to help oversee the five pages and fifty-seven guidelines on animal handling in film work.

Without the wolf, Sirtis did complete her own stunt for the "jump into space": leaping off a huge blue-screened platform onto air mattresses. The shot was matted in with the starfield, corridor walls, and computer-enhanced shadows and interactive light for both on and off the ship—a four-hour compositing job involving seven elements.

On the trivial side, we see Deanna's office is on Deck 8 and hear again she's "good with languages" ("11001001"/116); the Federation Council is mentioned, as is Data's dream program ("Birthright, Part I"/242, "Phantasms"/258). For Troi fans, much backstory is finally revealed here: Though Lwaxana once said Deanna's accent reminded her of him ("Haven"/105) he doesn't show it here, where he's seen to be a lieutenant in the gold-color duty division of the time—either engineering, helm, or weaponry. Taylor's injection of "Down in the Valley" being Deanna's favorite at bedtime fits with past facts that her father read Westerns to her ("A Fistful of Datas"/234) and sang to her ("The Host"/197). While her "Mr. Woof" for Worf is obvious ("Half a Life"/196, "Cost of

Living"/220), Lwaxana's nickname of "little one" for Deanna ("Manhunt"/145, "Ménage à Troi"/172, et al.) takes on new meaning; Ian's name was revealed earlier via his namesake, Deanna's "son" ("The Child"/127). The Trois' marriage on SD 30620 is an odd stardate compared to other timeframes dated, but the event works out to about 2328 reckoned with the clues given here. Deanna's "genetic bonding" mating at Wyatt Miller ("Haven"/105) likely occurred before Ian's death, when she was seven, circa 2343—and perhaps was what pushed Lwaxana to delete her seven years of log entries. In lines cut from the last scene, Lwaxana says Kestra was never jealous of her sister and she swore Ian never to mention her, while Deanna reveals she'd just received the photo from Homn after an update on her mother's condition.

ATTACHED

> Production No.: 260 ■ Aired-Week of November 8, 1993
> Stardate 47304.2 ■ Code: at
>
> ---
>
> Directed by **Jonathan Frakes**
> Written by **Nicholas Sagan**
>
> ---
>
> **GUEST CAST**
> Ambassador Mauric: **Robin Gammell**
> Security Minister Lorin: **Lenore Kasdorf**
> Kes aide: **J. C. Stevens**

In beaming down to meet with the Kes, a society whose bid to join the Federation is the first by a nonunified world, Picard and Dr. Crusher are intercepted and taken hostage by the Prytt—the Kes's isolated and xenophobic neighbors on Kesprytt—to discourage their suspected Kes-UFP union against them.

As Riker and Worf discuss their options with Mauric, the Kes begin to show a few paranoid signs of their own. Picard and Crusher escape with the help of a Kes agent but find they have been rigged with devices that open up uncontrollable telepathy between the two.

During their escape and flight toward the Kes-Prytt border, Picard and Crusher discover they become sick if they try to separate and regain some privacy. That closeness leads them to find that not only are they strongly attracted to each other, but that Picard was once in love with her yet repressed it because of Jack and his death.

Prytt guards cause a detour that delays their beam-up, leading Mauric to turn the tables and accuse Riker of a UFP-Prytt conspiracy. Riker beams Loric up against her will for a face-off, but the unending roadblock leaves him telling the Kes that their membership bid will be denied and that Prytt will be invaded by Starfleet investigators unless the two are returned.

Back aboard finally, Picard asks Crusher about their newfound feelings but she prefers to just stay friends—at least for now.

The long-hinted-at spark between Picard and Dr. Crusher is finally explored in this story from twenty-three-year-old Nick Sagan, son of well-known physicist Carl Sagan and a summa cum laude graduate of UCLA's film school. He won Gates McFadden's praise for "turning her season around." After an uneventful session with DS9's staff, the newest of TNG's favored freelancers recalled that his idea of Picard and Crusher kidnapped by a cult group and physically shackled together as in *The 39 Steps* was the last premise of twelve he'd pitched a year earlier; the telepathic link was added from an uncredited writer's premise. "He was one of the most comfortable freelancers we've ever had," Taylor said of Sagan, whose optioned screenplay for Orson Scott Card's Hugo- and Nebula-winning *Ender's Game* novel first impressed her.

Sagan, a longtime fan inspired to writing by role-play games and Patrick McGoohan's visionary *The Prisoner* series, welcomed the chance to finish Crusher's oft-interrupted tease "Jean-Luc, there's something I've always wanted to tell you" in times of peril (see "Remember Me"/179) and other close calls ("The Naked Now"/103, "Allegiance"/166, "Qpid"/194). Mauric's B-story aboard

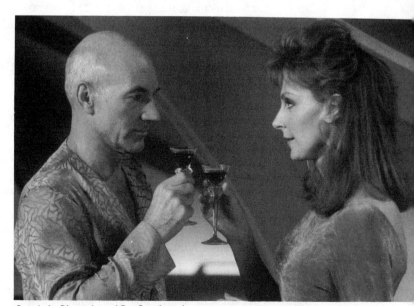
Captain Picard and Dr. Crusher share a romantic moment.

ship was originally more "an oblique cross between *Get Smart* and James Bond" in tone, Sagan recalled, but it was deemed too "over the top" and in Ron Moore's polish draft the gags were dropped—such as Riker being put on hold for twenty-fourth-century "elevator music" and an irritated Worf smashing a "sound-altering device" that makes such a racket that no one can hear himself think. Also cut was the fact that the link was drawing Jean-Luc and Beverly into an addiction to each other's brain waves and eventually a hive mind. Earlier, Sagan added, a shared kiss and a hint of possibly more by the duo around their campfire didn't survive the story break stage: Berman and Piller didn't want such a drastic change with the movies on the horizon.

Taylor recalled the fan buzz about the episode and spoke to the mail that poured in when the two leads didn't draw closer at the show's end. "Where do you go from there? It starts to become a soap opera, and Picard would be sealed off from other stories," she explained, praising the Stewart-McFadden chemistry. "Also it seems perfectly legitimate to me, emotionally, that two people who have gone that long without ever coming together—there must be a reason for that." Of course, fan demand for a Beverly/Jean-Luc tryst would soon get tweaked and then some in the show's final ("All Good Things . . ."/227–278).

Sagan's place names came from an original entry of a sign-board of more famous mythical places, such as Oz and Narnia, from his *Ender's Game* screenplay. A two-day return to the Bronson Caves area of Griffin Park near the Hollywood sign ("Darmok"/202, "Ensign Ro"/203, "Homeward"/265) provided the landscape; in fact, a gag photo was snapped with Stewart and McFadden in the foreground of the Tinseltown landmark. Science adviser Bormanis noted the Prytt mind-control devices should have been attached on the side of the head near the higher-reasoning center of the temporal lobe, but plot demanded that they be hidden on the back of the neck. We also learn that "associative membership" in the Federation is available, and that Ogawa had a late association with another crewman before being engaged to Andrew Powell ("Lower Decks"/267).

Trivially, Crusher's fear of heights was revealed once before ("Chain of Command, Part I"/236), as was her grandmother's story ("The Arsenal of Freedom"/121), with more to come ("Sub Rosa"/266); her pet phrase "Penny for your thoughts" is not new ("The Perfect Mate"/221). But this story raises a mystery: since Picard didn't know Beverly until after Walker Keel had introduced her ("Conspiracy"/125) to Jack, her remark that the trio spent more and more time together implies she was with Jack on the *Stargazer*, at least initially—unless it returned to base often, but that seems unlikely.

Though visual FX were not a big part of the story, they took a lot of time—including six hours of expensive blue-screen shooting for the fireball cave, which injected motion into the otherwise static lockdown of split-screen work with the "pan-and-scan" technique used when adapting a movie's anamorphic frame to the squarer television image. After director of photography Jonathan West was filmed walking through the cave with a bright photobulb for reference, the actors were shot running their action as live FX men Dick Brownfield and Will Thoms blew their hair with fans to match the fireball's close pass; the crew men were then erased from the shot. The fireball elements, rented from unused stock shot FX modeler Tony Doublin, were then composited with the live elements, with other details—shifting light intensity and the

images getting sharper when closer to camera—added digitally after that. Rare (for TNG) was the visible forcefield at the Kes border, complete with a costly and time-consuming nonstatic pan, after Stipes' coordinator Joe Bauer noted that the fugitives had no reason to recognize an unfamiliar planet's *invisible* forcefields. An unused DS9 element shot by Gary Hutzel provided the forcefield "hole."

FORCE OF NATURE

Production No.: 261 ■ Aired: Week of November 15, 1993
Stardate: 47310.2 ■ Code: fn

Directed by **Robert Lederman**
Written by **Naren Shankar**

GUEST CAST
Dr. Rabal: **Michael Corbett**
Dr. Serova: **Margaret Reed**
DaiMon Prak: **Lee Arenberg**
Computer Voice: **Majel Barrett**

While tracing the missing medical ship *Fleming* through the Hekaras Corridor—the only safe route through an area filled with tetryon particles, a hazard to warp-driven ships—the *Enterprise* is fired upon by a Ferengi ship that had seemed to be dead.

After DaiMon Prak asserts that an object presumed to be a Federation buoy emitted a disabling verteron pulse, the *Enterprise* helps the ship on its way—only to be attacked in the same way hours later.

A Hekaran brother and sister, Rabal and Serova, board the ship forcibly to explain their goal: to demand that the use of warp drive be halted before it destroys the fabric of space near their world—even if that means isolating it from the UFP.

An angry Picard softens after Data finds their theory merits study, but the impatient Serova sacrifices herself and her own ship to create a rift that sucks in the *Fleming* and threatens the *Enterprise*. A shaken La Forge, upset at the newfound dangers of warp drive, helps find a way to "coast" into the rift on a brief warp pulse and recovers enough to "ride" another wave out

DaiMon Prak (Lee Arenberg) refuses to help the *Enterprise* find a missing ship.

when the *Fleming* tries to restart its warp drive, damaging both ships.

With the UFP declaring a new warp five speed limit, La Forge consoles Rabal over his sister's sacrifice and joins Picard in mulling their careers' use of warp drive, resolving to put their new awareness to good use.

This disappointing though worthwhile "message" show finally beat the staff's so-called *Limits* Curse of Season 6, when Joe Menosky's environmental theme of warp-drive damage was tried but dropped from several stories ("Suspicions"/248). Or did it? Shankar, admitting "it wasn't one of my finer moments," was disappointed to lose his original version and its emotional underpinnings: a visit by Geordi's sister Ariana (only mentioned in "Interface"/255) to confront his emotional denial regarding their mother's death.

"I've been on enough series and tried to do environmental issues to realize that they are so hard to dramatize," Taylor said, "because you're talking about the 'ozone hole,' and . . . it's so, so hard to make it emotional and personal and give impact on that kind of level." Shankar agreed: "You oversimplify the issue, you oversimplify the solutions, and you end up with boilerplate and platitudes and nobody's happy."

Shankar, having championed the rebirth of the eco-premise

to Jeri Taylor after returning "galvanized" from an environmental film group breakfast, first wrote of Geordi as a "control freak" who was throwing himself into his work rather than mourn Silva's loss; the warp-drive revelations shook up the one thing he *had* been able to control—his engines—and led to much soul-searching. Taylor agreed with Piller that the Ariana plot was too forced and trite, though Shankar wished it had been worked out rather than dropped altogether; a conflict for Geordi with another crewmate didn't pan out, shooting deadlines approached, and the stripped-down script shows the padding of hastily written scenes concerning a rival engineer and Spot, of all things—in part thanks to the fast pace of editor-turned-director Lederman. "Somewhere about Act III the story finally starts, and by that time I don't think anybody even cared," added Taylor, who praised Shankar's attempts to deal in vain with a "doomed premise."

INHERITANCE

Production No.: 262 ■ Aired: Week of November 22, 1993
Stardate: 47410.2 ■ Code: ih

Directed by **Robert Scheerer**
Teleplay by **Dan Koepel and René Echévarria**
Story by **Dan Koeppel**

GUEST CAST
Dr. Juliana O'Donnell Soong Tainer: **Fionnula Flanagan**
Dr. Pran Tainer: **William Lithgow**

With the *Enterprise* on hand to help reheat the cooling core magma of Atrea IV, one of the married scientist team coordinating the project tells Data she was once married to Dr. Soong, his creator—and thinks of herself as his mother.

With no memory of her or a mention of her by Soong, Data takes a while to warm to Juliana Tainer, who had left the inventor after he became too immersed in his work. Data's memories of her and other early life events were erased when Soong and Tainer fled the Crystalline Entity on Omicron Theta, his creation place, and the colonists' logs were substituted. When pressed, she tearfully admits that she was against Data's creation and wanted him dismantled when they left, all because of fears he'd be like evil Lore.

Data finally accepts her as his mother but begins to sense other odd things about her. When her husband is injured in a plasma cave and

Juliana Tainer (Fionnula Flanagan)—Data's "mother."

Data joins her there, the instability forces them to jump from a cliff and her arm is severed, confirming his guess that she is an android.

Playing data from a chip found in her brain, Data sees Soong explain what happened: His wife really died after Omicron Theta, but he built his best-ever android to house her mind without her ever knowing the difference. Abiding by his wishes, Data opts to tell Juliana not of her true nature but of Soong's regrettedly unspoken love for her.

This simple yet beautifully mounted tale of yet another crewmember's "family" began as one more held-over pitch that got a second look during Season 7. As one of writer Echevarria's favorites, he acknowledged it was a real "insider's show" but was pleased with both its emotional tone and the chance to smooth out some rough spots from Data's backstory as it had evolved

("Datalore"/114, "Brothers"/177, "Silicon Avatar"/204, "Descent, Part II"/253). Also noteworthy is the much-praised performance by Flanagan, who'd already appeared on DS9's first-season "Dax."

Professional writer Dan Koepel's premise came in early enough that Echevarria was able to plan the idea of Soong's emotion chip having further memories—those wiped from his "childhood." The writer's first teleplay draft, differed in that Soong created the Juliana android so human-seeming merely out of his own drive, not due to his love for her, and it wasn't as clear on her "Sophie's Choice" guilt over dismantling Data rather than face another Lore.

Cut here was a scene in which Troi counseled Data to talk to his mother a reference to a hiccuping program that Soong could never make work. Only the bare-bones remains of another story line survived the cut too: Juliana's husband Pran is distrustful of androids like Data—a concept designed to raise the tension involved in his final decision. The cooling core "tech" was worked out by science adviser André Bormanis, who came up with the ship-based "chain reaction" method of reheating the plasma after the staff opted for the more visual symptom of earthquake shocks over rising radiation.

New background abounds here: Soong's jungle planet, unnamed in "Brothers," is here dubbed Terlina III; three failed androids preceded Lore; he apparently wore the same lab jacket all his adult life; Data had a childhood memory that was "wiped" and replaced with the colonists' logs, perhaps the reason for his "late" development; an isolinear chip can hold a smaller chip as an interface; and, in an Okudagram "Commercial Transport Database Achive" also filled with in-house joke entries, the Soongs stayed at Mavala IV four days when wed in 2328; one witness was a Corvallen (seen in "Face of the Enemy"/240). Other revisted references include the pattern enhancers ("Power Play"/215, "Time's Arrow"/226, "Ship in a Bottle"/238, "Frame of Mind"/247); magnesite ore (1967's "Friday's Child"); and phaser-bore drilling ("Pen Pals"/141, "A Matter of Time"/209).

Light on special visual FX, the show featured a Dan Curry matte painting for the phaser bore hole that Data looked up through. The pan-and-scan "cheat" was used again ("Attached"/260) to animate the split screen by following Brent Spiner as Soong back and forth around a stationary stand-in, with the crew directing the actor from a monitor, until Spiner/Data could be shot separately and matted in. As with the other violin scenes, the bowstrings are muted with wax so no sound covers the dialogue before music is looped later.

The hard luck extended to other areas as well, in small ways: "DaiMon" Prak has no Ferengi forehead military tattoo, while Mike Okuda said the Hekarras Corridor wall graphic title was misspelled and all but the last two incorrect letters were wiped out, leaving only "RS Corridor." Visually, though, the "space rift" was a success as FX supervisor Ron B. Moore augmented the standard liquid nitrogen/black velvet anomaly with added cans of dry ice dropped into boiling water. The distortion wave was the firestorm element again ("Lessons"/245), "stretched" and recolored.

The warp five cruising limit debuts here, designed with an "emergency clause" so it doesn't cramp future storytelling. The *Fleming* honors Alexander Fleming, discoverer of penicillin, while "biomimetic gel" (again in "Bloodlines"/274) was an item science adviser André Bormanis "created" from real news: a man-made material developed by scientists at Cambridge that creates small tubules than can mimic certain cellular-level biological activities and structures. We learn that warp drive is now three hundred years old, matching the dating of 1967's "Metamorphosis" despite the fact that the modern warp coil wasn't involved, since it wasn't developed until a century later ("A Matter of Time"/209). Also, the Ferengi Marauder, last seen in Season 2 ("Peak Performance"/147), is of the Dekora class with a crew of 450 and is seen to fire missiles from its rear arc but it is not clear how the Grand Nagus (DS9's "The Nagus" and "Rules of Aquisition") fits in with the "Ferengi Council." A cut line refers to Riker once surfing on Risa's Kattala Beach.

Other Trek bits return: verterons ("The Pegasus"/264); the ship's log recorder and delta rays, going back to original Trek's second pilot and "The Menagerie"; weather-modification systems ("True Q"/232, "Sub Rosa"/266, "Journey's End"/272); a glimpse of pinkish-white dilithium; the *Intrepid*, Sergey Rozhenko's ship ("Family"/178), which rescued Worf from Khitomer ("Sins of the Father"/165). Finally, though Spot's gender has changed ("Phantasms"/258), Geordi is the latest to discover that her disposition hasn't ("Timescape"/251, "Phantasms"/258, "Genesis"/258)—but her feline supplement (see "Phantasms"), now up to version 221, seems to have clicked.

PARALLELS

Production No. 263 ■ Aired: Week of November 29, 1993
Stardate: 47391.2 ■ Code: pa

Directed by **Robert Wiemer**
Written by **Brannon Braga**

GUEST CAST
"Lieutenant" Wesley R. Crusher: **Wil Wheaton**
"Dr." Alyssa Ogawa: **Patti Yasutake**
Gul Nador: **Mark Bramhall**
Computer Voice: **Majel Barrett**

Worf is nearly driven insane when, after returning victorious from a *bat'telh* competition, he realizes he is sliding from one alternate universe to another.

First the details of his unwanted surprise birthday party keep changing. Then the details of the sabotaged Argus Array—as well as his tactical console—are different too, resulting in La Forge's death during a Cardassian attack. At that point, Worf finds himself on an *Enterprise* where Ogawa is chief medical officer and he is married to Troi!

After Data points out that La Forge was nearby each time Worf sensed a change, his VISOR is activated and immediately makes the Klingon dizzy—and this time he wakes up on a Riker-led *Enterprise* as first officer, with Wes Crusher at tactical. Data has found that Worf's RNA shows quantum-level flux that is out of sync with the universe, and discovers with Wes a quantum fissure where many universes intersect—a fissure that trapped the original Worf and is aggravated by the VISOR's subspace pulse.

During the search for Worf's true universe, the warlike Bajorans of this one open fire, destabilizing the fissure so much that *Enterprise*s from the various universes begin popping in together—including a ragtag fugitive in a Borg-controlled galaxy that opens fire as Worf returns to his correct universe. That ship is neutralized, the quantum states are repaired, and once home Worf can't help but see his relationship with Troi differently.

From the briefest of premises, Braga developed the latest of his complex, high-concept stories that turned out to be one of Season 7's most popular—largely due to its unforgettable effects and the debut of what became known as the "Worf-Troi thing." "It's been kinda fun, but it infuriates some people," Taylor said of the dream-state romance. "Some people are so upset that we didn't put Riker and Troi together and just get it over with, and how *dare* we introduce this!"

Story needs and the nonpermanent formats of alternate universes were what tempted the staff to finally pursue the Worf-Troi romance they'd first toyed with in Season 5 ("Ethics"/216, et al.), after a plot based on Picard didn't pan out. "I think most people didn't pick up on the relationship we were trying to evolve, which was good—we wanted that surprise when we find out they're married," Braga said, noting its future incarnations ("Eye of the Beholder"/270, "Genesis"/271, "All Good Things..."/277-278). "This is a couple that only has relationships in alternate realities and timelines ... even as creatures. They make normal couples look boring by comparison!"

The story, which Taylor said "broke like butter" despite Piller's skepticism over its brief roots, is filled with other gems, as well: a Cardassian on the bridge in one universe, his people conquered by warlike Bajorans; another where Ogawa is a doctor and ship's medical officer; and still others where Picard is killed by the Borg and—most haunting—a fugitive *Enterprise* on the run from the all-victorious cyborgs. The last line "Champagne," originally unscripted, was written by Taylor at director Wiemer's request for a more definitive ending—after a huddle over just how direct Worf should be. Wiemer noted that even Worf's initial shuttle scene is not set in his "real" universe, but admitted the thought didn't occur

In an alternate universe, Worf meets Lieutenant Wesley Crusher.

to him until *after* he was done with the show! For the record, seven alternates are seen in all.

Braga also revealed that the throwaway Wes Crusher role was first written for Tasha but felt to be redundant ("Yesterday's *Enterprise*"/163); he would soon return in "reality" anyway ("Journey's End"/272). Worf's party song was to have been the traditional "Happy Birthday" in Klingonese—until producers learned the broadcast fee quoted by the copyrighted song's royalty holders. He made his nephew a namesake again ("Liaisons"/254, et al.) for Worf and Troi's "son," and he returned to the Argus Array ("Nth Degree"/193), a favorite design, just to have it break down again. The shuttle *Curie* was originally dubbed the *Borges*, after the one of Braga's favorite authors whose parallel-worlds story "The Garden of Forking Paths" greatly predated quantum mechanics as a science; the craft design is also finally given a name, Type 6. Bormanis said the "subspace pulse" of Geordi's VISOR is not a warp-like field but merely a computational speed accelerator, much like a transistor.

Also: Worf's birthday apparently fell on SD 47391.2, after a brief bio screen gave it as December 9 ("Conundrum"/214); his party featured a seventeen-candle cake, with twentieth-century balloons tied to chairs and poppers optically enhanced; Alexander is said to be visiting the Rozhenkos on Earth; the *Galor*-class Cardassian warship is mispronounced from its original "gay-ler" ("The Wounded"/186). Troi's chocolate fetish has a long history (see "The Game"/206, "Liaisons"/254) as does Worf's *bat'telh*, as well as a muddled spelling (back to "*bat'tehl*" of "Reunion"/181).

The alternate realities have a host of trivia, too: Troi's wardrobe

from the entire series (except for the buttoned-down Season 1, of course) is emptied here; set pieces from the alternate bridge would turn up in the finale ("All Good Things . . ."/277-278), while Barash's future comm badges with included rank bars ("Future Imperfect"/182) are worn here with pips. The fourth deep space station ever mentioned, DS5, is seen to be a Regula One design from the second *Trek* feature; the others besides DS9 are DS3 ("Inheritance"/262) and DS4 ("Suspicions"/248). "Starbase 47" is the redressed cryocapsule/relay station ("The Neutral Zone"/126, "Aquiel"/239), while we finally get a glimpse of Utopia Planetia's land-based facility, complete with surrounding red Martian terrain.

Recalling the earlier "cake crisis" ("Phantasms"/263), Braga early on contacted FX supervisor Ron B. Moore about a feasible way to create a "hundred *Enterprises*" to fill the screen after the fissure's collapse. Rather than using the "abomination" of stock shots with dozens of light-source angles, he and his coordinator Michael "B." Backauskas developed a motion control plan to film the model while rotating and lit in the same direction but from above and below and varying distances. The "multiple Worf" shuttle scene, conceived of as a clip sequence, was accomplished with split-screen shots, two with a stand-in in the back to allow more easy-to-matte crossing movement. Tossed in with a "less ominous" all-new anomaly and an old explosion effect ("Timescape"/251) for the Borg *Enterprise*, Moore was able to boast that his formidable segment's FX came out under budget and on time: "I don't know how many *Enterprises* are on the screen, but it's a good deal more than a hundred!"

THE PEGASUS

Production No.: 264 ▪ Aired: Week of January 10, 1994
Stardate: 47457.1 ▪ Code: pe

Directed by **LeVar Burton**
Written by **Ronald D. Moore**

GUEST CAST
Admiral Margaret Blackwell: **Nancy Vawter**
Admiral Erik Pressman: **Terry O'Quinn**
Commander Sirol: **Michael Mack**

Painful memories and choices are stirred up for Riker when his first captain, Erik Pressman, joins the *Enterprise* to lead a mission to retrieve their old ship, the *Pegasus*, before the Romulans can salvage the secrets it was testing.

Pressman, now an admiral, upsets Riker when he reveals his plan to salvage the ship and continue with the original test: a phased cloaking device that not only allows ships to pass through solid material but violates the original Treaty of Algeron with the Romulans.

Riker, ordered not to share the secret with Picard, is haunted when the frustrated former captain reveals that a cover-up muffled the news that Pressman's crew mutinied just before the ship was lost.

After a standoff with a Warbird looking for the Pegasus, Pressman orders Picard to take the *Enterprise* inside a fissure of the huge asteroid, where the Pegasus is eventually located. Aboard the ship, now phased partly into solid rock, Riker puts the loyalty he gave Pressman as an ensign behind him and defies the enraged admiral. But the two are suddenly beamed back with the salvaged phasing cloak as the Romulans seal the *Enterprise* inside the fissure. Riker reveals Pressman's secret as an escape option. Picard takes it—revealing the technology to the Romulans and arresting Pressman for the treaty violations, with the promise of an inquiry to expose his Starfleet allies.

Winning praise as LeVar Burton's second directorial stint and one of Ron Moore's finest efforts, the writer said this story began as a

bare-bones "Raise the *Titanic*" idea and struck paydirt when the conflict-torn Riker story was coined. Though it grew from the secret project, Riker's silence on the subject, and his "straight arrow" character as a young officer, Moore acknowledged a certain resemblance to the themes of honor and duty of his own "The First Duty" (219), where Wes Crusher didn't have the benefit of fifteen years' good record to minimize his early-career mistake. In contrast to Pressman, Picard is also portrayed as the type who'd pick his first officer sight unseen from resumes—a fact not explored since the pilot.

As a sidelight, Moore also jumped at the chance here to nail down the eternal question: Why not a Federation cloaking device? "I thought, let's sew this up," Moore explained, "not because it's the last season but because I'm sick of that question at the conventions! It's such a screamingly obvious thing to the fans, and I was just tired of it and wanted to put it to rest." After some thought, the treaty ban seemed to be the "cleanest" explanation, he added—and much better than the "bizarre theories" he'd heard in the past: " 'The cloaking device hurts humans but not Vulcans and Romulans,' or 'It wouldn't work on Federation starships because of their design' . . . or that the Federation wasn't smart enough to figure it out! Somebody also said, 'We don't sneak around'—and I thought that was kind of ridiculous too."

Ironically, the "phasing cloak" is the same concept that the "devious" Klingons and Romulans were known to be testing at one time or another ("The Next Phase"/224). Moore also wanted a lighthearted teaser to contrast with the coming heavy drama, but revealed that instead of "Captain Picard Day"—written to utilize Jonathan Frakes' never-aired Stewart impersonation—his first idea was a rehearsal of Shaw's "Pygmalion" performance shipboard directed by Crusher with Troi, Riker, and Data as Eliza, her father, and Professor Higgins. "After the [story] break, Michael kinda frowned and said, 'OK, give it a shot,' but it was just insane—it didn't fit at all," he said, hoping in vain that the scene could have been one of many saved and used later on.

The show debuts the first black Romulan, making it the latest Trek species to be depicted as multiracial, although not everyone got the message at first: actor Michael Mack—due back as the human Starfleet Ensign Hayes at tactical in the first feature—recalled that he was made up as a traditional Romulan with "lightened" skin for his first shooting! A second take with correct makeup had to be reshot a third time when the producers wanted his intensely menacing portrayal softened.

There's history of another kind in Act III, when longtime bridge extra Joyce Robinson—having finally gained a character name ("Phantasms"/258)—got to utter an uncredited reply to Picard. The line was written for Data but actor Brent Spiner—joined by the rest of the cast, when too late to change the setup—pointed out that the helm and not the ops officer should carry out the "course plotted" order.

Also for trivia hounds: Moore marks the difference here between Starfleet Security (internal) and Intelligence (external), noting that "There was a time when you couldn't even mention Starfleet Intelligence on the show—and I kept sneaking it into scripts—and finally people sort of stopped caring." His dating of the Treaty of Algeron puts in at the time of the never-detailed "Tomed Incident," the last Romulan-UFP encounter before TNG's first season ("The Neutral Zone"/125). Contest winner Paul Menengay was named for a friend of Brannon Braga's, although the

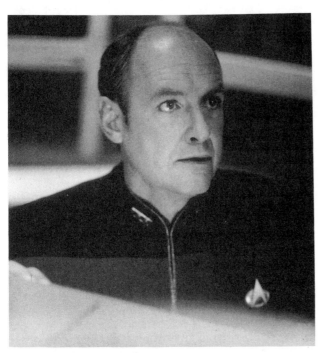

Admiral Pressman, former commander of the *Pegasus*.

Homeward

Production No.: 265 ■ Aired: Week of January 17, 1994
Stardate: 47423.9 ■ Code: hm

Directed by **Alexander Singer**
Teleplay by **Naren Shankar**
TV story: **Spike Steingasser**
Based upon material by: **William N. Stape**

GUEST CAST
Dobara: **Penny Johnson**
Vorin: **Brian Markinson**
Kateras: **Edward Penn**
Dr. Nikolai Rozhenko: **Paul Sorvino**
Tarrana: **Susan Christy**

entries actually came from two area elementary schools and prop man Alan Sims' own children. Science adviser André Bormanis was proud to contribute his first original "technobabble": a "duonetic field," coined from Daystrom's original duotronics ("The Ensigns of Command"/149) as the field equivalent of the fictitious verterons ("Force of Nature"/261 and DS9's "In the Hands of the Prophets," "Playing God," et al.) and tetryons, when factual forms became too awkward to say repeatedly.

Other past references include Admiral Shanti ("Redemption II"/201), the Excelsior-class *U.S.S. Crazy Horse* ("Descent"/252), the JAG office ("Gambit, Part II"/257), extending shields to protect another object ("The Next Phase"/224, "Final Mission"/183, "The Defector"/158, "Deja Q"/161), and the first emergency exception for exceeding warp five ("Force of Nature"/261). We learn that Riker trains for the *bat'tleh* with sticks and, curiously, says his beard is four years old; perhaps he shaved it after the second season!

Thanks to a convincing early test shot, the *Enterprise*-D for the first time was seen illuminated within the darkened asteroid with only its own sources and spotlights—actually, inexpensive focal spots attached to Image G's motion-control camera—to avoid what was facetiously dubbed "magic cave lighting." "To me, that's what really sold the show," FX supervisor David Stipes said. "I really wanted to get that creepy quality, dangerous and claustrophobic: Picard doesn't want to be there!" The five-foot carved-foam asteroid model and the many cave wall pieces were again Tony Doublin models, with the molten wall made of backlit paraffin and dissolvable styrene, plexiglass, and aluminum foil. Though Rick Sternbach readied sketches of a new ship based on *Enterprise*-"C"-era designs ("Yesterday's *Enterprise*"/163), budget forced the reuse of the Grissom model of *ST III* ("The Naked Now"/103, "The Drumhead"/195, "Realm of Fear"/228) in unaltered form with the "rock" simply pressed in around it; Richard James' interior set was tilted at a fifteen-degree angle.

Worf and his shipmates are disturbed to find that his foster brother Nikolai, a cultural observer on primitive Boraal II, has sheltered the natives in caves to protect them from the planet's suddenly dissipating atmosphere—an obvious Prime Directive violation.

Like Nikolai, Worf assumes Boraalan guise to blend in and assess the social damage. Picard insists on true noninterference under the Prime Directive, which would mean the Boraalans would perish along with their world.

But Nikolai won't back down, and he secretly creates a duplicate of the Boraalan caves in the holodeck. He transports them, planning to keep them safe until a new home planet can be found and the natives transported there, thinking only that the "storms" of their world have at last dissipated.

Picard and Worf are furious but feel forced to go along now, especially since Nikolai reveals he has fathered a Boraalan child and plans to stay with the people. In addition, one Boraalan, Vorin, is overwhelmed when he accidentally wanders out into the *Enterprise*; when he can't choose between staying or returning once he knows the truth, he kills himself.

Boraal's plasmonic storms harm the holodeck system so much it almost collapses, but before it does a new planet is chosen and reached, and the Boraalans transplanted. The brothers, despite their differences, finally come to value their cooperation and part on warmer terms. But for Picard and the others, the experience has left the pros and cons of the Prime Directive just as unresolved as ever.

———

Yet another celebrity fan, actor Paul Sorvino, appears in this story, which not only continued the season's "family" theme but re-aired the old Prime Directive debate ("Pen Pals"/141, "Who Watches the Watchers?"/152, et al.). Director Singer, working his sixth and last TNG outing, was concerned going in about working with well-known Sorvino and ensuring the Boraalan society was believable, but while those fears proved groundless he soon found his chief worry would be Mother Nature: surrounded by wildfires on location November 2 in the familiar Bronson Caves area of Griffith Park.

"We were simply told 'Finish, get out. No time to talk, get out'" he recalled. "The fire people said 'We can't protect you—there's only one way in and one way out and you're a sitting duck and the fires are out of control.'" He and line producer Merri D. Howard praised the crew for getting shut down and out in about forty minutes—and was thankful the area didn't burn after all, saving the extra expense of scouting a matching area. "It was exceptional—within two hours we were filming back here," Howard added. The schedule was reshuffled, only a half-day was lost, and the second time out proved more efficient with familiarity.

It was tough matching the outdoor camp on location, with the "fake" holodeck scene on stage, and then in the "real" nighttime scene shot onstage—a nightmare made even worse with the rescheduling due to the fire. "We had to go back in there, undress what we'd spent the whole day on before, put it up on the stage, and then undress it and bring it back to the park," set decorator Jim Mees recalled. "And it's a hundred degrees, and people are digging holes and building a stairway with seventy steps; my boys have not had a fun year!" Good thing the "village" included only fifteen actors and extras.

As for the story, Taylor had nixed as "strained credibility" Steingasser's premise about fooling primitives with a holodeck home mockup—until Echevarria had successfully married it to Stape's idea about finally seeing Worf's once-mentioned foster brother ("Heart of Glory"/120). "I do that with Michael," Taylor said of a writer's persistence. "He'll say no and I'll say, well, I'm gonna wait and maybe I can try this again—and I'm glad the boys do the same thing, because I am not the be-all and the end-all of knowing what will work." Still, the unanswered questions about the Prime Directive's application don't reflect well on the crew and Starfleet, Shankar noted; Echevarria wondered if the premise could even serve as a model for future such cases but recalled that Piller wanted to keep the status quo and the hard choices it forced: whether better to watch a planet die or incur the later suicide of those who could not handle the "change."

Though recalling that he was a bit more "temperamental" than TV actors, Taylor noted the nice serendipity of Sorvino asking to be on the series just as the teddy-bear-sized role of Nikolai came up—making him a believable echo of his "father," played by Theodore Bikel ("Family"/178). Nikolai's comment that Worf had "changed a lot in four years" implies they must have met at that time, possibly at Earth during the starship's post-Borg refit ("Fam-

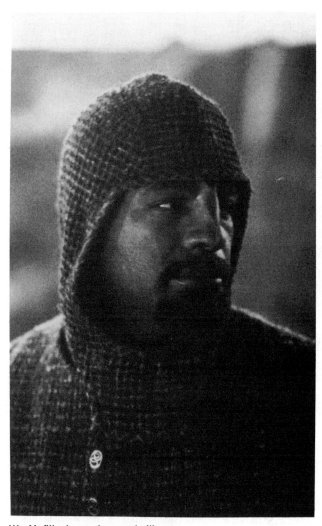

Worf infiltrates a doomed village.

ily"); in any case, actor Dorn got to go without his Klingon makeup for the first time, donning only a Boraalan nose.

On the trivia side, the *Enterprise* observes the warp five limit ("Force of Nature"/261); stellar cartography is seen again ("Lessons"/245, "Liaisons"/254, *Generations*); Dr. Crusher still hasn't got the hang of Pulaski's "memory wipe" ("Pen Pals"/141, "Who Watches the Watchers?"/152); and mention of "Holodeck 5" on Deck 10 implies that more than the first four on Deck 11 are now available, as with Holodeck 7 ("The Perfect Mate"/221). On location, a last-minute request for food on a spit for the Boraalans' camp was solved thanks to the day's catered set meal; prop man Alan Sims took the leftover chicken fillets, wrapped them on a stick, and charred the whole thing to look like rabbit!

Shankar was disappointed that budget limits prevented more FX shots from heightening the crisis of the failing holodeck, but FX supervisor Ron B. Moore did save time and money by using retouched old grid elements (shot at numerous angles for "Schisms"/231) for all the "signs of La Forge" save one—the grid in the water, which was done with a "live" grid under the small pond.

SUB ROSA

Production No.: 266 ■ Aired-Week of January 31, 1994
Stardate: c. 47500 ■ Code: sr

Directed by **Jonathan Frakes**
Teleplay by **Brannon Braga**
TV story: **Jeri Taylor**
Based upoin material by: **Jeanna F. Gallo**

GUEST CAST
Governor Maturin: **Michael Keenan**
Ned Quint: **Shay Duffin**
Ronin: **Duncan Regehr**
Felisa Howard: **Ellen Albertini Dow**

Following her grandmother Felisa Howard's funeral on Caldos IV, Dr. Crusher finds diaries revealing that the centenarian had a young lover named Ronin—and then fights off a friend, Ned Quint, who wants the doctor to throw away a candle he says has brought the Howard women bad luck for over eight hundred years.

Soon Ronin appears to her as an apparent "ghost" who has romanced her family's women for centuries. At the same time, malfunctions beset Caldos IV's weather-control net and it gets a power transfer from the *Enterprise*.

Ned warns Beverly about the candle and Ronin, but after some resistance—and odd nighttime sensations of pleasure—she is lulled by the loving "ghost" into resigning from Starfleet and taking Felisa's place there as a healer, joining him as his latest lover.

Ned, found trying to sabotage the weather net's power beam, shouts "He'll kill us all!" just before a green plasma bolt leaps out to kill him. The same kind of energy is traced to Felisa's grave, leading Picard to follow Beverly, confront Ronin about his mysterious origin, and order Felisa's body exhumed.

Ronin goes on a rampage, blasting Picard, Data, and Geordi in turn before reanimating Felisa's body and shocking Beverly with the truth: he is really an anaphasic plasma being who has used her family to stay alive and corporeal, via the candle and even the weather net.

She has no choice but to destroy the candle—and then his form as well.

As one of the most atypical TNG episodes ever, this lushly mounted "romance novel in space" was named the favorite of the year by the slightly biased story writer Jeri Taylor, a self-professed "addict of a number of trashy genres" such as gothic romances and historical novels. Actress McFadden, who called it a highlight of her own season, won kudos for her all-out performance: "The lovemaking without a partner—this is not easy stuff to do," Taylor said, "and she committed herself to it completely."

Still, Braga noted that the show was not a favorite of what he called "hard-core fans" but defended it as simply stretching the Trek envelope: "I've come to notice that whenever you infuse a show with sexual themes, some of these fans seem to short-circuit. I mean, the weather array malfunction causing thunderstorms—it was fun!" Countering some reports, though, Taylor said the story and its roots in fan Jeanna Gallo's year-old spec script was a nod to *The Innocents*, the film version of Henry James' *Turn of the Screw*—Braga's all-time favorite—and not the Scottish succubus Lasher of Ann Rice's *The Witching Hour*; the title is Latin for "under cover" or "not out in light." Gallo's Scot-based world focused on Beverly and her living grandmother, with aliens who had possessed humans for centuries as an explanation of paranormal activity. Attracted to and yet dissatisfied with the premise, Taylor recalled creating the unassigned story in a stream-of-consciousness session and then praised Berman and Piller for allowing the off-format show to go ahead.

The designers' showpiece featured a *Wuthering Heights*-like score by Jay Chattaway and an all-indoor set by Richard James, deceptively lit by director of photography Jonathan West and showcased by Frakes in his much-praised eighth turn as director. It came complete with a "raised" cemetery lawn to accommodate the buried casket and an organic tree assembled by greensmen working a solid weekend on Stage 16, using a real trunk anchored to the set and cutoff branches refastened and tied off from above; interiors were built within the cargo bay/shuttlebay set area. Look close and notice the art department's gag tombstones for the dead such as "Vader," "McFly," and others culled from the science fiction genre.

Set decorator Jim Mees recalled having to come up with a room full of camellias a month out of their season. The original order of three hundred silk camellias—clipped from their unconvincing wire stems and attached to real yet barren ones—was deemed not nearly enough on the Friday night before Monday's shooting, so the floral vaults of Paramount were opened up to fill the room with all manner of flowers, topped by the camellias for show. Propmaster Alan Sims had another surprise when "Felisa" turned out to be actress Dow, a college drama teacher he hadn't seen since 1972.

The Howard name, an homage to line producer Merri Howard, had actually first been glimpsed on Beverly's bio file ("Conundrum"/214); of course, given Terran paternal lineal naming, each "Howard woman" would have carried her husband's name unless Beverly was the first in a long line of feminists who chose not to! We've already learned back in Season 1 that she survived a disaster with her grandmother/healer ("The Arsenal of Freedom"/

Beverly is troubled by a ghostly presence.

contractors Joe Conti and Tim McHugh, was an effort to get more creative control in contrast to what visual FX supervisor David Stipes called the "act of God" luck of liquid nitrogen "smoke" filmed against black velvet. "The challenge really was to get the ghost," he said. "I thought everyone was really courageous in tackling this story. But if we didn't make that work, the whole story wouldn't sell: how to do purposeful, borderline-erotic ephemerals to look like it's caressing and hugging Beverly—without looking ridiculous or lewd?"

Lower Decks

Production No.: 267 ▪ Aired-Week of February 7, 1994
Stardate: 47566.7 ▪ Code: ld

Directed by **Gabrielle Beaumont**
Teleplay by **René Echevarria**
Story by **Ronald Wilkerson & Jean Louise Mattias**

GUEST CAST
Lieutenant (j.g.) Sam Lavelle: **Dan Gauthier**
Ensign Sito Jaxa: **Shannon Fill**
Lieutenant (j.g.) Taurik: **Alexander Enberg**
Ben: **Bruce Beatty**
Lieutenant [j.g.] Alyssa Ogawa: **Patti Yasutake**
Joret Dal: **Don Reilly**

121), while Braga revealed that he'd named Felisa after his own grandmother who'd died shortly before the story was written. In a scene cut for time, Beverly opens the show with the same eulogy Braga's own mother used for his grandmother: a recipe, recalling her love of cooking, for gingerbread baked in the "arms of a welcoming pan" in a "happily" heated oven. Another cut line tells us Beverly did not leave Caldos II for good until she wed Jack. Also, Braga took "Jessel" and "Ned Quint" from *Turn of the Screw* and was surprised to learn later that his made-up name "Ronin" was actually Japanese in origin.

The guest cast includes Regehr, a soap opera staple, and Keenan, best known as *Picket Fences'* first-season mayor who spontaneously combusted. We learn here that terraforming was new a century earlier when Caldos Colony was built, while weather control ("True Q"/232, "Force of Nature"/261, "Journey's End"/272) was at least that old. Also recalled here are the still-unseen Dr. Selar ("The Schizoid Man"/131, "Remember Me"/179, "Tapestry"/241, "Genesis/271, "All Good Things..."/277-78), Worf's *mok-bara* class ("Clues"/188, "Man of the People"/229, "Birthright, Part II"/243, "Second Chances"/250, "Lower Decks"/267, "Genesis"/271), and the drama masks in Beverly's room ("Suspicions"/248).

TNG's first use of the Amiga-based Video Toaster, provided by

Four young *Enterprise* ensigns find their friendship strained during personnel evaluations, as Sam Lavelle and Sito Jaxa learn they are both up for the same job as ops relief. Joined by their civilian waiter pal Ben, they learn that promotions seem assured for Nurse Ogawa and engineer Taurik—though the young Vulcan has his people's historic problem in reading his human friends and superiors.

Riker, blind to how similar he and Lavelle are, is not high on the young officer, while Worf has much faith in Sito—even though she receives a surprise tongue-lashing from Picard, who recalls her role in the cover-up by Wesley Crusher's Academy flight team.

The tension of promotions is abruptly broken by a baffling secret mission that all but Lavelle have a hand in: Ogawa must keep mum about a recovered Cardassian, and Taurik intentionally distresses a shuttle with phaser fire. Then Sito, after a lesson from Worf, stands up to Picard, giving him what he needed to see: the guts to volunteer to pose as a Bajoran captive taken by the Cardassians.

Sadly, Sito is lost on the mission, leaving behind only scattered escape-pod debris. Lavelle's promotion and new job leave him empty after her presumed death, but his spirits—and those of her mentor Worf—are bolstered by their friends' support.

Once again, Jeri Taylor regretted not being able to give veteran TNG freelancers Wilkerson and Matthias a shot at the teleplay of their "great, great concept" of the self-styled "little people"—which was so popular it fueled erroneous rumors that the junior officers were being primed for *Voyager*. The writing team presented this pitch—partly inspired by Wilkerson's love of the BBC classic *Upstairs, Downstairs*—in the unorthodox manner of fleshed-out character notes.

"Again, like our 'Lessons' [245], what was important was not the mission but the relationships of the people," Wilkerson said: "What it is like to work for Riker, to work for Worf, to wonder what goes on in secret briefings in the observation lounge"—and to put faces to the always-nameless crew. The lineup saw the writers return to the known character of Sito ("The First Duty"/219), develop TNG's first fully realized Vulcan (Matthias's favorite Star Trek race), create a "young Riker," and lean on an already established regular like Ogawa—Barclay having been considered but dropped as too well-known; a fifth, "nerdy" character was

scrapped. Echevarria added the civilian waiter Ben, perhaps the first ever in Ten-Forward besides Guinan allowed to speak, just to have a character "who hitched aboard the ship for fun, who's unconcerned about rank, and who passes along stupid rumors!"

For his part, Echevarria enjoyed getting more humor into less "buttoned-down" Starfleet characters with this story, which like his "Second Chances" (250) went practically unchanged from first to final draft. All the cast won praise, with Enberg's Taurik mentioned as a recurring guest had the series gone on; he had already played the reporter dogging Mark Twain ("Times Arrow, Part II"/227). Though the original name Sorik was changed to echo the new "T" Vulcan male name, as with Tuvok of the uncoming spinoff *Voyager*, all three writers' concept for Taurik matched: an odds-figuring "young Spock" barely concealing his pithy sarcasm as a junior officer.

Sito gained a first name unheard in her first appearance ("The First Duty"), while visual FX producer and martial-arts adviser Dan Curry marveled at actress Shannon Fill, a trainied dancer and acrobat but new to martial arts: "I've never seen anybody learn it that quickly and so convincing." After seeing the idea first nixed and then approved for development by Michael Piller based on Fill's performance, Taylor hinted that Sito may yet turn up on *Deep Space Nine* as a former Cardassian hostage. "I've gotten more mail on that—how could Picard send Sito to her death?" she said. "A lot of people were very upset by that and felt that was very inappropriate for him, and didn't behave as even the military now would behave."

Ogawa, who was almost cut from the story to make more room for the other characters, gets her personal life in order in a hurry: a new fiancé, only seven episodes after her last boyfriend ("Attached"/260), who conceives a baby only four episodes later ("Genesis"/271). Taurik's research guru was named for Cuban nuclear engineer Nils Diaz, Echevarria's true-life godfather and a

Worf trains Ensign Sito (Shannon Fill) to trust her instincts.

propulsion-system researcher. And for true trivia fans, Sam Lavelle's name can claim two sources: a close friend of Echevarria's and, initially, Wilkerson's Canadian labrador Samwell.

Though the segment is light on visual effects, supervisor Ron B. Moore singled out computer "Harry" artist Adam Howard's nice touch of dimming Taurik's phaser-rifle beam behind the smoked glass of the shuttle window in only the weapon's third appearance ("The Mind's Eye"/198, "Descent"/252). The tough *Curie* was Worf's quantum-crashing craft ("Parallels"/263), where it was seen to be Shuttlecraft 3—the same as the onetime *Justman* ("Suspicions"/248). Other notes: Echevarria originally had Sito not only track a lost puppy at ops but deal with a "turbolift traffic jam;" Worf adds a red lapel to his *mok'bara* gi here ("Clues"/188, "Man of the People"/229); Riker learned poker on the *Potemkin,* a stay of only six weeks ("Second Chances"); Cardassian dissidents would next be seen on DS9's "Second Skin"; and though the Klingonese *gik'tal* is not a *mok'bara* manuever, it does relate to death ("Firstborn"/273). This outing provides the first TNG mention of DS9's Bajoran religious vedeks, implies that Canada was still a Terran entity two generations earlier, recalls Riker's Alaska roots ("The Icarus Factor"/140), and reveals that a probe sent into Cardassian space is a treaty violation. Bridge duty shifts are apparently not long-lived: we see "alpha shift" with Worf and Data, while "beta shift" has Ensign Gates ("Phantasms"/258, "The Pegasus"/264) and extra Tracee Cocco's character—usually all seen working together. Also on ship, we learn that ensigns must share a cabin while junior lieutenants do not.

THINE OWN SELF

Production No.: 268 ■ Aired: Week of February 14, 1994
Stardate: 47611.2 ■ Code: th

Directed by **Winrich Kolbe**
Teleplay by **Ronald D. Moore**
Story by **Christopher Hutton**

GUEST CAST
Talur: **Ronnie Claire Edwards**
Garvin: **Michael Rothhaar**
Gia: **Kimberly Cullum**
Skoran: **Michael G. Hagerty**
Apprentice: **Andy Kossin**
Ensign Rainer: **Richard Ortega-Miro**
Computer Voice: **Majel Barrett**

Sent to retrieve radioactive debris from a downed probe on preindustrial Barkon IV, Data loses his memory and unwittingly spreads the fragments throughout a village, where radiation sickness begins to sicken the inhabitants.

Limited by the culture's unenlightened primitive science, the town's healer has no clue to the sickness, but all signs point to the odd-skinned man as the reason behind the outbreak. As it soon engulfs his befriended "family," a man named Garvin and his young daughter Gia, an angry mob confronts Data and reveals his inner circuitry, scaring them but intriguing the android, who was already far along in discovering a cause and cure.

The mob finally "kills" the "monster" and buries him, but with the starship's return Riker and Crusher arrive to locate and beam up the overdue android. Upon reactivation Data cures the villagers and finds he is now outranked by Commander Troi after she opted to take the bridge officer's test.

If moments of this story feel like an old Universal movie, it's no accident: Chris Hatton's "Data as Frankenstein" pitch, his second sell of the season ("Gambit"/256–257), quickly caught the staff's attention. "He wanders into the medieval village, is befriended by the little girl, and villagers come out and chase him with torches!" joked writer Ron Moore, who liked the show even though he never had a "close feeling" about it. Ironically, director Rick Kolbe felt it provided him a personal chance to improve on TNG's other "little girl" show, which he'd also helmed, "Pen Pals" (141): "I felt we had more character in there and didn't veer off into 'tech talk.'"

That welcome step was mostly due to Moore's avoiding a predictable "We've lost Data and we got to find him!" plot back on ship by reviving the B-story of Troi's test and promotion shelved earlier in the season ("Liaisons"/254). But Moore, who traced the idea of Troi's need for a stretch back to not only the mentioned roots ("Disaster"/205) but also Jeri Taylor's Pocket Books novelization of "Unification," wanted to correct the vague impression that in Starfleet one need only pass a test to get a commander's rank. "The action was an amalgam of both: if she became a bridge officer after the test, they'd also give her the promotion," he explained. Likening Crusher and Troi to today's naval medical officers of restricted line rank, he and the other writers posited that neither one initially attended Starfleet Academy despite Academy dates on their bio files ("Conundrum"/214)—a fact never addressed onscreen, aside from Troi attending "university on Betazed" ("Ménage à Troi"/172); a cut opening line had her returning from a class reunion of the unsited Carvin Institute for Psychological Studies. The backstory here explains Troi's standing watch later ("Genesis"/271) as well as Beverly's skills in "Descent" (252–53) and her future captaincy ("All Good Things . . ."/277–78)—and in hindsight backs Pulaski's comment that she was not a bridge officer despite her commander's rank ("Where Silence Has Lease"/128).

For what construction coordinator Al Smutko called a $104,000

Worf and Troi are stunned by the *Enterprise*'s strange transformations.

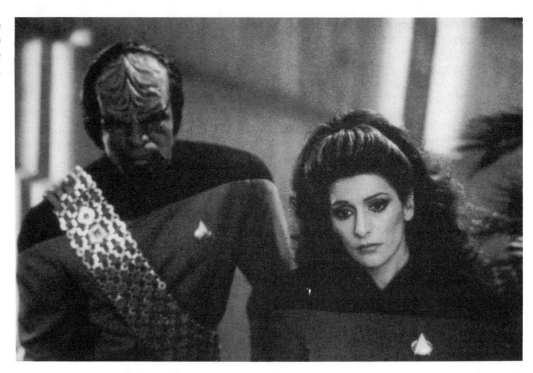

investment, production designer Richard James' Barkon IV village saw action many times throughout the spring, lasting through three major revampings for TNG ("Journey's End"/272, "Firstborn"/273, "Preemptive Strike"/276) as well as a shot on DS9's "Shadowplay." Among the segment's few visual effects, producer Dan Curry noted that computer "Harry" animator Adam Howard at Digital Magic designed the arcing around the pole spearing Data, while Harry animation and dry-ice elements provide the luminous cloth shimmers. Visual FX supervisor David Stipes joined Kolbe in seeking, for once, an *instantaneous* warp-core breach during Troi's crisis simulation—done inexpensively with a white-out wipe begun with blinding flash bulbs from onstage FX man Dick Brownfield.

For trivia hounds: "imzadi" is used—for the first time in a year ("Second Chances"/250) and the last time on the series—at Frakes' request, rewritten by permission from the original Act II line written as simply "ship's counselor"; his trombone playing is nothing new ("11001001"/116, "Future Imperfect"/182, "The Next Phase"/224, "Second Chances"/250).

Cut speeches specified that Troi passed the bridge test on her fourth try and, in the village, explained the roots of the name "Jayden"—Hatton's original premise title—as a handsome nobleman in a Barkon folktale, transformed to an ugly frog by a demon's spell. Also, the *U.S.S. Lexington* harks back to a Kirk-era starship in 1968's "The Ultimate Computer," while Data's once-secret on-off switch ("The Measure of a Man"/135, et al.) was already known to all those present in the last scene ("Datalore"/114, "Brothers"/177, "The Game"/206). That moment in sickbay features Patrick Stewart's only line of the whole show, a briefest-ever appearance arranged so he could perform his Olivier-winning *A Christmas Carol* in London during the segment's early December filming. Michael G. Hagerty earlier played a Klingon ("Redemption II"/201).

MASKS

Production No.: 269 ■ Aired: Week of February 21, 1994
Stardate: 47615.2 ■ Code: mk

Directed by **Robert Wiemer**
Written by **Joe Menosky**

GUEST CAST
Eric Burton: **Rickey D'Shon Collins**

A comet discovered by the *Enterprise* is found to be the "archive" of an ancient society. Unexpectedly, a sensor scan activates an odd replication program that begins converting areas of the starship to the Mayan-like culture of the archive's makers.

The program targets Data and deposits various iconic characters from the culture into him: baffling voices speaking of pain, death, and sacrifice. When areas of the ship actually begin to be transformed into foliage and jungles and Picard regretfully orders the archive's destruction, his command is cut short by the transformation of Main Engineering.

Eventually, Picard and the others deduce that Masaka, the most feared character, and "her" pursuer, Korgano, share a nip-and-tuck chase dynamic not unlike that of the Terran sun and moon. With time running out and direct override impossible, La Forge finally locates the archive's transformational program just in time for Picard to assume the "mask" of Korgano and "chase" Masaka off her temple throne.

Once Masaka is subdued, both the ship and Data return to normal—without the whole society of characters that were once within him.

Former staff writer Joe Menosky's second offbeat and long-distance script of the year, from an old premise off Michael Piller's suggested take on the "Lost Library at Alexandria," featured a large amount of well-done opticals but proved confusing to

Data is possessed by members of an alien civilization.

many—including several who worked on it! "I think a lot of people have been utterly mystified by it," admitted Jeri Taylor. "I loved the mythic aspect . . . how important that has been to so many cultures, and how we in contemporary days have strayed away from that."

"Joe has a magnificent imagination, he thinks in a deep way," agreed Naren Shankar, charged with clarifying some of the vagaries in his uncredited polish. "But in this case it was too much. . . . We had to make it more understandable, make the clues clearer. And the end result is . . . it's still kinda confusing!" Director Bob Wiemer, heading up his eighth TNG effort, was more to the point: "I didn't get it," he said, noting the extensive rewrite. "I always look and find a meaningful subtext of some kind in most every show I've done; more often than not they're little morality plays, and I was unable to find that in 'Masks' . . . it ended up kind of an exotic adventure story, but it didn't have any heart." Recalling a core element of the second Star Trek movie, science adviser André Bormanis said the script's original explanation of the archive was an "advanced Genesis device" that was to scout out a planet to re-create members of an old society kept "on file" and but mistook the *Enterprise* for such a world by a triggering malfunction.

Menosky's original use of purely archetypal forms were hard to conceptualize, Shankar recalled, and so they were changed to actual characters suggested by the archive's image files. That didn't help actor Brent Spiner, who made no bones about his concern in bringing off the various character extremes. "He said 'Dustin Hoffman took a year to figure out how to play a woman in *Tootsie*—how am I supposed to do it in two days?'" recalled Taylor. "But I thought he did an extraordinary job. . . . He's a fine actor and he needn't be so worried." Even so, Wiemer backed up Spiner's request for revoicing and, when refused, to have subtle effects done in post-production with Wendy Neuss's crews: raising the pitch of the child voice, lowering the man's, and adding reverb to the Ihat voice. The youngster Eric ("Liaisons"/254, "Firstborn"/273) returned as the lone guest actor.

Visually, the show was a clear triumph, with the props themselves featuring a hand-silversmithed mask for Picard and a sandstone-finished styrene version for Data. With Stage 16 taken up with the previous show's village, "Masks" saw Richard James' elaborate temple set built on DS9's Stage 18. Drawing from many ancients' design influences, it was later revamped on the sister show for the Albino's fortress interior on *Blood Oath*. We learn that Crusher took her test "eight years ago," before the *Enterprise* launched, and that perhaps antimatter pods can be ejected separately.

The visual effects crews had a field day, with supervisor Ron B. Moore praising the melting comet effect performed by Santa Barbara Studios, creators of the comet in DS9's main title sequence. This opening shot was such a hit that he won a costlier longer slot for the effect in the show's tightly budgeted running time—from six to nine seconds. The foot-high, primer red library model itself had been cobbled together from wood pieces by visual FX producer Dan Curry in the shop at Image G, where miniatures are filmed, and then digitized by Santa Barbara before the decision makers picked a texture to be applied.

Less splashy but more intricate were the onboard set transformations needed, a blue-screen dissolve overlaid with a visual ripple stemming from a water element much revamped from its initial use, the de-aging anomaly in "Rascals" (233). Both Curry and Stipes were amazed at another one of Patrick Stewart's feats: complete body control that allowed a blue-screen shot of his mask's final disappearance to be shot without a hokey "jump cut" when footage of it actually being removed is trimmed out. "You say 'stand still' and that guy's a statue!" recalled Moore, who tugged loose the mask's slip knot and let it fall while Stewart never budged nor blinked.

EYE OF THE BEHOLDER

Production No.: 270 ■ Aired: Week of February 28, 1994
Stardate: 47622.1 ■ Code: eb

Directed by **Cliff Bole**
Teleplay by **René Echevarria**
Story by **Brannon Braga**

GUEST CAST
Lieutenant (j.g.) Walter Pierce: **Mark Rolston**
Lieutenant (j.g.) Nara: **Nancy Harewood**
Lieutenant Daniel "Dan" Kwan: **Tim Lounibos**
Ensign Mattie Calloway: **Johanna McCloy**
Woman (Ensign Marla E. Finn): **Nora Leonhardt**
Man (Lieutenant William Hodges): **Dugan Savoye**

A suicide by promising young Lt. Kwan in the plasma stream of the isolated nacelle's warp coils is baffling to all those who knew him, but the first clue comes when Troi gets an overwhelming sense of panic and fear while visiting the site.

Guessing somehow she's detected an empathic echo, the counselor checks again with Worf as an escort. This time she suddenly sees the room in its unfinished state as it was back at Utopia Planetia eight years earlier, along with images of a terrified woman, her lover and a mysteriously menacing man—and Worf mysteriously disappeared.

Suspecting the empathic echo dates back to the *Enterprise*'s construction phase, a records check finds that Kwan and the mystery man, Walter Pierce, both were still aboard after having worked at the shipyard. Meanwhile, Troi and Worf find themselves drawing closer and actually consumate their newfound love, but she just

as suddenly succumbs to pangs of jealousy at the sight of Worf working with Kwan's girlfriend, Lt. Calloway.

Pierce proves evasive but fans Troi's jealously, tipping her off to catch Worf with Calloway in her cabin. Enraged, Troi shoots Worf and rushes to kill herself in the plasma stream—only to realize Worf, alive, is trying to stop her. The entire episode has been played out in her mind, a reaction to the echo left behind by the partly-empathic Pierce in his fatal love triangle at Utopia Planetia. But unlike Kwan, a partial empath, Troi had help in averting disaster.

Jeri Taylor recalled that this latest unreal chapter of the ongoing Worf-Troi "romance" was a brief year-old Brannon Braga "haunted room" idea, rushed directly from a memo to the story break as the late-season panic of dwindling premises set in again. Before he handed it off to Echevarria for the teleplay, Braga had already pegged the story to feature a rare suicide—albeit externally motivated—and a dramatic look inside the oft-discussed but never-seen nacelle tube, complete with warp coils and plasma stream.

Though happy with the mystery, the writers all worried the hallucination's beginning point might be a bit vague—including the fact that Worf's bumbling request to Riker for Deanna's hand came in *reality*. "That was confusing, even for the actors," Echevarria recalled. "They thought that was part of the hallucination; that's why Jonathan played it so broadly. . . . They thought they would have to reshoot it." The highbay door is already up for her second visit to the nacelle room; another clue, he said, is knowing that an external space shot such as the one following her first visit would be a Trek point-of-view violation never used during a dream or hallucination. Even so, he noted, a POV flaw occurs later when the camera cuts down to caller Beverly during Worf and Troi's "morning after."

The centerpiece is the nacelle set—a previously unconceived shipboard area that continuity tenders Rick Sternbach and Mike Okuda had to locate on their plans before consulting with Richard James for his designs; for the record, the room is at the nacelles' rear (in this case, the starboard) on Deck 25, accessible only via Jefferies Tube. Braga initially visualized a catwalk with plasma access the length of the nacelle, but Sternbach felt it took away from the "hot" feel of the engine and pushed instead for the isolation door approach—though he noted the flaw in not only a "one-way" forcefield but one more powerful by definition than the plasma itself!

Designed to give the leapers somewhere to fall from, James' cramped, two-level set created tension in more ways than one: director Bole, now on his 24th TNG outing, recalled the "endless" shooting day in the tiny room as the longest of his television career: The room cried out for a vista of the nacelle interior beyond, so with both time and budget in mind James huddled with the visual FX team to consider the varying angles of the view beyond. The two-step result: a distant Dan Curry background matte painting

Dr. Crusher examines Deanna, who is having strange visions.

representing the inside rear of the forward Bussard ramscoop ("Samaritan Snare"/143, "Night Terrors"/191, "Cost of Living"/220, "Liaisons"/254), and a 30-inch-long model of seven warp coils optically doubled to 14, built by Anthony Frederickson of the DS9 art staff. With no money to spare, his "quick and dirty" model was built around vacuum-formed styrene coils from a wooden proto-type and included foam coffee cups for dividers, blue-gelled plastic with black tape to set off the glowing nacelle "grills," and optical touch-ups of added "runway lights" lengthwise and a ceiling piece.

The plasma stream itself was more Video Toaster animation ("Sub Rosa"/266) with some elements taken from a WaterPik stream, noted visual FX supervisor David Stipes. Stunt coordinator Dennis "Danger" Madalone himself provided Kwan's suicide leap, but the shallow arc from his standing start was digitally stretched in post-production farther over into the bottom injector, which was reinserted after taking out the floor landing pads. The skeleton glimpsed behind the wall panel was none other than a "Visible Man" model FX coordinator Joe Bauer glued to a piece of glass, while the skeletal fragments in Sickbay are human remains obtained from India, complete with a hard skull that prop master Alan Sims had to bash when Bole wanted smaller pieces.

For true trivia buffs, a flurry of faces and names on briefly glimpsed bio file Okudagrams includes that of longtime Marina Sirtis stand-in Nora Leonhardt, who got a speaking credit as Ensign Marla Finn, the murdered woman; her lover, unidentified in the script, was labeled "Man" for the on-screen credits, dubbed "Indie" on production call sheets—for "N.D." or non-descript, the term used for unnamed extras—and given the name "Lt. William Hodges" on his file. Guy Vardaman, whose longtime extra finally gained the name "Wallace" last season ("Descent"/252), is an-other, here with the first name "Darien". Dan Kwan was an old family friend of Braga's, while the mentioned "Lt. Amanda" Ziff

and "Ens. Bruno" Salvatore, with surnames given only via bio screens, were named for Echevarria's friends Bitsy Ziff, a member of the all-girl band "Betty," and a bandmate's boyfriend Tony Salvatore.

Elsewhere, the story has the first permission granted to break the Warp 5 speed limit ("Force of Nature"/261) and recalls Worf's fire vision ("Birthright, Part I"/242, "Rightful Heir"/249), psilosynine ("Dark Page"/259), tea from the Yridians ("Birthright, Part I", "Sus-picions"/248, "Gambit, Part I"/256, "Preemptive Strike"/276), and the Utopia Planitia yards ("Booby Trap"/154, "Parallels"/263, et. al.). We also learn that Data's post-activation months were tough, Napeans are another partially empathic race, Lwaxana Troi's father looked down upon verbal communication, and Troi's secu-rity override at the time is "Troi delta 2-9."

Finally, although Kwan's suicide was not self-motivated, one wonders whether the late "Great Bird" Roddenberry would have sanctioned outright murder among his "flawless" Starfleet person-nel, such as Pierce. Ironically, that old GR dictum—usually ap-plied to only humans, amounting to a backlash Echevarria la-beled as a form of meta-racism—did survive in the guise of the alien junior lieutenant Nara, Kwan's superior. A human until she was described as perhaps jealous of Kwan's ambition, Echevarria noted, the character species was changed after Michael Piller memoed: "Make her an alien—that's not a Roddenberry thing to do." But humanity was uppermost when cast and crew took one morning to film a two-scene sketch written by Merri Howard assistant Dave Rossi for Comic Relief, the annual HBO benefit for the homeless co-hosted by recurring castmate Whoopi "Guinan" Goldberg—an irony that formed just one of the scene's many subtle funnies.

ENESIS

Production No.: 271   ▪   Aired: Week of March 21, 1994
Stardate: 47653.2   ▪   Code: ge

Directed by **Gates McFadden**
Written by **Brannon Braga**

GUEST CAST
Lieutenant (j.g.) Reginald "Reg" Barclay III: **Dwight Schultz**
Lieutenant (j.g.) Alyssa Ogawa: **Patti Yasutake**
Ensign Dern: **Carlo Ferro**
Computer Voice: **Majel Barrett**

During a shipboard lull, Picard takes Data along to retrieve a wayward demonstration tor-pedo. In their absence, with Data's cat Spot and newlywed Nurse Ogawa both recently found to

Lieutenant Barclay, part man, part spider.

be pregnant, Dr. Crusher routinely prepares a synthetic T-cell to help Barclay fight a flu bug he has no immunity for.

Soon the crew begin to exhibit odd symptoms: Barclay gets hyper, Troi becomes cold, Riker can't concentrate, and Worf becomes animalistic and withdrawn. Eventually he attacks Dr. Crusher with an odd venom sac, a new neck appendage, but by now Riker and the others are too far gone to send for help.

Upon their return, Picard and Data are shocked to find the ship slowly looping unpowered through space. Taking stock, Data soon discovers that a synthetic cell—which turns out to be Barclay's—has activated crewmates' dormant introns and changed them to various lower life-forms.

Oddly, though, the kittens of Spot are born normal, though their mother is now an iguana. That clue puts Data on the research trail for a cure as Picard—nervously feeling chills himself

now—takes on the chore of distracting the "de-evolved" and rutting Worf. Picard uses a power cable to stun the Worf-beast when he's cornered inside a Jefferies tube, but Data's cure allows a rapid return to normal for all—with Barclay as the disease's proud namesake.

This story, another creepy Brannon Braga reality-bender, will always be remembered as not only Gates McFadden's long-sought turn as director and Michael Westmore's most ambitious makeup show ever but also—by the crew, at least—the show that was struck by the Quake of '94. The Trek series and Paramount itself were very lucky, noted line producer Merri Howard, with only two days lost on TNG and minimal structural damage: just a sprinkler system wetting down a Jefferies tube set and a little broken shelf decor in the officers' quarters.

Braga had the idea of de-evolving the crew as far back as Season 4, but Rick Berman had objected to it until a plausible scientific explanation could be devised. Science adviser André Bormanis noted the reality of introns among many other types of dormant genetic material but said the non-fatal shock of the rapid body changes might be chalked up to it being an "alien" virus; even so, makeup designer Michael Westmore said a "reversal" sequence was readied for Ogawa's simian but never applied or shot.

Working closely with Westmore for the first time, Braga finished his teleplay two weeks early to give the makeup team more lead time for the enormous amount of research and design needed; the holiday break also came in handy. "Makeup was going to make or break this show," noted Braga, who forwarded examples of physiological details from his "Incredibly Weird" nature photo books as reference for Westmore. "Fortunately, [director] Gates has worked with Jim Henson and the Muppets, so that was good—she did some interesting things." The writer was also proud to use Spot—by now a confirmed female ("Phantasms"/258, "Force of Nature"/261)—as a plot point rather than a joke, although a scene with Data giving away the kittens was dropped in the final draft.

Westmore noted that all the actors wore their own makeup except for Worf stunt double Rusty McLennon; sculptors Michael Key, John Blake, and Michael Smithson handled the extra load, with the latter working over the holiday on Worf's creature and Barclay's "spider"—a fascinating partial design not seen as much as planned. His initial appearance that shocks Picard was to have been a drop downward but was cut for time; McFadden had wanted it and Schultz, appearing here for the first time this season, had agreed to do the stunt himself. Also cut was Troi's long and hard-to-film scene with waterproofed makeup in Trek's first-ever bathtub, showing her impatiently climbing in fully clothed. "I wondered about that bathtub; we've always seen a shower, but the writers wanted it," noted production designer Richard James.

Makeup was not the only department who had fun here, though. Along with Monster and Brandy again playing Spot the cat ("Descent, Part II"/253, et al.), Baja the iguana is voiced with the "reptilian purr" of a monitor lizard. "Our editors were real proud of that one," laughed post-production producer Wendy Neuss; Troi's amphibian sounds combined human noise and gill sound, while a monster specialist from her regular looping group did Worf's growls. "I knew we'd scored the show well," she added, "when the Barclay spider appears and my boss Peter Lauritson jumped out of his seat at the screening, even though he knew it was coming!" The actors all came in to try a few tracks making own noises, she revealed, but none were usable: "We tried them on the dubbing stage but there was too much extended laughter."

Among the FX-laden visuals was supervisor Ron B. Moore's last project before he left to work on the upcoming movie: the shuttle's approach of the looping, powered-down *Enterprise*, a long approach view, and a reverse shot outward from the bay. With the starship partly seen upside down, the shot also teases Rick Berman's visual dictum maintaining "upright" spaceships—and, surprisingly, required the first "new" shuttle flyby ever shot. The bay doors are seen closed and we know that shuttles can override them ("Coming of Age"/119), but both Moore and McFadden were disappointed that time ran out on finishing elements planned and filmed to show an exterior view of the door opening.

Worf's torpedo demonstration used numerous stock asteroid shots (including "Galaxy's Child"/190) with a new one of potato-sized foam chunks blown up on high-speed film, noted FX associate Michael "B." Baukaskas; the flammable explosions—illogical but visually satisfying, as visual FX producer Dan Curry had requested—were revamped gasoline-based elements salvaged by Curry from the TV *Buck Rogers* FX shop when it shut down. The departing shuttle's shadow cast over the saucer is dramatic but inaccurate. Caught too late to fix: the stunned, de-evolved Riker retains a glow longer than usual.

Worf's climactic "electrocution"—in a Jefferies tube with a floor of rubber, requiring the hatch unit—was erroneously filmed lighted from above before anyone realized the arcing would make it bottom-lit; the fix was made digitally. Showing cross-team cooperation, the arc animation was based on an element from videotape Joe Bauer shot of a Tesla coil at Los Angeles' Griffin Observatory; Peter Koczera and Joannie Jacobs at CIS did the animation as a warm-up to their feature work, although DM's Adam Howard diffused the arcs into the trademark *Star Trek* look. Finally, the first version of Worf's of the live venom spray was deemed unsuitable by Rick Berman, so FX associate Eddie Williams solved the minor last-minute crisis with a of couple hours' work using a tractor-beam element stretched and tinted green-yellow, with added moisture beads.

On the trivial side, Dr. Selar is paged again ("The Schizoid Man"/131, "Remember Me"/179, "Tapestry"/241, "Sub Rosa"/266, "All Good Things . . ."/277–78); T-cells had played a plot point before ("Identity Crisis"/192); Troi taking her first depicted bridge watch ("Thine Own Self"/268); Lieutenant Hayes is seen later (*Generations*); a Level I security alert may succeed the term "full alert" ("The Hunted"/159, "Power Play"/215); and Barclay wants to shut down nineteen decks' power for just a torpedo guidance check. We learn that an "Alpha 4-7" clearance is required for secure channel usage; Data's computer is independent of the ship's; Worf doesn't go for the standard hard Klingon bed ("Unification I"/208); the "Tarellian death syndrome" is for real (see note at "Liaisons"/254). Among many rooms here the arboretum ("Data's Day"/185, "Imaginary Friend"/222, "Dark Page"/259) is in Deck 17's Section 21-Alpha, Riker's quarters are Deck 08/Room 0912, Troi's are 0x/0910, Sickbay is 12/1631 with Crusher's office at 12/1629.

Sporting her new junior lieutenant's pips, Ogawa apparently opted to keep her last name after marrying Andrew Powell ("Lower Decks"/267), but her quick pregnancy would not end happily ("All Good Things . . ."/277–278); from original Trek comes the Symbalene blood burn—a fast-acting plague, suggested by Naren Shankar—and the K-3 cell count from 1967's "Immunity Syndrome" and "Operation—Annihilate!" "Dr. Hacopian" was Braga's chiropractor, Riker date Rebecca White was named for a friend of Rick Berman's wife, and the unspecified shuttlecraft was to have been named the Hypatia, after the female mathematician who was martyred at the sack of the Library of Alexandria.

Journey's End

Production No.: 272 ■ Aired: Week of March 28, 1994
Stardate: 47751.2 ■ Code: je

Directed by **Corey Allen**
Written by **Ronald D. Moore**
Based upon material by **Shawn Piller & Antonio Napoli**

GUEST CAST
Cadet 3/C Wesley Crusher: **Wil Wheaton**
Fleet Admiral Alynna Nechayev: **Natalija Nogulich**
Anthwarta: **Ned Romero**
Lakanta: **Tom Jackson**
Lieutenant Jack Crusher: **Jack Wert**
Gul Evek: **Ricahrd Poe**
Wakasa: **George Aguilar**
Traveler: **Erik Menyuk**

The downside of a historic UFP-Cardassian peace treaty becomes obvious when Picard is forced to evacuate Federation colonies outside the newly redrawn border. The case of one colony due for relocation, Dorvan V, is even more poignant because of the enclave of American Indians who settled there after a decades-long search, once they elected to avoid the cultural assimilation of Earth.

As the plainspoken Indians talk but resist—Picard pleads with Admiral Nechayev and the UFP Council in vain for a waiver—The tension mounts when a Cardassian team arrives to survey the planet, unconcerned about the Indians' refusal to leave.

Amid all this, a moody Wes Crusher arrives on leave from the Academy, unsure of his future but surprised to meet Lakanta, an Indian colonist who says he is destined to offer him help. When young Crusher encounters a vision of his father telling him to seek his own way, the cadet resigns from Starfleet before a stunned Picard, who'd been furious only a moment earlier after Wes warned the Indians of a planned surprise mass beam-up.

Lakanta later reveals himself to be the Traveler, the transdimensional being who offers to tutor Wes and thus fulfill his own prophecy of the young man's unique destiny. Meanwhile, Picard, Gul Evek, and the Indians finally strike a workable yet uneasy deal: the colonists stay put, trading Federation for Cardassian supervision.

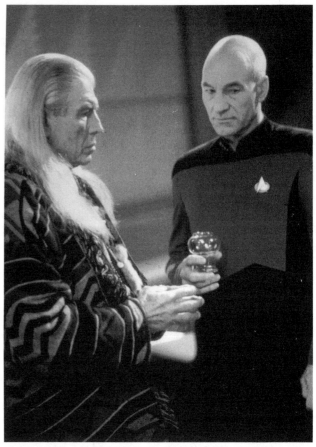

Captain Picard has been ordered to remove Indians from their homeland.

With a glimpse of the new *Star Trek: Voyager* due the coming winter, winding down episode returns to the "family" theme to reveal the fate of Wesley Crusher—a story that was not only a year-old story by producer Ron Moore but a personal one as well, echoing his own departure from an expected Navy career when he realized his yen to be a writer. "There were things in my life pointing me in that direction that I wasn't paying attention to, sort of like Wesley," said Moore. "I just thought that everything about this character said he did *not* belong in Starfleet. . . . It always seemed he was just doing things that were expected of him."

But the move did not sit well with everyone. "There was a lot of concern that this character, whom Gene created with his middle name, who *was* Gene Roddenberry—that it was doing him a disservice to have Wesley leave Starfleet," recalled Jeri Taylor. Finally, when Michael Piller held out for a unique destiny for Wesley, the Traveler reprise was developed as a fulfillment of his own prediction of the youth's Mozart-like giftedness ("Where No One Has Gone Before"/106, "Remember Me"/179). Even then, Moore dallied with having the Lakanta-to-Traveler transformation include a Boothby phase ("The First Duty") until Piller decided it would cheat Picard to make his mentor Wesley's as well.

Originally the cadet's aimlessness was to lead him into TNG's debut mention of the Maquis—pronounced "muh-KEE," for the French World War II resistance cell—in a plot by Taylor that would eventually be picked up for DS9's "The Maquis" two-parter and echoed on TNG ("Preemptive Strike"/276) as a well-laid setup for *Voyager*'s pilot background. Eventually the Maquis, and Wesley's short-lived involvement with them, became the Native American colony after the credited pitch by Napoli and Piller's son dovetailed with Taylor's desire to establish here the implied home of *Voyager*'s complex American Indian character Chakotay. The name "Maquis" itself isn't coined until the DS9 outing.

The rest of the story, Moore noted, involved finding the fine line of both fault and sympathy for all the depicted parties—including Picard, who had to have hard orders "without turning into Custer," and the Indians, who had been told not to settle so close to the border. At first, direct reference was made to the Hopi Indians and Tribes and others—with Picard's ancestor being Corporal Everett Picard, who had been with Kit Carson in 1875, destroying a Rio Grande village—but even with the series' use of advisers the tribes involved asked not to be depicted for fear of misrepresentation, so the terms were generalized: kachina dolls becoming mansaras, the ceremonial kiva now a habak, and so on.

For the art department, that meant the added burden of creating a very visual culture from scratch with the original village set of "Thine Own Self" (268) to build upon. "Nothing could have any [real-life] Indian indications, which immediately means that you can't rent anything," set decorator Jim Mees recalled. In fact, note that the tribal council's chairs bear a striking resemblance to those of a Romulan Warbird wardroom repainted ("Face of the Enemy"/240). Bularian canapés, for the record, are actually just odd crackers with Cheez-Whiz and olives, and propmaster Alan Sims recalled that Wesley's vision was to include an eagle until it was learned the only trainable one for rent, an endangered batalor eagle, was already booked. The show's major optical was the freeze-frame of time for Wes and Lakanta/Traveler, which again used an anamorphic lens to pan-and-scan motion into an otherwise static shot ("Attached"/260, "Inheritance"/262)—The foreground man shooting a beam the two walk through was shot against blue-screen and matted in, while his target was part of the live shot; the blasted chunk of building was likewise added with computer effects.

Returning here is Wert as Jack Crusher ("Family"/178, "Violations"/212), with the untold details of his demise now left up to future TNG movies. Moore said the ongoing use of Nechayev and Evek ("Preemptive Strike"/276 and DS9's "The Maquis") was a reflection of both continuity and the actors' work and the border setting of those stories; Nechayev's won a promotion of sorts, going from a vice-admiral to fleet admiral here. Initially he wrote the admiral as resisting Picard's overtures of detente in this episode, but later agreed with Piller that Picard actually could get through to her; her threat to temporarily remove him is not the first ("Chain of Command, Part I"/236). Picard in a scene cut for time mentions that he almost washed out in his sophomore Academy year, after his father's death, with Moore implying it was the incident Boothby once alluded to ("The First Duty"). Other cut scenes had Picard waking an oversleeping Wes, who'd turned away in "irritation" from Boothby, and the Indians criticizing artificial weather modification ("True Q"/232, "Force of Nature"/261, "Journey's End"/272).

For continuity's sake, Troi's knowledge of the Pueblo Revolt fits with her interest in Westerns ("A Fistful of Datas"/234), while Evek's sadness at his lost sons ties in with his people's high regard for children and family ("Chain of Command, Part II"/237, DS9's "Tribunal"). Rementioned are the Academy's Admiral Brand ("The First Duty"), the Federation Council, Dr. Vassbinder (see notes, "Timescape"/251), the latest Cardassian ship, the *Vetar*, and Picard's father ("Tapestry"/241), described as a great oral historian with family roots back to Charlemagne.

"Cochrane" is finally mentioned verbally as the unit of warp field stress for the first time Cardassian communicators are seen, mounted on their wrists. Also, Beverly apparently includes Wes's repeated year when she calls him a fourth-year cadet since he wears three pips, but Picard notes that he only left "three years ago"; perhaps Starfleet Academy offers a summer school. And the Katowa-led exodus of Indians from Earth occurred about 2170, or just after the Romulan War (from 1966's "Balance of Terror") and the Federation founding ("The Outcast"/217).

FIRSTBORN

Production No.: 273 ■ Aired: Week of April 25, 1994
Stardate: 47779.4 ■ Code: fb

Directed by **Jonathan West**
Teleplay by **René Echevarria**
Story by **Mark Kalbfeld**

GUEST CAST

K'Mtar/Alexander at 50: **James Sloyan**
Alexander Rozhenko: **Brian Bonsall**
B'Etor: **Gwynyth Walsh**
Lursa: **Barbara March**
Yog the Yridian: **Joel Swetow**
Gorta: **Colin Mitchell**
Quark: **Armin Shimerman**
"Kahless" Singer: **Michael Danek**
"Molor" Singer: **John Kenton Shull**
Eric Burton: **Rickey D'Shon Collins**
Computer Voice: **Majel Barrett**

When Alexander shows little interest in warrior training, Worf takes him to a Klingon outpost's colorful local celebration of their people's Kot'baval festival, marking the Kahless-Molor battle.

But the day almost turns tragic when the two are nearly killed by apparent assailants from the rival Duras family, anxious to kill Worf's only heir. Only the mystery appearance of K'mtar, a trusted family friend sent to avert such a surprise, saves the day.

Initially K'mtar helps the thankful father in piquing Alexander's interest in the warrior ethic, but Worf is angered and the boy driven away when K'mtar berates his lack of a killer instinct.

The starship meantime helps track the Duras sisters to accuse them of the incident directly, but the assailant's knife is traced to a child of B'etor's that she only just learned she was carrying. Going to confront K'mtar, Worf is shocked to see the man poised to kill Alexander in his sleep.

Finally, K'mtar reveals the odd truth that he is Alexander from forty years in the future, time-

Alexander participates in a mock Klingon battle ritual.

traveling back to change the upbringing that allowed him to become a pacifist diplomat duped into allowing Worf's eventual assassination on the Klingon Council floor. Worf, realizing he must change his own attitude, helps "K'mtar" realize that he can only die honorably if he allows Alexander to become his own person.

Helmed by "rookie" director Jonathan West, the series' two-year director of photography, this season's Klingon show returns to the family theme for Alexander's only appearance of the year. Kalbfeld's premise concerned only a Federation-marked Romulan ship from a supposedly peaceful future that turned out to be a Trojan horse whose time-travel and "future Riker" were both a hoax.

But the idea of a "future fix" hung on, and once Piller again nixed Joe Menosky's idea of an Alexander accidentally yet permanently aged thirty years in a time portal—"I think it's a hideous thing to steal somebody's youth from them," he said—the eventual *Back to the Future*–like plot evolved. It also reverberates with "Yesteryear," Dorothy Fontana's highly regarded 1973 animated *Star Trek* in which Spock restores a damaged timeline by saving himself as a child.

Jeri Taylor had been impressed with actor Sloyan ever since she screened "The Defector" (158) in her crash-course on Star Trek but had to fight for him as her first choice for K'mtar, over Rick Berman and Michael Piller's initial objection that he had portrayed Odo's Bajoran mentor on DS9 only weeks before. "I finally went to Michael and said, 'Look—we can take a lesser actor in this part or we can cast the actor who should be cast,'" she

recalled, arguing that the Klingon makeup would help "hide" him. It was during this show that Patrick Stewart was able to miss four days of shooting to host the February 5 *Saturday Night Live*.

Originally, Echevarria had also wanted to include K'Ehleyr ("Emissary"/146, "Reunion"/181) as young Alexander's climactic rescuer from K'mtar. Actress Suzi Plakson was interested in the reprise but declined on the timing, citing the beginning of hiatus after an exhausting year on her popular sitcom *Love and War*; a bedside photo had to make do. "The truth is, it was a blessing," Echevarria noted. "There was enough exposition to explain at the end of the show as it is!"

The wide-ranging story more than holds its own, switching from Klingon pageantry—with the tale of Molor and Kahless once touched upon ("Rightful Heir"/249)—to the chase for the Duras sisters ("Redemption I-II"/200-201) on the eve of their feature debut in *Generations*. That subplot opened up when Piller wanted a tougher search for the sisters, and actor Shimerman agreed to do a DS9 scene for "a very reasonable price"; with Quark's addition, the abandoned alien was switched from a Ferengi to a Dopterian, seen as their kin in DS9's "The Forsaken." The outing was the first for Brian Bonsall since his movie *Blank Check*, while Swetow had been Gul Jasad for DS9's pilot.

Visual FX coordinator Michael "B" Baukaskas, getting a supervisor's credit with Ron B. Moore's ongoing absence to work on the feature, had fun with the Klingons' holodeck fight with stunt coordinator. Dennis Madalone as the "frozen" assailant. Baukaskas recalled how West and the crew were "sweating it" late one day before young Brian Bonsall's time limit for work as a minor was running out; as it was, his parents acquiesced to go a few minutes over, and each of three angles needed was snared in one take without mishap. For VCR freeze-framers, watch the stilled fighter as K'mtar passes him: thanks to the interruption of the cutaway shot, the fighter had to be moved a few inches to the left for clearance after the planned pan-and-scan cheat ("Attached"/260) was abandoned for time. Also, live explosive "squibs" for the weaponry hits were eschewed in favor of optical add-ons ("Descent"/252, "Gambit, Part I"/256) to realistically tighten up the timing of the "speed-of-light" weapons.

Although the two actors playing the Klingon Kot'baval grunted their lines on stage, both were good enough singers to reloop and synchronize a new melody to their filmed mouthings when it was decided to make the Klingon opera more lyrical and composer Dennis McCarthy was called in. "We did some temporary tracks for the stage but we wound up doing the whole thing in post-production," said producer Wendy Neuss. "It was one of our biggest jobs all year—figuring out what the on-camera instruments would sound like, breaking down all the syllables, figuring where the offstage line would be."

Young Eric, given the surname "Burton" in the script, makes his third showing ("Liaisons"/254, "Masks"/269); his "Fullerene" water balloon, noted science adviser André Bormanis, comes from today's same-named synthesized molecule of carbon atoms that forms a hollow shell, named for geodesic dome designer Buckminster Fuller; the metallicized wax prop was actually thrown from off-camera for Worf's dunking by propmaster Alan Sims.

Thanks to TV magic, Worf's quarter-human son continues to mushroom; he's already age ten, though he was age three at K'Ehleyr's death only two seasons ago! Here he is said to have never seen the Home World and is said to be the only male-related heir of Kurn ("Sins of the Father"/165, "Redemption"/200-201). Other Klingon references include leader Gowron ("Reunion"/181, "Redemption"/200, "Unification I"/208, "Rightful Heir"/249), the annually marked Rite of Ascension and painstiks ("The Icarus Factor"/140), and the first-ever mention of Klingon currency, darseks. Whether intended or not, the trusted family adviser "Gin'tak" is also the word for a spear ("Birthright, Part II"); the Koh'manara block ("Second Chances"/250), the curse patahk for "animal," Qapla for "success," and gik'tal ("Lower Decks"/267) for "to the death"—the latter sung by the Kahless character—are also not new.

Trivia fans will note the mention of biomimetic gel ("Force of Nature"/261), bilitrium (DS9's "Past Prologue"), the Corvallens ("Face of the Enemy"/240, "Inheritance"/262), the inept Pakleds ("Samaritan Snare"/143), another Yridian ("Birthright, Part I"/242, "Gambit, Part I"/256, and DS9) and his wasplike ship ("The Chase"/246), and the flashy explosive magnesite—which dates back all the way to 1967's "Friday's Child." Echevarria not only created the U.S.S. Kearsage here after the historic Civil War ship but named the Vodrey Nebula after the fan who wrote in to suggest it. Finally, we learn that Riker is the only one at Quark's to ever win "triple-down Dabo" and was due gold-pressed latinum, the first TNG mention of either, while Lursa's offspring is not referred to again (Generations) but may yet be lurking out there for future sequels!

BLOODLINES

Production No.: 274 ■ Aired: Week of May 2, 1994
Stardate: 47829.1 ■ Code: bl

Directed by **Les Landau**
Written by **Nicholas Sagan**

GUEST CAST
DaiMon Bok: **Lee Arenberg**
Jason Vigo: **Ken Olandt**
Birta: **Peter Slutsker**
Lieutenant Sandra Rhodes: **Amy Pietz**
Tol: **Michelan Sisti**
Computer Voice: **Majel Barrett**

DaiMon Bok blames Picard for his son's death in the first UFP-Ferengi meeting, and emerges from prison to taunt the captain again—this time with news that he would kill the son that Picard never knew he had.

After the young man is hunted down, DNA tests prove that Jason Vigo is Picard's son, the apparent result of a long-ago brief fling with the now-dead sister of a Stargazer officer. Living a hard, troubled life after his mother's death, Jason approaches his newfound "father" warily and awkwardly. Bok then appears via a new long-distance subspace transporter to tease Picard all the more.

Bok eventually uses the device to kidnap Jason and threaten his life, but not before the young man's sudden attack of a genetic disease reveals Bok's ruse. Suffering from a syndrome that neither Picard nor his mother could have passed on to him, Jason is found to have had his DNA resequenced to match Picard's. Armed with that fact, the captain uses the risky subspace transporter, races to free the boy, and reveals Bok's profitless insanity to his mercenary crew, who depose him.

After Jason is cured, he and his would-be father acknowledge the bond they developed and agree to visit in the future, both having grown from the experience.

DaiMon Bok threatens the boy who may be Picard's son.

This story traces its roots directly back to a set visit during "Masks" (269). Brent Spiner and Patrick Stewart were asked about any hanging character threads that could be turned into stories. When Stewart recalled the unsatisfied vengeance of DaiMon Bok ("The Battle"/110), Taylor tossed the brief idea at writer Sagan, asking him ("Attached"/260) to flesh out his pitch about a "created" Picard son.

Sagan's first take emerged as the aired version after an uncredited polish by René Echevarria, but for a time it had been sent in another direction to avoid duplicating Trek novelist Peter David's script idea in development, about a woman who brings aboard Geordi's unknown son. Though intriguing, that intense emotional conflict never jelled to Michael Piller's liking, and Sagan's original plot was restored. His name of "Cristof" for the boy was changed by Echevarria to "Daniel," which then became "Jason" at Stewart's request to avoid using his own son's name ("The Inner Light"/225). Before the Bok angle is apparent, the tale of the unknown and somewhat hardened son is reminiscent of Kirk and David Marcus in the second and third Trek movies; as personal reference Sagan recalled drawing on his once-icy relationship with his own famous father.

Both writers were sad to lose the sentiment of the original ending, in which Jason and Picard confide mutually that they wish their newfound kinship were real—a moment likely muted to make way for Picard's "end-of-the-family" moroseness in the coming feature (*Generations*). While praising the freelancer's work and the sympathetic explanation Taylor created for Miranda Vigo's actions, Echevarria was also delighted that no one flagged Picard's self-deprecating line about his hairline—including Stewart, who loved it. Sadly, a funny line was cut when Picard realizes

Ferengi like Bok can "buy" their way out of prison and Birta shrugs it off: "He paid his debt to society."

Oddly, the Ferengi actors' fraternity is well represented here, but with a twist. Arenberg, who has played Prak ("Force of Nature"/261) and Gral (DS9's "The Nagus"), replaced the original Bok, Frank Corsentino, who later played Lwaxana Troi's suitor Tog ("Ménage à Troi"). Slutsker had appeared with him as Nibor before playing the tragic Dr. Reyga ("Suspicions"/248). Other Ferengi touches here include the reported debate on the Rules of Aquisition, the first TNG mention of that ubiquitous code created on DS9 and the first indication that they are amendable. Also we learn that the Maxia battlesite was in Ferengi space.

Vigo, of course, was the only *Stargazer* bridge crewman Picard called by name during the "ghost" sequence of "The Battle," and a cut line from Sagan's script actually made Miranda the weapons officer's sister; he must have been a longtime officer. She and Picard's involvement "twenty-four years ago" works out to be four years after he stood up Jenice ("We'll Always Have Paris"/124), or nine years before the Maxia incident. Miranda's birth "fifty years ago"—or in 2320, reckoned by the "2364" date of Season 1's "Neutral Zone" (126)—would have been seven years before Picard's Academy "Class of '27" graduation and made her twenty-six and he about forty-one. Her New Gaul birthplace is apparently not to be confused with New Paris (from 1966's "The Galileo Seven") or New France (DS9's "The Forsaken"), although the prior Bok-Picard confrontation was unknowingly changed in a late draft to Xendi *Kabu* instead of Xendi *Sabu*.

Sagan, another Trek baseball fan, named security officer "Garvey" after one of his favorites, Steve, while Jason's rare disease was dually named for Larry *Forrester*, the original writer of "The Battle," and *Trent* Reznor of the alternative rock band Nine-

Inch Nails, a favorite. The other guard's name, Lieutenant Sandra Rhodes, honored an Air Force officer and Trek fan whose family wrote Taylor and asked about the homage. Picard again here speaks wistfully of his and his father's estrangement ("Family"/178, "Tapestry"/241) and exceeds the warp five limit ("Force of Nature") for the first time without express approval—though it is a life-or-death matter. His Saurian brandy harks back to The Original Series (and "In Theory"/199), and—according to Echevarria—the Gorlan prayer stick among Picard's relics was not intended to be related to the Gorla Colony mentioned in 1967's "Mirror, Mirror," but it could be.

The show's few visual effects include David Stipes and Joe Bauer's "Princess Leia" hologram of Bok and the "battling transporters" effect; the Ferengi probe was fashioned by Dan Curry from an underground sprinkler sleeve.

Emergence

Production No.: 275 ■ Aired: Week of May 9, 1994
Stardate: 47869.2 ■ Code: eg

Directed by **Cliff Bole**
Teleplay by **Joe Menosky**
Story by **Brannon Braga**

GUEST CAST
Conductor: **David Huddleston**
Hitman: **Vinny Argiro**
Engineer: **Thomas Kopache**
Hayseed: **Arlee Reed**

A runaway train appears suddenly in Data's *The Tempest* program . . . the *Enterprise* suddenly goes into warp for no reason . . . and Picard is convinced he's lost control of his ship, especially after sensors show it would have exploded had the warp jump not occurred.

Amazingly, Data and La Forge discover a network of self-erected nodes cross-connecting ship's functions, much like a life-form's neural web. On the holodeck, the crew finds a train program running with a conductor, engineer, and characters from various existing programs— a hayseed, flapper girls, a hit man, a knight— that they realize represent different ship's functions.

But when the characters all stop Data from

shutting down the power grid within the program, he realizes that the ship is fostering its own embryonic intelligence. A molecular-like form is discovered "growing" in Cargo Bay 5, nurtured by the ship's arrival at a white dwarf star to "feed" it vertion particles via a tractor beam.

The whole process shuts down when the vertions are exhausted, and the crew must step in to help when ship begins a trip that will exhaust their life support. The colorful train "passengers" are finally convinced to try a nearby nebula as an artificial vertion source, but they disappear when the new life-form departs into space fully matured.

An actual Orient Express parlor car graced this wildly imaginative romp through the unconscious by Joe Menosky and Branon Braga, the series' lone joint effort by both its offbeat writers. It was "even weirder," in Jeri Taylor's words, before staff writer Naren Shankar pulled it back to a more produceable level in an uncredited polish. "Again, I thought Menosky mighta had a couple of mushrooms when he wrote the first script," laughed director Cliff Bole, preparing his record twenty-fifth and final TNG outing. "We all read it and thought, 'Jeeesus, you can't shoot this in thirty-five days!' I mean, marvelous crazy ideas, but it had to be downscaled."

Looking to include one more holodeck story, Braga said the staff discarded a final Dixon Hill adventure in development as "too familiar" in favor of this idea for the "ultimate holodeck show" he'd stewed on but only put into written form at the last minute. With Braga and Ron Moore busy on the finale, Jeri Taylor leaned again on Menosky, still writing from Italy, who took Braga's idea of the ship achieving sentience and added the concept of the new life-form's birth—almost a small-scale version of the Ilia/Decker/V'Ger creation from the first Trek feature.

The cast, which includes script coordinator Lolita Fatjo's husband, Arlee Daniel—previously seen as an alien terrorist ("Starship Mine"/244)—and the familiar face of character actor David Huddleston, also includes Patrick Stewart's longtime stand-in Dennis Tracy as the "man in the gray-flannel suit." The taxi driver is longtime TNG stunt man Nick Dimitri ("A Fistful of Datas"/234), here driving for the "Sunshine Radio System"—phone Circle 7-232—in location shots on Paramount's own New York Street, largely unaltered for this show.

Richard James' ambitious Art Deco designs for a scratch-built car were about to be reined in to save money when a shop carpenter mentioned he'd worked on the train car used for *Bram Stoker's Dracula* by Francis Ford Coppola. The car, rented and delivered to the studio's Stage 6 on a flatbed trailer, saved enough to still allow extensive refurbishing of its Edwardian interior to the desired 1920s look. "That train was marvelous," Bole said. "If we'd built that there would have been another 120 grand that would have been subtracted from everything else." Stock footage

Worf and Deanna on the malfunctioning holodeck.

from the classic *Murder on the Orient Express* in Paramount's vaults added an odd period mystique to the show, but Bole had to beg Rick Berman to get a close-up of the wheels braking and ignore the point-of-view logic that no one would be in the holodeck to see them. "The sparks coming and all that—I had to have it!" he said. "Sometimes for drama's sake you gotta break the rules, so I got away with it once."

Series visual FX coordinator Phil Barberio, this episode's fill-in supervisor for Ron B. Moore, opted to take Rick Sternbach's open-spaced design for the "helix" directly to computer creation to avoid a miniature's matting and mounting problems. Amblin Imaging, the Steven Spielberg auxiliary that handles the FX for *SeaQuest DSV*, brought it to live on a Video Toaster. The Mac-Pherson Nebula was taken from never-used elements Dan Curry shot years ago of lasers bouncing off plastics.

The show features the last Shakespeare theatrics of the series ("Hide and Q"/111, "The Defector"/158, "Devil's Due"/187)—shot here on a darkened corner of the late season's much-used village set (see "Journey's End"/272)—and the only TNG mention of vertions, another artificial kind of matter in the vein of verterons and tetryons.

PREEMPTIVE STRIKE

Production No.: 276 ▪ Aired: Week of May 16, 1994
Stardate: 47941.7 ▪ Code: ps

Directed by **Patrick Stewart**
Teleplay by **René Echevarria**
Story by **Naren Shankar**

GUEST CAST
Ensign Ro Laren: **Michelle Forbes**
Macias: **John Franklin-Robbins**
Fleet Admiral Alynna Nechayev: **Natalija Nogulich**
Santos: **William Thomas, Jr.**
Kalita: **Shannon Cochran**
Gul Evek: **Richard Poe**

Fresh from a year away at Advanced Tactical Training, newly promoted Lieutenant Ro Laren finds herself at the center of the growing Maquis crisis when Starfleet asks her to infiltrate the rebel colonists.

Gaining access to the Maquis in the guise of a Cardassian-killing Bajoran fugitive, Ro soon learns that the group suspects the alien empire of smuggling biogenic weapons into the Zone to use against the outsiders there. She gains the local cell's full confidence by staging a daring raid against the *Enterprise* for medical supplies—brought off with Picard's acquiescence, of course—but finds herself more and more sympathetic to the Maquis's plight.

Picard, the troubled officer's longtime supporter, is concerned to hear of Ro's new self-doubts about loyalty and sends Riker along with her on the next mission: a trap to lure Maquis in for capture. But when her elderly Maquis mentor Macias is killed in a surprise Cardassian raid at their base, Ro's mind is made up: during the mission she holds Riker hostage long enough to reveal the Starfleet ambush to her comrades.

Before leaving to go with them, she sadly hands over her Bajoran earring to Riker and lets him return, asking him to tell Picard her greatest regret is betraying the trust he put in her.

———

The long-awaited return of Ro Laren, with Patrick Stewart in his fifth turn at directing and the second this season, was another late-season tale borne of desperation for Jeri Taylor and the writing staff—but even more so it depended on a near-miracle that actress Michelle Forbes, who'd spurned a DS9 transfer to keep busy in films, would even consider it. After having one premise after another turned down by Michael Piller in search of the best final shows possible, Taylor found herself pursuing the

actress anyway just days away from prep—the design week before live filming—after coming up with a bare-bones Maquis idea to follow DS9's two-parter (see notes, "Journey's End"/272).

"Her agent had said last year 'Please leave us alone!'" recalled Taylor. "It came down to her agent and manager, saying, 'You—Jeri—get on the phone with Michelle and tell her what the story is, and if you can sell it she might do it.' So that was a phone call I really had a dry mouth about, because it was all on my shoulders. But I guess desperation and the clock ticking inspired me, because I just . . . spun gold out of straw—'a woman torn, and her choices are . . .'—and I knew I had her." Now all that had to happen was for René Echevarria, the only staffer with free time, to plunge directly from "Bloodlines" (274) into this teleplay. His first draft saw Ro pull off her trust-earning raid alone against a freighter, but just three days before filming Piller asked for a restructuring of Act III to its present form—both to make her task more credible and to get the regular cast more screen time.

One scene Echevarria was sad to lose from the first draft was based on the elder Macias being Bajoran and not wearing his people's traditional earring: after Ro's successful "raid" he asks her if she's ready to stop wearing hers because "you're not Bajoran, you're Maquis now." The moment was meant to add even more poignancy to her final request that Riker take her earring to Picard, which already harks back to her memorable run-in with Number One in Ro's very first time onscreen ("Ensign Ro"/203). Another rewrite change, he said, converted Macias' death from a greatly disfiguring one caused by the "mutagenic" weapons described previously ("Chain of Command, Part I"/236); when the staff didn't want Picard and Starfleet to be caught so "flat-footed," the filmed version mentions only a rumor of "biogenic" arms in the area and Macias' death is more routine. His name, though mispronounced from the namesake "mah-SEE-us," was inspired by a Cuban freedom fighter in that nation's War of Independence from Spain.

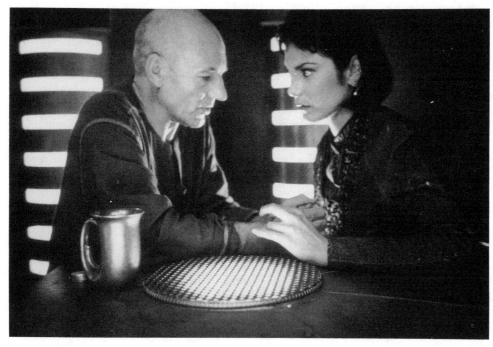

On an undercover mission, Captain Picard gets a report from Ensign Ro.

Along with yet another hair change, Ro herself—in her first real TNG role in two years ("The Next Phase"/224) after a brief turn last season ("Rascals"/233)—has jumped a whole rank to full lieutenant but is without the original Bajoran nosebridge piece she debuted and that Michael Westmore gradually phased out on DS9 due to the constant re-gluing needed. Her quarters are seen to be Deck 8/Room 4711; references to her father's death and her court-martial are now new ("Ensign Ro"). For the record, Forbes has told more than one interviewer she'd consider turning up as Ro again on DS9 if the story and role were up to par.

Nechayev and Evek, those denizens of the Demilitarized Zone, again lend continuity to the Maquis arc ("Journey's End"/272), while the village extras—as with DS9's "The Maquis"—include Klingons, Vulcans, and the Dorvan V Native Americans ("Journey's End") as subtle setup for the *Voyager* cast; the resigned lieutenant commander Ro speaks of from Tactical Training is a veiled reference to the new series' character Chakotay. Ongoing set-swapping between the sister series has DS9 art director Randy McIlvain's council room from the two-parter redressed for use here; the village itself, with an added catwalk to provide yet more depth of action, is the fourth revamping of Richard James' original Barkon IV community ("Thine Own Self"/268).

One of either series' largest space battles, storyboarded and supervised by visual FX associate Joe Bauer, featured many of the newer ship miniatures; its *Star Wars*-like conflict of smaller craft attacking the larger Cardassian Galor-class warship was a virtual first for any Star Trek, which tended to keep its rare space skirmishes to the ship-on-ship variety. DS9 illustrator Jim Martin designed both the Maquis fighter first seen on the DS9 two-parter, built by Tony Meininger, and Ro's fighter/transport debuting here as built by Greg Jein—with a cockpit window matching the regular "alien shuttle" interior set. Two Bajoran ships Meininger built for DS9's second-season opening trilogy, Kira's "attack ship" and a troop transport, are also in on the action here. The first-ever nighttime phaser fight also used more complex live interactive lighting from FX man Dick Brownfield's flashbulb arrays and live squibs fired from a converted paint gun, designed to spark on impact.

Trivia notes: Bajoran references include the belaklavion instrument Ro's father played and the foods foraiga and hasperat—which propmaster Alan Sims revealed was simply Armenian flat bread coated with cream cheese, lettuce, dried tomatoes, and black olive bits, then rolled burrito-style and cut in half to reveal the colorful cross-section. Also, "Type VIII" phasers are here said to be large and ship-mounted, in contrast to the long-established hand, pistol, and rifle phasers dubbed types I–III. Old references include the Pakleds ("Samaritan Snare"/143, "Firstborn"/273), the Yridians ("Birthright, Part I"/242, "Suspicions"/248, "Gambit, Part I"/256), and biomimetic gel ("Force of Nature"/261, "Firstborn"/273). Lastly, until someone realized that its title and the finale's both contained the same word, this episode was known as "The Good Fight."

ALL GOOD THINGS . . .

Production No.: 277 ■ Aired: Week of May 23, 1994
Stardate: 47988 ■ Code: ag

Directed by **Winrich Kolbe**
Written by **Brannon Braga & Ronald D. Moore**

GUEST CAST

Q: **John de Lancie**
Commander Tomalak: **Andreas Katsulas**
Admiral Nakamura: **Clyde Kusatsu**
Lieutenant (j.g.) Alyssa Ogawa: **Patti Yasutake**
Lieutenant Tasha Yar: **Denise Crosby**
Chief Miles O'Brien: **Colm Meaney**
Jessel: **Pamela Kosh**
Lieutenant Gaines: **Tim Kelleher**
Ensign Nell Chilton: **Alison Brooks**
Ensign: **Stephen Matthew Garvey**
Computer Voice: **Majel Barrett**

Picard is disturbed to realize, after several dizzying episodes, that he is slipping back and forth among three distinct time periods: the present; seven years in the past, when he first took command of the *Enterprise*; and twenty-five years into the future, when his crew has scattered or resigned from Starfleet.

The captain opts to keep his past crew in the dark, leading them to question their new leader's sanity, while those in the future think he's crazy due to Irumodic syndrome, a rare mental degradation of aging. Picard, amidst more unpredictable time travels, realizes that the link with his maddening situation is an odd anomaly in the Neutral Zone—and as Q makes a sudden reappearance. The superbeing admits to being the cause of Picard's time-shifting but insists that the captain, not he, is responsible for the impending doom of humanity. He even shows Picard how the first amino acids of life never connected under an anomaly-filled sky on primordial Earth.

The anomaly is the key, but the captain and his various crews can't figure out why it is larger in the past than in the present—or why it's

Worf decides to join his old comrades for one last mission.

absent in the future. Scanning with a tachyon pulse leads nowhere until Picard realizes the rift is a fracture of time and "anti-time" that enlarges into the past, by scanning the same point in 3 eras. The rift is healed after the apparent destruction of all three *Enterprise*s, but Q restores the present time by quietly telling Picard that his insight into the problem-solving was a mere glimpse of what humanity is truly capable of beyond mere space and science exploration.

With "reality" restored, Picard tells his officers of the future he glimpsed—Riker and Worf estranged when neither married Troi and Dr. Crusher a captain and his ex-wife. In the end he joins in the others' weekly poker game—to their surprise and delight.

This highest-rated and most complex TNG effort ever had anything but a smooth ride, as one might expect from its scope, humor, mystery, and surprises—with writers Ron Moore and Brannon Braga still dealing with their year-old *Generations* screenplay, a crew already exhausted by the long, ambitious season, a blaze of national media scrutiny, and a cast mindful of both the onrushing movie and their pending unemployment for the first time in seven years.

The studio had asked for a two-hour series-ender by December. When thoughts began turning to a plot, Michael Piller pulled elements from a "time-slipping" story by Braga (with Worf and Alexander) and followed Moore's suggestion to "bookend" the series by revisiting the "Encounter at Farpoint" courtroom with Q, while suggesting the three-era crew format with Picard as the conduit—an intentional homage to *Slaughterhouse Five*, an early personal influence. Jeri Taylor decided the movie duo would get enough of a break to do the finale's writing chores.

In a February 7 memo to the co-writers, Piller hit on two themes for the finale: the idea of "family" in each time period—as symbol of "the cast, the crew, the fans, the writing staff . . . all the families of *Star Trek: The Next Generation*"—and the realization that every moment is precious, affecting all those before or after (a theme he also explored in the DS9 pilot "Emissary"). "You can revisit it, you can remember it, laugh about it, hold reunions, go to conventions, show reruns forever, but you can never live that moment again," he wrote, leading to Picard's self-learned Q lesson that "if man is to evolve to the next level he must learn to explore the moment."

But Moore and Braga couldn't start until "Genesis" and "Journey's End" (271, 272) were put to bed. So, thanks to the due date being moved up a slot *ahead* of "Preemptive Strike" because of the finale's scope and complexity, the writers found themselves with only six days to finish a draft. "A two-hour show—they should have had a month to write it!" moaned Taylor. Originally, a *fourth* timeline was part of the mix: a revisit of "The Best of Both Worlds" (174-175).

Still, the finished product had a long way to go and became perhaps the mother of all TNG under-the-gun writing jobs. Director Rick Kolbe, here working his sixteenth and final TNG outing, recalled that "I don't think we ever had a production meeting with a full script. It always was 'Well we have Part I and an outline for Part II, we have Part II and an outline for Part I, we have everything but Act 10' . . . it was difficult."

"Everything that could go wrong went wrong," Braga said of the writing process. "We were running out of time; we couldn't get the story approved—and this was to be expected, since there was a great deal of scrutiny on everyone's part and rightfully so. But things were heating up with the movie, we had to rebreak the finale three times, we had to rewrite the whole script twice; Ron's dog got sick; we had a computer failure and lost an act. . . . There was a two-week period there where we wrote like three hundred pages! By the time it was over, I got some sort of carpal-tunnel syndrome between my thumb and wrist from hitting the space bar."

Cast and crew alike fell in love with that first draft, a "valentine to the characters" as Braga put it, but Piller caused a ruckus with a major restructuring of Part II that tightened up the story while

Q tells Picard the human race will be destroyed.

losing several character moments—including Picard's future crew "stealing" the mothballed *Enterprise* from a museum! The late rewrite led to unhappy actors and a weekend meeting requested by Patrick Stewart, when many of the character moments were restored amid the new framework.

"I knew there were problems, structural problems in Part II," Kolbe said. "But I think we might have gone a little too far in solving those . . . and it lost the charm and the freshness of the original." For his part, Piller agreed that the rewrite brought more "technobabble" to Part II and that the restored scenes helped "warm it up a little," but said his initial concerns about the weak, slow-developing second half still stand. "I won't argue at all with the fact that we lost some cute things, but it wasn't good storytelling," he said, noting especially the ship-stealing sequence. "The problem was, the future Picard needed a ship, and he got one by going to Beverly. . . . And just because the writers wanted to go and hijack the *Enterprise* because it would be neat—'OK, you've got the ship, now go get *another* one, too'—didn't make it good storytelling."

But getting a shootable script was just the beginning, recalled Kolbe—who had hoped for more than five days to prep his long-

sought Q show. Aiming to make this finale TNG's best-ever segment, he came to feel the project was taking a backseat to various unrelated distractions: the actors' ongoing contract negotiations for the movie, their anxiety about job hunting, and a revision to the already complex production schedule so Gates McFadden could leave long enough to shoot a new series pilot in Oregon—a change that led to an extra seventeenth shooting day only at Kolbe's insistence. "For a time I felt like I was the only guy doing anything, and it came to blows about halfway through—we had a big argument," Kolbe said. "And I said, You gotta focus on *this* show! . . . and then everybody—producers, cast, crew—just came together; it was amazing!" Adding to the frenzy was a virtual media circus tromping by the set daily to record the series' final days—promoted by the studio with the curious theme "Journey's End," a confusing overlap of titles (272)—and led to a couple of run-ins with camera crews by an exhausted Stewart, who never liked to be filmed while rehearsing anyway.

"I was at times anxious as to whether I would get through that last period of work, and I'm not being melodramatic," he said, noting his Christmas break spent onstage in London and his directing the previous episode. "This was followed then immediately by the final two hours, and I was in every single scene of the show. . . . Towards the end I just got so tired. . . . I was just trying to do the best job I could. And at the same time there were a lot of people with other needs and demands and I found it all just a bit distracting."

Fatigue was a concern for everyone, Kolbe added: "I was about as dead as you can be, which is not something I like to do, especially on a two-hour show. . . . It was the end of the season, everybody was basically tired and worn out, and tempers were short." But he gave credit to the stage crew, who not only supported his beyond-the-norm camera shots but gave a lift during the most hectic times—such as the last day of all, when eleven takes were needed to film Q's entrance on the floating camera crane while a second crane helped film it. Shooting's end for the whole cast together in their final scene—the poker game—was an emotional affair shot the Thursday before, which Kolbe recalled was slowed down by another brand of visitors—the Paramount brass. "I had the feeling that Sumner Redstone himself was in there," joked the director, referring to the chief of Viacom who had recently bought out Paramount. Ironically, with the Stage 16 courtroom not yet struck, the last first-unit shooting on April 5, 1994—the primordial Earth sequence—took place on DS9's Stage 18 cave set in the same soundstage where another famous Paramount swan song was filmed: Gloria Swanson's Nora Desmond uttering "I'm ready for my close-up, Mr. DeMille" from *Sunset Boulevard.*

The script that finally made it to film featured one big break from past Treks: a "future" that could be revealed on the pretense that no one wanted it to happen. "Since the feature's not anything like this, we had to get out of that by the end of the show," Moore noted. "Rick [Berman] felt very strongly about that—we have to keep our options open." But by doing so the door was open for all kinds of fun tweaking the known characters and background in two alternate timelines—"It was all about just playing with the audience's expectations," Moore said—and there was much throwaway that only a true fan could love: the Klingons' vengeful defeat of the Romulans ("Redemption"/200-201), with the subsequent end to the UFP's cloaking ban ("The Pegasus"/264); and the addition of a third nacelle to the future *Enterprise,* heretofore a design taboo, and its ability to go warp thirteen.

The characters themselves were affected even more, although some setup scenes were among those cut. One at least *referred* to in the aired version—Worf asking Riker's permission to date Deanna—was a straight rehash of the Klingon's earlier bungled try ("Eye of the Beholder"/270); in it Riker gives his consent, then thinks a moment before surprising both Worf and himself by withdrawing it. Another omitted scene saw Alexander tell his father he knew he'd just been with Troi because "you're always in a good mood after you see her" and in effect give his permission for them to go on; the future Worf was initially a Council member on the Home World. Still another scene, dropped even before the break session as "too contrived," Moore said, would have had Lwaxana Troi in the future bring the news via "long-range trans-porter" ("Bloodlines"/274) of Deanna's recent death—providing a shock to her old friends and a first step in the Worf-Riker thaw. Oddly enough, though the season-long Worf-Troi plot finally veers into "reality" here with their holodeck date, the subject is not dealt with at all in the upcoming *Generations.*

Another lost first-draft scene, setting up Geordi's surprise career as a novelist, saw him in the present confiding that he'd probably always be in Starfleet and disagreeing with Data over great literature, preferring holodeck versions to the original prose—a sly poke at today's nonliterate videophiles. For Geordi, the eternally disappointed dater, his passing reference to his wife "Leah" is a subtle sign that he and Leah Brahms somehow did get together ("Booby Trap"/154, "Galaxy's Child"/190)—though Moore revealed that the first thought was to have him wed Aquiel ("Aquiel"/239). "And everybody said, 'You *really* want to summon those bad vibes, the way that show turned out?'" he recalled. "And we said, 'Maaaaybe not!'"

Crusher's captaincy was another fulfillment of a season-long drive ("Descent, Part II"/253, "Thine Own Self"/268), while Moore noted that the writers were finally able to answer fan demands to *really* get her and Picard together ("Attached"/260)—only to turn that on its ear as well with their eventual divorce. Among the logical turns of Data's life were his easy use of contractions and his position as the Lucasian chair of physics at Cambridge—an homage to not only Isaac Newton but current holder Stephen Hawking, two of his famous holodeck buddies ("Descent"/252). For the record, Critters of the Cinema had ten of its cats on-set as successors to Monster and Brandy's "Spot" ("Descent, Part 2"/253, et al.): Bacall, Uma, Zeke, Bandit, Wendy, Shelley, and doubles Crystal, Sinbad, Sascha, and Justin filling in for Aspen, Caesar, Buffy, and Fido!

Though covering known territory, the "past" timeline provided almost as much originality. The only scene lost here, squeezed out in the later rewrite, would have had a conn officer named "Sut-cliffe" upset at the perverseness of that era's Picard and finally request a transfer—an homage, suggested by Piller, to the origi-nal "fifth" Beatle who likewise left his group on the eve of its greatness. Actor Christian Slater, a big Trek fan who'd cameoed in *Star Trek VI,* was up to play the part until it was penciled out; later tries at getting him in as the Romulan commander or other walk-ons didn't pan out.

Many of the "past" choices were dictated by visual needs, Moore said "Tasha was something that would tie us into the past,

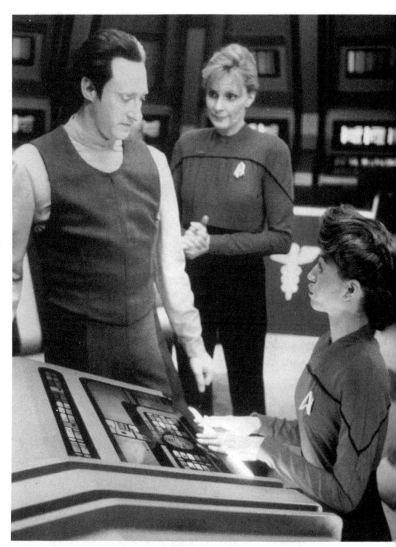

In the future, Professor Data and Captain Crusher discuss what Captain Picard has told them.

and so's O'Brien," said Moore, "and Troi's hair and go-go boots, and the ships on the wall in the obs lounge." Of course, here O'Brien—with Colm Meaney stealing a break from DS9 filming—is given a name and backstory with the *Rutledge* ("The Wounded"/ 186) and model-ship-building ("Booby Trap"/154) long before they were ever heard on the series; though his uniform is the command-division cranberry he first wore in "Farpoint," his pips show the revisionist rank of "chief" ("Realm of Fear"/228) and not ensign as they did then.

The past also recalls the early "babbling" Data—a fun re-creation for the writers as well as Spiner—and the first season's confusing lack of a chief engineer. A clip of "babyfaced" Riker from Season 1 ("The Arsenal of Freedom"/121) was inserted to provide a link to the period; a succeeding viewscreen moment between Picard and an uncomfortable Beverly was trimmed for time. There's also the bit that Picard's trademark "Tea—Earl Grey—hot" is not yet programmed, while the "future" includes the obvi-ous smart comeback to the command by Professor Data's house-

Back in the past, Data and O'Brien meet for the first time.

keeper Jessel—whose name is a repeat *Turn of the Screw* homage by Braga ("Sub Rosa"/266). Also, the "past" Troi recounts that she and Riker cooled off "years ago," although established dates ("Second Chances"/250) would make it only two years before this point.

Even Q's demeanor changed throughout the rewrites, with Berman pushing to pull back the sight gags so the tension would not be undercut by the alien's various guises as a croupier, the Grim Reaper with a scythe, and a game-show host flipping question numbers à la *What's My Line?* Still, de Lancie makes the most of all his chemistry with Stewart in his eighth and final TNG outing. "I did not want to make it a 'Q test,'" Piller said, wishing instead to echo the omnipotent being's observance of humans solving a problem as in the pilot. But Q's influence had to be injected when Stewart, as shooting commenced on the stage, pointed out the logic problem that the anomaly would not have occurred had Q not sent Picard in the time motion in the first place.

Visually, the production staff did all it could within reason to re-create the past *Enterprise*-D as well as postulate its future, such as returning the laid-back conn and ops chairs to the bridge; several details, such as set and carpet color, main viewscreen details, Q's courtroom chair, and so on, were not altered—although the "future" viewer used details from past "alternate" looks ("Parallels"/263, for one). The observation-lounge ships are the originals, safely stored ever since production designer Richard James opted not to return them when the set was rebuilt. Still, with a pricetag of about $281,000 for thirty-one sets to ready or revamp for the time-switches—including four all-new sets—construction chief Al Smutko recalled that his crews worked their fourth weekend in a row after a busy season windup to get the show ready.

Makeup wizard Michael Westmore regretted not being able to experiment more with aging and youthening the regular cast, but kept "the little things" of the cast's prior makeup jobs while opting not to shave Denise Crosby's hair as Yar.

A shuttle "07" named *Galileo* is the art department's parting homage to the original series craft, built for the namesake 1966 episode—though of course the Type 6 shuttle used here was not around at the time of the TNG pilot. The bridge plaque seen hung in the "past" is another Mike Okuda touch, replacing the original's production staff "admirals" with a design including only "authentic" Starfleet personnel mentioned in the series—including the Utopia Planetia technicians seen only weeks before ("Eye of the Beholder"/270).

The show was also a family affair for the visual effects team, with everyone divvying up the chores to have a hand in the last hurrah. With Phil Barberio handling some minatures and compositing, even Ron B. Moore took a moment from his *ST: Generations* duties to handle the transporters: "I can't possibly work on the series seven years and not be involved with the last one." Dan Curry created the "very radiant" anomaly and the primordial Earth, matting in backlit lava and rocks against actual ocean footage enhanced with "Boraxo spray." Artist Eric Chaubin, an Emmy winner for *The Young Indiana Jones Chronicles* and supplier of the Dyson Sphere interior ("Relics"/230), provided Data's futuristic Cambridge environs, one of this season's few matte paintings. Matte touch-ups also enhanced the "Picard" vineyards, shot this time near Temecula because the Lancaster area used previously ("Family"/178) was drably out of season.

The climax of the opticals featured Rick Sternbach's future Klingon ship, built by Greg Jein after a less inexpensive redress of the attack cruiser ("Reunion"/181, et. al.) almost had to make do, in a two-plane battle sequence intended as a Hans Solo-like homage by Moore and storyboarded by Joe Bauer. Beverly's medical vessel, the NCC-58928 *Pasteur,* was christened the Hope class after the World War II hospital ship, a suggestion of Don Beck with the series' previews-producing Beck-Ola. Bill George of ILM had already built the miniature in his spare time to TNG shooting specs for possible use, dubbing it Olympic class and basing it on an early original *Enterprise* concept by Roddenberry and Matt Jefferies, but the series' policy forbid accepting unsolicited models—that is, until Peter Lauritson won approval when a ship was needed in a pinch!

Among other scattered trivia, the first draft originally featured Admiral Blackwell and the Romulan Sirol ("The Pegasus"/264) until final casting of familiar faces Kusatsu ("The Measure of a Man"/135, "Phantasms"/258) and Katsulas, the latter making his first showing as Tomalak since Season 4 ("Future Imperfect"/182) and bringing some of the bravado of his *Babylon 5* ambassador to the part; he'd also appeared as the one-armed man in 1993's film remake of *The Fugitive.* A scene cut for time featured actress Martha Hacket as Androna, who would have been the first-ever depicted Terellian despite her having only two arms (see notes, "Liaisons"/254); as it was, Braga still inserted mention of the Terellian Death Syndrome, perhaps the same as the Terellian Plague

("Genesis"/271). Ensign Chilton was played by Alison Brooks, his girlfriend.

Also, Ogawa's baby dies an unborn hero ("Genesis"/271), with extra B. DeMonbreun finally seen as her elusive husband Andrew Powell ("Lower Decks"/267); Braga's USS *Bozeman* is back ("Cause and Effect"/218, *ST: Generations*), as is a mention of Dr. Selar ("The Schizoid Man"/131, "Remember Me"/179, "Tapestry"/241, "Genesis"/271, "Sub Rosa"/266), Admiral Satie ("The Drumhead"/195), the USS *Yorktown* (1968's "Obsession"), acetychloline (from 1967's "Immunity Syndrome"), a "fleetwide yellow alert" ("The Defector"/158), and Starbase 247 as Shanti's home ("Redemption"/200). Rigel III, Geordi's "future" home, is one of the few planets of that system not already mentioned as harboring a population.

"It's not like it's a perfect episode—it was done in quite a hurry—but I'm quite proud of it," Piller said, "and proud that we've done something very much Star Trek, very much that deal with this strange universe, the universe of ideas." "It's the kind of show that only be done now, and by people who know it forward and backwards—and have done it for a long time," Moore said. "It was a tall order but I think we pulled it off by the skin of our teeth," Braga agreed. "And I got to blow up *three* Enterprises in this one!"

PRODUCTION STAFF CREDITS-SEASON 7

(In usual roll order; numbers in parentheses refer to studio's episode numbers.)

EMMY NOMINEE: **Best Dramatic Series**
Casting: **(*)Junie Lowery-Johnson, C.S.A.; ****Ron Surma**
Music: **John Debney (264); ***Jay Chattaway (253, 255–257, 259, 262, 266, 267, 270, 272, 275, 276); (*)Dennis McCarthy (254, 258, 260, 261, 263, 265, 268, 269, 271, 273, 274, 277–78) (EMMY NOMINEE, music/composition/dramatic underscore, series: "All Good Things . . ."/277–278).**
Main Title Theme: **(*)Jerry Goldsmith, (*)Alexander Courage**
Director of Photography: ********Jonathan West (all but 272, 273); Kris Krosskove (+/*******) (272, 273)**
Production Designer: ****Richard D. James (EMMY CO-NOMINEE, art direction: "Thine Own Self"/268)**
Editor: *****J. P. Farrell (253); ****Steve Tucker (every third episode, 255–276); ******David Ramirez (every third episode, 254–278); Daryl Baskin (every third episode, 256–277); (latter two: EMMY CO-NOMINEE with supervising editor, single-camera editing, series: "All Good Things . . ."/277–278)**
Unit Production Manager: ********Brad Yacobian (+/***)**
First Asst. Director: **Jerry Fleck (all odd-numbered episodes, 253–277 except 275, plus 278); ******Adele G. Simmons (+/*) (all even-numbered episodes, 254–276); Richard Wells (275)**
Second Asst. Director: ********Arlene Fukai**
Costume Designer: *****Robert Blackman (EMMY CO-NOMINEE, outstanding costumes, series: "All Good Things . . ."/277–278)**
Co-Costume Designer: **( )Abram Waterhouse (272–278) (EMMY CO-NOMINEE, outstanding costumes, series: "All Good Things . . ."/277–278)**

Set Decorator: ****Jim Mees (EMMY CO-NOMINEE, art direction: "Thine Own Self"/268)**
Visual effects Producer: **(******)Dan Curry (+/*) (EMMY CO-WINNER, with staff, visual effects: "All Good Things . . ."/277–278)**
Visual Effects Supervisor: ********Ronald B. Moore (+/*) (all odd-numbered episodes, 253–269, plus 277–278); ******David Stipes (all even-numbered episodes, 254–278 except 276, plus 277) (EMMY CO-WINNER, with staff, visual effects: "All Good Things . . ."/277–278; Michael Backauskas (+/******) (271, 273); Philip Barberio (+/******) (275); Joe Bauer (+/******) (276).**
Post Production Supervisor: ********Wendy Knoller (+/***)**
Supervising Editor: **(******) J. P. Farrell (+/***) (EMMY CO-NOMINEE with editors: single-camera editing, series, "All Good Things . . ."/277–278)**
Senior Illustrator/Technical Consultant: **(***)Rick Sternbach (+/*)**
Scenic Artist Supervisor/Technical Consultant: **(***)Michael Okuda (+/*)**
Makeup Designed and Supervised: **(*)Michael Westmore (EMMY CO-NOMINEE, with crew, makeup: "Genesis"/271)**
Art Director: ********Andy Neskoromny (+/****) (EMMY CO-NOMINEE, art direction: "Thine Own Self"/268)**
Set Designer: *****Gary Speckman**
Visual Effects Coordinator: ********Phil Barberio (253–263, then "series"); Michael Backauskas (all odd-numbered episodes, 253–269, plus 277–278) (EMMY CO-NOMINEE with staff, visual effects: "All Good Things . . ."/277–278; Joe Bauer (all even-number episodes, 254–274, plus 277–278); Edward L. Williams (+/******)(275, 277–278)**
Visual Effects Series Coordinator: **Philip Barberio (+/*******) (264–278)**
Visual Effects Associate: ********Edward L. Williams (253–274, 276); Frederick G. Alba (277–278)**
Script Supervisor: **(*)Cosmo Genovese**

Special Effects: (*)**Dick Brownfield**
Property Master: (*)**Alan Sims**
Construction Coordinator: (*)**Al Smutko**
Scenic Artist: ********Jim Magdaleno (all odd-numbered episodes, 253–277, plus 278); Wendy Drapanas (all even-numbered episodes, 254–278, plus 277)**
Hair Designer: ********Joy Zapata (EMMY CO-NOMINEE, with crew, hairstyling: "Firstborn"/273)**
Makeup Artists: ***June Abston-Haymor; Gil Mosko (EMMY CO-NOMINEE, with crew, makeup: "Genesis"/271)**
Hair Stylist: ********Patti Miller; Laura Connolly (258–278) (both EMMY CO-NOMINEES with crew, hairstyling: "Firstborn"/273); Michael Moore (253–55); Lee Crawford (256–257)**
Wardrobe Supervisor: ****Carol Kunz (+/**)**
Sound Mixer: **Alan Bernard, C.A.S. (EMMY CO-WINNER, with crew, sound mixing: "Genesis"/271)**
Camera Operator: **Kris Krosskove (+/******)**
Chief Lighting Technician: ********R. D. Knox**
1st Company Grip: ********Steve Gausche**
Key Costumers: **Kimberley Thompson (all odd-numbered episodes, 253–277, except 257, plus 278); Deborah Hall (even-numbered episodes, 254–276); ******Dave Powell (all even-numbered episodes, 254–276); ******Matt Hoffman (all odd-numbered episodes, 253–273); Carol Kunz (+/****) (257); Maurice Palinski (275, 277–278)**
Music Editor: *Gerry Sackman; E. Gedney Webb (277–278)**
Supervising Sound Editor: ********Mace Matiosian (+/*) (EMMY NOMINEE, with crew, sound editing: "Genesis"/271)**
Sound Editors: ********Miguel Rivera; ******Masanobu Tomita; ******Guy Tsujimoto; ******Ruth Adelman (all EMMY CO-NOMINEES, with crew, sound editing: "Genesis"/271)**
Re-Recording Mixer: **Chris Haire, C.A.S., Doug Davey, Richard Morrison, C.A.S. (all, credited only 277–278) (EMMY CO-WINNERS, with crew, sound mixing: "Genesis"/271)**
Post Production Sound: (*)**Modern Sound**
Production Coordinator: (*)**Diane Overdiek**
Post Production Coordinator: ********Dawn Velazquez**
Assistant Editors: **Lisa de Moraes, Michael Westmore, Jr. (both 277–278)**
Visual Effects Assistant Editor: **Arthur J. Codron (277–278)**
Production Associate: ********Kim Fitzgerald (+/****); Kristine Fernandes (+/****); Dave Rossi, Cheryl Gluckstern, Zayra Cabot (all 277–278)**
Pre-Production Associate: ********Lolita Fatjo (+/**)**
Casting Executive: (*)**Helen Mossler, C.S.A.**
Stunt Coordinator: (***)**Dennis Madalone (253, 254, 256–260, 262, 266–278)**
Location Manager: ( )**Lisa White (253, 256, 260, 265, 277–278)**
Original Set Design: (*)**Herman Zimmerman**
Science Consultant: **Andre Bormanis**
Filmed with PANAVISION Lenses and Cameras: (**)
Monitors: (**)**Sony Corp. of America (253, 256–257, 271, 272–278)**
Special Visual Effects: (*)Industrial Light and Magic (ILM), a division of Lucasfilm Ltd.
Motion Control Photography: (*)**Image "G" (253–276); Erik Nash (277–278) (EMMY CO-WINNER, with staff, visual effects: "All Good Things . . ."/277–278)**
Video Optical Effects: **Digital Magic**
Special Video Compositing: (*)**CIS Hollywood (253–276); Don Lee (277–278)**
On-Line Editing: **John Carroll (277–278)**
Editing Facilities: (*)**Unitel Video (253–276)**

The number of * denotes a returning company or staffer's initial season of credit in that position; ( ) denoted they are an original credited or co-credited person in that position; a (+) following indicates prior TNG work in another position

STAR TREK GENERATIONS

"Rumor Becomes Reality"

Between March 28 and April 15, 1994, the unimaginable happened: three versions of the *Star Trek* universe converged. As *Star Trek: Deep Space Nine*, gained momentum in its sophomore season, *Star Trek: The Next Generation* ended its seven-year run on TV and launched its first widescreen spin-off.

The series and its theatrical successor filmed practically side-by-side as the feature got a head start by shooting scenes that didn't feature TNG regulars. These sections were numerous thanks to a plot that focused in part on Captain James T. Kirk.

Star Trek Generations benefited from the proximity and wisdom of many active creators well versed in Roddenberry's world. Unfortunately, these talented people didn't have much time to recharge their creative energy. Paramount's November 18 release date left only six months between the last hurrah of the series and the movie's debut.

Why the rush? "We were told to" was the simple answer of Rick Berman, executive producer of *Star Trek*s across all formats. "Originally they wanted us to have it out in March. Then they wanted us to have it out in March. Then they said Christmas, and then Thanksgiving. It just kept creeping up on us." But Berman didn't argue. Considering the gulf between the television and film camps in Hollywood, he faced a new world where the stellar success of the TNG series did not automatically guarantee him a blank check.

"The television studio people knew me and how I worked, and trusted me after seven years. But the feature film people didn't, and I had to develop that rapport with them," he said. Apparently something clicked, since Berman was able to provide many of the series' talents with their first feature credentials: director David Carson, post-production producer Peter Lauritson, costume designer Bob Blackman, composer Dennis McCarthy, and especially co-writers Brannon Braga and Ronald D. Moore.

Others from *Star Trek* past and present had already worked in features and were asked aboard again. Production designer Herman "Z" Zimmerman took a sabbatical from DS9 to work on *Generations*. Zimmerman had not only created the look of TNG in the first place, he also worked on the fourth and fifth *Trek* films. Other TNG staffers with feature credits prior to *Gener-*

307

Captain James T. Kirk
and his old friend
Scotty on board the
Enterprise-B.

ations included make up guru Michael West-more, visual effects supervisor Ron B. Moore, hair designer Joy Zapata, graphics scenic artist and *Star Trek*–film veteran Mike Okuda, and set decorator John Dwyer, who had worked on classic *Star Trek* the *Star Trek* films and the debut season of TNG itself. Executive producer Bernie Williams' film and TV credits were particularly impressive, ranging from *Ragtime* to *The Bounty* to the classic British TV series *The Prisoner*.

The TNG movie rumor mill had been working for years. But Berman recalled being formally approached by Paramount motion picture executives Sherry Lansing and John Goldwyn about the film in late 1992, four months before it was announced. Including the first *Star Trek* cast was not part of their original plan, but Berman and the eventual story developers ultimately agreed that including Kirk & Co. "seemed like a good way to pass the baton," as he put it—despite that cast's supposed swan song in 1991's *Star Trek VI: The Undiscovered Country*.

In the interim, a period he recalled as the film's "most delightful part," Berman had begun working on stories with former TNG co-producer Maurice Hurley—who favored a plot in which

Kirk alone is propelled forward to Picard's time—as well as Ron D. Moore and Brannon Braga. (Berman's fellow TNG executive producer Michael Piller turned down the opportunity, objecting to what he viewed as a "competition" for the assignment.)

"Rick called Brannon and I over for a meeting," Moore said, "And there was all this speculation—we thought we were being fired or the show was being cancelled; Brannon was convinced of it, and by the time this meeting came around, I started to believe it too. And we went in and sat down, and Rick got up and was very serious and started to pace a bit, and he said, 'Well, I've just completed two months of negotiations with the studio . . .' and I thought, 'This is it! It IS being cancelled—I don't believe this!' And he went on, '. . . and I've just been asked to produce the next two *Star Trek* movies, and I want you boys to write one of them.' And we just sat there and stared at him, and he went on, and we finally looked at each other out of the corner of our eyes—we were totally blown away, we had no idea. . .! We walked around the studio lot for twenty minutes just to get over our initial shock."

"We were prepared for the worst . . . and Rick Berman has a talent for making you squirm in anticipation," Braga agreed. "But we were thrilled . . . it was like walking on air. And from that day on, it was a pure joy to work on."

With the simple direction to "make a good one" in their initial meeting with the studio's Goldwyn and Don Granger, Moore recalled, he and Braga spent a few more weeks fleshing out their story with Berman. Then they took their TNG hiatus in May for a month-long working vacation in Hawaii. The writers completed a first-draft screenplay dated June 1 before diving back into the hectic series.

Throughout that stage, the bare bones of the plot came together. The original series cast would be used in a prologue, bridged to the TNG era only by Whoopi Goldberg's Guinan and a mystery that engulfs them all. The script also called for the destruction of the *Enterprise* with a climactic saucer landing planetside. And finally, Kirk would die after he helped "save the galaxy" one last time. The writers received one studio directive: write for an audience who isn't necessarily familiar with the TV series and its backstories.

The saucer crash sequence, inspired by a drawing from the *ST:TNG Writer's Technical Manual*, had first been proposed as the cliff-hanger for Moore's original version of "All Good Things. . . ," a proposed sixth-season-ender. Kirk's death came out of the early brainstorming between Moore, Braga and Berman. "We wanted to aim high, do something different and big, and set ourselves apart," Moore recalled. "We knew we had to have a strong Picard story arc, so what are the profound things in a man's life he has to face? Mortality tops the list." But who? The idea of killing off a TNG cast member was nixed, and then someone brought up the notion of Kirk's *death*. "I don't remember who said it," Moore added, "But we all sorta looked around and said, 'That might be it.' "

Surprisingly, the studio had few qualms about this turning point in *Star Trek* history. They only asked if William Shatner had been consulted about Kirk's demise. "We first met with him, and he only brought it up once," Moore said, referring to the point that would cause controversy when news of it leaked out to the fans. "We explained how it worked into the story, the theme of mortality, and giving Kirk his final moment . . . He nodded his head and said 'I see that'—and that was it! We kept waiting for him to drop the other shoe, but he never did."

Story development was fun. Production was work. Berman found himself addressing one problem after another. "There were a lot of budgetary battles that had to be fought in the early stages, people I was not used to working with," he recalled. After initial budgets had been run, the huge scope of the picture—with a wish list of true-life location shooting in Hawaii, Idaho and the Midwest—was soon pared down from well over $30 million to about $25 million.

Then there was fallout from negotiating with *two* eras of *Trek* actors. Early headlines jolted many fans with the news that Leonard Nimoy had not only turned down an invitation to direct the feature, but would not even appear as Spock. Soon afterwards DeForest Kelley also declined to appear. While Moore and Braga had provided for all seven of the '60s crew in the initial prologue, only Shatner's Kirk figured into the plot. "The way the story evolved had nothing to do with Leonard—it was just the way we put the story together," Berman said. "In the case of Leonard and De Kelley, they each thought they had made appropriate goodbyes in *Star Trek VI* and there was no reason to bring the characters back for this prologue." As Nimoy told the *Star Trek: The Official Fan Club Magazine*, "I told him [Berman] what my concerns were with the story and the script, and he told me there wasn't enough time left to do what I was suggesting . . . My response was 'I am sad about that; I wish I had been brought in earlier.' " The TNG cast also trod a bumpy road to the negotiating table. "All the actors wanted to do the movie," Berman recalled. "But here was a 130-page script with their character all throughout, and it put them in a very good position in terms of negotiating. It was very traumatic in terms of the pressure that went on both sides . . . It was a tense time for a while until all those deals were wrapped

Captain Kirk greets
Commander Chekov.

up, all the emotions and the pressures of the season and series wrapping up. But I always predicted they would all sign to make the movie, and of course they did."

Meanwhile, as of March 16, 1994 the script reflected not only budget and cast changes but producer, studio, director and actor notes as well. In the prologue of the first draft, an admiral presiding over 1701-B's commissioning ceremony warned Captain Harriman not to let the legend "get you in trouble out there." After a cute sequence during which older officers get trained by their "B" counterparts, the *Lakul*'s distress call forces Harriman to remind the oldsters that the ship is really his.

The writers felt that version of the scene was charming, but Shatner was concerned that the joke went too far. In response Moore and Braga devised another opening. This version featured the original cast crammed into an interminable turbolift ride. McCoy mutters to Spock, "I haven't been this close to you in years" and their one-time captain reminisces about his strenuous outdoor pursuits . . . again.

In the final script, Kirk was joined by only two former crewmates, Scotty and Chekov. James Doohan and Walter Koenig got to split the lines intended for others. McCoy's bit about an unstaffed sickbay went to the Russian, while Scotty's "I have a theory" exchange with Kirk was originally Spock's. Sulu's two lines were inherited by his daughter, Demora, who was originally envisioned as Chekov's daughter. In response to Shatner's notes about Kirk's overage exploits, the January 28 fourth draft had an even earlier scene depicting McCoy and Spock retrieving the orbital skydiver in an Iowa wheatfield. The location scene was shot, but dropped later due to editing problems.

Among the TNG characters, Picard's personal tragedy was initially limited to Robert's heart attack. But then Patrick Stewart suggested that a horrific fire killing both brother Robert and nephew René ("Family"/78) would add emotional impact. Picard's initial Nexus sequence then became a Christmas fantasy, rather than a clandestine meeting with a 12-year-old Robert at home.

As for Data, Moore said the team had done "so much with him" over the series' course that they had to take the next logical step. "It *is* the movies; we don't have to worry about protecting the character on a weekly basis anymore. And giving him the emotions chip opens new doors for us," he explained. "It's Pinocchio moving a big step forward, but he's still not quite human." A sequence the writers considered but dropped before the third draft revealed Data giggling during a holodeck version of *Romeo and Juliet*'s suicide scene while Geordi tried to adjust the quirks of the chip.

Moore also thanked TNG collegaue Jeri Taylor for early notes that led to the entire holodeck boat scene. Originally, the film's 24th century era opened at the observatory with two Rosencrantz-and-Guildenstern type ensigns lamenting their boredom. Their ennui is shattered as a Warbird decloaks and its crew invades the station. Just as one ensign is about to be killed by a Romulan soldier, Picard's *Enterprise* emerges from behind the sun's corona, and the cavalry comes to the rescue again. "Jeri felt it wasn't charming enough—just another big action sequence," Moore said. He recalled that she suggested an opening with "something fun"—such as "Picard pushing an egg across the floor with his nose in some crazy games in Ten-Forward."

Berman agreed on the light approach, and the co-writers brainstormed again, coming up with the nautical setting that harkens back to *Star Trek*'s roots. Worf's promotion was conceived as the reason all were gathered on the ship. In early drafts he was merely made to walk the plank and was pushed in, but TNG's cast grew concerned about their characters' dignity and the current version was added. Worf was still wearing his 19th century outfit while he dispatched a Romulan until the third draft; Riker was accidentally stepping on Spot in the holodeck through the fourth draft.

A ten-page sequence that followed the crew after the saucer crash was not trimmed until the fourth draft. The well-armed Duras sisters and a few surviving henchmen turned up to demand a shuttle after they fled their ship in escape pods. Riker responded to the theft by sending Data to deal with the sisters, since only an android could

survive their sexual omnivorousness. A bedraggled Data finally emerged to announce that "I believe I have opened negotiations" just as one of his arms fell off. He is later disassembled to help repair the shuttle systems and computer. Though he and Moore were sorry to lose this story arc, Braga noted that its demise paved the way for more mountaintop introspection between Soran and Picard, the screened and cloaked launcher, and Lursa and B'Etor's supposed "death." "In the end, everything helped fine-tune the script," he said. "I feel real good about it."

Meanwhile, Nimoy's decision to pass up the chance at directing allowed Berman to offer Carson his first shot at a theatrical feature. Carson's *Star Trek* résumé already included the two-hour DS9 pilot "Emissary" as well as prior stints with TNG characters Guinan ("Yesterday's Enterprise"/63) and the Duras sisters ("Redemption II"/101). He also had experience in theater, documentaries, news, music videos, and dramatic programs in both his native England and the U.S., including *Sherlock Holmes*, *L.A. Law*, and *Northern Exposure*. "My guess will be that David Carson is probably going to have a major film career available to him very, very soon, based on what he's done with this picture," Berman predicted. Carson enlisted Berman's aid to talk the studio into backing his costly choice for cinematographer—John Alonzo, the Oscar-nominated Hollywood veteran of *Chinatown*, *Scarface* and *Blue Thunder*. Alonzo was a self-professed late convert to *Star Trek* fandom. "My wife and I sat down one weekend to watch about 15 episodes of *The Next Generation*, and I really got hooked!" admitted Alonzo, who called the two lead captains "Billy" and "Patty" around the set.

The two worked well with Zimmerman, who was given total control over all visual elements "except the actors," he said. "It's been a real treat for me," Zimmerman commented. "I've had more freedom to design this show, the seventh feature, than I've had on any of the other features, or even on the original designs for *The Next Generation*." Prior to *Generations*, he had been working with leftover sets from the previous *Star Trek* films. This time, he and illustrator John Eaves were allowed to design the solar observatory and the *Lakul* from scratch. They also customized the *Enterprise-B* by adding teal-green accents.

From the start, both the writing and the design teams aimed to stay true to the feel of TNG. At the same time, they wanted to make a film that could stand on its own for an audience that included people unfamiliar with the series. To maintain that balance, they took several visual liberties with the sets, which no longer needed less realistic and flatter light colors to speed the work of time-conscious TV lighting crews. 1701-D's main bridge received a copper ceiling and darker brown walls with silver metallic accents. The facelift also included the aft consoles' extension over the emergency wall storage bins. Wide ramps were installed at those points, halved to provide two more seated consoles. In addition, the ready room received a wider window and a bigger aquarium.

"I remember David and Herman talking about changing the bridge and someone said, 'Gee, the Trekkies are used to it this way,'" Alonzo recalled. "And I said, 'Maybe the Trekkies when they see it in big scope will say, 'So that's what it's supposed to look like!'" Zimmerman echoed that view, noting the new level of detail added to the bridge and a resculpted ceiling frame required by cinema cameras' higher level of resolution. "I hope the fans will say, 'Oh that's what I've been seeing on that little TV screen all these years!'"

One unintentional change on the "D" bridge was the captain's chair—after crews discovered, 50 hours before filming, that it had been stolen! With no time to lose, shop crews worked 18 hours straight to fashion a new chair out of fiberglass molded over foam built on an old first-season frame. Luckily, the thief had left behind the chair's cast-iron base.

The budget played a big role in the sets' design—but not always in a negative way. As director Carson recalled, the deflector room scene actually benefited from financial constraints: the long horizontal set Zimmerman had envisioned was turned on its end into a two-story area. "That gave us the most wonderfully interesting camera angles," Carson said. "Making the approach different, from horizontal to vertical, meant dealing with the budget in a creative way like that." Dwyer added, "Herman had a good time designing that; he ran through it about four times by himself just to make sure he had plenty of stuff for Shatner to do."

Likewise, the solar observatory's Ops area was designed to be built from the shell of the "B" bridge, itself redressed from the old *Excelsior* bridges. The spacedock foyer had its windows filled in and wall logo removed to become the "B" sickbay, featuring all-new biobed designs and a return to futuristic thermal materials for linens instead of Nick Meyer's wool blankets from *Star Trek VI*. The gunner's chair and a few wall pieces were all that remained of the *Star Trek V* Klingon bridge, which featured a captain's chart for each Duras sister and ten feet more forward space. This set also included the same floor grating used in the walls of the *Enterprise* transporter room and Q's court. The bunkroom support columns, with a new paint job and

Scotty finds a way to save the *Enterprise-B* from the Nexus.

graphics, became small probes at the observatory.

Along with Dwyer and Sandy Veneziano, reprising her role as TNG's first-season art director, Zimmerman also benefited from the work of graphic artist Mike Okuda. "We had more video monitors on the bridges in this movie than in all of Star Trek V and VI combined," he noted. Some 35 monitors lined the "B" bridge conoles alone.

That bridge's design, Zimmerman noted, incorporated many touches intended to indicate the concept evolution from Kirk's first *Enterprise* through to Picard's. For example, weapons control was placed behind the captain for the first time, and there were refinements in the split Ops and Con stations as first seen on the *Excelsior* in Star Trek: VI.

Zimmerman said he conceived the new, enlarged stellar cartography lab—trimmed from three to two stories in the early planning—as the "jewel" of the *Enterprise*-D. "It's only one scene, but it's where we discover all the astronomical facts that we have to know to understand the end of the picture," he noted. "The story has great scientific appeal, and it needs visual support—and where it gets that support will be here."

Coordinating with visual effect supervisor Ron B. Moore, Zimmerman also put series illustrator Rick Sternbach's cosmic art on display, as well as three huge panels sporting Okudagram star charts that hung from the stage rafters with the lights. The panels would easily switch out when the huge bluescreen panels required for optical animation had to be used. "We shot that sequence in three days," recalled Ron B. Moore. "Nobody thought we'd be able to do it, but with these lights and rigging it just worked!"

With energetic FX house ILM handling the exterior space scenes under the direction of John Knoll, Moore was able to oversee nearly half the film's opticals at the series' regular vendors like CIS—even on a tight five-month schedule—thanks to the sophistication of the processes developed for the TV series. Along with stellar cartography, the non-ILM "routine" effects included a new 3-D transporter, the various phasers, cloaks and forcefields, the Picard Christmas ornament, and a subtle enhancement of Data's emotion program.

One of the last decisions to be firmed up before shooting was the chief villain and supporting cast, since so many roles were, in effect, pre-cast by *Trek*'s regulars old and new. "We went through many, many conundrums before we came to him," Carson recalled of the casting of Malcolm McDowell, whose credits included *A Clockwork Orange* and *Time After Time*. "*Star Trek* scripts are not full of grunts and groans; they're quite literate, and you need actors who can use those words. And he's one of those very fine actors who can turn a word into something very special by the way he treats it. He's absolutely a match for them all."

The director also revealed an even later decision. Practically on the eve of filming, the feature's think-tank opted not to use Blackman's new Starfleet uniforms. The new design featured the three duty colors in a two-piece outfit with a jacket-flap motif reminiscent of the movies' maroon tops. An earlier Blackman creation, the DS9 jumpsuit, was chosen instead. "When we eventually saw all of the costumes together," Carson recalled, "we decided that perhaps with the bridge and the other refurbished sets, we needed to strengthen those ties to these characters that people have seen for seven years, to keep that familiarity, and we decided changing the costumes might be too much of a jump."

"Heat and Harshness"

As rewrites wrapped and cameras readied to roll the cast and crew of *Generations* got a lesson in the differences between TV and film media, recalled Ronald D. Moore. "It was like the script we did for television in a *month*—it was just intensely focused and we kept doing it and churning it out—I've never written so many pages in such a short amount of time as I did on the final episode," he said. And then the feature, for a *year* . . . they were two very different experiences, as far as development and getting them done. And the irony is, they were both shooting at the same time there for a week or so."

STAR TREK GENERATIONS

Stardate: 48632.4 ▪ Code: ST:G
TNG Story #177 ▪ Opened November 18, 1994

Directed by: **David Carson**
Story by: **Rick Berman & Ronald D. Moore & Brannon Braga**
Screenplay by **Ronald D. Moore & Brannon Braga**

CAST
Capt. Jean-Luc Picard: **Patrick Stewart**
Cmdr. William Thomas Riker: **Jonathan Frakes**
Lt. Cmdr. Data: **Brent Spiner**
Lt. Cmdr. Geordi La Forge: **LeVar Burton**
Lt. Cmdr. Worf: **Michael Dorn**
Cmdr. Beverly Crusher, M.D.: **Gates McFadden**
Cmdr. Deanna Troi: **Marina Sirtis**
Dr. Tollan Soran: **Malcolm McDowell**
Capt. Montgomery "Scotty" Scott: **James Doohan**
Cmdr. Pavel Andreivich Chekov: **Walter Koenig**
Capt. James Tiberius Kirk, ret.: **William Shatner**
Capt. John Harriman: **Alan Ruck**
Ensign Demore Gulu: **Jacqueline Kim**
1701-B Science Officer: **Jenette Goldstein**
1701-B Com Officer: **Thomas Kopache**
1701-B Navigator: **Glenn Morshower**
1701-B Lieutenant: **Tim Russ**
Journalist No. 1: **Christine Jansen**
Journalist No. 2: **John Putch**
Journalist No. 3: **Tommy Hinckley**
Ensign Hayes: **Michael Mack**
Lieutenant Farrell: **Dendrie Taylor**
Lt. Alyssa Ogawa, R.N.: **Patti Yasutake**
Transporter chief: **Granville Ames**
Decurity officer Paskall: **Henry Marshall**
Girl with teddy bear: **Brittany Parkyn**
Computer voice: **Majel Barrett**
Lursa: **Barbara March**
B'Etor: **Gwyneth Walsh**
Klington guard: **Rif Hutton**
Klingon helmsman: **Brian Thompson**
El-Aurian survivors: **Marcy Goldman, Jim Krestaiuce, Judy Levitt, Kristopher Logan, Gwen van Dam**

Picard's "wife": **Kim Braden**
René Picard: **Christopher James Miller**
"Matthew Picard": **Matthew Collins**
"Mimi Picard": **Mimi Collins**
"Thomas Picard": **Thomas Alexander Dekker**
"Madison Picard": **Madison P. Dinton**
"Olivia Picard": **Olivia Hack**
Stunts: **John Nowak, Don Pulford, Randy Hall, Bernie Pock, Pat Tallman, Eric Stabenau, Michael Haynes**
Stunt coordinator: **Bud Davis**

Interrupted during a Holodeck party for Worf's promotion aboard a 19th century sailing vessel, Picard is stunned to learn that his brother and nephew on Earth—his only blood relatives—have been killed in a fire. The shock leads him to ponder his life choices as "the last Picard," but there's little time for grieving: Romulans have attacked an unarmed stellar lab, and Starfleet needs to know why.

La Forge and Data—who is at times to be overwhelmed by the long-delayed installation of his emotions chip—soon unravel the mystery. The Romulans' target is trilithium, a potential super-explosive that Dr. Tolian Soran has secretly stabilized for use on the station. The scientist is a long-lived El-Aurian like Guinan—and a survivor of a temporal energy anomaly that claimed the life of Starfleet's legendary James T. Kirk some 78 years earlier.

Soran is rescued by the Duras sisters, his backers, who are hoping to use the weapon to control the Klingon Empire. On their ship he tortures hostage La Forge to get him to reveal what Picard knows about his incredible project—the systematic destruction of whole stars to reroute the energy ribbon so that Soran can be reunited with the part of him retained in its "nexus," a joyful otherworld of eternal fantasies.

When the *Enterprise* heads for Soran's next target, the populated Veridian system, Picard exchanges himself for La Forge, who unknowingly allows the Duras sisters to penetrate the starship's shields. In a brief battle the Klingons' vessel is destroyed, but Riker must order the drive section evacuated and separated when the *Enterprise* suffers a warp core breach. In turn, the shock wave from that explosion slams the saucer section into Veridian III's surface, where the survivors pick up the pieces after a nerve-wracking ride.

Meanwhile, Picard confronts Soran one-on-one on Veridian III where the manic scientist has built another star-killer. Shocked, Picard can't stop the weapon and is swept away with Soran as the planet and 1701-D's survivors perish in the stellar cataclysm.

But Picard finds himself in the nexus, barely able to shake off the seductive Christmas scene of a family he never had in real life—including a still-healthy nephew René. A shadow of Guinan then helps him find none other than Kirk, who himself must be convinced to abandon numerous happy "what-ifs" to help Picard defeat Soran by leaving the nexus. They do, but Kirk gives his life in the struggle. Though their ship cannot be salvaged, the now-safe 1701-D survivors are rescued—and Picard comes to measure his life with less regret.

Captain John Harriman and Ensign Demora Sulu man the helm.

Even with the early budget scale-back, *Generations* still made heavy and effective use of location shooting, perhaps more so than any prior *Star Trek* film including the dramatic climax filmed over eight days atop a rise in the remote "Valley of Fire" north of Las Vegas, a harsh site that director Carson recalled all too well. "At one point we got blown off the rock by a very fierce dust and sand storm, and I got a piece of it in my eye and cut my cornea," he said. "So I had to spend a day directing with a patch over my eye. Fortunately a cornea heals very quickly. I'd hoped a little John Ford might rub off on me if I wore it a few more days, but I thought I'd rather see properly out of both eyes on that ledge!"

From the highest plateau accessible by truck, the slope climbed about 70 feet to a staging area, then another 25 feet at a 40-degree slope to the launcher site before the final, nearly vertical climb of 160 or so feet to the peak, requiring ropes and a full-time safety crew. Everything from sun shade, to film equipment, to liquids for rehydration had to be hauled or carried up. Most in the cast and crew carried umbrellas or wore hats as protection against the blazing sun, with the three actors involved in the sequence doffing

their hats only to shoot takes atop the bare upthrust of rock. The costumed actors were especially uncomfortable in the 110-degree heat, especially Shatner in his all-wool maroon uniform.

On top of all that, the Gatorade some crew members drank began attracting bees. "The heat and harshness slowed us down a lot, but it was a very beautiful place to be," said Carson, whose production office back at the headquarters hotel in Las Vegas just happened to be based out of one Room 1701.

Shooting at other locations proved more comfortable, but still challenging. Picard's chalet was actually a private house in Pasadena, where all but three items were moved in for the feature, including the custom-built carousel. The barn and horse jump was filmed at actor Noah Beery Jr.'s ranch, and Kirk's cabin, whose owner gained a new kitchen and staircase built for the movie, sat atop a one-lane road that got so clogged that the plan to use a hawk in the shots was cancelled when the trainers' vehicle got blocked out of the area.

Also memorable was the TNG cast's first sequence, shot on the *Lady Washington*, docked at

Captain Picard on the holodeck.

Marina del Rey in the Los Angeles area. For five days the ship—*a full-scale replica of the first American ship to explore the Pacific Northwest and visit Japan*—set out before sunup to drop anchor for filming a few miles offshore, with the filming and nautical crews totalling 50-plus. Dwyer and Zimmerman covered signs of the boat's actual name on its bell and stern. The on-screen wheel was a phony that replaced the ship's real steering tiller. Troi turned the wheel over to the boat's real chief, Captain Bill, whose crew appeared on camera and lent a few more authentic terms of nautical slang to enhance Navy-vet Moore's dialogue.

To cover a fogged-in day offshore, Ron Moore devised a way to film scenes wth the holodeck arch on the dock rather than aboard the cramped ship—but he still had to overcome the rocking motion of the boat when matching up the live and matted-in footage! The cast and crew's equipment and personal effects were stored in bags decorated in period decor. Each bag read "Doohan (Dwyer's wife) & Dwyer, Ship's Chandlers, Est. 1840, Fine India Hemp Lashings."

"Trivial Matters"

Despite its feature-film proportions, Dwyer still applied the austere approach throughout *Generations*: Geordi's torture chair was a redecorated birthing chair, with hand props from "dirtied up" nosehair clippers and little flashlights. Kirk's deflector room components were highly modified back massagers; Starfleet sickbay items were coin-changers, remote control units and back massagers attached to small thermos bottles; barbell-shaped neck massagers became Klingon bunk "headrests"; and—in the finest tradition of the original series as well as TNG—packing for resistors and TVs, and radiator covers became set decor forms, especially on the Klingon bridges. "That is standing operating procedure around here, dating back to Matt Jefferies," Dwyer noted.

Dwyer and Okuda couldn't resist adding touches only a longtime fan could detect, thereby paying homage to Matt Jefferies, the original *Star Trek* art designer. Along with a display of old phasers mixed in with antique guns—and "1701" plates originally designed to be Cardassian dishes in DS9's first season—Kirk's rustic cabin featured a three-panel backlit showcase displaying an original *Enterprise,* a replica of its simple bridge dedication plaque, and photo of his crew from the film era. The cabin also sported an original painting of a cowboy on horseback at night, watching a shooting star in the background while looking out over the real-life Alabama Hills adjacent to the location site; the cowboy's face looked surprisingly like James T. Kirk's! And in Picard's "chateau," an artist was commissioned to create three of Picard's heroic forebears: one in the flowing locks of a Trafalgar-era French officer, one in an old Starfleet uniform, and a third naval Frenchman with a burr cut and Prussian spiked mustache from World War I—this was the portrait Dwyer said Stewart liked the most. All three used the actor as a model, and he got permission to keep his choice while auctioning the other two off for charity.

The "B" sickbay included animated computer recreations of the original series' sickbay bed monitors, complete with floating indicators and blinking red pulse lights. Meanwhile, the "B" bridge monitors not only carried the red-alert graphic of its *Star Trek: The Motion Picture* forebear, but featured its round monitors as

well—this time, Okuda noted, *without* square-format readouts.

Another Okudagram data scroll revealed the *S.S. Lakul* as registry NFT-7793, a Warp-4 rated craft of Whorfin class with "YPS" pulse fusion (*Buckaroo Banzai* in-jokes) with a flight start of SD 9683.3, while its doomed sister ship of 267 passengers and crew setting out SD 9683.7 was NFT-1327, the *Robert Fox.* The latter was named for the ambassador of 1967's "Amageddon Game," as suggested by writer Moore.

Trivia-minded old-timers will also note the observatory's placards in '60s *Trek* type, perhaps including some marked "duotronic systems" (from 1968's "Ultimate Computer" and "The Ensigns of Command"/149), and perhaps even the curve-neck Dickey brewery "Saurian brandy" bottle from the original series, used in the space-dock banquet.

However, some choices were still a matter of budget, not sentiment. Though all may not show up on camera, the stellar observatory debris included many props familiar to faithful TNG viewers—the lab elevator that housed Lal ("The Offspring"/164) and Locutus ("Best of Both Worlds, Part 2"/175), a nacelle plasma injector

The Klingon Captain Lursa threatens Dr. Soran.

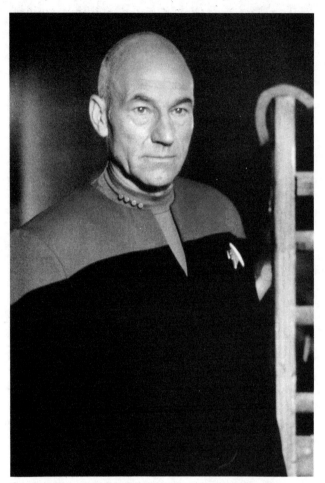

Captain Picard in Captain Kirk's farmhouse in the Nexus.

("Eye of the Beholder"/270), and the original small-scale Galactic Cartography bubble console (see in "Lessons"/145), which in its larger format is still labeled for Deck 12 ("Liaisons"/154), in Room 1072.

The shuttlecraft is new to TNG but not *Star Trek*: it's the stunt double exterior used in the *Star Trek V* hangar deck crash of that film's large *Galileo 5* craft later cut down to become TNG's Type 6 shuttle ("Darmok"/202, "Parallels"/263, etc.) Here it's lettered as the *Hawking*, once again honoring the onetime real-life guest star ("Descent"/252).

To fill a late request by Carson for some probe "guts," estimated at about $4,000 each, DS9 art staffer Anthony Frederickson cobbled together painted and striped plastic funnels, bowls and piping—all for about $150 total. The rockets they

adorned—and the ones fired—were actual civilian products built to Zimmerman's specs by Public Missile, an East Coast firm. A primary and two backups were ordered, with a full-blown launch landing so far away, Dwyer recalled, that the park ranger standing by ordered its remains "from four canyons over" be retrieved. "We only needed it to go 60 or 70 feet out of frame," the decorator chuckled.

The cast was peppered with familiar *Star Trek* faces and other notables, including actors Ruck, perhaps best remembered as put-upon best friend Cameron in 1986's *Ferris Bueller's Day Off*, and Russ, who had not only played a terrorist ("Starship Mine"/144) and a Klingon (DS9's "Invasive Procedures") but would soon join the *Voyager* cast as *Star Trek*'s first regular cast Vulcan since Spock. Lursa and B'Etor, of course, were old vets ("Redemption"/199–200, "Firstborn"/274, and DS9's "Past Prologue"); actor Mack had previously been a Romulan ("The Pegasus"/264) while his character had already been mentioned ("Genesis"/271). Also appearing were TNG returnees Putch ("Coming of Age"/119, "A Matter of Honor"/224), Kopache ("The Next Phase"/224, "Emergence"/275), Morshower ("Peak Performance"/147, "Starship Mine"/244), Braden ("The Loss"/84), and Thompson ("A Matter of Honor,"/234 and a Dosi in DS9's "Rules of Aquisition").

Ironically, the players also included Goldstein, the actress whose performance as the tough space marine Vasquez in *Aliens* inspired Tasha Yar's character in TNG's embryonic days. In addition, the special TV/film production continuity allowed many of the series' extras and stand-ins to find work here—including felines Brandy and Monster as "Spot" (see "Descent, Part II"/253)—to lend even more subtle links to the series.

In case there's any doubt, Moore confirmed the movie is set within a year of "All Good Things . . ." (277-78), around 2371. That puts the 1701-B's christening at 2293. This estimate is backed up by Data's 34-year "search for humanity," with TNG's eight-year run added to the 26 mentioned in "Datalore" (114). This reckoning means that Demora Sulu was born circa 2270, or during the time of the *Enterprise* refit before the V'ger incident (*Star Trek: The Motion Picture*), after her father's first missions with Kirk.

At last, much of Guinan's elusive past is nailed down, although writer Moore admitted some of it is "shaky." Her people are distant enough to be dispersed by the Borg, but near enough for their ships to be bound for Earth, which remains unaware of the attackers ("Q Who"/142). However, Guinan had earlier said she was not on her homeworld at the time of the Borg attack, which may explain why her arrival in 2293 with other refugees is much less than the century span she dated the tragedy back to in 2365 ("Q Who"/242). It is known that she was on Earth earlier ("Time's Arrow"/126) and clashed with Q a century before the Borg's overrunning of her people, when she went by a different name ("Q Who"/142). Interestingly, while Guinan's bio file was accessible enough, she had apparently managed to keep her origins a secret to all but old friend Picard ("The Child"/127). By the way, the set identified her quarters as Deck 08/Room 3150, which have an ethereal look with floating and multiple candle wicks, designed with Whoopi Goldberg's input.

The writers revealed most of the proper names were of nondescript origin with a few exceptions: the El-Aurians are named for the ancient Hebrew "angel of flame," while Kirk's would-be wife Antonia comes from Antonia Napoli, a former intern and co-story writer on "Journey's End" (272). Kirk's dog Butler was originally Jake, named for Moore's elder pooch who later died during filming, but Shatner changed it on-set to honor his own dog who had just died. Finally, Soran early on was "Moresh," later changed to avoid any perceived parallels with the late David Koresh, another fate-obsessed charismatic leader. The script is filled with trivia, beginning with the Dom Perignon bottled dated "2265," for the first year of Kirk's mission; the 1701-D's rescue ship, the *Farragut*, was named for his first post-Academy assignment. Though actor Shatner's equine hobby is well known, Kirk's horsemanship was not revealed until *Star Trek V*—unlike Picard's ("Pen

Pals"/141, "The Loss"/184, "Starship Mine"/244); Data's emotions chip finally found a home ("Brothers"/177, "Descent"/252, "Inheritance"/262). We learn also that the Ktarians ("The Game"/206, "Birthright, Part I"/242, "Timescape"/251, "Liaisons"/254, "Phantasms"/258) are known in Federation circles as far back as Kirk's time, while the Picard at the first Martian Colony harks back to an historic legal document (1966's "Courtmartial") and at least one variety of the Klingon Bird of Prey is the Class D-12.

We see another bathtub on the *Enterprise* ("Genesis"/271), though Dwyer noted Roddenberry's original dictum about water storage problems leading to the use of sonic showers (*Star Trek: The Motion Picture*, "Naked Now"/103, "The Game"/206). Also, the Amargosa star was located within the same-named diaspora ("Schisms"/131). Hayes was previously mentioned ("Genesis"/171) as was Forkas III, Worf's *bat'telh* tournament site ("Parallels"/163). The never-depicted Breen ("The Loss"/84, "Interface"/155) used disruptors on a par with the Klingons and Romulans ("Hero Worship"/111), here labeled up to Type III. And the *Bozeman* appeared to have been returned to active duty, judging by a graphic that mentions Captain Bateson ("Cause and Effect"/118).

Other fun graphics include the journalists from "FNN" (Federation News Network), "SFB" (Starfleet Broadcasting), and "EBC" (Earth Broadcasting Co.); the various photon-tube probes labeled as *Mark B*, *Mark IV*, *Mark V*—and *Mark VI*, as with Spock's "casket" tube from *Star Trek II* and *Star Trek III*.

Finally, ILM's visuals provided some of *Star Trek*'s most extensive all-computer opticals; no miniature was ever built for the *Lakul*, for instance, and it and the entire energy ribbon/*Enterprise*-B sequence were all computer-generated images (CGI). So were the 1701-D's warp effect, the stellar collapses, and the Veridian III planet itself. (Though the model for the planet was digitally wrapped with a very organic basic element: a square-yard sheet of copper etched with various acids for several days and then retinted after scanning.)

Dr. Soran threatens
Captain Picard on
Veridian III.

Meanwhile, tradition held for the observatory model, built by model shop foreman John Goodson, as well as the revised *Excelsior*-class 1701-B with add-on pieces per Zimmerman's design. While the Klingon Bird of Prey was used intact, the crew rebuilt the spindly 1979 *Star Trek: The Motion Picture* spacedock, heavily damaged after years of storage, and flattened it to better fit the *Excelsior*-style shape. They also covered its old orange paint job with a new gray one.

Because of the ship-sep filming required, the ILM's original six-foot 1701-D model was hauled out for the first time since the Borg attack ("The Best of Both Worlds, Part II"/175). Stripped down to its frame, it was heavily rewired and noticeably resurfaced to stand up to the level of detail that movie lighting reveals. A special 12-foot saucer was built for the crash sequence on a 40-by-80 foot planet-surface model, enchanced by bluescreened trees and distance matte paintings, with its extreme lip close-ups shot using an 18-inch-wide edge piece.

After the crash, members of Knoll's ILM team got on camera as the uniformed crew evacuating on the saucer top. This involved a matte-in shot for bluescreen in their parking lot, with the matted-in "Farragut rescue shuttles" culled from TNG's model as well as the bubble-domed *Star Trek III* spacedock vehicle and the executive shuttle from *Star Trek VI*, the basis of the *Jenolen* ("Relics"/130).

"A Few Missions Longer"

For any feature-film franchise, the box office books tell the tale, and though no plans were immediately spelled out before *Generations'* release, the short term all but assured the continuation of the TNG films. The feature capped an incredible year for Gene Roddenberry's one-time "failure"—but all booms come to an end. Or do they? "People ask, 'Can you make too many trips to the well?'" Rick Berman said in May 1994. "I think the answer is yes, you can. But I think we've been very careful that the most recent trip, *Voyager*, won't be that one-too-many-trips. We try to keep all these series different and that's not only good for the writers, it's good for the producers. It's good for everybody to skew a little differently on each of the series. And as long as we can keep them interesting to us and keep them challenging to us, I think they'll work with the audience."

So the familiar stars' trailers along Avenue P outside Stages 8 and 9 departed for the first time in seven years—an eternity in the entertainment world—though they'd soon be replaced by those of another *Star Trek* incarnation. In late May, with live filming wrapped and the future vague, the 1701-D's bridge was smashed apart by wrecking crews, with no fanfare, with no audience. But the "bones" of Ten-Forward and the sickbay/engineering/corridor complex would be retained and refurbished for *Voyager*, ensuring that "Hollywood's oldest standing sets"—and a chunk of one of its most enduring and successful stories—will be around a few missions longer.

ST: TNG Episode Index

Epis.	Air No.	Title	Code	Stardate	Aired Week of:	Page
721/101–102	1	Encounter at Farpoint	ef	41153.7	9/28/87	23
103	2	The Naked Now	nn	41209.2	10/5/87	32
104	3	Code of Honor	ch	41235.25	10/12/87	33
105	10	Haven	hv	41294.5	11/30/87	34
106	5	Where No One Has Gone Before	wn	41263.1	10/26/87	36
107	4	The Last Outpost	lo	41386.4	10/19/87	37
108	6	Lonely Among Us	la	41249.3	11/2/87	38
109	7	Justice	ju	41255.6	11/9/87	40
110	8	The Battle	ba	41723.9	11/16/87	40
111	9	Hide and Q	hq	41590.5	11/23/87	42
112	15	Too Short a Season	ts	41309.5	2/8/88	43
113	11	The Big Goodbye	bg	41997.7	1/11/88	44
114	12	Datalore	da	41242.4	1/18/88	46
115	13	Angel One	ao	41636.9	1/25/88	47
116	14	11001001	oo	41365.9	2/1/88	48
117	17	Home Soil	hs	41463.9	2/22/88	49
118	16	When the Bough Breaks	wb	41509.1	2/15/88	50
119	18	Coming of Age	ca	41416.2	3/14/88	51
120	19	Heart of Glory	hg	41503.7	3/21/88	52
121	20	The Arsenal of Freedom	af	41798.2	4/11/88	53
122	22	Skin of Evil	se	41601.3	4/25/88	54
123	21	Symbiosis	sy	unknown	4/18/88	55
124	23	We'll Always Have Paris	wa	41697.9	5/2/88	56
125	24	Conspiracy	co	41775.5	5/9/88	57
126	25	The Neutral Zone	nz	41986.0	5/16/88	59
127	26	The Child	tc	42073.1	11/21/88	66
128	27	Where Silence Has Lease	ws	42193.6	11/28/88	67
129	28	Elementary, Dear Data	ed	42286.3	12/5/88	68
130	29	The Outrageous Okona	ok	42402.7	12/12/88	69
131	31	The Schizoid Man	sm	42437.5	1/23/89	71
132	30	Loud as a Whisper	lw	42477.2	1/9/89	72
133	32	Unnatural Selection	us	42494.8	1/30/89	73
134	33	A Matter of Honor	mt	42506.5	2/6/89	74
135	34	The Measure of the Man	mm	42523.7	2/13/89	76
136	35	The Dauphin	dp	42568.8	2/20/89	78
137	36	Contagion	cg	42609.1	3/20/89	79
138	37	The Royale	ro	42625.4	3/27/89	80
139	38	Time Squared	tm	42679.2	4/3/89	81
140	39	The Icarus Factor	if	42686.4	4/24/89	82
141	40	Pen Pals	pp	42695.3	5/1/89	84
142	41	Q Who	qw	42761.3	5/8/89	85
143	42	Samaritan Snare	ss	42779.1	5/15/89	86
144	43	Up the Long Ladder	ul	42823.2	5/22/89	87

Epis.	Air No.	Title	Code	Stardate	Aired Week of:	Page
145	44	Manhunt	mh	42859.2	6/19/89	89
146	45	The Emissary	em	42901.3	6/26/89	90
147	46	Peak Performance	pk	42923.4	7/10/89	91
148	47	Shades of Gray	sg	42976.1	7/17/89	93
149	49	The Ensigns of Command	ec	43133.3	10/02/89	100
150	48	Evolution	ev	43125.8	9/25/89	101
151	50	The Survivors	sv	43152.4	10/09/89	102
152	51	Who Watches the Watchers?	ww	43173.5	10/16/89	103
153	52	The Bonding	bo	43198.7	10/23/89	104
154	53	Booby Trap	bt	43205.6	10/30/89	105
155	54	The Enemy	en	43349.2	11/6/89	106
156	55	The Price	pr	43385.6	11/13/89	107
157	56	The Vengeance Factor	vf	43421.9	11/20/89	109
158	57	The Defector	df	43462.5	1/1/90	110
159	58	The Hunted	hu	43489.2	1/8/90	111
160	59	The High Ground	hi	43510.7	1/29/90	112
161	60	Deja Q	dq	43539.1	2/5/90	113
162	61	A Matter of Perspective	mp	43610.4	2/12/90	114
163	62	Yesterday's Enterprise	ye	43625.2	2/19/90	116
164	63	The Offspring	of	43657.0	3/12/90	118
165	64	Sins of the Father	sf	43685.2	3/19/90	119
166	65	Allegiance	al	43714.1	3/26/90	120
167	66	Captain's Holiday	cp	43745.2	4/02/90	121
168	67	Tin Man	ti	43779.3	4/23/90	122
169	68	Hollow Pursuits	hp	43807.4	4/30/90	124
170	69	The Most Toys	mo	43872.2	5/7/90	125
171	70	Sarek	sa	43917.4	5/14/90	126
172	71	Ménage à Troi	me	43930.7	5/28/90	127
173	72	Transfigurations	tf	43957.2	6/4/90	129
174	73	The Best of Both Worlds	bb	43989.1	6/18/90	130
175	74	The Best of Both Worlds, Pt. 2	b2	44001.4	9/24/90	138
176	77	Suddenly Human	sh	44143.7	10/15/90	139
177	76	Brothers	br	44085.7	10/8/90	140
178	75	Family	fa	44012.3	10/1/90	142
179	78	Remember Me	rm	44161.2	10/22/90	144
180	79	Legacy	le	44215.2	10/29/90	145
181	80	Reunion	re	44246.3	11/05/90	146
182	81	Future Imperfect	fi	44286.5	11/12/90	147
183	82	Final Mission	fm	44307.3	11/19/90	148
184	83	The Loss	ls	44356.9	12/31/90	150
185	84	Data's Day	dd	44390.1	1/7/91	151
186	85	The Wounded	wo	44429.6	1/28/91	152
187	86	Devil's Due	dv	44474.5	2/4/91	153
188	87	Clues	cl	44502.7	2/11/91	154
189	88	First Contact	fc	unknown	2/18/91	155
190	89	Galaxy's Child	gc	44614.6	3/11/91	156
191	90	Night Terrors	nt	44631.2	3/18/91	157
192	91	Identity Crisis	ic	44664.5	3/25/91	158
193	92	Nth Degree	nd	44704.2	4/1/91	159

*The stardate for "The Next Phase" [224] was derived from an on-screen graphic.

Writers

ST: TNG Guest Stars and Their Roles

All numbers refer to studio episode numbers; an asterisk (*) indicates an uncredited role/actor; (**) denotes voice work only. In case of long role names, the billed name is underlined; parentheses or quotes indicate additional material or insight from episode context. Evolving names, ranks, etc., are first given with the episode of source.

Aguilar, George / Wakasa: je/272

Alaimo, Marc / *Badar N'D'D: la/108; Cmdr. *Tebok:* nz/126; Gul Macet: wo/186; *Gambler* (Frederick La Rouque): ta/226

Aldridge, Rhonda / "Secretary" (bg/113) Madeline: mh/145, cl/188

Allen, Chad / Jono: sh/176

Allen, Richard / Kentor: ec/149

Allin, Jeff / Ensign *Daniel Sutter:* pm/221

Allport, Carolyn / Jessica Bradley: bg/113

Altshuld, Alan / Pomet: st/244; Yranac: g1/256

Ames, Granville / Transporter chief: ST:G

Amick, Mädchen / (Anya as) *Teenage Girl:* dp/136

Anderson, Erich / "Cmdr. Keiran MacDuff": cn/214

Anderson, John / "Kevin Uxbridge": sv/151

Anderson, Sam / "Assistant manager: ro/138

Anderson, Steven / Dr. Nil!rem: fc/189

Arenberg, Lee / DaiMon *Prak:* fn/261; DaiMon *Bok:* bl/274

Aresco, Joey / Brull: vf/157

Argiro, Vinny / Hitman: eg/275

Armagnac, Gary / Lieutenant McNary: bg/113

Armstrong, Vaughan / Commander *Korris:* hg/120

Arnemann, Dawn / Miss Gladstone: tc/127

Arnet, Cameron / Ensign Mandel: di/205

Aron, Michael / Jack the Bellboy: ta/226, (Jack London), t2/227

Arrants, Rod / Rex: mh/145

Ashmore, Kelly / Francine: wa/124

Astar, Shay / "Isabella": pm/221

Avari, Erick / B'ljik: ul/208

Bader, Dietrich / Tactical Crewman: em/146

Bakke, Brenda / Rivan: ju/109

Barlow, Jennifer / Ensign Gibson: dp/136

Barrett (Roddenberry), Majel / Lwaxana Troi: hv/105, mh/145, me/172, hl/196, cs/220, dk/259; **Starfleet *Computer Voice* (uncredited in many earlier episodes): mi/198, rd/200, er/203, ul/208, ng/210, vi/212, cn/214, pw/215, cs/220, pm/221, t2/227, mn/229, rl/230, sc/231, ra/233, fs/234, ql/235, cl/236, c2/237, sb/238, aq/239, fe/240, tp/241, st/244, 1n/245, cha/246, su/248, rh/249, pa/263, hm/265, to/268, ge/271, fb/273, bl/274, ag/277-278, ST:G.

Barry, Carolyne / "Female Engineer": hs/117

Bastiani, William / Omag: u2/207

Bauer, Robert / Kunivas: hg/120

Bayle, Hayne / Ten-Forward Crew: of/164

Baxter, George L. / *David: us/133

Beacham, Stephanie / *Countess* Regina Barthalomew: sb/238

Beatty, Bruce / Ben: 1d/267

Becker, James G. Ten-Forward Crew: of/164

Beecroft, Gregory / Mikey D: ro/138

Belgrey, Thomas / *Yosemite Crew member:* rf/228

Bell, Michael / Groppler *Zorn:* ef/101-102

Benjamin, Zachary / *Young Ian* Andrew Troi, Jr.: tc/127

Bennett, Fran / Fleet *Admiral* Shanthi: r2/201

Benton, Craig / Ensign "Crewman" Davis: vi/212

Benzali, Daniel / Surgeon: ss/143

Berryman, Michael / Captain Rixx: co/125

Bethune, Ivy / Duana: wb/118

Bicknell, Andrew / Wagnor: hu/159

Bikel, Theodore / *Sergey* Rozhenko: fa/178

Billings, Earl / *Admiral* Thomas Henry: dr/195

Birk, Raye / Wrenn: hv/105

Birkin, David Tristin / René Picard: fa/178; Young Captain Picard: ra/233

Boen, Earl / Nagilum: ws/128

Bofshever, Michael / Romulan/Alien: tms/251

Bonsall, Brian / *Alexander* Rozhenko: ng/210, et/216, cs/220, pm/221, ra/233, fs/234, fb/273

Boone, Walker / Lieutenant Commander Leland T. Lynch: se/122

Boryer, Lucy / Ensign Janeway: rf/228

Bova, Jessica and Vanessa (twins) / Alexandra: wb/118

Boyer, Katy / Zero One: oo/116

Boyett, William / Lieutenant Daniel Bell: bg/113; Policeman: t2/227

Directors

Numbers refer to studio episode numbers

Allen, Corey: ef/101–102 (721); hs/117; fm/183; gm/206; je/272

Beaumont, Gabrielle: bt/154; hi/160; sh/176; di/205; im/222; fe/240; ld/267

Becker, Robert: wa/124; ok/130

Benko, Tom: tf/173; dv/187

Bole, Cliff: la/108; hq/111; co/125; ro/138; em/146; ec/149; hu/159; mp/162; hp/169; bb/174; b2/175; rm/179; fc/189; qp/194; rd/200; si/204; u2/207; pm/221; rf/228; aq/239; st/244; su/248; li/248; li/254; eb/270; eg/275

Bond, Timothy: vf/157; mo/170

Bowman, Rob: wn/106; ba/110; ts/112; da/114; hg/120; tc/127; ed/129; mt/134; dp/136; qw/142; mh/145; sg/148; br/177

Burton, LeVar: sd/250; pe/264

Carson, David: en/155; ye/163; r2/201; np/224; ST: G

Chalmers, Chip: cp/167; ls/184; wo/186; et/216

Colla, Richard: lo/107

Compton, Richard: hv/105

Conway, James L.: ju/109; nz/126; fr/247

Curry, Dan: bi2/243

Frakes, Jonathan: of/164; re/181; dr/195; ce/218; ql/235; cha/246; at/260; sr/266

Iscove, Robert: if/140

Kolbe, Winrich: ws/128; pp/141; ul/144; ev/150; bo/153; al/166; gc/190; ic/192; dm/202; ms/213; cs/220; mn/229; bi/242; rh/249; to/268; ag/277

Landau, Les: af/121; sm/131; ss/143; sv/151; dq/161; sf/165; sa/171; fa/178; fi/182; cl/188; nt/191; hl/196; er/203; ul/208; cn/214; ta/226; t2/227; c2/237; tp/241; dk/259; bl/274

Lauritson, Peter: il/225; gl/256

Lederman, Robert: ib/223; fn/261

Legato, Robert: me/172; nd/193

Livingston, David: mi/198; pw/215

Lynch, Paul: nn/103; oo/116; us/133; ma/209; fd/219

Manners, Kim: wb/118

Mayberry, Russ: ch/104

McFadden, Gates: ge/271

Nimoy, Adam: ra/233; tms/251

Phelps, Wyn: sy/123

Rhodes, Michael: ao/115

Rush, Marvin V.: ho/197

Scanlan, Joseph: bg/113; se/122; cg/137; tm/139

Scheerer, Robert: mm/135; pk/147; pr/156; df/158; ti/168; le/180; ng/210; oc/217; tq/232; cl/236; ih/262

Shaw, Larry: lw/132

Singer, Alexander: rl/230; sb/238; de/252; d2/253; g2/257; hm/265

Stewart, Patrick: it/199; hw/211; fs/234; ph/258; ps/276

Vejar, Michael: ca/119

West, Jonathan: fb/273

Wiemer, Robert: ww/152; dd/185; vi/212; sc/231; ln/245; in/255; pa/263; mk/269